Having worked in the law, journalism and numismatics, K. J. Parker now writes and makes things out of wood and metal (including prototypes for most of the hardware described in this book).

Parker is married to a solicitor and lives in southern England.

By K. J. Parker

THE FENCER TRILOGY
Colours in the Steel
The Belly of the Bow
The Proof House

THE PROOF HOUSE

VOLUME THREE OF
THE FENCER TRILOGY

K. J. PARKER

An *Orbit* Book

First published in Great Britain by Orbit 2000

Copyright © K. J. Parker 2000

The moral right of the author has been asserted.

A CIP catalogue record for this book
is available from the British Library.

ISBN 1 85723 966 0

Typeset by Solidus (Bristol) Ltd
Printed and bound in Great Britain by Creative Print and Design, (Wales)

Orbit
A Division of
Little, Brown and Company (UK)
Brettenham House
Lancaster Place
London WC2E 7EN

For GoE
(The world's shortest giant)

And the essential Jan Fergus

Author's Note

I couldn't have written this without the help of Roger Lankford, who taught me how to make armour, and in doing so pretty well gave me the book on a sixteen-gauge steel plate. Needless to say, the sloppy and inefficient working practices of the Imperial arsenal don't necessarily reflect the techniques Roger uses at Lancaster's Armoury, where he makes the finest steel leisurewear that money can buy. My thanks are also due to Michael Peters, of the Black Hydra (no, I'm not making that up) Armory for further expert advice ('hitting your thumb at this point is *not* a good idea'), and to Thomas Jennings, who lent me his factory to play in when I needed somewhere to bash metal without aggravating the neighbours.

CHAPTER ONE

It's customary to die first; but in your case we'll make an exception.

Bardas Loredan was in the new spur when the main gallery caved in. He heard the squeal of straining timbers, a volley of cracks and snaps, a blunt *thump* that knocked him off his knees into the loose clay, and then nothing at all.

He lay still and listened. If the spur was going to cave in as well, it might not happen immediately. It all depended on whether the arch at the junction of the gallery and the spur had survived. If it hadn't, the load of the spur roof would have nothing to support it except force of habit and the plank struts that lined the walls; it might come down all at once, or it might think about it, slowly and painfully calculating the stresses and forces like a backward schoolboy and finally coming to the conclusion that it had no right to be there. If that was how it was going to be, the first sign would be the harassed groaning of the timbers, a few handfuls of soil dropping down as the roof-boards bowed under the weight and opened up the cracks between them. It was, of course, academic; with the gallery blocked behind him and a solid wall of clay in front, he had nowhere to go in any event. Unless someone managed to dig through the obstruction in the gallery, reprop, cart out the spoil and find the mouth of the spur before the good air ran out, he was as good as buried.

It's customary to die first; but in your case, we've made an exception.

For the first time in months he was aware of the darkness. After three years in the saps, the endless maze of tunnels dug by besiegers and besieged under the walls of the city of Ap' Escatoy, he could go weeks at a time without seeing a light

1

and not realise it; it was only in moments of cold terror like this that the instinctive need to see reasserted itself.

You want light? Tough. His hands were full of loose, crumbled clay; he could feel it against his cheek, cold and dead, and the texture disgusted him. Curious; three years in the mines and he could still feel that strongly about something. He could have sworn he'd grown out of that sort of thing.

Well; no going back. At a guess, he had enough air for the best part of a shift, something of a mixed blessing under the circumstances. Men who'd long since lost the capacity to fear anything else were still terrified of death by suffocation in the aftermath of a cave-in. No going back, and staying put was a mug's game. The only option he could think of was to go forward, in the fatuous hope that the enemy sap they'd been trying to break through into was close enough that he'd be able to reach it (alone, single-handed) before the air ran out.

Put another way, the choice was: dig or stay put. After a moment's thought, Loredan decided to dig. If nothing else, it'd help use the air up more quickly and get it all over and done with.

It hadn't taken the Great King's sappers long to realise that the seam of heavy clay that lay under Ap' Escatoy was more than they could handle with ordinary tools and techniques. They'd broken their hearts and blunted their spades at the seam for three or so months when an old man had wandered across from the supply train and told them what they should be doing. He explained that before the war he'd been a clay-kicker, a specialist in cutting tunnels through clay-beds. He'd spent thirty years helping to dig the sewers of Ap' Mese (sacked and razed to the ground in six days by the Great King's army in the first year of the war) and what he didn't know about making holes in the ground wasn't worth spit.

To dig in clay, he told them, you need a stout, square wooden post, something like a farm gatepost, with a ledge dowelled to it about six inches from the base. You wedge this post (called a cross in the trade) diagonally-backwards between the roof and the floor of the tunnel, with the base a foot from the clay-face; then you perch your bum on the ledge, flatten your back against the post and use your feet and legs to kick the spade into the clay. Once the blade's gone in, a sharp upwards jerk with the knees ought to free a spit of solid clay; you pull it out and dump it for the scavengers behind you to clear away with a long-shafted hook and carry to the spoil-dolly, a little flat cart on wheels with ropes and pulleys fore and aft that whisks the clay out into the main gallery, where it's loaded on to the dog-carts that trundle up to the lift and back all day long. Behind the kickers and the scavengers come the chippies, the carpenters who cut and fit the boards that line the floor, walls and roof of the sap. Except for sawing the boards, every part of the job has to be done in pitch darkness, because even a closed lantern would be enough to set off the pockets of explosive trench-vapour that are all too common in the mines.

Bardas Loredan was too tall to be a good kicker. His knees were almost round his chin as he drew his legs back to punch against the crossbar of the spade. It was a job for short, squat men built like barrels, not long, lean ex-fencers. Unfortunately, if he didn't do the job, nobody else would. He steadied the spade, lightly pressing the point of the broad leaf-shaped blade against the wall in front of him, and stamped hard, so that the impact jarred his bones from his ankles to his neck.

Of course, the kicker isn't expected to work alone; the back-breaking chore of hauling out the chunks of compacted clay as the kicker boots them off the spade falls to the scavenger with his hook. But Loredan's scavenger was some-where back down the tunnel under a few hundred tons of cave-in and therefore excused duty, even in the Great King's army; which meant that after every three or four spits he had to wriggle off the cross, drop forward on to his knees and scrabble the spoil away behind him with his feet, like a rabbit digging in a flower-bed.

Give it up, Bardas, give it away. Quit burrowing like a mole and suffocate with dignity. It was all pretty ludicrous, really. He was a leathery little chick desperately trying to peck his way out of a marble-shelled egg. He was the prince of tightwads, baron marshal of cheapskates (every man his own gravedigger; why waste money on exorbitant sextons' fees when you can do it yourself?). He was the littlest ever worm in the biggest ever oak-apple. He was a dead man, still kicking.

Suddenly, the feel changed. Instead of the solid slice, a bit like a butcher's cleaver in a stringy old carcass, it was hammering into resistance, as it might be the compacted clay of a tunnel wall. More of the jar and shock was coming back up his ankles and shins than before. It was different, and anything different was hopeful. He bent his knees till he felt them brush the corners of his mouth, and kicked. Something was about to give; something had given way rather than hold still and be cut. Not bothering to clear away he carried on kicking, obstructed by the prised-out spoil but too pre-occupied to spare the time to do the job properly (*that's so like you, Bardas; be the death of you, one day*) until a ferocious stomp of his heels drove the spade forward into nothing, and he was jolted forwards painfully on to the base of his spine.

Through, by the gods. I've found the damn sap. That's handy. There was no light, needless to say, but the change in the smell of the air was extraordinary. Coriander; the tunnel he'd broken into reeked of coriander. Cautiously he wiggled his left foot into the breach he'd opened with the spade until he felt the flat of a board against the sole of his boot. He couldn't help grinning; what if he kicked this board away, and it brought the roof down on him? Die like that, you'd wet yourself laughing.

Coriander; because the enemy's bakers seasoned their bread with coriander, while the Great King's bread was made with garlic salt and rosemary. In the wet air of the mines, you could smell coriander or garlic on a man's breath fifty yards away; it was the only way to know he was there and which side he was on. Coriander, and pepper-sausage for the officers, smells death and danger. Rosemary and garlic are for home, rescue or the relief shift crawling up the spur towards you. Loredan pressed his boot flat against the board and exerted slow, even force, until he felt the nails draw out of the battens. Through, but into coriander. One damn thing after another.

Shuffling along on his arse, feeling his way with his heels, he edged through the breach in the wall until he came up against floorboards. One hell of a racket; but maybe it wouldn't matter. It hadn't occurred to him before now to wonder why the gallery had caved in; galleries cave in, it happens. But sometimes they cave in because the enemy undermines them, digging a spur of their own directly underneath and cutting out a chamber, called a camouflet, where they pile up barrels and jars of fat and rancid tallow, all hot, combustible stuff. As the fire burns it dries out the roof of the camouflet, the clay shrinks and suddenly there's an unsupported hole in the gallery floor into which the whole gallery tries to pour itself, like water draining from a sink. The gallery caves in. Job done.

Well, then; if the enemy, coriander, is off down some spur of its own, it's less likely to be tramping up and down its native gallery. A man, garlic, might slip through a breach in the wall and go unnoticed for quite some way before some bugger bumps into him and cuts his throat.

'Gods know.' (Voices coming, coriander; two men in a hurry, knees and palms bumping over the floorboards.) 'Maybe we're so close to their gallery that our wall's subsiding into the hole. In which case we'll get the whole bloody lot round our ears if we don't get it shored quick.'

Bardas Loredan felt himself nodding in agreement; here was a man who knew his mines all right, the sort of man you'd want on your shift, except that he was the enemy. Two of them, and still coming on; hadn't they got noses, he wondered, and then remembered that his shift hadn't eaten for two days, what with one thing and all. No bread, no garlic, no smell to give you away. Stop eating and live for ever.

'It's a bugger, whatever it is,' said the voice that went with the other pair of knees. Bardas felt in the top of his boot for the hilt of his knife; if the first one really was scent-blind, he'd have him, definitely. It'd be the second who'd have Bardas. Sacrifice your knight to take his rook; no fun at all if you're the knight. But: the hell with it. It's every soldier's duty to seek out and destroy the enemy. So, let's do that, then.

He let the first voice go by, and when the second voice was almost past him, he reached out carefully with his left hand, hoping for a chin or a jaw. Of course, this was the bit he was good at. His fingertips brushed against a man's beard, long enough for him to wind his fingers into and get a good grip. Before the man had a chance to make a sound, Bardas had stabbed up into the triangular cavity at the junction of neck and collar-bone, where death can come in quicker and quieter than anywhere else. The fashion in the mines was for short knives (short knives, short men, short spades, short lives; you got nothing for tall down the mines). He was in and out so smoothly that there was a fair chance the other man hadn't even noticed.

Nevertheless; 'Thank you,' Bardas muttered as he twisted the knife to free the blade. It was an unbreakable rule of the mines that you thanked the man who died in your place, when one or the other of you had to go. By speaking aloud he'd announced his presence in unmistakable terms, but he still had the advantage. The man, coriander, in front of him hadn't a hope of turning round in the cramped shaft of the gallery, which meant that his options were to hold still and try to kick backwards with his heels like a mule, or to rapid-crawl on his hands and knees like a little child scurrying under a table, in the hope of finding a spur to crawl down before his enemy realised he'd gone. Then it'd be the other way round, of course; no fun, so let's not allow that to happen.

With a soft grunt of revulsion Bardas Loredan crawled over the body of the man, coriander, he'd just killed, feeling the palms of his hands and the caps of his knees digging into the soft flesh of the dead man's belly and cheeks. He sniffed like a polecat to get a fix on his quarry, heard the scrape of a wooden clog-sole on a stone – almost close enough but not quite – so he hopped along, hands outstretched, shoving himself forward with his legs like a rabbit until he knew his face was within a few inches of the other man's heels. The spring, when he made it, was more froglike than feline; he landed heavily, jarring his elbows on the man's shoulder-blades. Afterwards, he thanked him.

Now what? Of course, he hadn't a clue where he was. In his own tunnels he could find his way easily enough; in his mind's eye he had a picture of a whole honeycomb of galleries, shafts and spurs he'd never actually seen but knew intimately nonetheless. He didn't even have to count the movements of his knees as he crawled forward to know where the spur gates were, or where the spur ended and the gallery began. He simply knew where they were, like a juggler with his eyes shut. But in these mines, coriander, he had no idea. The darkness here was genuinely dark to him, and he felt the lowness of the roof and the narrowness of the space between the walls as if it was his first day out of the light.

Common sense, common sense. If this is a gallery (too wide and high to be a spur), chances are it runs to the face from the lift-shaft – which begged the questions: which way is which, and which way did he actually want to go? Avoiding the enemy was definitely a priority, but not if it meant heading deeper and further into exclusively hostile ground. To the best of his knowledge, the only interface between his tunnels, garlic, and the enemy's was the hole he'd just wriggled through, so no way back. Forward – either direction – would sooner or later bring him up against an enemy camp or working shift, and even he couldn't kill them all.

It's customary to die first ... If only he could smell fresh air, he'd know which end was the lift-shaft; but he couldn't, only a stale, lingering flavour of coriander and the heavy scent of the dead men's blood on his clothes and hands. If he didn't do something soon, fear would catch up with him and he'd be paralysed – he'd come across men, coriander, in that state before now, crouched against a wall with their hands over their ears, unable to move. Left, then; he'd go left, because if he was still in his own tunnels he'd go right to get to the lift-shaft. Totally flawed logic, but he couldn't hear anybody objecting. Exactly why he should want to make for the lift he didn't know. Just supposing he was able to creep into one of the spoil-baskets and get lifted up out of the mines without anybody noticing, once he reached the surface he'd be inside the enemy city, a dirty, bloody man marinaded in the wrong herbs and spices. But if he went the other way, to the face – where would the face be, now? Presumably, at the end of the spur where they'd laid their camouflet. Effectively, he'd have gone round in a circle, but there might be a chance of breaking through, if (say) the spur, coriander, ran closely parallel with the gallery, garlic, to any extent. Even if that worked out, of course, there was the intriguing risk that he'd come though into his native gallery at some point after the cave-in, where he'd be just as trapped as he'd been in the spur. Only one way to find out. He'd go right, and see what happened.

'It's one of those moments, isn't it?' said a voice beside him.

He knew perfectly well that the voice wasn't really there. It hadn't been there for years.

'You tell me,' he replied, keeping his own voice down to a soft whisper. 'You're supposed to be the expert.'

'So people keep telling me,' the voice replied ruefully. 'I've always maintained that I'm like a man who's just bought an expensive new machine; I know how to use it but I haven't a clue how it works.'

'Well,' Loredan replied distractedly, 'you know more about it than I do, anyway.'

The voice sighed. It wasn't a real voice; it was make-believe, like the imaginary friends of children. 'I think it's one of those moments,' it repeated. 'A fateful choice, a cusp – is that the right word? I've been talking about cusps for thirty years and I don't actually know what a cusp is – a cusp in the flow, a crossroads. Apparently the Principle simply can't function without them.'

'All right,' Loredan muttered, squeezing himself through a tight spot where a side-panel had come adrift, 'it's a cusp. Do whatever it is you do. And if it's all the same to you, I'll just carry on with what I'm doing.'

'You always were sceptical,' said the voice. 'I can't say I blame you. There's a lot of it I have trouble believing in myself, and I wrote the book.'

Loredan sighed. 'You were rather less irritating when you were real,' he said.

'Sorry.'

Everbody heard imaginary voices after a while. Some people heard them as dwarves and gnomes, kindly creatures that warned about vapour-pockets and cave-ins. Others heard them as dead family or friends, while bad men heard them as the people they'd murdered or raped or mutilated. Some people put out bowls of bread and milk for them, as children do for hedgehogs. Others sang to drown the voices out, or yelled at them till they went away; others talked to them for hours, finding that it helped pass the time. Everybody knew they weren't really there; but in the mines, where it's always dark and everybody, real or not, is nothing but a disembodied voice, people learn not to be quite so dogmatic about what's actually there and what isn't. For better or worse, Bardas Loredan heard his voice as Alexius, the former Patriarch of Perimadeia, who he'd known for a short while years ago and who was now quite probably dead. Except here, of course, where the living are buried and the dead live on bread and milk, like invalids.

'If I were you,' Alexius said, 'I'd go left.'

'I was just about to,' Bardas replied.

'Oh. That's all right, then.'

He went left. The gallery was narrower here, the floorboards rougher, not yet polished by the passage of gloved hands and copped knees. It was hot, which suggested there might be vapour.

'Not that I'm aware of,' Alexius said.

'Good. I've got enough to contend with as it is.'

'But unless I'm very much mistaken,' the Patriarch went on, 'there's someone up ahead of you, about seventy-five yards – sorry I can't be more exact, but of course I can't see a damned thing. I believe he's stopped and he's fixing something; a board that's come loose, probably.'

'All right, thanks. Which way's he facing?'

'No idea, I'm afraid.'

'Not to worry. Is he a cusp too?'

'That I can't tell you. He might be a cusp, or he might be purely serendipitous.'

'Right.'

He slowed down, carefully shifting his weight with each knee-stride forward so as to make no sound at all. He smelt of blood, of course, and probably sweat, too. The man smelt of pepper and coriander.

'That's it, you've got him. Now do be careful.'

Bardas didn't answer, not this close. *Where were you just now, when I could have done with someone to talk to?* He could hear the man's breathing now, and the very faint creak of the leather cops on his knees as he worked.

'He's got his back to you.'

I know. Now please go away, I'm busy. He moved closer (couldn't be more than a yard now) and reached towards the top of his boot for his knife-hilt. Sometimes the blade made a very slight hissing noise as it rubbed along the cloth of his breeches. Fortunately, not this time.

Afterwards, he thanked him—

'Why do you do that?' Alexius asked, puzzled. 'I'll be straight with you, I find it rather morbid.'

'Do you?' Loredan shrugged (pointless gesture in the dark, where not even people who weren't there could see him do it). 'Personally, I think it's a nice tradition.'

'A nice tradition,' Alexius repeated. 'Like blackberry-picking or hanging bunches of primroses over the door at Spring Festival.'

'Yes,' Loredan said firmly. 'Like putting out saucers of milk for the likes of you.'

'Please, don't trouble yourself on my account. If there's one thing I can't abide, it's soggy bread in sour milk.'

'Well, you wouldn't have us waste the good stuff, would you?'

He crawled over the dead man; still no clue what it was he'd been doing there, so quiet and meticulous. Unimportant. Couldn't be much further now and he'd be at the face.

('Then how come,' he'd asked once, 'if you're wholly imaginary, you keep telling me things I don't know, like the enemy's up ahead or vapour-pockets? And you're nearly always right, too.'

Alexius had thought for a moment. 'Possibly,' he'd said, 'you're unconsciously picking up clues that are so slight your mind can't take notice of them in the usual way - tiny noises you don't know you've heard, just the faintest taste of a smell, that sort of thing - so it invents me out of thin air as a way of getting the information to you.'

'Possible, I suppose,' he'd replied. 'But wouldn't it be easier just to admit that you exist?'

'Maybe,' Alexius had replied. 'But just because a thing's more likely doesn't necessarily mean it's true.')

Sometimes he tried to picture it all in his mind; where he was in real terms, in relation to the city and the Great King's camp and the river and the estuary. He still believed in them, just about, though at times his faith was sorely tried. Maybe it would help if he left them the occasional bowl of milk.

He could hear digging; four, possibly five distinct noises. He could smell coriander, and sweat, and steel, freshly cut

clay, a very faint trace of vapour, not enough to be dangerous; leather and wet cloth and urine, and the blood on his
own hands and knees. For some reason he was having difficulty estimating the range – it could well be because he
was near the face, where the solid wall of clay ahead soaked
up the sound, or perhaps the roof was higher than usual,
creating a slight echo. Five men digging, so there'd be a
scavenger to each man, and at least two chippies – but he
couldn't hear scavengers' hooks or carpentry tools, implying that they'd only just started work, and if that was the
case, pretty soon a man would come up the gallery with the
rope to pull the spoil-dolly. He listened, but Alexius wasn't
there (typical; but everybody knew you couldn't rely on the
voices). Trying not to worry, he felt the side-walls carefully
for a spur, a lay-by, a point where the gallery widened
enough for him to tuck in out of the way and let the rope-
bearer go by – or failing that, somewhere he could turn
round and go back. If the worst came to the worst he'd have
to crawl backwards, but that was very much a last resort,
since there was always a risk of meeting someone, coriander, coming the other way.

As luck would have it there was a wide place, where they'd
had to cut through a rock when they'd built the gallery. The
carpenters hadn't bothered to board over what was left of
the rock, and the cutters had split it so deeply with their fire
and vinegar that there was a crack wide enough for him to
squeeze into, if he wasn't too fussy about breathing.

He didn't have to wait long; he heard the rope scuffling
along behind the man, and not long after that he could smell
him. He let the man go a little way, and afterwards he
thanked him; if anyone came down the gallery, they'd
blunder into him and make a noise, enough to give notice. It
was a friendly thing to do, and in the mines you had to take
friends where you found them.

Four men digging, two scavengers, one carpenter; he
could hear the hooks and one saw. Short-handed, obviously;
overstretched, not enough experienced men to go round. It
was a common problem, garlic and coriander. The carpenter
was furthest back; he'd warn his friends when the sound of
his saw stopped before time, but the scavengers couldn't
turn round – he'd have them easily enough. The problem

would be the kickers, who'd use their crosses to swing round.

He'd forgotten about the spoil-dolly; only remembered it when he put his hand on it (he'd been following the rope, so there was no excuse). It was hard, slow work climbing over it, and for a moment he was tempted by the thought of lying flat on it and pulling himself towards the face by hauling on the aft rope; but the sound of the wheels would be their friend, not his, whereas if he left it there it would be another sentry for him.

With forefinger and thumb only, he drew out his knife. It was the only material object he thought of as his own, and he'd never seen it. He felt with his fingertips for the slight grooves he'd scored into the wooden grip so that he'd know he was holding it right, and closed his hand around it. Three men to kill, then four more; then he'd have the place to himself.

In the mines, of course, all advantages create risk; any-thing that can help is dangerous. The thick pads of felt he wore on his knees and the soles of his boots muffled the sound of his movement with almost total efficiency, as the carpenter discovered the hard, sharp way, but they robbed him of most of his sense of touch; he couldn't feel where the ground changed, where the boards ended and the loose clay spoil began.

He located the first scavenger by the end of the shaft of his hook; as the man pulled back, the shaft rammed Loredan squarely in the chest. The man knew there was something wrong by the feel, but there wasn't time for him to do any-thing about it. The technique was always the same: left hand over the subject's mouth, to stop him making a noise and to pull the head up, exposing the pit where the throat meets the collar-bone, the quickest and surest place for an incision. When it was done and he'd mouthed his silent thanks, he drew the dead body carefully back and laid it on the ground like a newly pressed gown.

The second scavenger was aware of a change, but he only realised that what he'd noticed was a silence where there should have been the sound of a hook dragging clay a moment before Loredan found him. It was long enough for him to drop his hook and reach for his own knife, and quite by chance he drew the blade across the side of Loredan's left hand, cutting a thin, deep slice. He died before he'd had a chance to interpret the meaning of the feeling of slight resistance, and Loredan caught the knife before it had a chance to fall on the ground and raise the alarm.

'Moaz? Moaz, you bastard, why've you stopped?' One of the kickers, shouting nervously back as he wriggled round the side of his cross. Nuisance, Loredan thought; that'll make him hard to find. Still, he won't find me so easily either, and I have the advantage.

He moved the knife to his left hand, the one that was bleeding. A drop of his blood falling on a man's neck as he was reaching out for his mouth and chin wouldn't be his friend, it could mean a quick, instinctive shy away, a missed grab, a mistake which could not be rectified later (as the stallholders in Perimadeia market used to say, before the city fell and they were all killed). It was a disadvantage; he didn't have the same feel in his right hand. Another variable to factor into the calculation, as if it wasn't complicated enough already.

'There's some bastard down here,' a voice said. 'Moaz? Levka? Say something, for gods' sakes.'

Loredan frowned. The voice was an advantage, because it gave him a precise position, but if he went straight towards it he'd be at a disadvantage, because the man would be expecting him to come from the front. If he tried to go round the side, though, there was a fair chance he'd bump into one of the other crosses, or come up against a pile of spoil that would get in his way and be an enemy. If he wanted the voice to be his friend, he'd have to try another approach.

'Help,' he said.

Silence. Then, 'Moaz? Is that you?'

Loredan made a groaning noise; it was quite a work of art. 'Stay there,' the voice said, 'I'm coming. Did you get him?'

The voice came to him, making a lot of noise. He felt splayed fingers on his face, made the necessary calculations and stabbed upwards. No doubt about it, he had a feel for this sort of work.

'Thank you,' he said aloud, then rolled sideways until he was tight against the wall.

'What the hell's going on back there?' demanded another voice. 'Moaz? Yan? Oh, fuck it, someone go for a light.'

'Hold on,' said another voice, 'I've got my box.' Loredan heard a soft scrape, consistent with the lid of a tinder-box being drawn back. That wouldn't be good at all.

'Wait,' he called out; then he made his best guess and jumped, pushing off from the wall with his legs like a swimmer. It was a good guess; his outstretched right hand brushed against an ear. Where there's an ear there's generally a throat, and so it was in this case.

A good guess but a bad move, albeit forced on him by circumstances. As he pulled out his knife he felt a blow diagonally across his back, enough to jolt his breath, and a small sharp pain on the left side of his collar-bone where the knife nicked it. Quickly he caught hold of the hand with the knife in it; assuming the man was right-handed, that gave him a good fix. He followed it up. Five down.

Number six died trying to squeeze past him in the narrow neck of the tunnel. Number seven died facing the wrong way, having lost track of Bardas' movements without realising it.

Job done.

Job done, and nothing left to do. When he tried a few kicks at the face it felt depressingly solid; even if the main gallery (garlic) really did run parallel to this sap, the dividing wall between them was apparently too thick for him to break through. He lay back on the cross and let his shoulders droop, wondering how he was going to explain to the men he'd just killed that it had all been a waste of time.

'That's all right,' they said (with his eyes closed he was able to see them for the first time). 'You weren't to know.'

'It's good of you to see it that way,' he replied.

'You were giving it your best shot,' they told him. 'When it comes down to it, that's all a man can do. You can't be blamed for that.'

They were smiling at him. 'I was just trying to stay alive,' he said. 'That's all.'

'We understand,' they said. 'We'd have done the same if we'd been in your shoes.'

Loredan shooed them away, knowing perfectly well that they weren't real but not saying so out loud for fear of hurting their feelings. As soon as he'd seen their faces, he'd known they were just some fantasy, a projection of his own thoughts. Anything you could see with your own two eyes in the mines didn't exist, by definition.

'Including me?'

'Including you, Alexius. But you're old enough and ugly enough to be told these things.'

'Oh. Well, I won't bother you any more, then. Thanks for the bread and milk.'

'You're welcome. And you don't bother me. I'm glad of the company.'

Alexius smiled. 'You know, that reminds me of one of my tutors, back when I was a very young student. He used to go around all day muttering to himself, and one day the others dared me to ask him about it. So I did. "Why do you talk to yourself?" I asked. "Because it's the only way I'll get a sensible conversation around here," he replied. A good answer, I always thought.'

Loredan shook his head. 'Donnish wit,' he said. 'Sometimes I wonder if that's all you academic types do all day, lurk about trying to lure each other into carefully planned verbal ambushes. Odd way for grown men to behave, if you ask me.'

Alexius nodded. 'Almost as odd as crawling about in narrow dark tunnels,' he replied. 'But not quite.'

'Alexius.'

'Hm?'

Loredan opened his eyes. 'Is there any way I can get out of here? Or am I through this time?'

He couldn't see Alexius any more, but the voice was clear and distinct. 'Not you as well,' he said. 'I've spent my life explaining this. I'm a scientist, not a fortune-teller. I have no idea.'

'You know,' Loredan said, 'you don't sound at all like the Alexius I used to know. You sound younger.'

'It's one of the nice things about being imaginary, I can be whatever age I like. I've decided to be forty-seven. I enjoyed forty-seven best.'

Loredan nodded. 'I've always had this theory,' he said, 'that we're all born with a certain optimum age, the age we're really meant to be, and once we reach it we stick there, in our minds, where it counts. Personally I've always been twenty-five. I was good at being twenty-five.'

Alexius sighed. 'Just as well that you found your true age while you had enough time to enjoy it, then,' he said. 'If it'd been forty-seven you'd have been out of luck, because I'm afraid you'll never get there.'

'Ah,' Loredan said. 'I'm forty-four.'

'No you're not. Forty-six. You've lost count.'

'Really?' Loredan shrugged. 'Been down here too long, I guess. And now I suppose I'm going to stay down here for good.'

'It saves your friends the cost and trauma of burying you.'

'True. I'd hoped I wouldn't get buried until I was dead.'

'Admittedly, it's customary to die first. In your case, however, they seem to have made an exception.'

'I think I'd like to go to sleep now,' Loredan said, yawning pointedly. 'I haven't been sleeping well lately.'

'As you wish.'

He closed his eyes again. How can a man die better, he thought, than in peace and tranquillity, with all his friends around him? Here they all were, come to see him off (or to welcome him in, depending on how you looked at it); rows and rows of them, filling the benches in the public gallery, spilling out on to the edges of the courtroom floor itself, while Bardas Loredan chose a sword from the bag his clerk was offering him. He didn't need to look up in order to know who his opponent was going to be.

'Gorgas,' he said, with a stiff nod.

'Hello,' his brother replied. 'It's been a long time.'

'Over three years,' Loredan replied. 'You haven't changed, though.'

'That's kind of you, but I expect I have really. Even less on top, a little more around the middle. It's all this good, starchy food I'm getting in the Mesoge. I'd forgotten how much I like it.'

Gorgas lifted his sword, a long, slender Habresche, worth a lot of money. Bardas discovered that he'd selected the Guelan, his favourite sword for lawsuits, which he'd broken some years ago in this very court. It too was old, rare and quite collectible, though not nearly as valuable as a late-series Habresche.

'Are you sure we've got to do this?' Gorgas asked plaintively. 'I'm certain that if only we sat down together and talked things through—'

Bardas grinned. 'Scared, are you?'

'Of course.' Gorgas nodded gravely. 'I'm absolutely terrified I might hurt you. For two pins I'd drop this ridiculous sword and let you kill me. Only you wouldn't do that, would you?'

'Kill an unarmed man who's kneeling at my feet? Not normally. But in your case I'll make an exception.'

Their sword blades met, as Gorgas lunged and Bardas parried, high right, forehand. 'I knew you'd meet that easily enough,' Gorgas was saying. 'If I'd thought you couldn't handle it, I'd never have made the stroke.'

'Don't patronise me, Gorgas,' Bardas warned. 'I'm a whole lot better at this than you are.'

'Of course you are, Bardas. I have complete confidence in your abilities. We wouldn't be doing this if I didn't.'

Bardas riposted, turning his wrist so as to lunge low, but Gorgas made the parry in plenty of time. His handspeed had never been this good.

'I've been practising,' he said.

'Obviously,' Bardas replied. He watched the blade come on as Gorgas lunged back, read the feint early and compensated, drawing his parry wide to cover the full zone of possibilities. Once he'd made the parry, he stepped across and back with his right foot to change the angle and flicked a short, powerful lunge at his brother's face. Gorgas only just parried in time, and the needle-sharp point of the Guelan nipped a small, thin cut just above Gorgas' ear.

'Very stylish,' Gorgas said. 'You're seeing it well today. By the way, did I tell you, Niessa died? My daughter Niessa, I mean, not *our* Niessa.'

'I never met her,' Bardas replied. 'Only her brother.'

'Pneumonia, of all things,' Gorgas said. 'She was only nine, poor little devil.'

'Did no one ever tell you it's bad form to talk while you're fencing?'

Gorgas disengaged and swished a diritto at the side of Bardas' head. Bardas took a standing jump backwards to get out of the way. 'Relax,' Gorgas was saying, 'this isn't real, you're imagining the whole thing.'

'That's no excuse for boorishness. If you're going to fight in my imagination, you'll abide by the house rules.'

'You were always a terror for making the rules up as

you went along,' Gorgas said with a sigh. He was clear for a counterthrust to the groin; if he'd made it, Bardas would have had terrible trouble stopping it. But he held back, giving Bardas the time he needed to adjust his guard. 'It's just like when we were kids,' Gorgas went on. 'The moment you realised you were losing, suddenly there'd be this brand-new rule.'

'That's not true,' Bardas protested. 'I may have made the odd professional foul, but I never *ever* cheated. More hassle than it's worth, trying to get one past you. The tiniest least thing and you'd go running off to Father sobbing, "It's not fair, it's not fair." And he'd always take your side against me.'

'You think so? I reckoned it was generally the other way round.'

Gorgas lunged. It was a short, quick lunge, opportunist, made *en passant* as he recovered from the last parry. There wouldn't have been anything Bardas could have done about it under any circumstances. He felt –

– He felt a slight vibration running through the cross, and opened his eyes sharply. Someone coming up the gallery, moving fast. *Damn*, he thought. *However ready you think you are, it isn't something you could ever prepare for.*

He fished in the top of his boot for his knife, but it wasn't there. He smiled. Three years in the mines and he'd never lost a knife before. Coincidence? And the rest.

He closed his eyes and concentrated. Whoever they were, they were making good speed up the gallery, trundling along on hands and knees as if they were in some sort of bizarre novelty race. It occurred to him that if they were coming up the tunnel simply in order to kill him, they were going about it in a decidedly clumsy way. No cavalry charges in the mines; if the job's done properly, the first the dead man knows about it is the gratitude of his killer. Now then; if they weren't coming for him, why would they be coming this way at all? If they were this shift's relief, they wouldn't be racing up the line as fast as they could go. Maybe, then, they weren't hurrying towards him but away from something else – such as a raiding party, or a cave-in about to happen.

Be that as it may; they were on their way here, and when they found him they'd kill him. He felt for the nearest of his seven dead friends, found the man's knife and took it for himself. Under normal circumstances, robbing the dead was slightly bad manners, but in this case he was confident they'd see their way to making an exception.

'Look out!' someone yelled – it was either Alexius or one of the seven dead men, he couldn't tell which – just as the whole gallery jolted, as if it had been dropped. Dust filled his nose and mouth, as a second tremor jostled him on to his knees, and a third brought the roof down on top of him.

Camouflet, someone said. *Big, big camouflet. We've undermined their gallery, hooray!*

'Wonderful,' Bardas said aloud, and the falling dirt filled the space like an hourglass.

CHAPTER TWO

Garlic.

'... Glorious bloody genuine hero of the war. Dug the bugger out like a truffle, we did. Thought he was one of them till someone noticed the boots.'

Bardas Loredan opened his eyes, and the light hit him. He closed them again, but not quickly enough. The pain and fear made him cry out.

'He's coming round, look,' said a voice from the light. Unbelievable, that living things could survive in that scorching, agonising glare; couldn't be real, had to be a hallucination. 'Absolutely fucking amazing. No way he should have survived that, should have been killed instantly.'

Shows how much you know; can't kill a man who's dead and buried. He tried to move, but his body was all pain. The light was burning its way through his eyelids.

'Sarge? Sarge, can you hear me?' The voice was vaguely familiar, which was odd. What were those funny little lizard things that lived in fire? Salamanders. Where on earth would he know a salamander from, and why would it be calling him Sarge?

'It's quite normal,' another voice said. 'He's just had a city fall on his head, it's hardly surprising he's feeling a bit groggy.' That voice was familiar, as well. Two salamanders.

Alexius? Alexius, is that you? Stop playing silly buggers and put that fucking light out.

'Sarge? Here, he's coming round, look. Who the hell's Alexius?'

Who are you? I can't see you so you must be real. Did I kill you just now, in the gallery?

'Dear gods,' said yet another salamander, 'he's well away. Crazy as a barrelful of ferrets.'

20

'Like I said, he just had Ap' Escatoy land on his nut, what do you expect? He'll be right as rain in a day or two.'

There was no getting away from it, he was going to have to open his eyes sooner or later. The light was seeping in under his eyelids anyhow, getting into his brain. *Did I die and turn into a salamander too, Alexius? You should have warned me.* He opened his eyes.

'Who the hell are you?' he asked, blinking.

All he could make out at first was a shape: a big brown oval, looming over him. This is how humans must look to a carp in a fish-pond. No wonder the buggers swim away.

'Sarge?' said the oval. 'It's me, Malicho. Corporal Malicho, you remember?'

Loredan shook his head; painful operation. 'Don't be ridiculous,' he said. 'You don't look anything like him.'

'It's me, Sarge, straight up. Here, Dollus, tell him it's me.'

There was another oval, on the edge of the salamander pool. 'Think about it, Malicho. He's never seen you before. Never seen any of us, come to that. And we'd never seen him before now, if you think about it.'

'Then how do we know it really is him?' someone else asked. 'Maybe he really is one of them. Hey, don't look at me like that, I'm just saying it's possible.'

'It's him,' said the salamander Malicho, firmly. 'I'd know that voice anywhere. Sarge, wake up. It's all right, it's us. It's seventh shift, what's left of us. You're going to be all right. We dug you out after the camouflet went up. The war's over. We won.'

The strain of keeping his eyelids open was unbearable; he could feel the muscles tearing like cloth. 'We won?'

'That's right. We brought down the bastion, the gate fell in, we stormed the city. We won.'

'Oh.' *What war would that be? I don't remember anything about any war.* 'That's good,' he said. 'Well done.'

'He hasn't got the faintest idea what you're talking about,' a salamander said. 'Come on, Malicho, let the poor bugger get some rest.'

The legate could recognise cinnamon, and cloves, of course; a trace of ginger, oil of violets, the tiniest savour of jasmine.

The one special ingredient eluded him, however. It was infuriating.

'The family,' the colonel was saying, 'is quite well known, apparently. There was a sister who ran the bank on Scona—'

'Scona.' The legate carefully put down the tiny silver cup. 'I think I've heard that name somewhere. Wasn't there a war?'

'Very small-scale,' the colonel replied. 'But it caused a brief flutter on the exchanges. There's also a brother who's some sort of minor warlord in a place called Mesoge. And of course, our man was in charge of the last defence of Perimadeia.'

'Really.' Honeysuckle? No, it was a different sort of sweetness; not as dry. 'Quite an illustrious family, then.'

'Actually, no,' the colonel replied, smiling. 'Their father was a tenant farmer somewhere. But that's all by the by. A remarkable man, for an outsider. We should do something for him. The army would like it.'

The legate inclined his head slightly. 'I'll have to think about that,' he said. 'The line between rewarding merit and fostering the cult of personality is painfully thin in these cases. As a matter of policy –' (Honey; it was honey flavoured with something. No wonder it was so elusive.) '– as a matter of policy,' he repeated, 'nowadays we prefer to put the accent on team effort and group achievement; and from what I gather, that would be entirely appropriate in this case.'

The colonel nodded. 'Of course,' he said. 'To a certain extent, that's precisely what we should be doing. But Sergeant Loredan has already become something of a legend in the army. If we don't recognise him officially, it may prove counterproductive to recognise the unit as a whole. The soldiers are very loyal to their own; that's what gives them their edge, of course.'

'Indeed.' The legate didn't frown, but he didn't much like what he was hearing. Nevertheless, it was a minor issue. 'Well,' he said, lifting the cup again, 'I don't suppose it'll hurt if we give this man his moment of glory. A laurel crown, I suggest, and a prominent place in the triumph, if he's going to be up to it. And then a promotion.'

The colonel acknowledged the suitability of the suggestion. A promotion meant a transfer, a transfer would take him away from the soldiers who'd chosen him as their immediate object of loyalty. 'Citizenship?' he asked. 'Or perhaps not. There are precedents, of course.'

'I shall have to refer that back to the provincial office,' the legate said. 'A precedent isn't the same thing as a rule, or even a custom of the service. Just because something's acknowledged to have happened once doesn't necessarily mean it has to happen again.'

The colonel didn't say anything, but he let the issue lie between them. The legate had his political masters, but he had an army to motivate. And after all, he had just taken Ap' Escatoy.

'Forgive me,' said the legate suddenly, 'but I really do have to know. Is it the honey?'

The colonel smiled. 'How extremely perceptive,' he said. 'Yes, indeed; it's quite rare, a speciality of this region. At least, it's not from here, they import it from away up in the north, but this is the only known outlet for it. It's the heather.'

'Heather,' the legate repeated, as if the colonel had suddenly started talking about sea-serpents.

'The bees feed on heather,' the colonel explained, 'and that's what gives the honey its distinctive flavour. On its own it's nothing special, but suitably blended, the effect is rather fine, don't you think?'

Heather honey, said the legate to himself, *whatever next?* It was almost worth a concession on the citizenship issue; but the provincial office wasn't that decadent. Not yet. 'Your sergeant,' he said. 'I'll tell you what I'll do. Probationary citizenship, conditional on length of service. I'd say that strikes the proper balance between recognition and incentive, don't you?'

The colonel smiled. 'Excellent,' he said. 'I'm sure it'll do wonders for morale.' He lifted the silver-gilt jug and refilled the legate's cup. 'It's very important, I've always found, to make sure victory doesn't get out of hand.'

The merchants of the Island reacted to the news of the fall of Ap' Escatoy, after three years of siege and attrition, with characteristic speed and decisiveness. They immediately raised the price of raisins (by a quarter a bushel), saffron (by six quarters an ounce), indigo, cinnamon and white lead. As a result, the markets steadied before they had a chance to go into freefall, and the base lending rate of the Shastel Bank actually ended the day up half a per cent. More people made money than lost it, and by close of trading it was safe to say that no lasting harm had been done.

'Still,' said Venart Auzeil, pouring himself another cup of strong wine, 'I don't mind admitting I was worried there for a while. We were dreadfully exposed. I suppose we should all be grateful it wasn't a lot worse.'

'It'll get worse,' muttered Eseutz Mesatges, wiping her lips on her wrist. The new look for lady merchants (basically the year before last's Warrior-Princess look, but with less gold and more leather) suited her very well, but there wasn't an obvious place for a handkerchief. 'There's absolutely no reason to believe they're going to stop there. Not unless somebody makes them,' she added firmly. 'They're a damned nuisance, and something's got to be done. And I don't know what you're grinning about, Hido. If the Imperial Army decides to go up the coast instead of down like everybody's assuming, you won't be able to give away those pepper concessions we're always hearing so much about.'

Venart frowned. 'That's not likely, though, is it? I mean, surely the whole object of the exercise is to secure their western frontier. If they go north instead of south, they'll be extending it, not consolidating.'

'Gods, Ven, you're so bloody naïve,' Eseutz said impatiently. 'Securing frontiers my arse; this is crude old-fashioned expansionism, as anybody with half a brain could have told you three years ago. No, we should have stopped them at Ap' Escatoy; dammit, we should have stopped them before that even, at Ap' Ecy or before they even crossed the border. The further they get the harder it's going to be, and that's just a plain fact.'

Hido Glaia yawned and helped himself to another handful of olives. 'If you'll just listen,' he said, 'you'll find I'm not disagreeing with you. I think they're worse than a pest, they're a serious danger, and thank the gods we live on an island. The comic part is you thinking we could do anything about it.' He opened his mouth and picked out an olive stone. 'Now possibly us, *and* Shastel, *and* Gorgas Loredan's merry band of cut-throats down in the Mesoge, *and* King Temrai's people – if anybody should be worried right now, it's them; if I was the provincial office, I know what'd be at the top of my shopping list – if all of us got together, pulled our fingers out, really got behind Ap' Seny and told them, that's it, no further—' He shrugged his broad shoulders. 'Well, it could go either way, depending on what other calls the provincial office's got on its resources right now (and that's something we just don't know, though we should, and it's a scandal we don't). But face facts, it ain't going to happen. No, the best thing we can do is start talking very sweetly to the provincials about non-aggression pacts and tariffs and possibly preferred-carrier status. They aren't savages, you know. If we could learn to love the plainspeople, we can get along just fine with these bastards.'

Venart's sister Vetriz, who'd been lying back on her couch pretending to be bored, sat up. 'You can't be serious about that, Hido,' she said. 'Us, get into bed with the plainspeople? After what they did to the City?'

Hido grinned. 'We trade with them. You trade with them. Even the Shastel Bank does business with them, and gods know, if anybody's got the right to bear a grudge, it's her.' He leaned forward and scratched the arch of his foot. 'Where is Athli, by the way? I thought she'd be here.'

Eseutz scowled. 'Oh, she's off being terribly high-powered somewhere. I don't know; she runs that office like she owns the whole damn bank.'

'Eseutz tried to get a loan to take up those spice options,' Hido explained, 'and Athli turned her down flat, bless her. I could have told you if you'd asked me,' he went on, treating Eseutz to a warm, patronising smile. 'Athli may dress like an Islander and talk like an Islander, she's got a better nose for a deal than most of us who were born and bred here, but when it comes to lending money, she's Perimadeian to her socks and always will be.'

Eseutz sniffed and reached across the table for the wine jug. 'It's all your fault for bringing her here in the first place,' she told Vetriz. 'Well, the hell with that. You can tell her I got my loan, and at only one per cent over base.'

'You had to put your ship up as security,' Hido pointed out. 'Definitely rather you than me. I think Athli was doing you a favour, personally. Who the hell's going to want to pay your prices for peppers and cinnamon once the provincial office starts dumping the stuff on the spot market at half what you're paying for it now?'

Eseutz growled and banged the jug down. 'If that's your attitude,' she said, 'you might as well start memorising the names of the Great bloody Kings right now, so you can reel them off to impress the provincial when he comes stomping in here with a garrison.'

Hido dipped his head. 'It might be a sensible precaution, at that,' he said. 'If we're going to have to do business with these people, as seems increasingly likely, it might be sensible to learn how to crawl to their officials.'

When the evening was over and their guests had gone home, Vetriz kicked off her shoes and poured herself the last of the wine. 'I can't figure those two out,' she said. 'Are they or aren't they?'

Her brother shrugged. 'Both,' he replied. 'Which is odd, I'll grant you. I mean, it's obvious what he sees in her but not the other way round. Not in a million years.'

Vetriz raised an eyebrow. 'Funny,' she said, 'I'd have said it was the other way round. Oh, well, I suppose that means they were made for each other after all. In which case, I can't help wondering why they spend so much of their time trying to do each other down in business.'

Venart yawned. 'Their way of expressing affection, I suppose,' he said. 'But what she was saying about the Empire, it makes sense, you know, in a way. Mind you, so does what Hido said. This Ap' Escatoy thing's really brought it home.'

'If you say so,' Vetriz replied, slowly getting up. 'I'm going to bed while I can still move.'

'All right.' Venart hesitated for a moment, then continued, 'When I was down at the Nails this afternoon, I did hear one thing about Ap' Escatoy.'

'Hm? Tell me in the morning.'

Venart shook his head. 'Really,' he said, 'I should have

mentioned it earlier, except of course it's just a rumour, and I haven't the faintest idea where it comes from or if there's anything to it. I was waiting to see if Hido or Eseutz had come across it too, but apparently not.'

Vetriz yawned. 'Oh, for pity's sake, Ven,' she said. 'Stop hamming it up and tell me.'

'All right.' Venart looked away slightly. 'What it is, someone was talking about the end of the siege, how it actually happened, and he said the man who finally broke through in the mines and brought down the wall was called Bardas Loredan.'

Vetriz didn't turn round. 'Really?' she said. 'That's interesting.'

'I thought you should know,' Venart said. 'Well, there it is. Like I said, there's absolutely no confirmation or anything like that, just a rumour.'

'Of course,' Vetriz replied. 'Well, I'm off to bed. Good night.'

After that snippet of information it was inevitable that her dreams should return to the mines – she knew every inch of them by now, so that her knees and the palms of her hands ached at the thought of them – and the darkness and the stale air and the smell of clay and herbs. Once again she was crawling blind towards the source of the noise, the indecipherable confusion of steel and voices; this time she hoped she'd be able to pick out one voice among them, but that was completely unrealistic. Perhaps what she'd learned explained why she had to keep coming back here, but nothing else made sense. It was just a dream where she crawled along tunnels in the dark, and sometimes the roof caved in on her and sometimes it didn't. Maybe she'd been right the first time, and it really was divine retribution for eating blue cheese just before going to sleep.

But this time she called out his name; though whether she was telling him she was coming to help him or asking to be rescued herself, she wasn't quite sure. All night she slithered and stomped and crawled her way through the galleries and spurs of her dream, sometimes having to squeeze past and crawl over men who'd been dead a long time, sometimes people she'd known all her life, sometimes people she recognised for the first time; but the noise never got any closer and the voices stayed confused. She woke up sweating, the bedclothes twisted round her, the pillow on the floor where she'd thrown it after thanking it for its forbearance.

When Temrai opened his eyes, the light appalled him.

He shook his head like a wet dog, as if trying to get the dream out of his mind. Beside him, Tilden grunted and turned over, pulling the covers off his toes. She could sleep through anything, even the stifled yell he'd woken up with. If Tilden dreamed strange and terrible dreams, they were of casseroles spoiled by overcooking, or long-awaited tapestries which, when they finally arrived, didn't go with the cushions after all. The thought made him smile, in spite of himself.

He sighed and sat up, carefully shifting his weight so as not to disturb her. In fact, the light was nothing more than a gentle smear of moonshine leaking through the smoke-hole; remarkable that it could have seemed so unbearably bright a moment ago.

Methodically, like a conscientious witness in front of the examining magistrate, he recalled the dream. He'd been in darkness, in some cave or tunnel underground; he'd been scrabbling frantically along, trying to get away from something, or someone, either the roof caving in or a man with a knife, and most of the time it had been both together. When his pursuer had caught up with him, and he'd felt a hand gathering his hair and pulling his head back to expose his throat to the cutting edge, he'd heard a voice thanking him, and another saying that the dead man was Sergeant Bardas Loredan, sacker of cities, bringer-down of walls, responsible for the deaths of thousands –

– Which was all wrong, of course. He, King Temrai the Great, was the sacker of cities and slayer of thousands; he was the one who'd brought down the walls of Perimadeia, after first burning to death all the thousands and hundreds of thousands of people trapped in there when he burst in. The wise and expensive Shastel doctor he'd sent for when the dreams he'd had since the fall of the City made him dangerously ill had told him that it was all perfectly natural, that it was hardly surprising that in his dreams he should put himself in the place of one of the people he'd burned to death; somehow, the wise and expensive doctor had left him with the impression that it was so normal as to be positively good for him, like drinking plenty of milk and taking regular exercise. He wondered what he'd have made of this new development; the caves, the man with the knife who was Bardas Loredan, the sacker of cities. He could work some of it out for himself; his guilt and self-loathing had made him identify himself with the most frightening and destructive man he'd ever encountered, so that in his mind he'd become Loredan, the ultimate degradation. No need to spend good money to be told that.

He yawned. Absolutely no chance of getting back to sleep; what he really wanted was company. Gently he slid off the bed, feeling with his toes for his soft felt shoes, pulled on his coat and crept out of the tent.

Who would be awake at this time of night? Well, the sentries, for a start (or else they were all in trouble) and the duty officer and the duty officer's friend – there was a specific military technical term, but he hadn't a clue what it was; basically, the job consisted of staying up all night playing draughts with the duty officer to keep him from falling asleep. Fairly soon the bakers would be up and about, starting off the next day's bread. Almost certainly, somewhere in the camp, there'd be a bunch of young fools who'd stayed up all night drinking, and here and there a few men unable to sleep for worrying about whether they were going to die in the battle tomorrow. Quite likely he wasn't the only man in twenty thousand who'd been turfed out of bed by a bad dream. A short walk through the streets of the camp would find him someone to talk to.

He yawned again. It was a warm night, with a smell of rain. To his surprise, he realised he was feeling hungry. What he really needed, in fact, wasn't human companionship or someone to pour out his troubles to. What he really needed was a couple of white-flour pancakes smothered in sour cream and honey, preferably with a sprinkling of redcurrants and nutmeg. For a king spontaneously accorded the epithet Great by a devotedly loyal nation, that oughtn't to be too much to ask.

He also had the advantage of inside knowledge. The best pancakes in the world, he happened to know, were made by Dondai the fletcher, a spry, toothless old man who spent his life pulling carefully selected feathers out of the wings of the increasingly resentful geese that formed the supplementary fletchings reserve. That was all he did. Someone else sorted the feathers into left side and right side; someone else again split them down the pith, trimmed them to shape and delivered them to the workers who actually served them to the arrowshafts with thin threads of waste sinew. When he wasn't pulling feathers, though, Dondai made an awesome pancake; and, being too old to need much sleep, there was a good chance he'd be awake right now.

Dondai's tent wasn't exactly hard to find, even in the middle of the night; all you had to do was follow the smell and sound of geese. Sure enough, at the entrance to the goose-pen there was a small fire, beside which a man sat, with a furious goose struggling in his large, capable hands. The man had his back to Temrai, and it was only after he'd tapped him on the shoulder and the man had turned round that he realised it wasn't the man he'd been looking for.

'Sorry,' he said. 'I was looking for Dondai.'

The man looked at him, frowning slightly.

'Dondai the fletcher,' Temrai repeated. 'Is he asleep?'

'You could say that,' the man replied. 'He died three days ago.'

'Oh.' For some reason Temrai was shocked, out of all proportion. True, he'd been eating Dondai's white-flour pancakes since he was a boy, but that was all the old man had meant to him, a sure hand with a pottery bowl and a flat iron pan. 'I'm so sorry.'

The man shrugged. 'He was eighty-four,' he replied. 'When people get that old, they tend to die. It's not as if it's unfair or anything. I'm his nephew, by the way, Dassascai. You were a friend of his, then?'

'An acquaintance,' Temrai replied. 'You haven't been in the army long, have you?'

'I'm not in the army,' Dassascai replied. 'Until recently, I had a stall in Ap' Escatoy market, selling fish. Lived there most of my life, in fact.'

'Really?' Temrai said. 'It must have been terrible, these last few years.'

Dassascai shook his head. 'Not really,' he said. 'It was a

port, remember, and the provincial office couldn't spare any ships. There were never any shortages, people were spending money; it was a good war as wars go.'

Temrai nodded slowly. 'So what happened to you?' he asked. 'I'd sort of gathered that not many people made it out alive.'

'That's quite right,' Dassascai said. 'Fortunately, I wasn't there when it happened; I was on my way here, to see my uncle like a good nephew and then on to the Island to buy salt cod. In fact, I left two days before it happened, so you can see I'm a very lucky boy. Except,' he added with a sour grin, 'that I never take my wife and family with me on business trips. Plus, there's the small matter of a lifetime's accumulated property, though you aren't really supposed to mention that in the same breath as family. But the truth is, I know which I miss more.'

Temrai sat down on the ground, keeping the fire between them. 'So what are you going to do? Follow in your uncle's footsteps?'

'Pulling wing-feathers out of live geese for the rest of my life? Hardly.' Dassascai stood up, a furiously struggling goose hanging upside down by its legs in one hand, a small bunch of feathers in the other. 'For one thing, goose down makes me sneeze. For another, they stink. I'm doing this now because if I don't work, I don't eat. But something else'll come along, and when it does I'll be on my way.'

'Fair enough,' Temrai said. 'Any idea what form this something might take? In my line of work I occasionally come across good opportunities that need good people; I could keep my eyes open for you.'

Dassascai looked at him through the flames. 'And your line of work is?'

'Administration, mostly,' Temrai replied. 'And I hang about at staff meetings. That sort of thing.'

'A man of power and influence,' Dassascai replied. 'Well, I'd better tell you what I'm good at. I can buy, and I can sell; I'm used to travelling, I can bargain, usually get a good deal. My mother used to say I've got an honest face. That's about it.'

Temrai smiled. 'You'd probably have made a good Perimadeian,' he said. 'Or an Islander. How did you come to be in Ap' Escatoy, anyhow?'

Dassascai made a sudden swoop and stood up again, cramping another struggling goose to his chest. 'I'm not sure,' he said, sitting down. 'When I was a kid I fell out with my father about something or other. He got angry, I walked away and kept going. Some time later I found myself in Ap' Escatoy, hiding behind a row of barrels with a basket of stolen crayfish. Next thing I knew, I'd sold the crayfish and bought some more at the wharf. After that it was all reassuringly boring for a while. I like life better when it's boring.'

Temrai rubbed the tip of his nose with his knuckle. 'Do you?' he said.

'You don't, obviously.'

'I'm very hard to bore,' Temrai answered. 'Nearly everything interests me. For instance, I'd find building up a fishmonger's business from scratch very interesting indeed.'

Dassascai shook his head. 'Don't be so sure,' he said. 'You stand behind a trestle in the market all day, wondering how the hell you're going to shift the stock before it starts to smell if nobody ever stops and buys anything. You do this for most of the day, even on days when you sell out. Your feet hurt. You stare at the faces of dead fish and they stare back at you. Ten years later, you rent a covered stall with a torn awning. Five years after that, you worry about how much money your wife's spending on carpets, and try and figure out how exactly the hired help's ripping you off without it showing up in the accounts. Five years after that –' he lifted his head and smiled '– some bastard saps the walls of your city and you get another job plucking geese. The boring bits were the best, no doubt about it.'

Temrai stood up. 'I think you may well be right,' he said. 'If I hear of anything really dull, I'll let you know.'

'Thanks,' Dassascai replied. 'I'd like that.'

When he got back to his tent, Temrai found Bossocai the engineer and Albocai the captain of the reserves waiting for him, sitting on little folding stools just outside the flap. 'Sorry,' he said, 'have you been waiting long?'

'No, not at all,' replied Albocai, who was a rotten liar.

'I've just been talking to a most interesting spy,' Temrai went on, pushing open the flap and waving them through into the tent. 'Keep your voices down, by the way, my wife's still asleep.'

'How do you know he was a spy?' Bossocai asked.

Temrai grinned. 'If he'd had SPY tattooed on his forehead it couldn't have been any plainer,' he replied. 'He was a nice man. I knew his uncle for years.'

Albocai frowned. 'Well,' he said, 'we'd better have him arrested. What's his name?'

'No need for that,' Temrai replied. 'It's not as if we've got any secrets worth stealing. In fact,' he continued, with a smile the other two couldn't understand, 'being a spy in our camp must be the most boring job on earth, so that's all right. I'm not sure who he's spying for, but my guess is that he's been sent by the provincial office. That's interesting, don't you think?'

'I think you're either wrong or taking this far too lightly,' Albocai said. 'Are you sure he's a spy?'

Temrai nodded. 'When a man passes himself off as the nephew of a man I've known all my life and who never had a brother or a sister, let alone a nephew, and sits there knowing perfectly well who I am while pretending he doesn't know me, and then, in a not-so-roundabout way, asks me to employ him as a spy, I draw the logical conclusion. That reminds me – Albocai, I want you to find out what happened to a man called Dondai—'

'The goose-plucker? He died.'

'Ah, right. Find out more about it, would you? If he was murdered, you can have your spy with my blessing, and the next time I see him I'll expect him to be in several pieces. Anyway, that's enough about that. What can I do for you?'

'Well,' said the engineer, and launched into a detailed technical enquiry about torsion-engine rope settings, a subject about which Temrai knew more than anybody else in the army; after he'd got his answer, Albocai chivvied him about finalising the order of battle for the reserve light infantry. When they'd both gone, Temrai looked at the bed and yawned; he felt sleepy, and it was far too late now to go to bed. He picked up his quiver, sat down on the clothespress and began whetting the blades of his arrowheads on a leather strop.

Back at the goose-pen, meanwhile, Dassascai the spy was plucking feathers and going over in his mind the first contact he'd made with the man he'd been sent to kill.

*

'Watch out,' the boy said. 'Go careful, or you'll—'

Too late. Gannadius tripped over the fallen branch and fell forwards into mud; nasty, thick mud under a thin layer of leaf-mould. He felt his legs sink in, right up to the knees, and he knew he wouldn't be able to free them but he tried anyway. All he succeeded in doing was to pull his foot out of his boot. The feel of the mud on his bare foot was disgusting.

(*Just a minute*, he thought.)

'Hang on,' the boy said behind him. 'Don't thrash about, you'll just make it worse.'

The boy grabbed him under the arms and lifted. He angled his other foot so as not to lose that boot as well.

(*Oh hell, I remember this. And I don't think I'm going to like . . .*)

'There you are,' the boy said. He could turn his head now; he was looking at a young man, no more than eighteen but enormously tall and broad across the shoulders, with a broad, stupid-looking face, wispy white-blond hair already beginning to recede, a small, flat nose, pale-blue eyes. 'You really should look where you're going,' he said. 'Come on, it's time we weren't here.'

Gannadius opened his mouth, but his voice didn't work. He stooped down and tugged at his boot till it came free. It was full of mud and water. The boy had started lumbering off through the undergrowth (*a dense forest overgrown with brambles and squelching wet underfoot; yes, definitely the same place*) and he had to hurry to keep up. By following the boy exactly and walking where he'd trampled a path, he was able to pick his way through the tangle.

'I don't like the look of this, Uncle Theudas,' the boy said; and a moment later, men appeared out of the mess of briars and bracken, stumbling and struggling, wallowing in the mud and ripping their coats and trousers on the thorns. It would've been hilariously funny to watch, but for the fact that in spite of their difficulties they were clearly set on killing him and the boy and, unlike the two of them, they were in armour and carrying weapons.

'Damn,' his nephew said, ducking under a wildly swishing halberd. He straightened up, took the halberd away from the man who'd been using it and smashed him in the face with the butt end of the shaft. Another attacker was struggling towards him, his boots so loaded with mud that he could only just waddle. He was holding a big pole-axe, but as he swung it, he caught the head in a clump of briars, and before he could get it free Theudas Junior stabbed him in the stomach with his newly acquired halberd; his opponent wobbled, let go of the pole-axe and waved his arms frantically for balance, then collapsed backwards, his feet now firmly stuck, just as Gannadius' had been, and lay helplessly on his back in the slimy mud, dying. 'Come *on*,' the boy said, leaning back and grabbing Gannadius' wrist while fending off a blow from a bill-hook with the halberd, gripped one-handed near the socket. 'Gods damn it, if you weren't my uncle I'd leave you behind.'

(*And that's all I can remember. Damn.*)

'I'm coming, I'm coming,' Gannadius panted. 'Wait for me, for pity's sake.'

'Oh, for—' Theudas Junior reached out over Gannadius' head to crush someone's skull with the halberd. 'I'm beginning to wish I'd stayed at home.'

There were four soldiers left; they were hanging back (for some unaccountable reason). 'Don't just stand there,' his nephew said irritably, 'get going. I'll hold them off.'

Yes, but go where? I'm lost. Gannadius dragged his heavy legs up out of the sticky mud and plunged forward, his head down. Behind him he could hear the crash of steel weapons. *Absolutely no point escaping from the soldiers if all I'm going to do is drown in the swamp.* He considered looking back, but decided not to; too depressing, probably. Not long afterwards he tripped over his feet and landed on his face in the mud. He stayed put, too exhausted even to try to stand up.

'Uncle.' Obviously that tone of voice ran in the family; he could remember his mother using it for the I-thought-I-told-you-to-pod-those-beans admonitory speeches. 'Uncle, you aren't helping. Get up, for gods' sakes.'

'I can't. Stuck.'

'All right.' Gannadius felt a hand attach itself to his wrist; then some dangerously powerful force was trying to pull his arm off his body, and making a pretty good job of it. Fortunately, the mud gave way before his sinews and tendons did, and another hand jerked him up on to his feet. 'Are you all right?'

'I'm fine,' Gannadius replied. 'Sorry.'

'Come on. Try to keep up.'

So much, Gannadius reflected bitterly, for blockade-running. So much for slipping unobtrusively through the line in the night and the fog, when they least expected it. Fine in theory, but the Imperial admiral's not a complete fool. If he keeps his ships close in on dark, foggy nights, it's for a reason, maybe something to do with the fact that anybody stupid enough to try to thread his way through the submerged rocks of the straits would be asking for trouble.

'Are they still following us?'

'No idea,' the boy replied. 'More fool them if they are. Watch your feet, it's a bit sticky.'

And now here he was, a man of his age, scrambling about in a swamp in enemy territory, with half the provincial's army after his blood. Anybody with half a brain would have stayed on the Island, if necessary got a job and settled down to wait until Shastel and the provincial office had resolved their differences and stopped playing soldiers all over the eastern seaboard.

'We'll stop here,' Theudas Junior said, 'give you a chance to catch your breath.'

'Thank you,' Gannadius replied, with feeling. 'Are you sure it's safe?'

'How the hell would I know? I've never been here before in my life.'

Gannadius rested his back against the trunk of a tree and slid down on to his backside. 'I know,' he said. 'But you seem to be quite at home doing this sort of thing.'

The boy shrugged. 'Not really,' he said. 'I'm just making it up as I go along.'

'Fine. And here I was, assuming this was all stuff you'd learned from Bardas Loredan.'

'Not really.' The boy smiled. 'We did get in some bother with some soldiers once, but we just hid till they went away.' He looked at the halberd in his hand, then put it down. 'I don't know, maybe I take after my father. You told me he's a pirate.'

'Was,' Gannadius said, 'not any more. He's a respectable freighter captain now.'

'I'll believe that when I see it,' the boy replied. 'Which reminds me. I don't suppose Director Zeuxis is going to be all that thrilled when we tell her we sank one of her ships.'

Gannadius couldn't help smiling, picturing the scene. 'It wasn't a very big one,' he replied. 'And besides, Athli's got so many of the wretched things these days, I don't suppose she'll miss one. And it wasn't us who ran the blasted thing on the rocks, it was that so-called captain of hers. I see us as very much the victims in all of this.'

The boy nodded, apparently reassured. 'So,' he said, 'now what do we do?'

Gannadius frowned. 'I thought you were the natural-born leader,' he said.

'Yes, but you're the wizard. Conjure up a magic carpet and get us out of here.'

'If only.' Gannadius sighed. 'Doesn't work like that.'

'Doesn't work at all if you ask me.'

'You're entitled to your opinion,' Gannadius said wearily. 'But no, you're quite right. I can't conjure up magic carpets or flatten the enemy with a fireball or turn them all into newts. A great pity, but there it is.'

The boy shrugged. 'All right then,' he said, 'we'll walk. It can't be that far to Ap' Amodi.'

'Actually,' Gannadius said, 'Ap' Amodi's in the other direction. I may not be a wizard, but I can read a map. Inasmuch as we're headed anywhere, we're heading straight for Ap' Escatoy, and I respectfully suggest we don't want to go there.'

'Ap' Escatoy,' the boy repeated. 'Isn't that where—?'

'Exactly. Like I said, not a place we really want to intrude on.'

The boy rubbed his chin with a muddy hand. 'But what if Bardas really is there? He'll look after us, I know he will. We'll be all right.'

Gannadius sighed. 'I wouldn't bank on it if I were you. Even if we were able to get to him before we were captured, or if we were able to get a message to him, there's no reason to believe he'd be able to do anything for us. There's no reason to believe he's an officer or anything.'

The boy gave him a rebellious stare. 'Bardas wouldn't let anything happen to us,' he said. 'Not if he knew we were in trouble.'

'Maybe not. But there's ever such a lot of ways we could die without his knowing a thing about it. I say we find a way of doubling back and heading up the coast, towards Ap' Amodi. Not too far up, mind, or we'll find ourselves in Perimadeia.'

The boy nodded. 'And you know the way, do you?'

Gannadius shook his head. 'I've got a vague mental picture of the map I looked at, and that's it. Don't ask me about distances, either. We could be a day away, or three weeks.'

'Oh.' The boy suddenly looked very young and frightened, something which Gannadius found extremely disconcerting. 'And there's nothing you can do? I mean, with your ... powers?'

Gannadius smiled. 'Nothing at all, sorry.'

'Not much good for anything, are they?'

'No, not really.'

The boy stood up. 'Well,' he said. 'If they were following us, they'd have caught us by now. Which way? In general terms,' he added.

Gannadius thought for a moment. 'In general terms,' he said, 'I'd say north-east, which ought to be over there. Unless there's a mountain or a river or something in the way. Cartography's not exactly a precise science in Shastel.'

The boy studied the undergrowth for a moment, then took a mighty swing at the dense brambles with the halberd. 'Oh, well,' he said, as he jerked the snagged blade loose again. 'Better make a start, I suppose.' He swung again, then gave up. 'Let's go back the way we came, see if we can pick up that path we were following.'

'All right,' Gannadius said. 'What if we run into more soldiers?'

'Then we're stuffed,' the boy replied. 'But there's no earthly way we're going to get through this. It'd take twenty men a week just to get as far as that tall tree over there.'

Gannadius sighed, and followed. *Alexius*, he thought, *where the hell are you when I need you? Can't you find me, tell me what to do?* But of course, it didn't work like that, as he knew perfectly well. He could speculate all he liked about why, three years earlier, he'd seen that short, rather ludicrous battle in the mud-patch in some sort of random, Principle-induced vision. The fact was that the Principle wasn't a tool, something you could use. It was something that happened to you, like bad luck or rain. He trudged forward, fitting his feet into the boy's deep footprints. *Too old for this. And at this rate, unlikely to get any older.*

'The path should be here somewhere.' The boy's voice, bouncing him out of his enclosed train of thought. 'We must have missed it.'

'Quite likely,' Gannadius replied miserably. 'It's getting too dark for this. I say we stop here and wait till morning.'

'All right.' The boy flopped down where he stood, dropping the halberd in the mud. 'I'm hungry,' he said.

'Tough. If you want, you can go and see if you can kill something. If there's anything to kill in this horrible swamp except soldiers, which I doubt.'

The boy shook his head. 'Haven't seen any sign of anything,' he replied.

'Then we'll just have to make do without, and try not to think about it.'

'All right.'

A few minutes later the boy was fast asleep. Gannadius closed his eyes, but it didn't do him any good, not for a long time. When at last he did fall asleep, he had the dream again, and that was worse.

Gannadius?

He was in the dream: burning thatch, falling timbers whipping up clouds of sparks as they crashed to the ground, smoke and confused shouts. 'Alexius?' he asked. 'What are you doing here?'

There he was, standing in front of him. *I don't know. I haven't been here for a long time. Where are you?*

'I was hoping you could tell me,' Gannadius replied. 'What can you see?'

Well, this, Alexius replied. *The Fall of Perimadeia. What did you want me to see?*

Gannadius frowned. 'My nephew and I are lost in a swamp somewhere between Ap' Escatoy and Ap' Amodi. I was hoping you could tell me what to do.'

Sorry. Alexius shrugged. *Did you say Ap' Escatoy? That's curious. That's where I keep going lately.*

'Fascinating. I look forward to reading your monograph on the subject. Can't you make an effort and see if you can find out where we are? It'd be a tremendous help, you know.'

I really wish I could help, but you know how it is. Just out of interest, what are you doing in a swamp in the disputed territories, anyway? Last I heard, you had a nice, comfortable job in Shastel.

Around him, Perimadeia continued to burn. Gannadius tried not to watch. 'I hope I still do,' he said, 'though if I don't get back there soon they'll assume I'm dead and give it to somebody else. No, I went to the Island to see my nephew.'

Your nephew – oh, yes, I remember. The boy Bardas Loredan rescued from the City and took with him to Scona. Now that's a curious thing, as well.

'Quite,' Gannadius said, with a hint of impatience. 'The idea was, Athli Zeuxis – you remember her?'

Of course. Bardas' clerk. She's a merchant on the Island now, isn't she?

'That's right. Anyway, she brought the boy with her to the Island when Bardas went through that bad patch a few years ago, around the time she got the Island franchise for the Shastel Bank. Well, she's done very well for herself since then, to the extent that she needs to open a corresponding office back at headquarters, on Shastel; and she thought it'd be a good idea all round if young Theudas—'

Your nephew.

'That's right. Named after me in fact—'

Your original name was Theudas?

'Yes. Theudas Morosin.'

Good gods We've known each other all these years and I never knew that. Sorry, please go on.

'Athli thought it'd be a good idea,' Gannadius continued patiently, 'if young Theudas spent some time in Shastel with her agent there, setting up the office, learning the trade, and spending some time with me, of course, since I'm practically his only living relative – apart from his father, of course, but he's disappeared again, and he never was any sort of father to the boy.'

It sounds like a splendid idea. What went wrong?

Gannadius sighed. 'It was just my luck,' he said. 'A day or so after we left the Island, Shastel picked a fight with the provincial office over some wretched little island or other – really, it's all to do with this Ap' Escatoy business; obviously Shastel is scared stiff about what's going to happen next – and now the provincial fleet's blockading the Straits of Escati. If we'd had any sense we'd have turned back and gone the long way round – they haven't closed that off, as far as I know – or at the very least we could have sat tight in Ap' Amodi until the sabres stopped rattling. But no, we had to be clever and run the blockade. And instead, we ran on to the rocks, and then we ran into a patrol, and here we are. In a swamp.'

I see. What rotten luck. I really do wish I could help.

'So do I,' Gannadius said. 'But you can't, so that's that. Anyway, how are you keeping? All well with you?'

The figure of Alexius (not really him, of course; not in any comprehensible sense, though of course he was there) shrugged its thin shoulders. *Not so bad.* A dying spearman staggered toward him; he stepped sideways to let him through. *I haven't been sleeping at all well, though. Bad dreams, you know.*

'You as well? This one?'

Not lately; in fact, not since the last time I saw you here. No, I fancy I've been dreaming the siege of Ap' Escatoy. The Loredan connection, I suppose, though I can't remember having seen him. Just a lot of very unpleasant dark tunnels, with the roof caving in and people fighting in the darkness. Now the siege is over, perhaps they'll stop.

'Let's hope so,' Gannadius said, trying to sound properly sympathetic. 'I'm glad to say I haven't—'

'Uncle?'

Gannadius opened his eyes. 'What? Oh, it's you.'

The boy looked at him. 'You were talking to somebody,' he said.

'Was I?' Gannadius looked vague. 'I must have been dreaming. Um, what was I saying?'

The boy smiled. 'I haven't the faintest idea,' he said. 'You were mumbling, and I think it was some other language. Do you do that a lot? Talk in your sleep, I mean.'

Gannadius frowned. 'I have no idea,' he said. 'You see, even if I do, I'm asleep and don't know I'm doing it.'

CHAPTER THREE

'So you're him, are you?' the clerk said, looking sideways along his nose. 'The hero.'

There was a scorpion on the window-ledge; a female, with her newly born young clinging to her back. Bardas counted nine of them. She skittered a few steps, stopped and froze, her pincers raised. The clerk either hadn't noticed or wasn't bothered.

'That's me,' Bardas said. 'At least, I'm Bardas Loredan, and I've been called a lot worse.'

The clerk raised an eyebrow. 'Well, now,' he said. 'A sense of humour, too. You'll get on all right with the prefect, he's got a sense of humour. At least,' he added, 'he makes jokes. More a producer than a consumer, if you take my meaning.'

Bardas nodded. 'Thank you,' he said.

The clerk dismissed the thanks with a small gesture of his long, elegant fingers. 'We've heard all about you,' he said. 'Of course, you're an interesting man.' He swatted at a fly without looking at it; got it, too. 'The prefect collects interesting men. He's a student of human nature.'

'It's an interesting thing to study,' Bardas said.

'So I'm told.' The scorpion set off again; but the clerk spotted her out of the corner of his eye, picked up a half-round ebony ruler from the folding desk in front of him, leaned across and dealt her a devastating smack with the flat side, crushing her and her nine children into a sticky, compacted mess. 'It's all right,' the clerk went on, flicking the remains off the ledge, 'they're not nearly as dangerous as people make out. Sure, if they sting you, chances are you'll swell up for a day or so, and it hurts dreadfully. But it's quite rare for anybody to die.'

'That's good to know,' Bardas said.

The clerk wiped the ruler against the wall-hanging and put it back on his desk. 'So you used to be a law-fencer,' he said. 'I've heard about that. You used to kill people to settle lawsuits.'

'That's right,' Bardas said.

'Remarkable. Well, I suppose there's something to be said for it, as a way of dealing with these things. Quicker than our way, probably fairer, undoubtedly less painful and gruelling for the participants. Not how I'd choose to earn a living, though.'

'It had its moments,' Bardas replied.

'Better than digging mines, I expect.'

'Most things are.'

'I believe you.' The clerk picked up a short, thin-bladed knife and started trimming a pen. 'You'll find the prefect is a pretty fair-minded sort of man; remarkably unprejudiced, really, for an army officer. You play straight with him and he'll play straight with you.'

'I'll definitely bear that in mind,' Bardas said.

Through the window came the scent of some strong, sweet flower – a pepper-vine, at a guess; he'd noticed that the walls of the prefecture were covered in them. There was also a lingering smell of perfume, the sticks they burned here to mask out the other strong, sweet smells. A bird of some description squawked on the parapet above the window.

'Of course, most of the senior officers—' The clerk never got to finish his sentence, because the door opened and a man in uniform (dark-brown gambeson, steel gorget, dress dummy pauldrons, vambraces and cops) walked past without looking at either of them. 'He'll see you now,' the clerk said, and turned his attention to the papers on his desk. Bardas got up and walked into the office.

The prefect was a big man, even by the standard of the Sons of Heaven; darker than most of those Bardas had come across at Ap' Escatoy, which suggested he was from the inner provinces, a man of consequence. His head was bald and his beard was cropped short and close. The top joint of his left little finger was missing.

'Bardas Loredan,' he said.

Bardas nodded.

'Sit down, please.' The prefect studied him for a moment, then nodded towards the empty chair. 'Presumably you have a certificate from your commanding officer at Ap' Escatoy.'

Bardas pulled the little brass cylinder out from his sleeve and handed it over. Carefully the prefect popped off the caps and poked the curl of paper out with the tip of his mutilated finger.

'Please bear with me,' he said as he unrolled it, and as he read it his face was a study in concentration.

'A fascinating career,' he said at last. 'You were second in command of Maxen's army.'

Baras nodded.

'Remarkable,' the prefect said. 'And then your years as a law-fencer – a most intriguing occupation – followed by your brief service as colonel-general of Perimadeia.' He looked up. 'I've read about it, of course,' he said. 'A fine defence, under the circumstances. And the final assault really only made possible by treachery, so hardly your fault.'

'Thank you,' Bardas said.

'And after that,' the prefect went on, 'a somewhat shadowy role in the war between the Shastel Order and Scona; well, we won't go into that, it was a most unusual sequence of events by all accounts.' He paused, but Bardas didn't say anything, so he continued, 'After which you enlisted as a private soldier with the provincial office and spent – let's see – three years, give or take a week, in the saps at Ap' Escatoy, a most distinguished tour of duty by any standards.' He looked at Bardas again, with no perceptable expression. 'Very much the stuff of legends,' he said.

'It didn't seem that way at the time,' Bardas said.

The prefect considered for a moment, then laughed. 'No, of course not. Now then, what else have we got here? Ah, yes, your brother Gorgas; the same Gorgas Loredan who staged the military coup in the Mesoge. Clearly soldiering runs in the family. Another remarkable career, by all accounts. And very shrewd, strategically speaking. The importance of the Mesoge as a potential theatre of confrontation has been sorely underestimated, in my opinion.'

Bardas thought for a moment. 'That's Gorgas for you,'

he said. 'Though my sister's the smart one in our family.'

The prefect smiled again. 'Do you really think so?' he said. 'To build up a thriving business and then lose it so quickly, over such a trifling series of incidents? Well, of course I can't claim to know all the facts.' Again he paused, then continued, 'All in all,' he said, 'an impressive résumé for a sergeant of engineers. I confess, I'm curious as to how you came to join the provincial office, a man with your talents and experience. I'd have thought you'd have found something rather more challenging.'

'Well, you know how it is,' Bardas said. 'Wars seem to follow me about, whenever I get myself settled. So I thought this time I'd go and find one, before it found me.'

The prefect looked at him as if he hadn't quite understood. 'An interesting perspective,' he said. 'In any event, your service in the siege of Ap' Escatoy certainly merits a tangible reward, and the provincial office knows the importance of looking after its own. It ought to be possible to find a situation that will prove rewarding to you and which makes rather better use of your talents than the mines.' He glanced back at the paper in front of him. 'I see you have practical experience in manufacturing,' he said.

'I used to make bows,' Bardas replied.

'You were good at it?'

'Fairly good,' Bardas said. 'A lot depends on getting the right materials.'

The prefect frowned, then nodded. 'Quite right,' he said. 'Our procurement office takes particular care to ensure that all our specifications are properly met. And of course,' he went on, 'we're equally thorough when it comes to quality control. Which is why the proof house is such an important part of our manufacturing procedure.'

'Proof house,' Bardas repeated. 'I'm sorry, I don't know what that means.'

For some reason, that seemed to amuse the prefect. 'There's no reason why you should,' he said. 'It's a rather specialised department. Essentially, the proof house is where we test the armour we issue to our soldiers. It's a subdivision of the district armoury at Ap' Calick, although we test samples from provinces all over the western Empire.' The prefect drummed his fingers on the desktop in a quick, orderly rhythm. 'There's a vacancy for a deputy inspector at Ap' Calick. The post is equivalent in rank to sergeant-of-fifty, so it would represent a significant promotion; obviously it's not a combat assignment, but I venture to suggest that after such a protracted tour of front-line duty, the change would not be unwelcome. Mostly, though, the combination of proven administrative skills and considerable first-hand combat experience that your record suggests make you a thoroughly logical choice for this duty. Provided,' the prefect added, with a smile, 'it meets with your approval.'

Bardas looked up. 'Oh, absolutely,' he said. 'Anything that doesn't involve killing people down dark tunnels will do me just fine. Thank you.'

The prefect looked at him, his head slightly on one side, with the air of a man reluctantly giving up on an insoluble problem. 'My pleasure,' he said. 'If you'd care to call back tomorrow, any time after midday, my clerk should have your certificate and transit documents ready. You can use the post to get there; not that there's any immediate hurry, but it can be an awkward journey by conventional means.' The prefect stood up, indicating that the interview was over. Bardas followed suit. 'Good luck, Sergeant Loredan. I'm sure you'll do an excellent job in Ap' Calick.'

'I'll do my best,' Bardas replied. He opened the door, then hesitated. 'Sorry,' he said, 'just one quick question. How do you go about testing armour?'

The prefect spread his hands. 'I really don't know,' he said. 'I assume by simulating the sort of strain and damage it's likely to undergo in actual combat.'

Bardas nodded. 'Bashing it with swords,' he said. 'That sort of thing. Should be fun. Thank you.' He closed the door behind him before the prefect could say anything else.

Of course, Bardas knew all about the post. Everyone in the Empire had come across it at some time, usually in the context of scurrying out of its way. The post-horses, as everybody knew, stopped for nothing; they were explicitly allowed to ride down anybody who couldn't get out of the road quickly enough, and the post-riders seemed to delight in taking every opportunity they could to exercise this privilege.

'Three stops a day to change horses,' the master courier told him cheerfully, 'and two more at night; we take our food and water with us, and if you want a pee, you do it over the side of the coach. This all the stuff you're taking?'

Bardas nodded. 'Just the kitbag,' he said.

'No armour?'

'Sapper,' Bardas explained. 'We never bothered with it in the mines.'

The courier shrugged and signalled to the outriders to mount up. 'Fair enough,' he said. 'Just for once there's a bit of space on the coach; nothing much going up the line today. You can sit on the box with me, or lie down in the back if you can find room; your choice.'

Bardas climbed up, stepping on the horizontal spoke of the front wheel as he'd seen the courier do. 'I'll ride up front to start with,' he said, 'it'll give me a chance to admire the scenery.'

The courier laughed. 'You're welcome,' he said. 'Hope you like rocks, 'cos that's all you'll see till we're past Tollambec.'

The coach was a wonderful piece of work; wide and low at the front, enormous back wheels with thick iron tyres fitted front and back with sheaves of steel springs the size and thickness of crossbow limbs to float the chassis off the axles. 'Corners a treat,' the courier told him. 'Next best thing to impossible to turn it over, unless you're really trying hard. Built to last, too,' he added, giving the side of the box a meaty slap with the side of his hand. 'Well, they need to be, the amount of work they do. Bloodstream of the Empire, they call us.'

Bardas nodded. In the back he could see jars of wine with fancy designs on the seals, bales of various expensive-looking fabrics, some pieces of furniture vaguely recognisable under the cloth they were wrapped in, one barrel of civilian-made arrows and three or four sealed wooden chests. 'Essential supplies, that sort of thing,' he said. 'I can see the need for a system like this.'

Once they'd cleared the camp, the courier whipped the horses up into a swift canter, which soon made the coach too noisy and uncomfortable for anything except sitting still and quiet. The scenery was, as promised, an endless array of rock faces. Just occasionally the coach would hurtle past groups of men and donkeys ostentatiously pulled in to passing places; they looked away and tried to flatten themelves against the rock as the coach went by, like sappers laid up in the mines.

'You're the hero, right?' the courier shouted.

'Yes, I suppose so.'

'What? I can't hear you.'

'Yes,' Bardas yelled. 'I suppose so.'

'Ah, well. Each to his own, I suppose,' the courier roared, and the rocks bounced his voice backwards and forwards like children playing catch. 'Wouldn't suit me, all that crawling about in the dark.'

'Nor me.'

'What?'

'I said it didn't suit me either,' Bardas shouted. 'Not my idea of fun.'

The courier pulled a face. 'You're not supposed to say that,' he roared. 'You're a bloody hero.'

Bardas didn't have the energy to rise to that. 'I think I'll lie down in the back,' he shouted.

'Suit yourself.'

It was delicate work, edging down from the box and crawling across the cargo until he found a man-sized niche he could crawl into. Amazingly, in spite of the noise and the jarring movement of the coach, it wasn't long before he was fast asleep.

When he woke up, the courier was standing over him, grinning. 'Wake up,' he said. 'First change. I'd stretch your legs if I were you; long haul, the next stage.'

Bardas grunted and tried to stand up, something that proved to be harder than he'd expected. By the time he'd got back enough feeling in his legs to scramble down off the coach, the stagekeepers had already outspanned the old horses and were spanning in the replacements, identical-looking animals with nondescript dun coats, their manes and tails docked short. Each one was branded with the provincial office's mark and a serial number, large enough to be legible from some way off.

The courier was splashing his head and shoulders with

water from a leather bucket. 'You want a wet?' he called out. 'Wash some of the dust off.'

Bardas looked down; he hadn't noticed how dusty and grimy he was. 'All right,' he replied, and the courier dipped the bucket in a water-butt and passed it to him. The water was slightly cloudy with disturbed sediment.

'Time to go,' the courier told him, then turned round to shout a message back to one of the outriders; Bardas didn't catch what he was saying. The stagekeepers had finished changing the horses and were crawling about under the coach, painting grease on the axles from large clay tubs and checking the cotter pins. 'You'd better climb up,' the courier went on. 'We leave as soon as they've done, whether you're on board or not.'

Bardas hauled himself up over the box. He was only just in position in his valley in the cargo when the coach started to move.

As the courier had promised, the next stage seemed to go on for ever. Imperial roads were famous for being straight and, where humanly possible, flat; the provincial office's engineers thought nothing of hacking a high-sided cutting through a substantial hill for no other reason, or so it seemed, than to prove that they could. Bardas considered the cargo piled up around him; jars of dates, figs and cherries preserved in honey, footstools and hat-boxes, book-boxes (a lot of those) and brass tubes that held rolled-up silk paintings; it seemed a lot of effort to go to, slicing the middle out of a mountain just so that a prefect could have fresh grapes and the latest anthology of occasional verse; but the Empire could do that sort of thing, so why not? It wasn't as if they were particularly attractive hills to begin with.

At the third stage of the day, the coach took on another passenger. 'Shift over,' she said. Bardas looked at her, and shifted.

'I brought my own food,' she went on, burrowing into a huge wickerwork basket that only just fitted into the gap between the piled and roped-down boxes. 'I've been on this run too often to poison myself with government rations.' She emerged, like a rat from a hole in the wall, with a squat, flat packet made of vine leaves. Honey oozed out between the folds. 'Of course, you need a digestion like a compost heap to keep anything down on a post coach,' she went on. 'All that bumping and lurching on a full stomach; it's far worse than being on a ship, I can tell you.'

She was small, grey-haired and dark-eyed, bundled up in a thick woollen coat with a high fur collar, secured at the neck with a huge, vicious-looking brooch. Bardas, who was already down to his shirt because of the heat, couldn't help staring; she wasn't sweating at all.

'You think I'm overdressed,' she said without looking up, as her small, bent fingers picked at the string of her packet. 'You wait till you've spent a couple of nights on the road, you'll wish you'd brought something a bit warmer than that. Military?' Bardas nodded. 'Thought so. Well, it doesn't take a great analytical mind to come up with that one, why else would – well, one of your lot be on a government coach? Not that it bothers me, needless to say. There just isn't any room for those kinds of attitudes now, not if we're really serious about being one Empire and all that sort of thing. I dare say in twenty years or so's time, people just won't think about it any more. And quite right too, if you ask me. It's like this whole Sons and Daughters of Heaven thing; we don't believe it any more, you don't believe it (or if you do, you're a sight more gullible than I gave you credit for) so really, where's the point? People are people, and that's all there is to it.' She stripped away the vine leaves to reveal a golden-brown slab of cake, dripping liquid honey and scattering crumbs of nut. 'There really isn't a polite way to eat this stuff,' she said, 'so the hell with it. Here goes.' She opened her mouth as wide as it would go, stuffed about a quarter of the cake into it, and bit hard. 'Not bad,' she went on, as soon as her mouth was clear enough of cake to let her speak, 'though I do say so myself. Properly speaking, that was meant for my son in Daic, but what he wasn't expecting he'll never miss. Don't talk much, do you?'

'I prefer to listen,' Bardas replied.

'Very sensible,' the woman said. 'One mouth and two ears, like my mother used to tell us when we were children. How far are you going?'

'Sammyra,' Bardas said. 'Apparently I change coaches there for Ap' Calick.'

The woman was chewing. 'Ap' Calick,' she said. 'I used to call there when I was younger. The manager of the government brickyard there was a very good customer. Perfume,' she added, by way of explanation. 'Twenty years in the trade, either side of when the children were small; took over from my father when I was seventeen, bought out both my brothers by the time I was twenty. I'm hoping my youngest girl will take over from me in due course; she's very good on the production side, but she doesn't like the travelling. With me, of course, it's the other way round, so we work very well together. My son hates me still being on the road, of course; I expect he thinks it makes him look bad, but who the hell cares? Still, I won't deny it's a great help having a son in the roads commission. For one thing, I can scrounge a lift on the post whenever I need to, and that's a real advantage. I'm not sure I'd be quite so keen on the road if I was having to slog across this lot on a mule. Have you been to Sammyra before?'

Bardas shook his head. 'Just a name to me,' he said.

The woman sniffed. 'It's nothing much, really; been going downhill ever since they lost the indigo trade. The baths are worth a visit if you get time, but I wouldn't bother too much with the market. You can get exactly the same stuff in Tollambec at about half the price.'

Bardas nodded. 'I'll bear that in mind,' he said.

'Now the best thing about Tollambec,' the woman went on, 'is the fish stew. How they ever got a taste for fish living that far from the sea heaven only knows, but the plain fact is I'd rather have salt fish Tollambec style than the fresh stuff any day, and I don't care who knows it. Do they eat much fish where you come from?'

'I used to live in Perimadeia,' Bardas replied.

'Perimadeia,' the woman repeated. 'So, plenty of cod and mackerel, some tuna, eels, of course ...'

Bardas shrugged. 'I don't know, I'm afraid. We used just to call it fish. It was grey and came in a slice of bread.'

The woman sighed. 'My son's just the same,' she said. 'Wouldn't know good food if it bit him. That's such a shame; I mean, so much of life's about eating and drinking. If you don't take an interest, it's such a waste.'

'I suppose so.'

51

Just as the woman had said, as soon as it got dark, it got cold. Fortunately, there was a spare oxhide folded up in a corner of the cart, and Loredan crawled into it. The outriders stopped and lit lanterns, then carried on at not much less than the pace they'd set during the day.

'One advantage of a straight, flat road,' the woman said. 'Doesn't really matter if you can't see where you're going.'

The government rations the woman had spoken so slightingly of turned out to consist of a long, flat coarse barley loaf flavoured with garlic and dill, some strong hard cheese and an onion. 'They say you can tell someone who's been on the post from several yards away,' the woman commented, 'just from the smell. You've got to admit, it's a pretty obnoxious combination.'

Bardas smiled, though of course she couldn't see. 'I like the smell of garlic,' he said.

'Do you? That's – well, each to his own, I suppose. Mind you, in my line of business, you pretty well live and die by your sense of smell.'

'That must be strange,' Bardas said.

'Oh, it is. I find it remarkable how most people just take it for granted. It's definitely the laziest of the five senses, though that's nothing a little training won't cure. My name's Iasbar, by the way.'

'Bardas Loredan.'

'Loredan, Loredan – I've heard that name, you know. Isn't there a bank with that name somewhere in the – out your way somewhere?'

'I believe so.'

'Ah, well, that explains it. Does everybody have two names where you come from?'

'It's quite common,' Bardas replied. 'Does everybody where you come from have just one?'

The woman laughed. 'Oh, it's a bit more complicated than that,' she said. 'Let me see, now. If I was a man I'd be Iasbar Hulyan Ap' Daic – Iasbar for me, Hulyan for my father, Ap' Daic for where my mother was born. Because I'm a woman, I'm plain Iasbar Ap' Cander; the same idea, but Ap' Cander because that's where my husband was born. If I'd never been married, I'd still be Hulyan Iasbar Ap' Escatoy, which was where I was born. Don't worry if it sounds confusing,' she added, 'it takes foreigners a lifetime to get used to the nuances.'

'You were born in Ap' Escatoy?' Bardas asked.

'Yes indeed, while my father still had his shop there. I kept meaning to go back, you know, but now of course it's too late. It was a strange place to grow up in.'

'Really,' Bardas said.

'Oh, yes. They had an absolutely incredible thick soup made with lentils and sour cream; we used to go down to the market with one of those big curvy seashells and get it filled up for a half-quarter, then we'd sit on the steps of the market hall and drink it while it was hot. There was something about it, some special secret ingredient, and I've never been able to figure out what it was. Of course, if only I'd thought to ask my mother I'd know what it was, but it never occurred to me. Well it doesn't, does it, when you're that age?'

Bardas fell asleep while she was still talking. When he woke up, she wasn't there any more and the coach was just pulling away from the first stage of the day. She'd left him half a slice of the sticky cake, still in its vine-leaf wrapping; but the jolting of the carrriage had knocked it down on to the floor, and it was covered in dust.

'Temrai?'

He came back in a hurry and opened his eyes. 'What?'

'You were dreaming.'

'I know.' He sat up. 'You woke me up just to tell me I was dreaming?'

His wife looked at him. 'It can't have been a very nice dream,' she said. 'You were wriggling about and making sort of whimpering noises.'

Temrai yawned. 'It's about time I was getting up,' he said. 'Kurrai and the others'll be here soon, and I always feel such a fool climbing into that lot with people watching.'

Tilden giggled. 'It's quite a performance,' she said. 'I don't know why you bother, really.'

'It's to keep me from getting killed,' Temrai replied, frowning. 'I don't wear armour for fun, you know.' He swung his legs off the bed and hopped across the floor of the tent to the armour-stand.

'People never used to bother with it,' Tilden pointed out,

'not before we came here. Not all that paraphernalia, anyway.'

Temrai sighed. He loathed wearing the stuff at the best of times; it made his movements slow and awkward, and that made him feel stupid. He was convinced he made more mistakes these days just because he was buried under all that metalwork. 'I don't know about you,' he said, pulling on the padded shirt that formed the first layer of his cocoon, 'but anything that increases my chances of not getting killed is just fine with me. Now, are you going to help me, or do I have to do it all by myself?'

'All right,' Tilden said. 'You know, I'd find it easier to take it seriously if it didn't all have such silly names.'

Temrai smiled. 'Now there I agree with you,' he said. 'I'm still not sure I know what all the bits are called, either. According to the man who sold it to me, this thing's a besegew, but everybody else calls it a gorget. Is there a difference, I ask myself, and if so, what is it?'

'I imagine a besegew's more expensive,' Tilden said. 'And why not call it a collar? That's all it is, really, it's just that it's made of metal. Here, hold still. Why they can't put bigger buckles on these straps I just don't know.'

The besegew – or gorget – made it quite hard to breathe. 'It wouldn't kill them,' Tilden observed, 'to put longer straps on.' Temrai could have pointed out that if it wasn't a tight fit there wasn't much point in wearing it, but decided not to. Eventually he'd be able to take the wretched thing off again, and that would be nice.

Kurrai, the chief of staff, and his fresh-faced young men arrived just as he was putting on his boots ('But you mustn't call them that, they're sabatons'). Kurrai wore his armour as if he never wore anything else; which, Temrai reflected, might well be true.

'They're still there,' Kurrai said. 'As far as we can tell, they haven't moved at all.'

Temrai frowned. 'I still reckon it's too good to be true,' he said.

Kurrai shrugged. 'I guess they're just refreshingly stupid,' he replied. 'Honestly, if it is all a wonderfully cunning ruse, I can't for the life of me see what it is. They're in the middle of a plain with no cover, nowhere they can have hidden a couple of squadrons of heavy cavalry or anything else that's going to put us off our stroke. As far as I can see, they're just sitting there waiting for us to come and get them.' He sat down on a chair, which creaked ominously. 'There's such a thing as being too cautious, you know.'

Temrai shrugged. 'Maybe,' he said. 'I've been trying to figure out what I'd do if I was in their shoes, and I admit, I couldn't come up with anything clever. Mind you, I hope I'd never have got myself into that position in the first place.'

'They believe in personal bravery,' Kurrai said, scratching his nose, 'and the justice of their cause. We'll slaughter them, you'll see.'

Temrai smiled weakly. Somehow, he found it hard to get excited about slaughtering a small band of people who had, until a few years ago, been as much a part of the plains federation as he was. They'd been there with him when he burned Perimadeia; they'd helped build the torsion engines, lost their share of friends and family when Bardas Loredan poured liquid fire on them from the walls. He still didn't really understand why they'd chosen to turn against him. For all he knew, they were right about whatever it was, and he was wrong. Like so many other things, it had changed once they'd burned the city and settled down on the comfortable pastures opposite the ruins; so it was his fault, when all was said and done. Somehow, that made the prospect of an easy victory rather unpleasant. The bit about the just cause bothered him a little, too; he'd won a great and famous victory a few years ago, and at the time he'd believed he had a just cause. Since then, he'd come to wonder if there was such a thing, and if so, if it had ever been known to prevail.

'Don't let's get cocky,' he said, standing up and feeling the weight of his armour across his shoulders. 'The worst words a general can ever utter are, *How the hell did that ever happen?*'

Kurrai smiled dutifully. 'I don't know,' he said. 'Between over-cautious and cocky, how do people ever manage to win battles?'

'They don't, usually,' Temrai replied. 'As often as not, it comes down to who loses first.'

*

Dear Uncle, she'd written. It had taken her a lot of time and effort, gripping the pen between the stumps of her fingers, and the writing looked like a small child's school exercise.

Dear Uncle. The thought made her smile. Mostly, she wrote to her uncle to annoy her mother, who wanted her to have nothing to do with any of her uncles; not the three recently come into a desperate hand-to-mouth kind of power in that place she'd never been to but which even her mother sometimes absent-mindedly referred to as home; certainly not to her other uncle, the one she was still determined to kill one day, when she got around to it. The fact remained: the nearest she'd been to feeling at home anywhere had been her uncle Gorgas' house on Scona, in that short space of time before everything had inevitably torn itself apart, with a little indirect help from herself.

Dear Uncle. She looked out of the small, narrow window towards the sea. It was getting harder to find messengers to carry her letters, what with her mother's attitude, various wars and the general stagnation of trade between the Empire and its prospective victims. While he'd lived, the truffle man had been the most reliable courier; but presumably he was one of the however-many-it-was thousand who'd died in the fall of Ap' Escatoy, when her other uncle, the bad one, tunnelled under the walls like a mole and pulled them down on top of him. Nobody seemed to want to take over the truffle run between the Mesoge and Ap' Bermidan; the great lords of the provincial office were getting their truffles from somewhere else now, cheaper, bigger and fresher. And without the truffle business, why the hell would anybody want to go from here to there and back again?

Dear Uncle, nothing much has happened here since I wrote to you last. Could she really be bothered to go to all the trouble it would take her to write that? She thought about it, and decided yes, worth it just for that worried sideways look her mother gave her every time she suspected her of having sent a letter (*What the hell could be in those letters? The little bitch must be spying on me, sending him secrets; but what* could they possibly be? I hadn't realised I had any secrets he might possibly want, but obviously I do or she wouldn't be writing him letters ...). And besides, it wasn't as if she had anything at all else to do.

Years and years ago, when she was a little girl, an old man who was a friend of the family (her other family, not this one; this family didn't have friends) had told her stories about beautiful princesses who were locked up in towers by their wicked stepmothers. Inevitably, as night follows day, there was always a handsome young hero who tricked or slashed his way into the tower and rescued the princess; that was the order of things, and it explained why the princesses stayed calm and stayed put, knowing that sooner or later the prince would turn up and everything would work out as it was supposed to. When she was a little girl, she'd thought to herself how jolly it would be to be one of those princesses, with her own tower (nobody to scowl at her and tell her to get it tidied) and the reassuring knowledge that her own designated prince was probably already on his way.

Stories like that had all died on the same day her bad uncle killed her other uncle, her father's brother, the man she'd been betrothed to since she was a little girl listening to fairy stories. She'd given them no more thought after that, until suddenly she'd found herself in this tower, a tower of her very own overlooking the dark-blue sea at Ap' Bermidan. Of course, properly speaking she wasn't a princess, nothing like; her mother was just another merchant, albeit a very rich one (or she assumed she was rich; she had no way of knowing, cooped up here like a man buried alive). The situation was close enough, however, to put her in mind of the stories, and a make-believe wish that had come horribly true. Perhaps that was why it was so important to write to her uncle; if anybody was going to come to rescue her, it would probably have to be him; and, since she was a realist, she wasn't holding her breath. Looked at dispassionately, the main motivation was annoying her mother. Anything else was just serendipity.

It was also stretching the point a bit to call Uncle Gorgas a prince. True, he fitted the description in some respects; he was the ruler of the country he lived in (though technically that made him the king, not a prince); but there were a lot of other, nastier words to describe what her uncle Gorgas was. Or what he was to everybody else. Normal people.

She heard footsteps on the stairs, and swore under her breath. With her mutilated hand it was painfully difficult to get the writing stuff out of sight in time; one slip and she'd drop the ink-horn, leaving a tell-tale splodge on the floor, or a pen would fall to the the ground – there were any number of ways she could slip up and give herself away, finally give her mother the excuse she'd been looking for to tighten the chain; no more visitors, no more merchants and traders allowed to come to see her – which would mean no more paper, pens and ink, no more books. She'd just managed to get the paper out of the way under her bed when someone knocked at the door.

'Just a moment,' she called out. Well, it wasn't her mother, at any rate. Mother never knocked before barging into a room. 'All right, come in.'

But it was just the porter; the big, dozy-looking man who sat between her and the rest of the world, when he wasn't cleaning her shoes or making her soup. He was harmless enough, too stupid to recognise an ink-horn or a penknife if he saw one. 'What is it?' she said.

'Man here to see you,' the porter replied; and over his shoulder she could see one of Them, the Children of Heaven, in a fancy dark-blue travelling cloak with a gold pin that told you his rank if you understood about such things.

'All right,' she said.

The porter got out of the way, and her visitor came in. He was old; long and thin, as many of Them were, with grizzled white hair sticking to his head like bits of cobweb. He looked round without saying anything, then sat down without being asked.

'Iseutz Loredan?' he said.

She nodded. 'And you are?'

'Colonel Abrain. I have a commission from the prefect of Ap' Escatoy.'

He didn't seem in any hurry to let her see it, and she couldn't be bothered to ask. 'You've come a long way, then. What does the prefect want from me?' she asked.

Her visitor looked at her again, as if she were a mathematical problem, a complicated diagram in algebra. 'You have an uncle,' he said, 'Bardas Loredan. You've repeatedly threatened to kill him. The prefect would like to know more about him.'

She frowned. 'I don't suppose you're going to tell me why,' she said.

'I'll tell you if you want me to,' the man replied. 'I assume you know about the fall of Ap' Escatoy, and the part your uncle played in it.'

'Of course. Everybody does.' She thought for a moment. 'Let's see,' she said. 'Uncle Bardas is now a war hero, and you don't want me to kill him after all. Am I warm?'

She watched him puzzle out the unfamiliar idiom. 'The prefect doesn't see you as a threat, if that's what you mean,' he replied. 'And although it's true that Sergeant Loredan did distinguish himself—'

'*Sergeant* Loredan.'

He looked annoyed. 'That is his current rank in the provincial office, yes,' he said. 'I suppose you're used to thinking of him as Colonel Loredan. Well, now, in the provincial office, rank is earned, not carried forward from an individual's last employment.'

'That sounds reasonable enough,' Iseutz said. 'So, what do you want to know about *Sergeant* Loredan?'

He shifted in his chair in such a way as to suggest that he had a bad leg; it could just as easily be arthritis as an honourable war-wound. 'The prefect would like to find out as much as he can about the relationship between your uncle Bardas Loredan and the barbarian King of Perimadeia, Temrai. He understands that their mutual antagonism dates back to before the Fall of the City. He is also interested in finding out about Bardas Loredan's service with General Maxen; it seems likely that his experience in fighting the plains tribes might be helpful to the Empire in the event of war between themselves and us.'

Iseutz shrugged her bony shoulders. 'Why ask me?' she said. 'If you think we've had long, cosy evenings of niece-and-uncle chats by the fireside with him telling me all about his interesting life, you've got the wrong family. I didn't even find out he was my uncle until after he did this.' She held up her ruined hand; the Son of Heaven looked at it and frowned a little. 'Yes, I know he fought against the tribes when he was in Maxen's army; Maxen did a lot of really terrible things to them, which was why Temrai hated us so much. And yes, I would think Uncle Bardas probably knows more about killing the tribes than anybody else in the whole world. But you knew that before you came here.'

The Son of Heaven nodded. 'And you have nothing further to offer by way of insights or additional data?'

'Sorry.'

The small, precise gesture of his hands suggested that he forgave her. 'I understand that you are on bad terms with your uncle Bardas,' he said. 'But I gather your relationship with your uncle Gorgas is rather better. You write to him regularly.'

'Yes. How did you know that?'

He indicated her hand with a tiny dip of his head. 'Writing is obviously difficult for you, but you make the effort. Clearly you're quite close to your uncle Gorgas.'

She smiled. Most people looked away when she smiled at them, but not Colonel Abrain. 'In a way,' she said. 'I'm the only family he's got, really, since my mother betrayed him and Uncle Bardas murdered his son. Oh, there's his other two brothers in the Mesoge, of course, I was forgetting them. They're very easy to forget.'

'Tell me about him,' said Colonel Abrain.

Iseutz shook her head. 'I don't think I will,' she said. 'Not unless you tell me why you're interested in him.'

'I find your entire family fascinating,' the Son of Heaven replied impassively. 'I'm a student of human nature.'

'Really.'

'It's something of a passion among my people.' He steepled his fingers. 'More to the point, he has approached us with a view to forming an alliance against King Temrai. Obviously we would wish to interview as many of his close associates as possible before reaching a decision on this proposal.'

Iseutz thought for a moment. 'Well,' she said, 'I don't suppose anything I can tell you about him can do him any harm. Tell you what; you tell me what you already know, and I'll fill in the gaps.'

The colonel smiled thinly. 'As you wish,' he said. 'We know

that when he was a young man, he prostituted his sister and then murdered his father and brother-in-law when they found out what he had done. He also tried to kill his sister, but failed. In the same incident, he murdered your father; isn't that so?'

Iseutz nodded. 'That's right,' she said. 'What a lot of things you people know.'

'We pride ourselves on attention to detail. After committing these murders, he escaped from the Mesoge and spent a while as a pirate and soldier of fortune, until his sister – your mother – established the Bank on Scona; he joined her there and worked for her as head of the Bank's security forces; in which capacity, we understand, he opened the gates of Perimadeia to the forces of King Temrai, allowing the city to be taken and burned to the ground. Three years ago, matters between the Bank and the Shastel Order came to a head; Gorgas Loredan conducted a brilliant defence, considering the disparity in size and quality between the armies of the Order and the forces available to the Bank, but in spite of two remarkable victories in pitched battle, the Order prevailed and Scona was captured. Your uncle deserted the island immediately before its fall, taking with him the remnants of the Scona army; he sailed directly to the Mesoge and seized power there. After a few initial incidents, his regime has apparently become stable, although reliable information from the Mesoge has become rather difficult to obtain.' He unfolded his hands and laid them palm down on his knees. 'Is that summary basically accurate?'

'I'm impressed,' Iseutz said. 'You people are good at this, I can tell. Well, you didn't mention that the reason why he gave up and let Shastel walk right into Scona was because just before he was due to fight their third army – he'd annihilated the other two, as you know – Uncle Bardas killed his son, and my mother skipped out and left him; what with one thing and another, he couldn't see any point in prolonging the agony.'

The colonel nodded. 'Thank you,' he said. 'Now, what else can you tell me about him?'

Iseutz thought for a long while. 'I suppose you could say he's an uneasy mix of idealism and pragmatism,' she said.

'The idealism bit is this notion of family that he's got buried deep down inside; he's convinced that he believes in family as the most important thing. I don't think that's actually the case; what I mean is, I think he's fooling himself when he thinks that, but it's what he sincerely believes. I think.' She paused for a moment, her lips pressed to the back of her hand. 'The pragmatism bit's the other side of the coin. His philosophy is, what's done is done, no point crying over spilt milk, the thing is to make the best of the situation you find yourself in and not to let the past get in the way of the future.' She grinned. 'I guess you could say he takes that particular philosophy to extremes rather. But he's a pretty extreme person.'

The Son of Heaven stirred a little in his chair; cramp, possibly. 'Why do you think he seized power in the Mesoge?'

'Lots of reasons, probably.' Iseutz sighed and looked out of the window. 'He saw a good opportunity and took it. The Mesoge was his home; no other way he could ever go back after what he'd done, except at the head of an army, so he took an army. And I expect if you asked him, he'd say he did it for the good of his people. Probably believes it, too, somewhere inside him. That's another talent he's got - he can believe almost anything if he has to.'

'Why would he want to make war on the tribes? He helped them destroy Perimadeia.'

'Ah.' Iseutz nodded. 'That's a good one, but if you'd been paying attention you'd have figured it out for yourself. Betraying the City was one of the things he did that made Bardas hate him; so he reckons that if he fights the plains-people and kills Temrai, that'll make it up to Bardas. At the same time, it'll please you people, and if he's serious about being a king in the Mesoge, he's going to need friends - like you, for instance. But the political stuff is only the trimmings. Bardas is the reason. Bardas motivates most of what Gorgas does, when he isn't under orders from my mother.'

Colonel Abrain frowned. 'Explain,' he said.

'The two people he hurt most,' Iseutz replied. 'Well, three, really: my mother, Bardas and me. In that order. So, he's been trying to make it up to us ever since; he made it possible for my mother to play God Almighty in Scona, he's going to kill Temrai for Bardas, and – well, he'll get around to me later.' She yawned and stretched like a cat. 'Really, if you are a student of human nature, he's a real collector's item. He's either an evil man who spends his life trying to do right by his own family, or a good man who did one very evil thing. Or both. Like I said, he feels the greatest obligation to my mother, because she was the one he hurt most (apart from the ones he killed, of course, but they're dead, so he can't help them). But Bardas is the one he really cares about.'

'Even though Bardas killed his son?'

Iseutz shrugged. 'Uncle Gorgas has an infinite capacity for forgiveness. Which argues against the evil-man hypothesis, just as the killing-and-betraying-cities thing argues against the basically-good theory. We're a complicated lot, us Loredans. Almost but not quite more trouble than we're worth.'

The Son of Heaven stood up, slowly because of his bad leg. 'Thank you,' he said. 'You've been most helpful.'

'Oh, that's all right.' Iseutz stayed where she was. 'But do me a favour, if you would. See if you can't find some way of making life difficult for my mother – currency regulations, customs, import licences, something along those lines. She hates things like that.'

'I'm sorry,' the colonel said austerely. 'The provincial office doesn't work like that.'

'Really? Forget it, then. Goodbye.'

When he'd gone, Iseutz sat on the floor, her back against the wall, her arms tight around her knees, thinking about the recurring dream she had in which the Patriarch Alexius told her that, if she wanted, he could take a sharp knife and cut off the Loredan half of her, leaving only the Hedin half behind. Invariably she woke up just before he started to cut. She'd never been able to work out whether it was a nightmare or not.

'Who was that?'

She looked up. 'The rat-catcher,' she said. 'I sent for him. Place is swarming with rats.'

Her mother sighed impatiently. 'He was from the provincial office,' she said. 'What did he want?'

'If you're going to answer your own questions, what do you need me for?'

Niessa Loredan walked over to where her daughter was sitting and kicked her hard in the ribs, enough to wind her. 'Who was he,' she asked again, 'and what did he want?'

Iseutz looked up. 'He wanted to know if you like mushrooms,' she said. 'I said yes.'

Niessa kicked her again, rather harder, and pulled her foot away before Iseutz could grab hold of it. 'I haven't got time to bother with you now,' she said. 'I'll send Morz up to take away your books and your lamp, and don't think you'll get anything to eat.'

'Good. I'm sick of soup.'

Niessa bent down. 'Iseutz,' she said, 'don't be tiresome. What did he want?'

Iseutz sighed. 'He wanted to know about Uncle Bardas and Uncle Gorgas. I told him - well, all the stuff I knew he knew already. That's all I could tell him. I don't know any more.'

'Well.' Niessa straightened up. 'You told him what he wanted, then? We have to co-operate with these people; we depend on their goodwill.'

'I told him everything I know.'

Niessa nodded. 'And you weren't rude or difficult? Well, of course you were. But you didn't attack him or anything?'

'Mother!' Iseutz said angrily. 'For pity's sake. You make me sound like I'm mad or something. What do you think I did, chase him round the room on all fours trying to bite his ankles?'

Niessa walked to the door and opened it. 'We have to co-operate,' she said. 'It hasn't been easy since we moved here; I've had to work very hard. I won't have you spoiling it for me. Understood?'

'Perfectly.'

That sideways look again - *fear, she's worried. I love it when she's worried.* 'Iseutz,' Niessa said, 'one day, everything I've worked for, everything I've built, will come to you. You're my daughter, the only family I've got left. Why must you always be trying to *spoil* things for me?'

Iseutz laughed. 'You're going to die and leave me all your

money? Fat chance. If I thought you were mortal, I'd have bitten your throat out in the night.'

Niessa closed her eyes, then opened them again. 'You come out with things like that, and then you wonder why I keep you here. I know you don't mean it, you're just trying to shock me. You should have grown out of that when you were ten.'

CHAPTER FOUR

There wasn't much wrong with Sammyra that an earthquake wouldn't fix, except for the smell. The post coach had broken a wheel on its way down the mountains, which meant it was late getting in; the connecting coach to Ap' Calick was long gone. There would be another one through in the late afternoon. Until then, Bardas was at liberty to wander about the town and absorb its unique ambience.

'Thanks,' he said. 'Can't I just sit here and wait?'

The posthouse keeper looked at him. 'No,' she said.

'Oh.' He looked up the street and down again. 'Can I have a drink of water, please?'

'There's a well just down the road,' the keeper replied. 'There, on the left, by the burned-out mill.'

Bardas frowned. 'No offence,' he said, 'but is the water here all right to drink?'

'Well, we drink it.'

'Thanks,' Bardas said, 'but I'll see if I can find some milk or something.'

There were plenty of inns and taverns in Sammyra. There were the uptown inns, cut into the rock of Citadel Hill or amplified out of natural caves; most of them had signs by the door saying 'No Drovers, Pedlars or Soldiers', with a couple of large men leaning in the doorway to explain the message to any drovers, pedlars or soldiers who weren't able to read. There were the middle-town taverns, an awning giving shade to a scattering of old men sitting on cushions on the ground, with a dark doorway behind. There were the downtown booze-wagons, drawn up in a circle on the edge of the horse-fair, with a hatch in the side into which money went and from which small earthenware jugs

66

emerged. Bardas chose one of the middle-town awnings at random; it doubled as a knife-grinder's booth and doctor's surgery, and there was an old woman sitting at the back singing with her eyes shut, though Bardas didn't know enough about Sammyran poetry and music to tell whether she was an attraction or a pest. The song was something to do with eagles, vultures and the return of spring, and a lot of it appeared to be mumbling. Bardas didn't care for it very much. He sat down in the opposite corner; the old men stopped what they were doing, looked round to stare at him, then turned away. A very short, bald man with a long beard suddenly appeared behind his left shoulder and asked him what he wanted to drink.

'I don't know,' Bardas replied. 'What've you got?'

The old man frowned. '*Echin*,' he said, as if answering a question about the colour of the sky. 'Do you want some or not?'

Bardas nodded. 'Go on, then,' he said. 'How much?'

'Don't ask me,' the man said. 'You can have a cup, a flask or a jug. You choose.'

'Sorry,' Bardas said. 'I meant, how much money?'

'What? Oh. Half-quarter a jug.'

'I'll have a jug, then.'

The old man went away and came back a moment later, sidestepping the shower of sparks from the grinder's wheel and the patch of blood left behind by the doctor's last patient. 'Here,' he said, presenting Bardas with the jug and a tiny wooden cup. Bardas gave him his money, half-filled the cup and sniffed it. By now he was too thirsty to care.

Echin turned out to be hot, thin, sweet and black; an infusion of herbs in boiling water, flavoured with honey, cinnamon and a little nutmeg and used to dilute a heavy raw spirit that'd undoubtedly be fatal if drunk on its own. It was dangerously good for the thirst. Bardas nibbled down a cupful of the stuff and settled down to wait till his head stopped spinning. The old woman stopped singing. Nobody moved or said anything. She started again. It sounded like the same song, but Bardas couldn't be sure about that.

Some time later a large party of men appeared and sat down in a big circle in the middle of the tent. They were noisy and cheerful, ranging in age from seventeen to about sixty; not Sons of Heaven but not dissimilar either; clean-shaven, with very long hair plaited into elaborate pigtails. They wore very thin white shirts that reached down to their knees, and their feet were bare. Presumably, Bardas guessed, they were drovers; almost as bad as pedlars and soldiers, to judge by the notices uptown, though none of them appeared to be carrying any sort of weapon. They drank their *echin* sparingly from a huge brass cauldron in the middle of the circle, paid no attention to the old woman's singing and struck Bardas as reasonably harmless.

Some time after that (time passed slowly here, but steadily) a group of five soldiers wandered in. They weren't Sons of Heaven either; it was hard to say where they were from, but they wore the light-grey-faded-to-brown gambesons that went under standard-issue infantry armour and issue boots, brightly polished belts and the little woollen three-pointed caps that formed the padding for the infantry helmet. Four of them were wearing their swords; the fifth, the corporal of this half-platoon, had a square-ended falchion tucked under his belt. They walked straight across the circle of drovers, who got out of their way, and went into the back room. The old woman stopped singing, opened her eyes, got up and limped quickly away.

There was an old man sitting next to Bardas with his mouth open, a very small cup of *echin* going cold on the ground in front of him. Bardas leaned over. 'Trouble?' he asked.

The old man shrugged. 'Soldiers,' he replied.

'Ah.'

Inside, something smashed, followed by the sound of laughter. The drovers looked up, then carried on with their conversation. One or two of the other customers got up and walked away without looking round.

The soldiers came out, holding big jugs of something that wasn't *echin*, and stood looking down at the drovers. The conversation in the circle died again. The old man Bardas had spoken to left just as the man who'd brought Bardas his drink came out with a tragic expression on his face. Everything seemed to suggest that the tavern was a good place not to be for a while. Bardas would have left, but he hadn't finished his drink.

Thus saith the Prophet: do not start fights in bars. Do not interfere in other people's fights in bars. As religions went, it had a lot going for it, and Bardas had always kept the faith. When the fight started, he did as he usually did on these occasions; sat very still and watched carefully out of the corner of his field of vision, taking care not to catch the eye of any of the combatants. Taken purely as an entertainment, it had its merits; the drovers had the numbers, while the soldiers had the weapons, together with a rather more robust attitude as to what constituted a legitimate degree of force. When one of the drovers went down and didn't get up, the fight stopped; instead of a confused pool of action, there was a tableau of fifteen men standing quite still and looking very embarrassed. Nobody spoke for a while; then the corporal (who'd done the actual killing) looked round and said, 'What?'

One of the soldiers was looking at Bardas; at the dull brown of the tarnished bronze flashes on his collar, four for a master-sergeant. Actually, it wasn't even Bardas' own coat; it was something he'd picked up in the mines (nearly new, one careless owner). But everybody seemed to have noticed the little metal clips now. Bardas wondered what they all found so interesting.

The little man who'd brought the wine was standing over him now. 'Well?' he said. 'What are you going to do about it?'

Bardas looked up. 'Me?' he said.

'Yes, you. You're a sergeant. What are you going to do?'

Of course, he's right. I'd clean forgotten. 'I'm not sure,' he replied. 'What would you suggest?'

The little man looked at him as if he was mad. 'Arrest them, of course. Arrest them and send them to the prefect. They just killed someone.'

Thus saith the Prophet: when asked to arrest five armed men after a bar fight, leave at once. 'All right,' Bardas said, getting slowly to his feet. He looked at the soldiers for a moment without saying anything, then directed his attention to the corporal. 'Names,' he said.

The soldiers told him their names, which he didn't catch;

they were long, foreign and complicated. 'Unit,' he said. The corporal replied that they were the Something regiment of foot, such-and-such a company, such-and-such a platoon.

'All right,' Bardas said. 'Who's your commanding officer?'

The corporal gave him a look of misery and fear, then shouted and came at him, the falchion raised. Before he knew what he was doing, Bardas had caught him by the elbow with his left hand and driven his knife into the hollow at the base of the corporal's throat with his right. He hadn't remembered the knife getting into his hand, or being on his belt in the first place; but after three years in the mines, his knife was like his hands or his feet, it wasn't something you ever had to remember.

He watched the corporal die, then let his body slump to the ground. Nobody else moved. A great place for still people, Sammyra.

'I'll ask you again,' Bardas heard himself say. 'Who's your commanding officer?'

One of the soldiers said a name; Bardas didn't catch it. 'You,' he said to the little innkeeper, 'run to the prefecture and fetch the guard. The rest of you, get lost.' A moment later, he was alone with the four surviving soldiers and the two dead men. It was easy to tell them apart; the soldiers were the ones standing up.

After what seemed like a very long time the guard arrived, led by an unmistakable Son of Heaven in a gilded helmet with a very tall feather on top.

'Bar fight?' he said. Bardas nodded. 'And this one –' he prodded the dead corporal with his toe. '– this one took a swing at you?'

'That's right,' Bardas said.

The guard commander sighed. His collar made him out to be an ordinary sergeant, so Bardas outranked him. 'Well, then,' he said. 'What's your name?'

'Bardas Loredan.'

The guard commander frowned. 'I know who you are,' he said. 'You're the hero, right?'

Gannadius?

Gannadius pulled a face. 'Not now,' he said.

Gannadius? You're very faint, I can hardly—

'Oh, for pity's sake.' Gannadius opened his eyes. Alexius was standing over him, looking worried. 'No offence,' he said, 'but would you mind pushing off for a bit? I'm dying, and I'd hate to miss anything.'

What? Oh. Oh, yes, you are, aren't you. My dear fellow, I am most terribly sorry. How did it happen?

Gannadius shrugged. 'Oh, little things, really. I think it started with a fever and went on from there.' He paused for a moment. 'Am I dying?' he asked. 'Really?'

Alexius looked thoughtful. *Well, I'm not a doctor or anything, but—*

'I'm dying.'

Yes.

'Oh.' Gannadius tried to make himself relax. 'How can you tell?'

Well – just trust me.

Gannadius tried closing his eyes again, but it didn't seem to make any difference. He waited. Nothing much seemed to be happening. 'So,' he said, 'what's next? Any hints?'

No offence, Gannadius, but I wouldn't know. If it's any consolation, it's a perfectly natural thing. He could see Alexius ransacking his brains for a valid but not too alarming analogy. *Like childbirth* was, apparently, the best he could come up with.

'Really?' he couldn't resist saying. 'Seems to me there's at least one major difference.'

You know what I mean. Does it hurt?

'It did,' Gannadius said. 'Like hell. But not so much now. In fact, it doesn't hurt at all.'

I see.

'That's bad, is it?'

On the contrary, it's good. I mean, you wouldn't want it to hurt, would you?

'That's not what I ...' Gannadius sighed. 'So now what? Any idea what the drill is? Am I meant to do anything, or do I just lie here and wait?'

You tell me.

'Right; and then you can write it up as a nice prize-winning paper for the next big conference you go to. Sorry,' Gannadius added, 'that was small of me.'

I quite understand. In your position . . .

'I don't think I'm going to like this, Alexius,' Gannadius interrupted. 'In fact, if it's all the same to you I think I'd like to stop now and have another go some other time. I have the feeling that if I try to do it now I'll make a mess of it, and since it's something you only ever get to do once . . .'

Ah. But how do we know that?

Gannadius scowled. 'Oh, for gods' sakes,' he said. 'This is hardly the time to discuss bad doctrine.'

Sorry. I was only trying to be upbeat.

'Well, it's not helping. Alexius, can't you do something?'

I . . . What did you have in mind?

'I don't know,' Gannadius snapped. 'You're the bloody wizard, you think of something.'

It doesn't work like that. You know that as well as I do.

'Yes, but—' Somehow, he didn't have the strength to get angry; he didn't even have the strength to be properly frightened. Not being able to feel frightened – now that was frightening. 'I was going to say,' he went on, 'that you're the Patriarch of Perimadeia, there must be something you know that the rest of us don't, some special secret that only the Patriarchs are allowed in on. But that's not true, is it?'

I'm afraid not.

'I knew that, really. It's just that when you're – well, like I am now, you'd rather go with the hope than the logic, just in case. No hard feelings, old friend.'

Thank you. How are you feeling?

'Strange,' Gannadius admitted. 'It really isn't the slightest bit like I thought it'd be.'

Oh? In what way?

Gannadius thought for a moment. 'I don't know,' he said. 'I was expecting – well, theatre, I guess. Melodrama, even. Mystical stuff: bright lights, swirling mists, shadowy figures draped in shining white. Either that or pain and fear. But it isn't like that at—'

His eyes opened; really opened this time.

'It's all right.' A woman was standing over him. 'It's all right.'

'Alexius?' Gannadius tried to move his head to look round,

but couldn't. He didn't know whether that was bad or good. He'd been able to move quite freely before.

'He's coming out of it,' the woman was saying to someone he couldn't see. 'Whatever that stuff was, it worked.'

'That's all right, then,' said a man's voice behind the woman's shoulder. 'Usually a dose like that'd kill you. I'm glad it works.'

The woman looked unhappy. 'You mean you'd never tried it before?'

'Like I said, it's usually a deadly poison,' the unseen man said. 'Been wanting to try it out for years, but this is the first one we've had where it really didn't matter – I mean, properly speaking he was dead already, so what the hell?'

Gannadius realised what was so odd about the woman. Well, not odd; unexpected. She was a plainswoman – eyes, skin colour, bone structure. He felt an instinctive wave of panic – *Help, I'm in the hands of the enemy!* The woman saw him shudder and try to move, and smiled.

'It's all right,' she said. 'You're going to be all right.'

So you keep saying. '. . .' he said, then realised he'd forgotten the rest.

She was a round-faced, stocky woman in her late forties, with short grey hair, bright black eyes and a prominent double chin. 'You've been very sick,' she went on, 'but the doctor's given you something that'll sort you out, just you wait and see.'

Gannadius felt annoyed at that; *bloody doctor's been using me to try out his lethal new remedies*, he wanted to say. *Dangerous clown, he shouldn't be allowed near a patient.* 'Thank you,' he croaked. 'Where . . . ?'

The woman smiled. 'This is Blancharber,' she said. 'Have you heard of it?'

Gannadius thought for a moment. 'No,' he said.

'Ah. Well, it's a little village about half a day's walk inland from Ap' Amodi'. She pronounced the name as one word, not two. 'Roughly the same distance from Ap' Amodi and the old City.'

'Where . . . ?'

'Perimadeia. You're in King Temrai's country,' she added. 'You're safe now.'

*

Eseutz Mesatges, free trader of the Island, to her sister in commerce Athli Zeuxis; greetings.

This is a horrible place, and the people are loathsome. On the other hand, they surely do have a lot of feathers.

Which is where you come in. I'm now in a position to supply, FOB the *Market Forces*, sixty-seven standard volume barrels of premium white goose-wing feathers, all graded by wing polarity – to be precise, thirty-five barrels of right-wing, thirty-two of left-wing – suitable for fletching all standard-spine military arrows, at the ridiculously low price of twelve quarters (City) per barrel – well, almost. There's just one trivial shard of detail standing between me and this fantastic opportunity. I'm as broke as a dropped pot.

But I wouldn't be, beloved sister in commerce, if you supplied me with a letter of credit drawn on that bank of yours in the paltry sum of 268 quarters (City); then I'd have my feathers, you'd have your usual one-third cut, these people here would have an incentive to set up a regular, ongoing deal and everybody would be happy. Except the geese, of course; but I don't think they were planning on going anywhere.

Now then: if the *Squirrel* gets in as per schedule, you should be reading this on the sixth – plenty of time for you to scribble out the magic words and send the letter round to the master of the *King of Beasts*, which I happen to know is expected here on the seventeenth (so presumably it's not leaving the Island till the eighth at the very earliest). Provided you do your stuff with all due diligence, I can close the deal on or before the twentieth and be home on the *Market Forces*, with feathers, by Remembrance. As simple as that.

Well, that's it, really; but there's still plenty of space left on this sheet of high-quality paper, so I might as well fill it with something.

Let's see; what sort of thing do you want to know? Of course, you've actually been here, as I recall – didn't you come here with your friend the fencer, before the coup and all? I don't suppose it was much better then; worse, probably. Say what you like about the military regime and Butcher Gorgas, they give every impression of being good for business. If they made or grew anything at all worth selling (except, of course, for these utterly magnificent feathers you're getting a vicarious slice of), there'd be some nice opportunities here in the import/export line, since there's basically zip local competition; no merchant venturers, no producers' cartels, no aristocratic or royal monopolies, and even the government tariff is only two and a half per cent. It's what comes of having a government run by amateurs, I suppose.

It makes me wonder, though. Why did Gorgas Loredan go to all the trouble of taking the place over if he's not going to do anything with it now he's got it? After all, it's such an extreme thing to do, steal a country from the people who live there. Usually, of course, it's pretty obvious – someone wants the iron ore, or the warm-water port, or the osier beds, or the growing timber or the saffron plantations, or to stop someone else having it, or just so as to be able to draw a nice straight line down the map, or to have the complete set of islands. And when it isn't something blindingly obvious like that, you can bet it's a steady source of revenue – poll taxes and sales taxes and import taxes and road taxes and spice taxes and wedding taxes and taxes on every third heifer and scutage and heriot and tithes in ordinary. There's always a *reason* – except in this case, and it's bothering me to bits trying to figure it out. For one thing, a cool, calculating type like Gorgas Loredan doesn't do anything without a reason. What's he up to, Athli? You know about this sort of thing. Won't you let me in on the secret?

Anyway; 268 City quarters on the *King of Beasts* and that'll be the feather trade sewn up. Best investment you'll make this year, and that's a promise.

Yours in friendship and fair dealing,
ESEUTZ

'To summarise—' he was saying.

Alexius stopped and blinked, as if he'd just emerged into the light after a long time in pitch darkness. *Oh, no, not again*, he thought.

Old age, just old age; a tendency to wake up, as it were, to find that he was in the middle of doing or saying something but couldn't remember how he'd got there or what he'd said. A dreadful handicap for a lecturer, suddenly finding yourself standing in front of a thousand reverently silent young faces, without a clue as to what you were saying or what you're going to say next.

(Before that, he'd been in a dream, a daydream about a long, dark tunnel full of strange noises and smells, where people were killing each other by feel and instinct. Why he had to keep going there he didn't know, and no amount of speculating would make it any easier to stop.)

'To summarise,' he could hear himself saying, 'if we truly understand the nature of the Principle, we cannot fail to have our doubts about the existence of death. It becomes a shadowy, almost mythical thing, something we used to believe in when we were very young and impressionable, when we still believed in dragons and the Remembrance Fairy. If we truly understand the Principle, and the way its operation affects both the world about us and our perceptions of the world, we are led to the inescapable conclusion that death as we are taught to understand it is, quite simply, impossible. It can't happen. It's against all the rules of nature. If we choose, in spite of all the scientific evidence, to persist in believing in it – well, that must be a matter for faith and conscience, which have no place in scientific argument. But if we confine ourselves to those things which are susceptible to proof – and what is science, what indeed are learning and understanding and knowledge but those things which can be put to proof? – if we restrict ourselves to those things which have passed proof and not been found wanting, we must put aside this notion of death as, at best, not proven and not capable of being proved, with the overwhelming probability that there's no such thing. The Principle, on the other hand—'

(*'How is he? Can I talk to him?'*)

'The Principle,' Alexius heard himself continue, 'is proven, beyond any shadow of a doubt. The Principle, in fact, is proof; it's the very process by which we test those things that we do not already know, when we wish to come to the truth of a matter. And, if anything of what I've told you today has made an impression on you, if you even begin to understand—'

(*You can try. But I don't think you'll get much sense out of him. Later on, maybe; he's better in the afternoons.*')

Alexius opened his eyes. 'Athli?' he said.

Athli smiled at him. 'Hello, Alexius,' she said. 'How are you feeling today?'

'Fine.' Slowly and painfully, Alexius sat up. 'I was dreaming,' he said.

'Nice dream?'

He shook his head. 'Not really,' he replied. 'More of a nightmare, really. It was the one where I'm standing in front of a crowded lecture hall and I've forgotten the lecture.' He smiled. 'The good doctor Ereq would like me to believe it's because I will insist on eating cheese, in spite of his dire warnings. I'm inclined to look for a rather more metaphysical explanation,' he went on. 'But only so as to be able to carry on eating cheese.' He lowered his voice. 'It's the only food in this place they don't boil to a mush.'

Athli frowned. 'I don't think you can boil cheese,' she said, 'it'd melt.'

Doctor Ereq gave his patient a ferocious medical scowl and left, whispering in Athli's ear as he went. When the door was shut behind him, Alexius asked, 'What was all that about?'

'I'm to call him if you get upset and start talking nonsense. Oh, and I'm not to overtire you.'

Alexius shrugged. 'It's a bit hard if I've got to give up eating cheese *and* talking nonsense. I've been doing both ever since I was a little boy, and I'm far too old now to change.'

Athli perched on the edge of the bed. Outside, the rain was tapping against the shutters. 'You're not too old to fish for compliments, though, are you? We both know that talking nonsense isn't a fault of yours. Talking, yes; but you generally make sense, at least when I'm around. You don't like Doctor Ereq, do you?'

'No,' Alexius admitted. 'Which is wrong of me, I know; he's an excellent fellow, wonderfully good at his job, and when I think of how much all this must be costing you—'

'Oh, don't start,' Athli said. 'And besides, I write it all down to expenses in the accounts, so really it isn't costing *me* anything.'

Alexius looked intruiged. 'Expenses?'

'Oh, yes. You're employed by the Bank as a technical consultant; didn't I tell you? Well, you are. Valued member of the team.'

'Really?' Alexius raised an eyebrow. 'Am I any good at it?'

Athli waggled her hands in an equivocal gesture. 'I've come across worse,' she said. 'Seriously, though,' she went on, frowning a little, 'you shouldn't kid about with the doctors. They haven't got senses of humour like normal people do, and they'll assume you've gone funny in the head. Doctor Ereq's convinced already.'

'Oh, him.' Alexius pulled a face, like a little boy. 'What it was, I tried to explain to him about the Principle and being able to talk to people who aren't necessarily there. He wasn't listening, of course; he'd made his mind up I was off my head as soon as I mentioned the subject. You'd think a Shastel man'd know better.'

Athli grinned. 'Between you and me,' she said, 'I don't think he's from Shastel at all. Oh, he says he studied there, but I asked and nobody remembers him. He's colonial Shastel all right; I think he's third or fourth generation Colleon. Actually, that'd make him a much better doctor, even if it does sound a bit hayseed. The Colleon medical schools teach a lot of Imperial stuff.'

'Oh, well,' Alexius said. He tried to stretch, but a sudden cramp caught him and made him wince. 'Anyway, enough about him. How are you? How's business?'

'Could be worse.'

'I see. Is that *could be worse* meaning awful or *could be worse* meaning you're making money hand over fist?'

'A bit of both,' Athli replied. 'Things are terribly quiet still, but the ventures that are going out are doing quite nicely.'

'Such as?'

Athli thought for a moment. 'Well,' she said, 'the *Squirrel*'s due in any day now from the Mesoge with blueberries and honey; that'll tie in very nicely with the Molain people having landed a big order from the Bathary—'

'The who?'

'The Bathary. They make uniforms for the Shastel army, who (as I'm sure you know) wear dark-blue greatcoats.'

Alexius nodded. 'Which are dyed with blueberry juice. I see. Very clever.'

'Fortuitous,' Athli replied. 'And honey's fetching a good price, now that none of it's coming in from the Empire. For once, I think Venart Auzeil may have stumbled across a good solid proposition.' She frowned. 'With a little help from Gorgas Loredan,' she added. 'Nobody'd heard of the Mesoge three years ago, and now here we are looking at sourcing two staple commodities there. I just wish I could believe it's a solid place to do business.'

Alexius was silent for a while. 'The Loredan boys again,' he said. 'They do tend to crop up all over the place, don't they?'

Athli looked at him. 'You want to know if there's any more news about Bardas, don't you?' she asked.

'Yes.'

'Well.' She put her hands on her knees and looked at the shuttered window. 'I did happen to run into Lien Mogre this morning, and her brother's on the staff of the Shastel trade delegation that's just got back from the latest round of talks with the provincial office—'

'You mean he's a spy? That sounds promising.'

Athli nodded. 'Yes,' she said, 'but not a very good one. That's the trouble; the Shastel people are such very bad spies, they make it so painfully obvious what they're about. But I know for a fact that they do get fed lots of unimportant stuff just to keep them happy, so there's a good chance it might be reliable information. Anyway, he told me Bardas has been posted to a nice, quiet administrative job somewhere inland; production manager at a factory, he seemed to think.' She smiled. 'Well, you can't get more prosaic than that, can you?'

'Depends,' Alexius replied. 'There's factories and factories.'

'Yes, but even so.' Athli stood up and crossed to the window. 'I know you have this theory all about the Loredans and the Principle and how everything's tied up together in knots; but I don't really see how he's going to divert the tide of history sitting behind a desk cutting tallies and balancing ledgers.' She sighed. 'And if it keeps him out of harm's way, I think it's just fine, for all of us.'

A heavy gust of rain shook the shutters, rattling the catch. 'You're angry with him, aren't you?' Alexius said. 'Are you ever going to tell me why?'

'I'm not angry at all,' Athli answered, with her back to him. 'These days I don't give him a moment's thought from one day's end to the next. I'm pleased to say I've moved on since I was a fencer's clerk; I've made something of my life, thank you very much, and I've done it without hurting anybody or causing any fuss. I reckon that's something I can be proud of, don't you?'

Alexius lay back and closed his eyes. 'Of course,' he said. 'When I think of all the people you've helped and looked after since you first came here - me, Gannadius, his nephew; Venart and Vetriz—'

'Oh, that's all right,' Athli said quietly.

'I'm sure it is,' Alexius went on, 'but you didn't have to, and you did. But it's almost as if you've taken it on yourself to go around - well, tidying up after him, I suppose you could say. Here are all these people who've been left behind in his wake, and here you are, trying to give them back some semblance of a normal life. I find that interesting.'

'Really?' Athli carried on looking at the shutter. 'Well, it's a funny way of looking at things.'

'That's my job,' Alexius replied, with a hint of amusement.

The night after the fight in the bar, as he bounced and bumped about between the packing-cases and barrels in the back of another post coach, Bardas remembered the mines for the first time.

It began as a dream; but he got out of it as quickly as possible, wrenching his eyes open and hoping to see light. There wasn't any; there was a heap of roped-down luggage between him and the courier's lanterns, and it was a dark night. He could hear the crash-bump of the coach blundering down the rutted road. He could smell rosemary—

Rosemary? That's not right. He reached out to feel open space, but he'd slipped down into a crack between two large boxes, and all he could feel on either side was a rough wooden wall (*been here before, then*) and an obstruction against his feet. He kicked, heard and felt something splinter and crack. Of course, he knew he wasn't in the mines any more, but that didn't help a great deal; he'd known all sorts of things while he was down there, and very few of them had been true. He kicked again, and the world was flooded with the smell of roses.

The movement was all wrong, though. The mines didn't bump up and down and jar your spine (*wonderful; I've managed to find somewhere that's worse than the mines*) and the smell was wrong and there was way too much air. He was on a cart, or a ship. *Alexius?* No, then; not in the mines, at any rate.

He was on a coach, on the road from Sammyra to Ap' Calick; he was going to the proof house at Ap' Calick, where he was going to learn how to kill armour, suits of armour with nobody in them. It was all right; he wasn't in the mines any more (*except that once you've been in the mines, you'll always be in the mines*). He was going to be all right. He was deep inside the territory of the Sons of Heaven. He was safe.

It's customary to die first, but in your case we've made an exception.

Feeling a little foolish about the panic attack, he braced his hands against the sides of the coach and shoved himself up into a sitting position, his back to a tall barrel. The smell of roses was horribly strong; he'd put his foot through something fragile, broken something containing essence of roses. That might prove embarrassing in the morning, when the coach made its first stop. He leaned forward and sniffed; his legs reeked of the stuff, as if he'd died and been embalmed –

(That was what they used the stuff for; he remembered now. Strong essence of roses – it was so overpowering that it could even mask the smell of a body that's a week late for its funeral. He remembered the stink at Sammyra, when they'd taken the body of the dead corporal to the camp mortuary. They used a lot of rose essence there; burial detail was once a week, if you missed the detail you had to wait for the next one.)

– and rosemary; they used that for flavouring and preserving meat. They were clever that way, the Children of

Heaven; give them something dead and they could keep it sweet for ages, with herbs and spices and perfumes and essences. They could make rotten meat taste better than fresh; they'd hang up perfectly good carcasses and wait till maggots formed in them, just so they could get that perfect flavour. There was life after death in the Empire; of a sort.

Thinking about such things, he fell asleep. The courier woke him with a gentle nudge from the toe of his boot. It was broad daylight.

'Melbec,' he said, as if that meant anything. 'You can stretch your legs if you want to.'

Bardas stood up; pins and needles in both legs. He sat down again.

Change of horses at Melbec; another at Ap' Reac, where they parted company with the outriders. Ap' Reac was too small to be Ap' now; once, according to what the courier told him when they stopped there, it had been a city 'twice the size of Perimadeia', but that was before the Empire extended this far. When the frontier reached Ap' Reac there was a great war, a long and terrible siege. No more Ap' Reac.

That prompted Bardas to ask a question that hadn't occurred to him before: how old was the Empire, and where did it start?

The courier looked at him as if he was simple. 'The Empire is one hundred thousand years old,' he said, 'and it started in the Kingdom of Heaven.'

'Ah,' Bardas said. 'Thank you'

From Ap' Reac to Seshan (wherever Seshan was), the road went up a steep mountain and down into a deep canyon, with cliffs on either side. It looked for all the world as if the earth had been pulled apart; the road followed the bed of a long-dead river, which had cut the canyon and then dried up. Still thinking about the mines as they rumbled along under the shadow of the cliffs, Bardas couldn't help being reminded of the galleries, the main thoroughfares of the underground city under Ap' Escatoy. That city, with its complex grid of painfully cut roads and alleys, was all gone now; ruined and lost, like Ap' Reac or Perimadeia, except in his memory, where it was still vivid, more real than this improbable and unconvincing place he was in now, which smelt of rosemary and roses and was soaked right through with light.

Absolutely ideal place for an ambush, Bardas reflected. *Just as well we're deep inside the Empire; you'd get twitchy in here otherwise.*

Up above somewhere, the sun was high and hot. Under the eaves of the cliffs, it was dark and cool. The road seemed to stretch on for ever. There was next to no wind to take away the smell of roses. In a way, it was like being in the mines. In a way, everything would always be like being there.

The coach had stopped. Bardas hauled himself up and peered over the luggage.

'Is this Melrun?' he asked.

'No,' the courier replied.

They were in the ravine. The road ahead was empty. 'So why've we stopped?' Bardas asked.

'This isn't right,' the courier replied, standing up on the box.

'I don't understand,' Bardas said. 'What's wrong with it?'

The courier frowned. 'I'm not sure,' he said; at which point an arrow hit him just below the ear. He fell sideways off the box and hit the ground with a thump.

Oh, for pity's sake. Bardas dropped down, landing awkwardly among the packing-cases. The heart of the Empire; slap-bang in the middle of the shadow of the Children of Heaven, where (as everybody knew) you could leave a cartload of diamonds unattended all night in the market square and be sure nobody would steal them.

Whoever the unseen archer was, he was a cautious, methodical type, content to wait until he was sure the coast was clear before giving away his position. Bardas found this degree of professionalism highly aggravating; he was crouched down in a murderously uncomfortable position, from which he dared not move for fear of giving himself away and getting an arrow in his own neck. *This is ludicrous,* he thought. *It's not as if I'm likely to lift a finger to stop the Imperial post being looted; they can have the lot, and welcome, if only I could move my feet.* The thought of dying, from an arrow or thirst, or being fried by the savage heat of the sun, for the sake of twelve crates of rose essence and the Imperial mail was little short of insulting.

Nothing happened. He tried thinking it through. When was the next coach due? He ought to know how often they ran along this road. Someone had told him, but he couldn't remember. Presumably the cautious man up in the rocks knew the timetable, he didn't seem the sort to be slapdash about important stuff like that. He'd have to allow enough time to get the coach unloaded and haul off the stuff he wanted, that'd take time (unless he was planning to drive the coach to the end of the ravine, he was going to have to haul it up the sides with ropes). How many friends and relations did he have with him? Most important (and unfathomable) of all, did he/they know he was here, or was a long wait-and-see standard operating procedure when robbing the post?

Just as he was sure he couldn't stand the cramp in his legs any more, he heard the sound of someone scrambling about on loose rocks. Daren't look up, of course, so he couldn't see what was going on, but at least something was happening. No weapons, of course, except a short knife stuck down the side of his boot, as in the mines. *Been in worse scrapes than this.* Really? Name three.

'All right.' A man's voice, badly out of breath. 'You two, start unloading. Gylus, hold the horses. Azes, where's your damn brother with those hooks?'

'*I* don't know, do I?' replied a child's voice, with the eternal put-upon whine of the younger brother.

'Don't be cheeky. Gylus, lend me your knife. Bassa, for crying out loud be careful with that, it's fragile.'

The family business, obviously. *Families that loot together take root together.* 'It's not fair,' said another childish voice. 'You said it was my turn to have the boots.'

'You've already got a pair of boots. Why can't you do as you're told, just for once?'

– And there he was, standing on top of the luggage, his back to Bardas, directing his obstreperous workforce. All Bardas could see was the back of a bald head, wreathed with a few wisps of greying hair, and a shabby military-issue coat with a suspicious-looking hole, scrupulously darned, between the shoulders. *Go away,* Bardas thought, but the

man didn't seem to be in any sort of a hurry. 'Bassa! *Bassa!*
Put it down, you'll cut yourself and then I'll have your mother
on at me. Oh, for—'

He's seen me.

The man stood and stared for a full heartbeat, then groped
for the hilt of the cavalry scimitar that dangled incongruously
from his shoulder on an excessively long belt. *Damn*, Bardas
thought; his legs were too cramped for sudden, energetic
movement, else he'd have run away; but that option wasn't
available. The man had found his sword-hilt (round, jowly,
harrassed face; used to know a man who looked quite like
him, had a stall selling candles in the Chandlers' quarter)
and was struggling to draw it, hampered by the long belt and
his own extreme terror. The knife was in Bardas' hand (*here
we go again*), its pommel finding its own place in the hollow
of his palm, his thumb pressing down on the middle of
the handle, feeling for the slight groove that marked the
right spot, the fingertips resting lightly on the quillons; arm
back behind the ear, cock the wrist back and flick as the
arm comes forward, to keep the knife upright as it leaves
the hand, so that the shifting weight of the hilt guides it and
powers it – you have to do this instinctively, if you think
about it you'll miss, or the knife'll hit side-on. It's second
nature or it's impossible (it had always come naturally to
him in the mines, throwing his knife at a noise in the dark,
knowing where to find it again).

A good solid hit; not the ten, but cutting the edge of the
nine, slicing into the adam's apple and severing the windpipe,
so that there wasn't any air available for the curse or the
famous last words or whatever it was the man was about to
say; but his mouth opened and closed and nothing came
out, and then his feet slipped from under him and he went
crashing down on to a crate (marked *fragile*, inevitably)
which burst dramatically open, drenching Bardas in the
scent of dawn-plucked roses. A moment later, the dead
man's boot skidded past his ear.

'Dad?' No time for anything now; Bardas reached awkwardly over the body with his left hand and fished out the
cavalry sword (horrible, evilly balanced things, the pommel
nips your wrist and you'd have to be a triple-jointed cortor-
tionist to thrust effectively), then used his left hand to push

himself up on to his feet – left foot still numb, pins and needles in the right, what a stupid reason for getting killed ...

'Dad!' There was an edge of panic in the young voice. 'Bassa, what's happened to Dad?'

'Hang on.' A head popped up over the rampart of luggage – a girl, about nine years old, squat pudding face (obvious family resemblance). 'Dad?' Now she was staring at him, and at the dead body lying face down in the ruins of the crate. '*Gylus!* He's killed—'

The knife was in his hand again, but he was a bit too late; the head bobbed down again before he could throw. *I wish I wasn't here*, he thought, as he tried to shuffle along the ledge of exposed crate he was standing on; but his knees still weren't working properly, he lost his footing and stumbled, bashing the side of his head against a sharp wooden corner. *Ouch, that hurt*, he noted, trying to get the knee working so he could get up. Someone was swearing at him; he looked up and saw a boy, twelve or thirteen, resting a clumsy and crude-looking crossbow on the edge of the crate rampart. He could only see the eyes, the forehead, the clump of scruffy ginger hair, over the arched steel bow and the sun glinting on the honed edge of the arrow-blade. *Instinct*, he thought, as his wrist flipped over; and then, since instinct was running the show, he said, 'Thank you,' aloud, as the head snapped back and disappeared, taking his knife with it.

He heard the girl scream as he shifted the scimitar across to his right hand. *If she picks up the bow I'm still not out of this*, he thought, wincing at the pain as he put his weight on his left foot. *Come on, leg, this is no time for hissy fits.* Maybe that's all there were, father, son and daughter; or maybe there's the rest of the gods-damned extended family crouched up there in the rocks – brothers, sisters, uncles, aunts, nephews, nieces, fifteen different degrees of cousin, grandpa and grandma and a picnic lunch in a hamper. *What I'd really like is to be somewhere else; but I'd settle for my knife back.*

Azes. There'd been another kid, called Azes; a boy's name, presumably. Now what would a good boy do, in the circumstances? Would he scoop up his kid sister and get the hell out? That's what I'd do (only it's not what I did) or would he come after the monster, the destroyer of his family and his home and his life – *Oh I hope not. I really, really—*

In the mines, you knew when someone was behind you. As the boy jumped down, Bardas was already twisting around, trying to get some sort of balance so he could use his feet. It would have been nice to sidestep, hop lightly out of the way while bringing the sword up in a universal backhand parry – that's what he'd have done if he wasn't stumbling about in a narrow space between crates of perfume and biscuits in the back of a coach, with two clumsy, painful feet and the sun in his eyes as he looked up. As it was, he saw a blur and he hit it as hard as he could, relying on instinct (again) and basic timing. The boy's blood hit him in the face, suggesting he'd slashed through the jugular vein. A ten, and wrong-footed.

A good ten; he'd nearly cut the boy's head off. *I hope you were Azes*, he thought, turning round again. *I'd really hate it if there were more of you.* There was still the crossbow, spanned and cocked and with an arrow in the nut, somewhere up above his head on top of the luggage. Just as well Azes was as thick as a brick, trying to jump him from behind with a little wood-cutter's hatchet when there was a perfectly good crossbow lying about; not that intelligence seemed to run in this family, or they wouldn't have chosen this particular method of earning a living.

I've had enough of this. Let's get out of here. A gap where the roped-down crates had shifted was just enough of a toehold to allow him to scramble up on top of the luggage, past the crossbow, past the dead boy with the knife between his eyes, and down on to the box. If there'd been a third cousin twice removed up among the rocks with another crossbow he'd have been in trouble; but there wasn't, so that was all right. He grabbed the reins and the whip, trying to remember how you went about driving coaches – *can't be all that different from a hay-wagon, though I haven't driven one of them since I was – oh, Gylus' age.* Nobody shot at him, or tried to cut his throat from behind, or rolled rocks down on top of him, so that was all right.

'You're not the usual courier,' said the man at Melrun station, as he reached up to take the reins.

'The courier's dead,' Bardas explained. 'Someone tried to rob the coach.'

The man looked shocked. 'You're kidding.'

'Straight up. Jump up and count the bodies if you don't believe me.'

'You fought them off?' the man asked. 'On your own?'

Bardas shook his head. 'It's all right,' he said, 'I'm a hero. And besides, most of them were just kids.'

CHAPTER FIVE

The battle was effectively over. It had been short, one-sided and rather bloody, mostly because of the rebels' distressing reluctance to call it a day, even when it was obvious that they'd lost. Fighting to the last drop of blood sounds all very well in theory, but it's really only ever worth the effort when you're winning.

Temrai's handling of the battle had been textbook perfect, from the initial skirmisher attacks that had drawn the main rebel force out of position and into the killing zone, through the flawless enveloping manoeuvres of the main cavalry wings down to the perfectly conceived and executed pursuit and mopping-up of the enemy survivors. It was a pity, General Kurrai remarked afterwards, that such a masterly battle should be wasted on a bunch of malcontents and losers who'd never stood a chance anyway. A few volleys of arrows and a simple charge would have done the trick in a matter of minutes, and the cavalry could simply have ridden them down as they ran. Simple, efficient and there wouldn't have been that embarrassing business at the end ...

At the death, when the encircling horns of horse-archers and lancers had met up to complete the ring around the zone and it was all over bar the actual killing, one of the enemy ringleaders had caught sight of the pennants of Temrai's bodyguard and committed what was left of his forces to a suicide attack against that part of the line. Needless to say, only a handful of rebels actually made it through the shield-wall as far as the edge of the guard cordon, and nearly all of them ended up spitted on the pikes and halberds of the guards. No more than four men out of a whole double company came within striking range of Temrai himself; and of those four, just the one man actually managed to land a blow on the king's person. A thumbnail's width to the left, and all that effort would have been entirely justified.

Whoever he was, this one man out of so many, he must have been very angry. By the time he barged his way past the inner ring of guards, he'd already taken enough damage to stop a normal human being – two pike-thrusts puncturing his stomach, a glancing blow across the right side of his head that sprayed blood everywhere, as deep scalp wounds tend to do, a cut on the point of his left shoulder that lost him the use of that arm. But he was still on his feet and right-handed; and the backhand scimitar-cut he managed to loose, in the half-second or so before someone split his skull from behind, slammed into Temrai's neck on the very edge of his gorget, where the lip of the metal had been curled up and back. As it was, the shock of the blow sent Temrai sprawling, the impact enough to crush his windpipe and stop him breathing for long enough to make him believe it was all over. He dropped suddenly to his knees, in time for his head to get in the way of another guard's backswing which clattered across the front of his helmet like a blow from a smith's hammer. He landed at a hopelessly contorted angle down among the forest of legs and ankles, and lay curled and choking to death for a very long time, until a couple of guardsmen found out where he'd disappeared to and hauled him back on to his feet before anybody else could tread on him.

By the time he was up and breathing normally again, the meaningful part of the battle was already over, leaving only abattoir chores. Some guardsmen hustled Temrai out of the crowd and back to the calm and quiet of the tents, where an armourer had to cut through the straps of the dented and misshapen gorget before he could get the thing off. A surgeon examined the ugly swollen bruise, dabbed it with witch hazel and assured Temrai that there was no permanent harm done.

'Just as well you were wearing the thing,' Tilden said later. She was holding the twisted, mutilated gorget and looking at it thoughtfully. 'If it wasn't for that little raised bit round the edge, you'd be dead. I suppose the raised bit's there for precisely that reason.'

General Kurrai shook his head. 'Actually, no,' he said. 'It's just to stop the edge rubbing against your neck and cutting you to pieces.'

'Oh,' Tilden replied. 'Well, in that case it was definitely a slice of luck.' She put the gorget down with a little squeamish shiver, as if it had been covered in blood. 'Do you really need to do this?' she asked. 'Go to all the battles, I mean. Can't you stay near the back or something and let someone else do the actual charging about? After all, you're the King, heaven only knows what'd happen if you got yourself killed. And it's not as if you're a mighty warrior or a crack shot or anything.'

'Thank you,' Temrai said gravely. 'I'll bear that in mind.'

Tilden frowned. 'Well, you're not,' she said. 'And don't look at me like that. You know I'm right really.'

'Of course you are,' Temrai replied with a sad little smile. 'You could also point out that every time I get myself into trouble in a battle, it means other people have to risk their lives getting me out again, which is dangerously irresponsible behaviour by any standards. Unfortunately, there's nothing I can do about it.'

'Isn't there?' Tilden stood up, her arms filled with the heavy wool blanket she'd been darning. 'I'm terribly sorry, I mistook you for the King. My mistake.'

Temrai sighed. 'Yes, I'm the King,' he said, 'that's why I haven't got any choice in the matter. The people need to see me in there with them, fighting beside them, sharing the same dangers ...'

'But you aren't,' Tilden pointed out, the middle of the blanket tucked under her chin as she stretched it out to fold it up. 'You're surrounded by bodyguards. You're dressed head to foot in expensive imported armour. And besides, what makes you think that everybody's got their eyes glued to you all the time? If I were a soldier, I'd be watching the enemy, not peering over my shoulder to see if I can just make out the top of the King's head over the crowd. I don't suppose for a moment that anybody except you gives it a moment's thought.'

'That's not really the—'

'And anyway,' Tilden went on, 'if I were a soldier I wouldn't want my King and commander-in-chief stuck down in the front line, where he might easily get himself killed and where he hasn't got a clue what's going on. I'd want him to be standing on top of a hill somewhere, where he can see the whole of the battle and give the army its orders.'

'All right,' Temrai said. 'Point taken. It's not a very sensible way of doing things. But it's the way *I* do things, and I can't stop now without giving everybody the wrong message. You think I enjoy being the mark for every suicidal lunatic in the enemy army who wants to be a hero and end the war at a stroke?'

Tilden arched an eyebrow at him. 'Just because you don't enjoy it doesn't necessarily mean you have to do it,' she said. 'Look, if you're so worried about what people think, why don't you get one of the generals to make a public appeal to you, in front of the whole army so everybody can hear, and implore you not to take unnecessary risks? Then you'd say something like it's terribly sweet of everybody to be concerned, but you feel it's your duty and all that nonsense; then they'll all turn round and say, No, the general's right, you ought to take better care of yourself. And then you'd be off the hook and doing what your people want you to at the same time. Simple.'

Simple, Temrai reflected as he lay awake in bed that night. *Simple; and the truth is, I'm so terrified these days that it's all I can do to keep myself from running away as soon as I set eyes on the enemy. Ever since – well, ever since the burning of Perimadeia, when I was on the wrong end of Bardas Loredan's sword.*

He closed his eyes, and there was the image again; Colonel Bardas Loredan staring at him down the length of a sword blade, his eyes reflected in the brightly polished metal. All that was a long time ago now, and the last he'd heard was that Colonel Loredan was a sergeant in the army of the provincial office, on his way to some administrator's desk deep inside the Empire. *Out of my life for good*, he tried to tell himself, but he knew he was wasting his time. *I burned Perimadeia just because I was terrified of one man, and he's still out there, and here I am, waiting for him to come and get me.* Temrai couldn't help smiling at that; rebellions at home, the Empire pressing on the borders of his territory, the sort of threats that were worth losing sleep over, and he was so preoccupied with the phantom of Bardas Loredan that he scarcely had the time or the energy to be frightened of anything else. *The silly part of it is, I won; I destroyed the biggest city in the world, and I'm the one who's too scared to close his eyes. I don't suppose he's lying awake obsessing about me –*

'Gannadius,' the boy whispered, loud enough to be heard in the next valley. 'Are you awake?'

Gannadius rolled over and opened his eyes. 'No,' he said.

The boy glared at him. 'How are you feeling?' he asked.

'Awful,' Gannadius replied. 'How's yourself?'

He looks annoyed, Gannadius thought. *I expect I'd have been the same at his age. Flippancy really aggravated me when I was young.* The boy's scowl deepened.

'You do realise, don't you?' he said. 'These people are plains, they're the *enemy*. Just our luck, to be rescued by *them*.' He winced and pulled a face, as if a wasp had just stung him. 'What are we going to do now?'

Gannadius rolled his eyes. 'Speaking purely for myself,' he replied, 'I'm going to lie here till I'm better. You can do what you like.'

'Gannadius!'

'I'm sorry, Theudas.' Gannadius lifted himself awkwardly on to one elbow. 'But the fact is, there's not a lot we can do. I'm in no fit state to get out of this bed. You can try to get home if you like, on your own, but don't ask me how you'd go about it, because I haven't a clue. Besides,' he added, 'I like it here. Nice women bring me food and ask me if I'm feeling better, and I don't have to do any work.'

Theudas Morosin turned away sharply; too well brought up to be rude to his elders and betters. Where did he learn such good manners? Gannadius wondered; probably not from Bardas Loredan, so presumably from Athli Zeuxis, on the Island.

'All right,' Theudas said, 'if that's your attitude. I just hope you still find it all so wonderfully amusing when they realise who we are and stick our heads up on poles in the middle of the camp.'

Gannadius sighed. 'Right,' he said. 'So who are we, exactly? What are these dreadfully secret identities we've got to hide from them at all costs?'

Theudas winced. 'We're Perimadeian,' he hissed. 'Or had you forgotten?'

Gannadius shook his head. 'You may be,' he said, 'I'm not. I'm a citizen of the United Maritime Republic, more usually referred to as the Island, just like you. And last time I heard, relations between the Island and King Temrai have never been better. That's the lovely thing about belonging to a neutral country, people tend not to kill you just for where you live.'

Theudas opened his mouth and then closed it again; Gannadius could almost see the thought crossing his mind, like a big flock of rooks going home to roost. 'Actually,' he said, 'that's not right. You're a Shastel citizen, aren't you? Not that that matters in this instance,' he added.

'Wrong. I became an Island citizen the moment I started owning property there. So long as I've got a credit balance at Athli's bank, I'm a genuine, solid-gold citizen. Besides, you don't think foreign trash like me are allowed to join the Order just like that, do you?'

Theudas shrugged. 'Anyway,' he said, 'that's beside the point. And yes, I suppose you're right. I was panicking. Sorry. It's just,' he added, grimacing as if he'd just burned himself, 'I *hate* these people. I don't think anything'll ever change that, not after what I saw when I was a kid. You weren't there, Gannadius, you didn't see ...'

'True,' Gannadius replied firmly, 'for which I am duly thankful. And I'm not saying don't hate them; but as long as we're their guests, do it *quietly*. All right? That way, we stand a fair chance of getting put on a ship and sent home.'

Theudas hung his head. 'I'm sorry,' he said. 'And I know, I'm not fit to be out on my own.' He lifted his head and smiled. 'Just as well I've got you to look after me, really.'

'Works both ways,' Gannadius replied, lying back and closing his eyes. 'I don't know how far I'd have got after the wreck without you, but you could probably have measured the distance with a very short piece of string.' He breathed out, making himself relax. 'If you want to make yourself useful,' he went on, 'go and look for that nice lady doctor, see if you can get her to send a message to the coast, find out if any of our ships are expected, and if so, when. Try to be nice, will you? Don't call her a blood-soaked murderer or anything like that; you know the drill.'

'Yes, Uncle.'

When the boy had gone, Gannadius closed his eyes and tried to go to sleep. Instead, he found himself back in the awkward part of the scenario, the bit where the plains warrior was climbing in through the window of his room, marking the sill with blood.

'What the hell are you doing here?' the warrior said.

'I don't know,' Gannadius replied. 'I don't want to be here.'

'Tough.' He was squeezing his broad shoulders against the window-frame, trying to force it away from the wall so he could get through. He looked strong enough to be able to do it. 'You belong here,' he added with a grin.

'No I don't.'

'I beg to differ. You should have been here. And now, here you are. Better late than never.'

Gannadius tried to get out of bed, but his legs weren't working. 'I'm not really here,' he protested. 'This is just a dream.'

'We'll soon see,' said the warrior, and grunted with the effort. There was a sound of wood cracking. 'The way I see it, this is where you are, and where you'll always be. Properly speaking.'

Reaching behind him, Gannadius caught hold of the headboard and tried to pull himself backwards. 'I'm just making you say that,' he said, 'because I feel guilty. You don't even exist.'

'You watch your mouth,' the soldier replied. 'I exist all right. Give me a minute and I'll prove it to you.'

With an extreme effort, Gannadius pulled himself up into a sitting position and tried to swing his legs out of the bed, but they were completely numb.

'And besides,' the soldier went on, 'I'm telling you the truth, aren't I? Here you are, back on Perimadeian soil, where you belong. The truth is you never really left. And you know it.'

'Go away. I don't believe in you.'

The soldier laughed. 'Your prerogative,' he said. 'But you're wrong, and you can't kid yourself. You know too much about it. Agrianes' *On Shadow and Substance*, book three, chapter six, sections four to seven; I only know about it because it's right here in your mind for anybody to see.' He heaved and the central pillar of the window-frame tore loose. 'In which Agrianes postulates that whenever there's a serious dichotomy between perceived reality and the course of events that best accommodates the workings of the Principle, the latter interpretation is to be preferred in the absence of positive evidence to the contrary. In other words, proof. You prove you're not here and I might just let you go. Otherwise—'

'All right,' Gannadius whispered. 'What kind of proof do you need?'

'Proof—' the soldier repeated; and became Doctor Felden, the nice lady he'd just sent Theudas to find. She had a worried frown on her face.

'Are you all right?' she said.

Gannadius looked her in the eyes. 'Where am I?' he asked.

'It never rains,' said the courier sadly, awkwardly holding a sack over his head with one hand while grasping the reins in the other. 'Well, once or twice a year, and then it *rains*, if you see what I mean. Not like this.'

Bardas, who had no sack, pulled his collar round his neck. 'I'd say this is rain all right,' he said.

The courier shook his head. 'No way,' he said. 'Well, yes, obviously it's *rain*; but it's not the sort of rain you get here when it's raining. Comes down in sheets, it does; before you know it, the coach is full of water. Can't see ten yards in front of your nose. This is just – well, ordinary rain, like we used to have in Colleon.'

Bardas shivered. The ordinary rain was running down his forehead into his eyes. 'Well,' he said, 'this is rain like we used to get it in the Mesoge; about a third of the year, all spring and a bit of the late autumn. Bloody good weather for staying indoors in.'

'We're here,' the courier said. 'Ap' Calick. Where you're headed, remember?'

'What? Oh, yes. Sorry.' Bardas blinked rain out of his eyes, but all he could see was the vague, rain-blurred shape of a big, square, grey building in the valley below the hill they'd just come round. 'So that's Ap' Calick?' he said, for no real reason.

'That?' The courier laughed. 'Gods, no. Ap' Calick proper's another half-day on up the road. That's Ap' Calick armoury. Quite different.'

'Ah.' Bardas let go of his collar just long enough to draw a sodden cuff across his eyes. It didn't make much difference to the way it looked; a dim grey block, precisely square. 'That's all right, then,' he said.

'Dismal bloody place,' the courier went on. 'Mate of mine was posted there once; nothing there, he told me. Nothing to do; miserable little canteen where they water the booze. No women except for the godawful specimens who make the chain-mail, they've got hands like farriers' rasps, and talk about strong—' He shuddered, tilting rain out of a fold in his sack on to Bardas' knee. 'And the dust,' he went on, 'the dust's the real killer. A month in there, you'll be spitting up enough grit to polish a breastplate. No wonder they all die.'

'You don't say,' Bardas replied.

'That's if the noise doesn't drive you crazy first,' the courier went on. 'Three shifts a day, see, *clack, clack, clack* all the damn time. If you're really lucky, you'll go deaf. The heat's another killer,' the courier continued. 'I mean to say, typical provincial office, builds the biggest forge in the west in the middle of a bloody desert. You get blokes going crazy because they drink the brine.'

'The what?'

'Brine,' the courier repeated. 'Salt water, for tempering in. They get so thirsty in there on a hot day, they drink the salt water out of the tempering vats and go crazy and die. Three or four of them, every year. They know it'll kill them, but after a bit they just don't care.'

Bardas decided it was time to change the subject. 'I didn't know that,' he said. 'About tempering in salt water.'

The courier shook his head. 'Temper in all sorts of things,' he said, 'depending on what they're making. Salt water, oil, lard, plain water; molten lead they use for some things; or is that annealing? Can't remember. My mate didn't talk about it much. Made him depressed even thinking about the place.'

'Is that so?' Bardas said.

A few hundred yards further on, Bardas could hear the

noise. It was just as the courier had said, the clack-clacking of countless hammers, all out of sync, like massive raindrops on a slate roof. 'Worse inside,' the courier informed him. 'Big rooms, see; the sound bounces off the walls and the ceiling. You can always tell a man who's worked in one of these places, he doesn't talk, he shouts.'

Bardas shrugged. 'I don't mind a bit of noise,' he said. 'Where I was before, it was always a bit too quiet for my liking.'

The courier was quiet for a while. Then, 'Another thing that happens to them,' he went on, 'they lose the use of their left hands – the hand you hold the work in, right? All that constant shock and jarring, it kills the nerves. It gets so you can't hold anything. Once that happens, they ship 'em out to the desert forts. Be kinder to knock 'em on the head, really.'

The courier dropped him off at the gate (there was only one; high, nail-studded double oak doors, strong enough for a city), turned round and vanished into the rain. Bardas banged on the door with his fist and waited, until he could feel rainwater seeping down the insides of his boots.

'Name.' A panel had opened in the door while he'd been looking the other way. 'Yes, you. Name.'

'Bardas Loredan. You should be ...'

A sally-port in the main door swung open. 'Adjutant's expecting you,' said a voice from under a deep, sodden hood. 'Across the courtyard, third staircase from the right, fourth floor, left at the head of the stairs then right, sixth left, fourth door down on the left. Ask if you get lost.'

The hood darted away into a niche in the gatehouse wall, and Bardas, who was in no mood to stand about, scuttled across the courtyard, which had been baked earth but was now a thick grey mud the consistency of mortar; it sucked at his boots as he crossed it. In passing he noticed a series of massive timber A-frames, in pairs, linked by crossbars; they could have been anything from component parts of siege engines to production-line gibbets. There was nobody else to be seen, and all the windows overlooking the yard were shuttered.

The building on the other side of the yard was a half-hearted attempt at a tower; it was square, ten storeys tall, with a dozen staircases opening on to the yard. On either side of it were galleries, shuttered windows and no doors, like the galleries that ran along the other three sides; two storeys, or else one high-ceilinged storey and a loft. He counted off three from the right and started to climb the tightly curled spiral staircase. It was dark, slippery underfoot (how the rain was managing to get through he couldn't see), the pitch of the stairs was disconcertingly steep and there was no rail or rope to steady himself by; not the sort of stairs you'd want to meet anybody on, unless you relished the prospect of walking backwards down to the floor below. There was a certain similarity to the mines that wasn't lost on him (except, of course, that about the only way you couldn't die in the mines was by falling backwards down a flight of stairs).

Left, right, sixth left, fourth door left; he caught himself mumbling it under his breath like some protective spell, such as the hero in a fairy tale uses to get past the gatekeepers of the kingdom of the dead. He chided himself for thinking negative thoughts: *Don't be so silly,* he told himself, *it'll probably turn out to be a whole lot of fun once you're settled.*

There were lights in the corridors; little oil-lamps that flickered shyly in deep alcoves in the walls and provided almost enough light to see the way by. It was more reliable, Bardas found, to use the sappers' method of closing your eyes and finding a turn by waiting for the tickle of a draught on your face. *Just one of the many useful skills I've learned since I've been in the army,* he reflected, ducking just in time to avoid an invisible low doorframe.

There was a problem with finding the fourth door on the left: there were only three doors. He knocked on the third door, and waited. Just when he'd reached the conclusion that he'd come the wrong way after all, the door opened and he found himself looking up at a very tall, broad-shouldered, rather round-faced man, a Son of Heaven with wispy white hair on either side of a bald head and a little tuft of beard just under the curl of his lower lip.

'Sergeant Loredan,' the man said. 'Come in. I'm Asman Ila.'

The name was completely unfamiliar, but Bardas didn't mind that. He followed the man into a narrow, dark room, no wider than the corridor he'd just left. What light there was came from four tiny oil-lamps on a spindly iron frame that stood about as tall as his shoulder; there was a window at the far end of the room, but it was shuttered and barred from the inside. Three of the walls were bare; on the fourth, above the bare plank desk, hung what was probably a breath-takingly lovely Colleon tapestry, if only there'd been enough light to see the colours.

'From the spoils of Chorazen,' the man said (Bardas had never heard of Chorazen before). 'My grandfather commanded the sixth battalion. Daylight fades it, so I keep the shutter closed.'

'Ah,' Bardas said, trying to sound as if he'd just been given a full explanation. 'Reporting for duty,' he added.

Asman Ila indicated a small three-legged stool with a delicate gesture. It tipped alarmingly when Bardas sat on it; one leg was markedly shorter than the others. 'From Ap' Seudel,' said Asman Ila, 'before the fire. My first posting. The local rosewood, with a charming niello inlay. Welcome to Ap' Calick.'

'Thank you,' Bardas said.

Asman Ila sat down – his chair looked even more uncomfortable than the stool, but if there was a provenance to it, Bardas didn't get to hear it. 'So,' he said, 'you're the hero of Ap' Escatoy. A remarkable achievement, by all accounts.'

'Thank you.'

'A fascinating city,' Asman Ila went on. 'I spent some time there – what, thirty years ago. I'll never forget the quite out-standing carved ivory furniture in the viceroy's state apart-ments – quite distinctive, nothing remotely like it anywhere else in the world, though of course they try to copy it in Ilvan. It's easy enough to tell, though; you can almost feel the clumsiness as soon as you walk into the room. A cousin of mine in the provincial office has promised me one of the triptych audience screens from the main reception chamber; too much to hope for the pair, of course.'

As his eyes became accustomed to the gloom, Bardas could make out the shapes of chairs, chests, book-boxes, lecterns, stools and any number of other small, portable items; they were stacked on top of each other up against the walls, covered in dull grey sheets. 'My duties,' Bardas prompted him hopefully, but Asman Ila appeared to have forgotten that he was there.

'Nearly everything in this room,' he said eventually, 'comes from fallen cities, places I or my ancestors captured in war. Unique, I should imagine, some of them; the lamp-stand, for example. I believe it's the only piece of Cnerian wrought iron left in existence. The city is gone, but part of its heritage lives on, here with me. Now then, your duties. It's all perfectly straightforward.'

Far away, Bardas could still just about hear the clacking of hammers, faint, only just loud enough to be intrusive. 'I'm ashamed to admit it,' Bardas said, 'but I've only got a very general idea of what you do here. I don't know if it's possible—'

Asman Ila wasn't listening; he was looking at the door. 'Mostly,' he said, 'you're here to supervise, which is where your extensive experience in the trade will prove so useful; of course, I can't so much as peen over a rivet or knock a nail in straight, and needless to say, they take advantage. Theft from the stores is our worst problem, followed by fluctuations in demand. There are times when I wonder whether the provincial office even knows the meaning of the term phased sourcing.'

Bardas shifted a little in his seat, which was rickety and appeared to have been made for a much smaller man, possibly even a child. He wondered if there would be any point in mentioning that he knew absolutely nothing about armoury work, and decided that there wouldn't.

'But,' the Son of Heaven went on, 'we cope. We're fortunate in having so many highly skilled tradesmen here at Ap' Calick; it means we have the flexibility. Are your quarters adequate for your needs? If you have any problems or queries, feel free to ask me, or the captain of operations. After all, there's no point being uncomfortable unnecessarily.'

Bardas, who didn't even know where his quarters were, nodded appreciatively. 'Thank you,' he said, and wondered what he could say to make the adjutant let him go. The stool was starting to get excruciatingly painful, and he had the feeling that a sudden movement would probably break it.

'On the technical side,' Asman Ila went on, carefully stifling a yawn, 'you can always consult the foreman, Maj. I can't say he's entirely trustworthy, though I dare say he's no worse than most, but he seems to know what he's doing.

He repaired a set of candlesticks for me; Riciden ware, missing the scrolled finials and the dished base. You can hardly tell the difference, except in a strong light. My great-grandfather took them from the library at Coil, so it's hardly surprising they were damaged.'

A strong light, Bardas reflected. *No danger of that here.* 'Thank you,' he said. 'Will that be all?'

Asman Ila sat perfectly still for a few moments, staring at something above and just to the left of Bardas' head. 'And remember,' he said suddenly, 'my door is always open. Far better to deal with a problem when it arises than to try to hide it away until everything starts going wrong. After all,' he added, 'we're all on the same side, aren't we?

'Maj,' Bardas shouted for the third time. The man shook his head.

'Never heard of him,' he shouted back. 'Why don't you ask the foreman?'

Bardas shrugged, smiled and walked away. *Going to have to find some way of coping with this noise*, he thought, as he threaded his way between the benches, doing his best to stay out of the reach of the machines and the swinging hammers. *Anyway, it makes a change after the mines.*

Eventually he found the foreman (who was called Haj, not Maj); he was curled up in a little niche in the gallery wall, fast asleep. Haj turned out to be a short, stocky man in his early sixties, with long, bony forearms and the largest hands Bardas had ever seen. His right shoulder was higher than his left, and his hair was bristly and white.

'Bardas Loredan,' Haj repeated. 'The hero. Right, follow me.'

Haj moved quickly, taking lots of short steps; he ducked and threaded his way through the crowded workshop without apparently looking where he was going, leaving the more cautious Loredan far behind, so that twice Haj had to stop and wait for him to catch up. Like everybody Bardas had seen in the workshop, Haj wore a long leather apron that started under his chin and ended just above his ankles; he wore big military boots with steel caps over the toes, and the pocket of his apron was stuffed full of small tools and bunches of rag.

'You coming, then?'

'Sorry,' Bardas said.

'This way,' said Haj; and a moment later he vanished. Bardas stood for a second or two, trying to work out where he'd gone; then he saw a little, low archway in the gallery wall, nearly invisible in the dim light. He had to bend almost double to get under it.

The archway led to a short, very narrow passageway that ended in another steep, scary staircase that spiralled four turns and emerged on to a plank catwalk, high above the shop floor. There was no handrail. *Fancy that*, Bardas reflected, glancing down. *Presumably I've been afraid of heights all my life and never realised it till now.* He fixed his eyes on the door at the end of the catwalk, which led into the back wall of the gallery. Unless Haj had fallen to his death or turned into a bird, he was beyond that door somewhere. Bardas sucked in a long, deep breath and followed, his hands clasped behind his back, taking care not to look at his feet.

Beyond the door there was another narrow corridor, which turned a right angle and then stretched on into the darkness. Doors opened off it at frequent intervals; one of them was open, and Bardas went in.

'There you are,' said Haj's voice in the gloom. 'Well, this is it. Nice room.'

Bardas felt his way along the wall with his hands until something blocked his way. He reached out and felt rough wood; flat planks and a bar. He lifted the bar, which slipped through his fingers and fell on the floor, then groped around until he found a handle, and pulled. The room flooded with light as the shutter swung back, revealing what looked depressingly like a prison cell. There was a shelf projecting out of the wall, with a single folded blanket and a single yellowing pillow; another ledge under the window, on which stood a plain brown pottery jug and a white-enamelled tin bowl. That was it.

'Thank you,' Bardas said.

Haj sniffed. 'You don't like it, I can tell,' he said.

'No, no,' Bardas said, 'it's fine. At least, I've lived in worse.'

'Really?' Haj said. 'Most of us sleep on the roof, or under our benches in the shop in the wet season.' He looked round, as if daring Bardas to criticise further. 'Has anybody told you what you're meant to be doing?' he said.

'Not really,' Bardas replied. 'The adjutant said something about supervising, but—'

Haj smiled. 'You don't want to bother too much about anything *he* says. It's the foremen who run this place, which is how it should be, of course.'

'I see,' Bardas said. 'And what am I? A foreman?'

Haj shook his head. 'Really, you haven't got a job,' he said. 'They do this from time to time, send us people they can't find places for anywhere else. Doesn't do any harm, usually, so long as they keep out of everybody's road. Basically, you do what the hell you like, just don't interfere, that's all. Let's see, pay call's last day of the month; you lose two quarters kit and uniform levy, three quarters wounds and burial club, two quarters retentions, and the rest of it's yours to spend, though if you've got any sense you'll keep it in the big safe in the back of the stockroom, like the rest of them do. Good rule of thumb: don't leave anything lying about unless you don't care if it gets stolen. Lot of light-fingered types here; nothing else to do, see. Right, mess call's an hour after each shift; you're entitled to use the officers' mess in the tower basement, but that comes expensive, a quarter a day not including wine or beer. Otherwise, you can muck in with the rest of us in the canteen; ask anybody and they'll show you where it is.'

Bardas nodded. 'Thank you,' he said. 'What's retentions?'

'Retentions,' Haj repeated. 'Two quarters a month. Don't you know what retentions are?'

'Sorry,' Bardas said. 'Not something we had in the sappers, or at any rate we didn't call it that.'

Haj sighed a little. 'Retentions is what's stopped out of everybody's pay for their demob. You know,' he added, 'when you leave the army. It's for your old age, that sort of thing; you get back what you put in, plus your gratuity, less stoppages, fines, levies, exemptions, stuff like that. Didn't you have that in the mines?'

'No,' Bardas said. 'I suppose the chance of any of us having an old age was too small to warrant the extra work.'

'Whatever,' Haj said. 'Well, we got it here. Now, is there anything else I've got to tell you? Don't think so. Anything you don't understand, just ask somebody, all right?'

'That's fine,' Bardas said. 'Thank you.'

Haj nodded. 'Right,' he said. 'Now I've got to get back down there, before the whole section grinds to a halt.'

When he'd gone, Bardas sat on the bed for a while, staring at the opposite wall, listening to the sound of hammers. *Just the ticket*, he told himself cheerfully; *no problem at all staying out of trouble. I'm going to like it here.* It didn't work. Above all, he could hear the pecking of the hammers; when he put his hands over his ears, he could feel them just as clearly. *It's higher up than the mines*, he tried hopefully. *And there's nobody trying to kill me; now that's got to be worth something.*

After an hour alone in his quarters, Bardas carefully picked his way back along the corridors, over the catwalk and down the stairs into the gallery. He stood for a moment, letting the noise overwhelm him, trying to savour it instead of shut it out. Then he marched over to the nearest workbench, where a man was cutting shapes out of a sheet of steel with a heavy-grade bench shear.

'I'm Bardas Loredan,' he shouted. 'I'm the new—' He searched his mind frantically for something that would sound authentic. 'The new deputy inspector. Tell me exactly what you're doing here.'

The man looked at him as if he was mad. 'Cutting out,' he replied. 'What does it look like?'

Bardas clenched his face into a frown. 'That's not the sort of attitude I want to see around here,' he said. 'Describe your working method.'

The man shrugged. 'I get the plates from the layout section,' he said, 'with the patterns scribed out and marked up with blue. I cut them out and put them in this tray here. When the tray's full, someone comes down and takes it over there.' He indicated the far side of the shop with a nod of his head. 'That's it,' he concluded.

Bardas pursed his lips. 'All right,' he said. 'Now let me see you do one.'

'Why?'

'I want to see if you're doing it right.'

'Suit yourself.' The man hefted another sheet, laid it face down on the bench and turned it round. Gripping the sheet with one hand and the long lever of the shear in the other, he fed the sheet into the cutting jaws and drew down the handle. The cut seemed to take far less effort than Bardas had imagined; it looked for all the world like cutting cloth, except that one jaw of the scissors was bolted down to the bench. To make the curves, he moved over to another tool mounted on the other side; this one had the same long handle, but instead of the top blade of the scissors there was a circular cutter with serrations round the edge of the blade.

'All right so far?' the man asked.

'It'll do,' Bardas grunted. 'Carry on.'

The man didn't quite smirk, but he didn't have to. 'So you don't want to see the third step, then?'

'What? Oh, well, yes, why not?'

The man took the cut-out pieces and clamped them in an enormous bench-vice, lining the edge up carefully along the line of the jaw so that only the edge, left slightly ragged by the shear, was exposed; then he picked a big, wide chisel out of the rack next to the vice, laid it level on the top of the leading jaw, right at the edge and at right angles to the sheet, and started whacking the back of the chisel with a huge square wooden mallet. The ragged edge was sliced away, leaving a smooth, perfect edge.

'Well?' he said.

'Do another one.'

The man did another one; and another, and then two more. 'There,' he said, 'that's a trayful. Did I pass?'

Bardas made the most non-committal noise he could manage. 'All right,' he said. 'What else do you do?'

'Come again?'

'What else do you do?' Bardas repeated. 'Other procedures, stages in the operation.'

Again, the man looked at him as if he was gibbering. 'That's all,' he said. 'I cut out tasset-lame blanks. Why, am I supposed to be doing something else as well? Nobody's ever said.'

Bardas picked up the tray. 'Carry on,' he said, and headed for the area the man had pointed to.

In the far corner, a man was feeding bits of metal that looked like the bits in the tray into a large contraption that was basically three long, thick rollers laid horizontally in a massive wrought-iron frame. One roller revolved as the man turned a handle; this drew the steel plate under the other two rollers (whose pitch and settings could be adjusted by turning the large set-screws at either end) and fed it out the other side, by which point it had been turned from a straight strip into a shallow, even curve, the shape of one of the small plates that made up an assembly of shoulder armour; which, presumably, was what the term 'tasset lame' actually meant. After rolling each piece he held it up to a curved piece of wood on a stand, the idea apparently being that if it fitted snugly against the wood, he added it to the pile of completed pieces; otherwise it went back under the rollers, and the man fiddled with the set-screws until it came out sufficiently curved to fit the wooden pattern.

Taking a deep breath, Bardas walked up to this man, put the tray of steel bits down on the nearest bench and went through the deputy-inspector routine again. This man seemed marginally less sceptical (or else he cared even less); he carried on with his work as if Bardas wasn't there, until his tray was full.

'Right,' Bardas said. 'Now where do these go?'

The man didn't say anything, but he nodded his head sideways in the direction of the west end of the gallery. Resting the tray against his chest (it was no lightweight; forty or so curved sections, neatly stacked together in concentric semicircles, like the flaky cross-section flesh of a slice of overcooked salmon) Bardas tottered across the shop, once again hoping he'd recognise someone working with something similar before he'd made a complete and utter fool of himself. Fortunately, the next stage in the process was reasonably easy to spot: a man with a hammer and a small hole-punch, knocking rivet-holes into a batch of sections identical to the ones he was carrying.

'Easy as pie,' explained the hole-puncher, who was more than happy to explain every aspect of his job to the deputy inspector. 'You look for the punch-marks where the layout boys have marked out where the holes've got to go; then you take the work in your left hand, like so, and press it against the bench so; then you get your punch in your left hand and your hammer in your right, and –' (*clink*, went the hammer) '– there you are. Simple, isn't it?'

Bardas nodded. 'Yes,' he said, because it was.

'Another thing; it's not only simple, it's fucking boring.'
'What?'

The man looked at him. 'You know how long I was supposed to be doing this for? Two weeks, until the new man came and I got moved on to planishing, like I was trained for. And you know how long I've been here now? Six years. Six *years*, dammit, doing this pathetically simple job over and over and over—' The man took a deep breath. 'Look,' he said, 'you're the deputy inspector, see if you can't put a word in for me, all right? I mean, the bloke who had your job before, he promised he'd put in a word for me, but that was two years ago and did anything come of it? Did it hell as like; and if I stay here much longer—'

'All right,' Bardas said quickly. 'Leave it with me, I'll see what I can do.'

'You will?' The man's face lit up with joy, then clouded over with suspicion. 'If you remember, is what you mean; if you remember and you can be bothered. Well, all I can say is, I've heard that one before and all I can say about *that* is, I won't be holding my breath—'

'I'll see what I can do,' Bardas repeated, taking a step back. 'Just leave it with—'

'You haven't even asked me my name,' the man called after him, angrily, but Bardas was far enough away by now that he didn't have to look back; he could pretend not to have heard. He walked away quickly, as if he knew where he was going, until he tripped over a large wooden block and had to grab hold of a workbench to stop himself falling.

'Watch it,' said the man behind the bench. 'I could have smashed my thumb, you doing that.'

Bardas looked up. The man was holding a piece of steel in one hand and a hammer of sorts in the other. It didn't look like an ordinary hammer; instead of a steel head, it had a tightly wound roll of rawhide jammed into a heavy iron tube, set at right angles to the handle. 'Sorry,' Bardas replied. 'It's my first day.'

The man shrugged. 'All right,' he said. 'But look where you're going next time.' On the bench in front of him was another block of wood, maybe a little larger than the one Bardas had just barked his shin on. In the middle of the block – Bardas recognised it as oak – was a square hole, in which sat an iron stake topped by an iron ball slightly smaller than a child's head. The piece of metal the man was holding over this ball was roughly triangular and looked like a shallow dish; it was a panel for a four-piece conical helmet, the old-fashioned kind that was still issued to some of the auxiliary cavalry units.

The man noticed that Bardas was staring. 'Do you want something?' he asked.

'I'm the new deputy inspector,' Bardas replied. 'Tell me about what you're doing.'

'Planishing,' the man replied. 'You know what planishing means?'

'You tell me. In your own words,' Bardas added.

'All right.' The man grinned. 'They send you people out here, don't they, and you haven't got a bloody clue. No skin off my nose, though. Right, planishing is where we hammer the outside of the nearly finished article to take out the bumps and dents, get it smooth for the polishers. All the actual shaping, see, that's done from the inside; so to finish off, we just go over it lightly from the outside, not enough to move any metal, really it's just to leave it looking nice. I wouldn't tell you that if you were a *real* inspector, or else I'd be out of a job. You want to watch how I do this?'

Bardas nodded, and the man carried on with what he'd been doing, angling the work down on to the ball and smoothing the marks out of it with a series of crisp, even taps, letting the hammer fall in its own weight and bounce back off the surface of the metal. 'The trick is not to bash,' the man explained. 'Bashing gets you nowhere fast, you just let the mallet drop and the weight does all the work. That's why I'm holding it just so, trapped between my middle finger and the base of my thumb, look.' He held up his right hand to demonstrate. 'Here, you want a go?'

Bardas hesitated. 'All right,' he said, and held out his hand for the hammer. 'Is that right?'

The man shook his head. 'You're gripping,' he said. 'You don't want to grip, you're not trying to strangle the bloody thing, you just want to hold it firm enough so you can keep control – there, you're getting it. Pretty simple once you know, but you'll never get there just by light of nature.'

'Strange,' Bardas said. 'I'd never have guessed a lot of

little gentle taps with a bit of rolled-up leather could actually shape a piece of steel.'

The man laughed. 'That's the whole point,' he said. 'Thousands and thousands of little light taps with the hide mallet make the thing so hard and close-grained that a bloody great hard two-handed bash with a six-pound axe just bounces off.' He lifted the piece of work off the steel ball and ran a finger-tip over it. 'A bit like life, really,' he went on. 'The more you get shit kicked out of you, the harder you are to kill.'

CHAPTER SIX

No, no, they'd told him - they'd sounded quite shocked - *you mustn't call it a civil war, it was a rebellion. It'd only have been a civil war if they'd won.*

It wasn't the sort of victory Temrai wanted to dwell on any more than he had to; but it was in order, diplomatically speaking, for his new neighbours in the provincial office to express their pleasure, now it was all safely over, that the best man had won. A simple letter would have done; or a messenger with his words written out for him in big letters on a bit of parchment; there wasn't really any need to send a full proconsular delegation (although strictly speaking, as Deputy Proconsul Arshad carefully explained, since the mission was to a recognised non-aligned friendly sovereign state, from a provincial directorate as opposed to a provincial governor, it being a directly governed province and therefore in theory under the direct supervision of the chancellor of the Empire, by way of his duly appointed delegates, protocol did require a personal attendance by the senior ranking diplomat; anything less, Arshad implied, would have been an insult, or at the very least a display of bad manners and ignorance).

'I see,' Temrai replied untruthfully. 'Well, it's very kind of you to have come all this way; but as you can see, I'm still very much in one piece, as are the rest of my senior officers and ministers; really, in fact, no harm done.' He stopped, unable to think of anything else to say. Of all the people he'd met in the course of his extremely eventful life, Deputy Proconsul Arshad was the most inhuman. Light seemed to fall away into his eyes like water draining into sand, and when he spoke, the words seemed to come from a great way off. Temrai felt compelled to carry on talking, in an effort to fill the gap in nature the man seemed to produce. 'Of course,' Temrai went on, 'it was a dreadful business; we were fighting people who we thought of as our friends – well, more than friends, family. I'm still not sure what it was all about, to be honest with you. It just happened, I suppose. One minute we were all on the same side, wanting the same things, just not completely in agreement about how to go about achieving them. Next thing we knew, we weren't talking any more, and they'd left the camp and gone off somewhere with their horses and sheep and goats. Well, that was all right, if they didn't want to stay here, that was up to them. But then they started making trouble; nothing terrible, just awkward, rude I suppose you could call it. They wouldn't let some of our people water their stock at a river they'd decided was theirs; stupid thing to argue over, especially since if our side had moved a couple of miles up river, they'd have been drinking exactly the same water (just a few minutes earlier) and everybody would have been happy.

'But it didn't turn out that way, worse luck; first there was a standoff, then there was a scuffle, you couldn't call it more than that, but a man was killed, so I had to get involved; looking back, I keep asking myself if I could have handled it differently, found some way not to make an issue out of it. But I found myself insisting that the man who'd struck the actual blow had to be sent back here to answer for what he'd done; they refused, so I sent some people to fetch him. There was more fighting—' He shook his head. 'It shouldn't have happened, gods know, but it did; and now here we are, looking back on our first civil war. I suppose it's a sign of how far we've come, in a way. I mean, it's things like this that sort of define a nation.' Temrai bit his lip; he couldn't believe some of the things he was hearing himself say. But Deputy Proconsul Arshad was just sitting there, drawing the words out of him like a child sucking an egg. Presumably that was what he'd come for. Even so, he couldn't really see the point of the exercise. It was like deliberately opening a vein.

'A most unhappy sequence of events,' Arshad said eventually, moving his head very slightly forward, though the rest of his body remained motionless. He had an ugly scar running from the corner of his left eye right down to the lobe of his ear, and it was all Temrai could do not to stare at it helplessly. 'Let us hope that by dealing with the problem so quickly and decisively, you've effectively forestalled any further opposition to what we consider to be a most welcome and positive program of social reforms. As you say, if your actions here have ensured that something like this is unlikely ever to happen again, you're entitled to feel a considerable degree of satisfaction.'

'Thank you,' Temrai replied, though he wasn't entirely sure what he was thanking this peculiar man for. What he really wanted, of course, was for the Son of Heaven and his grim-faced retinue to go away and never come back. Maybe there was a special way diplomats could say that sort of thing without giving offence or starting a war; but if there was, nobody had let him in on the secret. 'Personally, I've had enough of wars and fighting to last me a lifetime. I mean to say, just because you're really quite good at something, it doesn't actually follow that you like doing it. Definitely that way with me and fighting wars – well, not just me, all of us, really. I'd say that, as a nation, we've been through all that proving-ourselves stuff and now it's time to move on.'

Deputy Proconsul Arshad studied him for a moment in silence, as if making up his mind whether to knock him on the head now or throw him back and let him grow a little bigger. 'I most sincerely hope those aspirations will prove to be attainable,' he said. 'For the present, may I remind you of something from my people's most respected treatise on the art of war. To paraphrase – necessarily – it says that trying to make peace without total victory is like trying to make soup without onions; it can't be done.' He didn't smile, but there was a space for where a smile would have been, had he been human. 'You have work to do; I've trespassed on your time long enough. May I conclude by saying that the Empire is delighted that at long last we have you for a neighbour.'

When Arshad had gone – Temrai saw him leave, but he had a totally irrational feeling that he might still be there somewhere, lurking – he breathed a long sigh of relief and asked, 'Anybody care to tell me what all that was about?'

Poscai, the newly appointed treasurer (his predecessor had been on the other side in the civil war, and hadn't survived it), smiled ruefully. 'Welcome to politics,' he said. 'They say it gets easier as you go along, but I have my doubts. I think it gets worse and worse, until finally both sides give up and go to war, the way human beings were meant to.'

Temrai shook his head. 'Why on earth should they want to start a war with us? We haven't done them any harm. And I can't believe we've got anything they could possibly want. Do you really think they're going to attack us, Poscai? Maybe I wasn't listening properly, but I don't think I heard anything you could actually describe as a threat. Nothing so straight-forward,' he added.

General Hebbekai pulled the cushion off the chair Arshad had been sitting on, put it down next to Temrai's feet and sat on it. 'Oh, there were threats all right. If the provincial office tells you it likes the shoes you're wearing, that's a threat: they're going to kill you and take your shoes. If they say it's a nice day for the time of year, that's a threat too. If they don't say anything at all, just sit there and smile at you, that's a really bad threat. You don't think a man like that'd come all this way just to borrow a pair of shears.'

Temrai shrugged. 'I wouldn't know,' he said. 'And neither would you, come to that. Face it, Hebbekai, we don't know *anything* about these people, or at least not yet.'

Poscai shook his head. 'Speak for yourself,' he said. 'Here's a cold fact for you. At any one time, Arshad and his friends in the provincial office – that's just one province, remember, and by no means the biggest province in the Empire – they've got a standing army of at least a hundred and twenty thousand men, all highly trained and beautifully equipped, not to mention lavishly paid. Armies aren't for decoration; if they've got an army like that it's because they're going to use it. Can't do otherwise.'

'I don't follow,' Temrai said.

'Don't you?' Poscai frowned. 'All right then, picture this. You have a hundred and twenty thousand of the best fighting men in the world, and you tell them you don't need them any more. That's it, they've done the job, they're free to go. So what do they do? Remember, these are professional soldiers. After six months, you'd need another quarter of a million men just to get rid of them, kill them or chase them off your land. No, once you've got an army like that, you don't really have a choice. You've got to keep on going. And now,' he concluded sadly, 'they've reached us.'

'Poscai's right,' said Hebbekai. 'Basically, we now have two options: fight them, or pack up and get out of their way.' He shook his head. 'Sorry,' he went on, 'I thought you'd worked all this out for yourself. That's what we just had a civil war about.'

Temrai looked up, startled. 'Are you serious?'

'I thought it was obvious. They wanted to pack up and leave, after what happened to Ap' Escatoy, follow the old ways – and what that really meant was, go back to the plains, as far away from these people as we can get. You decided against it. Your call. So we had a civil war. Isn't that right? Poscai? Jasacai? You tell him, I can see he doesn't believe me.'

Temrai held up his hand. 'You're trying to tell me I've just fought a civil war and nobody thought to tell me what it was *about*?'

'We assumed you knew,' said the chancellor, Jasacai. 'After all, it's so obvious.'

Temrai slid back in his chair and let his chin drop on his chest. 'Not to me,' he replied. 'All right,' he went on, 'I want you to promise me something. Next time we go to war, will somebody please tell me why?'

Another Imperial diplomat, not quite so grand but nevertheless a thoroughly competent man with nearly twenty years' experience, landed from a civilian merchant ship at Tornoys, the free port through which passed most of the traffic to and from the suddenly relevant backwater of the Mesoge. His name was Poliorcis, and although he wasn't a Son of Heaven (originally he was from Maraspia province, right on the other side of the Empire) his appearance alone was enough to make him stand out among the usual crowd on Tornoys pier. Mesoge people, and the traders who did business with them, tended to be short, square and functional, as if someone had made a conscious effort to get as many of them as possible out of a limited quantity of raw material. By contrast, Maraspians came fairly close to extravagance verging on deliberate waste.

While the porters were unloading the cargo, near the bottom of which were the various barrels and bundles of trade-goods and junk that constituted his persona of itinerant textiles dealer, Poliorcis took the time to watch a mildly interesting and informative little scene being played out in the doorway of a ships' chandlery at the town end of the pier.

Blink twice, and you'd have missed it; more likely, you'd have seen it out of the corner of your eye and dismissed it as too commonplace to be worth eavesdropping on. Hence, among other reasons, the provincial office's habit of sending complete strangers when it wanted discreet observations made.

The old man was drunk; no question about that. Whether or not he was disorderly would depend on what passed for good order in any given place, and in Poliorcis' opinion this was the sort of place where singing and waving one's arms about in an exuberant but not overtly intimidating fashion would be, at worst, a nuisance and at best, ambience. Since the old man was quite decrepit, definitely not a threat to anybody but himself, and not that bad a singer if only he'd take the trouble to learn more than the first five words of any of the songs in his limited repertoire, Poliorcis was inclined to mark him down, in context, as ambience. At home, of course, it would have been quite different – ambience was about as popular as garbage from a fifth-storey window where he came from, and just as severely regarded by the authorities. But in a setting like this, you'd have expected no reaction beyond a tendency for passers-by to cross the road. Instead, a soldier coming out of a tavern stopped, reached out, grabbed the old man by the front of his disreputable shirt and cracked his head sharply against the doorframe, then let go and watched him slump to the ground, leaving a smear of blood on the timbers. At least four people must have seen the incident apart from Poliorcis, but none of them turned his head or gave any other indication of having noticed anything, whether from familiarity or policy the stranger wasn't sure. The old man lay still; the soldier went on his way. It had been neatly done, as if it was something they practised in the drill-yard, over and over again until they got it right.

Having digested the scene and committed it to memory, Poliorcis carried on down the street towards the timber exchange, where he hoped to absorb some more significant ambiance. He hadn't gone more than a yard or so, however, when someone tapped him on the shoulder, and he stopped and turned round.

'You look lost,' said the man who'd stopped him. He was large, commonplace-looking, bald, with friendly looking grey eyes; the height aside, he looked typically Mesoge. 'Are you looking for someone?'

Poliorcis thought for a moment. 'As a matter of fact,' he said, 'I am.'

'You've found him.' The man was wearing a light-brown quilted wool shirt, faded from grey and frayed across the shoulders; only someone as widely travelled and professionally observant as Poliorcis would have recognised it as Scona military issue, designed to be worn under the heavy mailshirt the Scona army had adopted in the days of their affluence, when they could afford the best; not cumbersome and hot, like the leather arming-jack or habergeon the provincial office specified to go with their lighter, short-sleeved hauberk, or fancy and impractical, like the padded linen gambesons produced by the Perimadeian state factories; whoever designed the Scona shirt had given it a degree of thought, and had done his job well. 'I'm Gorgas Loredan,' the man went on. 'If you're who I think you are, you've come a long way to see me.'

Poliorcis dipped his head in acknowledgement. 'Travel is one of the great pleasures of my trade,' he replied. 'It's not often these days that I can say I've come to a place I've never been before. You could say I collect places.'

Gorgas Loredan smiled. 'National pastime with you people,' he said. 'Let's go in the tavern there and have a drink.'

The tavern was large and busy; one main room with a high roof, filled with groups of three or four men standing and chatting amiably – farmers come to market, most of them, and a few merchants, corn-brokers, a handful of soldiers (allowed a certain amount of room by the other customers). At the back was a staircase leading to a gallery that ran round three sides of the building; there were chairs and tables up there, but only one or two of them were taken. Gorgas sat down with his back to the rail and pushed out the other chair with his foot for Poliorcis to sit on.

'Excuse the melodrama,' Gorgas said. 'I don't imagine for one moment that there's anybody following either one of us, or anything silly like that. But you never know.'

Poliorcis nodded. 'Actually, I think you're very sensible. I don't know what sort of intelligence service they've got—'

Gorgas pursed his lips. 'Better than you'd think, actually,' he said. 'I don't think they're great ones for sending out secret agents or anything like that, but they do seem to have the knack of asking the right questions when they're chatting to foreign visitors – traders, sailors, people on their way somewhere. I'm sorry,' he went on, 'I don't think I quite caught your name.'

'Euben Poliorcis.' He reached into his satchel and produced a small, crumpled roll of parchment that could easily have been a letter of credit or a bill of lading. 'I take it you're familiar with Imperial seals,' he said.

'Not as familiar as I'd like to be,' Gorgas replied with a grin. 'For a start, I'd love to learn the knack you people have of lifting a seal off a letter without breaking it and then putting it back again when you're done. Just an ordinary bit of thin wire, so I understand, heated red in a clean flame and drawn through the wax.' With the nail of his left little finger Gorgas picked off the seal like a scab and flicked it away. 'Now then, let's see what we've got here. Yes, that all seems to be in order. Marvellous handwriting you people have. Talking of which, next time you come, bring me a dozen or so sheets of that linen paper they make in Ap' Oezen. Can't get it for love nor money in these parts.'

Poliorcis smiled thinly. 'Of course,' he said, 'I'll make a note of it. Now, as I recall, it was you who wanted to talk to us.'

Gorgas shrugged. 'Someone had to make the first move,' he said. 'But it's pretty straightforward, isn't it? Our interests and yours coincide; let's do business.'

Three men appeared at the head of the stairs, saw Gorgas and retreated quickly. 'Interesting you see it that way,' Poliorcis said. 'Personally, I can't quite see your interest in this matter. Please don't take this the wrong way, but what harm has King Temrai ever done you?'

Gorgas shrugged. 'Oh, I've got nothing against the man; I met him once, he seemed pleasant enough. But that's hardly the point. I'm more concerned with what you people are planning, long term. As I see it, there's a gap waiting to be filled. I want my share of it. You could do with my help. Simple commercial relationship. Let's be straight with each other, and we'll get along fine.'

Poliorcis leaned back in his chair, making distance between Gorgas and himself. 'Indulge me,' he said. 'Looked at from one point of view, you're trying to persuade the Empire to make an unprovoked attack on a sovereign state. I'd like to know why.'

'Do you need persuading?' Gorgas grinned. 'I don't think so. With Ap' Escatoy out of the way, it's pretty obvious you'll keep on going till you reach the northern sea. Take Temrai out of the equation, and how does the picture look? There you are, right up against the coast, breathing down the neck of Shastel; the Island's neither here nor there, they aren't going to bother you, though I guess you could use their fleet. After that, sooner or later you're going to come west, and pretty soon after that we'll be neighbours. I'd far rather we had a good relationship when that time comes. So,' he went on, leaning forward across the table, 'here I am, coming to meet you. Makes sense, doesn't it?'

Poliorcis smiled pleasantly. 'I'd say you have a rather individual view of what our aspirations are. But,' he went on, 'let's assume for now that your interpretation's correct. Suppose we do have territorial ambitions in the peninsular; why do we need you? Haven't we got enough resources of our own, men and materiel, to do the job without indebting ourselves to you?'

Gorgas laughed. 'Of course,' he said. 'No question about it. But that's not your way. Never do a job yourselves if you can get someone else to do it for you. Sound business principles again, nothing wrong with that. With my army involved, it means you don't have to take so many units away from garrison duty in other parts of the Empire. Sure, you've got vast resources; doesn't mean to say you're not spread pretty thin, even so. And we both know our history; weaken the garrison in any of the eastern provinces, you're asking for trouble. Look what happened in Goappa, just recently, when you moved the seventh legion. Rather a close call, wasn't it?'

'Quite.' Poliorcis' smile didn't waver. 'How very well informed you are; I suppose it comes of running a bank. But I fancy we'd be able to scratch around and put together a large enough expedition without making a mistake like that again. We read the reports too, you know.'

'Of course.' Gorgas made a small gesture with his hands. 'But why go to all that trouble? The strength of the plains-people has always been their archers. To fight them you need to match their archers with your own. Most of your archers are stationed in the east. No earthly use sending a hundred thousand heavy infantry against Temrai; you'd be asking for a bloody good hiding. No, what you need is experienced, reliable longbowmen; and that's what I've got to offer.'

Poliorcis didn't reply immediately; he sat still with his hands folded in his lap. 'All right,' he said at last, 'just suppose you're right. Just suppose we do intend to attack Temrai, and we ask you for help. If it's a sound business proposition, as you assure me it is, what do you get out of it? Just money? Or did you have something else in mind?'

A fly landed on the table, flicking with its legs at a sticky patch of spilt beer. Gorgas flicked it with his fingers before it could take off, killed it. 'Depends,' he said. 'Money comes into it, certainly.'

'Implying you want something else as well. Such as? Territory? You want a slice of Temrai's land?'

Gorgas shook his head. 'Good gods, no. What use would that be to me? For a start, I haven't got the manpower, let alone the ships to keep darting backwards and forwards to protect my interests. Besides, that'd make us neighbours rather sooner than I'd like, if you don't mind me saying so.'

'All right.' Poliorcis nodded. 'You don't want territory; what does that leave? As I see it, there are only three things worth fighting for: money, land and people. Is that what you want? Slave labour to help you expand your economy here in the Mesoge?'

Gorgas scowled. 'Certainly not,' he said. 'Quite apart from anything else, it'd be far more trouble than it's worth. No, I don't want anything like that.'

'Then I give up,' Poliorcis said. 'Tell me what it is you do want.'

'Like I said,' Gorgas replied. 'Friendship. The beginning of a long, smooth and mutually beneficial relationship between the western provincial office and the republic of the Mesoge. What's so strange about that?'

'I see,' Poliorcis said. 'You're prepared to help us defeat the plainspeople so that we'll then owe you a favour. Am I right?'

'That puts it quite well, yes.'

Poliorcis rubbed his chin. 'Actually,' he said, 'I can see how that would be a tremendous advantage for you. I'm not sure it'd be worth our while, though. You see, we have an annoying habit of sticking to our treaties. If we were really as hell-bent on conquest as you seem to think we are, wouldn't we be making a rod for our own backs here? Hypothetically speaking, of course.'

'Up to you,' Gorgas said quietly. 'We have a saying here: don't kid a kidder. I'm making this offer in good faith, we both know perfectly well why. Now you can tell me what I can do with my offer and I'll just have to live with it. But it doesn't have to be like that. Whatever else I may or may not be, I'm a realist.' He smiled. 'That's what makes me such a pleasure to do business with.'

'So I gather,' Poliorcis replied. 'Well, I think that's about as far as we can get at this stage; I've got to go back to my superiors in the provincial office, give them my report, let them make up their minds.' He stood up. 'As you'll appreciate, I'm basically just here to find out a bit more about you and your people here, give the decision-makers back home a little bit more to go on. And I think I've got enough from our meeting here; with your permission, I'd like to have a look around before I go. Please, feel free to point me in any direction you feel I ought to be taking. For instance, I'd be interested to see these archers of yours. We have a saying of our own: always try the goods before you buy. Before I can make a valid report, I do need something a bit more solid to go on than what I've heard from you and what I've seen so far here in Tornoys. I'm sure you see my point.'

'Oh, absolutely,' Gorgas said. 'No, please, go right ahead. In fact, if you've got the time I'll happily be your guide for a day or so; the main garrison camp, that sort of thing. Or if you'd rather not – I mean to say, if you think having me round your neck all the time you're wanting to go see for yourself—'

Poliorcis smiled gracefully. 'A guided tour of the republic with yourself as my guide,' he said. 'What better way to find out about things could there possibly be?'

On his third day as deputy inspector of the proof house, Bardas actually managed to find it.

It was at the end of the longest gallery, down another of the speciality breakneck staircases, along a dark, narrow corridor, down another staircase, along another corridor, down another staircase; by which time Bardas could sense he was back underground where he belonged –

(*It's customary to die first, but in your case we've made an exception.*)

– Along another corridor, seventh on the left, third on the right, down another staircase, there you are, can't miss it. He stood outside the massive oak door feeling like a very junior clerk on his first day at a great merchant's counting house (which was silly, because he was in charge of the place. Or so they'd told him back among the ruins of Ap' Escatoy, above ground where the rules are subtly different).

He pushed the door with his hand, then pushed harder, then put his shoulder to it; it gave an inch or so, which encouraged him to keep shoving.

'It sticks,' said a voice as he tumbled into a cold, echoing room. 'But we keep it shut anyway, because of the noise. Who are you?'

At least there was a certain amount of light, coming from a row of oil-lamps up on a ledge over the door. The draught made their tenuous flames dance, swirling the light.

'My name's Loredan,' Bardas replied, trying to see who he was talking to. 'I've been posted here.'

'The hero,' said the voice. 'Come in. Shut the door.'

Bardas put his back to the door and managed to walk it shut; then he looked around. The room was lined with large, raw stone blocks, and the walls formed a high arch. In the middle was a pile of armour – breastplates, helmets, vambraces, gorgets, pauldrons, cops, cuisses, sabatons, gauntlets, all mangled and ruined, twisted and dented and crushed, pierced and skewed. The voice seemed to be coming from behind the pile; and when Bardas looked there, he found a little old man – a Son of Heaven – and an enormous boy of about eighteen. Both of them were stripped to the waist; the old man was all sticks and sharp edges pressing against the skin, while the boy was muscle and fat. Between them was an anvil on which sat a helmet. The old man was holding it down on the anvil with a pair of very long tongs. The boy was holding a huge hammer.

'Well,' said the old man, 'you found us all right. Pull up a helmet, sit down.'

The air in the room was cold, but both men were sweating. The boy's long, sandy hair was plastered round his forehead, as if he'd been dipped in tallow like a candle. The old man didn't have any hair at all, and the sweat sparkled on his egg-shaped skull. Bardas looked round, saw a pile of helmets, pulled one out and sat on it.

'I'm Anax,' said the old man. 'This is Bollo.' He smiled, revealing a dazzlingly wide array of teeth. 'Welcome to the proof house.'

'Thank you,' Bardas said.

Anax nodded politely (Bollo didn't seem to have noticed Bardas yet). 'You don't mind if we carry on, do you?' he said – his voice was refined, cultured, very Son-of-Heaven. 'We've got a lot to get through today, as you can see.'

'Please, carry on,' Bardas said; and at once Bollo hefted the hammer, swung it over his head and brought it down hard on the apex of the helmet. The clang made Bardas jump. Then the helmet rolled off the anvil and clattered on to the stone floor.

'No good,' said Anax sadly. 'You heard the harmonics? Garbage.' He stooped painfully, picked the helmet up and put it back on the anvil. There was a slight dent on the left side of the crown. 'You can tell everything from the sound,' Anax went on. 'Listen. This is what it should sound like.' He stooped again – bending down seemed to trouble him inordinately – and came up with another helmet, as far as Bardas could see identical to the first. Anax gripped it in the tongs, and Bollo thumped it.

'You hear that?' Anax said. 'Completely different. Good helmet. Well, good seam. The rivets are garbage.'

Bardas looked at the good helmet; it too had a slight dent in the crown. 'Sorry,' he said, 'but I don't see—'

'Really?' Anax nodded, and Bollo swung again. The sound hurt Bardas' ears. 'A fifth higher; sort of a purer, whiter sound. It's a bit flat, of course, because of the garbage rivets. Here, it's easier to tell on a cuirass.' He groaned this time as he bent down; he came up with a dull grey breastplate which he laid over the top of the anvil, having first swept the two dented helmets on to the floor with the back of his hand. 'Listen for the high note,' he said. 'You should hear it quite clearly.'

Bollo shifted his grip slightly on the hammer handle, then dealt the breastplate five enormous blows, two on each side and one on the ridge that ran up the centre. To Bardas, it sounded like an awful clanging noise.

'I see,' he said. 'Yes, quite different.'

The old man laughed. 'Fooled you,' he said. 'That one's garbage too. Not that it seems to matter any; I test 'em and reject the batch, they issue them anyway, but with a little stamp on the inside: FP. It stands for Failed Proof. Wonderful, isn't it?'

Bardas coughed. 'I'm holding you up,' he said. 'You carry on, I'll just watch for a bit.'

Anax laughed again. 'Don't worry,' he said. 'Took me fifteen years before I started hearing it. Till then, I just bashed 'em till they fell apart, and never knew what I was doing. Now, of course, I can tell instantly. But we still go on bashing, because that's what we do.'

Next on the anvil was a pair of clamshell gauntlets, a dull grey colour with flecks of rust. Bollo wrecked them both with seven blows, bursting the rivets and crushing the lames flat, while the noise bounced from wall to wall. 'Good,' said Anax, making a mark on a tally-stick with a small, thin knife. 'Pass them. Do the pauldrons next.'

Bardas didn't know what a pauldron was; it turned out to be a shoulder-guard, domed at the top to fit the ball of the shoulder, articulated with five lames to allow the arm to move freely. Bollo's hammer didn't seem to have much effect on it, but Anax didn't seem impressed. 'Fail,' he said. 'Sounds dull. Flaws in the metal, that's what does it; bits of coke and grit and copper, all sorts of rubbish. Comes of having to use what we can get. I know,' he added, his eyes suddenly lighting up. 'Bollo, fetch the Iron Man. Let's show our guest something a bit clever.'

Bollo let the hammer fall to the ground with a thud, then slouched away behind another stack of wrecked armour. He came back dragging a heavy iron trolley on which stood a lifesize human figure made of iron. It was red with rust; Bardas could smell the rust from where he was sitting. 'Properly speaking,' Anax was saying, 'we ought to use the Iron Man all the time; but after, what, a hundred and twenty years of being bashed around, he's getting a bit brittle. Aren't you, pal?' He patted the figure's thigh. 'See? No left hand. Snapped off. Won't weld. Too much bashing, see, it goes all hard – work-hardened, we call it, very important concept – and when it gets hard it gets brittle, and when it's brittle – that's it, finish. All right, Bollo, this time we'll use a number-four felling axe, let's show the gentleman how it's done.'

Bollo grunted, wiped his forehead with his leg-thick fore-arm – there wasn't a single hair left on it, Bardas noticed – and bent over, rummaging in a long metal box. Meanwhile Anax was strapping pieces of armour to the iron figure, carefully tightening buckles and adjusting the tension in the various straps. 'Got to be straight and true before we start,' Anax said, 'or it won't mean anything.'

The iron figure had vanished under the grey steel, not a square inch of rust to be seen; and in its place stood what Bardas would have sworn blind was a man in full armour. 'All right,' Anax called out, brushing powdered rust from his hands. 'Stand well back,' he told Bardas. 'Sometimes you get bits falling off and flying round the room. Depends a lot, of course, on who's bashing and who's getting bashed. Slowly now, Bollo, it's not a race. This is work, remember, not fun.'

How hard would he hit if it was fun? Bardas wondered, and braced himself just in time as Bollo swung the axe over his shoulder like a sack, then accelerated it as he bent his knees, throwing his entire bodyweight into the stroke. Bardas had been expecting an almighty clang, but the noise was different, more of a high-pitched clunk, as the force of the blow was transmitted through the thin skin of the steel knee-cop into the solid iron behind it; it was a musical, pulsating sound, short and clipped, the sound of extreme force being applied and turned back – Bardas heard the turning-back, and saw the axehead bounce off, all the force having nowhere to soak away into. The place on the armour where the axe-blade had hit was deeply scored but the steel skin was unbroken.

'Now that's bad,' Anax said. 'Hold that sound in your mind. All right, Bollo.'

The next blow landed on the point of the left elbow; and sure enough, the sound was a little different, just as the damage was evident and extensive, the steel being caved in and crushed. But Anax looked pleased. 'Good,' he said. 'Properly domed, the way it should be. Well, think about it, will you? You get hit very hard, where do you want the force of the hit to go, into the steel or into you? That's what good armour does, it takes the blow. Bad armour passes it on. Simple as that.'

Good armour takes the blow, Bardas repeated to himself, bad armour passes it on. 'So this is what you do here?' he said.

Anax grinned from ear to ear. 'I know,' he said, 'it's a bloody funny way to earn a living. I mean, take yourself, you're clearly an intelligent man, you've been around, been in the wars, I dare say – well of course you have, you're a hero, I was forgetting. You look at that –' he pointed to one piece of scrap armour '– and then you look at that.' He indicated another, just as badly mangled. 'And you say to yourself, they're both busted, I guess they both failed. Wrong. It's a philosophy, you see,' he went on, wiping his nose on the inside of his wrist. 'It all fails, you see; there's nothing, no piece of munitions-grade plate in the whole world, that can stand up to Bollo here and the big, big hammer. It's *how* it fails that matters. And that's what I can't get them to understand,' he added, a tiny spurt of anger showing in his pale eyes. 'Because unless you're me, or someone else who's been destroying and wrecking stuff day in, day out, all his life, long as he can remember, you can't even understand there's a good way to get smashed into scrap, and there's a bad way. Your generals, now, and your brass in the provincial office, they say, we want a pattern that won't fail, period. And I say, all right; I can tell them how to make it, specifications, gauges and angles and heat treatment and all the rest of it, but you couldn't afford it and nobody could ever wear it. You want practical armour, you've got to come to an understanding with Bollo here and the number-four felling axe. And he'll scrap it, every time.'

Bardas nodded, trying to look as if he'd understood something. 'And you say it's the sound it makes?' he said, but the old man just looked impatient.

'That's just one test,' he said. 'One criterion for one test. Believe me, we don't just bash on the stuff with hammers and axes. Oh no. We shoot at it with longbows and crossbows, we squash it between rollers, there's the puncture test, the shear test, the breaking-strain test, the crush test, the flex test – you don't want to know all the different ways we can prove a piece, if anybody ever gave us a piece that got that far. And the point I'm trying to make is, it always fails – if it didn't fail, it'd be a pretty useless test. We deal in *extremes* here, Mister Hero; otherwise there wouldn't be any point.'

Anax suddenly stopped talking; he was staring at something. 'What is it?' Bardas asked.

'Duff copper rivets,' Anax replied, as if drawing Bardas' attention to a widening crack in the sky. 'Look at that, will you?' He pointed with a long, brittle-looking finger. 'See there, the rivets in that cop. Shorn off.'

Bardas made a show of looking. 'All right,' he said. 'What's the significance of that?'

Anax sighed. 'It's the whole point of copper rivets,' he said. 'Your copper rivet, when you put it under a strain it can't handle, it stretches – look, here, like this.' He prodded a derelict gauntlet with his toe. 'That's what it's meant to do. Now look at these here, on the cop. Torn the heads off. So that lot's no good, not that anybody's going to want to know that. It'd mean junking the whole batch, probably a hundred thousand rivets; if we do that, there's some clerk in an office in Procurement who'll have to answer for it. But he doesn't want to do that, and nobody really believes me anyway, so they won't take any notice. I tell you, if this wasn't what I do, I wouldn't do it any more.'

Bollo, who'd been standing by with the axe over his shoulder, seemed to have lost patience; quite unexpectedly, he whirled the axe round and brought it down on the point of the Iron Man's shoulder.

'Sharp clunk,' Bardas said. 'Not good?'

'Terrible,' replied Anax sadly. 'But what they'll do is, they'll issue double padding to go inside the pauldron cup, and then it won't seem so bad; at least anybody who wears the stuff won't wind up with a smashed collar-bone. But it'll be wrong. And I'll know.'

'I suppose so,' Bardas said evenly.

'Well of course,' Anax said. 'I always know.'

Theudas Morosin had found a ship; that is, he'd spoken to a man, a dealer in bulk almonds, who'd been talking to the captain of another ship a week or so before, who'd happened to mention that once he'd found a buyer for his cargo of ebony baluster-rail blanks from Colleon (he had no idea how he'd come to have a hold full of thirty-inch sections of ebony suitable for making baluster rails out of, assuming you had a lathe and a market for ebony baluster rails; price had been a part of the equation, but there'd been more to it than that) he was going to use the proceeds to buy a consignment of seven hundred sacks of duck-belly feathers he'd been promised by a man he knew in Ap' Helidon; the deal being, he'd have to go to Perimadeia (what used to be Perimadeia) to collect them. 'Although,' (he'd said, apparently), 'it may not be that much of a deal, at that, because who's to say how big a sack is?' The man Theudas had been talking to had then asked this other man, he didn't say how big the sacks were? And the man had replied no, but it can't be that important, because unless he was saying sack when really he meant bag, seven hundred sacks, at that price, is still a lot of feathers.

'I see,' Gannadius replied when his nephew had finished explaining all this. 'And you're hoping that when this man, the one who's buying the feathers, comes to collect his cargo, he'll take us with him.'

'Yes,' Theudas said. 'And then we'll be home again. Well, what do you think?'

Gannadius considered his reply. 'It depends,' he said. 'If they're small sacks, maybe he won't bother. If they're big sacks, there may well not be room for us on the boat. And didn't you say all this depends on him finding a buyer for a shipload of ebony stair-rods?'

'Baluster rails,' Theudas amended. 'Oh, come on. I'd have thought you'd be pleased.'

Gannadius scratched his nose. 'I'm just trying to tell you not to get your hopes up, that's all. And didn't you say this man comes from Ap' Helidon? I don't remember you saying he was going to take the feathers to the Island when – if – he got them. I don't really want to go to Ap' Helidon, if it's all the same to you. If it's where I think it is, it's part of the Empire. We'd be worse off than we are here.'

'No, we wouldn't.' Theudas folded his arms and looked away. 'Anywhere would be better than here. Here is *nowhere*.'

Outside the tent somewhere a man was singing, while a couple of other men accompanied him on a pipe and some kind of stringed instrument. The words didn't seem to make much sense –

> *Grasshopper sitting on a sweet-pepper vine*
> *Grasshopper sitting on a sweet-pepper vine*
> *Grasshopper sitting on a sweet-pepper vine*
> *And along comes a chicken and he says, 'You're mine'*

– but the music was fast and cheerful, and the men sounded like they were enjoying making it; there were worse noises, both outside and inside Gannadius' head. 'There'll be a ship,' he said sleepily, 'sooner or later. We've just got to be patient, that's all. What we don't want to do is go blundering about the western seaboard just for the sake of doing something. For one thing, I might die, and how are you going to explain that to Athli?'

That just made Theudas more irritable. 'I don't see what that's got to do with anything. And what's all this stuff about dying? You aren't even ill, you're just lazy.'

Gannadius smiled. 'That nice lady doctor wouldn't agree with you. She says I still need plenty of rest, after what I've been through.'

'Oh really? And what was that, exactly? I don't seem to remember anything all that dreadful. I mean, I was there too, and I'm not lying on my back groaning all the time.'

'All right,' Gannadius replied, laughing. 'All right. If your duck-feather man really does show up, and if he's going our way and if he agrees to take us and if there's room on his ship, we'll go. It'll be a comfortable ride, sitting on all those feathers.'

Theudas stood up. 'I'm going for a walk,' he said, 'before I lose my temper.'

It was bright outside the tent; so bright and hot that nobody was moving about. Instead, they were lying in whatever shade they could find. The three men who'd been making that awful noise had stopped now, thank gods; they were lounging in the shadow of a large timber frame they'd been working on, passing a big jug of some sort of drink from hand to hand, and eating nuts from a pot.

'Your friend,' one of them called out as Theudas walked past. 'How's he doing?'

Theudas stopped. 'Oh, he's all right,' he replied awkwardly.

'That's good.' The man was beckoning him over; it would be difficult not to refuse. Hate them quietly, Gannadius had said. Theudas went over and sat beside them. 'Is it true what they're saying?' the man asked.

Theudas stiffened a little. 'I don't know,' he said. 'What are they saying?'

The man laughed and handed Theudas the jug. 'That he's a wizard,' he said. 'One of the Shastel wizards. Well, is it true?'

Theudas nodded. 'Though really they aren't wizards,' he said. 'Actually, there's no such thing as wizards. They're scholars.'

'Whatever.' The man seemed to regard the distinction as trivial. 'Then it must be true, what I've heard,' he went on. 'The Shastel wizards are going to help us win the war.'

Theudas frowned. 'What war?'

'The war against the Empire,' the man said. 'King Temrai and the Shastel wizards are forming an alliance, so that when the Empire attacks one of us, the other joins in too. It's about time,' he went on. 'I mean, fun's fun, but it's high time somebody took this thing seriously.'

Theudas' frown grew deeper. 'I didn't know there going to be a war,' he said.

'Of course there's going to be war,' said one of the other men, the one who'd been playing the pipe. 'Because they've taken Ap' Escatoy at last. Now they're coming after us.'

'Or Shastel,' the third man interrupted.

'Or Shastel,' agreed the piper. 'Which is why we need

to make an alliance with the wizards. Nobody else is going to help us, after all. Nobody else is left.'

Theudas handed the jug to the piper, hoping nobody would notice he hadn't drunk any of what was in it; cider, he suspected, and he'd always hated cider, ever since he was a boy. They'd drunk nothing else in Perimadeia, and now the plainsmen had taken to it as well. 'What's this you're making?' he asked, hoping to change the subject.

The men looked at each other. 'Oh, come on,' one of them said, 'it doesn't really make any odds. Besides, anybody with an eye to see can look at it and tell for themselves. It's a trebuchet,' he went on. 'Like the ones we made when we took the City. Same design, in fact; well, they worked all right then, so let's hope they'll work just as well against the Empire.'

'A trebuchet,' Theudas repeated. He could remember the day the trebuchets had appeared; the day the plainsmen appeared under the walls, on the other side of the narrow channel, with their barges of pre-shaped timbers, and all the noise and bustle of assembling the engines. Nobody had known what to make of them, whether they were a joke or a threat or both. 'And this is because of Ap' Escatoy,' he added.

The man who'd played the guitar-like thing nodded. 'Because of that bastard Loredan,' he said. 'He thinks long, that bastard.'

'Loredan? You mean Bardas Loredan?'

The guitar player nodded. 'Planned the whole thing, everybody knows that. Went away after the Fall, joined the Empire, took Ap' Escatoy for them so they'd come after us next. He's the one we should be looking out for. Gods, he must hate us a lot.'

There was an awkward pause. Then the man who'd been singing said, 'Well, fair enough. It was his city we burned down, of course he wants to get even.'

'But we burned it down because of what he did to us,' the piper answered. 'Him and his uncle Maxen. That's why Temrai had to do it. And now he's come after us again, only this time he's got the Empire with him. He won't rest easy till he's killed us all, you'll see.'

Theudas looked down at the ground. Irrational; but he had

the feeling that if they saw his face, they'd *know*. Also, he had a terrible, painful feeling of guilt – the things they were saying about Bardas, who wasn't like that, they were making him sound like the angel of death or something and he wasn't, he was a quiet, lonely man who just wanted to keep out of the way of trouble – but trouble would keep following him around, like a dog sniffing the trousers of a sausage-seller. But *he* knew that the last thing Bardas wanted was to get even, and that none of it was his fault.

'I've got to go,' he said, standing up. 'Thanks for the drink.'

'Don't worry about it,' said the banjo-man. 'And hey, calm down. He hasn't got us yet. And he won't, you can count on it.'

'I know,' Theudas said, and walked away.

CHAPTER SEVEN

'Well,' said Gorgas Loredan, 'you're pretty quiet. What do you reckon?'

Poliorcis thought for a moment. 'It's beautiful,' he said. 'Very green.'

'Green,' Gorgas repeated. 'You know, I'd never thought of it like that before. Yes, it's certainly green all right.'

The rain was slowing up; just a summer shower, more or less a daily occurrence at this time of year in the Mesoge. Rain dripped in fat splodges from the thatched eaves of the old linhay they'd taken shelter in; a typical Mesoge building, half derelict, probably been that way for a hundred years, probably be in more or less the same shape a hundred years hence. A little stream of muddy water trickled through the open doorway, across the floor and away into a damp patch in the far corner. Even inside, the walls were green with moss.

'So,' Gorgas went on, 'that's all there is to it, really. My work on Scona was over, I'd done my best, things hadn't worked out the way I'd planned, but there was no point going all to pieces over it. So I came home.'

Poliorcis nodded. 'With an army,' he said. 'And seized power. And set yourself up as a - excuse me, I don't mean to sound rude, but it's an awkward concept to put the right word to. King's not right, somehow, and warlord has such dreadful connotations. Military dictator, perhaps—'

Gorgas smiled. 'Prince,' he said. 'That's how I like to think of myself, anyway. Prince of the Mesoge. You're right, it's not big enough for a kingdom. I thought about duke, but that has overtones of being somebody's subordinate.' He yawned, then bit off another mouthful of cheese. 'So I guess that makes this a principality. Seems suitable to me, in terms of scale. Bigger than a county, smaller than a country; what do you think?'

'Whatever,' Poliorcis replied. The barrel he'd been sitting on all this time was wet, too (everything was wet in this – this *principality*). 'Now, I'll be straight with you, the thing that I couldn't understand was why you met with so little resistance. Please, don't take this the wrong way—'

Gorgas waved away the niceties of diplomatic language. 'No problem,' he said with his mouth full.

'Thank you; but for a – oh dear, vocabulary again – for an *adventurer* like yourself to come barging in, with only a few hundred soldiers to back him up, and take charge of a country that's never really had a ruler or a government before: you must admit, it's enough to make one curious. But now I've seen it for myself—'

Gorgas nodded. 'Apathy,' he said. 'Or you could call it being fatalistic, or demoralised (except that suggests there was a time when they were all moralised, and there wasn't, far as I know); basically, it's not giving a damn one way or another. You see,' he went on, breaking up a strip of dried meat with his fingers, 'all this lot, ever since it was first settled, the whole country was planted out as estates by rich City families – Perimadeians, absentee landlords, naturally – and the poor bloody peasants who actually grew stuff and lived here, we were only ever tenants, or hired men; no tradition of owning the land, you see. I suppose the City bailiffs were the government, which is to say that they'd come round and tell you what to do and you'd do it; not that they bothered us much, we didn't see them from one year's end to the next. Apart from that, we just got on with things.'

'Quite,' Poliorcis said. 'And the sort of things governments do – courts of law, for example, justice—'

Gorgas laughed. 'Weren't any. Didn't need any. You'll have noticed, there's no towns, no villages even; just farms. And on every farm, a family. If there's any ruling to be done, the farmer does it, same as he does everything else.'

'I see.' A rat scuttled across the floor, stopped, looked at Poliorcis critically, as if he was a picture hung slightly crooked, and vanished behind a barrel. 'And disputes between neighbours? Feuds, presumably, and long, drawn-out petty bickering.'

'That sort of thing,' Gorgas said. 'Usually quite harmless; and if not, well, nobody else's business. Besides, mostly there just wasn't the time or the energy.'

Poliorcis shook his head. 'So,' he said, 'the only question that's left is, why should anybody *want* a place like this?'

'It's my home,' Gorgas replied. 'And when the City fell, there was a gap; no more landlords, no *shape* to anything. People like to know where they stand. It's one of the things that makes life possible.'

Poliorcis didn't feel like replying to that. 'I think I've seen enough,' he said. 'And the rain's eased off. Shall we go back to Tornoys?'

'I was thinking we might go to my farm,' Gorgas replied. 'It's quite close. We can stay there tonight, and go back to Tornoys in the morning.'

'Very well,' Poliorcis said. 'Is there anything to see there?'

Gorgas shook his head. 'It's just a farm,' he replied. 'My brothers look after it while I'm away. They've always been there, you see.'

There was something that Poliorcis couldn't quite place, but he saw no point in making an issue of it.

Half an hour's ride from the linhay they came to a bridge, or the remains of one. The middle of the three spans was missing.

'Damn,' Gorgas said. 'We'll have to double back to the ford.' He frowned. 'It's a nuisance, this sort of thing. Somebody needed some blocks of masonry, so they broke up the bridge. I'll have to send someone to fix it.'

At the ford there was a gibbet, with a body hanging from it. Gorgas didn't comment, and Poliorcis didn't feel like asking. The body looked as if it had been there for a couple of weeks.

'One thing I've got to do when I have the time,' Gorgas said, as they rode over the ford, 'is to have these roads made up. It's pointless expecting people to do it themselves; all that happens is, they fall out with their neighbours over who's responsible for which part. I gather you have expert road-makers in the Empire, people who do nothing else. I'd be interested in hiring a few.'

An hour on from the ford, the road petered out in the middle of a crop of barley. It wasn't much of a crop; the rain had beaten down flat patches, and the pigeons and rooks had come in and trodden down as much again. Gorgas sighed and rode down the middle until he came to a tall thorn hedge. There was a gate, but it was tangled up in thirty years' growth of thorns and briars.

'I thought it'd been a while since I last came this way,' Gorgas said. 'Now you see what I mean about proper roads.' He jumped down from his horse and started slashing at the hedge with his sword; but the briars were too springy to cut. 'Sorry about this,' he said. 'We'll have to head back to the lane and go round through the farmyard. And while we're there, I'll give them a piece of my mind about this gate.'

Poliorcis sighed. 'As you like,' he said. 'I think it's coming on to rain again.'

It was dark by the time they came to what Poliorcis assumed was the farm; too dark to see anything except the silhouette of a roof and a vague smudge of branches against the sky. He heard his horse's hooves clatter on a paved yard, and Gorgas shouting; a thin wedge of light spilled out as a door opened, very pale, yellow light, the sort that comes from thick lard and sparingly trimmed wicks. Certainly, the place smelt like a farm. As he got off his horse, he felt his feet splash in a puddle. He wiped rain out of his eyes with his sodden cuff and followed Gorgas towards the light.

'There's nothing grand about it,' said Gorgas cheerfully, 'but it's home. Come on in, you'll soon dry off.'

Gorgas was right; there was nothing grand about it at all. The glow from the tallow-lamp was too dim to let Poliorcis see what he was walking on; it felt like old, sodden rushes, and it didn't smell terribly nice. In the large room he'd been led into there was a large plain board table covered with wooden and pewter dishes, each containing a few scraps of crust or rind. Two men were sitting beside it, each with a big horn cup in front of him. They didn't seem to have noticed he was there.

'My brothers,' Gorgas annouced, 'that's Clefas on the left and Zonaras on the right.' The two men didn't stir, except to move their heads a little to stare at him, and then back at each other. 'You'll have to excuse them,' Gorgas went on, 'I expect they're tired out after a hard day. It's a busy time of year; we're cutting reed down by the river and making up the cheese for the cider.'

Still no reaction from Clefas and Zonaras. Poliorcis sat down on a three-legged stool and perched his elbows on a clear corner of the table. Gorgas was standing on a chair, getting something down from the rafters. 'How's the reed shaping up?' he asked.

'Bad,' Zonaras replied. 'Too wet. We'll leave it a week, see if the river goes down, though with all this rain I wouldn't count on it.'

The thing from the rafters turned out to be a net bag containing a big round cheese coated in plaster. 'Clefas, is there any fresh bread?'

'No,' Clefas replied.

'Oh. Well, never mind, we'll have to make do. Any cider in the jug?'

'No.'

Gorgas sighed. 'I'll get some more from the cellar,' he said, picking up the jug. 'Won't be a moment.'

He seemed to be gone for a very long time, during which neither of his brothers moved perceptibly. When he returned, he had a solid-looking loaf under one arm and the cider-jug in his hand. 'Fire could do with another log,' he said, but nobody seemed concerned. It was cold, as well as damp. Gorgas was sawing at the loaf with his knife.

'Anyway,' he said, 'you wanted to see the Mesoge; this is about as typical as you're likely to get. Here.' He was holding out a plate with some bread and cheese on it. 'I'll get you a mug and you can have some cider.'

'No, really,' Poliorcis protested, but he was too late. There wasn't enough light to see the cider by, but he could make out a little wisp of straw floating on the top. 'You can sleep in my room,' Gorgas went on. 'I'll muck in with Zonaras.'

Zonaras grunted.

'Well.' Gorgas sat down and broke off a piece of bread, which he dipped in his mug. 'This is home,' he said. 'Take it or leave it. Personally, I don't think you can beat plain, old-fashioned Mesoge hospitality.'

Poliorcis reminded himself that he was a diplomat and said nothing; because he was decidedly hungry, he even nibbled at a corner of the cheese, which was very strong and rather disgusting. Gorgas was asking if there was any bacon left. There wasn't.

'Thatch on the trap-house needs looking at,' Clefas said. 'Won't have time now till after we've got the hay in. If the reed doesn't come to anything, we'll have to buy in. That's if anybody's got any.'

'Oh, well,' Gorgas said.

'Got to move the apples out,' Clefas went on. 'Damp's getting in; we'll lose the whole lot otherwise. I haven't got time,' he added.

'Don't look at me,' replied Zonaras. 'What do you think I've been doing all week, sitting on my hands?'

Gorgas sighed. 'I'll send some men down,' he said. 'You just tell them what needs doing, they'll see to it.'

'What we need is someone to push the rooks off the laid barley,' Clefas said. 'I counted a hundred and four in there the other day. If it gets any worse it won't be worth cutting.'

'Hasn't come to anything special anyhow,' Zonaras pointed out. 'Too damn wet. We need ten days' clear sun before it'll be anything like ready. We should have put the beans in there like I said.'

'We had beans there last year,' Clefas replied. 'And we needed them in the top five-acre to put some strength back in the ground. Might as well plough them back in, the way they're shaping up.'

It was as much as Poliorcis could do to stop himself laughing; but Gorgas Loredan, self-anointed Prince of the Mesoge, was nodding his head sagely and looking grave; *he's playing the part of a farmer*, Poliorcis realised, *but he hasn't quite got it right; he tries to think himself into all these various parts – farmer, prince, diplomat, hard-bitten professional soldier – but he never quite manages to get below the surface. I wonder who he really is. I expect he does, too.*

Gorgas' room (the master bedroom, so he'd been informed, where Father used to sleep after Mother died) turned out to be a small loft, up a set of steps that were more like a ladder than a staircase. There was a bed, a mattress stuffed with very old reed, no pillow, one vintage blanket that had been carefully turned sides-to-middle round about the time Poliorcis had just started shaving (that would be back before

Gorgas' mother died, unless it was the handiwork of Niessa Loredan, before she got involved in international finance). Poliorcis peeled off his wet boots, swung himself on to the bed and pinched out the wick of the lamp. He could hear something pattering about on the roof – not rain, because nothing was dropping into the half-filled pans strategically placed around the room to catch the drips. Cats? Squirrels, if they come out at night? It could be rabbits – the eaves of the house backed into the low hill. Whatever it was, it made enough noise to keep Poliorcis awake, even though he was painfully weary.

An alliance between the Empire and these clowns – it was ludicrous to think that he'd even considered it. At best, Gorgas had – what, a thousand men? Probably not that many, and how many of those would he be able to spare, being realistic, from the job of bullying and bashing his fellow peasants into line? It was a sad reflection on his own gullibility; he'd wasted time here, and most of what he'd found out was worthless. At best, he had an insight of sorts into this curious tribe, the Loredans, who'd somehow managed to involve themselves so deeply in matters that were significant enough to affect Imperial policy. As he shifted about, trying to find a level patch of mattress big enough to accommodate his back, he reflected on this strange phenomenon, trying to make sense of it.

Niessa Loredan, for example; no longer relevant, but for a while she'd been dangerous enough to destabilise the Shastel Bank, and the piddling little army that she'd paid for and Gorgas had trained had killed a few thousand of the Order's halberdiers (and every little helped, potentially). She was out of the picture now; and so, he was certain, was Gorgas; this peculiar little nest of bandits he'd scraped together for himself would keep the Mesoge depressed and unimportant for years to come – keeping it warm, so to speak, just in case it should ever suit the convenience of the provincial office to look this way. That in itself was unlikely – Tornoys might be a useful base for a squadron of galleys, if the Empire ever built up a *proper* fleet, as opposed to the disorganised clutter of hired and captured ships that was referred to in the supply ledgers as the Imperial Navy, but Gorgas palpably didn't control Tornoys;

if he tried to muscle in there, it would probably be the undoing of him.

Which left Bardas Loredan, once colonel, now sergeant; the hero of Ap' Escatoy, the last defender of Perimadeia, the angel of death as far as the plainspeople were concerned. Poliorcis frowned in the dark, trying to remember what little he'd understood of basic causality theory. In the end, he gave it up; he was a diplomat, and the Empire had plenty of professional metaphysicians without needing any input from him on the subject. But even he, relying on the scrapings of his memories of a two-week foundation course at the Ap' Sammas military academy, could tell that there was work to be done in this area before any long-term plans could properly be made; and the data he was gathering here would probably be important at that stage. The thought comforted him; it had been a maxim of his division tutor that the first and most essential stage in doing useful work is finding out what work it is that one is supposed to be doing. Well, now he knew. He was here to study the pathology of Bardas Loredan. So that was all right.

Eventually he fell asleep; and if he had bad dreams sleeping in that bed in that house, it was most likely because of the cheese.

Vetriz Auzeil sat on the front step of her house, watching a small boy in the street below. He'd gathered a substantial hoard of small stones, and he was throwing them, with great deliberation, into a clump of raggety, neglected ornamental shrubs that grew in the front yard of the house opposite. Nobody had lived in that house for years – it was only still empty because Venart, bless him, was trying to buy it (and, being Venart, was going about it in a counter-productively devious way, using phantom intermediaries supposedly undercutting each other's offers and pulling out just before an agreement was due to be sealed – it was costing him a fortune, but it made him feel cunning, which was the main thing); nevertheless, Vetriz had a feeling that small boys throwing stones were a bad thing on general principles, and that as (gods help her) a grown-up, she was invested with all due authority to tell him to stop – except that she couldn't make out for the life of her what he was throwing the stones at, with such care and deliberation.

Finally her curiosity reached torture levels, so she went down the steps and asked him.

'Spiders,' he answered.

'Spiders?'

'That's right.' The boy pointed; and, sure enough, just inside the tangle of bushes was a veritable city of spiders' webs, most of them with a big fat brown spider in the middle; they hung so still and moody that they reminded Vetriz of stallholders in a market on a quiet day, gloomily poised for the onset of any customers who might eventually appear.

'Any luck?' Vetriz asked. She detested spiders. When she was a little girl, it had been an entirely passive loathing, but now she was an adult, it had evolved into something more militant.

'Four so far,' the boy replied proudly. 'It only counts if you kill them dead; if they just fall off and run away you don't score anything.'

That was as much of an invitation (a challenge, even) as she needed; she selected a pebble from the munitions dump, made her best guess at elevation and windage, and let fly –

(– *Like the trebuchets at Perimadeia. In a way.*)

'Missed,' the boy said, perfectly expressing by tone of voice alone the eternal contempt of the male at womankind's ineptitude at missile warfare. 'My go.' He picked up a stone, looked at it between his fingers, looked at the spider of his choice, and launched.

'Missed,' said Vetriz.

'I never said it was easy,' the boy replied, scowling.

This time, Vetriz tried to be more scientific in her approach. She pictured in her mind the trajectory of the stone, the decay of its arc as its mass overcame the initial momentum of launch. With the picture clear in her mind as if it had been scribed on the back of her eyelids, she cocked back her wrist and let go –

'We shouldn't be doing this anyway,' she said huffily. 'It's cruel. Those spiders never did us any harm.'

'They're poisonous,' the boy replied. 'If they bite you, you swell up and go black and you die.'

'Really?' Vetriz said. 'I never heard that.'

'It's true,' the boy assured her. 'My friend told me.'

'Oh, well then,' Vetriz said, sneaking another stone. 'In that case, I suppose it's our duty – there,' she added. 'Direct hit.'

'Doesn't count,' the boy said. 'It wasn't even your go.'

Vetriz smiled. 'And you're just a rotten loser,' she said. 'Now stop doing that at once, before I tell your mother.'

The boy looked at her savagely, his eyes accusing her of treason in the first degree; then he kicked over the pile of stones and slouched away. Vetriz, unaccountably delighted with her prowess, went back to her step, where she'd been supposed to be double-checking the stock ledger. She was trying to puzzle out a double-looped squiggle (Venart was a sucker for fashionable new abbreviations, but he tended to forget what they meant the day after he started using them) when a shadow fell over the page. She looked up.

'Vetriz Auzeil?'

She nodded and looked away quickly, trying desperately not to stare. But it was hard; too hard for her. After all, she'd never seen a Son of Heaven before.

'I'm looking for your brother, Venart,' the man said. 'Is he at home?'

Vetriz shook her head. 'I'm sorry,' she said, 'he's away on a business trip. Can I help you?'

The man smiled, as if the offer had come from a six-year-old child. 'Thank you, but no. It's business.'

It was well known among her friends that you only ever patronised Vetriz Auzeil once. 'Then it's me you need to see,' she replied, smiling sweetly. 'Please come in. I can spare you a quarter of an hour.'

The man looked at her, but followed. She led him into the counting house, which she knew would be empty at this time of day, when the clerks were either at the warehouse doing the stock reconciliations or in the tavern. 'Please excuse the mess,' she said, indicating the immaculately neat desks with a sweeping gesture. 'Now then, what can I do for you?' She sat down behind Venart's desk, the one he'd been lumbered with as part of a mixed lot of Perimadeian war loot, bought sight unseen; it was huge, ornate and unspeakably vulgar, and Venart hated it. 'Sit down, please,' she said, knowing full well that the stool on the other side was so low that you had to sit on a cushion just to see over the desktop. Disconcertingly, the Son of Heaven didn't seem to have that problem; were they all this damnably tall? she wondered.

'Thank you.' She watched the man trying to squirm himself comfortable; impossible on that stool. 'My name is Moisin Shel, and I represent the provincial office. We're interested in chartering a number of ships.'

Vetriz nodded, as if this sort of thing happened every day. 'I see,' she said. 'What sort of ship, how many, and how long for?'

Moisin Shel looked at her, raised an eyebrow. 'You have a ship called the *Squirrel*,' he said. 'We understand it's a twin-masted square-rigger capable of sustaining six knots with a following wind, and that you're used to sailing a close-hauled course with the wind abeam, on coastal runs. It should be suitable for our purposes, if the capacity is adequate. Am I right in thinking the *Squirrel* is at least a hundred and thirty tons?'

'Oh, easily,' Vetriz replied, not having the faintest idea what the man was talking about. 'What cargo do you have in mind?'

Moisin Shel didn't seem to have heard her. 'A few technical points, before we go any further – I'm sorry if this sounds fussy, but we have to satisfy ourselves that your ship conforms to the provincial service specifications before we can enter a charter agreement. Are you able to answer such questions, or should I wait until your brother comes home?'

'No problem,' Vetriz replied firmly. 'Ask away.'

'Very well.' The man steepled his fingers. 'Are the garboard strakes mortised to the keel rabbet, do you know?'

To her credit, Vetriz managed to keep a straight face. 'The *Squirrel* is a working merchant ship, Mr Shel, not a pleasure yacht. I can assure you, you need have no worries on that score.'

The Son of Heaven nodded again. 'And presumably the stempost and sternpost are scarfed to the keel,' he went on. 'As I said, I'm sorry to have to trouble you with this sort of detail, but we have had some rather unfortunate experiences in the past when dealing with civilian shipowners.'

'I . . .' Vetriz took a deep breath. 'Offhand,' she said, 'I can't quite recall. I would imagine they are. After all, my father was ferrying bales of cloth from Colleon to Scona in the *Squirrel* when you were still learning to walk; if she's stayed in one piece that long, chances are she's not held together with waxed paper and glue. However,' she added quickly, as the Son of Heaven drew his breath in sharply, 'I can get confirmation of that as soon as she gets in; or you're welcome to look her over for yourself. I suggest we proceed on the assumption that she meets your requirements. What was it you said you wanted her for?'

The corner of Moisin Shel's lip twitched slightly. 'I didn't,' he replied. 'Well, I think it would be best if I do as you suggest and inspect the ship myself when she gets back. Can you give me any idea when that might be?'

'Hard to say,' Vetriz said. She'd decided that she didn't like Mr Shel very much. 'A week, maybe two. It depends on several things, you see—'

'Of course.' Moisin Shel stood up. 'I shall be here for another three weeks at least; as and when the *Squirrel* gets in, I'll be in touch again. Thank you so much for your time.'

'Um.' Vetriz jumped up too. 'If you'd just like to let me know where you're staying, so that when she does get in—'

'That's all right,' Shel said. 'I'll know. And I'll be back then. Good day.'

When he'd gone, Vetriz leaned back in her brother's chair and swore, something she didn't often do. As a merchant and a natural daughter of the Island, she knew, she should be thrilled at the thought of a good deal like this (at least, she assumed it would be a good deal; now she thought of it, the subject of money hadn't actually cropped up); but there was something about Moisin Shel that made her teeth ache. Not, she quickly assured herself, that Venart would have handled things any better – oh, he'd have smiled and fawned like an idiot, but she knew for a fact that her brother wouldn't know a garboard strake if it bit him on the nose. Well, if the wretched man did call back, Ven could have the pleasure of closing the deal, and welcome. She shook her head, left the counting house and went through into the small room that had been her father's office. There, if she remembered correctly, fifteen years ago there had been a small, fat, scruffy book with a name like *Vesano On Shipbuilding*; she might not have a clue right now what a garboard strake was, but by gods she'd know all about the wretched things by the time Ven got home; whereupon she could tell him, as if explaining to a small child – you know, Ven, the garboard *strakes*. I thought everybody knew *that*.

And find out she did; and remarkably boring it proved to be. But at least it meant that when Venart got home (the very next day, oddly enough) she was able to say, 'the long planks on either side of the keel,' as if she'd known that since before she'd started eating solid food.

'Oh,' Venart replied. 'Then why not call them that, instead of having some bloody stupid fancy name? And what about "mortised to the keel rabbet"? No, don't tell me, I don't want to know. If I really need to find out I can look it up in Dad's old book, same as you did.'

Vetriz frowned. 'Anyway,' she said. 'What do you think?'

Venart's look of annoyance faded into a smirk. 'Money for old rope,' he replied. '*Good* money for old rope, come to that; if they're paying a quarter a ton per week, it'd be like finding a silver mine under the kitchen floor.'

Vetriz's eyebrows shot up. 'Goodness,' she said, 'that sounds like an awful lot. Is it?'

'The *Squirrel*'s two hundred and fifteen tons,' Venart answered gleefully, 'do the sums. And you can forget about all that complying-with-specifications garbage. They're taking on anything that can float, down to and including upturned barrels. Why the hell do you think I came scurrying back here in such a hurry?'

It was (he explained) all over everywhere, from Ap' Imatoy to Colleon: the provincial office was getting ready to make its move against King Temrai, and the main invasion force was going to be carried round the Hook and through the Scona Straits to Perimadeia by sea, thereby avoiding a long and dangerous march overland and denying Temrai the chance of breaking up the attack with hit-and-run tactics. One consequence was that they'd patched up their quarrel with Shastel, whose waters they'd have to go through – aggravating, since he was now stuck with a shipload of overpriced Nagya cornmeal that he'd bought entirely on the assumption that the Shastel chandlers wouldn't be allowed to ship the stuff to Berlya, but undoubtedly good for business in the medium and long term. 'I'll just dump the stuff in the harbour if I can't offload it in the market,' he added. 'After all, with what we'll be getting from the imperials, the cost of a few sacks of flour is neither here nor there. Although I suppose I could offer it to the brewers on South Quay; they do use the stuff, and—'

'The Empire's going to attack Perimadeia?' Vetriz interrupted. 'Since when?'

Venart grinned and poured himself another drink, ladling in a second spoonful of honey by way of celebration. 'You should follow these things if you really want to be a trader,' he said insufferably. 'Think about it, will you? It's all to do with Ap' Escatoy, as anybody with half a brain ought to have worked out years ago. Thanks to our friend Bardas, bless his heart, the Empire's finally managed to do what it's been trying to do ever since we were kids - break through on to the western coast. Now they're here - well, the sky's the limit, really. Ironic,' he went on. 'Even if Bardas and the City people had managed to beat off Temrai and his lot, now they'd be facing the prospect of a full-scale invasion from the Empire - foregone conclusion, obviously.'

Vetriz frowned. 'Except,' she said, 'if the City hadn't fallen, Bardas wouldn't have been there to take Ap' Escatoy for them.'

'Oh, well.' Venart shrugged. 'Broad as it's long; if it hadn't been him, it'd have been someone else. It's always only been a matter of time. I mean, nobody beats the Empire, that's a fact of life.' He drank half his cupful and leaned back in his chair. 'And now Temrai's going to get a taste of his own medicine. Can't say I'm heartbroken; he's a bloodthirsty little brute, by all accounts. Still, you can't help feeling just a little bit sorry for anybody who's got the Empire snapping round their ankles. I guess it must be a bit like knowing you've got a fatal disease.'

'Don't.' Vetriz said, with a slight shudder. 'It's rather horrid, when you come to think of it. I mean, all those *people*. And now you're saying it was all pointless.'

'I suppose you could see it that way,' Venart replied. 'Or

you could say they were all for the chop sooner or later, so does it matter whether the plainsmen or the Empire actually do the business? Can't argue with geography; if you're mug enough to live on a strategically vital promontory, with the Empire bursting to get through a hundred miles or so to the south of you, it's wilful blindness to imagine you're going to live out your time in quiet and peace. I'm just thankful we live on a small rock in the middle of the sea.'

Vetriz looked up. 'Really?' she said.

'Well, of course.' Venart yawned. 'The Empire hasn't got a fleet; hence all this hiring ships business. Whatever happens, they're never going to come bothering us. So that's all right.'

'Oh,' Vetriz said, and changed the subject.

Alexius? Bardas called out, but he didn't appear to have heard.

Bardas had been having his usual dream, the one about the mines; and then suddenly, for no reason he could see, when the wall caved in he'd been standing at the back of the main lecture hall in the City Academy back in Perimadeia (a place he'd never set foot in, all the years he'd lived there; but he knew precisely where he was, and that he was actually there). On the rostrum at the front he could see his old friend Patriarch Alexius, wearing his best gown and academic robes; he was delivering a lecture to a huge crowd of students.

'A case in point,' Alexius was saying, 'is the fall of Ap' Escatoy, an incident with which you are all doubtless familiar. You will recall that in those days, the Empire had not yet penetrated to the western sea, let alone crossed the northern straits; hard to imagine, I know, but worth the effort nonetheless, since it's vital to bear in mind that the whole world as we know it today was arguably shaped by the actions of one man, at one turning point in history.'

Bardas scowled, trying to understand. He knew beyond a shadow of doubt that this wasn't a dream. He was standing in the Academy (which was fire-cracked rubble overgrown with bindweed now); but this was some time in the future, and here was Alexius, somehow not yet dead despite all his assumptions to the contrary.

'One man,' Alexius went on. 'One quite unremarkable

man, regarded objectively; certainly unremarkable enough to his contemporaries. A man who was never happier than when he was hedging and ditching on his father's farm in the Mesoge, or building bows on Scona, or planishing breastplates with the other workers in the armoury at Ap' Calick; hardly a man of destiny, you'd have thought. But consider; if Bardas Loredan hadn't accidentally broken through into the enemy's main gallery under Ap' Escatoy and brought down the city walls, what would have happened then? Let's imagine that the siege dragged on another year, or two years, even; then a revolt in a far province or a change in administration at the central finance office or a political squabble between factions at court – whatever – led to the siege being abandoned. So, Ap' Escatoy hasn't fallen – and the world is utterly different. One man. The different development of one moment in time. This, gentlemen, is the Principle. In that moment, in the darkness of the mines – and they were dark, I can vouch for that – everything changed. Everything was brought down, made small – so small that it fitted comfortably into a tiny cramped spur, hardly high or wide enough for a man to crawl down – and then enlarged again, made to expand like ripples in water. This is the action of the Principle for you; an effect that does away with all dimensions, a place where all places meet, a tiny pinhole at the end and the beginning, into which everything goes and out of which everything comes—'

Bardas found that he couldn't hear any more; it was as if his ears were blocked up with wax. He could see Alexius still talking, but he couldn't make out the words. When he stood up to shout out, *Speak up, we can't hear you at the back*, he felt his head crack against the low roof of the spur, just as the walls began to buckle and come in on him, like a tin cup being crumpled under the wheels of a cart.

'Sergeant Loredan?'

His head snapped up. 'Sorry,' he said. 'I was miles away.'

'As I was saying,' the adjutant went on, giving him an austere look, 'the situation in that part of the world is deteriorating steadily. Imperial interests are being directly threatened. We can no longer guarantee the safety of our citizens. Accordingly, central command is drawing up con-

148

tingency plans in case military intervention becomes unavoidable.'

'I see,' Bardas said, not having a clue what the adjutant was talking about. 'That's – disturbing.'

'Quite so.' The adjutant folded his hands on the desktop, leaned forward a little. 'Now, as you will appreciate, first-hand experience of these people will be of great value in planning our response, both long-term and tactical. Since you have fought in several wars against them—'

Gods. They're going to attack Temrai. 'I see,' he repeated.

The adjutant nodded. 'At the moment,' he went on, 'you've been ordered to stand by, pending a detailed debriefing by senior staff; I have little doubt, however, that as the situation develops, you will be reassigned to a more active role in the war. There may,' he added alluringly, 'be a further promotion, depending on the nature of the duties you are called on to undertake.'

A promotion. Gosh. 'In the meantime?' Bardas asked.

'As I said, at present you are to await orders and hold yourself in readiness. It would be in order, however, for you to conclude any unfinished business you may have here, and make arrangements for handing over to your replacement in due course.'

Bardas stood up. 'Of course,' he said. 'I'll get on to it right away.'

Beats me why they don't sling me out of this army, he reflected as he walked back down the endless corridors. *Disrespectful, insubordinate, generally sloppy; ah, but I took Ap'Escatoy for them. And now I'm going to take Perimadeia.*

He stopped.

'So you're going to take Perimadeia, are you?' the man said. Bardas couldn't see him very well; it was a dark point in the corridor, halfway between two sconces, and he couldn't make out his face; but he could smell coriander. He realised he'd stopped breathing, for some reason. Instinct, maybe.

'They want me to,' he replied. 'I do what I'm told. If I do a good job, they'll make me a citizen.'

'They'll make you a citizen,' the man repeated. 'Wouldn't that be just fine? Imagine that; you, a citizen. Bardas Loredan, there isn't a civilised society anywhere in the world that'd have you as a citizen.'

Bardas frowned. 'Excuse me,' he said, 'but do I know you?'

'We've met. In fact, we've been here before – here or hereabouts. Don't change the subject. You're going to take Perimadeia. Why am I not surprised? Enjoy your work, do you?'

Bardas thought for a moment. 'No,' he said. 'Well, it depends. I've done a lot of different things in my time. Some were worse than others.'

'Such as?'

'The mines,' Bardas said. 'I didn't enjoy them at all. And serving with Maxen, that was pretty grim, most of the time.'

'Fair enough,' said the man. He hadn't moved, and neither had Bardas. 'What about being in charge of the defence of Perimadeia? Was that nice or nasty?'

'I didn't enjoy it,' Bardas replied. 'I knew I was the wrong man for the job. I did the best I could, but someone else might have saved the city. And the experience itself was pretty wretched.'

'I see. And what about your career as a fencer? Was it exciting, thrilling? Did you relish the challenge? Did you feel good each time you won?'

'Relieved,' Bardas said. 'Glad I was still alive. But I did it because it was something I was good enough at to make a living. I needed the sort of money I could earn by fencing, you see, to send home to my brothers.'

'They frittered it all away, of course,' the man said, 'so it was all a waste of time. Well, that only leaves farming, teaching fencing, bowmaking and whatever it is you're doing now. How do you feel about them? Happier, I suppose.'

'Yes,' Bardas said. 'Farming was a hard life, but it's what I was born to do. Teaching fencing was better than fencing, and the money was adequate; I could have carried on with that quite happily. The same with making bows – living that sort of life, I didn't really need much money, and I like working with my hands. Same goes for this, I suppose, if only I could find something I could actually do here. Still, nobody's trying to kill me, so I'm that much ahead of the game.'

The man laughed. 'What an uncomplicated fellow you are, deep down,' he said. 'All you really want out of life is a hard day's work and a fair day's pay; and instead, you grind down tribes, defend and destroy cities, kill men by the hundred. Tell me; in all the fights to the death you've been in, all the him-or-me confrontations, why is it, do you think, that they all died and you're still alive? Is it just your superior skill and hand-speed? I'd be interested to hear what you make of it.'

'I prefer not to think about it,' Bardas replied. 'No offence, but what business is it of yours?'

'None,' the man replied. 'Except that I'm curious, as most people are. I just wanted to know what you were really like. It's so easy when you're reading or hearing about a great historical figure to get into the habit of assuming that they were completely different from the rest of us, that they lived by entirely different rules. Talking to you like this, just the two of us, I realise it isn't like that at all. It's obvious to me now; most of the time, you simply hadn't got a clue what you were doing; nothing more to it than that. But I'd never have seen that if I'd stuck to what it says in the books, or what Grandfather told us when we were kids. Well, I think that's all. Goodbye.'

'Wait,' Bardas said; but he was talking to half a shadow.

'Oh, and one last thing,' said a voice from the darkness where the man and the smell of coriander had been. 'Thank you.'

'You're welcome,' Bardas replied; then his knees folded up and he hit the ground.

When he opened his eyes again the light was horribly bright, and there was a ring of heads peering down at him.

'The heat, possibly,' a Son of Heaven was saying. 'They take time to get used to it. He comes from a cold, wet country.'

'Or the residual effects of being buried alive,' said someone else at the bottom edge of his vision. 'In cases of severe concussion, it can be weeks before the symptoms manifest themselves. That would account for the hallucinations.'

'So would heatstroke,' replied the Son of Heaven. 'In fact, hearing imaginary voices and talking to people who aren't there is rather more indicative of heatstroke than cranial trauma, although I grant you, it's common to both conditions.'

'I think he's awake,' said another voice. 'Sergeant Loredan, can you hear us?'

Bardas opened his mouth; his tongue and throat were stiff and dry, like leather that's got wet and been allowed to dry without being oiled. 'I think so,' he said. 'Are you real?'

The Son of Heaven seemed offended by the question; but the man who'd spoken to him smiled and said, 'Yes, we're real; real enough for your purposes, anyway. Can you remember what happened to you?'

'I fell over,' Bardas replied.

'Cranial trauma,' muttered the man with the buried-alive theory. 'Notice the slight aphasia, the obvious memory loss. Typical.'

'We know that,' said the man who was talking to him, slowly and gently, as if to a dying man or an idiot. 'You fell, and you bumped your head; nothing serious. But before that.'

Bardas thought for a moment. 'I was talking to someone,' he said.

That seemed to please the man who was talking to him, because he smiled a little. 'Aha,' he said. 'And can you remember who you were talking to?'

'My superior officer,' Bardas croaked. 'He was telling me I might get a promotion.'

Wrong answer, apparently. 'I meant after that,' the man said. 'After your interview with the adjutant, but before you fell over. Were you talking to anybody?'

Bardas tried to shake his head but it didn't want to move, so he spoke instead. 'No,' he replied.

'You're sure?'

'Yes. At least,' he added, 'as far as I can remember.'

'He's hiding something,' muttered the Son of Heaven. 'Evasiveness, slight paranoia. Obviously heatstroke.'

The man who'd been talking to him tried again. 'We're doctors,' he said, 'we're here to help you. Are you sure you weren't talking to anybody else?'

'Positive,' Bardas said; then, as the man's face creased into a disappointed scowl, he added, 'Of course, I imagined I was talking to someone, but I know it wasn't real. Just a hallucination or something.'

The man looked more annoyed than ever. 'Really?' he said. 'And how can you be so certain of that?'

'Easy.' Bardas' head began to hurt a lot. 'First he tried to make me believe he was someone I killed in the mines; then he wanted to make out he was a student of history from hundreds of years into the future. Also he knew too much about me; I must have imagined it.'

'I see,' said the cranial-trauma man. 'And do you talk to imaginary people often?'

'Yes,' Bardas replied; and the doctors vanished. When he opened his eyes again, he was still in the same place, but alone; and now it was dark, and he could smell onions and rosemary and blood and sweet marjoram and urine. For a while everything was quiet as the grave; then he heard a man groaning a few yards away. Hospital, he thought.

His head was still splitting, though the pain was rather different now. He savoured it for a while, trying to place it by its texture and intensity (if cranial trauma was medical for a bash on the head, he was ready to plump for cranial trauma; he'd been bashed on the head many times, and this was pretty much what it felt like).

Bardas?

'Shhh,' he whispered. 'You'll wake people up.'

Sorry.

'That's all right. How are you, anyway?'

Can't complain, Alexius replied. Bardas closed his eyes; he could see Alexius very clearly in the dark behind his eyelids. *So what have you been doing to yourself?*

'I don't know,' Bardas admitted. 'One moment I was walking down a corridor in the armoury building, now I'm here. It could be heatstroke, or cranial trauma.'

Cranial trauma?

'Bash on the head. Not that I've been bashed on the head recently, but apparently it can take a while to show up. Anyway, here I am; that's about all I know.'

What rotten luck, Alexius said sympathetically. *I hope you feel better soon.*

'Thank you.' The pain suddenly got worse, then better again. 'Was there something you wanted, or did you just drop by for a chat? Only, I don't want to sound unfriendly, but—'

Of course. I just wondered where you were, that's all. When I heard about Ap' Escatoy, I was worried; being buried alive and so forth, it sounds absolutely awful.

Bardas smiled. 'I can't remember much about it,' he replied. 'I went out like a light, and then they dug me out and I came to in a field hospital. How about you? What are you up to these days?'

Would you believe, I'm teaching again. It's almost like the old days. But so long as I take things a bit steady, it doesn't seem to be doing me any harm. And it's good to be doing something useful, instead of just sitting about.

'I'm pleased for you,' Bardas replied. 'So where are you doing this teaching?'

'Delirious,' said a man's voice, unseen, quite loud. 'A common enough effect in cranial-trauma cases. What would you suggest?'

Bardas opened his eyes. There was light, the soft flush just after sunrise, when the ground's still cool. A tall man, a Son of Heaven, was standing over him. A little further away was a group of young men, listening attentively. 'Rest,' said one of them. 'It's about all you can do, isn't it?'

'Good answer,' replied the Son of Heaven, 'but I think we can do a little better than that. Anyone?'

One of the young men cleared his throat. 'A sedative,' he said diffidently. 'Poppy juice, to keep the patient calm and let him sleep while he's healing. And a willow-bark infusion for the pain.'

'But not both together,' the Son of Heavem chided. 'Or else he might go so fast asleep that he'll never wake up. Besides, if he's asleep, he won't need anything for the pain. Very good. Right, let's move along.'

'Doctor.' One of the students had noticed that Bardas was awake, and nodded in his direction. The doctor looked back.

'He's awake,' he said, 'splendid. But we must keep this short for fear of overtiring him. Well now, how are we feeling today?'

'Awful,' Bardas croaked. 'Where am I?'

But the doctor was leaning over him, pressing his skull with the balls of this thumbs. 'Does that hurt?' he asked. 'And what about that?'

'Ow,' Bardas replied with feeling.

'As I thought,' the doctor said. 'The skull's too soft, and there are a number of dents and ridges that need to be taken out.' He turned away and looked at one of the students. 'The number-one planishing hammer,' he said, 'and the oval-head stake, if you please.'

Before Bardas could move or object, the doctor had forced his mouth open and shoved something into it; Bardas recognised it as one of the stakes that fitted in the slot on top of the armourer's anvil, used to beat down on when shaping work from outside. Then the doctor took the hammer from the student - it had two flat faces, one square and one round - and started tapping the top of Bardas' head with fast, even, pecking strokes.

'The purpose of this action,' he announced, 'which we term planishing, is to smooth out the finished work. In addition to this, it has two other important functions: to compress the metal and to close its surface pores, thereby imparting to the outside a level of work-hardening comparable to that imparted to the inside by the act of doming or raising. It is important not to overdo the planishing process, lest the metal be beaten thin or made too hard, in other words brittle. Should brittleness be imparted by excessive zeal at this juncture, the piece would have to be annealed by fire and worked again, both outside and inside.' Bardas wanted to shout, but his mouth was full of the oval-head stake; his head vibrated and echoed with the countless rapid blows, each one pinching his skull between the stake inside and the hammer outside. He tried to close his eyes; but the rivets around which the steel lames of his eyelids pivoted were slightly distorted, and the lids wouldn't shut properly—

He opened his eyes.

He was sitting bolt upright on his bed in his little room in the top back gallery, his mouth open in mid-scream.

'Steady on,' said a voice at the foot of the bed. 'Were you having a bad dream or something?'

Bardas closed his mouth - he felt that his jaw ought to pivot around two hardened steel pins, like the visor of a bascinet; but that was plainly absurd. 'I'm sorry,' he said.

'That's all right.' The man at the foot of the bed turned out to be the old Son of Heaven, Anax, who worked in the proof house. Just behind his shoulder, inevitably, was the enormous shape of Bollo, his assistant. 'Though I'll admit you startled the life out of me, shouting like that. Anyway, how are you feeling?'

Bardas shuddered and lowered himself carefully back on to the mattress. His head hurt.

'Excuse me if this sounds strange,' he said, 'but are you real?'

Anax smiled. 'You have trouble telling the difference, do you?' he said. 'I know the feeling. Yes, we're real; or as real as it gets around here. It's that sort of place, though, isn't it?'

Bardas thought for a moment. 'What's been happening to me?' he said. 'Last thing I knew, I was walking down a corridor—'

'And you flaked out, apparently,' Anax said with a grin. 'Dead to the world when they found you; couldn't wake you up. They tried prodding you, slapping you round the face, even emptied a jug of water over you. Then they sent for us. I guess they decided you were our responsibility. Anyway, we brought you up here – or at least Bollo did.'

'You're heavy,' Bollo said. 'Especially going upstairs.'

'I see,' Bardas replied. 'How long was I out for?'

Anax thought for a moment. 'Let's see,' he said. 'Half a day, last night and this morning; call it a round twenty-four hours, give or take half an hour. I don't know,' he went on, 'fainting fits, at your age. That sort of stuff's for old men and young girls who don't eat properly.'

'Maybe it was heatstroke,' Bardas suggested. 'Or cranial trauma.'

'Cranial what?'

'Trauma. A bash on the head.'

'Oh. So who's been bashing you on the head?'

Bardas shrugged. 'Nobody, as far as I know. But it could be a delayed reaction to what happened to me in the mines.'

'Nah.' Anax shook his head. 'That was weeks ago. Anyway, you seem to be all right now, which is the main thing. Tell you what; you stay in bed a day or so till you're quite sure you're all right; I'll send Bollo or one of the lads from the foundry shop to look in on you from time to time – make sure you haven't died or gone off your head. I'd stay myself, but we've got a lot of work on, and we haven't made much headway with it sitting here watching you sleep.'

When they'd gone, Bardas tried very hard to stay awake. He managed to keep going for an hour; then he woke up in a panic to find Bollo standing over him with a bowl of salt porridge and a wooden spoon.

CHAPTER EIGHT

Once the fire has been lit, the report said, *it must be kept going to maintain the necessary level of heat. Approximately twenty-four loads of charcoal are needed to produce eight tons of pig-iron.*

Athli closed her eyes, then opened them again. It was late, and she wanted to go to bed; but the report had been sitting on her desk for two days now, and she wouldn't have time to read it tomorrow – meetings all day, and the accounts to audit after that. She found the place again and tried to concentrate.

In refining the pig-iron into a bloom of plate, one ton in eight will be lost. Five hundredweight of plate will make twenty cuirasses, Imperial standard proof, with pauldrons. Four hundredweight will make forty sets of cuirasses, without pauldrons. Sixteen hundredweight will make twenty full suits of cavalry armour, Imperial standard proof. Four plateworkers will make up thirty-seven hundredweight of plates in a week, therefore one plateworker will make up nine and a quarter hundredweight in a week, or one and a half hundredweight a day, using a coal-fired furnace; where the fuel is timber or charcoal, the daily output is unlikely to exceed one hundredweight.

Athli yawned. At first glance, it had seemed like a sound enough proposition; with wars breaking out here and there, the Empire on the move, its neighbours panicking, generals and masters of ordnance everywhere looking to upgrade equipment, what better investment than an armour factory, either here on the Island or away in Colleon, where labour was cheap and raw materials conveniently to hand? But she was cautious, getting more so every day, and so she'd asked the librarian at the Merchant Venturers' Hall, who owed her a favour, to see if there was anything about the economics of running an armoury; and he'd found an old report by the warden of the city armoury of Perimadeia, compiled thirty years ago and more, which he'd had copied and sent to her wrapped in silk and tied with a broad blue ribbon. It was very kind of him, though it wasn't going to get him anywhere, if that's what he was thinking; but the very least she could do was read it, after he'd been to all that trouble.

She tried to focus, but her eyes slid across the page like a colt trying to cross a frozen river. Dry stuff; well, of course, what did she expect, a love interest? Concentrate, she urged herself, this is the good bit. If one man can make one and a half hundredweight of plate a day, and if five hundredweight makes twenty cuirasses (with pauldrons, whatever a pauldron was), but using coal, not charcoal; twenty-four loads of charcoal makes eight tons, of which one ton is lost; but how much charcoal do you get in a load? She scowled, and rearranged the counters on her counting-board.

Coincidence, she thought; apparently Bardas has been posted to the armoury at Ap' Calick. Hey, why don't I just go to Ap' Calick and ask him about all this stuff, instead of killing myself trying to understand it from a book? What a good idea. No, thank you. Not even if he knows what a pauldron is, or whether it's a good thing or a bad thing to have with a cuirass.

Who could she think of – who *else* could she think of who'd be likely to know what a pauldron was? On the Island, armour came in barrels stuffed with straw and sealed with the factory seal, and it stayed there until it was offloaded on the customer's dock and paid for. What was inside the barrel, nobody knew or cared. The Islanders knew a lot of things – they had a library, after all – but technical military information wasn't the sort of thing that interested them. Chances were, she could find ten people who could tell her how much a pauldron was worth, twenty who happened to know where there was a consignment of best-quality pauldrons, cancelled order, virtually at cost; forty who were crying out for pauldrons to meet an order, cash on the nail, good customer, but the stuff's never about when you want it. Show them a pauldron and they'd probably try to poach an egg in it. She shuffled the counters up and down the lines and wrote the result on the wax tablet next to the board. Good, solid, meaningless data.

Armour, she thought. Was there really going to be a war? Everybody seemed to think so; they were counting on it, planning ahead for it, stockpiling and getting rid - Maupas is buying arrowheads and selling paintbrushes, because nobody's going to want to buy brushes when there's a war on; Ren is buying Maupas' brushes, because the price is right and after the war is over, people will want brushes again; but in order to pay for the brushes, he's got to sell the two hundred thousand copper rivets he got cheap in Aguill all those years ago - but that's all right, because they use rivets to make armour, soon people will be crying out for rivets because of the war, so wouldn't he be better off keeping the rivets and passing on the brushes? It was an odd way to look at a war, purely in terms of all the things needed to make it work - all the arrows that would be shot off, armour that would be bashed up and mangled, all the hundreds of thousands of pairs of shoes and miles of strap leather, all the belt buckles and whetstones and cartwheel spokes and nails and pickaxe handles and parchment-roll covers and stockings and planks and feathers and axle pins and water bottles. You could take away all the people, and still a war is a massive thing, a vast collection of goods, an endless supply and demand of material, all being crammed into the mouth of the war; such a displacement of things. And why? Because war is inevitable. Fancy you needing to ask.

Perimadeia, displaced. The war had been inevitable. Likewise, presumably, the fall of Ap' Escatoy, brought low by one Bardas Loredan. Such a displacement of people; but things were easier to deal with, things were her business now. If I knew what a pauldron was, would it all suddenly become clear, would I truly understand? Possibly. Possibly not.

Once the fire has been lit, it must be kept burning to maintain the necessary level of heat. She pulled a face; read that bit already. Why couldn't these people want to make something she knew a bit about, like carpet?

The counting-house door opened; Sabel Votz, her chief clerk, in a hurry and a fluster.

'Visitors,' she said, as if announcing the end of the world. 'From the provincial office. Downstairs, in the hall.'

If Athli had taken her cue from her clerk's tone of voice, she'd have been in two minds whether to send for wine and cakes or barricade the doors. Fortunately she was used to Sabel by now. 'Really,' she said. 'Well, it's about time. Bring them up, wait two minutes, then fetch in a tray.'

Sabel looked at her disapprovingly. 'All right,' she said. 'And no interruptions?'

'Exactly.' Sabel went away again, and Athli looked round instinctively to make sure the place was tidy. A silly instinct, that; she wasn't a housewife suddenly descended upon by her husband's mother, she was the Island agent for the Shastel Order, and as such a person of consequence. At the last moment she caught sight of a pair of shoes, lying under the table where she'd kicked them off the night before. She just had time to scoop them up and hide them behind a cushion before the door opened, and Sabel ushered in two Sons of Heaven and a long, thin, pale clerk, who looked as if he'd been put out in the sun to dry and forgotten about.

Exceedingly polite, these Sons of Heaven (they were called Iqueval and Fesal, and both of them were lieutenant commanders in the Imperial Navy; this came as something of a surprise to Athli, who wasn't aware the Empire had a navy). Even sitting down, they seemed to loom over her, the way the towers of Commercial Hall looked down on all the houses in her street. Both had white hair and short tufts of beard on the points of their chins; but she could tell them apart because Iqueval's collar buttons were black lacquered horn, and Fesal's were silver plate.

'Yes,' she said, when they'd explained the purpose of their visit, ' I have two ships, and I'd be perfectly happy to—'

Fesal cleared his throat. 'Unfortunately,' he said, 'that's no longer the case. You now have only one ship. I'm sorry to have to tell you the *Fencer* ran aground on a reef while apparently trying to slip past an Imperial blockade. She broke up before salvage was possible, and sank. I do hope for your sake she was properly insured.' The Son of Heaven smiled consolingly, then added, 'If it helps at all, I can provide you with a certificate of shipwreck to prove the loss, in case your insurer makes difficulties over the claim. After all,' he added with a smile, 'knowledge is one thing, proof is another.'

'Thank you,' Athli said. 'Do you happen to know if there were any survivors?'

'Regrettably, we have no information one way or another,' Iqueval replied, 'beyond a report from one of our patrols in the vicinity who encountered unauthorised foreigners in a restricted area shortly afterwards. One of our men was killed in the encounter, I believe. The intruders escaped north, towards Perimadeia.'

Athli nodded. 'Thank you for letting me know,' she said. She felt slightly numb and rather dizzy, as if she had a bad cold; just disorientating enough to make communication tiresome. 'Well then, I've got *one* ship. I imagine you know all about that one, too.'

'Indeed,' Iqueval confirmed. 'The *Arrow*; sixty foot, two hundred tons burden, twin mast square-rigger, under the command of Captain Dondas Mosten, a Perimadeian; presently at anchor here, due to sail the day after tomorrow for Shastel with a cargo of mixed luxury goods, books and furniture. We would very much like to charter your ship, at a quarter per ton per week plus wages, provisions and damages.'

Athli thought for a moment. 'Starting when?' she said.

'That hasn't been decided yet,' said Fesal. 'Our intention is to start the charter, at full hire except for wages and provisions, some time before we actually start our work; this will be necessary to ensure that all the ships we're chartering will be available when we need them.'

'I see,' Athli said. 'And what would this work of yours be?'

Fesal smiled tightly. 'That's restricted, I'm afraid,' he said.

'Oh.' Athli looked him in the eye, but saw nothing there. 'I'm only concerned in case there's an element of risk. To be perfectly straight with you, I don't want to get involved in anything that would leave my ship at the bottom of the sea, particularly,' she added, 'now that it's the only one I've got. I do have certain commercial interests quite separate from the Bank, you see, and I need my ship—'

'In the event of damage,' said Fesal firmly, 'or indeed outright loss, we will pay you compensation in full, in

162

accordance with the market value of the ship as at the date of the charter, such value to be fixed by an independent local valuer. This will be a term of the charter. So really, you needn't be concerned.'

Athli frowned. 'What about lost earnings?' she said. 'Between you losing my ship and me getting another one, I mean. Is that included?'

Fesal was obviously impressed. 'I believe we can come to some agreement on that score,' he said. 'For example, we might take out insurance to cover such losses, in your name, of course. But we feel sure that loss and serious damage are unlikely to occur.'

'That's something, I suppose,' Athli answered. 'I don't suppose you'd care to comment about these rumours flying around, that you're hiring a fleet to carry your army to war against the plainspeople?'

'Is there a rumour?' Iqueval said.

Athli smiled. 'Oh, there's always a rumour,' she replied. 'But some rumours are more believable than others. Still, it's good money – well, you know that, I'm sure you're completely up to date on charter tariffs. You aren't about to tell me how long this job of yours is expected to take, are you?'

'You're quite right,' said Fesal, 'we aren't. That information is, obviously, restricted.' He made a placatory gesture with his long, fine hands. 'It goes without saying that entering into an open-ended arrangement of this sort is both unusual and, potentially, inconvenient. We believe that the level of payment we're offering is more than adequate compensation. Ultimately, the choice is yours.'

'Oh, quite,' Athli said. 'Well, I suppose I'd have to be an idiot to turn down an offer like this. About payment, though – will that be in advance or arrears? I'm sorry if that sounds fussy, but ...'

'There's no need to apologise for a firm grasp of the essentials of your profession,' Fesal replied. 'In advance for the first month, in arrears after that. We believe that's a reasonable compromise. Is that acceptable?'

'Method of payment?'

'By letter of credit,' Iqueval said, 'drawn on the provincial office, redeemable wherever you choose to specify. In your case, I assume, in Shastel; you can then write it directly to yourself here.' He smiled. 'I wouldn't be surprised if quite a few of your compatriots elect to have their payments written to Shastel, which ought to be good for business. You may care to put arrangements in hand, though of course it's not for me to tell you how to run your franchise. Still, with the Loredan Bank gone, there aren't that many banks outside the Empire for people to choose from.'

And only one inside the Empire, Athli didn't reply. Instead, she said, 'That'll be fine. And yes, I'll be happy to arrange exchange facilities for anybody else who wants to use us, though with the sort of money you're talking about floating around, it'll be quite an undertaking. I'll probably end up having to lay off some of the credit with other people here on the Island.'

Fesal stood up. 'You're going to be busy,' he said. 'Well, thank you for your time. We'll be in touch when we're ready to make a start. It's been a pleasure doing business with you.'

'Likewise.'

When they'd gone, Athli spent a fascinating few minutes with her counting-board and tablets, first making the calculations and then checking them three times to make sure she wasn't making some elementary mistake that made the sum she'd be due to receive seem much larger than it should be. But it worked out the same each time; good money, indeed.

So they're going to attack Temrai, are they? She should be pleased; delighted, in fact, that the monster who destroyed her home and butchered her people was only a few months away from defeat and death. The good man loves his friends and hates his enemies; wasn't that what she'd been taught as a child? My enemy's misfortune is my good fortune – confound it, if they'd come to her and asked for the loan of her ship, free of charge, for a holy war against the plainspeople, that'd have been straightforward enough; *Yes*, she'd have said, *with my blessing*. But this way, revenge and a substantial profit – somehow she wasn't sure the world worked like that.

Not that a substantial profit would go amiss; not if her poor *Fencer* was at the bottom of the sea, and Gannadius and his nephew with her. Even if they were still alive, lost somewhere between the Empire and Temrai, chances were she'd never see them again. She found it hard, almost impossible, to feel anything about that; not because she didn't want to, but simply because she couldn't. When Perimadeia had fallen and she'd come here, she'd started making herself armour, good armour proof against such things – a helmet of business, a breastplate of friends, pauldrons (whatever they were) of possessions, success, prosperity. When she'd taken Bardas Loredan aboard the *Fencer* to visit his brothers in the Mesoge, and had come back with his sword and his apprentice but without him, she'd closed up the rivets and planished the exterior, making this armour of hers good enough to pass any proof; the death of an old friend and the boy Loredan had given her to look after were blows she acknowledged but couldn't actually feel. That's the merit of good armour; the blows either glance off the angled contours or waste their energy against the internal tensions of the metal, which are so much more powerful than any force likely to be applied from the outside. To be good armour, to be proof, it must have its own inner stresses, those of constricted metal trying in vain to push outwards, so that pressure inwards is met, force against force, and repelled. She had those internal tensions, those inner stresses; now here was an act of proof, and look, her armour had turned the blows easily. The prospect of some money, some business, an opportunity to find more clients and increase her prosperity had quite taken away the force of the attack.

So that's all right, then. As for her ship, her poor little ship, the Son of Heaven was quite right: it was insured, so heavily that it was a wonder it had ever managed to float under all that weight of money. Once the insurers stopped squirming (only a matter of time, plus a certain amount of effort) she'd do rather well out of the loss of the *Fencer*.

Well, of course. That's what insurance is for, to turn the blow. And if she hadn't been expecting, deep in the darker galleries of her mind, to lose it some day, she probably wouldn't have called it the *Fencer* in the first place.

Being an orderly, methodical person (by practice if not by nature) she made a note of her meeting with the Sons of Heaven, filed it in the proper place and went back to reading the report, which was, of course, all about armour. She managed to get to the end of the seventh section before her eyes filled with tears, making it impractical to try to read further.

'Really?' Temrai stopped what he was doing and looked up. 'Perimadeians? I didn't think there were any left.'

'A few, here and there,' the messenger replied. His name was Leuscai, and Temrai had known him for years, on and off. How someone like Leuscai came to be running errands for the engineers building siege-engines down on the southern border he had no idea; chances were that he simply hadn't wanted to get involved. It was a problem with a lot of his contemporaries; though they'd never have considered supporting the rebellion, let alone joining it, they weren't happy with the direction Temrai seemed to be leading the clans in, and they manifested this unease by taking part as little as possible. It was profoundly irritating, to say the least. But Temrai couldn't be bothered to raise the issue with an old friend like Leuscai; it'd probably result in falling out, bad temper and the end of a friendship, and he had few enough of those left as it was.

'Oh, well,' Temrai said. 'Now then, how does this look?'

'Unintentional,' Leuscai replied. 'That is, I wouldn't insult you by thinking you meant it to look like that.'

'That bad?' Temrai sighed. 'I'm getting cack-handed in my old age, that's what it is. It's not so long ago I was able to earn my living bashing metal around.'

'In Perimadeia,' Leuscai pointed out, 'where presumably their standards weren't so high. All right, put me out of my misery. What's it supposed to be?'

Temrai grinned. 'There's a technical term for it,' he said, 'which escapes me for the moment. But basically it's a knee-guard. Or rather it isn't.'

'Not unless you've got really unusual knees,' Leuscai agreed. 'But it's just as well you told me, or I'd never have guessed. To me it looks like a slice of harness leather pretending to be a pancake.'

'Yes, all right.' Temrai let the offending item fall from his hand. 'It's frustrating, really,' he said. 'While I was in the City, I read about how you're supposed to do this, and they made it sound really easy. You just get thickish leather, you dip it in hot melted beeswax, you shape it, and there you are; cheap, strong, lightweight armour, made out of something we've got lots of. I don't know,' he went on, sitting on the log he'd been using to beat the thing into shape over. 'Making things used to come so easily to me, and now I seem to have lost the knack. Anyway, tell me more about these stragglers of yours. Any idea who they are?'

Leuscai smiled. 'You mean, are they spies? Well, it's possible. From what we've been able to gather so far, one of them was a wizard – well, assistant wizard – and they're both something to do with the Island and the Shastel Order.'

'Really?' Temrai sounded impressed. 'Wizards and diplomats. We're honoured.'

'That's not the best bit though,' Leuscai continued, the smile quickly fading from his face. 'The kid spent several years on Scona. He was Bardas Loredan's apprentice.'

Temrai sat perfectly still for a moment. 'Is that so?' he said. 'Then I think we've met. Briefly, but memorably. How do you know all this?'

Leuscai pulled up a log and sat down beside him. 'Pure chance, really. You remember Dondai, the old bloke who used to make the pancakes?'

Temrai nodded. 'He died a short while back,' he said.

'Apparently. And his nephew, you've come across him? Dassascai, his name is. Doesn't know a lot about pancakes, but he's surprisingly well informed about commercial activity on the Island. Says he has contacts from when he was in business in Ap' Escatoy, though if you ask me that doesn't quite tie up. Anyway, for some reason, this Dassascai—'

'He's a spy.'

'Oh, really? Well, that explains what he was doing snooping round our yard, where we're raising the trebuchets. This Dassascai, he happened to see our two guests, recognised them (so he says) and went to the camp commander about it.'

'Goscai.'

'That's right. Nice enough man, but he worries; and he got into an awful state over this, as you can imagine. First he was going to have them strung up on the spot; then he thought he'd better not, in case he started a war, so he was going to have them put in chains instead; then it occurred to him that they might be *our* spies (don't know where he got that from)

– finally, he got himself into such a tizzy he didn't know what to do, so we said the best thing would be to ask you. He hadn't thought of that; but as soon as we suggested it, he was delighted. So here I am.'

Temrai rubbed his forehead with the heel of his hand. 'Any idea how they got there?' he asked. 'Or did they just show up, saying, *Hello, we're spies, mind if we look around?*

'Hardly.' Leuscai laughed. 'Though if they had, I for one would've said, *Go ahead, help yourselves.* The way I see it, some solid intelligence work by the provincial office might do us a power of good.'

'Quite possibly,' Temrai replied, 'but let's not get into all that now.' He breathed in deeply, then breathed out again. 'How did they get there? Any ideas?'

'Some of our people found them in the swamp,' Leuscai replied, 'when they were out looking for ducks. In a pretty bad way, apparently. The wizard's no spring chicken. If they are spies, they went to a hell of a lot of trouble to look like dying men. Their story was that they were on their way to Shastel from the Island, got run aground by the Imperial coastguard and were on the run from the foot patrols. Plausible enough, I suppose.'

'All right,' Temrai said, picking up a bossing mallet and putting it down again. 'You send them here; I'll look them over, frighten them politely for a day or so and send them on their way. If they really are spies, I'll give them the guided tour; that'll confuse them so badly they won't know what to think.' He looked round at the mess left over from his experiment in armour-making. 'You don't happen to know of anybody who can do this?' he asked. 'It's got me beaten, but it can't really be all that difficult. It really annoys me when I know I'm on to something but I can't make it work.'

Leuscai shrugged. 'Can't help you there, I'm afraid. Of course, you could always write a letter to Bardas Loredan, care of the Imperial state armoury service. I'm sure he'd be delighted to help.'

Temrai scowled, then laughed. 'Do you know,' he said, 'he bumped into me in the street once, in Perimadeia. He was drunk, obviously he hadn't got a clue who I was. Everywhere I go, there he seems to be; and I can't figure that out for the

life of me. I mean, why should there be this horrible connection between us? He's a farmer's son from the Mesoge; by
rights he should be hoeing turnips in the mud right now, not
lurking in the shadows everywhere I go, waiting to jump out
at me. I wonder, what the hell could it have been that tangled
our lives up together like that?'

'You make it sound like you're in love,' Leuscai said. 'Star-
crossed lovers, like in some old story.'

'You think so? In that case, I reckon it's high time we got a
divorce.'

When the messenger eventually found him, Gorgas Loredan
was at the farm, helping his brothers patch up the floor of
the long barn.

'Bloody menace,' Zonaras had said in passing, when Gorgas
asked him why he wasn't using it any more. 'Planks rotten
right through. You could break your leg.'

'I see,' Gorgas had replied. 'So you're just going to abandon
it, are you? Let it fall down?'

'Haven't got time to fix it,' Clefas had put in. 'It's a big job,
and there's only the two of us.'

Gorgas had grinned at that. 'Not any more,' he'd said.

And so there he was, muddy and bad-tempered, standing
astride a newly felled sweet-chestnut tree with a hammer in
his hand, blood trickling down from his knuckles where he'd
scraped them carelessly while manhandling the timber.

'Who are you?' he asked.

'Sergeant Mossay sent me,' the messenger replied defensively. 'Letter for you, from the provincial office.' He held the
little brass cylinder out at arm's length. 'The courier arrived
last night at Tornoys.'

'Is he waiting for the answer?' Gorgas asked, wiping his
hands on his shirt.

'No,' the messenger replied. 'No answer expected, he
said.'

Gorgas frowned and took the cylinder, flipping off the
carefully fitted lid with his thumbs.

They'd started by felling the tree; the last of the stand
of chestnut trees that their grandfather had planted shortly
after their father was born. It hadn't been an easy tree to fell.
The wind had twisted it, so when they tried to saw through,

the timber clented on the saw-blade until finally it broke
(it was old and rusty, like all the other tools about the place).
So they'd got out the felling axes; and after they'd blistered
their hands, and Clefas had taken his eye off the cut and
knocked the head off his axe as a result, they thought better
of it and dug out the other saw, which was even older and
rustier. But Gorgas made them rope the tree back, and they
used a block and tackle to put some tension on it, opening
the cut to allow the blade to move freely. When they were
three-quarters of the way through, they realised that if they
carried on the line they were following, the tree would
drop on the roof of the old pig-house and flatten it. Of
course, the old pig-house hadn't been used for years except
as a miscellaneous junk store; but Gorgas made them drive
in another post and rope the tree back another way so
that they could chop a wedge out and alter the direction
of the fall. Eventually they cut through and the tree fell; not
the way Gorgas had intended, but it nearly cleared the
pig-house, only sweeping off a few cracked slates with an
outlying branch. It had taken them the rest of the first day to
trim the trunk and cart off the loppings to the woodshed (which was too damp to store wood in now that half
the thatch had blown away); now, finally, they were splitting the trunk to make the planks they'd need for the barn
floor.

'Bastard,' Gorgas said, scowling and crushing the letter in
his fist. 'You know what? That bastard Poliorcis, he's made
them reject the alliance.'

The messenger took a step backwards, trying to look as
if he wasn't there. Clefas and Zonaras stood still, apparently
unconcerned.

'No material advantage to the Empire,' Gorgas went on.
'Well, the hell with them. Come on, let's finish this. You,' he
added as an afterthought, as the messenger stood unhappily
by, waiting to be dismissed, 'you go back, find that courier
and bring him here. I've got a reply all right.'

The messenger nodded doubtfully. 'What if he's already
left?' he said.

'You'd better hope he hasn't,' Gorgas replied. 'Because if
he has, I might be inclined to ask why it took a day for this
to reach me, if the courier got in last night as you just told me.'

The messenger hurried away, his feet squelching on the waterlogged grass of the yard.

'Clefas,' Gorgas said, 'get the wedges. This stuff's knotted and twisted like you wouldn't believe.'

Clefas stood for a moment, then slowly walked away. Gorgas took a deep breath, then went back to what he'd been doing. He had a froe jammed in a lengthways split down the trunk of the tree, in too far to budge with the tommy bar, which he'd just contrived to break by jerking on it with his full weight.

'You'll never get that out,' Zonaras said.

'Watch me,' Gorgas replied. 'Here, pass me the side axe. I'll cut the bloody thing out if I have to.'

'Suit yourself,' Zonaras said, handing him the axe, which was bevelled on one side only for cutting at an angle. 'Watch the head on that, it's loose.'

'Really?' Gorgas said.

His brother nodded. 'Been loose for years,' he said. 'Needs the head taking off and a new wedge knocking in.'

Gorgas hacked away for a few minutes, trying to cut out a slot beside the jammed tool to free it. He hadn't made any significant progress by the time Clefas wandered back with the wedges. They were heavy and indescribably ancient, and their heads had been smashed into razor-sharp flakes by generations of Loredans pounding on them with big hammers. 'That's better,' Gorgas said. 'Right, Zonaras, bash in a wedge either side; that'll open it up.'

Zonaras picked up a wedge in each hand and nestled them in the crack fore and aft of the froe; then he bashed them home with the poll of the surviving felling-axe. The froe came out easily, but the wedges were stuck fast.

'Marvellous,' Gorgas said angrily. 'Solve one problem, make two more.'

Zonaras sighed. 'Grain's too twisted for splitting,' he said. 'I could have told you that before you started.'

Gorgas straightened his back, pulling a face. 'We'll knock in the axe-heads as wedges,' he said, 'that'll get these two out. We'll get there, don't you worry.'

Several hours later, when it was getting dark, they gave up for the day. They'd got the wedges out, and the froe (which they'd put back in, jammed solid and got back out again by bashing it to and fro with a hammer) but the axe-heads looked as if they'd never budge. 'What we need,' Gorgas said as they trooped back into the house, 'is a saw-pit. Then we could saw our planks instead of trying to split them.'

Neither of his brothers said anything. They kicked off their boots and sat down on either side of the table, clearing a space to lean on with their elbows. *Curious*, Gorgas thought, *they're Loredans too; but of course, they've never been away from the farm. They were the lucky ones.*

'We could build one down by the river,' he went on, 'near the ford, where the banks aren't too steep. Then we could have a water wheel driving a mechanical saw. I've seen them, in Perimadeia. Wonderful things, but it should be easy enough to make one.'

Clefas looked up at him. 'Down by the river,' he said.

'That's right,' Gorgas replied. 'Where Niessa used to do the washing. You know the place I mean.' *Of course they do.*

'I reckon so,' Zonaras replied. 'But we don't need a saw-mill. What'd we want one of them for?'

Gorgas frowned. 'I'd have thought that was obvious,' he replied. 'To saw planks, of course, instead of wasting three days bashing lumps of iron with hammers.'

'But we don't need planks,' Zonaras pointed out. 'Except a few now and then. And we buy them.'

'Waste of money,' Gorgas said impatiently, 'when we've got perfectly good timber on the farm. Besides, if we set up a powered saw-mill, we'd be able to supply planks for all the neighbours, at only a fraction of what they're paying now. It's a good business proposition.'

Clefas shook his head. 'And who's going to work it?' he asked. 'Zonaras and me, we've got our hands full just managing the farm. Are you going to drop everything and come running every time someone wants a few bits of wood cut up? Don't see it, myself.'

Gorgas waved the objection aside. 'As well as planks,' he went on, 'we could make our own fenceposts, gateposts, rafters, weather-boards, the lot. We could even build a ship if we wanted to. Yes, I think a saw-mill's a damned good idea. First thing in the morning, I'll get some of the men on to it. It'll give them something to do, at any rate.'

Clefas and Zonaras looked at each other. 'Well,' Clefas said, 'if you're going to do that, there's no point us killing ourselves tomorrow trying to split that log. When your mill's running, we'll get it sawn up there.'

'That's right,' Zonaras added. 'I mean, it's not like there's any rush. We don't use the long barn any more, anyhow.'

That night, Gorgas dreamed he was standing outside the gates of a city. It was dark, and he wasn't sure which city it was – could've been Perimadeia, or Ap' Escatoy, Scona even; any one of a number of places. The gate was barred, immovable, so he was trying to break it up by splitting it, using wedges and an axe. The wedges, he somehow knew, were his brothers; he was the froe, and the axes too, both when they were driven into the split as wedges or swung as hammers. He could feel the hammer-blows on the polls of the wedges (the hammer falls, the steel is compressed, and where does all the force go, pinched between steel and steel?) as surely as he could feel the tommy-bar twist in the socket of the froe. He could feel the unsustainable stresses in the wood, as the fibres of the grain were wrenched apart – wood's not like steel, if you torture it, eventually it fails and bursts. But steel, the more you hammer it, the more you compress and work-harden it, the harder and stronger it gets. And that, logically enough, is why the Loredan boys aren't like other people ...

Well, it was dream-logic, the sort that melts away as soon as your eyes open.

Gorgas woke up, realised he didn't stand a chance of getting back to sleep, and resolved to do some work instead. He'd insisted on having the one working oil-lamp in the place, and after a good deal of fumbling with flint and rather soggy tinder, he had light. He also had paper – a few sheets he'd brought with him, and the back of the letter he'd had about the refused treaty, quite serviceable once he'd smoothed it out over the table. He sat down and wrote three letters; one to his niece, one to an employee, giving him further orders, and one to Poliorcis the Son of Heaven, which he managed to make polite and friendly in spite of every-thing. After all, there was still time for them to change their minds, no point alienating them by being petulant just be-cause it'd feel good to vent his anger. Keeping his personal feelings out of the way of his business decisions had brought

Gorgas all the success he'd ever managed to achieve, after all. It was a rule he'd only ever broken where Bardas was concerned, and that one exception had cost him dearly enough, gods know. But Bardas was different; Bardas was his brother, Bardas was the only failure in a life full of remarkable achievements. And very few failures are definitely final, provided you're level-headed enough to keep your feelings at bay.

When he'd finished writing the letters, it was still dark, too early for anybody else to be up and about, so Gorgas decided to fill in the time with one other minor chore, a task he'd neglected for the past couple of days. In the corner of the room stood a fine embossed-leather bow-case. He opened it and took out his bow, the rather special bow his brother had built for him three years before. People who knew the circumstances behind the making of the bow were amazed, even horrified, to find that he still had it. They'd assumed that he'd got rid of it - burned, buried, thrown into the sea - long before. They couldn't understand how he could even bear to look at it, let alone touch it. But the fact remained, it was a very fine bow; and since it had cost him so much, the least he could do was use it and look after it - otherwise everything that had gone into making it would be wasted, all to no purpose.

First, he went over the back with a fine, stiff brush that lived in a pocket under the flap of the case, to remove all the loose dirt, mud and other rubbish. Then he sprinkled on to it a little of the special oil that he'd had specially mixed for this job, just enough to cover the fingernail on his left index finger; oil that kept the wet out and the sinew in. The oil had to be rubbed in until every last trace of it was gone, a job that called for thoroughness and patience. Finally, he waxed the string with a small block of solid beeswax. By then it was dawn; no sooner had he pushed the bow back into its case than the sun came up. Gorgas washed his hands carefully (the oil he'd used for the bow was poisonous), pulled on his boots and went to look for some more work to do.

An hour or two after Gorgas cleaned his bow, a ship limped into Tornoys harbour.

It had taken a pounding from a freak storm, the sort that

added an unwelcome degree of uncertainty to navigation at this time of year. The ship had coped pretty well, all things considered; it had taken on rather more water than was good for it, and the wind had damaged the rigging and put a crack in the mainmast that would have caused real havoc if the storm had lasted much longer. But she was still afloat and nobody had been killed or badly hurt. It was as much as anybody had a right to expect, fooling about in those seas at that season.

Because it was still early, there was nobody much about. The fishing fleet had already left, of course, apart from a few lazy oyster-boats, and the bigger ships that were due to leave that day wouldn't be ready to sail for another hour or so. They'd taken their cargoes on board the night before, so that the men could get a good night's sleep before catching the tide. One or two of Gorgas' men were hanging around the quay, but they weren't on duty; it was still the last knockings of the night before, and they were hanging around waiting until the taverns started breakfast, hoping that the cool dawn breeze would help clear their heads.

Pollas Arteval, the Tornoys harbourmaster – he was the nearest thing to an official that Tornoys had, and even then he was really nothing more than a chandler who kept a register and collected contributions from the waterfront traders' association – leaned on the gate outside his office and tried to figure out where the ship was from. It was old but soundly made, clinker-built, unlike the majority of the Colleon and Shastel sloops and clippers; certainly not from the Empire, with those sails. From the Island, possibly – they'd use anything that could float and a few that couldn't – but the rigging wasn't Island fashion somehow. He stared for a little longer, and realised what was bothering him. It was nothing really, a trivial detail of how the tiller bars of the rudders were socketed into the upper part of the loom, but he had an idea he'd seen something like it before, a long time ago. Still, he'd seen a lot of ships from a lot of places, with every possible contrivance for steering as for every other function. He made a note in his mind and started thinking about warm, fresh bread dunked in bacon fat instead.

The ship nuzzled up to the quay (if it'd had a face it'd have grinned with relief; Pollas fancied he could hear it sighing) and someone jumped down with a line and made her fast while others put out a gangplank. The men were like the ship, unfamiliar but faintly evocative of something he'd seen – what, twenty-five, maybe thirty years ago. Quite possibly, they were from some far-flung place that used to send ships here and then stopped doing so for some reason – war or politics, or just because there wasn't enough in it to justify such a long haul. Reasonably enough, the men looked tired and fraught – so would anybody after a long night in the squalls off Tornoys – but they didn't look like men who were expecting a well-earned rest. Rather, they had the resigned look of people who had most of their work still to do.

A crowd of them were ashore now, some fifty-five or sixty of them (a big crew for a ship that size, or maybe they were passengers). Then, in the time it took for Pollas to turn his head to smell the bread in the oven and then look back again, they'd drawn swords and axes and bows, put on helmets, uncovered shields. Suddenly Pollas knew where he'd seen a ship like that before. They were Ap' Olethry pirates, runaway slaves and deserters from the Imperial army who infested the southern coastline of the Empire, and the chances were that they hadn't come here for a hearty breakfast.

Pollas Arteval stood with his mouth open, horribly conscious that he hadn't the faintest idea what to do. The pirates were splitting up into three groups, about twenty in each party; all he could think about was his own house, his wife opening the door of the bread oven, his daughter slicing the bacon. He couldn't protect them, he didn't own any weapons and he didn't know how to fight. It wasn't a required skill in Tornoys, where there wasn't anything to fight about. He watched the small knot of soldiers to see what they were prepared to do about it, but they didn't seem to have realised what was going on. Maybe, he thought, it isn't really happening; maybe they're just *wearing* their swords and shields and helmets, rather than getting ready to use them.

Not wanting to turn away, he stepped backwards into his porch, still watching. Be logical, he told himself: they're here to steal, they won't hurt anybody unless anybody tries to fight them, and nobody would be that stupid—

It would have been some misinterpreted nuance of body-language, a movement just too quick, a gesture that reminded someone of something he'd seen before. In all likelihood, it was glimpsed out of the corner of an eye, acted on with instinct rather than thought. It can't have been an intentional act, for one of Gorgas' soldiers to draw his bow and shoot an arrow into a pirate, for the simple reason that contingents of six men don't pick fights with forces ten times their number, not even if they're heroes. If the arrow had missed, even if it had glanced harmlessly off the angled side of a properly contoured helmet or breastplate, things might have been different. But it didn't. The pirate was on his knees, screaming in terror, and instead of trying to help him, his friends were closing with the soldiers in a short, predictable mêlée. If they'd managed to kill all six of the soldiers it might not have been so bad, but they hadn't. One man got away, ran up the hill much faster than anyone would have expected just from looking at him in the direction of the billets where Gorgas had stationed a half-company of men to make his presence felt in Tornoys. Pollas could see how the pirates felt about it all by the way they moved into action. They were unhappy but resigned, as you'd expect from men who've just seen a simple job turn into an awkward one. *More fighting*, they were saying. *Oh, well, never mind.* They formed their shield-wall like weary hands in a factory who've been told they're having to work late.

They're coming, Pollas realised; but there still wasn't anything he could do other than get himself and his family out of the way; and he knew without being able to account for why that he'd left it rather too late for that. It was too difficult to accept the reality of the situation. A few moments ago, less time than it took to boil a pot of water, everything had been normal. He could see people he recognised, shopkeepers and dock hands and quayside loafers, running away from the shield-wall or stumbling and falling; but he'd seen roughly the same sort of thing in dreams before now, when the nameless-familiar enemy or monster was chasing him along an alley or searching for him in the house – there had been this same illogical sense of detachment (*it's all right really, you're asleep*), this feeling of being an uninvolved spectator—

Someone was tugging at his arm. He looked round and saw his wife. She was pointing with one hand, pulling at him with the other, and he couldn't make out what she was saying. He allowed himself to be pulled, and looked back as she hustled him away; they were using the bench from in front of the Happy Return to bash in the doors of the cheese warehouse. They were inside Dole Baven's house, because there he was, with no clothes on, scrambling out of the back window, but he hadn't looked to see what was underneath. He'd dropped down right in front of one of the other parties, and a pirate stuck him under the ribs with a halberd.

'Come *on*,' his wife was shrieking (basically the same intonation she used for chivvying him in from the barn when dinner was on the table, going cold), and he could see the sense in that; but they were killing his friends, the least he could do was watch. It would be terrible if nobody even knew how they'd died.

'Mavaut, come back!' His wife's voice again; she was watching their daughter sprinting away on her own, terrified, going the wrong way. Belis wanted to go after her, but he grabbed her wrist and wouldn't let her (she didn't like that). He watched as Mavaut bundled down the hill in a flurry of skirts, suddenly came up against the shield-wall, spun round and came scampering back.

They were coming up the hill now, this way. If they ran, they might still get out of the road. 'All right, I'm coming,' he said, and an arrow appeared in the air above him, hanging for a very brief moment before dipping and falling towards him. He could see it quite distinctly, down to the colour of the fletchings, and he watched it carefully all the way down and into his stomach, where it passed at an angle through him and out the other side, leaving six inches of shaft and the feathers still in him. Belis was screaming but after the slight shock of impact he couldn't feel very much, except for the strange and disturbing sensation of having something artificial inside his body. 'All *right*,' he snapped, 'don't fuss, for gods' sakes.' Time to be sensible, he decided, and led his family up the hill, then at right-angles along Pacers' Alley. As he'd anticipated, the pirates carried on up the hill. They had better things to do than break order to go hunting stray civilians.

He sat down on the front step of Arc Javis' house and looked at the arrow. There was blood all over his shirt, soaking into the broad weave of the cloth. There would be no point trying to stand up again now; his knees had failed completely, even his elbows and wrists felt weak and he was confused now, distracted, unable to concentrate his mind. The best thing would be to lean his head against the door and close his eyes for a while, just until he felt a little stronger.

His wife and daughter were arguing again – well, they always argued, Mavaut was at that age – and they seemed to be arguing about whether they ought to pull the arrow out or leave it in there. Belis was saying that if they took it out now it'd make the bleeding worse and he would die; Mavaut had to know different, of course, and she was nearly hysterical. With what was left of his consciousness, Pollas hoped his wife wouldn't give in, the way she usually did when Mavaut worked herself up into a state, because an overindulged child would be an awful thing to die of.

He must have been asleep for a while, though it hadn't seemed like it; he'd just closed his eyes for a moment. But he could hear different sounds; shouting, men shouting information backwards and forwards, like dock hands loading an awkard cargo. Orders; he could hear a man's voice telling someone to keep in line, another voice shouting, *Dress your ranks, raise your halberds*, or something along those lines. He raised his head – it had got very heavy – but there was nobody in the alley except Belis, Mavaut and himself; the battle, if that's what it was, seemed to be happening fifty yards or so away, on the main street. He applied his mind, trying to work out what was going on just by listening, but without seeing he had no idea which lot of foreigners were the pirates and which were Gorgas Loredan's men. Of course he knew nothing about the shape of battles, about how they worked; it was like trying to work out where the hands of the town clock were just by listening to it ticking. More orders, a lot of shouting; it hadn't occurred to him how busy the sergeants must be in a battle, how many things they must have to think about at once; like the captain of a ship, or the master of a work crew. He couldn't make sense of the orders, though; the technical stuff was outside his experience – *port your arms, dress to the front, wheel, make ready at the left there.* He could hear feet shuffling, the nailed soles of boots scraping on cobbles, a few grunts of effort, the occasional clatter of a dropped weapon; but not the ring of steel or the screams of the dying, the sort of thing he'd been led to expect. It was remarkably quiet, in fact, so presumably they hadn't started fighting yet.

He remembered something, and glanced down. The arrow wasn't there any more, and once he saw that he started to feel an intrusive ache, like the worst kind of bellyache. *Damn,* he thought, *they pulled the arrow out after all.* They were sitting quite still beside him, holding on to each other as if they were afraid the other one would blow away in the wind.

Then the noise started; and yes, a battle was pretty loud. It was the sound of a forge, of metal under the hammer, not ringing but dull pecks and clunks and bangs – he could almost feel the force of the blows in the sound they made, unmistakable metal-on-metal, force being applied and re-sisted, thumping and bashing. They were going at it hard all right, if the noise was anything to judge by. There was effort behind those sounds; it must take an awful lot of effort to cut and crush helmets and breastplates and armour. He closed his eyes, trying to concentrate, isolate sounds so as to inter-pret them better, something which is of course much easier to do in the dark. It was hard work, though; the shouting of the sergeants got in the way, drowning out the nuances of the metal-on-metal contact, blurring his vision in the dark-ness. *Typical,* he thought. *First time I'm ever at a battle and I can't see a bloody thing. Fine story this'll make to tell my grandchildren.*

Quite suddenly, the battle moved on. The likeliest thing Pollas could think of was that one side or the other had given ground or run away, because the noise was muffled and distant, but whether it was up the hill or down he couldn't make out. Down the hill was what he wanted, presumably, Gorgas' men driving the pirates back into the sea (unless they'd somehow changed places, so that Gorgas' men were attacking up the hill – all he knew about tactics was that they were complicated, like chess, and he couldn't even beat Mavaut at chess these days). Besides, he couldn't concentrate properly any more, the bellyache got in the way of his hearing and pretty well everything else, and his head was spinning as badly as if he'd just drunk a gallon of cider on an empty stomach. All in all, he didn't feel very well, so he was probably excused observing battles for now. Oddly enough, though, the pain didn't get in the way of falling asleep; so he did that –

– And then he was in a bed, his own; the room was dark and there was nobody else there, so he couldn't ask if he was dead or alive (and he had no way of knowing for himself). It followed, though, that his side had won; so that was all right.

CHAPTER NINE

In the courtyard below the prefect's office, a madman was reciting scripture. The words were right, as accurate as any scholar could wish, but the madman was howling them at the top of his voice, as if uttering curses. The prefect frowned, disturbed by the inconsistency; here was everything that was beautiful and good, unmarred by error or omission, and yet it was utterly wrong.

The district administrator paused in the middle of his summary, aware that his superior wasn't paying attention. Being slightly deaf, he hadn't found the distant noise intrusive, but now he could hear it too. The two men looked at each other.

'Shall I send the clerk for the guard?' the administrator asked.

The prefect shook his head. 'He isn't doing anything wrong,' he replied.

The administrator raised an eyebrow. 'Disturbing the peace,' he said. 'Loitering with intent. Blasphemy—'

'I didn't say he wasn't breaking any laws,' the prefect replied with a smile. 'But it's every man's duty to preach the scriptures. It's just a pity that he's choosing to do it at the top of his voice.'

(But it wasn't that, of course; it was the tone of voice that was so disturbing, the savage anger with which the fellow was reciting those calm, measured, impersonal statements of doctrine, those elegantly balanced maxims, so perfectly phrased that not one single word could be replaced by a synonym without radically altering the sense. It was like listening to a wolf howling Substantialist poetry.)

'Sooner or later,' the prefect went on, 'someone else will

call the guard, the wretched creature will be taken away and we'll have some peace again. Until then, I shall pretend I can't hear it. I'm sorry, you were saying—'

The administrator nodded. 'The proposed alliance,' he went on, 'is of course out of the question; this man Gorgas Loredan is nothing but an adventurer, a small-scale warlord who's set himself up in a backwater and is desperately trying to enlist powerful friends against the day when his subjects get tired of him and throw him out. Doing anything that would appear to recognise his regime would reflect very badly on us. Quite simply, we don't do business with that class of person.'

'Agreed,' replied the prefect, trying to concentrate. 'But there's more to it, I can tell.'

The administrator nodded wearily. 'Unfortunately,' he went on, 'the confounded man has had a quite extraordinary stroke of good luck. Two days ago, the small port that lies on his border - Tornoys, it's called - was raided by a pirate ship. One ship, fifty or so men; they were after the despatch clipper from Ap' Escatoy, which they'd been stalking all the way up the coast until it was driven into Tornoys by a sudden storm on the previous day. They followed it in, got badly knocked about by the storm themselves, and spent the night riding it out before coming into harbour just after dawn. Now I'm not sure what happened after that, but Gorgas Loredan and his men arrived before they could do anything about the clipper and engaged them in battle; half of the pirates were killed, and Gorgas has the survivors locked up in a barn somewhere. He's also holding on to the clipper, though he hasn't given any reasons.'

The prefect was scowling. 'It's Hain Partek, isn't it?' he said.

The administrator nodded. 'And Gorgas knows precisely who it is he's got hold of,' he went on. 'Well, he'd have to be singularly ill-informed not to; after all, we've been offering large sums of money for him and posting his description up all over the province these past ten years; and of course it's wonderful news that he's been caught, I suppose. I just wish, though, that it had been somebody else and not this Gorgas person.'

'Quite.' The prefect leaned back in his chair. 'Had we told him we weren't interested in his alliance?'

'Unfortunately, yes,' the administrator said, picking up a small ivory figure from the desk, examining it briefly and putting it back. 'The timing couldn't have been worse. As soon as he got our response, he sat down and fired off a reply; most extraordinary letter I've read in a long time, a thoroughly bizarre mixture of obsequiousness and threats – you ought to read it yourself, if only for the entertainment value. My assessor reckons he's off his head, and after reading this letter I'm inclined to agree with him. Apparently, when the letter telling him we didn't want the alliance reached him, he was in a farmyard splitting wood.'

'Splitting wood,' the prefect repeated. 'Why?'

'I get the impression he likes splitting wood. Not *per se*; he enjoys making believe he's a farmer. He comes from a farming family, apparently, though he had to leave home in something of a hurry. So far, the only possible explanation I've heard for what he's done in the Mesoge is that it was the only way he could ever go home.'

'He does sound deranged, I'll admit.' The prefect made a slight gesture with his hands. 'Insanity isn't necessarily an obstacle to success in his line of work, though,' he observed. 'Frequently, in fact, it's an asset, if properly used. Has he said what he wants from us yet?'

The administrator shook his head. 'All we've had is a terse little note saying he's got Partek in custody and would like us to send someone to discuss matters with him. I imagine he'd far rather we made the opening bid; which is reasonable enough, I suppose, from his point of view. I mean, all he knows is what we've said openly, he's got no way of knowing how important to us Partek really is.' The administrator hesitated for a moment, and then went on. 'To be honest,' he said, 'I'm not entirely sure myself. What's the official line on that these days?'

The prefect sighed. 'He's important enough,' he said. 'Not as important as he was five years ago, but he's still a damned nuisance; not because of anything he's done or anything he's capable of doing, it's more the fact that he's still out there, and we haven't been able to do a damn thing about it.' He frowned, and scratched his ear. 'It's amusing, really; the less he actually achieves, the more his legend grows. In some parts of the south-eastern region, they're firmly convinced he's in control of the western peninsula and he's raising an army to march on the Homeland. No, we need to be able to point to his head nailed to a door in Ap' Silas; if we could do that, it'd be a good day's work.'

'Which means,' said the administrator, 'we have to give Gorgas Loredan what he asks for?'

'Not necessarily.' The prefect paused for a moment. He couldn't hear the madman any more; someone must have come and dealt with him. 'There's no reason why we should necessarily replace a big problem with a smaller one. Now then,' he went on, 'if I remember correctly, this Gorgas Loredan's the brother of our own Bardas Loredan.'

'The hero,' replied the administrator with a grin. 'That's right. Extraordinary family; if only the Mesoge produced more men like that, it might be - well, interesting to have an alliance with them. They're both barking mad, of course, but you can't help but admire their vitality.'

'I can,' the prefect said, 'when it causes me difficulties. Let's see, then. We need Bardas Loredan to be the figure-head against the plainspeople, so presumably we can't play rough with Gorgas Loredan, for fear of offending him—'

'I don't know about that,' the administrator interrupted. 'By all accounts, Bardas hates Gorgas like poison - there's a really wonderful backstory to all that, by the way, remind me to tell you about it when we've got five minutes - so I wouldn't worry too much about that. But Gorgas, apparently, dotes on Bardas—'

The prefect held up his hands. 'This is all a bit much,' he said. 'I'm sorry, please go on. I just find all this a trifle bewildering, that's all.'

'So do I,' the administrator replied with a smile. 'But you must admit, it's rather more intriguing than the quarterly establishment returns.'

The heavy clouds that had been masking the sun lifted, and a blinding beam of amber sunlight dazzled the prefect for a moment. He shifted his chair a little to avoid it. 'At my time of life I can manage quite well without being intrigued, so long as I don't have to deal with messy little people living in obscure places,' he said grimly. 'On the other hand,' he went on, lightening up a little, 'I must confess, Bardas Loredan was something of a collector's item. He obviously didn't have a clue who he was talking to, which was really quite refreshing. Anyway, where were we?'

The prefect leaned back, his fingertips pressed against his lips. 'We need Bardas because of Temrai, and now Gorgas has got Partek; but we don't want to be seen to be friends with Gorgas, and Bardas won't mind if we aren't friends with Gorgas ... What was that you said about the clipper?' he added, leaning forward again. 'He's detaining it, you say?'

The administrator, who had been studying the floral designs carved along the edge of the desk, nodded. 'And that's awkward too,' he said. 'You see, there's quite a lot in despatches about the Temrai business; all the paperwork for the ships we've been chartering, letters of credit, signed agreements, draft schedules – put them together and you'd have a fairly clear picture of what we're proposing to do, provided you had the wits to understand it all.'

'Which Gorgas clearly does, even if they're addled,' the prefect said. 'That's awkward. I was considering rattling a sabre at him for detaining our ship, perhaps frightening him into giving us Partek that way. But that would only draw his attention to what he's got hold of.'

The administrator pursed his lips. 'I'd tend to look at it the other way round,' he said. 'How would it look to you if you were illegally detaining the provincial office's despatches courier, and they *didn't* make an almighty fuss about it? In fact, I suspect that's precisely why he's doing it, to see how we react. Otherwise, he's got no possible motive for pulling our tails in this way.'

'That's a very good point,' the prefect conceded. 'Oh, damn the man, he's giving me a headache. At this precise moment, I think I could easily do without the vitality of the Loredan brothers, thank you very much.'

'Ah.' The administrator smiled. 'That's where we might be able to do something. I'm thinking about the Loredan sister.'

The prefect turned his head sharply. 'Do you know, I'd forgotten all about her. Niessa Loredan, who ran the bank on Scona that so annoyed our friends in the Shastel Order.'

'That's the one,' the administrator said. 'Currently enjoying our hospitality, of course.'

'That's right. Now then, how do the brothers stand as far as she's concerned? They either love her or hate her, I'm sure, but which is it?'

The administrator folded his hands neatly in his lap. 'Gorgas loves her, I think,' he said, 'although she did rather leave him in the lurch at the fall of Scona when she skipped off with all the money and left him to do all the fighting. But I don't think Gorgas holds that against her; he's very forgiving when it comes to family.'

The prefect raised an eyebrow but didn't take the point. 'And Bardas? He loves her too?'

'I don't think so,' the administrator replied. 'I don't think he hates her, either. But her daughter has made a public vow to kill him, if that has any bearing on matters.'

'Oh, for pity's sake.' The prefect shook his head. 'Never mind, I expect it's all in the files somewhere. In fact, I must have read about it all before I interviewed the man. So, I take it you've got something in mind.'

Beautiful, though rare, are the smiles of the Children of Heaven. 'Not really,' the administrator said. 'Little more than a notion that she might come in handy, if the situation looks like getting out of hand. But it'd be as well to secure her – both of them, actually, the daughter as well as the mother. We'll hold them as illegal aliens and leave it at that for now.'

The prefect stood up and walked to the window, under which grew a fine old fig tree. From the window he could almost but not quite reach the topmost fig. 'For now, I'm afraid,' he said, 'getting hold of Partek must have priority. If I lose him now, I'll have some difficult questions to answer. Do what you can; obviously I'd prefer to avoid any kind of alliance with that man, but I'm sure you can find some form of words that'll satisfy him and not commit us to anything. Next priority is the Perimadeia business, though it's not in the same league as Partek, so be a bit careful where Bardas Loredan is concerned. Otherwise, I'm quite happy for you to use your own judgement.' He turned away from the window, so that his face was in shadow, and frowned. 'There's always a danger when we start looking at these sort of people on an individual level of losing our sense of proportion. Aside from Partek, none of the individuals here is even remotely significant at a policy level. It's only when we come down to strategic – lower than that, even; tactical – that they begin to look important.' He shrugged and sat down on the corner of his desk. 'I mean to say,' he went on, 'if you come to the conclusion that the best way to get hold of Partek is to take two divisions and some of these ships we've been chartering and annex the Mesoge, then by all means do it. I'm not suggesting you should,' he added, before the administrator could say anything, 'I'm just pointing out the need to focus on journey's end, not the scenery along the way. The same goes for Shastel, or any of these petty little kingdoms. If they've got to go, they've got to go. All we're concerned about is cost-efficiency and economy of effort.'

The administrator stood up to leave. 'A valid point,' he said. 'I'll bring in Partek, have no fears on that score. But you won't object if I try to do it neatly and elegantly, will you? After all,' he added with a grin, 'it doesn't take much imagination to send in an army. It's sending in an army under budget that gets you noticed by the provincial office.'

'This is appalling,' muttered Eseutz Mesatges, easing her shoulder-strap where it was biting into the side of her neck. 'All these people wanting to buy, and nothing to sell to them.'

Another quiet day on the Span. Usually it took half an hour to thread one's way the hundred or so yards across the bridge; today it had taken a few minutes. Hido Glaia, desperate for three bales of green velvet to make up an order he'd assured the customer he'd despatched a week ago, nodded sadly. 'If this incredible opportunity of a lifetime goes on much longer,' he said, 'it'll ruin us all. That's if we don't all die of boredom first.' He picked up a sample of cloth, the same piece he'd examined and rejected yesterday, and the day before, and the day before that. It was the only green velvet on the Island. 'I'll be so desperate I'll come back for this tomorrow,' he said, 'and by then someone'll have bought it. Come on, let's have a drink. Assuming there's still some booze left on this miserable rock.'

In the Golden Palace, they found Venart Auzeil and Tamin Votz, sitting gloomily over a half-empty jug. As soon as they walked in, Venart looked up hopefully.

'Hido,' he said, 'my axe-handles. Have you got them for me?'

Hido pulled out a chair and sat in it, stifling a yawn. 'Oh, come on,' he said, 'what do you take me for, the tooth fairy? Or do you think I was down on the beach at first light, whittling them out of driftwood?'

'I take it that means you haven't,' Venart replied miserably. 'Which means I've now got to go to the Doce brothers and try and explain to them—'

'That my ship and your ship and everybody else's ship is tied up at the quay,' Hido interrupted, 'along with all of theirs. I think they probably already know. Relax, Ven, the Doce boys know the score, you're all right. You're not the one with a ferocious Colleon fabrics cartel breathing down your neck and threatening you with penalty clauses. Talking of which,' he added, 'you wouldn't happen to have such a thing as three bales of green velvet, Island standard fine?'

Venart frowned. 'Not me, no,' he said, 'but you might try talking to Triz. I know she bought a whole load of stuff a few months back – you know, when they sold up Remvaut Jors. I have an idea there was some green velvet in with it, though whether—'

'God bless you,' Hido said, jumping up. 'You wouldn't happen to know how much she paid for it, would you?'

'Hido! She's my *sister!*'

'Can't blame a man for trying. Thank you.'

He bustled away. Eseutz emptied his cup into hers. 'Well, you never know,' she explained, as Venart looked at her. 'They may be rationing the stuff tomorrow, if things go on like this.'

Tamin Votz laughed. 'What I don't understand is,' he said, 'I know why none of our ships are coming in or out, but why aren't any foreign ships coming here? Do you think the Empire's chartered them too?'

'It's possible,' Venart said. 'Well, it is,' he added defensively as Eseutz giggled. 'Gods alone know how big this army of theirs is going to be, and it goes without saying they've got the money.'

'Really?' Tamin Votz smiled as he emptied the last few drops from the jug into his cup. 'You know, the thing that's come out of all this that I find most interesting is how little we actually know about the Empire. Oh, we think we know, but that's not the same thing at all. It's like looking at the sky. I mean, we all see it every day, it's just *there*. But we don't know how it works, or what it's really for, or even what it actually *is*. Same with the Empire, if you ask me.'

Eseutz had found a discarded bowl of olives on a neighbouring table. 'I was reading a book,' she said with her mouth full, 'and it said the sky's really just this enormous piece of blue cloth, and the stars are little holes where the light comes through. And the rain, too, although that bit strikes me as a bit far-fetched. Because if that was the case, every time it rains you'd expect there to be dirty great big puddles right under the Pole Star. I wonder if anybody's actually checked to see if they line up. The rain, I mean, and the stars.'

Tamin raised an eyebrow. 'I didn't know you read books, Eseutz,' he said. 'Come wrapped round something, did it?'

'Oh, very funny,' Eseutz replied, spitting out an olive stone. 'I'll have you know I've got a whole box of books in my warehouse. This big, it is. And even now I can't shift them,' she added wistfully. 'Hey, Ven, I don't suppose you'd be interested—'

'No.' Venart swirled the last of his wine round the bottom of his cup. 'But I suppose you're right,' he went on. 'No, not you, him. About the Empire. I haven't got a clue how big it is. I just know it's - well, big.'

'It's that all right,' Tamin said. 'Too big, if you ask me. I've been hearing stories about a civil war, even.'

'Really?' Eseutz lifted her head. 'Oh, wait. Do you mean the Partek rumours? Because I happen to know for a fact ...'

Tamin shook his head. 'I mean a real civil war,' he said, 'not just random acts of meaningless violence by a bunch of pirates. No, this is supposed to be a showdown between the Imperial family and some warlord or other, far away to the south-east. The whole thing's probably been exaggerated way out of proportion, but I do believe there's at least a small grain of truth in it. And that's my point, you see,' he went on. 'I simply don't know how these things work. If there's a civil war, a real one, will they suddenly put everything else on hold and hurry back home to take part? Or do things like that happen every day?'

Venart shrugged. 'Does it matter?' he asked. 'One thing we can all be sure of, the Empire's never bothered us. And I don't believe it ever will.'

'Oh, yes?' Tamin enquired. 'What makes you so sure?'

'Well,' Venart said, 'for one thing they don't have a fleet, and this is an island after all. Or had you always assumed we were on a mountaintop and it'd been raining a lot?'

'They do have a fleet, though,' Eseutz put in. 'Ours.'

'All right, but they're hardly likely to use our own fleet against us.'

'Oh, I don't know. More to the point, they don't need a fleet to use against us if ours is out of the running.'

'And how are they going to get here without any ships? Walk?' Venart shook his head. 'The point is, I can't see the Empire ever attacking us. It doesn't make any sense. It's not how they go about things.'

'As far as you know. And, as I think we've all agreed, we know spit about the Empire.'

Venart sighed patiently. 'They're only interested in securing their borders,' he said. 'We're in the middle of the sea. End of story.'

'Maybe you're right,' Tamin said. 'I just feel we ought to know more about them, that's all. For example, the amount of business we do with them is pretty well negligible – and that does concern us all right. We could be missing out on some amazing opportunities.'

Venart scratched his ear. 'My guess is, they don't need anything we sell. They can get everything they want from inside the Empire. And I'm not sure I'd be all that keen to trade with them anyway. I don't know what it is, but they give me the creeps.'

'Ah,' Tamin said, 'that's more like it. We don't do business with them becasue we're afraid of them. Or we just don't like them, whatever. That's a pretty juvenile attitude for a trading nation, don't you think?'

'I don't know,' Venart replied. 'Maybe it's just me. But they're so big, and—'

'Scary?'

Venart nodded. 'All right,' he said, 'scary, yes. I feel on edge dealing with them. I can't help it, it's just the way I feel.'

'Because you don't know about them,' Tamin said, smiling. 'I'm sure if you understood them better, you wouldn't be so apprehensive.'

'Quite,' muttered Eseutz. 'I bet they're really sweet once you get to know them.'

Gannadius?

Gannadius sat up. It was dark; he was faintly aware of Theudas, stirring in his sleep in the bed next to him. Someone had called his name.

Gannadius. It's me.

'Oh,' he said aloud; then he closed his eyes.

He was back in the City (oh, not *again*), in the ropewalks this time; on either side of the enormously wide street, houses and warehouses were burning, brightly enough for him to be able to see as if it was daylight. He was standing in the middle of the road, which was fortunate; all the fighting and killing was taking place on the edges, under the eaves of the burning buildings.

'Sorry,' Alexius was saying. 'I don't like it here much, either; it's just where I happened to be.'

Gannadius shivered; he couldn't feel the heat from the fire all around him, although he knew he ought to. 'Charming place you've got here,' he said. 'Actually, I haven't been here before, I don't think. And I've been to most parts of the Fall at one time or another.'

Alexius pointed, though Gannadius couldn't quite make out what he was supposed to be looking at. 'Over there,' Alexius was saying. 'See that man there, the plainsman with the long hair? Any moment now the roof of that shed's going to slide off, and he'll be trapped under it and killed. That's the point of all this, why it's important. There it goes, look,' he added, as a small building collapsed in a shower of sparks, and someone Gannadius couldn't see screamed. 'It took me ages to work out what was important about this, but finally I tracked it down. If he'd lived, he'd have taken part in an archery contest; he'd have shot an arrow that bounced off the edge of the target frame – real million-to-one stuff – and hit Temrai's wife in the eye. Well, not his wife then, and she never would have been his wife; instead he'd have married someone else, and things would have been a whole lot different.'

'I see,' Gannadius said, inaccurately. 'And that's what you wanted to tell me, was it?'

Alexius shook his head. 'Good gods, no. Like I said, this is just where I've been spending time lately. No, it's much more important – for you, that is. I need to warn you—'

'Excuse me,' Gannadius said. He'd just noticed that he'd trodden on a dying man. He knew, of course, that there was nothing he could do to help, since all this had already happened and besides, he wasn't really there. But it went against the grain just to walk on.

'I'm sorry,' he said, kneeling down, but the man didn't show any signs of having heard him. His wounds were spectacular – a deep slicing cut running diagonally from the junction of the neck and shoulders, following the line of the collar-bone, and a massive stab-wound, as broad as Gannadius' hand, just under the arch of the ribs.

'Halberd wounds,' Alexius remarked, above him and out of sight.

'Halberds? I didn't know the plainsmen used them.'

'They don't,' Alexius replied; and when Gannadius looked up, he realised that he wasn't in Perimadeia any more. 'Scona?' he asked.

'That's right,' Alexius confirmed. 'What you're seeing is the sack of Scona by the Shastel Order.'

Gannadius frowned. Behind him, though he couldn't see it, all the warehouses that lined the Strangers' Quay were on fire, and people were fighting each other to get to the head of the line to board ships that had already left, and been sunk in the harbour by the catapults mounted on the decks of the Shastel barges. 'But that never happened,' he said.

'Strictly speaking, you're right,' Alexius said. 'Bardas Loredan prevented it; he put Gorgas out of action, making him give up the war, so there never was a siege, or a sack. Nevertheless, this is here. Ask your friend there if you don't believe me.'

'You're saying that this is what should have happened.'

'Good gods, no. You've been reading too much Tryphaenus. I never could see any sense in dragging value judgements into the study of the Principle. It's like saying the sun rises in the east because it's a better neighbourhood. All I'm saying is, this happened too. In a sense.'

Gannadius stood up. 'You've lost me,' he said. 'And please, don't try to explain. My thirst for pure knowledge isn't what it was, I'm afraid. What were you about to say? About a warning?'

'Oh, yes.' Alexius pointed. 'There, look.'

Somehow, while Gannadius wasn't looking, Scona had gone. Instead, they were standing in the middle of what Gannadius assumed was a plains encampment; a large one, with tents and temporary stockades all around them in every direction. Someone was attacking it; many of the tents were on fire, and there were horsemen riding up and down between the rows, setting light to the waxed felt or hacking at random at the people trying to slip past. Directly ahead, Gannadius saw a wagon. The felt cover had almost burned away, leaving the hoops sticking up like ribs, and underneath it, Gannadius could see the face of a boy peeping out between the spokes of the offside front wheel at a horseman, who was looking back at him. Because of the angle, and because the horseman's visor was down, Gannadius couldn't see his face ...

'Who's that?' he asked, redundantly

'Guess.'

'I see,' Gannadius said. A man was trying to sneak past the horseman, squeezing himself against the side of a row of barrels. The horseman caught sight of him and leaned forward in the saddle, bending from the waist. His blow landed on the flat top of the man's head. 'So this is how it all started, I suppose.'

Alexius smiled. 'There's more to it than that, I'm afraid. You're assuming that this is one of Maxen's pre-emptive raids against the tribes, the one in which young Temrai saw his family killed. Yes?'

Gannadius nodded. 'Isn't that him under the cart?' he said.

'Of course. But,' Alexius went on, 'this is also what's going to happen. Observe the armour and kit the horsemen are wearing.'

Gannadius looked annoyed. 'I'm sorry,' he said, 'I'm not what you'd call a military buff. What's so special about the armour?'

'It means they're Imperial heavy cavalry,' Alexius said. 'What you're watching is the annexation of what used to be Perimadeia by the provincial office. And yes, the man on the horse over there is Bardas Loredan; and yes, the boy under the cart is King Temrai. Of course, *boy* is stretching it a bit now, he must be twenty-four or five by now; but he looks young for his age, especially when he's terrified. And the cart helps, too, putting him in shadow.'

Gannadius looked round again. 'All right,' he said, 'if that's so, how come I can't see the City? Or the ruins, at least.'

Alexius smiled. 'King Temrai decided it would be suicide to stay put and fight the Empire,' he said, 'particularly when he heard who was nominally in charge of the army. If they want Perimadeia, he said, they can have it; he ordered his people to pack up their things and led them back to the plains, where they'd come from. But the provincial office wasn't impressed. If they can go away, they argued, they can also come back. Best to deal with them now. So they sent Bardas and the army out into the plains, relying on Bardas' local knowledge and long experience. Sure enough, he led them to where he reckoned the tribes would set up camp as soon as they felt they were out of danger and could relax. There was a bloody massacre – exhibit one – and thousands of the plainspeople were killed. Thousands weren't, however. So Bardas spent the rest of his life hunting them, until he died of pneumonia and his second in command – a man called Theudas Morosin, if that rings any bells with you – led the army home. By then, the Empire had rebuilt Perimadeia, and Morosin settled down there, although he didn't have much of a life, poor fellow. Then one day the tribes suddenly appeared on the border, led by a strong young king who'd been no more than a boy on the day Bardas burned the camp and killed his family. He knew there'd never be peace so long as the City stood. Fortuitously he was some kind of military genius; Theudas Morosin, hastily recalled and put in charge of the defences, did an outstanding job in the face of fecklessness and apathy unusual even by Imperial standards, but the City fell, and Theudas was one of only a handful of survivors ...'

Gannadius was clapping his hands, slowly. 'Very good,' he said. 'A splendidly neat and well-crafted piece of work. I don't believe a word of it.'

'You don't?' Alexius raised an eyebrow. 'Oh, come on, Gannadius, since when were you so critical? Look.' He pointed, and Gannadius was back where he'd started, in the burning ropewalks of Perimadeia; only this time he could see himself, a very old man with a dazed, sleepy expression on his face, being hustled down the street by—

'Theudas Morosin,' he said, in the tone of voice of a conjuror's stooge who's just had a bunch of roses pulled out of his ear. 'And yes, I'll grant you, he looks just like Bardas in all that gear.'

'It's even the same sword,' Alexius said. 'The Guelan broadsword Gorgas gave Bardas the day before the sack. Bardas gave it to Athli Zeuxis to keep for him. Athli gave it to Theudas when Bardas died. Here it is again – they really made them to last in those days. It's that kind of attention to detail that really impresses people.'

Gannadius closed his eyes; which was a mistake, because now he was in the mines under Ap' Escatoy, undoubtedly his least favourite hallucination of all—

'*Not* a hallucination,' Alexius corrected him. 'Not an optical illusion, trick done with mirrors, anything like that, as you know perfectly well. Whatever you see is real; the only thing here that isn't real is you.'

Gannadius opened his mouth to object, then hesitated for a moment. 'That sack of Scona we saw,' he said. 'That's in the future too, isn't it?'

'Ah!' Alexius beamed. 'Eventually, after all this time, you've got there. I knew you would. Exactly so; it hasn't happened yet. Just because you haven't read the last page of a book, it doesn't follow that the story hasn't been written.'

'Actually,' Gannadius confessed, 'I always read the ending first. I find it helps me to appreciate the nuances. You're saying that just because none of this has happened here yet, it's already happened –' He paused, frowning. 'Somewhere else?'

Alexius leaned his back against the panel wall of the gallery. He smelt of coriander. 'Now you're getting somewhere,' he said. 'Now, at long last, you're beginning to see how simple the Principle really is. I can't really blame you for not understanding before, I suppose. It's taken me this long to work it out for myself, and you simply won't believe the trouble I've had to go to ... You remember how we used to speculate whether we could find a way to use the Principle to see into the future? We should have realised, only we were too criminally stupid to understand the painfully obvious – we can see the future because it's all already happened.'

'You've lost me again,' said Gannadius sadly.

'Oh, for pity's sake.' Gannadius could feel the whole gallery shaking, and the air was thick with loosened dust. 'We can watch Theudas killing the tribes because we can watch Bardas doing the exact same thing. We can watch the fall of Imperial Perimadeia because we've already seen Perimadeia fall. We can see everything that way, because it's all the same event. We can even see our own deaths, if we're that morbidly inclined. Of course, it's customary to die first ...'

The roof collapsed, filling the gallery with dirt. It was like being inside an hourglass as it's turned upside down. Gannadius choked, felt a timber crash into the side of his head and opened his eyes.

'Uncle?'

'Theudas,' he said. 'What's going on? Where are we?'

'You were having a nightmare,' Theudas said, bringing the lamp close. 'It's all right. We're with the plainspeople, remember? Temrai's summoned us, and he's going to send us home.'

Gannadius sat up, shaking his head. 'He was wrong,' he said. 'You can change it, if you find the right place and sort of *push*. We did it ourselves, with Bardas and that girl.' He looked up at Theudas' face, as if examining whether it was genuine. 'Coriander,' he said. 'Doesn't that mean the enemy?'

Theudas put down the lamp. 'Stay still,' he said, 'I'm going to see if I can find that lady doctor. You'll be just fine, you'll see.'

Gannadius sighed. He'd woken up with a splitting head-ache. 'It's all right,' he said, 'it was just some leftovers from the dream I was having, I haven't gone mad. Sorry, did I frighten you?'

Cautiously, as if afraid of an ambush, Theudas came back. 'It was another one of *those* dreams, was it?' he said. 'I thought the silverwort tea had sorted them out.'

'Not really,' Gannadius said. 'But it tasted so disgusting I stopped telling you about them, so you wouldn't make me drink it any more.' He breathed out and lay back on the bed. 'Now that I think of it, I seem to remember reading somewhere that silverwort's a slow poison. Well, it's bad for you, at any rate. Does things to your kidneys.'

Theudas scowled. 'Go back to sleep,' he said. 'We've got a long day tomorrow, and you need your rest. In fact, I'm going to have a word with the drover; you can't be expected to rattle along in a cart all day at your age.'

'Oh, I wouldn't fret about it.' Gannadius smiled bleakly. 'I happen to know that I survived to a ripe old age, all my hair fell out and half my teeth as well. So did you; survive, I mean. Probably you died of pneumonia, but don't hold me to that; I'm extrapolating from associated data.'

'Uncle—'

'I know, I'm talking crazy again. I'll stop.' Gannadius yawned conscientiously and turned over, his eyes still open. 'Put out the lamp,' he said, 'I promise I'll try to get some sleep.'

Theudas sighed. 'I worry about you, I really do,' he said.

'So do I,' Gannadius answered, trying to sound drowsy. 'So do I.'

'You're cured then, are you?'

Bardas smiled. 'Apparently,' he replied. 'At least, I'm no crazier than I was to start with. Also, I was making the infirmary look untidy, so they threw me out.'

Anax, the ancient Son of Heaven who ran the proof house, nodded sagely. 'It's not the sort of place you'd want to hang about in,' he said. 'What they're best at is sawing off limbs - they make a wonderfully neat job of it, probably because the surgeon used to be the foreman of the joinery shop, until he got too much seniority and had to be promoted. You should see some of the false legs he's fitted; they turn them out of whalebone on the big pole lathe they've got down there. Works of art, some of them.'

'I shouldn't wonder,' Bardas replied.

While Bardas packed his few belongings into a kitbag, Anax sat perched on the end of the bed, reminding Bardas of a pixie in a story he'd heard when he was very young. To the best of his recollection, the pixie occupied its time by making marvellously detailed and complicated lifesize mechanical dolls that were well nigh indistinguishable from real boys and girls, and substituting them for the children he stole from poor families in the dead of night. The story had horrified him so much that he hadn't slept for weeks afterwards, and (rather illogically) had got into the habit of tapping his arms and legs to make sure they weren't made of metal.

'So you're off, then,' Anax said, after he'd been silent for a while.

'Apparently,' Bardas replied. 'It's a shame, really. I was getting used to being here.'

Anax smiled. 'Getting used to,' he said. 'That's about the furthest anyone could ever go, unless of course they happened to love bashing sheet metal with hammers. Don't laugh, some people do. Bollo here, for instance; don't you, Bollo?'

Anax's enormous young assistant pulled a face. Bardas laughed.

'Don't let him fool you,' Anax went on. 'Secretly he loves his work. When he was a child, he was always getting yelled at for breaking things – and something that size in a small peasant cottage is bound to break something every now and again, it's inevitable. Here, he can break things all day long and get paid money for it.' Anax looked down at his fingers, then up again. 'If you're going to the wars, what are you going to do for equipment? You don't seem to have much kit of your own.'

Bardas shrugged. 'They'll issue me with some, I suppose,' he replied. 'At least, I assume—'

'Seems a bit long-winded,' Anax interruped. 'After all, we make the stuff here. Why take pot luck with some provincial quartermaster's clerk when you can have the pick of the production run? Better still,' he added, hopping down from the bed, 'you could have some made bespoke. At least that way you'd know it was proof.'

'I haven't really given it much thought,' Bardas replied, holding a shirt against his chest to fold it. 'From what they've told me, my main function's going to be to stand up on a high point where Temrai can see me and look terrifying. Which'll suit me fine,' he added. 'Gods know, I'm in no hurry to get involved in any fighting.'

Anax sighed. 'He hasn't given it much thought,' he repeated. 'Deputy inspector of the proof house, or whatever he calls himself, and he's prepared to make do with any old piece of junk off the shelves in the QM stores. We can't have that, can we, Bollo? Imagine how it'd reflect on us if he got himself killed, or lost an arm. Some people just don't think, is their trouble.'

'All right,' Bardas replied, smiling. 'You choose some for me, then I'll know who to blame.'

'We'll do better than that,' Anax replied. 'We'll make it for you, ourselves.'

Bardas raised an eyebrow. 'I thought you only smashed it up,' he said. 'I didn't know you could make the stuff too.'

Anax made a show of looking affronted. 'Do you mind?' he said. 'I was a tin-basher for twenty years.'

'Until you got too much seniority and they had to promote you?'

Anax slapped him on the back. 'It's a pity, you know,' he said. 'The man's just starting to get the hang of how this place works, and he's getting posted. It's a waste, if you ask me.'

Before Bardas could object, Anax had marched out of the room. He walked so fast that Bardas had trouble keeping up with him, especially in the maze of corridors and galleries under the main shop, which was where he was headed. Bollo lumbered along some way behind; he wasn't built for speed or agility, and he knew the way already.

'Good,' Anax said, peering in through a doorway, 'nobody's found it yet. One of these days I'll come down here and it'll be full of equipment and people working, and that'll be my private workshop gone. Where's Bollo with the lamp? We need to get a fire going so we can see what we're about.'

When there was light, Bardas was able to look round. In the middle of the floor stood an anvil, the full-sized three-hundredweight type, bolted to a massive section of oak beam to dampen the shock of the blows. Next to it on the beam was a swage block, a large square of heavy duty iron into which were cut holes and grooves and cups of various sizes and profiles, half-round and square and three-square; into these recesses the sheet metal could be hammered, to mould a variety of shapes, such as flutes and raised edges. At the end of the beam a cup-shaped hole had been chiselled out, about half a thumb's length deep at its deepest point (it was shaped rather like a scallop shell, sloping gently at one end, steeply at the other). Bardas noticed that the fibres of the wood had been hammered smooth, hard and shiny.

'Dishing stump,' Anax explained. 'For dishing and hollowing. And that's the folder,' he went on, pointing to a contraption mounted on a stout workbench at the far end of the room, 'and next to that's the rollers and the shear. All there is to it, really. Now then, let's see what we've got behind here.' He knelt down and reached behind the workbench. 'Unless somebody's been in here and found it, we should have – yes, here we are.' He hauled out a sheet of steel, dull brown under an even layer of rust. 'I put this aside – what, fifteen years ago it must be, just in case I ever wanted to make some good stuff. I watched it being drawn down out of a single bloom of proper Colleon iron – lovely clean material, not full of bits of grit and rubbish like the garbage we use for work. There's half a hundredweight here, plenty to be going on with if we cut neatly.' He bit his lip, then went on, 'You know, this probably sounds silly to you, but I knew when I saw it that I'd find a use for it some day.'

Bardas felt vaguely uneasy about this. 'Are you sure you can spare it?' he asked. 'I mean, if it's such good material—'

'That's all right,' Anax replied with a slightly cock-eyed grin. 'So long as it's going to someone who'll make proper use of it.'

'I'm not sure I like the sound of that,' Bardas said.

From a shallow box in the corner Anax produced a set of patterns cut out of thin wood. 'Breastplate,' he said, handing up the largest of them. 'Backplate, gorget, vambraces, helmet panel, cheekpieces, neckguard – damn it to hell, where's the neckguard? Ah, got it. All seems to be here; cuisses, greaves, cops, rerebraces – are we going to bother with sabatons? No, I don't think so, you'll hardly be able to move as it is. Taces?'

'What's a tace?' Bardas asked.

'All right, no taces. That'll do. Bollo, get the sheet up on the bench so I can start marking out.'

Carefully, while Bollo held the sheet still, Anax drew round the patterns with chalk. 'It's just as well for you that you're a decent height,' he said. 'I cut these patterns for us – the Sons of Heaven, I mean. Most of you outlanders are funny little short people.'

'Like you,' Bardas pointed out.

'Precisely,' Anax agreed. 'But then, I'm different. Luckily for you. All you'd ever get free from the rest of us'd be your three days' rations. Keep the damn sheet still, Bollo, you're wobbling it about.'

It took a long time to mark the patterns out, and longer still to cut out the sections on the shear. Bollo cut the straight lines, pulling down the long lever effortlessly, his mind obviously elsewhere; Anax cut the curves, something which Bardas would have sworn was impossible to do, since the shear was nothing more than a giant version of a pair of snips, one jaw bolted to the bench, the other fitted with a three-foot handle. 'You're worried,' Anax said between grunts of effort, 'that I can cut this stuff like paper. You think it must be too thin to be any good. Well, all I can say to you is, have faith.'

'I wasn't worried, actually,' Bardas said, but Anax didn't seem to have heard, because he went on, 'The point is, steel is wonderful stuff. I can cut it and bend it and shape it like it was parchment or clay; and then when I've finished with it, Bollo and his biggest big hammer won't be able to make so much as a dent in it. And you know what the secret is? Stress,' he went on, before Bardas could answer. 'A bit of stress, a bit of tension, maybe just a little torture even, and suddenly you've got good armour, the genuine proof. Ouch,' he added, as he cut his finger on a sharp sliver of swarf. 'Serves me right, I wasn't thinking about what I'm doing.' A drop of blood plopped like a single raindrop on to the surface of the section he was cutting out and stood proud, like the head of a rivet.

'Stress,' Anax repeated, putting a steel plate into the folder. It was an odd-looking thing – two square frames, like window-sashes, one fixed, the other pivoting at right angles. Anax trapped the plate between the two frames and pushed down on the pivoting arm, neatly folding the plate down the middle like a sheet of card. Next he transferred it into the roller, which reminded Bardas of the big iron mangle they used in the laundry round the corner from his apartment in the island-block in Perimadeia. Anax adjusted a set-screw to allow a little play between the rollers, then turned the handle with a sharp, jerking motion and the sheet fed through, coming out the other side with a pronounced curve; the right-angled edge that the folder had put in had become an arched rib, running up the centre-line of the sheet. 'Stress,' Anax said again. 'This bit here,' he went on, running a finger along the rib, 'is stressed outwards, like an arch; bash on it from the outside and you'll have a devil of a job to move it. So it becomes your first line of defence, see; it follows the line of your leg-bone up the piece, and no matter how hard you get clobbered, that force won't come through and smash your leg. You'll thank me for that when someone feints high and then sweeps low across your shins.'

Bardas smiled politely. 'Thanks,' he said. 'That's a leg-guard, is it?'

'Greave,' Anax corrected him, 'don't show your ignorance. It covers you from the knee down to the ankle.' He was holding the piece up between his hands, squeezing the edges gently together, lifting it up so he could see along it, pulling it apart a little, repeating the process. 'Just adjusting it to fit,' he went on, 'not too tight and not too loose. It doesn't look it, but you're watching pure skill here.'

'I'm sure,' Bardas said.

When he was finally satisfied (Bardas couldn't tell the difference from when he'd started) Anax went over to the anvil and picked up a hide mallet. Propping the piece at an angle against the horn, he tapped and pecked at the edge, raising and curling it around the radius to form a lip. The hand holding the mallet rose and fell in a quick, impersonal rhythm; with the other hand he fed the piece along, making sure that the blows fell evenly spaced. 'More stress,' he explained, a little breathlessly. 'Once the lip's curled, you can't just go bending it between your hands like I've just been doing; it's stiff and inflexible, like provincial office regulations. There,' he added, as he finished drawing the lip round, 'we'll call that done and do another one, while we still remember how. Planishing can wait till we've finished.

'Hollowing, now.' Anax was making cops, the cup-shaped pieces that covered the knees and elbows. 'Hollowing's where you really put in the stress.' He was standing in front of the dishing stump, holding the truncated-diamond-shaped section over the scooped-out hole at an angle so that the middle of the plate was directly above the deepest part. 'But you've got to understand stress really well to do this,' he went on, 'or you'll ruin everything.' With the edge of the mallet-head he started to peck at the plate, pinching it between the mallet and the wood. 'Bash it too hard in the middle and you'll make it thin, you'll squeeze the metal out of it, like wringing out a wet cloth. Bad stress, that; too much, too soon. So instead you come at it gently, starting on the edge of where you want the hollow to be, and you work in from the edge to the centre – that way, you're squeezing thickness out of the sides into the top of the dome, where you need it most.'

He stopped, wiped his forehead with the back of his wrist and grinned. 'Sneaky, I call it,' he said. 'But nobody ever said this business was fair.' His right hand rose and fell quickly and precisely, so that the hammer dropped in its own weight and bounced itself back up off the metal – minimal effort, the effect being achieved by accuracy and persistence, the sheer number of precisely aimed blows. 'As well as stress,' he went on, 'there's compression, you're crushing the inside up tighter than the outside, making more stress; and stress is strength, to all intents and purposes. It's what we call work-hardening, and it's a wonderful thing, except when you overdo it. You want to remember that, my friend; stress on the inside is strength on the outside, and hardness comes from getting bashed a lot. Understand that, and you're pretty much there.'

The orange light of the fire rolled in the steel-burnished brightness of the plate, like the last of the wine in the bottom of a silver cup. 'I think I see what you're getting at,' Bardas replied. 'But doesn't bashing it sometimes make it weak?'

'Ah.' Anax nodded his head. 'That's something different. That's fatigue. That's when you've stressed it so many times that it can't take any more. Bad stress. Or there's brittle; brittle is when you make it so hard it's got no give. You make something too hard and when you drop it, the damn thing shatters like glass. Very bad stress. You don't want to worry about that; we take stuff like that out in proof. That's what proof's for.'

When he'd finished, the piece of sheet had gone from flat to perfectly domed, without any flat spots or wrinkles. 'Got to be smooth,' he said. 'Unless you get it smooth, you'll have weak spots. That's why you've got to bash every last bit the same.' He held the cop up, to see if any flaws caught the light. 'Bashing gives shape,' he said. 'Shape is strength, too. Look; that's the shape it wants to be. The God of our forefathers could jump up and down on that all day in heavy boots and he'd never so much as mark it.'

Bollo was feeding the biggest section through the rollers, applying so much force that the handle flexed. 'Memory,' Anax went on, 'that's how you achieve stress. Give the metal a memory, a shape it'll return to when something tries to distort it; then, when it flexes, it'll try to get back to that shape, which is what gives it the strength to resist. Memory is stress, stress is strength. It really is remarkably straightforward once you understand the basics.'

'The Sons of Heaven,' Bardas asked, as Anax carefully bent a curve into the breastplate blank, holding it by the edges and pressing down the middle on to the horn of the anvil. Bollo had already folded in a ridge up the middle line and rolled it into its basic shape; Anax was adjusting it, a series of careful, controlled distortions. 'I'll be straight with you, I've never really managed to figure them out. You don't mind me asking, do you?'

Anax looked up at him and flashed him a rather terrifying smile; a controlled baring of the teeth. 'You're asking me,' he said. 'I suppose that's a compliment, by your standards. You said to yourself, the Sons of Heaven are bastards, but he's not like them, he's almost normal.' Anax applied pressure and the metal obeyed him. 'Which only goes to show, you don't know spit about the Sons of Heaven. Nobody knows anything about us,' he said, pressing a little more, 'except us; and we're not telling.'

'I see,' Bardas replied. 'I'm sorry, I didn't mean to be offensive.'

'Nothing offensive about ignorance,' Anax replied pleasantly. 'Not to an enlightened mind, that is; and we're enlightened, you see, that's what gives us our edge. But I'll tell you what I'll do: I'll give you a few hints. Armour for the soul, that's what inside information is.'

'Thank you,' said Bardas gravely.

'The Sons of Heaven –' Anax was hammering a lip around the edges of the breastplate; he raised his voice a little and Bardas could hear him clearly, in spite of the shrill, crisp noise of the mallet '– well, the Sons of Heaven are this.' He stopped the mallet halfway down in its descent and held it still for a moment. 'And you're this,' he added, nodding at the plate. 'Or you're the Sons of Heaven, and this breastplate is you. Has it ever occurred to you that everything in the world might possibly have a meaning? Well, I'm not saying that's so, that'd be a really stupid generalisation. But if it's true, in whole or in part, then the Sons of Heaven are the meaning, or at least they're what everything is about. We're the axle,' he went on, turning the metal a little, 'and everything else is the wheel. Basically, the whole world's here for our benefit, to make it easier for us to do our job.'

'I see,' Bardas said. 'And what would that be?'

Anax smiled. 'Perfection,' he said. 'We perfect. We make everything we touch perfect. Well,' he admitted, shifting his grip slightly on the mallet handle, 'that's the theory. In practice, we also smash up a lot of things and do a great deal of damage. Do you see what I'm getting at, or do you want me to explain a bit more?'

'I think I get the idea,' Bardas said. 'You're proof.'

Anax stopped what he was doing and grinned broadly. 'Bless the man, he *has* been listening all this time. That's right, we're proof. We perfect by testing to the point of destruction. What passes proof, we add to our collection;

what fails, we junk. Like absolutely *everything*, it's totally simple once you start thinking about it the right way.'

After the armour had been shaped and planished, Anax punched holes for the rivets, cut the straps and fitted the buckles, put all the parts together. 'There you are,' he said eventually. 'You can try it on now, if you like.'

It was, of course, a perfect fit. It covered Bardas like a second skin; the strength on the outside, the stress inside. 'What about proof?' Bardas asked with a smile.

'Proof?' Anax pulled a face. 'Huh. What do you think *you're* for?'

CHAPTER TEN

The war between the plainspeople and the Empire started late one afternoon, on the edge of a lake in the marshy region between Ap' Escatoy and the Green River estuary. It was started, somehow appropriately, by a duck.

The party of trebuchet builders to which Temrai's old friend Leuscai was assigned had run out of timber; accordingly, Leuscai was put in charge of a small scouting expedition and sent off to find tall trees suitable for shaping into the main arms of trebuchets. Straight, fast-growing pines were the best bet, though occasionally it was possible to find an unusually straight fir or spruce in the forests to the south. When Leuscai reached the region he'd been told to try first he found plenty of evidence of pine, fir and spruce: a considerable number of stumps, carefully sawn off close to the ground by generations of Perimadeian shipwrights, rough-hewn on the spot and shipped back to the City to be made into masts. Time was pressing; there weren't enough suitable timbers in the store to furnish arms for the current production run, let alone the fifty extra trebuchets Temrai had just commissioned.

On the other side of the Green River, Leuscai knew, there were a fair number of suitable trees; he could see them as he sat on an ivy-covered pine-stump and gazed at the bank opposite. Technically, however, the southern bank of the river was Imperial territory – at least, it had been until recently part of a long, narrow tongue of land claimed by Ap' Escatoy, although the claim had been unenforcible for at least forty years owing to the general decline in the city's fortunes. Leuscai considered the risk; invading the Empire hadn't been part of his mission briefing and he

208

didn't really want to do it, but he badly needed the timber, and he assessed the chances of being noticed, let alone challenged, by Imperial personnel as too slight to worry about, compared with the reception he'd undoubtedly face if he went back home, or even returned to the camp, without any timber. He took a deep breath and started thinking about how he was going to cross the river, which was wide, deep and fast.

After a long, irritable day of brainstorming, he rejected all the ideas so far canvassed and led the way downstream in the hope of finding a natural ford of some description. As luck would have it, he didn't have to look far; he'd come out only a few miles up from a treacherous but passable shallow point just above some rather spectacular rapids. The crossing itself was tense and not particularly pleasant, but they made it without loss of life or any essential equipment. What they did lose were half a dozen supply mules which were carrying the food.

This stroke of bad luck changed their immediate priorities. Leuscai, who'd been brought up on the principle that starving in a forest or beside a river takes a deliberate act of will, split his group up into a number of hunting parties, told them when and where to meet up, and set off into the forest.

He was quickly disappointed. The forest turned out to be a swamp with trees growing in it, and what little game there was saw or heard him coming. He came back empty-handed to find that nobody else had done much better; but one party reported that they'd stumbled on a lake about a mile due south that looked promising for duck.

Leuscai wasn't enthusiastic. He'd had enough of duck a few years back, when he'd been one of the men Temrai had sent to hunt the wretched creatures for food and feathers during a hiatus in supplies just before the attack on Perimadeia. He'd been a victim of his own success; they'd found what seemed like an inexhaustible supply of ducks and proceeded to exhaust it, grimly and piecemeal, with nets, slings, throwing sticks, arrows – in some cases, where they'd found a strain of particularly trusting, stupid ducks, their bare hands. For weeks on end he'd done nothing but wring necks and pull out feathers, with nothing but duck to eat (fishy and stringy) and the creatures' obnoxious smell always in his nose. He'd come to loathe the sensation of killing them, gripping the neck tight just below the head and swinging the body round and round in circles until the bird suffocated – but you kept getting ones that were the next best thing to immortal, that carried on living even after you'd broken their necks and crushed their heads into the ground with your heel; nothing on earth is harder to kill than a horribly injured duck, not even a bull buffalo or a man in full armour. And here he was again, about to kill and eat yet more ducks if he wanted to stay alive. Maybe, he speculated, he was really the Angel of Death for ducks, and killing them was what he'd been put into the world to do (he thought of Colonel Loredan and the plainspeople); if so, there wasn't any point trying to avoid the inevitable. Yes, he said, by all means; let's go and scrag some ducks. So they went.

Inevitably, it seemed, they got lost; the lake had moved, because it wasn't where the scouts said it was. They spent most of the day hunting for it, dragging through the wet, dangerous swamp, losing boots and getting filthy, having to pull each other out when they suddenly went in up to their thighs. When at last they stumbled on the lake, Leuscai was pretty sure it wasn't the one they'd been looking for – the scouts had mentioned a hill at the southern end that rose above the tree line, and there was no sign of anything like that. But it was a lake, and it was unquestionably covered with ducks. Thousands of them, floatng in enormous black and brown rafts, like the garbage flotsam washed down into a lake by the first storm rains of summer. They showed absolutely no inclination to go away when Leuscai and his men poked through the trees on to the shore; they quacked and steered away a little, obviously not aware that Death himself was watching them. Foolish, objectionable ducks.

Leuscai convened a brief ways-and-means conference. They had no nets, no slings, no throwing sticks, no dogs and no boat, which ruled out most of the conventional ways of slaughtering waterfowl. They had their bows, but not enough arrows that they could afford to waste any, sinking into the still water spitted through a dead duck. 'We'll just have to throw stones,' someone suggested; and since there were no better suggestions, the motion was carried.

Leuscai, of course, was a master of the art of stoning ducks. They found a handy supply of stones in the bed of one of the streams that ran into the lake, and agreed their strategy. There was a small spit of dry land sticking out into the lake, and a particularly dense mob of ducks bobbing up and down in the horseshoe-shaped bay it created. They'd be able to bombard the ducks from three sides; they'd have about twenty seconds of extreme activity before the whole flock got up off the water in an explosion of wings and spray, leaving their dead and wounded behind. If they didn't manage to get enough the first time, they'd undoubtedly get another chance next morning, and next evening too, if need be. It would be rather like the bombardment of Perimadeia, with Leuscai and his men being the trebuchets (ironic, given what they'd originally come for).

Since Leuscai had absolutely no wish to repeat the performance, he took special pains in deploying his artillery; spook one duck, and there was a faint but disturbing chance that the whole lot would get up before a single stone could be dispatched. So the hunting party set off from well inland and crept up slowly and painfully to the shore, taking great care not to make a noise or a sudden movement. The plan was tactically sound and would surely have succeeded if one of the party hadn't slipped and gone down in a boggy patch, grabbing at his neighbour as he went and pulling him down as well. As luck would have it, there was a single adventurous duck nosing about in the bushes at the edge of the lake a few yards away fom where the men went in, and their sudden, pitiful yells of distress sent the duck rocketing into the air, like a stone from a torsion engine. At once the whole flock rose with it, blotting out the sun like a huge volley of arrows lobbed over a city wall at extreme range. Leuscai howled with rage and frustration and hurled the stone he'd been gripping in his hand; he was well out of range, of course, and the stone splashed noisily into the water. The ducks swung and lifted over the trees, then swung again and headed out towards the middle of the lake, putting up other flocks until the whole surface of the lake seemed to be standing up, like a man getting out of bed.

The Imperial patrol, which had taken the afternoon off to go wildfowling on the other side of the lake, were furious. They'd been looking forward to their evening's sport all week; they'd smuggled nets and slings and gunny-sacks out under their armour, trudged all the way across the swamp to get here, and just as they were about to set up and take their positions, something had spooked the birds and ruined everything. The sergeant's first guess was a fox; but it was just too early for foxes to be about, and what else would panic the best part of five thousand ducks? The only other creature fearsome enough was a man, and that couldn't be right, since this was a restricted area. A thought occured to him, and he snapped at his men to shut up and keep still.

Sure enough, his fears were justified. On the far shore he saw men moving about. He couldn't make out much in the way of detail, but he didn't really need to; there were too many of them for their purpose in being there to be legitimate. For a while he simply couldn't decide what to do for the best. He was outnumbered (nearly two to one, if his estimate of their numbers was at all accurate), but he had the element of surprise, and of course his men were Imperial heavy infantry, which put rather a different complexion on the matter. Received wisdom had it that a force of Imperial regulars facing only twice as many opponents could quite reasonably be held to be outnumbering them ... That was all very well, and it did wonders for morale if you could actually get the men to believe it; as their sergeant, it was his job to preach one doctrine and believe another. The only alternative was to go back to the camp, a day and a half away through the marshes, and hand the matter over to Captain Suria - three, maybe four days' delay, by which time finding the enemy again certainly wouldn't be a foregone conclusion. In the end, the deciding factor was the thought of explaining to Captain Suria how they'd come to be at the lake at all, since it was quite some way from their designated beat; it'd be much easier to handle the interview if he'd just driven off an enemy invasion of Imperial territory and become a hero. True, that wasn't necessarily a good thing (the Empire approved of heroism but generally despised heroes); but so far, in its thousand-odd years of history, the

Empire had never court-martialled a hero for netting a few ducks.

Once he'd made his mind up, he gave the order to advance. With every squelching, bogged-down step closer to the enemy, the sergeant questioned his decision; there were even more of them than he'd thought there were, and they were quite definitely plainsmen, and they were armed with bows (and what else would plainsmen be armed with?) – he'd stumbled across a major raiding party, possibly the skirmisher line of a whole invading army, and he was proposing to give them battle with one platoon of heavies. The only way to avoid being shot down like – well, ducks, say – was to get very close very quietly, and rush them before they even had a chance to get their bows out of their cases.

Fortunately (the sergeant couldn't fathom why) the enemy seemed determined to make his job as easy as possible. There were no pickets, no sentries; they appeared to be arguing violently among themselves, with their backs to the likeliest vector of attack. For the first time since he'd embarked on this idiotic venture, the sergeant began to feel just a little hopeful. One statement of official doctrine about the plainsmen that wasn't just good-for-morale was that they were warriors rather than soldiers, basically undisciplined and disorderly.

Most of the way he was fairly sure of staying out of sight as long as he kept his men just inside the tree-line. He'd chosen to follow the western shore of the lake, and the choice turned out to be a good one; the trees grew close enough together on the western side that it was possible to hop from tree-root to tree-root, avoiding the boggy leaf-mould pits. By the time they reached the southern side, where the trees were older and more openly spaced, they were no more than a couple of hundred yards from the enemy. Still, it might as well have been a mile for all the good it did him, because the going became horrendously wet and sticky and nobody, not even Captain Suria and the Sons of Heaven, can wade up to their knees in thick black liquid mud and be unobtrusive about it. He called a general halt and tried to hustle his brains into coming up with a better strategy – unfair and uncalled-for, since he was only a sergeant and neither trained nor expected to be a battlefield tactician.

When he gave the order to go back, he could tell the men weren't happy about it, but it was an order, and that was all there was to it. They hopped back about fifty yards; then he led them at right angles deeper into the woods, striking in about a hundred and fifty yards. His reasoning was simple: if he was going to have to make a noise, it'd be sensible to make it as far away from the enemy as possible for as long as he could. He'd swing round behind them and then make the best job he could of charging, or at least squelching quickly, into the enemy's rear. He had no idea whether it'd work or not, but he was wet, muddy, extremely weary and very frightened, and he couldn't think of anything else.

In retrospect, it would probably have been a very good strategy in the circumstances, if only they hadn't got lost in the wood. But both distance and direction are notoriously hard to keep track of in a wood unless you happen to be an experienced forester; when the sergeant launched his charge, he found out the hard way that he'd come too far, as his breathless and dishevelled command burst through the undergrowth at the edge of the lake to find that instead of being behind the enemy, they were alongside them, about forty yards to the east.

A mistake; but in the event not a wholly decisive one. When Leuscai first became aware of an Imperial patrol materialising beside him, his first instinct was to hide weapons rather than ready them. The way he saw it, he'd been caught trespassing and poaching; his mind was busy trying to find a plausible lie to explain why he and his men were there (we got lost in the forest; excuse me, but are we right for the Green River?) and it didn't occur to him that he was going to have to fight anybody until two of his men, who'd been trying to hide their bows behind their backs, were speared like fish by a couple of legionaries.

Without any conscious effort on the part of either commander, they'd managed to hit on the optimum conditions for bloodshed. There was just enough time for the majority of Leuscai's men to get their bows out, nock and draw, and just enough time for the Imperials to close with the plainsmen nearest to them. It was a short battle and extremely uncharacteristic; neither side could very well avoid killing the enemy, or being killed themselves. Leuscai's archers were loosing at point-blank range, easily punching their bodkin-head arrows through plate and into muscle and bone. The patrol were thrusting and slashing at effectively unarmed men, without armour, shield or sword to ward off the blows. Interestingly enough from a theorist's point of view, the casualty ratio more or less validated provincial-office doctrine (one Imperial footsoldier to three plainsmen) to the extent that if the fighting had carried on to the point of annihilation, there should have been four Imperials left standing, and no plainsmen. Unfortunately for military science, the experiment was abandoned early, with the survivors of both parties giving up as if by mutual agreement and pulling back; so the data, although persuasive, cannot be taken to constitute proof.

Leuscai died in the brief third phase of the engagement, when the Imperials closed for a second time after taking the plainsmen's one devastating volley. He'd been rushing to get a second arrow on to the string; he fumbled the nock, dropped the arrow in the mud and was reaching over his shoulder for another one when a man he hadn't even seen wedged a spearhead between his ribs. The blade was too broad to penetrate any further and too firmly stuck to be withdrawn, so its owner wisely abandoned it and tried to finish the job with his sword. But he was rushing things, too; instead of a clean, coaching-manual, skull-splitting blow, all he managed was a cack-handed slash that scived half the scalp off the left side of Leuscai's head and toppled him into the oozing leaf-mould. As the mud covered his raw flesh like a poultice, he was aware of the man for the first time, putting one heavy boot on his chest as he tugged at the shaft of his spear, vainly trying to get it unstuck. After three goes he gave up and went away, leaving Leuscai to bleed peacefully to death. It turned out to be not nearly as traumatic as he'd imagined it would be. Ironically, the last sound he was aware of hearing was the distant quacking of ducks, cautiously drifting back to the middle of the lake.

*

'Wonderful,' said Eseutz Mesatges. 'Now we can have the war, get it over with, get our money and have our ships back.'

She'd met Athli Zeuxis in the street outside a dressmaker's shop, one of the best and most expensive on the Island – one of the few things left to spend money on was clothes, and for some unaccountable reason there had just been a wave of seismic activity in women's fashions; the warrior-princess look was out, stale and dead as last night's scraps, its place triumphantly usurped by the nomad-caravan look, all cloudy silks and bare midriffs. This suited Eseutz perfectly – warrior princess had placed what she felt was an unhealthy emphasis on cleavage, and the leather made her sweat.

'We won't have the details for a day or so,' Athli said. 'That'll have to wait until I get the official despatch from head office in Shastel. But their reports are always pretty reliable.'

Eseutz thought for a moment. 'Short term, it's going to create havoc,' she said. 'It'll be the same as it's been since this started, only worse, too much money chasing too few opportunities, everybody desperate to buy before prices soar, but nothing to spend the money on.'

'Except futures,' Athli replied. 'Which is an area I've always tried to keep out of, since I don't happen to be a qualified fortune-teller. If I were you, I'd hang on to my money until things start getting back to normal; pretty soon, everybody who's overbought in the first rush of excitement is going to want to sell, and that'll be the time to buy. Sadly,' she went on, 'I haven't got the luxury of following my own advice; everybody's going to be wanting their money so they can start spending, which means that unless I can arrange cover from head office, I'm going to be in an awkward position for a week or so.'

Eseutz held a spangled slipper up to the light. 'Give 'em paper,' she said. 'They'll grumble, but they'll take it. After all, everybody knows Shastel scrip is good; mind you,' she added, with a grin, 'that's what they used to say about Niessa Loredan.'

'Quite,' Athli said, looking down at a tray of silver ankle-bracelets. 'And if I start flooding the Island with paper, it won't be long before it's "that's what they used to say about Athli Zeuxis". No, thank you. I'll just have to write some of it off with Hiro and Venart. It shaves my margins, but at least I'll still be here this time next year.'

One of the dressmaker's girls appeared from the back room and started fluttering round Eseutz with a measuring tape. Eseutz didn't seem to have noticed she was there. 'I wouldn't object to a bit of that, if there's any to spare,' she said innocuously. 'Bear me in mind, will you?'

Athli smiled. 'No,' she said.

'Ah well, no harm in trying,' Eseutz replied. 'Actually – no kidding – just at this precise moment in time I'd be good for the money.' She frowned. 'That's what's bothering me; I'm not used to being in credit. Being in credit is nature's way of telling you you're missing out on an opportunity somewhere.'

'Maybe,' Athli said. 'But your opportunities have an unfortunate habit of sinking.'

'That's an exaggeration. It was just the one time ...'

'Or getting impounded by the excise,' Athli went on, 'or stolen by pirates, or infested with weevils, or repossessed by the original owner ...'

'It's true, I do like to go after investments with a certain element of risk. They don't all turn yellow on me, you know.'

'All the ones I ever backed did.'

'Oh, come on. What about those seventeen barrels of turmeric?'

Athli wrinkled her brow. 'Oh, yes,' she said, 'I'd forgotten that. I'll admit, that turned out all right in the end, after I bought out that other partner of yours you hadn't got around to telling me about, and paid off the import duty you'd forgotten to mention. The profit I made on that deal kept me in lamp-oil for a week.' She winced slightly, as the girl with the tape started on her. 'No offence, but I'll take my chances with Hiro and Venart, thank you very much. Hey, what do you reckon?' she added, holding up an amethyst-and-silver pendant. 'Will it go with the mauve silk, do you think?'

Eseutz shook her head. 'Overstated,' she said. 'You want something small and intense with that, like diamonds.

So, how long do you think the war will last? You ought to
know about these plainspeople, if anyone does.'

'Depends.' Athli carefully gathered up the pendant chain
and put it back. 'An all-out assualt, and it ought to be over
quickly. If they let themselves get bogged down, it could drag
on for months.'

'This man Loredan,' Eseutz went on. 'What's he like? You
knew him for years, didn't you?'

Athli nodded. 'I worked for him,' she said, 'as a clerk. Gods,
that seems like another life. Somewhere at home I've got
a sword that used to belong to him. I wonder if I should
send it on.'

Eseutz examined her carefully for a moment, as if she were
an investment with a certain element of risk. 'You've gone
all woolly,' she said. 'Well, none of my business—'

'Actually, you're wrong. But yes, it's none of your business.
I thought you were asking for my opinion of him as a military
leader.'

'Mphm. Any good?'

Athli nodded. 'He did amazingly well, considering what he
had to put up with from the City authorities. But I don't
think he'd have been able to save the City, even if he'd had
a free hand. He doesn't really have the single-mindedness
you need to be a high-class general.'

'But this thing he's supposed to have over the plains King,'
Eseutz said. 'Is there any truth in that?'

Athli shrugged. 'There was something there, I'm pretty
sure. But he never talked about that stuff, so I wouldn't know.
Besides, from what I've gathered, he's only going to be a
sort of figurehead; it's the provincial office commanders
who'll actually be running the war, and I don't know the
first thing about any of them. If they're provincial office staff,
you can be sure they're competent, at the very least. The
job will get done, one way or another.'

On her way home, Athli couldn't help thinking about the
war, and her tiny part in it. Had there ever been a time,
she wondered, when she hadn't been in the business of
making money out of other people's deaths? That's what
she'd done as Bardas' clerk, that's what she was about to
do now. Yet she'd never seen herself in those terms, as some
kind of carrion-eater circling high over plague-pits and

battlefields. All she'd ever set out to do was earn a decent sum, on her own merits, living an independent life. And she'd succeeded, going from strength to strength; except that so many people had to die to keep her in the manner to which she'd become accustomed. It was the Loredan factor – in spite of all her efforts, everything she'd ever been was by and through him; as his clerk in Perimadeia, now this war – and she'd only got her start here on the Island through Venart and Vetriz Auzeil, who she'd met because of Bardas. What was it, she wondered, about these damned Loredans that meant that they started everything, finished everything, ran through everything like a bloodstain saturating cloth? She thought of Alexius, and the Principle; she missed Alexius.

As if to confirm her musings, she found Vetriz Auzeil waiting for her at home, wanting to know if she had any news about the war.

'You mean any news about Bardas,' she replied, because she was tired and fed up. 'No, sorry. If there's anything in the despatches from Shastel, I'll let you know.'

'Oh.' Vetriz smiled. 'That obvious, is it?'

'Pretty well,' Athli replied, wondering just what Eseutz had meant by 'woolly'. An odd term to use. 'If you're that bothered, why not just write him a letter? I'm pretty sure the Shastel courier would pass it on; there's a regular diplomatic bag now between Shastel and the provincial office, and once it's there, the Imperial post is excellent.'

'Thanks,' Vetriz said, 'but I don't really have anything to say. I was just curious, really; you know how it is, when someone you know is mixed up in something important. You take an interest.'

Hanging around in someone's porch waiting for them to come home just in case they had some news struck Athli as rather more than just taking an interest; but it wouldn't help matters to point that out. 'Coming in?' she asked.

'Why not?'

Athli opened the door. 'Actually,' she went on, 'I did hear something that might interest you, since you spent all that time as a guest of the other Loredans. Gorgas is making trouble again.'

Vetriz caught her breath. 'Really?' she said. 'Why am I not surprised?'

'I'm going to pour myself a drink; can I get you anything? Apparently, he wrote to the prefect offering an alliance against Temrai. The prefect turned him down flat.'

'Well, he would,' Vetriz said. 'Who'd want to be associated with the likes of Gorgas Loredan?'

Athli smiled. 'Ah,' she said, 'but it gets better. A day or so after Gorgas got the get-lost letter from Ap' Escatoy, he managed to capture a man called Partek—'

'Now that name's familiar.'

'It should be,' Athli said. 'He's been on the Empire's Most Wanted list for years. He's some kind of rebel leader, apparently.'

She handed Vetriz a cup of sweet cider, spiced Perimadeian style with honey and cloves. Vetriz managed not to pull a face when she sipped it. 'Really? I didn't think the Empire had rebels.'

'Well, it does,' Athli said, dropping on to a couch and kicking off her slippers. 'Though they hate admitting to it; the warrants always say *pirate* or *highway robber*. But it's common knowledge that they'll do whatever it takes to get hold of Partek.' She closed her eyes. 'I must admit, I resent it when people like Gorgas get strokes of luck like that. I mean, it's not as if he'll do anybody any good with it; probably not even himself, if his record's anything to go by.'

Vetriz had become uncharacteristically quiet; she was staring at the wall a foot or so above Athli's head as if something was written there. Athli decided to change the subject—

But Vetriz wasn't listening. *Oh, damn*, she thought, *I thought I'd seen the end of this sort of thing.* Apparently not; she was standing in some kind of workshop or factory, and the first thing she noticed (couldn't help but notice) was the noise. Men were bashing bits of metal with hammers. The light slanted in from high, tall windows, marking out silver squares on the floor and making the rest of the building seem dark and gloomy by comparison. In the middle of the floor she could see a pile of what looked like body parts: arms, legs, heads, torsos, heaped and jumbled up - it was in the dark part, and she couldn't see clearly, only a flash of metal and the evocative shapes of joints and limbs. The men at the benches were bashing away at more of the same, hammering a leg or a torso or a hand, then adding it to the pile. Why were they doing this, she wondered? There didn't seem much point, bashing a limb that was already severed; or maybe this was a factory where they made mechanical men, like the ones in the fairy tale she remembered from when she was little. Then the angle of the light shifted a little, and she saw that they were making armour –

(*Same thing, really; perfect steel men, can't be broken or damaged from the outside. If only these people were a little bit more clever, maybe they could find a way of doing without the soft, fallible bit that goes on the inside.*)

– And there was someone she knew; they were building him, piece by piece from the feet up, and when they put the head on, it had his face (*but there's nothing inside. There was something inside once, it's customary for there to be something inside. Maybe in his case they've made an exception*) –

'Triz?'

'Sorry,' Vetriz said. 'I was miles away. What were you saying?'

The battle wasn't going well.

Temrai leaned away, settling his weight over the heel of his back foot, and kept his guard up, his wrists low, watching his enemy along the outstretched, upwards-tilted flat of his sword. He was completely out of his element here, of course, struggling to remember position one from fencing lessons fifteen years ago. He'd just about got the hang of position one when the camp was raided and there was no more time for education; so as far as scientific swordfighting was concerned, that was it.

Don't look at your sword, look at me, they'd told him – encouragingly, patiently, angrily, loudly, until he'd made himself do what he was told just so he'd be allowed to lower his guard and ease the pain in his wrists. Now he could see what they'd been getting at; but it was too late now to ask what he should do next.

All he could see in the other man's eyes was intense, single-minded concentration, something he found infinitely more disturbing than mere hatred. It was as if he could see the lines, angles, geometric projections that he was calculating behind his expressionless steel face; it was like trying to stare down pure mathematics. Just as he was thinking seriously about dropping his sword and running away, the other man made his move; a wonderfully co-ordinated manoeuvre involving a long step forward with the front foot, a powerful swivel of the waist, a minimal-backlift sideways cut with the bend of the wrists accelerating the blade swiftly and smoothly through the arc of the swing. In reply, Temrai jumped backwards with both feet and pushed his sword at right angles towards the other man's face, as if urging him to take it from him. He felt the shock of the blades colliding run up past his wrists into his elbows; it was a dull, bone-jarring pain, like hitting your own thumb with a hammer.

It had all gone wrong so quickly. First, a volley of arrows dipping down at them out of the sky – it was like the time he'd been cutting ferns for the horses' litter and inadvertently sunk his hook into a wasps' nest, the same be-wildering, unexpected suddenness. The column was still bucking and scrambling and rearing and picking itself up off the floor when the heavy infantry had erupted out of a small copse the scouts had certified as clear only a few minutes before; they made contact while the last of the arrows were still dropping in and pitching (like pigeons or rooks on a patch of rain-flattened beans, with a swirl and a flourish). They pulled the men on the outside down from their horses and trod on them as they squashed their way in, pushing men and horses out of the way with their shields, slashing at exposed arms and legs and knees as if they were trimming back a hedge. Temrai had just worked out who they were and where they'd come from when the pikemen slammed into the column from the rear; then he'd been knocked off his horse by the man next to him, toppling out of the saddle like a badly secured sack of flour, and for a while he'd seen nothing of the battle except the hooves of spooked horses, trampling the ground all round his head.

Apparently, he'd parried the first blow; but even he could see that he'd done it the wrong way, got himself deeper into trouble. With a small, precise movement, the other man disengaged his sword from the block, made a slight adjustment of angle and lunged, far too quickly for Temrai to do anything about it. The swordpoint hit him at the top of the arch of his ribs; but amazingly the angled contour of the breastplate turned it, made it slide away across his chest and under his armpit. Without really knowing what he was doing, Temrai slammed his own sword across the other man's forehead, making a terrible thumping noise. The other man took a step back, put his heel down on the head of a dead man behind him, turned his ankle over and went sprawling down on his backside, his legs lifting up in the air so sharply that Temrai would have had his teeth smashed in if he hadn't managed to dodge the flailing sabaton.

Unfortunately, in all this excitement he'd dropped his sword. By the time he'd stooped awkwardly down and picked it up out of the mud the other man was sitting up, backing away, scrabbling for his own sword. Temrai hit out at him and managed to connect with the side of his helmet, the force of the blow glancing off the sloped plate; and the grip was so slippery with mud that he couldn't hold on to it, and it slipped through his fingers like the first trout he'd ever managed to tickle off the bed of a stream and then didn't dare hold on to. The other man was on his knees, swishing at him with his sword – easily avoided by taking a step backwards, but that was a mistake, since his own sword was now about five yards away, behind his enemy.

The hell with this, Temrai said to himself; and he jumped over the flailing arc of the sword blade, landed with his knees round the other man's neck and went over, grabbing at the top of his head as he fell. His shoulder hit the ground first; then he felt a screaming pain in his knee where he'd twisted it round almost half a turn. Without thinking much about what he was trying to achieve, he got his fingers under the bottom rim of his enemy's helmet and dragged upwards as hard as he possibly could. He could feel the other man twisting and struggling between his legs, hands trying to grab his; so he tugged harder, shrieking as the pain from his knee surged up through his whole body. It hurt so much that it was several seconds before he realised that the other man had stopped moving, strangled by his own chinstrap.

Temrai realised that he couldn't let go; if he did, all his

weight would fall on his dislocated knee, and he couldn't bear the thought of that. 'Help!' he yelled, but of course nobody could hear him - half the men within a five-yard radius were the enemy, and all of them were dead. Fat lot of use they were to a man in a nasty spot of trouble.

Wonderful stuff, armour, he thought, in the small part of his mind that wasn't saturated with pain. *Mine saved me, his killed him. Pity we can't train it to fight on its own; then we could all stay at home.* Then the pain leaked through into that compartment as well. He closed his eyes and tried to numb out the ache in his fingers, which were starting to slip. He could feel the sharp edge of the helmet rim methodically cutting the skin on the inside of his top finger-joints. If he held on long enough, say for a week, would it eventually slice through the bone?

'Temrai? Is that you?'

He opened his eyes. He couldn't see who it was talking to him, and he couldn't quite place the voice. 'Yes, of course it's me. Help me up, I'm stuck.'

'What seems to be - oh, right, I see. Hold still. This'll probably hurt.'

'Mind what you're—' he said, and then screamed and let go with his fingers. The next thing he was consciously aware of was the feeling of the flat ground under his back and head, and a slightly different modulation of the pain in his knee. 'Thank you,' he said, and opened his eyes.

'That's all right.' It was Dassascai, the spy. 'Now then, how the hell am I going to get you out of this?'

Temrai breathed in as far as he could manage. 'What's happening?'he said.

'We counter-attacked,' Dassascai replied. 'It wasn't the cleverest move in the world, but we got them beat by sheer weight of numbers. You don't want to know any more, for now.'

'Don't I? Oh, right. Can you get me out of the way somewhere, and then find Kurrai or someone—'

'Not Kurrai,' Dassascai said. 'He wouldn't be much use.'

'Oh,' Temrai repeated. 'Damn, I can't remember who's next in seniority. Find someone, anyhow. I need to know what's going on.'

'First things first,' the spy said. 'I'm going to try dragging you over to that tree – oh, of course, you can't see it from there. It'll probably hurt a lot.'

'All right,' Temrai said. It did.

A little later, Dassascai knelt down beside him and asked, 'Do you still want me to go to look for someone, or would you rather I stayed here? The last I saw we pushed them back, but I haven't a clue whether we made it stick; they could be through here any minute. I really don't want you to be lying here like this if they come back.'

Temrai shook his head. 'You'd better go,' he said. 'Send someone to fetch me when you get the chance. And thank you.'

Dassascai nodded his head. 'That's all right,' he said.

'Excuse me asking, but are you really a spy?'

Dassascai looked down at him, smiled and shook his head. 'No,' he said. 'All right, stay there. I'll be as quick as I can.'

Temrai closed his eyes; above all, he realised, he was completely exhausted. It'd be very easy right now just to drift off to sleep. But that wouldn't do, not in the middle of a battle. He thought about what Dassascai had just told him – not the cleverest move in the world, got them beat by sheer weight of numbers. *I bet you really are a spy*, he thought, and passed out.

When he came round, there were voices talking overhead.

'—Wasn't meant to be a decisive battle; just a probe, that's all, to see what we're about and slow us down a little. Gods help us when they really come after us.'

'Quiet. He's awake.'

He opened his eyes, and at first it was as dark as if he was underground. Then a lamp flared as someone lifted it over his head and put it down nearby.

'Temrai?' He recognised the voice and the face, but the name escaped him, which was odd, since he knew the man well. 'Temrai, it's all right. You're back at the camp.'

Temrai tried to move his lips, but his palate was dry and numb. 'Did we win?'

'Sort of,' the man replied. 'We made them go away, at any rate. Now we're falling back on Perimadeia.'

'Basically,' said the other voice, which was equally familiar, 'basically, they've cut us off from the plains, it's like they're trying to bottle us up in the Perimadeian delta with our backs to the sea. Latest reports say they've got three separate armies in the field now. If we try to get through, they'll come at us from both sides.'

'I see.' He thought of Tilden, his wife, back at the main camp. 'Is Kurrai dead?' he asked.

The second man frowned. 'You are in a bad way, aren't you?' he said. 'Do I look particularly dead to you?'

'Oh.' Temrai closed his eyes and opened them again. 'Sorry, yes. I'm a bit confused. Someone told me you were dead.'

'A lot of people seem to have thought so,' Kurrai replied. 'I just hope they aren't too disappointed.'

'Casualties,' Temrai said, remembering a time when he wouldn't have used the word; he'd have asked, *How many of my people were killed? How many of my people were badly hurt?*

'Not good,' said the other man, the one who wasn't Kurrai.

It cost him a good deal of effort, but Temrai managed to scowl. 'Define a good casualty,' he said. 'How many did we lose?'

The two men looked at each other. 'Over two hundred,' Kurrai said. 'I think it was two hundred and thirty, something like that. Plus another seventy-odd wounded. We got about thirty of them.'

Temrai nodded. 'I see,' he said. 'Two hundred and thirty killed out of a column of five hundred. What are we going to do?'

The man he hadn't identified yet frowned. 'I don't know about the rest of us,' he said, 'but you're going to get some sleep. Doctor's orders.'

'Oh. Are you a doctor, then?'

'What do you mean, am I a doctor? Dammit, Temrai, I was your doctor before you were even born.'

Temrai smiled weakly. 'Just kidding,' he said.

'Like hell you were,' the doctor replied. 'Did you get bashed on the head during the battle?'

'Can't remember.'

'Well no, quite possibly you don't. It's my fault, I should have examined you more thoroughly. Feel sick at all? Head-ache, lights flashing in front of your eyes?'

'You think I've lost my memory,' Temrai said.

'Bits of it,' the doctor said. 'It happens that way sometimes.'

Temrai smiled, and the smile widened into a broad grin. 'If only,' he said cheerfully. 'If only.'

Poliorcis the diplomat shivered and wiped rain out of his eyes with the back of his hand.

'Are we nearly there yet?' he asked. The carter grunted without looking round. The rain was dripping in soft, fat drops off the broad brim of his leather hat. He didn't seem to be aware of it. Quite probably, by his standards, this constituted a sunny day.

Usually Poliorcis trusted his sense of direction, a valuable attribute for a man who spent so much of his time travelling in unfamiliar places. On this occasion, however, he was completely lost. The route the carter was taking was completely different from the one Gorgas Loredan had taken; either because Gorgas had been showing him the scenic route, or because Gorgas wasn't aware of the short cut. He'd also lost track of time, which was most unlike him. He put it down to the effect this country had on him. It reminded him rather of swimming in the lagoon off Ap' Sendaves; floating on his back in still water, gradually ceasing to be aware of his body, of anything around him, until he was nothing but a consciousness without context, an awareness with nothing to be aware of. That had been a bizarre feeling but a pleasant one. The Mesoge, in his opinion, certainly wasn't pleasant, and it didn't strike him as interesting enough to be bizarre; but it left him feeling disorientated in much the same way.

He even felt too bemused to rehearse what he was going to say, or run through in his mind the arguments he was going to use. That was unfortunate – he felt more uneasy about this meeting than any number of far more important negotiations he'd been involved in – but the harder he tried to pull himself together, the more his mind wanted to wander. If it wasn't for the rain he could close his eyes and get some sleep; but nothing helps you stay awake better than the feeling of rainwater seeping under your collar and down your back. He pulled the sodden wreckage of his own hat a little further down and gave up trying to think; instead he gazed sullenly at the wet green all around him, the hedges dripping rain, the pools of brown water filling the wheel-ruts in the track ahead, the leaves of the docks and ferns glistening. The air was moist and tickled his throat, and he was painfully cold.

Must be easier ways of making a living, he muttered to himself, *a man of my age.* It was ridiculous for one of the provincial office's senior departmental negotiators to be squelching and bumping along in a carrier's cart in the rain, risking pneumonia and pleurisy at the very least, on his way to try to reason with a lunatic who had no official standing, whose authority wasn't even recognised by the Empire, in order to secure the person of a minor trouble-maker who'd happened to be taken up and turned into some kind of popular hero by a bunch of malcontents who probably wouldn't recognise him if he was sitting at their kitchen table.

The cart had stopped. He lifted his head and looked up, but all he could see was rain.

The carter didn't move. 'Stay here,' Poliorcis said. 'I'll need you to take me back to Tornoys.'

He started to ease himself down off the cart, but with a movement faster than anything he'd have imagined the man was capable of, the carter grabbed him by the elbow.

'Two quarters,' he said.

Poliorcis nodded and burrowed about in his drenched sleeve for the money. 'Stay there,' he repeated, and tried to reach the ground with his feet. He was too high up; but the hem of his robe caught in something, and he ended up kneeling in the mud. 'Stay there,' he said, one more time; then he got up, muddying his hands in the process, and headed for the gate he could just make out through the rain. While he was grappling with the catch (which was rusted up – presumably Gorgas and his brothers clambered over, and never bothered opening the thing; that would explain why it sagged so desperately on its one good hinge and the tangle of coarse hemp twine that did service for the other one) he heard the reins crack behind him, and the sound of wheels slowly rolling through a puddle.

The farmhouse door was open, but there didn't seem to be anybody about. 'Hello?' he called out. Nobody answered. He stood for a moment, watching rain drip off him and on to the stone flags, then decided that this simply wouldn't do.

He might not be a Son of Heaven, but he represented the Empire; the Empire doesn't stand dripping in doorways, it marches in and puts its feet up on the furniture.

At least it was dry inside the house, and what remained of the fire gave off a little warmth. He parked himself in the chimney corner, still wrapped up in his travelling coat, which was now three parts water to one part cloth. The settle was more comfortable than it looked. He let his head rest against the back and closed his eyes.

He woke up to find Gorgas Loredan leaning over him, a slightly scornful expression on his face. 'You should have let us know you were coming,' he was saying, 'I'd have sent a carriage for you.'

'Doesn't matter, really,' said Poliorcis, who'd just realised that he'd woken up with a splitting headache. 'I'm here now.'

'Good.' Gorgas Loredan sat down next to him on the settle, so close that he had to budge along a little to avoid being in contact with him. 'In that case we can cut the small talk and get down to business. I assume you're here to make me an offer.'

'Well, yes,' Poliorcis mumbled. 'And no.' His mind was foggy and furred up, and he couldn't remember a single one of the principal bargaining positions he'd been working on over the last few days. 'It's more a case of asking what you want from us. I think you'll find we're willing to consider any reasonable proposals.'

Gorgas sighed and shook his head. 'I'm sorry,' he said, 'I must have misunderstood. You see, I was under the impression that we were going to work this thing out together in a constructive and sensible fashion, instead of playing games. Goodbye.'

'I see.' Poliorcis stayed exactly where he was. 'After I've come all this way, you're throwing me out.'

'I'd never dream of being so rude,' Gorgas replied. 'Still, since you don't appear to have anything to say to me, I must confess I can't see any point in your being here; and since you've already seen all the sights, and our climate doesn't seem to agree with you—'

'All right.' Poliorcis had an unhappy feeling that he'd given away the initiative in the negotiations before they'd even begun, and had no real chance of getting it back. 'Here's a firm offer, no ambiguities at all. Money: how much will you take for your prisoner?'

Gorgas laughed. 'Please,' he said, 'let's at least pretend to respect each other. You've seen the Mesoge; what possible use would money be to me in a place like this?'

Just outside the back door, a dog was barking furiously. The noise picked at the pain in Poliorcis' head like fingers plucking harpstrings. 'Very well then,' he said. 'Not money. What else? Something we have, presumably, that you need. Tools? Weapons? Raw materials?'

Gorgas shook his head. 'You're making fun of me,' he said. 'Personally, I don't regard that as very diplomatic. Tell me, do you really despise us that much? Do you really think we're nothing but bandits and thieves, little better than the gangs who go around fishing through open windows with a hook on the end of a pole? I thought you'd have understood, when I took the trouble to show you; we're farmers, peaceful people who want to make friends with our neighbours. Show us just a little respect and I'll give you your damned rebel for free.'

'You're talking about the alliance,' Poliorcis said. 'I can only say that I'm extremely sorry, but the provincial office feels that a formal alliance at this time would be inappropriate.'

'Inappropriate.'

Poliorcis felt as if he was slowly sinking up to his knees in mud. 'I'd just like to point out,' he said, 'that what you're asking is entirely without precedent. We have no formal alliances with anybody; not Shastel or the Island or Colleon. Please try to understand our concerns; if we made an alliance with you, what sort of message would that send to them, after we've turned down overtures from all of them? Quite simply, it's not the way we do things.'

'All right.' Gorgas yawned. 'If there's one thing I pride myself on, it's flexibility. Flexibility, realism, always look for the deal that's good for both sides. Now, you're telling me the Empire doesn't have any allies, and I'm sure you'd never lie about a thing like that. Well then, we'll forget all about an alliance, and I'll tell you straight exactly what's in my mind. The truth is, whether or not we're formal allies, all

I want is for you, the provincial office, to give me a chance to do something I need to do; you think about it and tell me if you can see a way it can be done. After all, you're the diplomat; I'm just a soldier and a farmer and I'm really out of my depth here. I need to pay off an old debt – no, that's not it. I need to set right a really bad thing I did once. You see, I made it possible for Temrai to sack Perimadeia. Does that shock you?'

Poliorcis looked at him. 'I know,' he said.

'Oh.' Gorgas sat still, expressionless. 'What do you think about that?'

'I don't,' Poliorcis replied. 'That is, I know why you did it, what your reasons were; it was because your sister owed a lot of money to rich individuals in Perimadeia, and she knew she could never pay them back. It was a business decision. Now, I can give an opinion as to whether that was wise or unwise from a commercial point of view, but if you're expecting me to say whether I think what you did was right or wrong, I'm afraid I can't. I don't think in those terms; it's as if I was colour-blind and you wanted my opinion about a certain shade of green. So,' he went on, 'what has that got to do with us?'

Gorgas breathed out, rubbed his chin. 'I suppose I'm the one who's shocked,' he said. 'I'm not colour-blind, as you put it. I can see that what I did was terribly wrong. I knew my brother was fighting for the City; I ruined his life and nearly got him killed. That's what I've got to put right. I have to kill Temrai and destroy the plains tribes, fighting side by side with him, paying my debt. Can you see that? Even you must be able to see that. Now, I don't care what my official standing is, I just need to be there and to do my share, otherwise I won't be able to live with myself. Because of what I did, I'm already responsible for the death of my own son; I owe it to him as well. Can you see how simple and straightforward this all is?'

Poliorcis thought for a while. 'One thing I'm sure about,' he said, 'you're an interesting man. And if there's one thing the Sons of Heaven are interested in, it's interesting people. But let's think this through, shall we? With all due respect, we already have all the military resources we need. When we first met, you were talking about archers, how we don't have enough. The fact is, we do. We have whole nations of archers in the Empire – longbow, short recurve, long recurve, horse archers, crossbowmen, you name it. Our factories can deliver twenty thousand bows and two hundred thousand arrows a week, all made to specification, identical, though the factories might be a thousand miles apart. So really, we don't need any more archers. Now, you've told me why you feel you need to fight this war. Let me tell you why we're fighting it. We have more regular full-time soldiers than there are men, women and children in all of Shastel and the Island and Colleon and Perimadeia and all the other places you've ever heard of put together. We built that army so that nobody – nobody – could ever be a threat to us. Between the Sons of Heaven and the remotest possibility of danger there's a wall of steel and muscle so thick that nothing on earth could ever break through it. If the ground suddenly opened and swallowed our homeland up, we could fill the hole with human bodies and rebuild our homes on top of them. No, we make war because we need to find our army something to do, to keep them from getting bored and restive and out of shape; so you see, we really don't want anybody else fighting our battles for us – it'd defeat the whole object of the exercise. I'm sorry, but there it is. I can't help you.'

Gorgas nodded slowly, as if he'd just had a difficult calculation explained to him. 'I understand,' he said. 'And sooner or later you'll come here, walking the dog, so to speak; and it'd be embarrassing for you to be seen to pick a fight with people you once treated as friends and allies. That's sound enough reasoning, I can accept that. But it doesn't solve my problem. Poliorcis, I'm asking you because you're the expert: how can we arrange it so that you get what you want, this pirate of yours, and I get what I need? There has to be a way. All we've got to do is figure out what it is.'

Poliorcis frowned. 'I must say,' he said, 'you're dealing with the news of your impending conquest and subjugation very well. Most people would probably have got angry, or frightened.'

'Pointless,' Gorgas said. 'You weren't telling me anything I didn't know. It's obvious enough; you said it yourself, that's one of the reasons I wanted the alliance. But you're too smart for me, and I accept that; there's still no reason why we can't put our heads together and find a way of making the inevitable a little bit less painful than it'll otherwise be. Flexibility. Realism. That's what it's all about.' He bit his lip, then clapped his hands together so loudly that Poliorcis jumped. 'I know,' Gorgas went on. 'I know exactly what we can do. I hereby surrender the Mesoge to the Empire, and throw myself and my people on your mercy.' He smiled beautifully. 'And as a gesture of goodwill, it'd be really appreciated if we could take our place as auxiliary soldiers in your expeditionary force against Temrai. There, doesn't that cover everything beautifully?'

It had been a long time since Poliorcis had been shocked by anything, and he wasn't sure he remembered how to deal with it. 'You're joking,' he said.

Gorgas shook his head. 'No, I'm not,' he said. 'I'm practising what I preach. I'm sparing my people the horrors of a war we could never hope to win, and getting to pay my debt off at the same time. If you want me to abdicate, I will – well, look, you can see for yourself, I'm not exactly comfortable as a military dictator. All I want to do once I've settled that old score is to live here and work my farm; I'm sure the provincial office won't mind me doing that. Now then, you think of the advantages; think of Tornoys and the Mesoge as a base for your conquests in this region, how much easier it'll make it to pick off the neighbouring states one by one. Think of what it'll mean to you personally – you came here to get a rebel, you succeed, and you take home a new province for the Empire into the bargain. Can you possibly imagine a better outcome? Well?'

It was the enthusiasm, above all; the waggy-tailed-dog boisterousness of the man. It was almost more than Poliorcis could bear. But, 'No,' he replied, 'I can't say that I can. Well, you've certainly given me a lot to think about. Will it be all right if I rest here tonight and start for home in the morning?'

Gorgas gave him a smile as big and bright as sunrise. 'Whatever you say,' he replied. 'After all, you're the boss.'

CHAPTER ELEVEN

They woke Temrai up in the middle of the night to tell him the news. The messenger had ridden all the way from the battlefield to the camp beside Perimadeia; he was exhausted, and his boots were full of blood from the halberd cut in his groin. Chances were he'd be dead by morning.

Temrai woke up in a panic, grabbing wildly at the covers and wrenching his damaged knee. They told him it was all right, there was nothing to worry about; then they brought in the messenger, all bloody, hanging off the shoulders of two men. Temrai was still groggy with sleep and shocked by the pain in his leg, and he couldn't quite make out everything the dying man was saying; he heard words like *ambush* and *seventy per cent casualties* and *driven back in disorder* and *hit again before they could regroup*. It was only when Kurrai started chattering excitedly about making the most of the opportunity and following up with a massive counter-attack that Temrai realised he'd just been told about a substantial victory, not a catastrophic defeat.

'We won,' he mumbled. 'I'll be damned. So how did that happen?'

By this time the messenger had passed out; they took him away and wrapped him in blankets, and he died just after dawn. Instead, Temrai heard the story from Kurrai, with the added benefit of the general's strategic and tactical insights.

It had all started when the Imperial army, carefully mopping up after their victory in which Temrai had been hurt, stumbled across a small party of plains renegades who'd been running from Temrai's men ever since their side had lost the civil war. To the provincial office, however,

234

plainsmen were plainsmen. Their cavalry chased the renegades, pinned them down in a high-sided canyon and sent
for substantial infantry reinforcements.

It was hot and dusty; there was water in the bottom of the
canyon, where the renegades were, but not higher up, where
the Imperial stakeout was settling in. The messenger sent to
the Imperial field HQ made a point of stressing the urgency,
and a column of just under two thousand men, led by a Son
of Heaven, set out the same day.

Their own remarkable stamina and fitness caught them
out. If they'd been slower, or not following the optimum
route, it's unlikely that they'd have run into Temrai's reserve
mounted infantry, who'd broken, run and been cut off from
the rest of the army at an early stage in the first battle
and had only just managed to find their way out of Imperial
territory. The two forces coincided in a valley between a
forest and a river, and purely by chance the plainsmen found
themselves in a position that gave them an overwhelming
tactical advantage. The Imperial infantry were hemmed in by
the river, which was in spate and impassable; a bend in
the river closed off one of the plainsmen's flanks, the forest
masked the other. The Imperial commander was left with a
choice between sitting still and being pecked to death by
hit-and-run attacks from the enemy archers or mounting a
direct frontal assault against volley fire. Basing his decision
on the superior quality of his men's armour, he opted for the
assault.

In his defence, the other option would probably have been
equally disastrous. Doubtful, though, that this was much consolation, as he watched his advancing lines crumple up, like
flawed metal under the hammer. After four detachments had
failed to get within seventy-five yards of the enemy before
collapsing in a tangle of metal and bodies, he fell back on the
river in the wild hope that he might prompt the plainsmen to
charge and give away their advantage. It didn't work. The
plainsmen held their position and sent out small parties to
harass and disorganise the men on either flank. Eventually, in
spite of all their training and discipline, the Imperial soldiers
started to edge away from the attacks towards the perceived
safety of the centre, opening gaps between themselves
and the river bank wide enough for a sudden encircling rush.

With mobile archers now surrounding them on all four sides, all they could do was huddle behind their shields and watch the arrows slant in at them. They made a few half-hearted attempts at sorties to break through the cordon, but it was pointless; the archers in front drew back as they approached, while those behind closed in, and the sortie parties were shot down before they could lumber more than a few yards.

The battle lasted six hours, five of them in the circle. If the Imperial commander had hung on for another half-hour, the plainsmen would have run out of arrows and pulled out, but of course he had no way of knowing that. He surrendered and his men were marched away, leaving twelve hundred of their number behind.

(A day or so later, a party of itinerant pedlars wandered on to the battlefield, stared in wonder at what they'd found, and spent the next two days stripping armour off the dead, beating out the holes and dents and cramming it all on to their wagons. In the end they sold the whole consignment to a scrap dealer in Ap' Idras for more money than they'd ever imagined existed; in turn, the dealer sold it on to the Imperial armoury at Ap' Oule at a hundred and fifty per cent mark-up, proving that even the most dismal tragedy is somebody's opportunity of a lifetime.)

'We won,' Temrai repeated, when Kurrai had finished. 'That's amazing.'

'Don't sound so surprised,' Kurrai replied. 'And whatever you do, don't start thinking our problems are over, because they aren't. I don't want to worry you unduly, but are you aware that every single nation that's managed to inflict a significant defeat on the Empire over the last hundred and fifty years is now effectively extinct? They get awfully upset when they lose. There used to be a saying among the Ipacrians: the only thing worse than getting beaten by the Empire is beating them.'

Temrai nodded slowly. 'Thank you very much,' he said. 'One more victory and we're done for, is that it?'

Kurrai looked uncomfortable, and shrugged. 'I just feel it's important not to let one success go to our heads, that's all. And we have to remember, fighting the Empire isn't like fighting anybody else.'

'I think I get the message,' Temrai said.

By now, of course, he was far too wide awake to go back to sleep. Under normal circumstances he'd shake off the fit of depression by getting up, bustling about, finding something to do; but of course, he didn't have that option. Tilden wasn't there; she was on the other side of the straits with the rest of the non-combatants, camping out among the ruins of the City. The more restless he became, the more his knee hurt. Finally, he gave up even pretending to rest and yelled for the sentry.

'Go and wake somebody up,' he said. 'I'm bored.'

The sentry grinned, and came back a little while later with a couple of very sleepy-looking council members, apparently chosen at random – Joducai, in charge of the transport pool, and Terscai, deputy chief engineer. Then he saluted and returned to his post.

'Temrai, it's the middle of the night,' Joducai said.

Temrai frowned at him. 'I can't help that,' he said. 'Now then, those two Islanders, the old wizard and the boy—'

'Islanders?' Joducai looked confused, reasonably enough. 'Sorry, you've lost me.'

'We picked up a couple of Islanders wandering about down south,' Temrai explained. 'They said they'd been shipwrecked and just wanted to go home, but they could be spies, so I had them brought here.'

Terscai grinned. 'Since when have you been bothered about spies?' he said.

'Since a spy saved my life, I guess,' Temrai replied. 'I'm thinking of recruiting my bodyguard exclusively from spies. Do me a favour, go and round them up and bring them here.'

'Why us?' Joducai asked.

'You're up and about,' Temrai said. 'Everybody else is asleep.'

Joducai sighed. 'You're feeling better, I can tell,' he said. 'It was wonderful when you were dying, a man could get a good night's rest around here.'

A little later they came back with the two Islanders, Gannadius and Theudas Morosin.

'Morosin,' Temrai repeated. 'That's a Perimadeian name, isn't it?'

The boy said nothing. 'That's right,' the older man

replied. 'We're both Perimadeians by birth. I'm his uncle.'

Temrai thought for a moment. 'Gannadius isn't a City name, is it?'

'It's the name I took when I joined the Perimadeian Order,' he replied. 'It's traditional to take another name, usually borrowed from one of the great philosophers of the past. My given name was Theudas Morosin.'

Temrai raise an eyebrow. 'The same as him?' he asked.

'That's right. Morosin's the family name, and Theudas is a name that runs in the family, if you follow me.'

'Not really,' Temrai admitted, cupping his chin in his palm. 'It strikes me as showing a lack of imagination.'

'Like having everybody's name ending in *ai*,' Gannadius replied. 'It's just the way we did things, that's all.'

Temrai nodded slowly. 'And you used to be Perimadeians,' he said, 'and now you're Islanders. I see. I imagine you feel pretty uncomfortable here.'

Gannadius smiled. 'He does,' he said. 'I'm a philosopher, so I don't worry about that sort of thing.'

Temrai muffled a yawn – a genuine one, though it was well timed for effect. 'Really,' he said. 'And what was a philosopher doing wandering about in our territory?'

'We were shipwrecked,' Gannadius said.

'I see. On your way where?'

'Shastel.' Gannadius suddenly realised that he couldn't remember what relations were like between the plainspeople and the Order; he couldn't think of any reason offhand why there should be bad relations, or indeed any at all, but rationalising isn't the same thing as knowing. Temrai, however, didn't seem concerned.

'And may I ask why you were going to Shastel?' he said.

'I live there, ' Gannadius said.

'Oh. I thought you said you were an Islander.'

'I am. I'm a citizen of the Island.'

'A citizen of the Island, born in the City, living in Shastel, with two names. You must find life confusing sometimes.'

'Oh, I do,' Gannadius replied. 'As I think I may have mentioned, I'm a philosopher.'

Temrai smiled, as if conceding the match. 'What about him?' he said. 'I'm asking you, because he doesn't seem very keen to talk to me.'

'He's shy.'

'I see. Does he live in Shastel too?'

Gannadius shook his head. 'On the Island. He works for a bank.'

'Really? How interesting. And before that, did he go straight to the Island from the City after the Fall?'

Gannadius' expression didn't change. 'Not exactly,' he said. 'He spent a few years abroad before that. You know all this, don't you?'

Temrai nodded. 'He was Bardas Loredan's apprentice,' he said. 'Colonel Loredan rescued him from the sack of Perimadeia; from me, in fact, personally.' He turned his head and gave Theudas a long, hard stare. 'You've grown,' he said.

For the first time, Gannadius' air of affable rudeness waned a little, but not by much. 'So what are you going to do to us?' he asked.

'Send you home, of course,' Temrai answered, with a brilliant smile. 'Though in your case, Mr Philosopher, I'm going to have to ask you to specify which one. You seem to have so many.'

'The Island will do fine,' Gannadius replied quickly. 'Or Shastel. Whichever's the most convenient, really.'

'Anywhere but here, in fact?'

'Yes,' Gannadius admitted.

'I quite understand.' Temrai winced, as his knee twinged. 'Please excuse me,' he said. 'I managed to damage my knee the other day.'

Gannadius nodded. 'Strangling an Imperial trooper with your bare hands, so I gather,' he said. 'No mean feat, I'm sure.'

'With a helmet strap, actually,' Temrai replied. 'Well, I think that's everything. I believe there's a ship sailing for the Island in a few days' time; I don't know the name offhand, I'm afraid. I strongly suggest you get on it; sea traffic's more or less at a standstill at the moment, ever since the Empire hired all the ships on the Island.'

Gannadius clearly hadn't heard about that. 'Really?' he said. 'May I ask, do you know why?'

'They're going to attack us by sea,' Temrai replied, 'and the Islanders are lending them the ships to do it with, since the Empire hasn't got any of its own. Sorry; hiring, not lending. I'd hate to offend your Island sensibilities by suggesting you'd ever do anything like that for free.'

'That's quite all right,' Gannadius replied. 'As you know, I'm really a Perimadeian, so I don't mind.'

Temrai looked at the young man, Theudas (strange to be able to put a name to the face after all these years of nightmares). He was as white as a sheet, his hands balled into tight fists. 'If you should happen to see Colonel Loredan before I do,' he said, 'please give him my regards and tell him to keep as far away from me as possible.'

Theudas was about to say something, but Gannadius was quicker. 'We'll be sure to deliver your message if we see him,' he said, 'though I would think that's quite unlikely, really. After all, the only reason we're here - no offence to you or your admirable hospitality, your people couldn't have been kinder - is that the Imperials were trying to kill us.'

Temrai smiled. 'Because they mistook you for Shastel.'

'Oh, we are. At least I am. At least,' Gannadius added gravely, 'some of the time.'

'It must be wonderful to be so many different people,' Temrai said. 'I've only ever been me. I envy you.'

'Really?'

'Absolutely. If I'd been able to choose my identity, I wouldn't have had to do the things I did, and I wouldn't be faced with the problems that are facing me. Everything I've ever been or done or had to suffer's been because of who I am; but you - well, you're lucky.' He beckoned to the guard, who opened the tent-flap. 'Thank you for stopping by,' he said. 'It's been interesting talking to you.'

'Likewise,' Gannadius replied. 'It was a pleasure meeting you, after all this time.'

'Ap' Calick?' said the Son of Heaven. 'Then you probably met my cousin.'

The column had pitched camp for the night, and the cooks were starting the evening meal. They'd just killed and paunched a sheep the foragers had brought in, and were putting up a trestle to hang it from. Being a Son of Heaven, Colonel Estar was taking a personal interest.

'Your cousin,' Bardas repeated.

'His name's Anax,' Estar replied. 'He runs the proof house. Short, bald chap in his late seventies. You'd remember him if you'd seen him.'

Although Bardas hadn't been in the Imperial army for very long (at least, not by Imperial standards) he had an idea that it was unusual, to say the least, for the commanding officer of a column to sit under a tree beside the cooking-fire chatting amiably with an outlander, even if the outlander was nominally his co-commander. Either he was bored, or he found Bardas an unusually fascinating companion, or he was taking an opportunity to assess the army's secret weapon in plenty of time before actually deploying it against the enemy. From what little he'd been able to gather about the Sons of Heaven, it was most likely a combination of all three.

'Oh, yes,' he replied, 'I met Anax all right. He made me the armour I've been wearing today.'

'Really?' The cooks had managed to get the trestle to stay up, and were threading a rope between the bone and the sinew of the sheep's back legs, just above the ankle. 'I haven't seen him in years. Really, I ought to make the effort and go to visit him next time I find myself out that way. How's he keeping?'

'Pretty well,' Bardas replied. 'Remarkable, for a man of his age.'

'Good,' Estar said, his eyes fixed on the work in progress before him. 'He's - let's see, he's my father's mother's eldest sister's son. I expect you were surprised to find - well, one of us, working with his hands for a living.'

Bardas nodded. The cooks had strung up the dead sheep and were starting to skin it; one of them knelt down and pulled on its front legs, while the other made a delicate cut around the leg just below the point where they'd passed the rope through, taking care not to nick the tendon. 'I assumed it's what he likes doing,' Bardas said. 'I can't imagine any other reason.'

Estar smiled. 'Not really,' he said. 'The truth is, Anax has led what you might call an interesting life, one way and another. At one time he was a deputy prefect in the commissioner's department, right in the heart of the Empire. That was when he made a mistake.'

Now the cooks were slitting the skin down along the legs, following the bone with the specially shaped points of their knives until they reached the wide opening they'd made in the belly when they scooped out the guts. 'Mistake,' Bardas repeated. 'I'd better not ask about that.'

'Oh, whyever not?' Estar grinned. 'I'm not so cruel as to drop a tantalising hint like that and then leave you hanging, so to speak. He was in charge of a district, and a rebellion broke out. Well, it wasn't even a rebellion, properly speaking; there was a tax-collector who was a bit too heavy-handed in his methods, and he came to a bad end. It should have been perfectly possible to sort it out. But for some reason, Anax got it wrong; first he let them get away with it for far too long, and then he sent in a platoon of soldiers to demolish the village. After that, there really was a rebellion.'

Now they were cutting away round the vent; one of them caught hold of the tail and twisted sharply, until the bones cracked. 'I see,' Bardas said. 'What happened?'

'It dragged on for ages,' Estar replied. 'Anax sent more troops, the rebels burned their village to the ground and hid in the woods. The soldiers tried to bring them out by attacking the other villages in the district, but that just made matters worse, because all the people they displaced went to join the rebels. It wasn't long before there were several thousand men in the woods; enough to inflict a serious defeat on us if we tried to go in after them and messed it up. On the other hand, Anax couldn't just ignore something like that, and in the end he had no option. The whole thing was a disaster from beginning to end, really.'

They were peeling the skin off the sheep's back, pressing down into the opening flap with their fists to keep the flesh from being torn off. There's no other sound like it. 'I assume he won, though,' Bardas said, watching the cooks as they worked. 'In the end, I mean.'

'Well, of course. The Empire always *wins*; what matters is how it wins. And in this case, we didn't win well. I forget how many men he lost crashing about in the woods before he finally managed to pin them down, but it was a couple of hundred; that's pretty disastrous in any context, but for a police action in a supposedly quiet and peaceful inner province—' Estar shook his head. 'He had to burn them out in the end; he cleared firebreaks right the way round the part of the wood they were ensconced in, stationed guards in the drives and set fire to everything in the middle. None of them even tried to come out. Apparently the smell was quite revolting.'

To get the skin off the ribs without tearing it, the cooks were shaving the membranes between the hide and the bone, going carefully so as not to nick the skin and start a tear. 'I can imagine,' Bardas said, pulling a wry face. 'So what happened to Anax after that?'

Estar poured himself a drink from the little cherrywood flask Bardas had seen tucked into his sash. 'They were going to put him on trial,' he said, 'but the family pulled some strings; instead, he was officially censured and posted to the western frontier – what was the western frontier then, forty years ago; of course, it's moved on since then, but Anax stayed where he was. Officially he was the deputy master of the proof house; in reality, he was shoved in there and told he was never coming out. And there he's been ever since, amusing himself as best he can. He brought it on himself, I suppose, but I can't help thinking it was a pretty harsh way to treat a man for what was, after all, an error of judgement.'

With the points of their knives, following the bone by feel, they were slitting down the line of the front legs. 'It's not for me to comment,' Bardas said. 'I suppose you have to live with the risk of something like that, once you start taking responsibility for other people's lives.'

'Oh, it's everybody's nightmare, isn't it?' Estar answered, pulling a sad face. 'You're the man in command when everything starts going wrong; or you're the man who has to fight the battle that can't be won, attack the impregnable city, hold off the unstoppable horde. You could say he was just plain unlucky. I mean, who's to say you or I would have done any better, in his position?'

– And finally, with much effort and exertion, they pulled the skin over the shoulders and away from the severed neck, so that it came off whole and undamaged, clean on the inside, without spoiling either the hide or the carcass. The flesh glistened slightly in the glow of the fire, like a newly born baby, or a man shiny with sweat as he takes off his armour on a hot day. Then they started to joint it, while the kitchen boy set about breaking open the head with a big pair of shears. 'I'm going to pull rank and ask for the brains,' Estar said with a smile. 'Straight from the bone, simmer for half an hour in brine, add a couple of eggs and some lemon juice; there's nothing to beat it. Some people reckon you should sauté them, but to my mind that's sacrilege.'

Bardas shrugged. 'My mother used to cook them when we were kids,' he said, 'but I can't remember what they were like. Everything she cooked tended to taste the same, anyway. Since then, I've never been all that interested in food.'

Estar laughed. 'I pity you,' he said. 'One of the great pleasures of life you've missed out on there, and now I suppose it's too late for you to learn to appreciate it. That's a shame.' He watched the kitchen boy attentively. 'And I thought Perimadeia was famous for the variety and quality of its cuisine.'

'It was,' Bardas said. 'Or so people told me. I was quite happy to take their word for it.'

'And what about the wine, then?' Estar asked. 'Or don't you drink, either?'

'Mostly we drank cider,' Bardas replied. 'Cheap, and it did the job. Better for you than the wine; at least, the sort of wine they sold in the sort of places I used to go. I don't think you'd have liked it very much.'

They were cutting through the breastbone with a saw. 'Oh, I've drunk my fair share of rotgut,' Estar said, 'when I was a penniless student. Remarkable how quickly you can get used to it, if there isn't anything else.' Bardas noticed how intently he was watching the cooks. It was more than the obsessive attention to detail of the true gourmet. Maybe Estar was aware of his interest, because he smiled and said, 'All this is part of a boy's education, back home. At the same time as we're learning spelling and basic algebra and geometry, we're being taught the one true way of jointing and dressing meat. The idea is that by the time a boy's ten years old, you should be able to give him a dead sheep and a sharp knife, go away for a couple of hours and come back to a perfect meal of roast mutton, seasoned with rosemary and bay and served in the proper manner, according to the specifications set down in the Book. If I were at home right now, I'd be doing all this

- it's the host's privilege to prepare food for his guests; we take that sort of thing very seriously. Good food, good wine, good music and good conversation. Everything else is just a necessary evil.'

'That's an interesting point of view,' Bardas said diplomatically. 'Of course, it does rather depend on having something to eat in the first place.'

Estar frowned for a moment, then laughed. 'You're missing the point,' he said. 'The very essence of luxury is simplicity. Luxury's not really got anything to do with being rich and powerful; it's just that the two are often found together, like horseflies and dung. Suppose that all you've got is a slingshot and a handful of pebbles; you can walk up the mountain and kill a sand-grouse as easily as walking down the mountain and killing a rabbit; as you go, you gather a few essential herbs and seasonings, and when you get back you take a little more care and trouble over cooking the meal than you absolutely have to. Good wine's made from the same materials as bad wine; as for good music and good conversation, they cost nothing.' He sighed and put his hands behind his head. 'You should read some of our great poets, Bardas,' he said. 'Dalshin and Silat and the *Rose-Scented Arrow*. They're all about the simple life, an ideal existence from which everything gross and intrusive has been purged away - refined, in the true sense of the word. That's the very root and source of our culture; it's who we are. "No man can fold a bolt of silk as perfect as a rose"—'

'I see,' Bardas interrupted, before Estar could get any further. 'So what are you doing here?'

Estar closed his eyes. 'Necessary evil,' he replied. 'To live the perfect life, you must first have stability, security. How can you possibly concentrate on the essentials of existence if there's any possibility of danger from outside? The army, the provinces - they're a wall we've built around us, they're the armour we need to protect us; strength outside, sweet simplicity within. Sadly, it means that some of us have to turn our backs on the important things for some of the time; it's worth it, though, because we know the simple perfection will always be there, waiting for us when we come home.' He opened his eyes and sat up. 'You're smiling,' he said. 'Obviously you don't agree.'

Bardas shook his head. 'Actually,' he said, 'I was thinking of my home – well, my original home; I've lived all over the place. But what I was thinking about was where I grew up, in the Mesoge. That's about as simple as you can get.'

'Oh yes?'

'Definitely.'

Estar raised an eyebrow. 'Have you been back there recently?' he asked.

'About four years ago,' Bardas replied. 'I didn't enjoy the experience much.'

'The Mesoge,' Estar repeated. 'Isn't that where your brother—?'

Bardas nodded. 'Now, Gorgas would probably agree with you,' he said. 'About home and the simple things being the most important. With him, I think, it's always been home and family, or at least that's what he's always chosen to think. I did too, for many years, until I actually went home and saw my family again.' He smiled. 'That's what made me join the Imperial army,' he added.

'Sorry, I don't follow.'

'The Empire's a big place,' Bardas replied. 'And I wanted to put as much distance between myself and my home and family as I possibly could.'

'Oh.' Estar's expression suggested that here was a concept he'd have difficulty grasping. 'Well, your misfortune is our good fortune, I suppose. Are you happy doing this?'

Bardas frowned. 'I don't know,' he said. 'I mean, I'm not sure. It's – well, as far as I'm concerned, it's an unusual criterion to judge anything by, whether it makes you happy or not. It's a bit like asking a man who's clinging to a piece of driftwood in the middle of the sea whether he likes the colour.'

Estar folded his eyebrows in a mock scowl. 'Oh, come on,' he said, 'that's a bit melodramatic, surely. Here you are, a strong, healthy man in the prime of life. Sure, you have to work to make a living; but wouldn't it be just as easy to make that living doing something you enjoy, or at least something that isn't actively offensive to you? It's like the imaginary hunter with the slingshot I was talking about just now; he may only have a sling and a stone, but he still has the choice to go up the hill. If you don't like being a

soldier, go away and do something else; weave baskets
or turn bowls or scare crows. Or make yourself a sling and
gather a handful of pebbles.'

Bardas smiled. The boy had finally managed to crack open
the sheep's skull, and was scooping the white, sloppy brains
out into a bowl with a tin spoon. 'Ah,' he said, 'but before I
could do that I'd need a suit of armour, like you said yourself.
I'd need to be safe from all my enemies.'

Estar shrugged. 'Come and live inside the Empire,' he said.
'Once you get in deep, past the outer provinces, everybody's
safe there. You could get right away from all these enemies of
yours, and even if they did track you down and find you,
they'd never dare to make any trouble inside the Empire.'

'It's a tempting offer,' Bardas replied, remembering the man
and his children who'd tried to rob the post coach. 'But I'd
think twice before making it, if I were you. You see, wherever I go, this dangerous, bloodthirsty troublemaker keeps
following me, and I'm not sure you'd be all that keen on
having him around.'

Estar furrowed his brow. 'You mean your brother?' he
asked.

Bardas watched the kitchen boy shaking the last scrap
of white jelly out of the skull. 'My own flesh and blood,' he
replied.

'What do you think?' Iseutz said.

'You look ridiculous,' her mother replied without looking
up from her chequer-board. 'Fortunately, nobody's going
to see you in it, so it doesn't matter.'

Iseutz frowned. 'I think it suits me,' she said.

In the corner of the room, her mother's cat was eating
a bird, rather noisily, not particularly concerned that the
bird was still alive. Iseutz recognised it as next door's pet
mynah bird. 'It could do with taking up a little here, don't
you think?' she said, twitching the hem of the skirt with her
left hand. 'I'm not sure. Should it be on the knee or an inch
above?'

Niessa Loredan scowled at the counters spread out before
her. 'Who cares?' she said.

'I care.'

'Since when?' Niessa laughed unpleasantly. 'And besides,'

she added, 'if you knew even the slightest bit about fashion, you'd know that look's over and done with now. You're just doing this to annoy me, the same reason you do everything.'

Iseutz took no notice; she sat down in the window-seat, her back to the blue sea, and studied the stumps of her fingers. 'If nobody's ever going to see me,' she said sweetly, 'what does it matter if it's gone out of fashion?'

'I've got to look at you,' Niessa replied sourly. 'And I've got enough to put up with without you prancing round dressed like that.' She looked up. 'This is because I stopped you writing to your uncle Gorgas, isn't it?'

That's what you think. 'It's nothing to do with that,' Iseutz said. 'You think everything I do has somehow got to be about *you*.'

Niessa folded her arms. 'If you were really interested in how you look,' she said, 'if you were really interested in anything normal, it'd be different. But you aren't. Look at you. You're a freak.'

'Thank you,' Iseutz replied gravely.

'And now,' her mother went on, 'you insist on dressing like a freak as well. And that's too much. I won't have it in this house, and that's final.'

Iseutz glanced over her shoulder at the sea. 'I'm not a freak,' she said, 'I'm a Loredan. The difference is small but significant.'

Niessa shook her head. 'For one thing,' she said, 'isn't it horribly uncomfortable? It looks like it should be.'

It was, of course; that was one of the reasons why the warrior-princess look had died the death in other, more rational places. Here in Ap' Bermidan, it was little short of torture; the leather was stiff and clammy with sweat, and the sheer weight of the chain-mail top pressing on her neck and shoulders was giving her spasms of cramp up and down her back. 'It's fine,' Iseutz said. 'Much more comfortable than all those dreary long skirts.'

'Then why do you keep massaging your neck when you think I'm not looking?' Niessa demanded. 'I can see from here, it's rubbed a big red sore patch. Serves you right.'

Iseutz drummed her heels against the wall. 'I like it,' she said. 'I think it's *me*.'

Niessa grinned. 'I won't argue with you there,' she said. 'But the whole point of putting clothes on is to try to disguise what *you* are.' She clicked her tongue, something that grated unbearably on her daughter. 'And you say you can't understand why I don't let you out in public.'

Disguise what I am, like cooking herbs with tainted meat. You haven't said what you think I should do about the skirt,' Iseutz said. 'On balance, I think I'll leave it as it is; after all, I'm not terribly much use with a needle.'

'Or without,' Niessa sighed. 'Now shut up or go to your room. I've got work to do.'

Iseutz smiled, and shifted a little so that she could look out of the window without craning her neck. Blue sky and blue sea, with a spit of white sand dividing them. It was a very boring view, but there wasn't anything else.

'What was that?' Niessa said, lifting her head sharply. Someone was bashing at the door down below. 'Startled me.'

Iseutz pretended to take no notice. She hoped it was the Ap' Muren courier; a bulk garlic merchant from Ap' Muren sometimes bought from an Islander who occasionally went to the Mesoge for dried wild mushrooms and isinglass. But her mother hadn't had dealings with Ap' Muren for ages, so it wasn't very likely.

The door opened, but the man who walked in wasn't the porter; he was hovering behind the newcomer's shoulder, looking agitated. The newcomer was a soldier.

'Niessa Loredan,' he said. It was a statement of fact, not a question.

'What do you want?'

'You're coming with us,' the soldier said, as two more, apparently identical in every respect, barged past the porter into the room. Their armour made them look huge and bulky.

'Like hell,' Niessa said, but a soldier grabbed hold of the back of her neck, like a man picking up a small dog, and shoved her towards the door. 'What is this?' Niessa squawked. 'Where are you taking me?' The soldier didn't seem to have heard. Iseutz slid down off the window seat.

'Can I come too?' she asked.

The soldier looked at her. 'Iseutz Loredan,' he said. 'You too.'

'My pleasure,' Iseutz replied. 'Have we got time to pack a few things, or—?'

Apparently not; the soldier caught hold of her arm and hustled her out of the room, down the spiral staircase, shoving her so hard she nearly slipped and fell. At the foot of the stairs he stopped, pulled the little toy sword out of its scabbard at her waist and dropped it on the floor. 'This way,' he said.

'What, down the path? I'm so glad you told me, I'd never have guessed.'

No sense of humour, soldiers; for that, she got a shove on the shoulder that nearly sent her sprawling. But she managed to keep her balance long enough to catch hold of the man's wrist with her left hand and flip him across her back and over her shoulder. Judging by the noise he made, he didn't land very well.

'*Iseutz!*' her mother screamed, angry and terrified and embarrassed. One of the other soldiers was drawing his sword – instinct, probably, or conditioned response, but Iseutz wasn't at her most rational, either. Skipping forward a step or two she kicked the fallen soldier in the face before he had a chance to get up (she heard the bone in his nose snap), bobbed down, slid his sword out of its scabbard left-handed and advanced. Both of the remaining soldiers had their swords drawn now, but they didn't know what to do – fighting one-handed girls who were wanted alive by the prefect's office and were also capable of throwing lance-corporals of the guard around like rose-petals was definitely not something they were willing to undertake without first being told the rules of engagement by a senior officer.

'Iseutz,' Niessa wailed, beside herself with fury, 'what the hell do you think you're doing? Put that down immediately, before you get us both—'

If her mother hadn't interfered, Iseutz might well have dropped the sword; she was, after all, in a completely untenable position. As it was, she gripped the hilt even more firmly, and prayed silently to Fool's Luck that the soldiers wouldn't guess that she couldn't fight southpaw worth spit. As she advanced, they backed away; she circled, gradually edging them round until she had her back to the road. Then she turned round and ran as fast as she could. They followed, the two squaddies close behind her and gaining, the lance-corporal lagging behind. This wasn't any good; too long spent cooped up in her mother's house, not enough exercise. So she waited till they were almost on to her, then spun round, swishing the sword at shoulder height in a flat circle. The soldiers pulled up sharply. One stumbled and slipped on to his face and hands, the other took a defensive guard and stared at her with a horrified why-me expression in his eyes. Iseutz grinned at him and lunged. It wasn't a good lunge – Uncle Bardas wouldn't have approved – but the soldier wasn't a particularly good fencer; instead of parrying he got out of the way by jumping backwards, almost landing on his colleague's outstretched hand.

Give it up, she thought. *They aren't going to hurt you.* Instead she lunged again; a truly sloppy lunge this time, head not still, balance nowhere. The soldier's parry was worse, a typical fumbled response by a right-hander against a southpaw. She made a half-decent recovery, feinted low and came up into a short backhand cut that caught the soldier's sword on the fort of the blade, a finger's breadth below the quillons, and knocked it out of his hand. He stood perfectly still, staring at her; beside him, his colleague was scrabbling up on to his feet. Iseutz turned and ran.

A little better now. The soldier had stopped to pick up his sword, his mate who'd fallen over had turned his ankle and was hobbling, and the lance-corporal was still well behind. Nevertheless, it was only a matter of time and distance, and she knew that. What the hell; it'd be amusing to see just how far she could get. '*Iseutz!*' her mother was shrieking in the distance. Probably no other incentive could have made her force her numb-weary knees to carry her up the scarp and down into the dip on the other side –

– Where (*there is no god but Fool's Luck, and I am his chosen one*) she found herself in the arms of an extremely startled man who was standing beside a perfectly good horse, tight-ening the girths of his saddle. Iseutz squeaked with shock, turned the squeak into a growl and waggled the sword in the air; the man reeled backwards, slipped and staggered away. *But I hate horses*, Iseutz thought as she jammed her foot in the stirrup and launched herself on to the animal's back, trying to catch hold of the reins with the stumps of her right-hand fingers and failing. She slid the sword between the saddle and her right thigh, pressing hard to keep it there, caught hold of the reins and dug her heels in.

Of course, she hadn't the faintest idea where she was going; she'd hardly been outside the door ever since they'd arrived in this godforsaken place. But it didn't matter. She was going to get caught sooner or later, so there wouldn't have been much point in planning an itinerary. The horse, on the other hand, seemed to have views of its own; no matter how hard she tried to pull its head round, sooner or later it returned to its default course – if pressed, Iseutz would have hazarded a guess that they were running due west, but her sense of direction had never been her strong suit. The sword and a raised seam in her idiotic leather skirt were digging into her quite excruciatingly. All in all, she felt, she wouldn't be too sorry when it was all over.

(*Spur-of-the-moment actions, quick reflexes, snap decisions; then grab somebody else's horse and get the hell out, fast as you can. It's the Loredan way. Uncle Gorgas will be so proud when I tell him …*)

And then, quite suddenly, there was nowhere else to go. The sea sprang out at her from under the lip of a patch of dead ground. She'd come to the edge.

The horse wanted to go left, following the coastline up towards Ap' Bermidan. Iseutz had no strong feelings on the matter either way. They turned left; and before long they were on the outskirts of the town, passing the square wooden frames where the fishermen hung up their catch to dry in the sun and the wind. She took note of the fish as she rode past, contorted by death and desiccation into melodramatic writhing shapes, stiff as boards and flaking loose scales. Dipped in olive oil or smeared with a little garlic butter, the stuff tasted like greasy firewood, and none of the locals would touch it. Instead they shipped it inland, where it was reckoned a delicacy.

As she reached the edge of the harbour, a shallow half-moon enclosed by a long artificial spit extending from a projecting spur of rock, she saw that there were only two ships tied up at the quay. One of them was a short, stubby galley, the pitiful excuse for a ship that was all the Imperials knew how to build. The other was completely different;

curved and tapered at each elevated end like a slice of melon, with small castles fore and aft standing high above the water. She hadn't been a merchant's daughter very long, but even she could recognise a Colleon long-haul freighter. She reined in the horse, frowned, then grinned. It was pointless, of course; they'd never go for it, and besides, the timing would be all wrong – they'd probably only just arrived and would be in no hurry to leave. Nevertheless, she couldn't see any reason why she shouldn't give it a try. All she could do was fail.

There was a small gang of men loading barrels on to the ship with a block and tackle. 'Hello,' she said. They stopped what they were doing and looked at her.

'Where are you headed?' she asked, hopping down from the horse.

There was a long pause, then one of the men said, 'The Island.'

'That's a bit of luck, then,' Iseutz replied cheerfully, 'because that's where I'm headed.'

The man who'd spoken looked her up and down. 'Merchant?' he asked.

Iseutz realised that her ludicrous outfit was just the sort of thing an Island merchant might be wearing. 'Courier,' she replied. 'For the Shastel Bank. Just letters,' she added with a smile, 'no cash money, so there's no point throwing me overboard as soon as we're out of sight of land. I missed my connection a few days back and I'm running really late, so if you could possibly help me out, I'd be very grateful. And so would the Bank,' she added.

'Not up to me,' the man replied.

Iseutz nodded. 'Then if you could possibly see your way to telling me where I can find whoever it is up to—'

The man jerked his head up at the ship. 'Captain Yelet,' he said. 'You got much stuff to take? We'll be off soon as this lot's loaded, or we'll miss the tide.'

She smiled, shook her head, unfastened the saddlebag and slung it over her shoulder. It was surprisingly heavy, and as she held it against her cheek, she thought she could hear the chink of money.

'Captain Yelet,' she repeated. 'Thanks ever so much. See you later.'

The captain wasn't hard to find; but by the time she tracked him down, checking the fastenings in the cargo hold, she'd had a chance to peek inside the saddlebag. Fool's luck: there was a small fortune in there.

'You want to be careful,' the captain warned her gravely as she counted out two gold quarters into his huge round hand. 'Travelling on your own with that much money.'

Iseutz shrugged. 'I manage,' she said.

Dear uncle -

She'd never even tried to write left-handed before. It was still a mess, but much better than she'd ever managed with the stumps of her right.

As the sun set, so the wind had dropped, and at last the ship was holding still long enough for her to be able to put her ink-horn down beside her on the deck with a reasonable chance of it staying there. Quite the treasure trove, that saddlebag; as well as the money she'd found this adorable little traveller's writing set, pens, powdered ink, a dear little penknife, ink-horn and stand, all in a flat box you could use to rest on. And her fool's luck didn't end there; after Captain Yelet concluded his business on the Island, he was heading for Barzea, where he was sure he'd be able to find a jute-dealer headed for Tornoys who'd be only too pleased to deliver her letter. It was turning out to be a good day after all.

Wasn't over yet, of course. There was still a drop or two of blood to be squeezed out of the sun before it set, enough time for the soldiers' galley to show up and arrest her, assuming that they'd heard about this ship and figured it right. That was what ought to happen; but in the other pan of the scale was the luck of the Loredans—

(*After all, Uncle Gorgas managed; I wonder how he did it. Did he ride to Tornoys, that day I was conceived, and just happen to find a ship on the point of sailing for Perimadeia? Did he open the saddlebags on my father's horse and discover a fat purse of money, enough to buy him his passage across the sea? Did he stop to wonder how much further he could get before the rope ran out?*)

She thought for a moment, trying to find the right words. Never an easy job at the best of times; when the course of one's entire life may hang on a misunderstood nuance, decidedly ticklish.

Dear uncle, would it be all right if I came to stay with you for a bit? Things have been a little fraught just recently –

(No need to specify further.)

– and I think a change of scene would do me good. Needless to say, I promise I'll behave –

(Or would that strike the wrong note? A lot would depend on whether the letter reached him before the official pronouncement that she was a wanted fugitive, and that in turn would depend on whether Captain Yelet was going straight to Barzea after stopping at the Island or working his way up the coast making deliveries and running errands, and whether the price of jute was good enough at the moment to justify the Barzea ropewalk owners buying in raw materials from the Mesoge. On balance, better to leave it out; he wouldn't believe her anyway, or care particularly much.)

– A change of scene would do me good. I feel as if I've been cooped up in this dismal place for simply ages; and besides, it's been years since I last saw you. How are Uncle Clefas and Uncle Zonaras, by the way? You realise, I've never met them, so that'd be something to look forward to. So if you could see your way –

(No. Don't plead.)

– Oh, one other thing. According to the captain of this ship I'm on, there's not much leaving the Island right now – something to do with the provincial office chartering anything that'll float; I'm so behind with the news that I've probably got that all mixed up – so if by any chance you happen to know of any ships sailing to the Island from the Mesoge and back again, could you possibly ask the captain to look me up and take me back with him? I don't quite know yet where I'll be staying; I don't know anybody on the Island, so I expect it'll be an inn somewhere –

(The right degree of pathos there, or should she stress it a little more? No; being obvious would most likely prove counterproductive.)

When she'd finished writing the letter, she sealed it up with a drop of the rather splendid blue sealing-wax in the writing set – she was just about to press down on the little cornelian seal when it occurred to her that Uncle Gorgas might just conceivably know the man she'd stolen it from, and that could cause problems; so she marked a big L for Loredan with her thumbnail instead – and took it to Captain Yelet, who made a great point of putting it away safely in his own document case, neatly curled up in a smart brass tube. Apparently the captain had formed the impression that she was the daughter of some prosperous Island family, sent abroad on her first errand, who'd made a mess of things and missed her boat, so that helping her out would quite probably pay dividends in the future. She hadn't said anything to him herself; so presumably it was the chain-mail blouse and daintily embossed hardened leather cuisses of the warrior-princess look that misled him.

CHAPTER TWELVE

'It only goes to prove what I've always maintained about us,' said Eseutz Mesatges, watching the tenders loading up beside the City Wharf. 'We aren't really businessmen, we're romantics. We play at commerce because it's fun, the same way other countries play at war. We aren't in business to make money; it's just an excuse for a good time and exciting adventures.'

'Now that's not—'

'Ignore her, Ven, she's just being perverse,' Athli interrupted, before Venart Auzeil could reply. 'Aren't you, dear?'

'Certainly not.' Eseutz perched on the edge of a large bale of Ap' Imaz wool and rested her elbows on her knees. 'I meant every word of it. If we really cared about money, we'd be sad right now, because it means this wonderful deal is drawing to a close; but I can feel the waves of relief wafting over from you lot like cooking-smells on a hot afternoon. You were bored just sitting still and taking the prefect's money for nothing. Now something's happening, you're all looking forward to watching a cracking good war, then getting your ships back so you can get off this poxy little island and out into the big wide world again. Admit it,' she said with a grin, 'I'm right. Probably,' she added, 'sheer force of habit.'

'Yes, Eseutz,' Athli said severely, 'anything you say.' But she had to admit, there was a certain degree of truth in what Eseutz had just said. As a non-Islander she could see it; they, of course, couldn't, as was only to be expected.

City Wharf derived its name from the traffic it had been built to serve, the regular exchange of goods between the Island and Perimadeia. When the wharf was built, there hadn't been any need to specify which city, just as when you talked about the sky, you didn't have to identify which sky you were

257

referring to. Since the Fall (on the Island, the word Fall was
equally unambiguous), business on the Wharf had dropped
by over a third. Only Colleon freighters called there now; the
Islanders' ships sailing for Shastel, the Empire and the west
started their journeys from the Sea Dock or the Drutz. It was
like old times, people were saying, to see the Wharf crowded
again; a sign of things to come, they added hopefully,
as and when the provincial office rebuilt Perimadeia and
reopened her countless factories and workshops.

'It's about time they dug out the Cut,' said Venart, who'd
been following this line of thought. 'Ever since the Fall it's
been silting up. If people are going to start using the Wharf
again—'

Athli smiled. 'Rather a big if, don't you think?' she said.
'The fleet hasn't even sailed yet, and already you're dreaming
about new business opportunities.'

'You're putting words in my mouth,' Venart replied grump-
ily. 'I'm just saying, the Cut needs some work doing on it, and
the longer we leave it, the worse it'll get.'

The Cut had been a thing of wonder in its day, a canal
dug across the Island from the Wharf to the Drutz in a dead
straight line, right through the low hills just above Town and
(thanks to the team of Perimadeian engineers who'd built the
thing two hundred years earlier) under the White Mountain
by way of a mile-long tunnel chipped out of solid rock.
Compared to the Cut, the small man-made harbour on the
other side was a fairly ordinary achievement; but it was
the harbour that bore the name of Renvaut Drutz, the chief
engineer, not the canal that was undoubtedly his greatest
achievement, both in terms of magnitude and utility. That
was the Island for you.

'Well,' said Vetriz Auzeil, who'd been sitting quietly in the
shade of her small painted parasol, 'I agree with Eseutz; at
least, I think I do. The sooner they've had their blasted war
and we get our ships back again, the sooner Ven can get back
to work and I can have a little peace around the house.
He's been insufferable these past weeks with nothing to do.
The day before yesterday, he spent three hours making a
written inventory of the linen-closet—'

'Only because you never—'

Vetriz ignored him. 'You should have seen him, it was

comical. "Item, one sheet, worn, sewn sides to middle, white, discoloured. Item—'"

Eseutz giggled. Athli smiled and said, 'How very practical of you, Ven. Now if ever there's a fire, you'll have a record for the insurance.'

'No, he won't,' Vetriz objected. 'When he'd finished it he put it in the document cupboard in the counting house. It'll get burned to a crisp along with everything else.'

'My mother used to do that,' Eseutz said. 'Patch up old sheets, I mean. By the time she died, pretty well every scrap of cloth in the house had been mended so many times it was more twine than cloth. The whole lot ended up going to the paper mill. And it wasn't that we couldn't afford to buy new; she was just compulsive—'

'Just as you are,' Athli observed, 'only the other way round. All the times I've been to your house, I'll swear I've never seen the same wall-hangings twice.'

'That's business,' Eseutz retorted. 'Stock in trade. Anything I haven't got room for in the warehouse I hang on the wall. Then when people come by and say, *My dear, where did you get those divine hangings?* I make a sale.'

The tenders were the traditional Island pattern, not found anywhere else; long, clinker-built barges with impractically high keels that served no known function and added days to the time it took to build one. From the front, they looked for all the world like a black swan landing on the water. Now they rode low in the water, wallowing under the weight of the bales of supplies and provisions that were appearing as if by magic from the lofts and doorways of the warehouses that faced the Wharf. The warehouses were probably the most beautiful and imposing buildings on the Island; built in imitation of a hundred different architectural styles from a hundred different places, no two of them were the same. Merchants who were happy to live in small, cramped apartments and drafty attics behind inconspicuous doors in the ramshackle streets and alleyways of Town had spent fortunes on decorating the façades and metopes of their warehouses, arguing that they spent more time there than they did at home and met their customers there. The Great House of the Semplan family was seven storeys high, had solid brass doors twelve feet tall and three inches thick, and was faced with Colleon marble decorated with bas-reliefs depicting ancient sea battles; a hundred years ago, every detail of the sculptures had been carefully picked out in red, blue and gold paint, which the salt sea air stripped away within a matter of a few months. Nobody had the faintest idea whose the ships were, or what battle was recorded; Mehaut Semplan had taken them in settlement of a bad debt from a customer in the City, and spent as much as she'd originally lost on the deal getting them home and putting them up. The Semplan House, in the lower end of South Town, was hidden away behind a bonemeal store.

'Where did all this stuff come from?' Venart asked. 'Presumably they bought it from us, but I don't recognise any of it.'

'Wretched, isn't it?' Eseutz agreed. 'If you look closely, you'll see provincial office batch numbers and store tallies stencilled all over everything. It's all stuff from abroad; they've been taking delivery here and storing it for free in our warehouses, and now they're sending it home on our ships. They don't need us for anything.'

Athli grinned. 'They may have been using your warehouse for free,' she said. 'But that's your fault for not paying attention. You were too busy daydreaming about what you were going to do when you got your ship back.'

Eseutz scowled, then relaxed again. 'Oh, well,' she said. 'But I still say they've got a nerve, doing their buying and selling and storing here as if they owned the place, while we've been sitting on our hands all this time with nothing to do. It makes one feel useless, somehow. I'll be glad when this is all over and they've gone home, and the hell with the money.'

'I'm with you there,' Venart said. 'To be honest with you, they give me the creeps. Anybody who's so cold-blooded about starting a war—'

'Best way to be, surely,' Athli said, expressionless. 'Most efficient, anyway; make your preparations early, be sure you've got all your supplies and equipment in hand before you start, think out your plan of campaign well in advance. Look how well it worked for Temrai, after all. Don't suppose I'd be here now if he'd just blundered up to the City gates and waited for someone to let him in.'

Understandably enough, there was an awkward silence.

When it was starting to get embarrassing, Eseutz smiled brightly and said, 'While I think of it, Athli, have you reached a decision about going into the armour business? I know you were thinking about it a while back.'

Athli sighed. 'Not going into it myself,' she said. 'Just investing in someone else's concern. And yes, it all checked out. Gods know, there's enough demand for the stuff.'

Venart frowned. 'I wouldn't if I were you,' he said. 'As soon as this war's over the market's going to be flooded with war surplus and loot; it always is, after a war. I remember a few years back after the Scona thing – and that was only a little war, mind – there was so much looted and stripped chain-mail floating about, you couldn't give it away. And halberds – they were cutting them down for bill-hooks or selling them by weight for scrap. And as for arrows—'

'Ah,' Athli interrupted, bright red in the face, 'but that was different. The Empire's going to win this war, and they never sell off equipment, they just put it into store. And once they've won and got control of the City – sorry, the place where the City used to be – everybody west of the straits is going to start wondering who'll be next, and there'll be a demand for armour and weapons like you can't imagine; not that it'll do them any good, but that's none of my business. Next to shipbuilding, armour's the best possible area to invest in at the moment.'

Venart lifted his head slightly. 'Shipbuilding?' he said.

'That's right,' Athli replied, looking out over the Wharf. 'For when they realise the armour won't help and they start evacuating.'

Dassascai the spy (so called to distinguish him from another man with the same name who repaired tents) sat beside his fire next to the duck pen and sharpened a knife. It had a long, thin blade with a clipped back, the sort used for cutting meat off the bone. He'd finished with the oilstone and the water-stone and was stropping it slowly on the untanned side of a leather belt.

He was possibly the only man sitting still in the whole camp; Temrai had decided to move the clans south-east, towards the Imperial army approaching from the direction of Ap' Escatoy. After nearly seven years in one place, the plainsmen were moving stiffly, like someone getting up in the morning after too little sleep.

Half the workforce had left at first light to begin the awkward job of rounding up the herd. After seven years of continual grazing, there was barely a blade of grass left in the immediate vicinity of the camp. Instead of being close at hand, therefore, as it always used to be in the old wandering days, the herd was split up and scattered across thousands of acres of the eastern plain. Many of the boys riding with the herding party had never seen a full-scale roundup and weren't quite sure what to do; for the most part, they were sensibly treating the whole thing as an adventure, and their enthusiasm was enough to stop the men from thinking too hard about the implications of Temrai's decision. Each rider had his goatskin provisions bag over his shoulder, a bow and quiver on either side of his saddle, his coat and blanket rolled up and stowed behind the crupper. A few of the men wore helmets and mailshirts, or carried them wrapped in waxed cloth covers or wicker panniers; nobody knew for certain where the enemy might suddenly appear – they'd already taken on many of the attributes of fairy-tale sprites and demons, who lurk in dark woods and pounce unexpectedly from the shadow of tall rocks.

The other half of the clan were busy breaking the camp; uprooting tent-poles, folding felts and carpets, trying to stow seven years' worth of sedentary life into panniers and travoises designed to hold only the essentials. Many people were discarding the wondrous but useless treasures they'd looted from the sack of the City – up and down the rapidly vanishing streets of the camp there were bronze tripods and ivory tables, huge bronze cooking-pots, an incongruous assortment of bits of bronze and marble statue (a head here, an arm or a colossal booted foot there; not a single complete piece anywhere, so that the camp field looked like the aftermath of a battle between two tribes of giants). Wherever possible, they were dismantling the machines and tools they'd built over the years, sawbenches and lathes and water-powered grindstones, trebuchets and mangonels, presses and winches and treadmills and watermills, dismembered like carcasses in a butcher's store and loaded on to flat-bed carts, but far too much would have to be left behind, either for lack of transport or for sheer size and weight. The enormous butter-churn, for example, that Temrai himself had helped design and build, was set in brick foundations to keep it from toppling over. They had already stripped the giant looms and dismantled the shed they'd stood in for the lumber; now the frames stuck up from the ground like the bones of dead men buried in thin soil, while women cut up the huge carpets that had been woven on them into small, practical squares. They'd tried to salvage the fish-weirs, but most of the main timbers were already too badly rotted to be worth taking; and on the high bank where they'd built permanent butts for archery practice, the great round woven-straw target-bosses lay on their faces, too big to carry, their frames broken up and used to make improvised rails for the carts. Already, the camp looked as if it had been overrun by an enemy; on all sides lay spoil and waste, disregarded wealth and broken equipment, while the banked-up fires where they'd burned off the surplus hay and provender added an evocative stench of smoke.

'You're not going, then,' someone said, as Dassascai flicked his blade backwards and forwards across the strop.

'Of course I'm going,' Dassascai replied. 'But my stuff won't take long to get ready. No point rushing to pack everything away and then sitting on my hands for a couple of days waiting for the rest of you.'

'Won't be a couple of days, if Temrai's got anything to do with it,' the man replied. 'We're out of here at dawn tomorrow; anybody and anything that isn't ready, stays.'

Dassascai smiled. 'We'll see,' he said. 'I think he's forgotten exactly what's involved in moving this camp. It's not like we've only been here a week; you can't just bundle seven years in a bag and sling it over your shoulder.'

'That's what he said,' the man answered. 'You want to take the matter up with him, you go ahead.'

'No need,' Dassascai said. 'All I've got to do is fold the tent, catch up the ducks and I'm ready to go. You get practice moving on at a moment's notice when you're a refugee.'

The man grinned. 'I'm sure,' he said. 'Here, is it true what they say? About you being a spy?'

Dassascai inclined his head. 'Of course,' he said. 'Pulling feathers off ducks is just a hobby.'

The man frowned, then shrugged. 'Ah, well,' he said. 'If you really are a spy, stands to reason you wouldn't admit it.'

'Do you think I'm a spy?' Dassascai asked.

'Me?' The man thought for a moment. 'Well, people say you are.'

'I see. So who am I spying for? The provincial office? Bardas Loredan? The Bad Tooth pixies?'

'How should I know?' the man replied, irritated. 'Anyway, whoever it is, won't do them any good. Temrai'll keep one step ahead, just you see.'

'So I should hope, if he's supposed to be leading the way.'

When the man had gone, Dassascai carefully wrapped the knife in an oiled cloth and put it away in his satchel. Then he pulled out a little brass tube, tapped the roll of paper out of it and spread it over his knee. There was nothing written on it. Having first looked about him to make sure nobody was paying him any attention, he reached down and fished a thin piece of charred wood out of the dead edge of the fire. He tested it on a corner of the paper. It wrote well.

He didn't start off with the name of the person he was writing to; only one person would ever see it, and that person didn't need to be told his own name. Instead, he wrote, *For gods' sakes, tell me what you want me to do*, rolled the paper up again and stuffed it into the tube. Then he reached into the duck pen, pulled out a large, fat drake and broke its neck by gripping it just below the head and whirling the body round fast, like a man with a slingshot. When it was dead he picked a little folding knife out of his sash, opened it and slit the duck from just under the ribs down to the vent. With a sharp turn of his wrist, almost gracefully easy from long practice, he flicked the stomach and intestines out through the slit, slipped the message tube in their place, and quickly stitched the slit up with horsehair and a steel needle that lived buried in the fabric of his coat collar. That done, he walked away from the camp towards the mouth of the river, where a single ship was tied up to the remains of the old Perimadeia wharf. He was just in time to intercept the two people he wanted to see.

'Excuse me,' he said.

Gannadius looked up. 'Yes?'

'Sorry to trouble you,' Dassascai said, 'but I need to send

someone a duck. Would you be kind enough to take it to the Island for me?'

Gannadius looked at him. 'You're sending somebody a duck?'

'That's right.'

'Alive or dead?'

'Oh, dead.'

Gannadius frowned. 'But that's silly. You can buy a duck from any poulterer's stall.'

'Not like this duck you can't. It's a sample. Special order.' He smiled. 'Got the delivery instructions today. If he likes the sample, he'll take them a thousand at a time. You'd be doing me a real favour.' Dassascai smiled pleasantly and pulled the duck out from inside his shirt. 'See?' he said. 'Now admit it, that's a real honey of a duck.'

'I suppose so,' Gannadius said doubtfully. 'But won't it have gone - well, you know, bad?'

Dassascai shook his head. 'Don't you believe it,' he said. 'Four days is just about perfect to bring out the flavour. My friend'll see you right for your trouble, if that's what you're worried about.'

'Oh, no, that's all right,' Gannadius replied quickly. It was a matter of honour with Islanders that they always carried and delivered letters if they possibly could; an essential ethic for a commercial nation. Expecting a reward for doing so was considered extremely bad form, like asking a drowning man for cash in advance before rescuing him. 'It's just - well, all right.'

'Thanks,' Dassascai said, beaming. 'That's a great weight off my mind. I've been trying to close this deal for ages, but there've been so few ships going your way I was worried sick my man'd lose interest and the whole thing would fall through.'

He handed Gannadius the duck, head upright. Gannadius looked at it with faint disgust. 'No offence,' he said, 'but it looks just like an ordinary duck to me.'

Dassascai nodded. 'Exactly. But it's a *cheap* duck. They're the rarest and most sought-after variety there is.'

'Fair enough,' Gannadius replied dubiously. 'But wouldn't it be better to send him a live one? Then he could kill it himself and there'd be no risk of it going bad.'

'Ah.' Dassascai furrowed his brow and grinned. 'And suppose somebody else gets hold of it and starts breeding from it; that'd be the end of my business opportunity, for sure. If you knew ducks, you'd realise what you've got there.'

'If you say so,' Gannadius said, wishing he hadn't got involved in the first place. 'All right, who's it to go to?'

'I've written it down,' Dassascai answered. 'Don't look so surprised,' he added with a smile. 'Some of us can read and write, you know.'

'Of course. I didn't mean to imply—'

'That's all right then.' Dassascai pushed a little scrap of parchment into his hand and curled his fingers over it, squeezing so hard that Gannadius flinched. 'I really appreciate this,' he said. 'Something like this could be good news for both our countries.'

Nation shall send ducks unto nation, Gannadius thought. 'Splendid,' he said. 'Well, I'd better be getting on board; I don't want to miss the boat.'

'What was all that about?' Theudas asked as his uncle joined him on deck. Theudas had reserved a place for them both among the coils of anchor-rope at the stern. 'And what are you carrying a dead duck around for?'

'Don't ask,' Gannadius replied. 'I'm delivering it. Apparently it marks the dawn of a new era.'

'Really? By the time we get there it's going to smell awful.'

Gannadius dropped the duck into the hollow middle of a pile of rope and dumped his satchel down on top of it. 'Nonsense,' he said. 'Four days old is the prime of life for a dead duck. Well, prime of death. Whatever. Stop looking at me like that, will you? It's just a perfectly ordinary commercial sample. If it was a bit of carpet or a bag of nails, you wouldn't think twice about it.'

Theudas sighed and squatted down on top of the rope. 'All right,' he said. 'Only this strikes me as a funny time to be sending trade samples from here to the Island, what with this war and striking camp and everything. You'd think they'd have other things on their minds.'

'Apparently not.' Gannadius leaned his back against the rail. He knew he was going to be seasick sooner or later, so being as close to the side as possible was a necessary precaution. 'Nothing wrong with optimism,' he continued, provided nobody expects *me* to invest money in it. It's almost uplifting in a way, this faith in the future of his people.'

Theudas shook his head. 'Either your man's as mad as a hare,' he said, 'or they're playing a funny joke on you. Either way, if I were you I'd chuck the thing over the side now, before it stinks the whole ship out and *we're* the ones who get put over the side.'

'Don't be such a misery,' Gannadius told him. 'We're finally getting out of here, aren't we? I'd gladly festoon myself from head to foot with putrescent ducks if it meant getting away from here and back to civilisation. Not,' he added, 'that it was anything like I expected – well, for one thing we're still alive, which is considerably more than I expected when we were squelching about in that foul muddy swamp, being chased by the provincial office. Actually, they've been extremely decent to us, according to their lights. Lugging about the odd dead waterfowl is probably the least we can do in return.'

'Decent?' Theudas looked at him with disgust. 'You really don't care any more, do you?'

Gannadius was silent for a long time. 'You know,' he said, 'I'm not sure that I do. Probably it's because I wasn't actually there – for the Fall, I mean; I didn't see the same things you did. Oh, I know what I've been told; I believe it too, in a way. But all that happened to me, personally, was that I moved from the City to the Island, then from the Island to Shastel – where I've got a good job, people treat me with respect, and damn it, yes, I'm happy. I thought seeing all this again –' He waved his arm in the direction of the ruined City, without turning his head '– would make it all different, make me start hating them again. But it didn't, somehow. When I look at them now, all I can see is a bunch of people who are so worried by the threat of being invaded that they're packing up their lives in barrels and sacks and moving on. Exactly what I did. Somehow, I can't hate people who're so like me.'

Theudas smiled grimly. 'I can,' he said.

'Yes, but you're young and full of energy.' Gannadius shifted slightly; his back was getting uncomfortable, pressed against the rail. 'When you get to my age, you'll find it's fatally easy to forget to hate all your enemies all the time; and once you've slipped up and not hated one of them, it makes it almost impossibly hard to hate the rest of them.

You allow yourself to start thinking things like, *The ordinary people are all right, it's their leaders who're responsible for all the evil stuff they do*; and then one day you meet one of their leaders and he turns out to be almost human, and that's a cruel blow, like a broken finger would be to someone who plays the harp for a living.' He shifted his back again. 'It was odd seeing Temrai,' he said. 'Reminded me of once when I was young and I saw a shark that had got itself caught up in some mackerel-fishers' nets; they had it strung up by its tail, all stiff and dead, and they were cutting it up. It looked a whole lot smaller than I expected it to be.'

Theudas closed his eyes. 'Odd you should say that,' he said. 'I thought the same thing, seeing him again. Of course, when you see someone when you're a kid and again when you've grown up, that's often the way. Still, I wouldn't mind seeing Temrai strung up. I think I could get to like him hanging by his feet.'

'Your privilege,' Gannadius replied, muffling a yawn. 'I never said you should stop hating him; after all, you've got cause. All I'm saying is, I'm not so sure as I was that I have.'

'You could hate him for my sake. Isn't that what we're taught, love your friends' friends and hate their enemies?'

'Oh, all right,' Gannadius said. 'For your sake I hate him and I hope his pet lizard dies.'

(*A curse*, Gannadius realised; *I'm laying a curse on someone I don't hate for the sake of someone young and soaked through with the lust for revenge. That's what Alexius did once, and look what happened. Gods, I hope this headache I'm getting is just a headache* –

– And he saw behind his eyes the shark, the fat and flesh flayed away from the framework of its bones, like the frames of a ship before they start planking up the sides. A fine feast they were preparing, these cooks he could see; shark and bear steaks, and eagles cooked whole on spits like chickens, slowly turning in front of the heat of the fire, wolves roasted and stuffed with apple and chestnut, great snakes gutted and made into the skins of blood sausages, a flitch of smoked lion hanging from a hook in the ceiling, a whole dinner of predators – he could see them laying strips of tenderloin of leopard in the bottom of the pie-dish, and bottling giant Colleon spiders like fat plums –)

'What do you mean?' Theudas said. 'Temrai hasn't got a pet lizard.'

'You see?' Gannadius replied. 'It's starting to work already.'

Bardas Loredan was sure he'd watched the arrow all the way, from the moment it appeared as a tiny speck in the sky until it actually hit him; an unbearably long time, but not long enough for him to move a foot to his right and get out of its way, although he did his best. Curious, he thought, at the moment of impact, how time can work like that. It's enough to make a man believe in the Principle.

When the shock of the arrow on the cheekpiece of his helmet pushed his head round – it was like being slapped hard across the face – he was sure he must have died (*it's customary to die first*) but apparently he'd made a mistake (*in your case we'll make an exception*). Instead, he could feel a sharp pain in his temples; and if he understood the rules correctly, the dead are excused pain, as a sort of consolation prize. As he turned his head back again, he was aware of the jagged edges of the small hole the arrow had punched in the steel slicing painlessly along the line of his jaw to the edge of his lip, and the hot trickle of blood inside the padded helmet, quite remarkably like the warm, wet feel of piss running down his leg when he was a little boy. Delayed shock; he staggered briefly, found his feet and stood up straight again.

They'd attacked without warning; a distant hiss, like oil in a hot frying pan, and a quite lovely pattern of arrows rising against the noon sun, like a large flock of doves put up off a stubble field. It had taken him a few moments to work out where the arrows were coming from – a fold of dead ground between the column and the opposite ridge of the valley. This was advanced archery, shooting extreme-range volleys at a target they couldn't even see, something the provincial office's auxiliary bowmen didn't have the skill or the confidence to do. For the rest of the column it had been terrifying, heartstopping, this business of being killed by an enemy you hadn't even seen. In Bardas' case, it only made him slightly nostalgic for the mines.

He looked around for Estar but couldn't see him. Nobody seemed to be giving orders, and the patient, disciplined ranks of Imperial infantry were standing still, like carthorses in heavy rain. *Damn*, Bardas thought. He stepped forward out of line and started shouting military stuff like *Left wheel* and *Dress to your front*, the sort of thing he'd learned in Maxen's army and thought he'd forgotten. The Imperials weren't like Maxen's men, though; they were a joy to drill, smart and precise, men who didn't just obey the words of command but actually believed in them, as if they were the holy words of some religion. It was unnerving, this total and unthinking obedience, with all its connotations of responsibility and trust. *Don't say I'm getting involved again*, Bardas thought resentfully; but unless somebody got these men out of the line of fire, there would be avoidable deaths and injuries; Estar nowhere to be seen, the other officers standing by as faithfully as the men. The blood had reached his collar-bone; the lapel of his habergeon was soaking it up like a sponge, and the sharp edges were cutting more deep, thin slices, precise as the leaf-thin blades of the cooks' knives as they dressed out the sheep. *Almost proof, but not quite; a small puncture hole on the outside, a series of bloody gashes within.*

He'd brought the army out of column into line, and gave the order to advance. For this sort of situation the Imperial writers on the art of war recommended a manoeuvre they called the 'hammer and anvil': invite the enemy to concentrate their fire on an apparently suicidal infantry advance, the main body of the army apparently walking directly into the hail of arrows (but that's what armour's for) while wings of cavalry and light infantry hook round the back and drive the enemy headlong on to the men-at-arms' pikes. It was a sound enough tactic provided you could rely on your cavalry officers to do their job. Bardas had seen them move off as soon as he started to turn the line, riding away from the enemy before describing a wide arc and appearing unexpectedly behind them. On this ground they'd have to ride all the way round to the other side of the far ridge if they wanted to stay out of sight. It'd be a long time before they were in position, which meant the armoured infantry were going to have to stay out in the rain getting soaked. It was a wager, the lives of thousands of men riding on a bet, their archers against our armourers. *Welcome back to the proof house, Bardas Loredan; we knew you wouldn't be able to stay away.*

What the hell had become of Colonel Estar? Common sense suggested that he'd gone down in the first volley of arrows, though Bardas hadn't seen him fall. It was inconceivable that he'd run away. He was, after all, a Son of Heaven, and even Bardas Loredan needed to believe in something. If Estar was dead – things like that don't happen, commanders-in-chief of mighty armies don't die in the first volley of the first battle they fight in. But if he was dead (and Maxen died, remember) command of the army would pass to Sergeant Loredan, until such time as another Son of Heaven arrived from Ap' Escatoy. The thought made Bardas shudder.

Here was an interesting problem, an examination question in the art of command. To reach the enemy they were having to march down a steep slope. It was essential that they keep in line; but the sheer weight of the armour on which everything depended was making them tend to hurry, almost to the point of breaking into a run. Bardas was having to drive his heels into the dry, crumbling turf just to keep his balance. In his mind he could clearly see the ludicrous image of an army in full plate tobogganing down the slope on their backsides, skidding and crashing into each other, tumbling head over heels into a tangled heap of steel and flesh – that was just the sort of thing that happened in a war, it was the way disasters came about and wars were lost. In a moment of great clarity he could see it, as if it had already happened; a mighty trash-heap, like the pile of pieces that had failed proof (men as well as armour that had failed proof; welcome home), with the plainsmen standing on the top of the little rise shooting at will into the mess and laughing so hard they could scarcely draw their bows. The image was so strong that it was almost impossible for him to distinguish between it and what he could actually see. He shouted back to his officers, invisible behind him, to keep the line, to slow down the advance – well, anybody could say the words, but turning the words into action, making the words come true, was a job for a real commander; he could only hope that there were a few of those in the ranks behind him. The arrows weren't helping, either; they were on the skyline now, shooting down at almost their maximum reverse elevation; the arrows were

271

glancing off the artfully angled surfaces of the plate and skidding away in all directions, smacking sideways into the faces and bodies of the fourth and fifth ranks. There was nothing to be done about them, they had to be ignored, as if they were horseflies on a hot day. The one thing the line couldn't do now was stop and go back; if they tried that, they'd be tumbling down the slope in no time.

There was nothing for it but to trot the last few yards. A few men did go down, and each man that fell took two or three with him, with a thump and a crash like an accident in a smithy. No time to see to the fallen, they'd have to sort themselves out if they were still capable of doing so; there were living men pinned down under dead men, he knew, like miners trapped by a cave-in, and there they'd have to wait, depending on the general, on Sergeant Loredan, to win the battle and survive; otherwise they'd stay there till they died, or until the scrap-metal people came with their sharp knives to collect the spoil and skin the carcasses. Never should have let command fall into the hands of an outlander. Obvious recipe for disaster. He could hear them saying it now.

They'd managed to get down the slope; now came the tricky part. They didn't have far to climb, but the gradient was steep and there were enemy soldiers at the top of it. *This isn't on; if I'd wanted to work this hard I could have stayed on the bloody farm.* It was worse than carrying the grain-sacks up the ladder to the loft, or manhandling heavy timbers up scaffolding. With every step he was sure his knees would burst or the muscle would break out through the back of his calf; he could feel his muscles taking damage (*this isn't very clever, Bardas, you'll do yourself an injury*) and the thought of having to fight someone if he did manage to scramble up to the top was enough to make him laugh out loud. If they wanted to fight him, they'd have to help him up the last few yards, as if he was an old man, getting tottery on his pins.

The sound the arrows made as they deflected off the plate was extraordinary, a whistling scream of frustration. Not that all of them were being turned; because they were being shot at from above, the angles were all wrong, there were flat spots where an arrow could strike fair and square. Every man shot took two or three more with him as he toppled backwards and rolled down the hill (if the enemy had any

sense they'd be rolling rocks and logs) and that wasn't helping either. The pace had slowed right down, it was as if
time had stopped (the arrow coming towards him) and
there was still nothing he could do except force himself to
climb another step, then another. Just breathing was next
to impossible now. This is how battles are lost, this is how
disasters happen; the trash-heap, the pile of parts that failed
proof.

He was staring directly at a pair of boots. They were
old boots, scuffed, one toe mended. *I had a pair of boots like
that once*, he thought; and just as he remembered the dead
man he'd taken them from after a battle on the plains, the
owner of the boots kicked him in the forehead. That was
a mistake, too; boots not sturdy enough to go kicking steel
with. In spite of everything, Bardas couldn't help grinning –
no breath to laugh with, can only grin – as he heard the
howl of pain. Then (he could still only see as far as the man's
knees) he lunged upwards with his pike, the bloody heavy
piece of kit he'd lugged all this way and might as well use,
and cut the howling short.

*Fighting. Well, we know where we are with that. At least it's
something I know how to do.* Following up the slight momentum of the thrust he hauled himself the last step or so on to
the crest of the rise, managing to step over the dead man
who'd pulled the pike out of his hands with his stomach. As
he lurched forward someone hit him across the shoulders
(wasting his strength, trying to bash on the junction of
pauldrons, backplate, gorget) but Bardas didn't have the time
or the energy to deal with him; he walked past as if ignoring
a drunk in the street, and his whole body heaved as he drew
in a breath – it caught in his throat, it was like trying to
swallow a whole apple. Some fool was bouncing an axe off
the top of his helmet; that one didn't last long – all Bardas
had to do was lift his arm and let it fall in its own weight,
allow the mass of vambrace, cop, pauldron and gauntlet to
force the sword blade down through bone and flesh, the
armour doing all the work, the man inside having little to
do with it. *It's happened*, Bardas thought, as he wrenched
his sword free from the severed collar-bone, *the armour's
grown round me and sealed me in, like the rings of a tree; only
the outside, the steel part of me, is alive.*

They tried various tests – swords, spears, axes, even big stones and heavy clubs, but they couldn't make the armour fail proof. They weren't in the same league as Bollo and his big hammer when it came to crushing and bashing sheet metal. Their flesh and bone, on the other hand, was no good at all; the whole batch failed to pass, apart from a few pieces that were withdrawn from the test at the last moment. When the session was over, there was the big trash-heap he'd been seeing all along, the pile of arms and legs and heads and trunks and feet and hands that hadn't succeeded in passing proof. Little wonder, now that he saw them close to; they were made of some material other than steel, which was crazy.

When the cavalry finally deigned to show up there was nothing left for them to do. It was clear they weren't pleased about it, or about finding that they were now under the command of an outlander infantry sergeant. Their captain turned out to be a Perimadeian by the name of Olethrias Saravin. Bardas tried to turn over command to him, but to no avail. 'Not bloody likely,' Saravin said. 'You made a hash of it the last time you fought these people, now's your chance to put things right.' There didn't seem to be any point arguing with him, so Bardas let the matter drop and ordered him to take out three companies and scout ahead, this time (if at all possible) keeping an eye out for any substantial numbers of enemy archers that might be roaming about the place. Saravin galloped off with a very bad grace, and Bardas gave the order to pitch camp for the night.

They found Estar's body and brought it to him. There wasn't a mark on it, apart from a few footprints. By the looks of it he'd fallen off his horse and given himself a heart attack trying to get back up again, unassisted, in full armour.

'We could try the Honour and Glory, I suppose,' Eseutz Mesatges suggested. 'Shouldn't be too crowded at this time of day, and they do a passable fish soup.'

Vetriz nodded. She wasn't particularly bothered where they sat down so long as they sat down; she'd made the mistake of wearing her new sandals (hard leather straps and two-inch heels, as required for the nomad-caravan look) before breaking them in properly, and the straps were cutting into her like a bowsaw.

The fish soup turned out to be mediocre, not helped by the fact that the cooks had left the mussels and oysters in their shells –

'Which is supposed to denote freshness and back-to-essentials simplicity,' Eseutz commented, ducking a floating mussel under the surface of her soup and watching it bob up again, 'but as far as I'm concerned it means the cook thinks scraping shellfish out of their armour is a rotten job – a view I wholeheartedly share, let me tell you. The really sordid part is, you end up with a great big trash-heap of bits of discarded shell on the edge of your plate, which really isn't the sort of thing you want to be looking at while you're eating.'

Vetriz smiled distractedly; she had something of a headache, and she wasn't really in the mood for Eseutz Mesatges. 'Leave them, then,' she said. 'Just eat the soup.'

'What, and waste stuff I've paid good money for? Not likely.' Eseutz grimaced and ripped apart a mussel. 'Worst of all is those little pink beetle-things, all curled up in a ball like a dead woodlouse. I defy anybody to prise one of those things open without a crowbar and a big hammer.'

Somebody Vetriz thought she knew had just walked in; she caught sight of the back of a bald head, a pair of broad shoulders. 'You know,' she said, 'I'm really not hungry. I think I'll go home now.'

'Oh, don't be silly,' Eseutz said. 'Look, if you really don't like the fish soup, we'll order something else. What about the curried mutton?'

'Really,' Vetriz said, rather more loudly than she'd intended to, 'I'm not hungry.'

Several people looked round, including the man with the bald head and the broad shoulders. He looked at her for a moment, grinned, and walked away towards the table under the window. Vetriz sat back in her chair, feeling rather sick.

'It's not the fish soup, is it?' Eseutz said.

'No,' Vetriz replied. 'It's not the fish soup.'

Eseutz studied the retreating back for a moment. 'It's none of my business, right?'

'You're right,' Vetriz said. 'It's none of your business.'

'Fair enough. If you're really not hungry, do you mind if I pinch your bread?'

Gorgas Loredan stopped and looked round until he saw what he was looking for. No mistaking those thin, hunched shoulders. He stepped up close and put his arm round them.

Iseutz Loredan squirmed like a fish, then saw who it was and relaxed a little, though not completely. 'Uncle Gorgas,' she said.

'I got your letter,' he said, straddling the bench and sitting down beside her. He looked too big in such an ordinary place. 'In fact, it reached me just as I was setting off for a meeting here. So naturally, I thought I'd offer you a lift.'

Iseutz smiled at him. 'That's wonderful,' she said. 'Thank you.'

'My pleasure,' he replied. 'Really, I ought to have invited you over long before this, but I wasn't sure how things stand with your mother and me. That soup looks good.'

'You have it, then,' Iseutz said. 'It's disgusting.'

Gorgas shrugged. 'By the way,' he said, 'is it true you nearly killed that soldier? Left-handed, too. You really do have a gift for this swordfighting stuff, don't you?'

'Must run in the family,' she said, expressionless. 'So you know all about that, do you?'

'Mphm.' Gorgas had his mouth full of soup. He opened his lips and fished out two mussel shells, which he dropped on to the table. 'Dirty trick, if you ask me. You see, I've got something they want, but they don't want to pay my price – stupid if you ask me, because they really need what I've got and what I want will cost them nothing, but there you are. I imagine you and your mother were going to be their counter-offer. It's a sad thing when you can't try to do business with people like the provincial office without having your family kidnapped and held to ransom. If it wasn't for the fact that they've still got your mother, I'd scrub round the whole deal and let them go to hell.' He picked up the soup-plate and tipped the rest of the soup into his mouth.

'I know about the deal,' Iseutz said. 'I wasn't sure we'd be worth that much to you.'

Gorgas frowned. He chewed for a moment, making a loud

crunching noise, then swallowed. 'Don't be ridiculous,' he said, 'you're family. Nothing's more important than family. But I got the better of them in the end – or I thought I did. I gave them the Mesoge.'

Iseutz opened her eyes wide. 'You did what?'

'I handed it over to them, free, gratis and for nothing.' He grinned. 'The look on that oily bastard of an envoy's face – well, he looked just like you look now, like he'd swallowed a doughnut and found it was a hedgehog. On reflection,' he added, 'it may be that they tried to grab you as security for the deal, in case I changed my mind. Anyway, whatever they did it for, it isn't on. If they want their damned pirate they'll have to give me Niessa *and* what I originally asked for. In fact,' he added, frowning a little, 'you've just given me an idea. This trip might turn out to be more useful than I'd thought.'

Iseutz smiled. 'Glad to have inspired you,' she said. 'Look, I don't want to rush you or anything, but is this business of yours going to take awfully long, because I'd really like to be on my way as soon as possible. I'm sure all these soldiers have much more important things on their minds than stray prisoners, but they make me nervous.'

Gorgas nodded. 'You'd be surprised,' he said. 'If there's one thing the provincial office truly despises, it's losing a prisoner. No, you're right to be worried. The best thing would be to get you safely on board my ship and off this island. I'll tell them to come back for me.'

'Are you sure? I don't want to be a nuisance or anything.'

Gorgas looked at her. 'There's no need to overdo it,' he said. 'Come on, you can be straight with me, I'm your uncle. I'm the one you spat at when you were in that prison on Scona. That's why we get on so well together; we haven't got any illusions about each other. It's how it should be, between family.'

Iseutz scowled at him, then shook her head. 'I'm sorry,' she said. 'I didn't mean to be insulting.'

'Ah well, I'm insult-proof,' Gorgas replied with a smile. 'Look, I'll be straight with you, the way I want you to be with me. I want you somewhere safe where the prefect's bogies can't get to you, because I don't want to let them have another hostage. If that means I've got to spend five days here instead of two, that's no big deal; it'll give me time for this other little job I've just thought up for myself. You're doing me a favour – two, actually, because you gave me that idea – and I'm doing you one in return. And we're both happy, and that's good. Now then, you've had your dinner, so let's get you down to the dock. Is there anything you want to take with you, or are you ready now?'

'Ready as I'll ever be,' Iseutz replied. 'I don't suppose you're going to tell me what this great idea is, are you?'

'No, I'm not. Come on, let's be on our way. Actually, the soup wasn't half bad, I must remember this place. We'll go out the back way.'

As they passed the table where Vetriz was sitting, Gorgas stopped, nodded politely and went on.

'Who was that?' Iseutz asked.

'Friend of your uncle Bardas.'

'Oh,' Iseutz said.

Meanwhile, Eseutz Mesatges was leaning forward and asking, 'Come on, who *is* he?'

'Like I said,' Vetriz replied angrily, 'none of your—'

'You're upset,' Eseutz went on, 'because he had a girl with him. Young enough to be his daughter, too. You're well rid, if you ask me.'

'I don't,' Vetriz said, 'so shut up.'

'Not another word. But I thought you were still hung up on this Bardas Loredan character; you know, the one who made a hero of himself at Ap' Escatoy—'

'Eseutz.'

'Sorry.' Eseutz grinned and held up her hands. 'Change subject. Didn't mean to pry. Only you're no fun at all in that direction, you're never interested in anybody, so you can hardly blame me if – all right,' she added, as Vetriz glared at her. 'Completely different subject. Did you buy those shoes you were telling me about? Only I tried a pair of them myself and they cut my heels to ribbons. Talk about an instrument of torture – forget your red-hot irons and your thumbscrews, five minutes in those sandals and I'd tell you anything.'

When she finally managed to get rid of Eseutz, Vetriz went straight home and put the bolt on the door. It was a pointless gesture, and Venart would be furious when he got home and found he was locked out, but it went a little way towards making her feel better. She went up to the first-floor balcony and sat behind the curtain, watching the street, until it was too dark to see.

For her part, Eseutz dropped in at the wool exchange, where there was nothing doing, called on Cens Lauzeta, the fish-oil baron, who wasn't at home, bought a sea-bass and an inkstone in the Salvage Market and stopped off at the jeweller's to see if they'd mended her grasshopper brooch yet, which they hadn't. Then she went home.

There were two men sitting in the porch when she got there. One, annoyingly, was Cens Lauzeta. The other one she recognised, though she didn't know his name.

That, however, was quickly remedied, because as soon as he'd chided her for staying out late, Cens introduced him. His name, apparently, was Gorgas Loredan, and he had a business proposition.

CHAPTER THIRTEEN

'I'd find it downright funny if I wasn't scared out of my brain,' Temrai said, letting go of the saw-handle and sitting down on the beam. 'Here I am building fortifications for Bardas Loredan to come and lay siege to.' He wiped sawdust out of his eyes, then went on, 'It's like when we were kids and took it in turns to be the good guys and the bad guys. Unfortunately, I seem to have lost count, so I'm not sure which I am at the moment.'

They had almost reached the Grey Slate River by the time the news reached them: Cidrocai's army wiped out, Bardas Loredan in command of the enemy column following the death of the Imperial colonel. ('Just my luck,' Temrai had said when he heard about it. 'We kill a colonel, and look what happens.') Temrai had halted the march immediately (*into the jaws of death; yes, certainly. Into the arms of Bardas Loredan; no*) and sent out scouts to find a place he could fortify, with extreme prejudice, against the inevitable confrontation.

As it turned out, he couldn't have chosen better if he'd been planning to dig in all along. An hour's march away the scouts had found a steep-sided plateau rising out of a flat, dry plain, with a wood below it on one side and a lively little river curling round it on the other. When he first saw it, Temrai couldn't help grinning; with time and a certain amount of work, it could be made into a fairly passable replica of the Triple City.

'At least it gives us a pattern to follow,' he'd pointed out to his engineers. 'We'll just copy what they did as best we can in the time we've got. We should be able to get quite a bit done if we all knuckle down and get on with it.'

No question; one thing the plainspeople did know how to

do was work. There had been no complaints or objections when he sketched out the first phase for the council of war - dig a channel to divert the river so that it surrounded the plateau on all sides; fell and dress up all the usable timber in the forest; fetch bastions out of the sides of the plateau to make platforms for the artillery. Effectively he was asking them to rebuild Perimadeia in a month; so far, nobody had even suggested it was going to be difficult, let alone impossible.

The man on the other end of the saw (a distant relative by the name of Morosai; elderly, short, bald-headed and with about five times his stamina) yawned and passed him the water bottle. 'Going well,' he said.

'Isn't it?' Temrai replied. 'Better than I expected, to be honest with you.'

'They're glad to have something to do,' Morosai said. 'When people are doing something, they don't feel quite so helpless. The harder the job is, the better it makes them feel.'

Temrai shrugged. 'I wish it worked that way for me,' he said.

'Ah.' Morosai nodded, doing his familiar imitation of a Wise Old Man. 'It doesn't have that effect on you because you know the truth.'

'Do I?' Temrai paused to rub sawdust out of his eye. 'First I've heard of it if I do.'

'You know,' Morosai went on, 'that if we go to war with the Empire, we don't stand a chance. Even beating them does more harm than good. It's their policy; kill one of them and they guarantee to send five more in his place. That's why you were all set to run away, until *he* stopped you.'

'Really?' Temrai said irritably. 'I know all that, do I? Fancy.'

'Of course you do,' Morosai answered, apparently oblivious of how aggravating he was being. 'I wouldn't insult you by suggesting otherwise.'

'Fine. And do I know a way of getting us out of this mess? One which doesn't end with us all being killed?'

Morosai nodded. 'Course you do,' he said. 'You'd have to be stupid not to.'

Temrai stood up and took hold of the saw-handle. 'Let's do some work,' he said, 'instead of sitting around nattering all day. We're supposed to be setting an example.'

'You're supposed to be setting an example,' Morosai pointed out. 'I'm old enough to be excused duty, but I could see you weren't going to be able to manage this on your own.'

When he was a boy, Temrai remembered, he'd always hated cousin Morosai. 'Very true,' he said. 'All right, are you ready? From your end, then.'

They worked the saw for a while, until the wood started to clent on the blade. 'Hold it,' Morosai said, frowning. 'You'll break the saw if you try to force it.'

Temrai let go and leaned against the beam. 'All right,' he said. 'So now what do we do?'

'We don't do anything. You hold still while I free up the blade with the bowsaw.'

Morosai started to cut a wedge out beside the cut. Working the saw didn't seem to bother him in the least, whereas Temrai's wrists and hands were hurting. 'Go on, then,' Temrai said. 'What's this blindingly obvious way out we both know?'

'Surrender,' Morosai replied; he was three finger-breadths down into the wood already, and no sign of being short of breath. 'They only want the land; give it to them. Then we go back to the plains, where we belong. Really, it's the same as what you were planning to do.'

Temrai nodded slowly. 'So we pack up and move on again. And Colonel Loredan's just going to stand by and let us go past, without raising a finger. Sorry, but I can't see it.'

The object of the exercise was to convert the corpse of a mature beech tree into a pile of neatly sawn planks, which would form part of the swinging bridge across the river. Temrai's design for the bridge called for about a hund-red nine-foot planks. So far, he and Morosai had spent three hours sweating and straining at the big saw, and they hadn't even produced one plank yet.

'Would you rather I came up top?' Morosai asked. He was down in the saw-pit, while Temrai was up top (traditionally the young, fit apprentice went down in the pit, while the decrepit old man stayed topside; the significance of this wasn't wasted on Temrai). 'Better still,' he went on, 'why don't you shove off and find someone else to do this with me. I know you're doing your best, but you really aren't very good at it.'

Temrai sighed. 'All right,' he said. 'Point taken. But just answer my question, will you? What makes you think Bardas Loredan will let us walk peacefully away?'

'Because his superiors will tell him to,' Morosai replied. 'The prefect doesn't want to fight if he doesn't have to; our dead bodies aren't any use to him, unless he's found a way of tanning human skin into usable leather, or gone into the bonemeal business. What he wants is the land. If he can get it with vacant possession, so much the better. And even if Colonel Loredan does want to kill us all – which I doubt, incidentally – if the prefect tells him to let us go, he'll let us go. Simple as that. You were on the right track, young Temrai, and then you had to stop and play at soldiers. Still, you know I'm right.'

'On balance, I think you are,' Temrai said, standing up and dusting himself off. 'But I can't take the risk.'

'I know,' Morosai said. 'A pity, isn't it?'

Having sent Morosai a competent replacement, Temrai walked up to the highest point of the plateau and looked down, trying to visualise what it would all look like if and when it was finished. Here where he was standing would be the citadel, separated from the rest of the plateau by a ditch and a bank topped with a stockade. There'd be another stockade round the whole of the plateau, with towers at regular intervals for archers and catapults. Halfway down the steep sides there'd be the bastions for the big trebuchets, built on top of platforms made from thick piles packed close together and rammed down hard. At the point where the single narrow, winding path reached the plain would be the swing-bridge and the pump – a grandiose name for the array of buckets on ropes that would carry water up to the top. The pump would be housed in a heavily reinforced plank shell and guarded by towers on either side; it was a naturally vulnerable feature, so it made sense to position it alongside the other weak point, the bridge. What he'd really prefer to do, if there was time, would be to enclose the pump and the bridge-house in a brick or even stone tower, thereby making the weakest point into the strongest (just as the head, the most vulnerable part of the body, is protected by the helmet, the most strongly built piece of armour).

Well; it was all very fine in theory. How well it would do in practice, when it was put to the test, remained to be seen. Morosai was right, of course; pinning their hopes on fortifications, on armour, wasn't the right thing to do. It was the enemy's way of doing things, not theirs; and no matter how strong armour may be, it's bound to fail if it's bashed with a big enough hammer. But the thought of walking towards the enemy, towards Bardas Loredan, and hoping that common sense and expediency would prevail was something he couldn't do – and that was, as Morosai had said, a pity, because the army and the man who'd managed to bash down Ap' Escatoy were unlikely to have much trouble smashing up a few palisades of green timber. *Here I am, waiting for Bardas Loredan, Sacker of Cities; only seems like yesterday that I was Temrai, Sacker of Cities, knowing in my heart that even the walls of Perimadeia weren't strong enough for me and my big hammer.*

Nevertheless; knowing something is all very well, but it doesn't count for anything until it's been proved, and proof – well, they hadn't reached that point yet. In the meantime, they had plenty to keep themselves amused with.

He wandered back down the path, stopping halfway to watch the men who were digging out the moat and banking up the spoil on the inside to make yet another line of defence. Mostly they were working in silence, which was unusual for plainspeople, but here and there he could catch bits of old songs, concurrent and discordant. They were deep enough down now to need derricks and winches to haul the baskets of dirt out of the canal bed; he could see the occasional group of carpenters shaping them out of springy green timber. Further off he watched the long timber-wagons rolling towards the plateau, massive logs stacked unnervingly high and lashed down with miles of the coarse grass-fibre rope that the women (nominally under the command of his wife, although Tilden had never made a rope in her life and didn't care who knew it) were busily plaiting in their improvised ropewalk, a hundred yards or so off the road, opposite where the bridge would be. He could hear the crisp, cold chink of hammers on steel, steel on anvils, as the smiths bashed out nails by the thousand, mattock-heads, axe-blades, bill-hooks, hammer-heads, shovels, axle-pins, iron bands for barrels and rims for cartwheels. Next to the makeshift smithies he watched the coopers and wheelwrights, busy with drawknives and adzes and froes. Beside them, in a neighbourly sort of way, were the basket-weavers, working quickly and steadily and with no apparent sign of concern, while their children scampered to and from the wood with enormous armfuls of twigs and shoots. Level with where he was standing on the path, they were digging into the side of the escarpment to make the footings for a trebuchet position; one man wielding the big hammer, the other steadying the drill, giving it a sharp twist after every hammer-blow. In the distance, he could see the saw-pits, the repeating flash as the sun glanced off a saw-blade rising on the draw-stroke. So much activity and work and creation and goodwill, so many different things being made by the exercise of so many and such diverse skills; he couldn't help thinking of the first day he'd spent in Perimadeia, a wide-eyed boy walking dazzled through streets alive and pulsating with the activity of countless workshops and factories. *One day*, he'd thought then, *I'd like my people to be like this.*

And now, thanks to him, they were.

'Excuse me,' Gannadius said, 'but are you expecting a duck?'

The man turned round.

'You've brought it? Splendid.' He was wearing a hat; that's why Gannadius hadn't recognised him, seen from behind. 'It's Dr Gannadius, isn't it? Of course, I don't suppose you remember me.'

'Gorgas Loredan,' Gannadius replied.

'You do remember me.' Gorgas smiled. 'I'm flattered. Well, this is a pleasant surprise. Please, sit down, let me buy you a drink.'

Gannadius smiled nervously. 'Actually—' he began, but it was too late. Gorgas had already tipped the big cider-jar and was pushing a horn cup across the table at him.

'Not quite up to City standards,' he was saying, 'but palatable nevertheless. You should try some of the stuff we're making in the Mesoge these days, though; it'd bring back pleasant memories, I'm sure.'

'I always thought beer was your speciality,' replied Gannadius, who neither knew nor cared what they drank in the Mesoge. 'Is this an innovation of yours, then?'

Gorgas shook his head. 'We've always made cider there,' he said. 'I remember spreading the cheese when I was a boy; the smell literally made your head spin. But yes, I've been encouraging it; something we can sell abroad, you see. I have a notion there's a lot of City expatriates out there spreading a taste for good cider, and I want us to be the ones who supply it. Your health, anyway.'

'And yours,' Gannadius replied dutifully. The cider was sharp and rancid, like vinegar.

'Thank you for bringing me my duck,' Gorgas said solemnly. 'That's another line we're very interested in right now. This new breed they've come up with over there – do you know much about ducks, Doctor?'

Gannadius shook his head. 'Only how to eat them,' he said. For some reason, Gorgas seemed to find that hilariously funny.

'Ah, well then,' he said, when he'd recovered from his out-break of mirth, 'you're helping me prove my point. I'm pre-pared to bet you there's an almost unlimited demand for quality poultry, not to mention the eggs and the feathers.' He held the duck up by its feet, so that its head swung to and fro. 'Yes,' he went on, 'I think we're well on the road to success with this one. So, how have you been keeping? And what, if you'll excuse my curiosity, were you doing with the plainspeople? Hardly the place I'd expect to find a world-famous philosopher.'

Gannadius explained – not very well, but he got the impression that Gorgas knew all about it already. When he'd finished, Gorgas nodded and refilled his cup for him. 'It's an awkward situation there, no doubt about it,' he said. 'I have the feeling that Temrai and his people aren't long for this world – sad, in a way; you've got to admire them for their courage and initiative, the way they've bettered them-selves over the last seven years or so. Oh, I'm sorry, I hope you didn't think I was trying to be offensive. I got so used to thinking of you as a Shastel academic during our little pocket war on Scona, I forgot that of course you're Perimadeian.'

'It's all right, really,' Gannadius replied, thoroughly alarmed at the thought that Gorgas Loredan had been thinking about him in any context. 'And yes, to a certain extent I agree with you. I found it very hard not to like them when I was over there.'

Gorgas smiled. 'Still,' he said, 'it's an ill wind, and so forth. As far as I'm concerned, the good thing is the opportunity it gives my brother Bardas to advance his career with the Empire. I know it must sound silly, but I worry about him; well, he's my brother, I'm entitled. You see, ever since he left the army – the City army, I mean, after Maxen died – well, he's just been marking time, drifting aimlessly along without any real purpose in his life, and it's such a waste. I really thought I might have been able to get him involved with what we were doing on Scona – give him my job, basically, after all, he'd have done it much better than I ever could; and all I've ever wanted is to go home to the Mesoge and mess about playing at farming. And now,' he continued with a sigh, 'I've got what I want, and where's Bardas? Serving time as a sergeant, for gods' sakes, when he isn't risking his neck down some hole in the ground, or slaving away in some miserable factory, when he should be making something of his life, achieving something he could be proud of. No, if Bardas beats the plainspeople and kills Temrai, coming on top of what he did at Ap' Escatoy, he's got to be in line for a proper job somewhere, possibly even on the fast track to a prefecture somewhere, even though he's an outsider.' He smiled again, and leaned back. 'So, and I know this must sound a bit callous, I'm sorry for Temrai and his lot, but I really *want* this war, for Bardas' sake. It could be the answer to a lot of things for him.'

Gannadius took a sip of his cider. It still tasted just as foul, but his mouth was painfully dry. 'As you say,' he murmured, 'it's an ill wind. Well, I hope things work out for you with the duck project.' It occurred to him that if the plainspeople were massacred, there wouldn't be any duck project; in which case why was Gorgas bothering with it? But he decided not to raise the issue. Instead, he stood up, smiled, and walked away, rather more quickly than was polite.

And that, he reflected as he crossed the Market Square, ought to be the end of my grand adventure; home again (well, it counts as home for all practical purposes), safe and sound and none the worse for wear. But it didn't feel like the end of anything; rather, it was as if he was hanging around waiting, like an athlete at a country fair who's been knocked out of one event and has several hours to kill before he's on again.

So, instead of heading for Athli's house, where Theudas would be waiting and Athli would be inexplicably delighted to see him safe and well, he crossed over to the south side of the Square and headed inland, without knowing why, in the general direction of the brickyard and the wire mill.

Why a nation that adamantly refused to make anything it could buy or sell abroad had decided to make an exception in the case of bricks and wire, nobody knew. There weren't even any theories (and Islanders had theories about *everything*); it was just a freak accident of commerce, to which no particular significance should or could be attached.

Unusually, the big double doors of the wire mill were open, and Gannadius stopped for a gawp.

At first, he couldn't make out what they were doing. They'd set up a series of posts, in pairs, about four feet high and two feet apart; through each pair of posts ran a thin steel rod about half the thickness of the tip of his little finger. Each rod was as long as he was tall, and had an L-shaped handle at one end and a slot in the other. The factory hands had threaded wire through the slots and were turning the handles, wrapping wire tightly round the rods like the serving on the handle of a bow. When there was no more space on the rod for any more turns of wire, they lifted it up and off by way of a slot cut in the side of each post and carried it over to an anvil, where two men with cold chisels worked down the length of the rods, cutting off the loops of wire so that they fell to the ground as split-ended steel rings, which a couple of young boys scooped up in large baskets and carried into the back of the shop.

It reminded Gannadius of something. He thought for a while and then remembered the wire factories of Perimadeia, where they'd used something similar but much larger to form the links of chains. Once he'd found that mental image, he knew what they were doing: they were making armourers' rings, for chain-mail. For some reason, Gannadius found the idea disturbing. No question but that the stuff was for export; he didn't know a single Islander who owned a mailshirt (he knew several who owned *thousands* of mailshirts, carefully packed in oil-soaked straw and ready for shipping; but such ownership was intended to be as temporary as possible) or a sword that wasn't a fashion accessory, or a bow or a spear or a halberd. As a nation the Islanders acknowledged the existence of war only as something that happened far away between two rival groups of potential customers. A unique mindset, simultaneously endearing and reprehensible, like so much about these people ... He shook his head, as if making himself wake up. There was no real likelihood of the Islanders taking up arms and going off to war, even if the rest of the world seemed determined to do so. Far more than mere water separated the Island from everywhere else, and for that Gannadius was extremely grateful. Nevertheless, he didn't feel like wandering about any more. It was high time he went home, even if (like every other place he'd thought of as home for as long as he could remember) it was somebody else's.

The armies of the Sons of Heaven sang as they marched; and generally speaking, they did it well. In addition to the signallers who blew their bugles for the charge and the retreat, there were any number of soldiers who carried flutes, rebecs, mandolins, fiddles and small drums along with their blanket rolls and three days' rations; when the mood took them, they would hand their pikes to their neighbours in the column and accompany the singing, so that from a distance the approach of the army sounded more like a wedding than the onslaught of the Empire.

Bardas Loredan, who had no ear for music, had been rather taken with this apparently uncharacteristic frivolity; and besides, even he liked the tunes, which were either fast and lively or fast and sad, but never droopy like the refined fugues and motets they were so fond of in Perimadeia, or tuneless and interminable like Mesoge folk-songs. He couldn't sing and could barely whistle, but he hadn't been with the column long before he found himself humming, bumble-bee fashion, when the soldiers struck up one of his favourites.

But he couldn't understand the words. They were in a language that was entirely unlike anything he'd ever come across; not the highly inflected sing-song Perimadeian that was the standard in most places, from the Mesoge to the plains; or the attractively rounded-and-crisp language of the trading nations, Colleon and the Island (and, by default, Shastel and Scona), which nobody had ever set out to learn deliberately but which everybody acquired, like a sun-tan, after any sort of regular contact with the people who spoke it; or the hammered-flat Perimadeian dialect that was the second language of all the western provinces of the Empire. When he finally got around to asking someone, he was told that the soldiers' songs were in the language of the Sons of Heaven, and that nobody had a clue what any of them meant.

To Bardas' mind, this spoiled the effect of the marching minstrel show, to the point where it started to get on his nerves. The idea that twenty thousand men could march along singing a song they didn't understand struck him as rather distasteful; for all they knew, they could be singing graphic accounts of the defeat and subjugation of their own native cities, with detailed descriptions of what the victorious Sons of Heaven had already done to the men and were intending to do to the women and children. He asked the man he'd been talking to if it bothered him, and the man replied, no; the songs and singing them were an ancient tradition of the service, and traditions are what hold a professional army together. A man should be proud to be allowed to learn the words and join in singing them; they were a secret, a mystery that came with being accepted, becoming part of something great and invincible. The ordinary soldier didn't need to understand the words of the song, the plan of campaign or the reason for the war; he was there to put into effect what the Sons of Heaven, in their absolute wisdom, decided should be so. And that was all there was to it.

In spite of the disillusionment, Bardas couldn't help humming one tune that had burrowed deep into his mind. It was one of the fast, lively ones, generally accompanied with drums and flutes – the words, of course, were just a blur of noise but it had to be a marching song, if only because it was so difficult not to hum it when marching ... Its shape was an endless loop, so that unless you made a conscious decision to abandon it there was no reason why you'd ever stop.

As easily as he'd taken to humming the tune, Bardas got into the habit of commanding the army. As much as anything, it was a matter of convenience and habit. He'd learned a long time ago that the easiest way to do anything is properly; it was less effort to tell the officers and sergeants the right way than have to sort out the mess they made if they tried to work it out for themselves. Every morning, just before daybreak and reveille, he held a staff meeting, told the heads of department what he expected them to do and questioned them about the things they'd done wrong or hadn't got around to doing the previous day. He interrogated the quartermaster and the colonel of foragers about supplies and materiel, the colonel of scouts about the terrain they'd be crossing in that day's march, the captains of each division about the state of their commands, the captain of engineers about how he proposed to deal with any natural obstacles or obstructions; if they gave the wrong answers he told them the right ones, the first time patiently. It was so much less effort than discussion, canvassing opinions, arguing merits; and since he'd been here before and done very much the same things, there wasn't really any point in pretending to listen to the views of men who knew less about the subject than he did. Anything else would be like discussing the letters of the alphabet with a bunch of children who couldn't read yet, rather than simply chalking them on a slate and saying, *Learn this.*

And he had been here before; it was strange how easily it came back to him, across over twenty years of deliberate forgetting. They passed the place where Maxen had won an incredible victory, five hundred heavy cavalry against four thousand plainsmen; he'd almost expected to see the bodies still lying where they'd left them, but there was nothing to mark the spot apart from a cairn of stones he'd ordered built himself to cover their own trivial losses. They crossed the Blue Sky River by the ford where Maxen had finally caught up with Prince Yeoscai, King Temrai's uncle – the river had been in spate and when they found him, Yeoscai was sitting on his horse staring at it, as if he couldn't believe in such gratuitous spite from something that wasn't even human. They camped one night in the little valley where Maxen died; his cairn was still there, but Bardas was content to look at it from a distance. And from that point on, it was simply a matter of remembering; no more thought needed.

Two days on from Maxen's cairn (*if I'd been Temrai I'd have pulled it open and flung his bones to the wild dogs years ago*) they were held up by another river; the Friendly Water, which had dammed up in the hills and flooded the Longstone Combe. The easiest solution was to build a bridge at the head of the combe, but the nearest timber was a day's cart-ride behind them. He emptied the supply wagons and sent them back with the pioneers and the foragers, armed with detailed specifications of the amount and dimensions of timber they'd need, and settled down to wait. There was no reason why the army should be idle while it was waiting; there was kit to overhaul and inspect, armour to repair, boots to patch up and renail; archery practice and weapons drill and parade drill, an opportunity to train the soldiers in specific techniques they'd need against the plains cavalry and archers, tactical seminars for the captains and lieutenants, a few disciplinary tribunals that had been too complex to decide in an evening session on the march, a chance to update and correct the provincial office's rather vague maps. By the time he returned to his tent, well into the second night of the delay, he was rather more weary than he'd have felt if they'd been on the road. He took off his armour – it was a second skin to him now, and he felt strange and uncertain on his feet without the weight of it on his shoulders; first, unbuckle the chausses, followed by the gorget, then the pauldrons, followed by the cops and vambraces, followed by the cuirass, finally the mailshirt and habergeon, and he was a little white worm again, a snail out of its shell – then kicked off his boots and lay down on the late Colonel Estar's foldaway rosewood camp bed.

As soon as he closed his eyes he found himself in a place he knew well, almost as well as the plains. It was dark there, and he couldn't see the walls or the roof; it was a tunnel under a city, garlic and coriander together, a cellar under a factory, the proof house. He turned round – that involved kneeling down, feeling for the plank walls of the gallery – and saw that Alexius had got a fire going; he saw the smoke rising straight up into the vent-hole in the roof, with its blackened edges.

'You're early,' Alexius said.

'We've been making good time,' he replied. 'Is there a lot to get through?'

Alexius shook his head. Oddly enough, he wasn't wearing Alexius' body this time, or rather he'd put on another man's face over his own (like a visor) so that he'd become Anax, the Son of Heaven who had failed. 'Shouldn't take long,' he said. 'Fetch the hammer and we'll make a start.'

He remembered the feel of Bollo's hammer in his hands – big, heavy, definitive, the measure of all things – but for the first time (and how many times had he been here? He'd lost count) he noticed that the hammer was in fact the Empire, because of course nothing can survive Bollo's hammer, it's just a matter of seeing how long it continues to offer resistance and the manner in which it eventually fails –

The first piece to be tested was an arm; a low-specification, munition-grade arm, made of ordinary flesh and bone, not expected to pass above the first degree of proof. Anax laid it on the anvil and Bardas reduced it to pulp with a few well-placed blows.

'Fail that,' Alexius said. 'All right, next.'

He put a torso up; it was quite well made, with skilfully formed pectorals and well-defined ribs, and it was stamped with the plainsmen's mark, usually a guarantee of quality. Bardas started with a couple of heavy bashes across the breastbone – 'Thought so,' Anax commented, 'fancy decoration on top of poor material' – then methodically broke the ribs, easily as snapping off icicles. 'Fail that,' said Anax, and Bardas swept it off the anvil into the scrap.

'Next,' Alexius said, and Bardas put up a head. 'Collector's item,' he said, because it was the head of a Son of Heaven, the late Colonel Estar. 'Always wanted to see how well one of these would do,' he said, and swung the hammer, putting a lot of left elbow and right shoulder behind the blow. The skull crumpled but stayed together – 'That's quality for you,' said Anax – and it took him seven blows to wreck it completely. 'It's the bone structure that does it,' Anax pointed out. 'That high-domed forehead, see, and those cheek-bones. I'll pass that in the second degree; still not good enough for the purpose it was made for.'

Another torso; female this time, with small round breasts and sloping, rounded shoulders. It had been made in the Perimadeian style but the patina on the surface suggested the sunlight of the Island. Breaking the ribs and collar-bone was easy enough; but the flesh was soft and springy, like the quilted silk armour of the far-eastern provinces, easy to bruise but next to impossible to crush, the force of the hammer blows just seemed to soak away into it, like water into sand. In the end, Bardas managed to ruin it by trapping it between the hammerhead and the edge of the anvil. 'Third degree pass,' said Anax. 'Impressive.'

'Cheating, if you ask me,' Bardas replied.

Next was a hand; a girl's hand with long, slender fingers. Instead of the hammer Bardas used the eight-pound axe, and the fingers came away quite cleanly. 'Now the hammer,' Alexius said, and Bardas smashed it across the back, expecting it to pulp. It didn't. 'Ah,' said Alexius with a smile, 'that's a genuine Loredan, you see. Tough as old boots, they are.' By the time he'd wrecked it to his satisfaction, Bardas had worked up quite a sweat.

'Let's have that head there,' Alexius said. 'Now,' he went on, turning it round in his fingers, 'here's a challenge for you. Let's see just how strong you are.'

Bardas grinned; the head was bald, with a strong jaw and a big, soft mouth. 'Leave it to me,' he said; but the first, second and third blows glanced harmlessly off the curved surface of the skull, and the head, opening its eyes and winking, forgave him.

'I'll pass it if you like,' Alexius said sardonically. Bardas didn't reply; he laid the head on its side and hammered on the jaw until the hinge cracked, then attacked the temples. He made some inroads but had to give up when he hit short, caught the shaft of the hammer on the side of the anvil and broke off the head.

'Damn,' he said. 'I'll use the axe.'

'All right,' said Anax, 'but it's not the right tool, so it won't be a fair proof.'

'So what?' Bardas replied. The axe made a better job; but by the time he was satisfied there wasn't much edge left on it, and the blade was notched where he'd hit directly on one open, winking eye. The head forgave him again as he shoved it off the anvil. 'Fifth degree proof,' Alexius said. 'They don't make 'em like that any more.'

Bardas was tired. He wiped away the sweat from his forehead with the back of his wrist and asked, 'Is that it?'

'Almost,' said Anax. 'One more head, and then we're done.' And he reached under the bench and produced the head of Colonel Bardas Loredan. 'All right then, Mister Clever,' he said. 'Crack that if you can, and I'll buy you a jug of cold milk.'

Bardas frowned. 'What with?' he said. 'I've bust the hammer and the axe is useless.'

Alexius scowled at him. 'Don't be so pathetic,' he said. 'When I was your age we proved *everything* with our bare hands, we didn't faff about with hammers. Stop mucking about and get on with it.'

So Bardas hammered on the piece with his clenched fists, which were of course harder than any axe and heavier than any hammer; but try as he might, once he'd battered away the skin and the flesh, he couldn't make so much as a little dent in the skull. 'Quality,' Anax muttered. 'Don't think you'll ever crease that, not even with a drop-hammer.'

'Rubbish,' Bardas replied irritably. 'I can break anything. Bloody fine assistant deputy viceproofmaster I'd be if I couldn't. Here, give me that.' He pointed to an arm which Anax had picked out of the pile; it was Colonel Bardas Loredan's sword-arm, neatly sawn off at the elbow. He cut off the hand with his thin-bladed kitchen knife, the one he used for jointing and skinning the carcasses, and swung the massive bone round his head with all the strength he could muster. Steel on steel, the noise was; because Colonel Loredan's head was a helmet and his sword-arm a vambrace, cop and lames. 'You can always tell the quality by the sound it makes,' Anax reminded him. 'Listen to that, best Mesoge steel. When you've done with that skull, I'll have what's left for a planishing stake.'

'There won't be anything left,' Bardas grunted; and he attacked the piece as if it was an enemy and his life depended on the outcome. In the end, honours were roughly even between the arm and the skull; both were dented and twisted, but nothing a good armourer couldn't mend by beating out over an anvil. Quality like this can always be mended by hard, skilful bashing between hammer and anvil; no reason why it shouldn't go on for ever.

'Give up?' Alexius asked, and the skull's eyes opened –

– 'What?' Bardas asked. There was a man standing over him. 'Gods, is it morning already?'

'Staff meeting,' the soldier replied. 'Then weapons training; it says on your schedule you're doing wounds and death with the ninth, tenth and twelfth platoons.'

Bardas yawned. 'I'd completely forgotten. All right, tell 'em I'll be out in a minute or two.'

Another agreeable thing about the Imperial army was its eagerness to learn. Two centuries ago, the Sons of Heaven had hit on the happy notion of performance-related bonuses for field armies. These awards were calculated at platoon level (to take it further down the command structure would be to risk encouraging soldiers to place individual opportunity above corporate goals) and were based on the number of confirmed kills attributable to each platoon during a battle. Naturally, any kills achieved in the face of or to the prejudice of explicit orders from an officer were discounted; only the platoons that saw action were eligible, which had the beneficial effect of making each unit eager to take its turn in the front rank. In consequence, combat tutorials from an expert like Colonel Loredan were regarded as a genuine opportunity to increase a platoon's earning power, and were very well attended.

'Today,' Bardas said, looking over the top of the mass of attentive faces, 'we're going to look at the mechanics of killing; this is all about making your blows count, doing as much damage as you can with as little exposure and risk as you can get away with.'

You could have heard a coin drop. Bardas suppressed a grin. *If you could see me now, Alexius; a college lecturer.*

'Quite simply,' he went on, 'there's two ways of doing damage with the sword and the halberd, namely thrusting and cutting. Now then, hands up anybody who's studied fencing or something similar outside the service.' A couple of hands appeared; Bardas nodded. 'Well, first thing you'll be doing is forgetting everything you were taught in fencing school about thrusts being better than cuts. Sure, thrusts kill better than cuts, but they kill slowly. You're in a battle and the other man's trying to kill *you*: you don't just want him dead, you want him dead *now*. Most of all, you want to stop him being able to hurt you; which is why a cut that does relatively little damage – snips off a thumb, say – is quite likely going to be more use to you than a neat thrust through the lung that'll drop him dead as a stone in ninety seconds' time.'

The audience shifted a little in their seats. Bardas knew why; they weren't sure which they were more interested in, staying alive or racking up a healthy body-count. Very good; let them keep that division of priorities firmly in mind.

'If you're going to kill a man or take him out of play, you'll need to damage either the works or the pipes; works are things like muscle, sinew and bone, pipes are veins and arteries. But damage isn't everything; you can do fatal damage and still not do the job. Just as important as damage is shock. Always remember that, if you can.'

Bardas paused and took a sip of water.

'For a good military kill with a thrust, don't bother with the head too much. Skulls are thick; unless you're lucky enough to get a fluke shot in through the eye, the ear or the mouth, chances are that all you'll do is make your enemy even more bad-tempered than he was before. Necks are good, especially if you twist the blade once you're in, but the neck's a damn fiddly small target; so's the heart, come to that. If you go for the heart, ten to one you'll get tangled up in the ribs, which are springy and a right pain. You can make a real mess of someone's chest and still not stop him; it's a low-return shot, not something you want to muck around with in a serious battle.

'If you're fighting cavalry, of course, you've got the option of a thrust up under the ribs – also if you're kneeling to receive an infantry charge. As well as the heart, you've also got a clear shot at the liver and a big fat artery. Gut-shots are probably the easiest kind of thrust; but you'll be amazed at the amount of junk there is inside there that you've got to get through before you reach anything worthwhile. Also bear in mind that the stomach muscles convulse when they're cut, enough to move your shot off line. By the way; when you prick a stomach, it goes pop as all the air comes rushing out; it'll startle the life out of you the first time you hear it, so be prepared for that.

'Actually, if you're thrusting you can do a lot worse than go for the arteries in the groin, the small of the back, upper arm, armpit, knee and so forth. Lay one of those open and you'll almost certainly have a kill; but please, always bear in mind the fact that bleeding to death takes its own sweet time, during which he's still armed and dangerous. Even if you've got him fair and square in a good place, always follow up, preferably with a big cut, just to make sure he ends up on the deck. Same goes for kidneys, lungs, all that stuff. If all you're interested in is killing, get a job in a slaughterhouse. If you want to be a soldier, concentrate on killing *quickly*.'

He paused for breath. Still got their attention? Good.

'Cutting, on the other hand,' he went on, 'is as much about shock as damage. Cut a man's hand off and suddenly he's not a threat any more, even if he lives to be a hundred. Remember, pain is your friend, it'll stop him trying to get you; a perfectly lethal thrust might not hurt enough to notice, and if a man doesn't know he's dead, he might not stop attacking you until it's too late. Now, the choicest cuts are to the head and neck; but don't fool about trying to chop the other man's head off when a nice crunching slash across the neck artery will do just as nicely. For one thing, while you're swinging your sword up for the really big hit, you're the next best thing to an open target yourself. Short, meaty cuts across bones are what bring home the bacon; so long as you stop him cold, you can always finish him off with the next one.

'Finally, people will tell you the thrust's quicker than the cut; maybe so, but that sounds to me like you're taking too big a swing. Get close first, then take your shot; use your feet to close up the gap, move your body and your arm at the same time, and you won't need to worry too much about slow cutting. Do it right and they'll never know what hit them. All right, any questions?'

There were questions, plenty of them and for the most part intelligent and informed. Once again Bardas reflected on what a pleasure it was to work with people who really cared about technique and craft. If only he'd had a few students of this calibre (instead of only one) when he was running his fencing school, perhaps it might have worked out a whole lot better.

Later that day, the first timber wagons rolled back into camp, and the tempo changed noticeably. In no time at all the lumber was unshipped and hauled to where it was needed, giving the engineers barely enough time to finish their designs. As he watched the teams of men dragging the heavy logs into position, he couldn't help remembering the spectacle of Temrai's men as they shifted lumber and built their trebuchets and catapults under the walls of the City. No matter which side you're on, there are few sights more inspiring than a large number of men working well together on a big, ambitious project; watching them lever and winch huge bulks of timber about as if they weighed nothing at all, even hoist them into the air on cranes and pulleys, is enough to make a man feel proud to be human. *Is this how Temrai felt?* he wondered. *He'd have been entitled to, no question about that.* It was odd; being back here, doing this sort of thing, was almost enough to make him feel young again.

Young and in charge, like Temrai against Perimadeia. Young and supremely confident, like Bollo starting to swing his hammer. Young and with a lifetime of opportunity ahead of him, like Bardas Loredan leading Maxen's army home from the wars. He thought for a moment about the young lad who'd briefly been his apprentice on Scona, when he'd been trying to make his living as a bowyer. He remembered what it had felt like, on the night of the Sack, twisting Temrai's arm behind his back with one hand, holding the cutting edge to his throat with the other. That had been one of the most intimate moments of his life.

As they worked, the soldiers of the Sons of Heaven sang the appropriate working songs, taking them on trust, as always. It must be wonderful, Bardas thought, to have that kind of faith; so comforting, so much easier, like a log running on rollers instead of being dragged along the ground. Trust, believe, and it'll make you young again – that's what a sense of purpose can do for you. If only there wasn't always some older, wiser man to hold a sharp edge to your throat and take the faith away, like Bardas Loredan during the Sack.

*

'Asking for trouble, I reckon,' Venart protested, yet again. He'd said it so many times that it was rapidly turning into a joke.

'We'll see,' someone replied. 'We've got them over the proverbial barrel. They need us; it's business, pure and simple.'

'They're late,' someone else commented. 'They've never been late before.'

In the Long Room of the Island's Chamber of Commerce, fifty or so representatives of the Island's Ship-Owners' Association (founded a week previously) were waiting to meet with a delegation from the provincial office, on a matter (as the invitation to the meeting had phrased it) of some urgency and delicacy.

'It's hustling, that's what it is,' Venart persevered, 'and you know it as well as I do. You can call it what you like, but that's what it is.'

Runo Lavador, owner of seven ships, sat on the edge of the President's desk, swinging his legs like a small boy. 'All right,' he said, 'it's hustling. Perfectly legitimate business practice. We've got what they need – ships. They've got what we want – money. It's for the parties to the deal to make their own bargain.'

'We made a deal, though,' said one of the few people in the room who agreed with Venart. 'Going back on it – well, it doesn't seem too clever to me. We've got a pretty good deal already, if you ask me.'

Runo Lavador shrugged. 'If you don't want to be here,' he said, 'then by all means bugger off. Nobody's forcing you to do anything. Besides, you simply don't understand the nature of the charter business. All along, they've been entirely at liberty to call it a day and walk away if they found a better deal somewhere else. They chose not to. Now we're making a choice; we want more money. They can still walk away, any time they want. To listen to you, anybody'd think we were holding a knife to their throats.'

The tall, heavy doors at the other end of the hall swung open, and the Sons of Heaven made their entrance. Hard not to think in terms of pageantry and theatre when a party of them entered a room; first, an honour guard of halberdiers in half-armour, then a secretary or two and a couple of lesser clerks carrying desks and chairs and ink-horns; then the

300

delegates themselves, both of them a head taller than any-body else in their party, and scurrying behind them, three or four unspecified attendants, cooks or valets or personal librarians. *Look out*, Venart thought, *here come the grown-ups*. He hoped they weren't going to mind too much. They wouldn't, would they? After all, it was only money that was at stake here, and so far the Sons of Heaven had given the impression of valuing money the way sailors value seawater.

Cens Lauzeta, the fish-oil baron, was sitting in the President's chair. Nobody could remember electing him chairman, but nobody minded very much if he wanted the job. He stood up and nodded politely as the delegates processed (no other word for it) down the hall and sat down at the far end of the long table.

'Good of you to spare the time to see us,' said Cens Lauzeta, sounding even more cocky than usual (what was it about the fish-oil trade that brought out the boisterous-ness in people?). 'We represent the Island Ship-Owners' Association,'

'Excuse me,' interrupted one of the delegates. 'I don't seem to recall having heard of your organisation before.'

'I don't suppose you have,' Lauzeta replied cheerfully. 'We haven't been in existence for terribly long. Up till now, there hasn't been a need. But here we are; so, if it's all right with you, we might as well get on with the negotiations.'

'By all means,' replied the Son of Heaven. 'Perhaps you'd care to tell me what we're here to negotiate.'

Lauzeta smiled indulgently. 'Money,' he replied. 'So far, you've chartered ships belonging to our members – no complaints on that score, by the way, you've been perfectly straight with us and we've been straight with you. But now,' he went on, sitting on the arm of the President's chair, 'things are about to change. You're going to take our ships off to a war; we don't know how long this war's going to last – well, how could anybody know that? – we don't know when we're likely to get our ships back, or whether we'll get them back at all. No offence, my friend, but we're businessmen, and we've been hearing reports about the way this war's going that put a whole new perspective on the deal.'

'Is that so?' replied the delegate coolly. 'Please enlighten me.'

'If you like,' Lauzeta said. 'One column effectively wiped out; the colonel in command of another column killed in action; the enemy have mobilised and are on the move, taking the offensive - this isn't what we all had in mind when the deal was struck. Those invincible armies don't seem quite so invincible any more, and we think that changes things quite a bit.'

'I see,' said the Son of Heaven. 'But you're not disputing the fact that we have binding agreements with the members of your Association?'

Lauzeta shook his head. 'Not the way we see it,' he said. 'What we're saying is, one of the assumptions on which the contracts were based has changed. I've spoken to some of our leading commercial lawyers and they all tell me the same thing. A contract's like a house; if the foundations collapse, the whole thing falls to the ground. As we see it, the contracts are null and void.'

The delegate raised an eyebrow. 'Really,' he said. 'As far as my layman's understanding of Imperial law goes—'

'Imperial law, maybe,' Lauzeta interrupted. 'But the charters were all signed here on the Island, so they're under the jurisdiction of Island law and Island courts; and I'm telling you, as of now the contracts are dead and buried. Fact.'

'An interesting line of argument,' said the delegate. 'In which case, assuming your interpretation is valid, I suppose you want us to withdraw our men and return the ships.'

Lauzeta shook his head. 'By no means,' he said. 'That'd put a serious crimp in your plans, and none of us want that. No, we're quite happy to carry on with the agreement just so long as the agreed levels of payment are revised to take into account the likely additional time and risk. After all,' he went on in a rather more conciliatory tone, 'the last thing we want to do is fall out over this; the Island and the Empire have always been close—'

('No they haven't,' Eseutz Mesatges whispered in Venart's ear, 'Even with a following wind, it's a two-day journey.'

'Shh,' Venart replied.)

The delegate frowned and smiled at the same time. 'You want to proceed with the existing agreement, but you want more money. Is that what you're saying?'

Lauzeta nodded. 'Bluntly, yes,' he said. 'I think it's entirely reasonable to factor in an allowance for depreciation of goodwill and loss of business opportunities. For one thing, what do you think is happening to our regular business while our ships have been standing idle? We do have competitors, you know.'

The delegate conferred briefly with his colleague. 'How much more money do you want?' he asked.

Apparently, Cens Lauzeta hadn't been expecting that particular question; he opened his mouth and closed it again, and said nothing. The delegate raised an eyebrow.

'What we need to do,' Lauzeta said at last, 'is agree some sort of formula that'll allow us to work this out scientifically. I mean, I wouldn't want you to think we're just pulling a figure out of the air.'

'You mean,' the delegate replied, 'you want more money, but you don't know how much more money.' He stood up, and the rest of his entourage immediately did the same. 'Perhaps when you've thought of a figure you'd be kind enough to let me know. In the meantime, I'd be grateful if you could tell me whether we should continue loading our ships, or whether you want them unloaded again.'

'I—' Lauzeta didn't appear to have anything to say. There was a moment of embarrassed silence; then Runo Lavador, who'd been sitting still and cringing quietly for most of the meeting, jumped to his feet. 'Probably it'd be best if you unloaded,' he said. 'I mean, until we've finalised this payment business—'

'Excuse me.' The delegate had spoken quite softly, but everybody in the room was looking at him. With a tone of voice like that, there wasn't really any need to shout. 'May I ask who you are, and what standing you have within the Association?'

A faint mist of panic clouded Lavador's face; he dispelled it with a visible effort. 'I'm Runo Lavador,' he said. 'And I'm just an ordinary ship-owner, that's all. But I'm pretty sure I'm speaking for all of us. Isn't that right?' He looked round at his colleagues, none of whom moved an inch. 'I'm sure you understand,' he said.

The delegate looked at him for a count of three. 'Very well,' he said, and walked briskly out of the room, followed in no particular order by the rest of the party. Lauzeta waited till the doors closed behind them.

'Well, how was I supposed to know?' he said, before anyone else could say anything. 'And you weren't helping,' he added, glowering at Lavador. 'A right bunch of fools you made us look.'

'*I* made us look?'

As the shouting match quickly gathered momentum, Venart slipped away as unobtrusively as he could. He was sorely tempted to run after the delegates and apologise; but that wouldn't help, either. In fact, he couldn't think of any sensible action except going straight home, so he did that.

'Well?' Vetriz called out from the counting house as he walked in through the front door. 'How did it go?'

'Terrible,' Venart replied, dropping into a chair. 'Couldn't have gone worse if we'd really tried.'

'Oh.' Vetriz appeared in the doorway and leaned against the frame. 'That well,' she said. 'Why aren't I surprised?'

Venart stretched out his legs and stacked his feet on a small, low table. 'I think now would be a good time to go abroad,' he said, 'until this whole mess has been sorted out. Unfortunately, we can't, of course, on account of not having a ship. Well, if ever I happen to meet Cens Lauzeta in a dark alley—'

'What happened?'

Venart told her. 'So,' he summarised, 'one way and another we've contrived to put their backs up something rotten. You should have seen the look of contempt on that man's face as he walked out. Never seen anything quite like it.'

'Oh, well,' Vetriz replied. 'They'll just have to sort it all out again, won't they? Look on the bright side; if they decide the deal's off, we'll still have the ship and the money we've already got out of them. If the worst comes to the worst, we'll just have to send Cens round in a hair shirt and make him do a bit of grovelling.'

Venart sighed. 'I suppose so,' he said. 'But I ask you, for so-called representatives of a commercial nation, we do know how to make ourselves look ignorant.' He reached over and pulled a handful of grapes off the bunch that lay in a shallow wooden bowl on the table. 'Getting things wrong is one thing,' he said as he munched. 'Getting everything wrong all at the same time, though; now that's a class act.'

Vetriz smiled. 'Well,' she said, 'if it's any consolation I've just been doing the books for this quarter, and we're down twelve per cent on this time last year, so I guess Cens did have a point, of sorts. Of course, last year things were unusually busy, so strictly speaking it's not a fair comparison. In any event, I reckon we should go out for dinner to celebrate.'

'Celebrate what? Doing worse than last year? Offending the Empire?'

'Why not? Who says you can only celebrate something nice?'

CHAPTER FOURTEEN

'Cinnamon,' said the prefect of Ap' Escatoy, after a long, tense silence. 'Cinnamon, but probably not the domestic variety. In fact, I'd say probably Cuir Halla. Am I right?'

'Close enough,' replied the chief administrator, with his mouth full. 'In fact, it's a new variety. My man on the Island sent me a box with the dispatches. I believe it comes from the south-west, but that's as much as he could tell me.'

'A new variety,' the prefect repeated, brushing crumbs off his fingertips. 'I have to admit, you surprise me. What are the prospects for securing a regular supply?'

The chief administrator nodded to the cooks, indicating that they could go. 'I'm not sure,' he said. 'The way the Islanders do business is so erratic, I can't tell whether it was a one-off purchase or part of a long-standing arrangement. They will insist on treating everything to do with business as a game. It's part of the childish streak that permeates everything they do.'

The prefect looked up. 'That sounds faintly endearing,' he said.

'Maybe. I just find it irritating, to be honest with you. Childishness is endearing in children. In grown-ups, it's annoying.'

'I suppose so,' the prefect said, putting down his plate. 'Still, it's refreshing to come across people who so obviously enjoy what they do. I imagine this is by way of introducing your report.'

'It's a good illustration, certainly.' The administrator sat down opposite his superior, his elbows on his knees. 'Personally, I don't find delaying the invasion and thereby possibly jeopardising our forces in the interior to be even

306

remotely endearing. We should have seventy thousand men in Perimadeia by now, and instead they're lolling about in the camp here, forgetting why they're there and what they're meant to be doing. To be frank, it's playing havoc with my budget and making the Empire look ridiculous.'

The prefect sighed. 'That's intolerable, I agree.'

'And that's by no means the worst part of it,' the administrator went on, fidgeting with a small brass dish he'd picked up off the table. 'Temrai's marching this way; what if he somehow manages to defeat our field army? How are we going to explain that?'

'Ah.' The prefect smiled. 'It's not as bad as that. Apparently he's stopped dead in his tracks and is building a fortress. Remarkably impressive rate of progress, I have to admit. Really, they're such an energetic people; quite unlike most nomadic tribes I've encountered. When this is over, I think I'd like to study them a little more closely. Part of the reason for having an Empire in the first place is to enjoy the strange people you come across, surely.'

'With respect,' said the administrator severely, 'I think the wine-tasting can wait till after the vintage. I agree, if Temrai's halted his advance it takes the pressure off us to a certain extent. But even so; if we'd been able to proceed according to thr original schedule, they wouldn't have got that far and we wouldn't be facing the prospect of digging them out of this new model anthill they're building. The plain fact is, these Islanders are going to cost us lives, money and time. We can't afford to let that go by.'

The prefect sighed. 'I suppose not,' he said. 'Something has to be done, I agree.' He closed his eyes as an aid to concentration. 'It's a nuisance that we can't crew the ships ourselves. Relying on their crews is going to slow things down even further. Can't we recruit sailors somewhere else?'

'I've considered that,' the adminstrator said. 'Unfortunately, it's not that simple. We might be able to find enough men to make up the numbers, but I couldn't guarantee the quality. Typically, those Island ships are difficult to handle unless you know what you're doing. I wouldn't want to take the risk of using inexperieced crews.'

'Really?' The prefect opened his eyes. 'It's not a long journey, is it?'

'I don't profess to know anything at all about ships and sailing,' the administrator said. 'I can only go on what my experts tell me; and of course, they aren't experts in this field, because the only people who really know about sailing Island-pattern ships are the Islanders. However—'

'I take your point.' The prefect stood up and looked out of the window. They were pruning the orange trees in the cloister below, and the symmetry of the pruners' work intrigued him. 'I think we may have to resign ourselves to a certain degree of delay,' he said. 'Or even a reassessment of our strategy. Fortunately, Temrai seems intent on making it possible for us to do just that.' He steepled his fingers, like a chess-player contemplating the move after the move after next. 'For now,' he said, 'I'll assign the sixth and ninth battalions to Captain Loredan's army; that'll give him another thirty thousand men. How many do you suppose you'll need?'

The administrator thought for a moment. 'One battalion ought to be more than enough. In fact, five thousand men should be plenty. It won't be a difficult job, provided you can let me have a half-decent commander.'

They were shaping the trees so that the pattern of branches formed a perfect sphere; quite an undertaking, considering the natural tendency of the trees to push out sideways. Art is the subversion of nature; discuss. 'I was thinking of Colonel Ispel,' the prefect said.

'He'd be ideal. In fact, he'd be wasted on a job like this.' The administrator frowned. 'I know,' he said, 'if Ispel's available, why don't you give him the army against Temrai and assign this Loredan to me? It seems faintly ridiculous to have one of our best officers conducting a routine police action, while a major field army's under the command of an outlander.'

The prefect shook his head. 'Normally, I'd agree,' he said. 'But the plain fact is, Temrai wouldn't be being so obliging if it wasn't for Captain Loredan. It was Estar's death and Loredan replacing him that frightened him so badly he abandoned his really quite sensible strategy of taking the war to us and made him start burrowing into the dirt like a groundhog. As a result, I need Loredan to stay where he is, and that means you can have Ispel. Assuming you do want him, that is. If you'd rather have someone else, please say so.'

'On the contrary.' The administrator seemed distinctly annoyed; probably, thought the prefect with a certain degree of malicious pleasure, because Ispel outranks him socially and he'll have to treat him as equal-and-above when they appear in public together. That'll be an interesting spectacle in itself.

'That's settled, then.' The prefect turned his head and consulted the large, exquisite glass water-clock that stood in the corner of the room. As transparent as the water it contained, the fabric of the walls was the next best thing to invisible, with only the calibrations etched on the two vessels betraying the fact that it was there at all. A gift from a wealthy manufacturer, angling after a contract to supply the army; he hadn't got the contract, but he hadn't asked for his clock back, so presumably he didn't mind. 'Shall we walk down to the Arcades?' he said. 'We can talk on the way. I make a point of going down myself these days; there's nothing like a controlled distraction to help maintain the concentration.'

The administrator smiled – genuine pleasure, the prefect noted, and was glad to see it. 'I was hoping I'd be able to find the time to drop by when the fresh stuff comes in,' the administrator said. 'But I've been so busy lately—'

'Really,' the prefect admonished him, 'nobody's too busy for really fresh bread. I make it a rule never to trust a man who can't make time to do his own shopping.'

The portico was busy, as was to be expected at this time of day. The booksellers and stationers had already set up their stalls, and the number of people walking along reading and therefore not looking where they were going made for slow, cautious progress. 'Remind me,' the prefect said, 'to call in at the flower market on the way back. I'm not at all satisfied with the roses they've been sending up lately, and there's few things as dismal to look at as half-dead roses.'

The administrator made a sympathetic noise. 'I've been saying for some time that we ought to look into buying the flowers for all the departments centrally, from just the one reliable supplier. As it is, quality's pretty much hit-and-miss. A few days ago our consignment at the State Office was white with mildew, and by then it was far too late in the day to get anything to replace them with.'

'That's a very sensible suggestion,' the prefect said, in a tone of voice the administrator couldn't quite interpret. 'You go ahead and let me know how you get on.'

Once they were past the portico itself, the crowds thinned out and it was possible to walk at a more comfortable pace. 'You'd never think that most of this was only ten years old,' the administrator went on. 'Tell me, has there been any word from the marshal's office about their plans for redevelopment? As far as I know, they haven't even confirmed that they're going to keep the administration here, now that the siege is over.'

The prefect smiled, acknowledging the skill (fairly minimal, in his opinion) with which the administrator had angled the conversation round to the topic he really wanted to discuss. 'I can confirm that the bulk of the administration for this prefecture will be staying here,' he said, watching his colleague out of the corner of his eye to see if he'd react. 'It was felt that since during the course of the siege we'd effectively built a small town of our own here – and done it pretty well, too – it'd be wasteful to up sticks and move away. As to whether they're going to rebuild Ap' Escatoy itself, they've referred that decision back to me.' He looked straight in front and waited for the administrator to respond; but he'd underestimated the man's patience. They were almost at the gate of the Arcades before the administrator spoke again.

'And have you reached a decision yet? I don't suppose you have, or you'd have mentioned it.'

The prefect stopped to examine a passing cart with an unusual arrangement for attaching the brake to the axle. Most of the time the administrator found his superior's ability to take an interest in virtually anything a harmless, even praiseworthy attribute; there were occasions, however, when it made him want to hit him.

'It all depends, doesn't it,' the prefect said, 'on what happens with Temrai and the war. If we can take possession of the old Perimadeia site fairly soon, with a view to getting major construction under way before the beginning of winter, then obviously I'd prefer to build there; it's a far better position and much better situated for communications and the like for when we begin the westward expansion. On the other hand, if we can't get in there in time to make a start in this fiscal year, I shall have to build here in Ap' Escatoy or else lose the provincial office funding I had to work so hard to get in the first place; it's a term of the grant that I commit to a scheme of works before the year end, and there's absolutely nothing I can do about that. If I lose the grant – quite apart from the frustration, after all I had to go through to get it in the first place – I'll have to finance the building work out of revenue income and plunder, which means I'll end up having to make a lot of compromises I'd really rather avoid if I can. You can see how awkward my position is.'

A glimmer of light began to shine in the administrator's mind. 'Of course,' he said, 'if you had a fairly cast-iron expectation of a substantial lump-sum receipt from revenues and plunder, it'd give you a degree more flexibility in your planning.'

'Indeed,' the prefect replied, his expression unchanged. 'In which case, I think I'd be even more likely to rebuild Perimadeia. After all, traditionally it's been the centre of gravity for this entire region; people naturally look to the City as their economic and cultural point of reference. It'll make the job of restructuring in the west that degree smoother if we can make it seem as if we're carrying on where they left off; restoring things to how they were, even.' He bent down, still apparently fascinated by the cart. 'But it'd still be preferable, I feel, if we could find a way to get the war back on schedule. This possible cash windfall is all very well, but wouldn't it be better to have the grant and the windfall as well?' He straightened up. 'In a sense,' he went on, 'Captain Loredan's already done what I needed him to do; we can have Perimadeia, with vacant possession, just as soon as we can land enough men there to hold it. Which makes this Island business,' he added, frowning a little, 'even more annoying. I do hope you'll be able to get it sorted out quickly. It'd be infuriating to miss a rather splendid opportunity because of some trivial obstruction.'

The smell of fresh bread, exquisite and unique, loaded the air with value, and the two men instinctively looked up. 'Our fault for dawdling,' said the prefect. 'And I refuse to be seen trotting through the streets like a runaway donkey. We'll just have to accept that we've missed the best of the day.'

They quickened their pace; but by the time they reached

the bakers' arcade, the pyramids of warm, pristine loaves were already looking battered and worn, like the walls of a city bombarded by heavy engines. 'When we rebuild Perimadeia,' muttered the administrator, scowling, 'we'll have at least five bakers' arcades, all baking at different times. That way, we won't have to be so very critical in our timing.'

The prefect grinned. 'But if you do that,' he said, 'you'll spoil the whole experience. If you guarantee satisfaction, you deprive yourself of the joy of uncertain attainment.'

'If you say so,' the administrator said, sounding less than convinced. 'Personally, all I want is to be sure of getting really fresh bread.'

'Of course. What on earth could be more important than that?'

The post-coach was running late; an extraordinary thing, only partly accounted for by the increased volume of traffic on the road caused by the war. In the back among the luggage, and feeling remarkably like a sack of turnips, Niessa Loredan nursed a bad headache.

She neither knew nor cared where she was. It was far too hot, the coach had managed to find every last pothole and rut with a diligence that would have been admirable in some other context, and her bladder was making her feel distinctly uncomfortable. As if that wasn't bad enough, she was cursed with a travelling companion who simply wouldn't stop talking, or rather shouting. It was enough to make her wish she'd stayed in Scona and taken her chances with the halberdiers.

The annoying woman had managed to get the impression, gods know where from, that Niessa wanted to know her name. 'You may find this rather complicated,' she was saying, 'being an outlander. Let me see, now. If I was a man I'd be Iasbar Hulyan Ap' Daic – Iasbar for me, Hulyan for my father, ap' Daic for where my mother was born. Because I'm a woman, I'm plain Iasbar ap' Cander; the same idea, but Ap' Cander because that's where my husband was born. If I'd never been married, I'd still be Hulyan Iasbar Ap' Escatoy, which was where I was born. Don't worry if it sounds confusing,' she added, 'it takes foreigners a lifetime to get used to the nuances.'

Niessa grunted and turned her head, trying to give the impression that she found the view (sandhills topped wth scruffy tussocks of dry white grass) unbearably fascinating. The annoying woman didn't seem to have noticed.

'Now I expect you're wondering,' she went on, 'what I'm doing hitching a ride on the post-coach; well, it's the last thing I ever imagined I'd do, but ever since my son – that's my middle son; my eldest is at home, of course, he inherited the estate when my husband died and he's a musician, people are beginning to think quite highly of him, and my youngest son's in the army, still quite junior, of course, he's *aide de camp* to this Colonel Ispel everybody's talking about as the new commander-in-chief in the west; but my middle son, Poriset, he's the chief administrator of the arms factory at Ap' Calick – not a particularly interesting job, as he's the first to admit, but he's the youngest man ever to be appointed to a position of such seniority so I suppose it's quite a feather in his cap, and if he does well there, increases output or cuts costs or whatever you're supposed to do if you run a factory, he did explain it to me once but I'm such a scatterbrain – and so of course he can arrange for me to ride on the post-coach whenever I go to visit him and his wife – did I mention he's only just got married? Quite a nice girl, though I don't really think he's ideally suited to someone that quiet; still, it was his choice and he's such a serious young man, I'm sure he gave it an awful lot of thought and weighed up the pros and cons—'

Niessa closed her eyes and tried to block out the noise. It was all wasted on her, of course; she'd been in the banking business long enough to recognise a spy when she saw one. The duty spy, presumably; doomed to bounce up and down this hateful road day after day, year after year, as a matter of standard operating procedure. She really wasn't very good at it; somebody's aunt, at a guess, for whom a job had to be found. For want of anything better to do, Niessa spent a few minutes assessing the feasibility of pushing her off the coach under the wheels – she ought to have enough physical strength to manage it, but making it look like an accident was problematical, at best. Telling her to shut up would be more straightforward, but she'd learned enough recently about the Sons of Heaven to know that offending any of them was a bad idea. *When I was afraid they'd torture me, I had no idea they could be so insidious. Or so damned thorough.*

'I need a piss,' she growled. 'Do you know how to make them stop the coach? Otherwise I'm just going to have to pee all over the floor.'

That shut her up, the miserable bitch. Niessa felt better already. If only they could have discussed things openly at the start, she could have pointed out that the homely woman-to-woman-chat approach was going to be counter-productive in her case; they could have chosen something far less tiresome from the woman's repertoire of personas, and it might even have been mildly entertaining.

'I'm afraid not,' the spy replied in a little muted voice that barely rose above a shriek. 'It's dreadful, the way they just don't think about such things. I mean, it wouldn't kill them to have a jerry or even just an old jar or something. I think I'll get my son to do something about it.'

In spite of herself, Niessa couldn't help admiring the fluency of her recovery. Maybe they did have something in common, professional to professional. Now if only they could talk on that level, one woman of the world to another, it might be quite interesting.

'So tell me,' Niessa said. 'How long have you been a spy?'

The woman stared at her, then shook her head. 'What an extraordinary thing to say—' she began, but Niessa was gazing straight into her eyes. 'You must be Niessa Loredan,' she said. 'I was told you'd be coming through at some stage.'

'You know about me, then.'

The woman laughed. 'The notorious witch of the outlands? I should say so. Not that I believe in all that stuff myself, but there are plenty who do. Outlanders, of course,' she added quickly. 'You're much older than I'd expected; I suppose that's what put me off.'

'Thank you very much,' Niessa replied. 'And for the record, I'm not a witch, I'm a banker. There's no such thing as witchcraft, as you well know.'

The coach went over a particularly deep pothole, and Niessa felt her teeth crash together. 'You must have offended somebody, to be given this job,' she said. 'Getting shaken to bits like this has got to be some kind of punishment.'

The woman shrugged. 'You're not that far off the mark, actually,' she said. 'Promoted sideways, at any rate. And to answer your question, five years. Before that I was an office manager in the prefecture at Ap' Escatoy. That was a good job, I didn't mind it at all, but I'd been in it too long; wouldn't do for a Daughter of Heaven with my seniority to be in a job where I might have an outlander for a superior. So here I am.'

'My sympathy,' Niessa replied. 'Now then, since you've been straight with me, was there anything specific you wanted to know? I don't suppose there was, since you say you didn't know who I was until just now. Or were you given a set of mission objectives for as and when you came across Niessa Loredan?'

'Only very vague ones,' the spy answered. 'And they're mostly to do with your daughter's escape – was it pre-arranged, did she have any help from any of our people, that sort of thing. If you'd care to tell me anything about that, I'd be grateful.'

Niessa wriggled her back into a crack between two barrels. 'By all means,' she said, 'but there isn't anything much I can tell you, or at least there's nothing you can corroborate, which is much the same thing. No, it wasn't prearranged – at least, not that I'm aware. You see, my daughter and I aren't exactly friends. In fact, we hate each other. Really and truly. Do you have any children?'

The spy shook her head.

'You're better off,' Niessa said. 'Anyway, it's just possible that Iseutz knew what was going on and cooked up some scheme behind my back, but I doubt it. Have you caught her yet?'

'I don't believe we have. The last I heard was that she was with her uncle in the Mesoge; but you'll appreciate that I haven't got any special clearances for restricted information; that's just the rumour that's going around.'

'I understand,' Niessa said. 'How's the war going, do you know? Where I've been they haven't told me anything.'

The woman narrowed her eyes. 'Presumably you know about your brother Bardas being in command of the field army.'

Niessa shook her head. 'Joint command,' she said. 'Meaning he's only there for show.'

'Not any more. Colonel Estar was killed; your brother's really in charge now. It's a strange thought, an outlander in command of four battalions. No offence, but I'm not sure I like the idea.'

'Given his track record, neither would I,' Niessa grunted. 'They've beaten him once; twice, really, since all he managed to do when he took over from Uncle Maxen was get the army out of there and back home again. He's a competent enough subordinate, our Bardas, but I wouldn't say he had what it takes to be a leader. The same's true of my brother Gorgas, to a lesser extent; he's a good soldier, but he has problems dealing with the larger issues. Basically that's what went wrong on Scona; he couldn't see that the game had stopped being worth the candle. Mind you, Gorgas has never known when to quit; it's his biggest problem, really.'

The coach lurched again, even more fiercely this time, and came to a sudden halt. A barrel of fancy biscuits was dislodged from the top of the stack and fell down, nearly hitting Niessa on the head. 'If I were you, I'd get this driver replaced,' she said; and then noticed that the spy was dead. There was an arrow right through the exact middle of her throat, pinning her to the barrel she'd been sitting against. As Niessa watched, the spy's head toppled sideways and flopped down on her right shoulder, eyes still open.

Now what? Niessa thought angrily, and she looked round to see where the arrow had come from. *And what's the point of having an Empire if you can't keep the roads safe?* Nothing seemed to be happening; but wherever they were, it was depressingly open and exposed. Trying to run would be suicide, if the bandits were inclined to kill witnesses, whereas staying put wasn't any better. No point trying to hide if they were going to steal the cargo; they'd find her sooner or later while they were unloading. *So that's it, then*, she thought. *All this way for nothing. What a waste of time and energy.*

A helmet appeared above the side-rail. Here at least was something she could vent her anger on; she picked up the barrel of biscuits and slammed it down on the apex of the helmet, where the straps that held the plates together met. The result was satisfying, if not downright comic; there was a sigh, and the helmet vanished in a shower of broken slats and biscuits. *That's what you get for tangling with one of the Fighting Loredans*, Niessa said to herself, grinning. *Just because I'm a girl doesn't mean I can't play rough games too.*

'Niessa Loredan?' The voice was behind her, and as she spun round she caught her ankle in a niche between two boxes. It hurt.

'Ouch,' she said. 'Yes, who wants to know?'

'We're here to rescue you.' Another damned helmet, with some sort of visor contraption that covered the man's face completely. Was it too much to ask to be allowed to talk to a human being, instead of all this ironmongery?

'What are you talking about?' Niessa said.

'Your brother's orders,' the helmet said. 'We've come to rescue you and take you home.'

Niessa scowled. 'Which brother?' she said.

The helmet looked bewildered; a difficult trick for a piece of iron. 'Gorgas Loredan,' it replied.

'Oh.' Niessa sighed. 'Well, you can jolly well go back and tell Gorgas that I don't need to be rescued, I don't want to be rescued and, if I did, the last person I'd want rescuing me is him. Have you got that, or shall I write it down for you?'

Now the helmet was looking utterly wretched. 'You don't understand,' it said. 'We're taking you back to the Mesoge. There's a ship waiting for us. But we've got to hurry, because there'll be a cavalry column along here in an hour, and—'

'It's all right,' Niessa said, 'I won't tell them which way you went, provided you leave now. Just do me a favour and steal some of this junk; try to make it look like an ordinary hold-up.'

Poor helmet, she thought as she said this. She could hear other voices of other helmets – they all had a booming, resonant quality, like a man down a well, or the way her late husband Gallas had sounded once when he got his head stuck in the whey bucket. The other helmets sounded agitated, which was reasonable enough. 'I'm sorry,' the helmet said, 'but I've got my orders. You're coming with me. Anything between you and your brother is no concern—'

'Hang on,' Niessa said. 'You're a Scona man, aren't you? Well, of course you are. Are you really going to use force to kidnap me? You do know who I am, don't you? Apart from being Gorgas' sister, I mean.'

'Yes,' said the helmet, rather panic-stricken, 'but it's not up to me. I've got to do what I'm told. Now stand up and I'll help you down off the cart.'

'Go to hell,' Niessa replied. 'In fact, you go back to Gorgas and you tell him I said to stop being such a bloody fool, because I've had enough of him and his ridiculous heroics. Go on, he won't bite you. Not if you tell him I said—'

At which point, the man who'd climbed up silently behind her dropped a sack over her head, flipped her carefully off her feet and knelt down beside her to do up the rope. 'About time,' the helmet said. 'Get all this junk off the cart, we'll use it to lay a false trail.' Inside the sack, Niessa was making the most extraordinary noises. Between them, they hoisted her off the cart without banging her about too much, while another man looked after the soldier Niessa had brained with the biscuit-barrel, and another finished off the driver, who'd been trying to crawl away in spite of two arrows in almost the same hole through his chest. They cut the guy-ropes and pulled off the barrels and boxes, letting them smash and roll; spices and perfumes and herbs and fine wine and scented oils for dressing salad – all mixed together, the smell was extraordinary, abstruse and exotic enough that even a Son of Heaven would have been hard put to it to identify all the ingredients.

'That'll do,' said the helmet, pulling up his visor to wipe his forehead. Under the metal he was a round-faced man with a little bobble for a nose. 'You two, take the coach, we'll meet you back at the ship.'

An hour or so after they'd gone, the cavalry column came through, just as the helmet had said. They found two bodies, one male and one female, stripped naked, and a large heap of smashed biscuits. No barrels or boxes – a bunch of opportunists had appeared out of the sand-dunes and dismantled them in a matter of minutes, prising out the nails to be straightened later, carefully lifting off the steel bands from the barrels and collecting the staves (unbroken ones in one bundle, to be used again; broken ones separate, for firewood) – and all the cargo had been looted, apart from the cinnamon and wild rose honey biscuits so highly prized by the prefect of Ap' Escatoy. Apparently the looters had tried a few of them, spat them out and jumped up and down on the rest, just in case any foolhardy souls might be tempted to eat them.

'That's the lot,' sighed Habsurai, gang-boss of the logging contingent, as the last lumber wagon rolled to a halt. 'I hereby certify that there's nothing bigger than a dandelion left standing between here and the Pigeon River. And if you want us to go further out than that,' he added, before Temrai could say anything, 'you're going to have to give us an armed escort, because from where we were felling yesterday we could see Loredan's scouts fooling about on the other side of North Reach ford. If you want any more timber, you're going to have to fight for it.'

Another hot day; there was a constant relay of weary-looking children struggling up and down the steep path with buckets, and the stonemasons had all but given up. Not that they were proper stonemasons; the clans didn't have any, never having had a use for large blocks of stone before now. Anybody who didn't have a hat was improvising furiously – a sack draped over the head and shoulders, secured with a piece of twine around the temples; the broad, flat wicker baskets the bakers carried their bread in; the gonfalon standard of the late City Prefect of Perimadeia, looted on general principles at the Fall and now at last coming in handy for something, wrapped round its new owner's head like a turban. Temrai was wearing his arming cap, the detachable liner that had come with the fine and completely unwearable barbute helmet he'd bought from an Island merchant before the civil war. The cap was made of thick, matted grey felt and was the only part of the ensemble that even remotely fitted.

He wiped sweat out of his eyes and shook his head. 'Which would defeat the object of the exercise,' he said. 'Well, if that's it, that's it; we'll just have to make do with what we've got. Thanks; you've done a good job.'

Habsurai's men had brought in a lot of timber – the stacks of trimmed logs looked like a small city in their own right – but it probably wasn't going to be enough. The lower and middle palisades were finished, the head of each stake dramatically sharpened to a point, and the swing-bridge, causeways and catwalks were nearly done, but the upper stockade wasn't a practical proposition any more, not if they wanted any lumber for all the other works that still had to be done. Temrai sat down on an upturned bucket and tried to think of an alternative. A simple ditch and mound – well, it'd be better than nothing, but not good enough, not if Bardas Loredan had taken to heart the valuable lessons he'd been given in the sustained use of trebuchets against a fortified position. Without timber, they had a choice between turf and stone; both labour-intensive, time-consuming, inefficient. It would take a lot of people a long time to cut enough turves to build a wall high enough and thick enough to be of any defensive value, but at least there was enough turf for the job. Stone – well, there were a few outcrops of weatherbeaten granite dotted about, enough at a pinch for a few towers and gateways, but if they wanted more than that they were going to have to dig for it and quarry it out.

Sitting still wasn't going to solve anything. He stood up (*since when did my knees hurt so much? I'm getting old*) and hobbled rather self-consciously across to the timber stack, where Habsurai's people were hoisting up the last few logs on the big crane. For all his weary, jaundiced mood he couldn't help stopping and gazing at the spectacle, a hundred-year-old oak trunk whisked up and flown through the air like a child's toy. *We can do this sort of thing now; how did we ever learn to do this? If only we had a future, what a future we'd have . . .*

Then the crane broke. Later, when the engineers examined it, they found that the strut that supported the beam that the counterweight hung from had been cut from wet, star-shaken wood, and the stresses of the crane had torn it apart; a real novice's mistake, if ever there was one. As the counterweight plummeted to the ground, the magnificent flying oak that Temrai had been admiring dropped sharply, slipped one of the two loops of its cradle and swung wildly, out of control on the remaining loop. It was coming straight at him and for some reason he was too astonished to move –

– Until someone jumped at him, like a cat pouncing, and pushed him off his feet just as the butt end of the log whirled above him, pushing aside the air in more or less the exact spot where he'd been standing. He tried to lift his head, but a hand thrust it down, grinding his nose into the dirt while the log lurched back again on its return swing; it crashed into the side of the crane, expending the last of its force.

'Are you all right?' The voice sounded anxious, and familiar. 'Temrai? Are you all right?'

'Mmm.' Using his arms, Temrai pushed himself up off the ground. His mouth was full of mud. 'Thank you,' he said, just as he was in the act of remembering who the man was. 'Dassascai? Is that you?'

'Yes,' Dassascai replied. 'I think I've put my shoulder out. That'd be a real nuisance; I've got a couple of hunded ducks to kill and pluck.'

Very cautiously, Temrai stood up. There were people running towards him from all directions. 'It's all right,' he told them, 'no real harm done—'

'Speak for yourself,' Dassascai muttered.

Temrai held out a hand and helped him up. 'That's twice,' he said. 'You seem to have a knack of showing up just when I'm about to get myself killed.'

'Really?' Dassascai wriggled his shoulders and cried out in pain. 'Well, you can show your appreciation by sending along a couple of men to kill my ducks. And a doctor wouldn't come amiss, either. Sorry, did I just say something funny?'

Temrai shook his head. 'You lived in Ap' Escatoy for years, didn't you?'

'That's right,' Dassascai replied. 'Most of my adult life, as it happens.'

'Thought so. I think you might find your idea of a doctor isn't the same as ours. I thought I'd better warn you, that's all.'

Dassascai grunted. 'Even your pig-ignorant medicine men ought to know how to put back a wrenched shoulder,' he said. 'If they want to slit open a few ducks while they're at it, it won't bother me.'

'That's all right, then. Just so long as you know what you're letting yourself in for.'

In the event, all it took was a sharp, controlled twist, enough to make Dassascai yell with pain but over in a moment. 'You'll live,' the sawbones said cheerfully. 'Get some rest if you can,' and, to Temrai, 'See to it he's excused duty for a day or two. What does he do?'

'Kills ducks,' Temrai replied.

The doctor nodded. 'Repetitive arm and shoulder movements, not a good idea. Put someone else on it, give this one
a break.'

'Certainly,' Temrai replied. 'It's the least I can do.'

For some reason he found it difficult to raise a volunteer
for duck-slaying duty; in the end he had to take a work detail
off ditch-digging, and even then they complained about it.
Then he went back to his tent, where he'd left Dassascai
lying on the bed. (Tilden was away supervising the felt-
makers) 'How's it now?' he asked.

'Evil,' Dassascai replied with a grin. 'Well, you wouldn't
expect me to say, it's fine, really; not when I've got a chance
of a lifetime to milk a genuine obligation on the part of the
head of state.'

Temrai smiled. 'Be my guest,' he said. 'Like I said, that's
twice now. Anybody'd think you were my guardian angel.'

'Enlightened self-interest. How else was I going to get out
of doing those goddamn ducks?'

It was cool and pleasant in the tent, and hot and
unpleasant outside; and Temrai remembered that he hadn't
stopped for a rest for almost thirty-six hours. 'Have a drink
with me,' he said. 'There's something I've been meaning to
ask you.'

'Oh yes?'

Temrai nodded as he unstoppered the jug. 'Pancakes,'
he said. 'You haven't inherited your uncle's recipe, by any
chance?'

Dassascai laughed. 'Oh, the recipe's plain enough – eggs,
flour, water and a little goose-fat to lubricate the pan. He
told me so himself, many times. Problem is, he never actually
followed it himself.'

'Oh.'

'He was that sort of man,' Dassascai went on, taking the
cup from Temrai's hand. 'He never could bear the thought of
anybody being able to do the one thing he was better at
than anybody else. Can't say I blame him, really; if you're the
undisputed master of a popular skill, what reason would you
ever have for teaching people how to replace you?'

'I suppose so,' Temrai said. 'But if I'd been him, I wouldn't
have wanted my discovery to die with me.'

'That's because you're not my uncle,' Dassascai replied. 'I'm sure that's exactly what he wanted, so that in years to come people would shake their heads and say, Nobody makes pancakes like the ones Dondai the fletcher used to make. People tend to remember things like that, you see; it's a shot at immortality, like being a great poet, only more so. After all, how many people really care about poetry, as against the number who really care about pancakes?'

'I see,' Temrai said gravely. 'So if I want to be remembered for ever, instead of conquering Perimadeia I should have learned to fry batter.'

Dassascai yawned. 'Quite possibly. For one thing, it's far less uncertain. No offence, but it's quite possible that you'll be remembered as the man who got comprehensively beaten by Bardas Loredan and the Empire; that's immortality, but not a very nice sort. Whereas if they remember you for your pancakes, it'll only be because they were the best there ever were.' He frowned slightly. 'Is that what you want?' he asked. 'To be immortal?'

'Not really,' Temrai replied. 'Oh, I'm not saying the thought hasn't crossed my mind; like it did just now, when I was watching people working. If a hundred years from now people remember me as the man who turned our nation into craftsmen and engineers, that'd be quite pleasing, if I were here to see it. But I won't be, of course. I'll be dead, and past caring.'

Dassascai yawned again, and winced. 'Very sensible attitude,' he said, 'in the circumstances. I wonder if Bardas Loredan thinks the same way. At the moment, he's down as the man who lost Perimadeia; do you think he's hell-bent on fixing that, or doesn't he care, either?'

'That's twice you've mentioned him,' Temrai said calmly. 'Why?'

'No reason.'

Temrai scratched the back of his neck. 'You're not trying to needle me, or anything like that?'

'Why should I want to do that?'

'No idea,' Temrai replied. 'Well, I suppose you could be probing me for weak spots, or trying to find out if I turn pale and shiver at the mention of his name – that's the sort of thing a spy might be interested in.'

'Not really.' Dassascai held out his cup for a refill. 'As far as I know, and I'm speculating here, all spies want are hard facts – you know, troop movements, disposition of forces, ground plans of the city defences, where the blind spots are in the field of fire. I can't see that the getting-to-know-you stuff ever won any battles.'

'That's all right, then. Are you a spy, by the way? Really?'

'No.'

'Fair enough. I'll take your word for it.'

Dassascai dipped his head. 'Thank you,' he said. 'Just out of interest, have you got any spies in the enemy army?'

'Not really,' Temrai replied.

'And if you did, you wouldn't tell me. In case I mention it in my next report.'

'Precisely. My turn: what made you come here, after Ap' Escatoy? It's obvious you don't fit in here.'

'Only because people won't accept me, because they think I'm a spy.'

Temrai pursed his lips. 'That's partly it,' he said. 'But it's true, you don't act like you belong here. You could have gone anywhere – the Island, Colleon, Ausira; you could've gone east, or stayed around Ap' Escatoy until they rebuild it. Wouldn't you have found a city a bit more congenial?'

Dassascai laughed. 'I don't know where you get this could-have-gone-anywhere notion from. For a start, I lost everything in the fall of Ap' Escatoy. I spent my last few quarters getting here, and even then I had a long walk because I couldn't afford the fare for the last leg of the journey.'

'All right,' Temrai conceded. 'But since by your reckoning getting anywhere at all was a real achievement, couldn't you have made your way – overcoming difficulties of heroic proportions, granted – to a city; somewhere you could get a bath and a shave without having had to carry the water in a goatskin bag for two days' march across the wilderness? What I mean is, you had to pass by several perfectly good cities to get from there to here. What was the big attraction?'

'Ducks,' Dassascai replied. 'All my life I've secretly yearned to spend my days up to the elbows in duckshit and blood.'

Temrai nodded gravely. 'That I can understand,' he said. 'This is no good. I should be out there working, setting an example. But it's too hot.'

'Take it easy while you've got the chance,' Dassascai agreed. 'But since you raised the subject, you should understand, because you made the same choice.'

'Did I?'

'Of course. You lived and worked in Perimadeia for a while; don't tell me you hated every minute of it and couldn't wait to finish the job and get out of there, because I don't believe you. I mean, if you'd hated it, how come you've spent so much time and effort since then trying to turn our people into replica Perimadeians?'

Temrai sat still and quiet for a while before answering. 'Do you know,' he said, 'I'm not sure. To begin with, it was just a side-effect – we had to learn how to build siege engines in order to take the City, so we taught ourselves the basics. Once we'd done that, though, it seemed a pity to stop there and go back to chivvying goats across the plains. And no, you're right; I didn't hate my time in the City, far from it. I enjoyed it, and by and large I liked the City people a lot.'

'And then you wiped them out? No offence, just asking.'

'It's a fair point. I suppose it's inevitable; if you want to harm your enemies, you'll always end up harming your friends as well. You can't keep war and destruction stoppered up in a little bottle, like vitriol or nitre; if you want to use them, you've got to slop them about.'

Dassascai shifted slightly and lay on his back. 'True enough,' he said. 'But this business of imitating the people you destroyed, what about that? Is it guilt, do you think? Or did you supplant them because you wanted to take their place?'

Temrai frowned. 'I don't think it was anything so deliberate,' he said. 'I think it's just the way things are; the more you hate an enemy, the more you come to resemble him. It's an extremely intimate relationship, hatred; it makes you very close to the person you hate. I sometimes think you can't really hate somebody unless you really understand them. Harming, yes; killing, even – you can do that with detachment, cold-bloodedly. But you don't hate ducks, quite likely you don't understand them.'

Dassascai smiled. 'What's to understand?'

'Ah, well, there you are. Now, when I was a kid and my

father and uncle took me out hunting the first time, they told me that a true hunter has to understand what he kills; and I honestly believe that they *loved* the deer and the boar we used to hunt. When they used to talk about them, it was all affection, as if they were talking about family. I suppose it's because they'd studied and observed them for so long they'd grown attached to them. They always made a point of saying thank you to anything we killed. Once when I was quite small, I asked my father if it bothered him, killing animals like that; and he said yes, it bothered him a lot, because every time he felt he'd just lost a friend. Now I never could make any sense out of that until I went to live in the City; I still can't explain it, but now at least I know what he meant.'

'It doesn't make sense,' Dassascai said. 'But then, neither does friendship, or love for that matter. I suppose it must be like those terrible family feuds that you hear about from time to time; they couldn't hate each other so much if they didn't love each other too. Like the Loredan brothers, for example.'

'Three times.'

'What? Oh, yes, sorry. But it's a good example.'

'You're right,' Temrai said, 'it is. Now there was a time when I hated Bardas Loredan, more than anybody else in the world. I can't say the same now. Maybe that's because he's hunting me, rather than the other way round.'

Dassascai looked at him. 'If he does kill you, will you forgive him?'

Temrai smiled. 'I already have.'

The first they knew of it was after breakfast, when they went out to do business; and even then, it took some time for them to notice.

There were Imperial soldiers in the streets; half-platoons standing about on street corners looking embarrassed more than anything else, like young men stood up by their girls. Venart was aware that something was different, but it was too early in the morning for him to consider the implications. Besides, groups of people standing aimlessly on street corners were a common enough sight on the Island. There was bound to be a simple, rational explanation; at least,

Venart was prepared to take it on trust that there was one.

It was when they reached the Market Square that they all started to feel uncomfortable, because there was a full company of soldiers there when they arrived, drawn up in parade order but with their weapons uncovered and drawn.

'Don't say somebody's tried to break into their treasury,' Eseutz said. 'Not tactful.'

'That man's pinning a notice on the Market Hall door,' Athli pointed out. 'Is he one of them?'

'No idea. Well, come on. Let's go and see what it says.'

The provincial office house style was brief, clear and businesslike; as from dawn on the seventeenth day of Butrepidon ('When's that?' Eseutz asked. 'Today,' Venart replied. 'Quiet.') the prefect of Ap' Escatoy, by the powers vested in him etcetera, had annexed the Island to the outer western province of the Empire. All property belonging to citizens of the Island would henceforth legally vest in the said prefect, in accordance with the practice of the Empire. There followed a list of regulations governing the transitional period leading up to full incorporation: nobody to enter or leave the territory without permission; no citizen to purport to make a binding contract with a foreigner; no public assembly or gathering to exceed ten people without previous consent; all arms and munitions of war to be surrendered immediately; all non-citizens to report to the commissioner for aliens forthwith; all buildings to be left unlocked to facilitate entry and inventory; sundry public order provisions; announcements of a census and interim taxation –

'But they can't,' Eseutz said. Nobody else spoke. The man who'd pinned up the notice put his hammer back in his satchel and walked away, exchanging a few words with the captain of the guard.

'It's all right,' said Venart, after a quick count. 'There's only four of us.'

'Shut *up*, Ven.' Vetriz was reading the notice for the third time. 'That's it, then. You and your bloody Ship-Owners' Association.'

'What?'

'That's what's done it,' she said, quietly and angrily. 'You thought you could pull their tails and stiff them for more money, and now look.'

Eseutz was pulling at her sleeve. 'Come on,' she said, 'let's move away. Those soldiers look very tense, if you ask me.'

'What? Oh.' Vetriz and the others followed her to one of the small colonnades behind the Market Hall, where there were already quite a few groups of up to nine agitated-looking citizens.

'Here's what we do,' Eseutz was saying, in a loud whisper. 'We go home, pack up as much money and valuable stuff as we can comfortably carry, and try and get to the ships. If only we can get off the Island, they can't follow us or anything, they haven't got any ships of their own. That's why they can never make this thing stick.'

Venart scowled at her. 'And how do you propose we deal with all the soldiers who're already on the damn ships? Or had you forgotten, they're going to invade Perimadeia with them. Athli, what about you? I can't remember, are you a citizen or a foreigner?'

Athli thought for a moment. 'That's a good point,' she said. 'Yes, I'm a citizen, because I own property here; but I might be able to kid them into thinking I'm Shastel. But how's that going to help you?'

'Well, somebody's got to go and get help,' Venart said. 'Raise an army, throw these bastards into the sea. That's why you've got to go and raise the alarm—'

Athli looked at him. 'Don't be silly,' she said. 'Who on earth is going to come and rescue us?'

Venart hadn't thought of that, obviously. 'Mercenaries,' said Eseutz. 'We could hire mercenaries – the hell with how much it costs, we've got to get them off the Island. Once we've done that, we'll be safe.'

Athli shook her head. 'You're dreaming,' she said. 'There must be – what, fifty thousand men in the expeditionary force? You'd need at least three times that for a disputed landing. Where are we going to find—?'

'No,' Eseutz interrupted, 'you're wrong. Right now there's fifty thousand; but when they've gone off to attack Temrai there'll only be a little garrison. That's when we get them.'

Athli closed her eyes and opened them again. 'When they've got our ships,' she said. 'Not a very sensible suggestion, is it?

As soon as they hear what we've done, they'll come storming back and we won't stand a chance. Have you any idea what they do to rebels?'

'There has to be *something* –' Eseutz stopped in mid-sentence; five soldiers and an NCO were heading towards them. Venart looked as if he was about to run away, but his sister grabbed his arm. 'If you run, they'll kill you,' she whispered.

The soldiers came nearer, stopped. 'Venart Auzeil,' the NCO said. 'Eseutz Mesatges.'

Venart took a deep breath. 'I'm Venart Auzeil,' he said. 'What—?'

'Eseutz Mesatges.'

Athli, Vetriz and Eseutz stayed perfectly still. The NCO waited for a few seconds, then nodded. 'All right,' he said, 'we'll take them all and sort it out later. You're under arrest,' he added, as an afterthought. 'This way.'

CHAPTER FIFTEEN

'I hate getting arrested,' Eseutz said. 'It's so boring. You sit around for hours in cells and interview rooms and waiting rooms and anterooms, with nothing to do and nothing to read, and it's always either too cold or too hot, and the food—'

That morning, it had been the guild secretary's office, tucked away discreetly at the end of a corridor leading off the gallery that ran round three sides of the Merchant Venturers' guild house. That morning, it had been a place you dreamed of being invited to; a big, fat office hidden down a little, thin passageway, a monument to the fusion of discretion and conspicuous display. Secretary Aloet Cor was known to be a fanatical collector of furniture, in particular the delicate, expensive and entirely impractical bone and ivory chairs and tables made by the Arrazin family of Perimadeia for six generations; she didn't like them much, so they said, but she collected them because they were rare and horrendously overpriced, and likely to appreciate in value considerably now that the supply had been made finite following the death of all the Arrazins in the Fall. It was worth sitting on the hard marble bench outside for an hour or so, they said, just for a glimpse of the bizarre and rather grotesque lampstand carved by Leucas Arrazin a hundred and fifty years ago out of a single piece of whalebone.

'Get arrested often, do you?' Venart asked. 'Sorry; I'm just curious.'

Eseutz shrugged. 'It depends where you go,' she said. 'In some places it's accepted, like their way of saying hello, welcome to our fair city. There was a time when I used to go to Burzouth a lot, I was on first-name terms with all the

330

warders at the excise guardhouse. We used to play chess or I'd sew buttons on for them—'

'You?' Vetriz interrupted. 'Since when have you been able to sew on a button?'

Tonight it had become the office of Major Javec, the newly appointed sub-prefect of the Island; and somehow the corridor was darker and colder, the marble bench was harder, and seeing the famous Arrazins wasn't quite the priority it would have been a few hours earlier. In fact, Vetriz had a horrible feeling that she had just been added to a collection, and had been dumped in a stockroom waiting to be catalogued, stamped and put in a cabinet. She'd known a man once who collected the skulls of birds; he'd described to her the method of skinning them, boiling out the brains and flesh, bleaching the bone and mounting the finished exhibit; she'd actually found it rather fascinating, in a disgusting sort of way.

'The point I was trying to make,' Eseutz said, 'is that different people mean different things by arresting you. For all we know, it could just be a getting-to-know-you thing, nothing more sinister than that.'

Venart sighed. 'Then how would you account for the fact that we're the only ones here?' he said. 'Do you think that, as far as they're concerned, we're the only people worth getting to know on the whole island?'

Eseutz made an exasperated gesture with her long, thin hands. 'All right,' she said, 'be miserable, see if I care. Personally, I don't see the point. After all, it's not going to make things any better, you sitting there worrying yourself to death. But if that's your idea of a good attitude, then you go ahead—'

'Eseutz.' Athli lifted her head and looked her in the eye. 'Shut up. And you, Ven. I know it's only because you're scared, and bickering makes it easier, but you're starting to annoy me. All right?'

'Speak for yourself,' Eseutz snapped. 'I'm not in the least scared—'

The door opened and the two guards who'd been standing like architectural features behind them, blocking their way back down the corridor, motioned to them to get up and go in. 'It'll be all right, you'll see,' Eseutz whispered. The others ignored her.

Sub-Prefect Javec was a round man, short for a Son of Heaven, bald as an egg on top but fringed round his multiple chins with a little curtain of woolly beard. He looked neither threatening nor friendly; mostly, in fact, he looked very tired, which was of course perfectly understandable. Annexing a whole country is hard work.

'Names,' he said; not to the four Islanders but to his clerk, a young outlander with curly brown hair. The clerk read the names off a list. His pronunciation was awful; Eseutz Mesatges became Ee-soo Muzzertgees, while Venart and Vetriz both found that their family name was now Orzle. He was rather better at Perimadeian names, because apart from putting the stress on the wrong syllable of Zeuxis, he managed it quite competently.

'Thank you,' the sub-prefect said, and the clerk sat down and started to sort through a tray full of wax tablets, the sort that Imperial NCOs were issued with for filing reports. 'And thank you,' the sub-prefect continued, apparently noticing the Islanders for the first time. 'I hope this isn't too inconvenient for you, but these things have to be done. You are all friends of Captain Bardas Loredan—'

'Excuse me,' Eseutz interrupted. 'I'm not.'

Javec moved his head a little so that he could see her without getting a crick in his neck.

'Oh,' he said. 'Is that right?' he went on, facing Athli, who nodded. 'You two, is that right?'

Venart took a deep breath. 'Yes, sir,' he said. 'I don't think she's even met him once.'

'I see,' Javec said. 'Well, can't be helped; you'll have to stay with these three until the war's over. Now,' he went on, 'you're Vetriz Auzeil.'

'That's right.' She was impressed; Javec's pronunciation was flawless.

'And about seven years ago you had an affair with Gorgas Loredan.'

Vetriz sighed. 'That's right,' she said, before Venart could deny the statement on her behalf. Pity; she'd managed to keep it from him this long. 'Though *affair* is probably an overstatement. I believe the usual expression is one-night stand.'

Javec nodded. 'I stand corrected,' he said. 'That is what it says in the file. Well, I'm sorry about this but I'm going to have to put the four of you under house arrest for the time being - I'm sure you're all harmless enough, but as long as Captain Loredan's in command of a major field army, anybody who could be used against him as a hostage - well, we'll feel happier if we know you're out of the way and safe. I'm sure you'll see the logic behind it if you think about it for a moment.'

Nobody said anything.

'We'll try to make this as painless as possible. You'll be confined to the Auzeil house – that's number sixteen in the fourth transverse alley, yes? I'll be posting a guard, obviously; they'll have their own bivouac and wash-house and cook and everything, so you won't have to fetch and carry or feed them. You can receive visitors for an hour a day, but of course there'll have to be soldiers present. Any questions?'

Out of the corner of her eye, Vetriz caught sight of what had to be the notorious lampstand. She turned her head a little for a better view; it was every bit as hideous as she'd imagined.

'Overrated, if you ask me,' the sub-prefect said. 'Of course, I'm not an expert by any means, but I find the late-period Arrazins are almost like parodies of the products of the classic period. There's this unfortunate tendency to try to do things on a massive scale that are better suited to small work. Take the big two-handed cup, for instance; over there, look.'

They looked in the direction he was pointing, and saw what looked unpleasantly like a human skull, mounted on a small ivory pedestal. The top had been sawn off, turning the brain cavity into a cup, and two handles, made of cunningly spliced finger-bones, had been inserted into the ear hollows. 'That's an interesting piece, isn't it?' Javec went on. 'I believe it was originally the head of a rebel prince of the plains tribes; he lost a civil war about a century ago, and his victorious rival sent it to the City to be mounted. It was part of the loot brought back by Captain Loredan, when he was a young man. Probably a unique example, although I have a stag's head that's generically similar in my own collection at home; Suidas Arrazin, quite early.'

Vetriz felt slightly sick.

'Is it valuable?' Eseutz asked. 'Only, I know where there's one just like it, if you're interested.'

(*That's Eseutz*, Vetriz thought.)

'Really?' Sub-Prefect Javec leaned forward a little. 'A genuine Arrazin? With a provenance?'

Eseutz frowned. 'I think so. I'd have to check, obviously. If it is genuine, roughly how much are we talking about?'

'Money isn't really an issue,' Javec replied. 'If you'd care to give me the name of the person who has this thing, I'll follow it up; thank you.'

'Jolay Caic; he's got a stall down by the long quay, anybody'll tell you how to find it.' As she spoke, Eseutz realised just what Javec had meant by, *Money isn't really an issue*. A pity; she'd known Caic for a good few years, and he'd never done her any harm. 'But it's been a while,' she added quickly. 'For all I know, he may not have it any more.'

Javec shrugged. 'I'm sure I'll be able to track it down, if it does turn out to be a genuine piece. But that's by the way.' He moved his head slightly and fixed his eyes on Athli. 'Now then,' he said, 'I imagine that you're about to point out that I have no jurisdiction over you because you're a Shastel citizen, and by detaining you I'm risking a diplomatic incident. Well, for a start I think that at best you've got dual nationality and in all likelihood you're just as much of an Islander as these three; but I'm not going to get involved in that, because I just don't have the time or the energy. Let me put it this way: I'd suggest to you that staying put where we can keep an eye on you and protect you is very much in your best interests, just as it's in the best interests of your ward, Theudas Morosin. You two are probably closer to Captain Loredan than anybody else outside his family, and naturally that puts you at risk. If you accept what I'm saying – and you're a sensible young woman, so I'm sure you do – these tiresome issues of citizenship and jurisdiction simply don't arise, and we won't have to waste time on them. Do you agree?'

Athli looked at him; it was like looking at her own reflection in the polished visor of a helmet, for all the good it did her. 'I suppose so,' she said quietly. 'After all, I don't imagine I'd be doing any business even if you let me go.'

Javec smiled. 'Thank you for reminding me. For what it's

worth, the provincial office has taken over the Shastel Bank franchise here – we've written to the Order to regularise the position, and I'm sure there won't be any difficulties. I should congratulate you on the clarity and thoroughness of your records, by the way. When things have settled down a bit, I'm sure they'll be glad to have you back as chief clerk.'

Athli looked at him for a long moment, and nodded. 'That's very kind,' she said.

'Unless,' Javec went on – he was watching her very closely – 'unless you feel you might be interested in joining Captain Loredan's staff, wherever his next posting happens to be. It'd be just like old times, don't you think?'

'I don't think so,' Athli replied. 'I don't know a thing about military administration, I'm afraid.'

'Well, you don't have to make your mind up right away,' Javec said. 'We'll see how things turn out, shall we? And now, if you'll excuse me – thank you for your time; and for the tip about that possible Arrazin head-piece. I'll most certainly follow that up.'

The two guards took a step forwards, and the Islanders stood up quickly. 'Just one thing,' Athli asked.

'Yes?'

'You mentioned Theudas – Theudas Morosin? What's going to happen to him?'

Javec smiled. 'Once again, thank you for reminding me. I've already talked to him; he's going to join Captain Loredan. Interestingly, it sounds as if he might have some really rather useful local knowledge, following his recent detention by the plainspeople. I'm sure he sends you his best wishes.'

Athli frowned. 'He's already left, then?'

'Either that or he's on his way.'

'I see. It's just that I've got something that belongs to Bardas – to Captain Loredan; a sword, as it happens, rather a fine one, and I was wondering if Theudas could take it to him when he goes.'

Javec nodded. 'The Guelan,' he said. 'Superb example, isn't it? And the sentimental value as well, being a gift from his brother. It's all right, we've already seen to that. But thank you for raising the matter.'

He nodded to the guards, and a moment later the four Islanders found themselves back in the corridor, having to walk faster than they'd have liked just to keep up. In due course they arrived at the Auzeil house, hot and out of breath. The front door was open, with a soldier standing on either side of it.

'Excuse me,' Eseutz started to say, but a hand in the small of her back propelled her into the house, and the door closed behind her. There were two more soldiers in the hall, and a further three in the courtyard. One of them, a long, skinny man in his early fifties, declared that he was Sergeant Corlo, and provided they didn't give him any trouble, everybody was bound to get along just fine.

'I don't think I like him very much,' Eseutz whispered, as she went with Vetriz into the south back bedroom. 'In fact, I don't think I like any of them.'

Vetriz didn't answer; she'd been very quiet, in fact, for some time.

'I don't know,' Eseutz went on. 'I can't see how this is going to work out. I mean, what about our ships? Or the rest of our property? They can't just *take* it; what're we supposed to live on, for gods' sakes? And what are we supposed to do? Really I'd prefer it if they looted the place, so long as they went away afterwards and left us in peace. Being robbed is one thing, but—'

'Eseutz,' Vetriz interrupted, dropping heavily on to the bed, 'please. I've got the most dreadful headache and I need to lie down for a while.'

'What? Oh, all right. I'll go and see if I can at least get them to bring me some clothes; assuming they haven't confiscated them all.'

Has she gone?

Vetriz closed her eyes and nodded. 'Yes, thank goodness. She's a nice enough person, I do actually like her a lot, but the thought of being cooped up with her indefinitely is fairly horrifying.'

I can imagine.

Vetriz smiled. 'Being cooped up with anybody's bad enough, I suppose,' she said. 'But I'm sure that's going to be the least of our problems. What's going to happen, do you think? Seriously.'

I wish I knew.

'Oh.' She sighed. 'When that horrible man mentioned

Gorgas Loredan, I thought I was going to die. I suppose I'll
have to talk to Ven about it, and he'll be all pompous and
aggravating. When I think of some of the specimens he's got
mixed up with—'

*Perhaps you should have told him. But I can see why you
didn't.*

'Oh, I can handle Ven. Alexius, what *do* you think's
going to happen? It looks like a ghastly mess to me, and
it's all our own fault. We shouldn't have provoked them like
that.'

*Well, it's done now. Once they've finished with this war, I
expect they'll go away. Then it'll be up to you to try to make
the best of it. Of course, they'll keep the ships, and the crews
too, until they can train crews of their own. If I were you, I'd
be thinking about where you can go.*

'Oh,' Vetriz repeated. 'Leave the Island for good, you mean?
I've never ... Oh, this is awful. They can't do this to us, surely.'

*Don't count on it. They don't need you. They'll probably want
the Island itself as a naval base, so there'll be a need for inns,
shops, things like that. But they tend to prefer their own people,
in which case they might well evacuate all of you and send you
somewhere else inside the Empire. It's one of the things they
do; it's a very good way of keeping control.*

Vetriz lay quiet for a while. 'So where do you think we
should go? Colleon, maybe – but it's so hot there, I don't think
I'd be able to cope. And what would we do for a living? I
suppose it depends on whether we're able to take anything
with us. I think we'd be all right running a shop, especially if
Athli comes in with us – now there's a born survivor, if ever
there was one. I think Ven has friends in Colleon who'd
help us out.'

*Possibly. Of course, it won't be long before the Empire
annexes Colleon. Personally, if I were you, I'd be looking to go
a long way further out than that.*

She shook her head. 'Now you're really starting to depress
me,' she said. 'Not that I'm saying you're wrong. I just wish I
knew how all this happened so quickly.'

*Simple. It's because Bardas Loredan made it possible for
them to take Ap'Escatoy. They'd been stuck there for ten years;
there was no reason to assume they'd ever succeed. Arguably,
if it hadn't been for Bardas they never would. Ap' Escatoy*

was impregnable, there was no way round it, and the Empire doesn't have a fleet. Now Ap' Escatoy's fallen and they've got a fleet. As a study in how one man can affect the whole direction of the flow of the Principle, it's absolutely fascinating. If only I were still alive, I could write a book about it.

For a long time, nobody spoke.

'What the hell—' Iseutz finally broke the silence. 'What the *hell* is *she* doing here?'

Gorgas frowned. 'That's no way to talk about your own mother,' he said. 'Come on, this is a historic occasion, our first proper family reunion in – what, how long is it now, Niessa? Must be over twenty years.' He thought for a moment, then clicked his tongue. 'Of course, we know exactly how long it's been. How old are you now, Iseutz? Twenty-three?'

In the exact middle of the table was a cup, which Clefas had put there to catch the drips from the roof. Their father had dished it out of a piece of plate steel cut from a helmet his father had picked up on the site of the last major battle fought in the Mesoge, over a hundred years ago. As the raindrops fell into it they made a plinking noise, like a light hammer bouncing off an anvil.

'Twenty-three,' Gorgas repeated, when it was obvious that nobody else was going to contribute to the conversation. 'Which makes it nearly twenty-four years since the last time we were all together around this table. Well, nothing much seems to have changed around here, I'm glad to say.'

Clefas and Zonaras were sitting perfectly still, like mechanical iron figures in a clock-tower that haven't been wound up. Niessa was sulking, her arms folded, her chin jutting as she stared out of the window at the driving rain. Iseutz was pulling a piece of cloth into strips, one end gripped between her teeth. Nobody had bothered to clear away the cups and plates from the last three meals, though Clefas had at least taken the time to squash a couple of cockroaches. Gorgas was sitting at the head of the table. He'd put on a new shirt and trousers for the occasion – Colleon silk with brocade – and he was wearing his father's ring, which had been in the family for generations.

'You'll find your room's pretty much the way it was,' he told his sister. 'Same old linen-chest, same old bed. Of course, you and Iseutz are going to have to share, but that shouldn't be a problem. Maybe we should think about turning the old apple store into another bedroom, though; it's going to get a bit cosy otherwise.'

'Where are you sleeping?' Niessa asked, without moving her head.

'In father's room, of course,' Gorgas replied.

'I thought so.'

Iseutz had finished tearing her bit of rag into strips; now she started tearing the strips into squares. 'Go on, then,' she said, 'say it, and let's get it over with.'

'Say what?'

She rested her hands on the table. 'Any minute now,' she said, 'you're going to say something like, *It's just a pity Bardas isn't here, then we'd all be together again.* Well, aren't you?'

Gorgas frowned a little. 'All right, yes, it would be nice if Bardas was here, but he's not. He's got a life of his own now, he's making something of himself. He knows this house will always be here for him, as and when he needs it.'

'Oh, for gods' sakes.' Iseutz banged the table with her mutilated hand. 'Uncle Gorgas, *why* did you have to bring her here? Well, I'm not sharing a room with her, and that's that. I'd rather sleep in the trap-house.'

'Fine,' Niessa muttered. 'You do that.'

'Niessa!'

Dear gods, Niessa thought, *he sounds just like Father. Now that's . . . worrying.* Gorgas was glowering round the table, his arms folded ominously. *Any minute now he's going to tell me to eat up my porridge.*

'And the rest of you, for pity's sake. We've had our differences, gods know – and yes, before anybody else says it, yes, a hell of a lot of them were my fault, I'm not trying to pretend they weren't. But that was then and this is now; and let's be absolutely straight with each other, none of us is exactly perfect.' He stopped, glowered again, and went on, 'I didn't want to have to do it this way, but I think it's necessary. Let's start with you, Niessa; you're self-centred, completely amoral, you've never really cared about anything or anybody but yourself; when things got too hot for you on Scona you just walked away, leaving for dead all the people who depended on you - I was the only one who even tried to do anything; I managed to get some of them out and I brought them here, but you didn't give a damn. You betrayed a city - a whole city, all those hundreds of thousands of people you practically sentenced to death, just so you wouldn't have to pay your debts.

'And the way you've treated your own daughter is little short of abominable. When I brought her home to Scona, what did you do? You threw her in jail, for pity's sake. And don't you start looking all smug and self-righteous, Iseutz, you're the last person - you tried to kill your own uncle - no, you be quiet and let me finish. You tried to kill Bardas for something that wasn't his fault. He was only doing his job, he had no way of knowing that man was your uncle, he didn't even know you existed. I'm sorry for what you've been through, but really, you're just going to have to come to terms with it and start acting like a sane, normal human being while you can still remember how.

'And as for you two,' he went on, swinging round and scowling at Clefas and Zonaras, 'you're every bit as bad, if not worse. You had everything; you had the farm, dammit, you had Bardas sending you all that money, every quarter he could scrape together by risking his life, and what did you do? You squandered it, threw it all away. Dear gods, when I think what I'd have given to have what you had; to be here, at home, doing what we were all meant to do, instead of wandering around the world fighting and cheating and screwing other people just to make a living - you know, I don't get angry easily, but that really does annoy me.' It was very quiet now; even the rain seemed to have stopped dripping into the steel cup. 'About the only one of us who can honestly say he's always tried to do the right thing, always put other people before himself, is Bardas - and he's the one who can't come home, because of what *we've* done to him. Isn't that right, Clefas? Zonaras? He came here, when he needed somewhere clean and safe to go to, and as soon as he saw what you two had done, he was so disgusted he couldn't bear to stay here, so he went off again - and now look where he is, practically an exile; and it's you two who're to blame for that, and I'm really finding it hard to forgive you for it - although I do forgive you, because we're family, we've got to stick together no matter what we've all done. But for heaven's sake, why can't you all just make a bit of an effort and stop *bickering* with each other like a lot of spoiled kids? That's not so much to ask, is it?'

For a long time, nobody spoke. Then Iseutz giggled.

'I'm sorry,' she said, 'but it's comical, honestly. All those terrible things we've all done, and it's supposed to make us all one happy family. Uncle Gorgas, you're one of a kind, you really are.'

Gorgas turned and stared at her, making her shiver. 'And what's that supposed to mean?' he said.

'Oh, come on. Listen to yourself. And just out of interest, has it slipped your mind that Uncle Bardas murdered your son and made his body into a—'

'Quiet.' Gorgas took a deep breath, making himself stay calm. 'If we keep on bashing ourselves, bashing each other, over what we've all done, then we might as well all give up now. It's not what we've done that matters, it's what we're going to do – just so long as we all *try*. At last we've got everything we need – we've got the farm, we've got each other, there aren't any landlords or outsiders breathing down our necks—'

'What about the provincial office?' Niessa interrupted, still staring out of the window. 'I suppose they just melted away into thin air.'

'I can handle them,' Gorgas replied. 'They're nothing to worry about. Really and truly, there isn't anything to worry about any more, just so long as we're together, as a family. We've done the hard part, we've all been through the bad times; it's been a long haul, we've all had to go miles out of our way just to get back here again, but it's all right now, we're *home*. And if you could all just understand that—'

Clefas stood up and walked towards the door.

'Where are you going?' Gorgas demanded.

'To see to the pigs,' Clefas said.

'Oh.' He breathed out, as if in relief. 'Tell you what, why don't we all go and see to the pigs? Do some useful and constructive work for a change, instead of sitting round here moping like a lot of owls?'

His tone of voice suggested that participation wasn't optional.

Outside, it was beginning to get dark. The rain had turned the bottom end of the yard into a swamp; the drainage ditch was blocked with cow-parsley again, and nobody had got around to clearing it out yet. Niessa, who only had the sandals she'd been wearing in the desert, could feel the mud between her toes.

'How much longer do you think we'll have to put up with this?' It was Iseutz, whispering in her ear. 'Does he really think we're going to stay here and play let's-pretend-nothing-happened for the rest of our lives?'

Niessa turned her head away. 'I don't care what he thinks,' she said out loud, 'or what you think, for that matter. This is obviously ridiculous. Now go away and leave me alone.'

Iseutz grinned. 'You think you'll be able to snap him out of it,' she said. 'Pull rank on him, as if you were both still on Scona. Well, I don't think it's going to work, he's way too far gone for that. Still, look on the bright side; as I understand it he's practically given this horrid country to the Empire; sooner or later they'll round him up and put him out of his misery, and then we can get on with what we're supposed to be doing.'

The pig house smelt bad. Nobody had got around to mucking it out for a week and the rain was pouring through a hole in the roof and flushing a stream of slurry under the door and out into the yard. Gorgas didn't seem to mind the rain; his new silk shirt was probably ruined already, but he hadn't noticed, or he didn't care. *He's like a young kid, all excited at being allowed to help,* Iseutz thought. *Too bad. On balance, it* would *be fun to have Uncle Bardas here as well. He and Uncle Gorgas could bash each other to death, knee-deep in pigshit.*

'Come on, Zonaras, get me the rake,' Gorgas was saying. 'Niessa, you get the shovel.' (Niessa stayed exactly where she was.) 'Clefas, where's the wheelbarrow? Oh, for crying out loud, don't say you haven't mended it yet, I thought I told you to do that last week. Doesn't anybody else do any work around here, except me?'

'Family reunion,' said Bardas Loredan, staying where he was. 'I suppose I ought to say *haven't you grown*, or something like that.'

Theudas Morosin stopped dead in the doorway of the tent. 'I thought you'd be pleased to see me,' he said.

Bardas closed his eyes and let his head loll back. 'I'm sorry,' he said. 'I didn't mean it like that. I just wish you hadn't come here.'

Theudas stiffened. 'Oh?'

'If I said I hoped you were out of my life for good,' Bardas went on, 'you'd think I was being horrible. What you probably wouldn't understand is, I hoped it for your sake.' He opened his eyes and stood up, but didn't approach the boy. 'I'm really pleased that you're safe and well,' he went on, 'you've got to believe me when I say that; but you shouldn't be here, not getting mixed up in this war. You should have stayed on the Island, you've got a future there.'

Theudas was about to say something, but changed his mind. *He looks different*, he thought. *I was expecting he'd look different, probably older, thinner, I don't know, but he doesn't. If anything, he looks younger.* 'I want to be here,' he replied instead. 'I want to see you defeat Temrai, pay him back for what he did. I know you can do it, and I want to be here when you do. Is there anything terrible in that?'

Bardas smiled. 'Yes,' he said, 'but don't let it worry you. You're here now, we're together again; I suppose you might as well make yourself useful.'

Theudas grinned with relief; it was the tone of voice when he said *make yourself useful*, just like the old times. He should have known there wouldn't have been any show of emotion, no hugs or tears; he wouldn't have wanted that anyhow. What he really wanted was for things to pick up where they'd left off, that day when the Shastel soldiers broke into their house and everything changed. 'All right,' he said. 'What do you want me to do?'

Bardas yawned; now he did look tired. 'Let's see what Athli's taught you about keeping books,' he said. 'If you've been paying attention, you could come in quite handy. And nobody could ever make sense of paperwork like Athli. How is she, by the way?'

There was something in the way he'd said that – *he hasn't heard yet. Why? Why haven't they told him?* 'She was fine,' Theudas said cautiously, 'the last time I saw her.'

'That's good. And what about Alexius? How's he doing? Have you seen him lately?'

This time Theudas didn't know what to say. He really didn't want to be the one to tell him – not if he also had to break the news about what had happened on the Island. But he'd have to do it sooner or later, and he didn't want to have to lie ... 'Alexius,' he repeated. 'You haven't heard.'

Bardas looked up sharply. 'Haven't heard what? He's not ill or anything, is he?'

'He's dead,' Theudas said.

Bardas sat very still. 'Both of them,' he said.

'What?'

Bardas shook his head. 'Nothing,' he said, 'sorry. I just heard yesterday, another friend of mine's died, a man I used to work with at the proof house. When did he die?'

Theudas' mouth was dry. 'Quite some time ago,' he said. 'I'm really sorry, I thought you must have known.'

'It's all right,' Bardas said (*it's customary to die first after all, even if there are exceptions*). 'He was an old man, these things happen. It's just – well, odd. I'd have thought I'd have known, if you see what I mean.'

'You were quite close at one time, weren't you?' Theudas said, knowing as he said it that he couldn't have put it much worse if he'd really tried.

'Yes,' Bardas replied. 'But I haven't seen him for years. If you remember exactly when he died, I'd be interested. Now then, let's find something for you to do; or do you want to have a rest? I suppose you've been travelling all day.'

'That's all right,' Theudas said. 'Did you say you wanted me to do the accounts or something? I suppose there's a lot of paperwork and stuff, running an army.'

Bardas smiled. 'You wouldn't believe it,' he said. 'Or at least, there is with this army; somehow we never seemed to bother with it when I was with Maxen's crowd. These people, though, they need dockets and requisitions and reports and gods know what else, or nothing gets done.'

Theudas sat down behind the small, rickety folding desk, the top of which was covered with bits of paper and wax tablets. He hadn't served any formal apprenticeship or term of articles while he'd been on the Island, but he knew enough about clerkship to recognise a pig's ear when he saw one. 'I can make a start on reconciling your sun-and-moon ledger if you like,' he said. 'Have you got any counters?'

'In the wooden box,' Bardas replied. 'What's a sun-and-moon ledger?'

Theudas smiled. 'Sorry,' he said, 'it's what they call standard double-entry format where I come from – I mean, on the Island.' The smile was still there on his face, like the visor of a bascinet, a false steel face. 'You know, receipts and expenditures. We draw a little sun on the left-hand side and a little moon on the right.'

'Ah. Well, yes, by all means. That'd be a great help.'

Theudas opened the box; it was cedarwood, sweet-smelling, pale with a faint green tinge. Inside was a little velvet bag, drawn tight at the neck with silk braid. He loosened the knot and shook out a handful of the most exquisite counters he'd ever seen – butter-yellow gold, Imperial fine, with allegorical figures in high relief on both the obverse and reverse. Neither the figures nor the legends in the exergues meant anything to him, of course; these were Imperial make, illustrating scenes from the literature of the Sons of Heaven and inscribed in their script.

'They belonged to a man called Estar,' Bardas said. 'I inherited them, along with this army. You can keep them if you like; I hate doing exchequer work.'

'Thank you,' Theudas said. In the box with the counters was a small piece of chalk, which he used to draw his lines – full lines for full tens, broken lines for the intermediate fives. 'But are you sure? They look as if they're pretty valuable.'

'Never given it any thought, to be honest with you,' Bardas replied. 'Once you've spent time with these people, you start assessing value in a different way, if you see what I mean.'

Theudas didn't see at all, but he nodded anyway. 'If you're sure,' he said. 'It's a pleasure to use them.'

Bardas smiled. 'I think that's the general idea,' he said. 'Look, we're getting ready to move on – we've been stuck here for far longer than we'd expected, and we're horribly behind schedule. I've got to go and see to a few things. Will you be all right here on your own for a bit?'

'I should think so,' Theudas replied, setting out counters

on the lines. 'I've got plenty here to keep me busy for a while.'

For an hour or so the work more or less filled his mind, as he wrestled with divisors, quotients and multiplicands, traced misplaced entries, struggled to make sense of Bardas' handwriting. It was enough to feel the textile-soft texture of the counters between the tips of his fingers, or hear the gentle click they made as he dropped one back into the bag. But as he was drawn deeper into the calculations, so the images embossed on the counters began to assert themselves in the back of his mind, like splinters of metal thrown off the grindstone embedding themselves in your hand. There was an army marching to war; in the foreground a Son of Heaven on a tall, thin horse, behind him a sea of heads and bodies, each one no more than a few cursory strokes of the die-engraver's cutter. There was a trophy of captured arms, set up on a battlefield to celebrate a victory – swords and spears, helmets and breastplates and arms and legs heaped up, and at the summit, like a beacon on a mountain, the radiate-sun standard of the Empire. There was a city under siege; high towers and bastions in the background, and at the front of the field, engineers digging the mouth of a sap, sheltered from the arrows and missiles of the defenders by tall wicker shields. There was an armoury, where two men raised a helmet over a stake while a third watched. Because he couldn't understand the words, Theudas didn't know which wars and sieges and cities were being commemorated here, but it didn't really matter; they could be any war, any siege or city you wanted them to be (since all wars and sieges and cities are pretty much alike, seen from a distance, from outside the field). For all Theudas knew, it might have been deliberate; since the Empire is eternally at war, eternally celebrating some new victory, it was sound practical sense to keep the celebrations of victory vague and generic, whether they be the images on counters or the marching-songs of the army.

He remembered that he'd forgotten something; on the floor, where he'd dumped it, was his luggage – one small kitbag and a long parcel wrapped in oiled cloth. Fortuitously, that was when Bardas walked in.

'I've just remembered something,' Theudas said. 'I'm sorry, it slipped my mind. I've brought something for you.'

Bardas raised his eyebrows. 'Really? That's nice. What is it?'

Theudas knelt down, picked up the parcel and handed it to him. Maybe his face changed a little while he was picking at the knots in the twine; it was completely free of any sort of expression when he pulled out the Guelan broadsword.

'I see,' was all he said; then he put it back. 'How are the books coming along? Made any sense of them yet?'

'Of course you're perfectly at liberty to leave at any time,' the man in the department of aliens had told him. 'As a citizen of Shastel, you're unaffected by what's happened here.' Then he'd gone on to point out that there weren't any ships leaving for Shastel, now or in the foreseeable future – in other words, if he wanted to exercise his undisputed right to leave the Island, he was going to have to walk home across the sea to Shastel.

So he went back to Athli's house, which was empty. They'd come and collected all the files and papers, not to mention the ten massive cast-iron strongboxes in which she kept the Bank deposits; they'd cut the chains and bolts with cold chisels and big hammers, leaving behind them scars in the walls and floors like the cavities left behind when teeth have been pulled. They hadn't touched anything else, however; this was an annexation, not a fall or a sack. Much more polite than either of those, and for obvious reasons; after all, where's the point of stealing your own property?

But they hadn't taken the food; so he cut himself a thick slice out of the new loaf, and a big square of cheese, and took them over to the window where it was pleasantly cool but he could still see the sunlight. From where he was sitting he could just make out the tops of the masts of ships, riding at anchor in the Drutz. Any day now, they'd be going where he'd just come from, to take the war to Temrai and avenge Perimadeia. Or something of the kind.

He closed his eyes; and then he was somehow underneath the town, directly under Athli's house, in a tunnel, the usual tunnel, that reeked of coriander and wet clay. 'Look, is this really ... ? he started to protest, but the floor of the tunnel was giving way under his feet, and he was falling –

– Down into another tunnel (the usual tunnel), where they were scooping up the spoil and loading it on to the dolly-trucks; and mixed in with the spoil he could see all manner of artefacts and curios from a time several hundred years ago. Some of the pieces were familiar; others weren't, and some of the unfamiliar ones were a very strange shape indeed – parts of suits of armour for creatures that were far from human, or part human, part something else.

You again.

Gannadius looked round. There wasn't anybody there that he could see, just helmets and pieces of armour –

Over here. That's it, you're looking straight at me.

An elegant, if somewhat battered, barbute sallet, the sort of helmet that covers the face completely apart from narrow slits for the eyes and mouth. 'Is that you?' Gannadius asked. 'You remind me of someone I used to work with, but I can't quite ...'

Well, of course I do. It's me. Here inside this blasted tin hat.

No great mystery; they'd run the tunnel through the middle of a burial ground, a mass grave for the losers of some battle long ago; or else they'd reopened a tunnel from some previous siege, where a cave-in had buried an assault party. 'Just a minute,' Gannadius said, 'you aren't Alexius, you don't sound a bit like him. Who are you?'

Does it matter?

'It matters to me,' Gannadius replied, turning the helmet over. It was empty.

Alexius couldn't make it, so he sent me instead. I'm a friend of Bardas Loredan's, if it actually matters at all. And you're Gannadius, right? The wizard?

'No, I ... Yes, the wizard.' Gannadius couldn't sit down, there wasn't room, so he leaned his back against the curved, damp wall of the tunnel. 'Is there actually a point to this, or is it just that big hunk of cheese I ate?'

You wound me.

'I'm sorry,' Gannadius replied, feeling rather self-conscious about apologising to a hallucination. 'So I take it there is a reason for this?'

Of course. Welcome to the proof house.

Gannadius frowned. 'The what house?'

This is where you come to be bashed and buried, though it's considered good form to die first. Still, you weren't to know that; we can make allowances. Now then, let's see. If asked to identify the Principle with one of the following, a river or a wheel, which would you choose?

'I'm not sure,' Gannadius replied. 'To be honest with you, I don't think either comparison is a perfect fit. Besides, why are you asking me this?'

Answer the question. River, wheel; which?

'Oh ...' Gannadius shrugged. 'All right, on balance I'd say the Principle is more like a river than a wheel. Satisfied?'

Explain your reasoning.

Gannadius scowled. 'If I treated my students like that, I'd be out of a job.'

Explain your reasoning.

'If I do, can I wake up?'

Explain your reasoning.

Gannadius sighed. 'All right,' he said. 'I hold that the Principle flows like a river along a bed of circumstance and context; it goes where it goes because the landscape takes it there. I hold that it flows from a beginning to an end, and as and when it reaches that end, it'll stop. I hold that the course of the Principle can be deflected, but only by diverting it from one set of circumstance and context into another; further, that only the future course can be diverted – it's impossible to change the past. How am I doing?'

Now explain why the Principle resembles a wheel. In your own words.

'If you insist. I hold that the Principle revolves, like a wheel, around an event; but, like a wheel, as it turns on firm ground it pulls itself forward, thereby moving its own axis forward with it – which explains why we don't live the same day over and over again. The analogy breaks down because the events that form the axis, or do I mean axle, are constantly changing, but the wheel continues to revolve around them without loss of continuity – which is why it's better to think of the events as the bed and banks of a river, in my opinion. I'll admit, though, that the wheel analogy is preferable because it brings out the repetitive aspect of the Principle, something which is rather understated in the river image; it's still there, of course, because a watercourse only comes into being after hundreds of years, when countless cycles of rain and flood have eroded a channel for it to run down. Actually, both images are misleading; the Principle doesn't repeat itself, it just tends to make the same sort of thing happen over and over again. Anyway, to get back to the wheel, you can't divert the wheel itself – it can only go round – but by shifting the axle you can steer those revolutions on to a different road. In theory, that is. In practice, anybody fool enough to try interfering will probably get run over – or drowned, if you prefer. There, will that do?'

It's adequate.

'Adequate,' Gannadius repeated. 'Well, thank you ever so much.'

Adequate isn't good enough; you're our man on the spot at a crucial turning point in history. Adequate won't make head or tail of this –

– And the roof caved in, and the town came crashing down through it, and after that the whole world; but not enough to fill the tunnel. For a moment Gannadius could see it all – cities and roads and towns and fortresses, villages and fields and forests, tumbling into the hole like milk through a tin funnel and soaking away into the black clay. There was a rich stench of garlic, and all around him Gannadius could see the Sons of Heaven, watching in silent, detached appreciation, as if this was a ballet or a lecture. He could see ships, vast fleets of them spilling infinite numbers of steel men on to all the beaches and headlands in the world, until the steel men covered the face of the earth –

'As if the world was wearing armour,' he said aloud. 'Nice touch.'

– and under every city and town and village he could see tunnels and galleries and saps, where steel men burrowed and hammered and bashed steel limbs and heads over anvils, until all the cities and towns were undermined and fell down into the camouflets, and the skin of steel closed over where they'd stood. In the mines, the steel men skinned the steel off the bodies of the dead, cutting the straps with thin-bladed knives, peeling away the steel plate to reach the flesh beneath; the steel went into the scrap, the trash, piled up in pyramids that touched the roof, while the hammers bashed and pounded the flesh, breaking up the fibres to make it easier to cook. And all the flesh went into the mouths of the Children of Heaven, and all the steel went back into the melt, to be drawn off in blooms, hammered into billets, hammered again into plates, hammered again into the shapes of limbs, hammered again by the sword and the axe and the mace and the flail and the morningstar and the halberd and the long-shafted war-hammer, at every stage put to proof (*proof, if proof were needed*) and hammered to the point of failure, which is the point at which the chrysalis fails at the seams and bursts open, releasing the butterfly.

'That's an interesting hypothesis,' Gannadius murmured.

Then the images merged, as all the cities became one city, all the countries one country, all the steel one suit of proof, all the people one man; and he was standing over his anvil swinging his hammer, letting it fall in its own weight, pinching the metal between the hammer and the anvil so that it flowed like a sluggish river, or the stream of lava from a volcano.

'Alexius?' Gannadius asked.

But the man shook his head. 'Close,' he replied, 'but no grapefruit. Alexius is dead, I'm afraid – we just couldn't make an exception for him any longer – and so is Anax, Bardas Loredan's friend, and a lot of others too. They went in the scrap, and the scrap went into the melt, and the melt became billets, and the billets become me. You're seeing me as Alexius because of your basic human need for a reassuringly friendly face.'

'Ah,' Gannadius said.

'Which is misleading, of course,' he went on, 'because I'm not reassuring and I'm sure as hell not friendly. You see, the Principle is the Empire; it's the melt and the anvil; it's a river that drowns you, or a wheel that runs you over. The lava stream is a good image too, as far as it goes. But personally, I like the idea of the Principle being the proof house, because for every inch of development there has to be a crumpled and wrecked yard of destruction; otherwise, how do you ever get on to the next stage?'

'I'm not sure I follow,' Gannadius said.

'Fair enough,' he replied, as his hammer distorted the metal. 'It's because you can't see the beginning, the points it started from. You see, every act of destruction begins with a first small moment of failure – the first point where the metal stresses and tears, the first crack, the first place where the material is beaten thin. Once you have that, everything around it fails and everything falls in – it's like the one prop you pull out to set off a camouflet, and then the city falls through the hole. Gorgas Loredan was a point of failure, where the stress became too much; there were others – centuries ago, some of them, like the moment when the Sons of Heaven first broke through, or very recent, like the Empire getting its hands on a fleet of ships, which is the failure that'll pull down the cities across the sea. There was a moment of failure when Alexius stupidly agreed to place the curse on Bardas, and that ripped open a whole seam. You could say it was like splitting a log – one wedge opens a crack to put the next wedge in. That's the progressive element of the Principle.' He laughed. 'Definitely not reassuring,' he said with a smile. 'And definitely not friendly. Another really major failure was the moment when you agreed to carry the duck from Perimadeia to the Island; that was a disaster from which the world may never recover. But try not to feel guilty about it; you weren't to know. Quite probably, you were only trying to be helpful.'

'That's right,' Gannadius said. 'I was.'

He nodded. 'Comic,' he said, 'in a grotesque sort of a way; destruction and ruin swoop down on the west, sewn up in the crop of a duck. Well, that ought to have given you plenty to think about. Thanks for watching.'

– And his eyes were open again, as the plate toppled off his knees and the crusty end of the bread rolled under the chair. *Damn*, he thought. *But I'm not sure I'm convinced. It's a specious enough theory, but I'd like to see some hard proof.*

Someone was hammering at the door; he stood up, brushing away crumbs, and answered it. There were two soldiers standing in the doorway, and a clerk.

'Doctor Gannadius?'

'That's me.'

'The sub-prefect's compliments,' the clerk said, 'and he thought you might be interested to know there's been an unscheduled arrival, a ship from Shastel. It was blown off-course and put in here. The sub-prefect has asked them to hold over until tomorrow morning so they can carry some letters for him, and he thought you might like a berth on it.'

'That's very thoughtful of him,' Gannadius said. 'I'd like that very much. What's the ship called?'

'The *Poverty and Forbearance*; the master's name is Hido Elan, and it's down on the Drutz. They've agreed to take you home for free, as a gesture of goodwill.'

'Goodwill,' Gannadius repeated. 'Well, isn't everybody being kind to me today.'

CHAPTER SIXTEEN

Colonel Ispel, in command of the provincial office's expeditionary force against Perimadeia, made an undisputed landfall and sent out his scouts. When they returned, they reported no sign of the enemy in any direction. Ispel pitched camp on the site of Temrai's recently abandoned settlement, spread out the maps on the floor of his tent and did his homework.

Because the enemy had abandoned their position and moved off inland, the reason for launching the offensive this way had become obsolete before he'd even embarked. Nevertherless, his situation was strong; he had just over fifty thousand men in arms, made up of twenty thousand heavy infantry, four thousand cavalry, sixteen thousand light infantry and ten-thousand-and-something archers, artillery-men, pioneers and irregular skirmishers. He left two thousand of the least useful irregulars to keep the crews of his ships from slipping away - they were, after all, Islanders, no threat but entirely untrustworthy - and set out with the main army to follow in Temrai's footsteps. In addition to the fighting men, he had a large but not unwieldy baggage and supply train, with enough supplies to see the army clear across the plains and back into Imperial territory - one thing he knew for sure about this country was that living off it was out of the question. Such a large encumbrance would obviously slow down the progress of his main force, but he resisted the temptation to send his cavalry too far ahead. The clans were extremely competent light cavalry and horse-archers, and what he'd read about them suggested that they would enjoy nothing more than an opportunity to harass a slow-moving column unprotected by cavalry, to the point where momentum broke down and the advance ground to a halt. Besides, he was in no great hurry; intelligence reports from Captain Loredan's army suggested that Temrai had dug in on top of some hill and was waiting for the end. If that was true, the only way this war could be lost was by making a stupid mistake, and he'd be far more likely to do that if he rushed blindly ahead into barren and largely unknown territory.

The plains turned out to be unlike any other country he'd served in. He'd fought in swamps and deserts and mountains, in hell and in paradise, in bleaching sun and driving snow, but this was the first time he'd had to march across a landscape that was utterly, painfully boring. It wasn't called the plains for nothing; once he'd left behind the little fringe of mountains that overlooked Perimadeia itself, there was nothing on either side but flat land covered in coarse, fat blue-green couch-grass for as far as the eye could see. Not that boring was necessarily a bad thing; in country this open an ambush was effectively impossible, and provided they kept to the road, they would be able to make extremely good progress. Off the road, of course, it was a different matter; the ubiquitous couch tended to grow in little tussocks about the size of a man's head, and trying to march an army across country would be courting disaster. Apart from the substantial monetary cost of keeping an army in the field (twenty thousand gold quarters a week), he wasn't facing any problems that called for forced marches and flying columns. The only niggling fear in the back of his mind was that Captain Loredan might have finished the job before he arrived, leaving him and his men with nothing to look forward to except a long, dull march home.

Nevertheless, he kept to standard operating procedures, just in case. Each morning he sent out scouts, in all directions except one, and every evening they came back with nothing to report. Every night he stationed sentries around the camp and pickets out in the open, so that he'd have plenty of warning if the enemy did somehow materialise and try a night attack.

The only direction he didn't probe with scouts was, of course, the one he'd just come from, and so the first he knew about the raiding party that had been following him all the way from the coast, riding at night and laying up during the day with sacks over their armour and weapons to stop them flashing in the sun, was a sudden explosion of activity at the one time of day when an Imperial army on the march was ever truly vulnerable: dinner-time.

It was, of course, the perfect time to attack. It was dark; the men were out of their armour, standing in line at the cookhouses; the pickets weren't in place yet and by the time the enemy rode down the sentries it was too late to raise the alarm. Quite suddenly there were armed horsemen inside the circle of firelight, galloping down the food lines slashing at hands and faces with their scimitars, spearing anybody who broke line and ran. The men who'd already got their food dropped their plates and cups and tried to get to the weapons stacks, but the horsemen kept pouring in, one unit crashing through the tents, another running off the cavalry horses, another rounding up the men in the queues like wild ponies in the autumn and driving them towards yet another unit, which surged forward to meet them. Ispel himself blundered out of his tent with his napkin still tucked in his collar, his sword-hilt tied to the mounts of the scabbard (to stop it falling out); by the time he'd picked out the knots there were horsemen in his street of tents, cutting guy-ropes and prodding the fallen heaps of canvas with long, narrow-bladed lances. He looked round and saw a gap in the line of tents which would let him through to the light-infantry camp, where the archers were quartered; archers and skirmishers, men who didn't fight in armour, were more likely to be able to cope with a sudden disaster like this. He plunged through and came out in the main thoroughfare of the light quarter, only to find it empty except for horse-men; the skirmishers, archers and mobile auxiliaries had used their mobility and quick reaction time to get out of the danger area and away from the camp and the sharp edges of the scimitars, and it was a sure thing that they weren't going to be coming back until it was safe.

Three horsemen saw him simultaneously; obviously they'd recognised him, which spoke highly of their intelligence work. Two of them dragged their horses round, making them turn almost on the spot, but it was the third man, who calmly put an arrow on his bowstring, aimed and loosed, who got the most coveted prize of the evening; the small three-bladed bodkinhead nuzzled between his ribs, through his lung and would have made it out the other side if it hadn't jarred against his spine. When they saw where he'd been hit, the other two horsemen let him lie; he'd keep, and there was plenty for everybody.

Ispel died in a sort of dream, slowly, as his lungs filled with blood. It was maddening to have to lie there and die – he couldn't move at all, even to turn his head – without knowing what was going on, exactly how much damage the raiders were doing to his army. When he could no longer see, he tried to keep track of what was happening by the noises; there was a lot of shouting and yelling, but whether it was his officers calling out words of command as they rallied the men, or just the inarticulate noises of the terrified and dying, he simply couldn't tell. Just as he was certain he could make out at least one coherent voice giving orders, a plainsman jumped out of the saddle and cut off his head; it took him five blows before he was through the bone, and Ispel felt them all.

In fact, he'd been mistaken; the voice he'd heard calling out commands was that of the leader of the raiding party, a distant cousin of Temrai's by the name of Sildocai, and he was trying to call off the attack before they pushed their luck too far. Nobody appeared to be taking any notice, however, and it didn't seem to matter; as soon as the enemy made any attempt at rallying or forming a coherent group, a party of horsemen was on top of them, cutting and prodding where the bodies were most closely packed together, until the blockage in the flow was cleared. It was, the raiders said later, like Perimadeia all over again; the few who tried to fight were killed quite early, and after that it was like chopping through brambles, hard work, heavy on the shoulders, arms and back. But they stuck at their work and cleared a lot of ground, and as the job wore on they got better at it, worked out the most efficient cuts and angles – waste of effort to slash away wildly at arms and legs; one carefully aimed blow to the head or neck gets it done, and don't hit harder than you have to, no point in wearing yourself out; try to get a rhythm going, it's easier that way.

In the end, the attack was only broken off because of a

silly misunderstanding. The cavalry horses, driven off at the beginning of the engagement, stampeded off into the couch-grass and stayed there for a while; but couch-grass didn't make good eating, being coarse and bitter, and they were getting hungry. Being used to moving together they headed back towards the camp in a herd, and when they were quite close a plains horse that had lost its rider blundered into them at the gallop and spooked them, sending them stampeding towards the light. A couple of raiders at the edge of the camp heard the thudding of hooves and assumed that it meant enemy cavalry; they raised the alarm and got out of the way, and within a few minutes the attack was over, although the Imperial army didn't realise until a while after they'd all gone.

It was one of the heaviest defeats ever inflicted on the Imperial army; fewer than four thousand killed outright in the raid (two thousand of them officers and sergeants), but over twenty thousand wounded, most of them slashed about the head and shoulders, losing too much blood from scalp and neck wounds. It was a long time before the NCOs could find an officer fit enough to take command, since the officers dined in separate messes in grander tents, and the raiders had found them quite easily. They'd also run off or killed most of the draught horses that pulled the supply wagons, and that was what caused most of the deaths.

Given a choice between carrying supplies or carrying their friends who were too badly cut up to walk, the soldiers decided to dump most of the provisions, on the grounds that they weren't too far from the ships and they'd have to make do until they reached them. With so many officers and NCOs dead, there was nobody to tell them otherwise; so, when the raiders came back the next day and attacked the column as it crawled back along its tracks, they met with only marginally more resistance than they had during the night. But what they did encounter was enough to persuade them against closing with the sword and the spear; instead, they held off at medium range and shot from the saddle, not the most efficient method in the short term, but extremely cost-effective as regards the casualty ratio. What was left of the imperial cavalry tried to shoo them away, but they didn't last long; there were only a few hundred horses among nearly four thousand men, and a horse is a large target. As for the light infantry and archers, whose job it ought to have been to swat flies in these circumstances, they'd made a serious error of judgement when they assumed that leaving the camp and plunging into the darkness was a safer option than staying put. It was the tussocks of couch-grass that did for them; they stumbled and fell, with twisted ankles and sprained knees, so that by the time Sildocai found them and put a cordon of archers round them, they'd more or less ground to a halt, sprawled on the grass and unwilling or unable to go any further. Most of them died where they lay, and the rest were pruned back later the next day.

Of the fifty thousand who disembarked from the ships, fifteen thousand made it back, with Sildocai's men coming down to the coast to see them on their way; of the other thirty-five thousand, at least half were left behind in the empty plains; Sildocai went home, the fleet sailed back to the Island, and there was, as Ispel had so acutely observed, very little to eat on the plains, if you had the misfortune not to be a goat.

Sildocai attributed his victory to a souvenir he'd picked up in the sack of Perimadeia; it was a small book, entitled *The Use Of Cavalry In Extended Campaigns In Open Country*, by Suidas Bessemin; one of the few City military historians ever to study in detail the campaigns of the illustrious Perimadeian cavalry commander, Bardas Maxen.

The prefect of Ap' Escatoy heard the news from the fastest, most experienced courier in the Imperial messenger corps, who left the island twenty minutes after the first ship landed. The prefect took the news calmly; having personally seen to it that the messenger was given the fastest horse in the cavalry stables for his journey to the provincial office in Rhoezen, he called for jasmin tea and honey-cakes, sent for his advisers, and sat down for a long day and night of sensible, hard-headed planning.

Bardas Loredan heard the news from the army courier sent out by the sub-prefect of the Island three hours after the news broke there. He had to be told the story three times; then he sent everybody away and sat in the dark all night.

When he finally came out, he didn't seem unduly worried or upset; he gave orders to step up the pace of the advance and post extra scouts and pickets.

Gorgas Loredan heard the news from his man in the Shastel proctors' office, who made sure the official courier took a detour on his way south with the commercial dispatches. After he'd seen the courier, Gorgas took the big axe, which he'd had to put a new handle on himself, and spent the morning in the woodshed, splitting logs. Then he sent out three messengers of his own; one to the Island, with lugubrious condolences and offers of assistance; a second also to the Island, accompanied by a party of fifty or so ferocious-looking men whose letters of transit identified them as trade negotiators; and a third, the best man he had left, towards Temrai's camp at the far end of the plains.

Temrai himself heard the news from Sildocai, as the raiding party returned home at record speed, even faster than the Imperial post-coach. He said '*How* many?' and shook his head when the figures were repeated. Then he went back to supervising the reinforcement of the inner gates, and was in a foul mood for the rest of the day.

The provincial governor heard the news on the morning of his eldest daughter's fourteenth birthday. He immediately cancelled all the scheduled celebrations, as was only fitting in the circumstances, and wrote a long letter to the prefect of Ap' Escatoy expressing his sympathy, his support, his unwavering confidence and his profound disgust, promising a new army of a hundred and fifty thousand infantry, sixty thousand cavalry and genuine artillery support, to be despatched within two months, and enquiring politely after a silk painting by Marjent which the prefect had promised to send him a month ago, but which didn't seem to have arrived yet. He then wrote another letter to the office of central administration, eight weeks' ride away in Kozin province, asking whether the prefect should be put on trial, merely replaced, or left where he was. Finally, being a kind-hearted man, he rescheduled his daughter's birthday by having the provincial astronomer-general insert into the calendar a special non-recurring intercalary month, to be named Loss-and-Reaffirmation, starting at midnight on the day the news reached him. It was generally agreed to be a particularly elegant and thoughtful gesture, and there was some talk of making it permanent.

Gannadius heard the news at dinner the day before the ships reached the Island; a survivor of the Imperial light infantry, striking out on his own for the coast, had lost his way and strayed north, where he ran into a party of Shastel commercial messengers returning home with important news about likely developments in the spot-market price of Bustrofidon copper. Because their message was so urgent, they'd taken the risk of riding overland through the war zone, and their first instinct on seeing an Imperial soldier running up the road towards them was either to shoot him or run away. When they realised what they'd stumbled across, however, they speeded up even more (they had to leave the soldier behind, not having any spare horses) and were thus able to bring the news to the Citadel before the close of that day's trading; an act of heroism on their part that paid dividends for the Order's commercial arm. Gannadius himself didn't seem unduly surprised by the news; it was almost, his colleagues at High Table whispered after he'd gone to bed, as if he'd already heard about it from somewhere else. This greatly increased their respect for and resentment of the Perimadeian scholar and suspected wizard, who carried on with his daily routine as if nothing had happened.

When the news reached Voesin province, it sparked off a minor revolt in that already unsettled and unreliable corner of the Empire. A man appeared out of nowhere in the town square in Rezlain on market day, announcing that he was God's chosen envoy, sent to lead the people out of slavery, and dragging along with him a startled and apparently half-witted young man who turned out to be the last descendant of the former royal house of Voesin. About six thousand people straggled into the rebel camp before the cavalry arrived; although a third of them were women, old men or boys, they managed to hold out for six days, until a full company of artillery was brought up from Ap' Betnagur and the camp was buried under a mountain of seventy-pound trebuchet shot.

The detainees in the Auzeil house were probably among

the last people on the Island to hear the news, which arrived in the early hours of the morning in the form of a bench, borrowed from outside the Faith and Integrity four doors down the alley, and which smashed a panel out of Venart's front door. The soldiers on duty scrambled out of their bivouac in the courtyard to investigate; but by that time the door was open and a dozen armed men were in the hallway. What followed wasn't a fight in any realistic sense; one soldier made it halfway up the main staircase before an arrow between the shoulders brought him down again, *bump-bump-bump* on his face, but otherwise it was all very controlled and efficient.

They found Venart hiding under his bed ('I told you that'd be the first place they'd look,' Vetriz commented as they hauled him out; she hadn't done much better, ducking behind the curtains) and told him that he was now the new leader of the Island resistance army, which was poised to retake the city and drive the enemy into the sea.

'Who the hell are you?' Venart demanded, trying in vain to tug his collar out of the grip of the man who'd thus hailed him. 'And what the hell do you think you're doing?'

The man grinned. 'We're your allies,' he replied. 'Gorgas Loredan sent us to rescue you. Look sharp, the glorious revolution can't hang about while you put your socks on.'

'Gorgas Loredan?' Venart managed to say, before they bustled him out of the house. Meanwhile, another of the liberators had caught Eseutz Mesatges trying to shin down a drainpipe, and brought her out too. 'Ask her,' the squad leader went on, 'she was one of the people he talked to when they had the meeting.'

'Eseutz?' Venart looked mystified. 'What meeting?'

Eseutz was struggling to get dressed (she'd grabbed the first thing that came to hand when she heard the door being smashed in; unfortunately it was the warrior-princess outfit, which properly speaking needed the help of a strong maid-servant to get into). 'I don't know what he's talking about,' she said.

'You're lying,' Venart replied. 'For gods' sakes, stop fooling about and tell me, what's been going on?'

'All right,' Eseutz admitted angrily, straining to reach a stray shoulder-strap that was dangling out of reach behind her back. 'Yes, I did meet Gorgas bloody Loredan; he was going around saying we should stick the provincial office for more money for the ships.'

'It was his idea?'

'I suppose so,' Eseutz said. 'Anyway, he was suggesting it to everybody in the Ship-Owners' who'd listen. Gods only know why.'

Venart shook his head. No, he couldn't make sense of any of it, but he had an uncomfortable feeling that there was sense in there somewhere, only he wasn't devious enough to understand it. 'So it was his fault,' he said, 'all this – the occupation and everything. Because he was stirring up trouble.'

'Give yourselves some credit,' the squad leader interrupted. 'Mostly it was you people's fault, because you're greedy and very, very stupid. But yes, Gorgas planted the idea in your pathetic little heads; and now that the army's been wiped out, he's going to help you get out of it again.'

Eseutz grabbed his arm. 'What do you mean,' she said, 'the army's been wiped out?'

'You haven't heard?' The squad leader laughed. 'You've got King Temrai to thank for your freedom,' he said. 'I'm amazed you don't know. There's been riots in the streets here pretty well non-stop the last two days, and the sub-prefect can't do anything about it, not with half his garrison all cut up from the battle and the other half on permanent guard to keep the ships from sailing away.' He nudged Venart painfully in the ribs and grinned. 'You'd better get a move on, illustrious leader, or you'll be late for your own revolution.'

'What do you mean,' Eseutz repeated, 'wiped out? That's impossible.'

'Wiped out. Forty thousand dead. Caught 'em on the plains and cut 'em to ribbons. I must say, I never knew they had it in 'em. I mean, taking Perimadeia, yes; but my old granny and her cat could've done that. Knocking off an Imperial army, though – that takes some doing.' He looked up; his men had found Athli and brought her out too. 'Makes four,' he said, 'right, that'll do. We'll head for the Faussa warehouse; there's ten thousand quarters' worth of halberds and partisans in there that old man Faussa somehow forgot to mention to the sub-prefect when they were doing the confiscations. Once we get that lot out on the street, things'll really start to happen.'

To Venart Auzeil it all looked worryingly familiar; he'd been in Perimadeia on the night of the Fall, and the sight of armed men running in the streets was something he found highly evocative. But he told himself that these were *our* armed men; and it was true enough, you only had to look closely at them to see they'd never handled a weapon before in their lives. But a poleaxe or a bardische isn't like a harp or a jeweller's lathe; you don't have to be terribly good at it to make it work in some fashion, and when the enemy aren't standing to face you, some fashion is good enough.

Apart from a few desultory foot patrols and the sentries posted outside some buildings, there weren't any soldiers to be seen. According to the squad leader, they were all either barricaded into the Merchant Venturers' Hall or crowded on to the ships down on the Drutz. Venart didn't like the sound of that.

'We can't just leave them there,' he said. 'How are we going to get them out?'

The squad leader smiled and picked a lantern off a wall-sconce outside a tavern. 'Easy,' he said. 'Watch and learn.'

The crowd surrounding the Merchant Venturers' was large and noisy, but standing back a respectful distance after the Imperial archers had given them a demonstration of the effective range of an issue crossbow –

('Lucky for us,' the squad leader pointed out. 'They sent all the longbowmen with the army, and they didn't come back; all they've got here are crossbows, and they can only shoot once every three minutes.')

– But the sheer number of them was what impressed Venart the most. He hadn't imagined that his fellow countrymen would be so quick and so eager to risk their lives for their liberty. On the other hand, it wasn't as if they had anything to lose.

'They're in there all right,' someone reported to the squad leader; another of Gorgas' men, presumably, since Venart had never seen him before, and he looked too fierce to be an Islander. 'Did you find any oil?'

The squad leader shook his head. 'Don't need any,' he

replied. 'All right, sort out a cordon; I want halberds and poleaxes in the front two ranks, axes and hammers behind. Keep 'em well back; for one thing, this is going to burn hot.'

He was right; oil or pitch or sulphur would have been redundant. As soon as the first few torches pitched in the thatch, the Merchant Venturers' burst into flames like a beacon, lighting up a circle as bright as noon as far as the buildings on the other side of the square. The Islanders were shocked to see it go up; for a hundred years it had been a source of civic concern to make sure the thatch didn't catch fire, and setting it alight on purpose would never have occurred to them.

For what seemed like an impossibly long time nothing happened, and Venart found himself wondering if the Imperials were in there, standing to attention as they burned to death at their posts – from what he'd seen of them, he wouldn't put it past them. Then the front and side doors seemed to explode outwards and the soldiers came pouring into the light, their armour and helmets dazzling; it was like watching molten metal glowing white as it runs from the crucible into the mould, and Venart couldn't see any way it might be stopped, not by his fellow citizens and a few spikes on long sticks. He didn't want to watch, he could feel his skin crawling at the thought of cutting edges on bare skin, but it happened too quickly for him to look away in time. At first, the fiery bright ram crashed into the line of points and rode it down; but the mass of bodies behind soaked up the momentum, as the soft padding inside the armour absorbs the blow; the charge slowed and came to a stop, cooling, solidifying into individual men; at which point Venart saw that the outcome was inevitable. Herded together, without room to swing their weapons, the soldiers were crushed down, like an egg in a man's fist – the brittle shell, the armour, not standing up to the soft pressure all around it, not coming up to this level of proof. They were pulled down, their helmets ripped off; they were bashed down with hammers and axes and spades, mattocks and bidels, until all the shining steel shapes were crumpled into a heap of scrap lying on the ground, under the feet of the people. When it was over, there was a long silence.

So that's that, Venart thought; and as the crowd surged away from the circle of light and down the hill towards the Drutz, he wondered how this strange creature, this soft and flexible anvil, had been subdued so easily in the first place, when the soldiers first came out on to the streets and the notice of annexation was pinned to the door. It was still there, or at least strips of it were, burning fast and turning into soft ash, but everything else seemed to have changed, and he couldn't quite work out what had made all the difference. But then he looked sideways at the squad leader, Gorgas' carefully selected emissary, signalling to his men at the edges of the crowd, effortlessly directing the mob; *the Loredan touch*, he said to himself; *of course, it makes all the difference.*

Lieutenant Menas Onasin, in command of the army because everybody else was dead, looked back over his shoulder at the sea. *Here we are, then*, he thought. *We can die on our feet, or we can drown. Spoiled for choice, really.*

They were throwing stones; big, jagged stones, chunks of pavement, arms and heads smashed off the statues that lined Drutz Promenade. The man standing next to him in the line had been killed by a marble head, a bizarre way to die, with undesirable overtones of comedy. Having no archers to return fire, he had no option but to stand and take it; he'd tried charging the mob five times, and each time he'd led out a company and brought back a platoon. It was like fighting the sea, or a sandstorm.

His principal mistake had been leaving the cover of the ships in the first place. At the time it had seemed like the sensible thing to do; ships, like thatched buildings, are inflammable, and he hadn't relished the prospect of fighting on two fronts (the mob on land, the mutinous crews below decks) while trapped between fire above his head and water under his feet. Face them on dry land, he'd told himself, where we can at least stand up straight and use our weapons.

Someone had set up one of the light trebuchets they'd mounted on the forecastles of the ships and was loosing off ranging shots; the first stone fell short, nearly creaming the front row of the mob, the second, third and fourth had gone splash in the water. If the man behind the arm was being at all methodical in his approach, number five was due to pitch into the exact centre of the army, and there was nothing that Lieutenant Onasin could do about it. It was like old times, standing still while quick learners lobbed rocks at his head; he was a Perimadeian, a refugee from the Fall, and he'd learned everything he knew about motionless cowering during Temrai's bombardment of the City.

For shot number five they used a torso, all that was left of Renvaut Razo's masterpiece *Triumph of the Human Spirit*, which had stood in the courtyard of the Copper Exchange ever since Onasin had first visited here as a boy of nine, brought along by his father as a special treat. He could remember the statue vividly; it was huge and dramatic, and the head was far too small for the colossal, mountain-breasted body; but when he'd pointed that out, his father had told him to be quiet, and he'd kept the secret to himself ever since. Now there were bits of the *Triumph of the Human Spirit* all around him – not just the torso, which had squashed seven armoured men like beetles, but arms and hands and drapery shrapnel too, not to mention the too-small head (which had flattened one man and wrenched the leg off another). He remembered eavesdropping on two earnest-looking women who'd stood for ages just staring at the statue; according to them, what made it so special was the ease and power of its movement. He'd waited twenty years to find out what they'd meant by that. They were right, too; hurled from the sling of a trebuchet, Razo's gift to the ages moved like shit off a shovel and packed a devastating punch.

They were setting up more trebuchets. It was a pity that the soldiers of the Empire were universally known not to surrender, not under any circumstances, because a few more direct hits were going to panic the men, and that would open gaps in the line; and when that happened, the sea in front of him would come rushing in and sweep him off the dock into the sea behind him, and he was too well armoured to swim. Surrender would be an excellent option right now; but he'd already tried it twice and they simply hadn't believed him.

Another charge would also break up the line; but on balance Lieutenant Onasin preferred the thought of dying fighting to either drowning or being squashed, so he yelled out the appropriate orders and the front three ranks dressed to the front. A stair, ripped out of the steps that led up to the customs house, enfiladed the front rank, knocking off heads. Onasin raised his arm and stepped forward, straight into the path of a brick. It bounced off his gorget, crimping the metal so that he couldn't turn his head. *Damn*, he thought, and dropped his arm to signal the advance.

After that, there wasn't any point in deluding himself that he had any control whatsoever. The momentum of the ranks behind him boosted him forward like driftwood on a wave, and all he could do was keep his legs moving, so that he wouldn't get shoved over and trampled. As he was propelled forward, he saw the spike on the head of the halberd dead ahead, but of course he couldn't slow down, or even move sideways. The man behind him rammed him on to the spike like a cook driving a skewer into a cut of meat; he felt himself being jolted forward as the spike finally burst through the belly of his breastplate, then the shock of coming to a sudden stop as the crossbar at the end of the spike held him back. The pressure on his backplate wasn't getting any less, which meant that his body was being crushed between the man behind him and the crossbar, the main effect being to drive the spike deeper into his compressed belly.

And there he stuck, because the momentum of the mob easily matched the momentum of the charge. He found that he was looking directly into the face of the man who was holding the halberd; he was wearing an expression of panic and what could only be described as acute embarrassment (which was quite understandable; after all, what do you say to a perfect stranger who's impaled himself on the spike you happen to be clinging on to?) and if he'd had any control over the muscles of his face, he'd have been tempted to smile, or even wink.

It was the trebuchets that saved him. There were ten of them in action now, and they all loosed in unison, suddenly flattening the men in the ranks directly behind him. With no more pressure from them he found himself being thrust back; then his feet caught on something, he stumbled and went down on his backside, wrenching the halberd out of the other man's hands. Now it was the other man's turn to be shot forward; Onasin felt the sole of the man's boot on the side of his jaw as he stumbled forward, then a savage pain in his shoulder as somebody else stood on that. Then he lost count, and fell asleep.

When he opened his eyes, he found that he was staring into another man's eyes; but this man was quite definitely dead. In fact there were dead men everywhere. Mass grave. He opened his mouth to scream, but only a little squeak came out, so he tried waving his arms and legs instead. They were scarcely more co-operative than his throat and lungs, but apparently he'd done enough, because he heard someone shout, 'Hold on, we've got another live one.'

He wasn't sure how they got him out again; the grave was pretty deep and sheer-sided, so he guessed someone had had to jump down in there, on top of all the really dead people. That didn't strike him as a pleasant thing to have to do – well, he wouldn't have fancied it himself – so he tried to say thank you as he swung face-down through the air; but if anybody heard him, they didn't acknowledge it.

'Will you look at that?' someone he couldn't see said as he was flipped over on to his back. 'He's never going to make it with a hole that size.'

'You'd be surprised,' someone else replied. 'I knew a man once who was gored by a damn great bull – when they got the horn out you could literally see daylight through him, poor bugger. He made it, though.'

'All right,' said the first voice, 'put him over there with the others. If there's a medic with nothing better to do—'

'You'll be lucky.'

But there was a medic, eventually, a sad-faced man who cleaned and bandaged the wound. Whether his sorrow arose from the horrors he'd seen or the remoteness of his chances of getting paid for his work, there was no way of knowing. By then, of course, the battle was over, the enemy had been killed or captured, the fires put out; and the Islanders were moving wearily about the streets, clearing up wreckage, repairing damage, stumbling over bodies that had been overlooked by the corpse details. After they'd filled up two deep graves, they stopped bothering with such niceties, loaded the dead on to two enormous grain freighters and dumped them in the sea.

Onasin ended up on a similar grain-ship, which had

been pressed into service as a prison hulk. It could have been
worse; it would have been far worse if it had been an Imperial
prisoner-of-war compound. From what he could overhear
of the guards' conversation, they explained away their
humanity by claiming that the men in their charge were
potentially valuable hostages, but by this time Onasin knew
them better than that. This was, after all, their first war; they
hadn't learned yet.

'A tragedy,' sighed the prefect of Ap' Escatoy. 'A tragic,
wretched waste. And so futile, too.'

The chief administrator nodded sadly. 'It is rather heart-
breaking,' he said, wiping honey from his fingertips with a
damp cloth. 'And, as you say, they've achieved nothing by it.
If anything, they've made matters worse for themselves.'

'Undoubtedly,' the prefect said. 'But I'm afraid they've
forfeited my sympathy, given what they've done. I know,
vindictiveness is an ugly emotion, but on this occasion I'm
going to allow myself that luxury. They will be made to
pay for what they've done.'

'Figuratively speaking, of course.'

The prefect smiled grimly. 'Unfortunately,' he said. 'I wish
it were otherwise, but it isn't.' He shook his head. 'No, the
fact must be faced, and we must come to terms with it: this
confounded battle has cost me my refurbishment grant, and
with it goes my best chance of rebuilding Perimadeia. All
gone, and no actual benefit to anybody. And on reflection
it isn't tragic; tragedy has a certain nobility about it that this
shambles lacks. It's waste, plain and simple.' He picked up
a corner of the tablecloth and rubbed it between the palms
of his hands, as if wiping away the unpleasantness of life. 'But
there, it's done, and now it's up to us to make the best we can
of the circumstances we're faced with. Practical, pragmatic
and positive,' he added with a little smile – it was obviously a
quotation or a reference to something (the prefect was an
inveterate slipper-in of apt but abstruse quotations, to the
point where it wasn't safe to assume that anything he
said was necessarily his own words) but the administrator
couldn't place it; so he nodded and twitched his lip in token
refined mirth. 'And we should start,' the prefect went on,
'with the war. The main thing is to make sure there aren't

any more defeats. Send a letter to Captain Loredan telling him to stay put and do nothing, just make sure Temrai doesn't slip past him and escape. I want the actual *coup de grâce* to come from the new army, the one the provincial office is sending. Just defeating them won't be enough; they have to be completely outnumbered and crushed if we're to put this mess into perspective.'

'Agreed,' said the administrator. 'Now then, what about the Island? That's going to be awkward, isn't it? We're going to have to get some ships from somewhere.'

The prefect shrugged. 'We'll need ships anyway, for the war. Potentially, of course, this Island business could be far worse for us than Temrai and losing an entire army.' He turned his head and sat still for a moment or two, watching a kestrel in a lemon tree in the courtyard below; it had a small bird, still alive, gripped in one claw and was trying rather awkwardly to kill it without letting go of the branch with its other foot. 'In a way,' he went on, 'a major setback like the one Temrai's given us needn't be an entirely negative thing. Once in a while, it can even be – well, almost desirable. The point is, there's no prestige to be gained from overrunning a weak and negligible opponent. A serious defeat, provided it's followed up in short order by a complete victory, serves to give the enemy a degree of stature. And, of course, it helps keep standards up in the army; nothing like getting your face slapped once in a while to stop you getting complacent. The Island business, though; as I said, there's nothing to be gained from that. There's all the difference in the world between a setback along the way to an inevitable triumph, and getting kicked out of a place we're supposed to have subdued and added to the collection, so to speak. What makes matters worse is that everybody *knows* that the Islanders aren't worthy opponents or formidable warriors, let alone noble savages whose primitive virtues we can admire, etcetera, etcetera; they're fat, smug, slightly obnoxious little men who make a living by buying cheap and selling dear.' The prefect was starting to get annoyed now; there was nothing to show it in his face or his voice, but he'd pulled the ring off his little finger and was twisting it round, as if tightening a screw. When he did that, wise men who knew the score found excuses to go elsewhere for a while. 'Still,' he went on, 'getting worked up about the situation won't help it, and it might lead us to make more mistakes. For that reason, I feel we ought to leave them alone for a while; at the very least, until the war's over.'

The administrator nodded. 'I agree,' he said. 'In fact, I've been giving the matter some thought; what I'd suggest is that we give them some time to reflect on what they've done and then send them a letter offering them a chance to buy their lives. Of course,' he added, as the prefect raised an eyebrow, 'they'd have to send us the heads of the ringleaders first, as a token of good faith – I always feel that getting rebels to execute their own leaders is far better than doing it oneself; you simply can't make a martyr of a man whose head you've cut off yourself.'

'An interesting point,' the prefect conceded.

'Then,' the administrator went on, 'we set the terms; we'll accept their abject surrender on condition that they put their fleet at our disposal, fully manned – after all, that's the object of the exercise, and that's what our betters in the provincial office will judge us by, at the end of the day. We need Islanders to crew the ships; if we slaughter them to a man, we'll have ships but no crews. If we do it my way, we'll have crews who are acutely aware that their familes and countrymen are hostages for their good behaviour and satisfactory performance—'

'Thereby,' interrupted the prefect, stroking his chin, 'turning this ghastly business to our advantage and making something good out of it after all. Thank you; I do believe you've restored my faith in the value of clarity of vision.'

'My pleasure,' the administrator replied. 'One of the pleasures of life, as far as I'm concerned, is taking a disaster and turning it into an opportunity.' He smiled. 'Fortunately, it's a pleasure I rarely have a chance to savour.'

The prefect tilted his head back and gazed at the ceiling. '"Lord, confound my enemies; or, if Thou must confound my friends, grant that I may be their salvation." Do you know, the older I get, the more I appreciate Deltin; but he's wasted on the young, and one must have something to look forward to.'

The administrator nodded. 'So,' he said, 'that's that settled.

This is turning out to be a productive morning. Now, if we can only devise some way of rebuilding Perimadeia after all, we'll have earned our lunch.'

The prefect opened his eyes and looked at him. 'Don't tell me,' he said. 'You have an idea.'

'Just an outline,' the administrator replied, 'slowly taking shape in my mind's eye. And no, I don't propose sharing it with you quite yet. After all, it wouldn't do to disclose it until I'm certain it has merit, otherwise I'll jeopardise my reputation for resourceful and imaginative thinking.'

'That's fair,' the prefect conceded with a wry grin. 'But you do have an idea. Or an idea for an idea.'

The administrator made a small gesture with his hands. 'Always,' he said. 'But I try to be like a careful doctor: I make sure my mistakes are buried before anybody sees them.'

The messenger set out that afternoon, with orders to reach Captain Loredan as quickly as possible. It was imperative, he was told, that he get to the captain before he had a chance to react to the news of the disaster. This was a matter of the utmost importance to the well-being of the whole Empire.

What the dispatcher meant by that was: get a move on, don't dawdle or stop to pass the time of day with any old friends you may happen to meet, no sightseeing or shopping, no detours to deliver private letters or trade samples. But the dispatcher was an eloquent man with a forceful turn of phrase, and the messenger was young and rather conscientious. As a result, he set off in a cloud of dust, a map stuffed into the leg of his boot and three days' rations bouncing against his back in a satchel.

There seems to be a law of nature that the more one hurries, the more ingeniously circumstances contrive to slow one down. He made excellent time as far as the Eagle River ford; but the river was in spate, the first time in thirty years it had flooded in the dry season, which meant he had to retrace his steps and head upstream to the Blackwood bridge. But the bridge wasn't there; some idiot had been robbing stones from the base of the nearside pillar, and the whole thing had slumped quietly into the river one fine morning, damming it up just long enough to accumulate a sufficient body of water to saturate the sandhills on the nearside bank when eventually the blockage was swept away. In consequence the Blackwood ford was impassable as well, something the messenger found out the hard way when his horse went in up to its shoulders in the newly created quagmire. He tried in vain to get the wretched creature out for the best part of a morning before abandoning it and setting out on foot for the nearest of the border outposts to the south.

By this stage he was almost out of his mind with rage and frustration, so he was immensely relieved when he came across a small caravan of mixed Colleon, Belhout and Tornoys merchants taking a short cut to Ap' Escatoy. It took him a further two hours of almost lethal frustration to persuade them to accept a provincial office assignat in payment for a horse, even though he knew he was paying nearly double what the animal was worth – it was just his luck that the only decent horse for sale belonged to a Belhout who, belonging to a nation who steadfastly refused on moral grounds either to read or to write, had extreme difficulty in relating to the concept of paper money. In the end he had to use his assignat to buy gold from a Colleon jeweller, at fifteen per cent over standard, with which to pay the Belhout; but the jeweller would only sell him gold by the full ounce, which meant he had to buy three quarters more than he needed ... By the time he was back on the road, he was a day and half a night behind schedule, and still on the wrong side of the Eagle River.

But he still had his map; so he sat down under a wind-twisted thorn tree with a piece of string for measuring distances, and looked for an alternative route. He found one readily enough; he could carry on following the west bank of the Eagle until it became the north bank, thereby avoiding the need to cross it at all. That was also a much more direct route, which would allow him to make up nearly all the time he'd lost provided he could keep up a good rate of progress. The problem was that it took him within an hour's ride of Temrai's fortified camp.

He considered the risks. If he arrived late, going on what the dispatcher had told him, he might as well not arrive at all. One man alone, riding fast; if he dumped his mailshirt and

helmet and wrapped his cloak round his head, riding a horse
with a Belhout saddle and harness, he reckoned he could
pass for a Belhout himself. The worst that could happen
would be that he'd be caught, and the message would never
get there – no worse than if he arrived late. Looked at the
other way round, if he didn't go this way, he'd most certainly
be late, whereas if he took the risk, there was a reasonable
chance he'd get there, and in time. From that perspective,
he didn't really have a choice.

He was a messenger, not a diplomat or a historian or a
scholar interested in abstruse facts about remote tribes; so he
couldn't be expected to know that a small element among
the plains tribes had a long-standing grudge against the
Belhout, arising out of a half-forgotten feud about a disputed
well.

The scouting party that ran him down, after a long and
exciting chase that lasted well over an hour, brought back his
head and stuck it up on a pole on the embankment they
were working on at the fortress, until Temrai saw it and made
them take it down. It wasn't until some time later that the
letter came to light, when the scouts were sharing out
the dead man's possessions; the man who received it took it
home to his wife and told her to use the parchment to patch
a hole in his wet-weather trousers. She couldn't read either,
but she happened to know that the three-headed-lion
seal meant provincial office, and nagged her husband until he
took the letter to his gang-boss, who took it to the head
of his section who took it straight to Temrai. When Temrai
read it he became angry, then very quiet.

'Marvellous,' he said, when they asked him what the
matter was. 'They order Loredan to leave us alone, and we
have to go and intercept the letter. Any more intelligence
coups like that, and we're finished.'

He explained what had happened, and read out the
relevant part of the letter. Nobody said anything for a long
time.

'What if we forwarded it on?' someone suggested. 'Close
up the seal with a hot knife; maybe nobody would notice it's
already been opened.'

Temrai laughed. 'Give the provincial office some credit,' he
said. 'Imperial couriers have to know five different levels

of security code, a different one for each class of message. If they can't give the right code when they hand over the message, they're strangled on the spot and the message is assumed to be a fake. Imperial seals are painted with lacquer after the wax has cooled; if you try to doctor them with a hot knife, the lacquer burns and makes a mess of the seal. I've even heard it said that for important messages they use a special kind of ink that changes colour once it's been exposed to light, so even if you get hold of a duplicate seal they'll know at a glance if the letter's been opened. No, we've done enough damage for one day, let's not make it any worse by giving him reason to think we're up to something.' He rolled up the letter, put it back in its brass tube and let it fall to the ground. 'If I were a superstitious man, I'd probably give up now. Opinions, anybody?'

'We could forget all about making a stand,' said Sildocai, the hero of the recent victory. 'If building this fortress makes them think we're staying put, then it'll have done its job. Meanwhile we pack up and slip away in the middle of the night, head north, try to get across the mountains before they catch up with us. They'd have to be crazy to follow us after that. Don't dismiss it out of hand, Temrai. I know, it's horrible country the other side of the mountains, cold and wet and bleak – that's why nobody lives there, it's not worth invading. But if we go, we'll still have some sort of a life. If we stay here, we'll probably die. As decisions go, I'd say that's an easy one.'

'It's what we were planning to do,' someone else pointed out, 'when we left the City plain. We all agreed on it then. Nothing's really changed since.'

Temrai shook his head. 'I don't agree,' he said. 'The difference is, Loredan and his army are just the other side of the Swan River; if we try to run away, he'll catch us. We'll be fighting out in the open; we won't be able to use the trebuchets.'

'But we outnumber them,' Sildocai pointed out. 'And let's face it, we've just proved that our horsemen can make monkeys out of their heavy infantry. That's assuming they catch us, which isn't certain by any means.'

'They'll catch us,' Temrai said. 'Count on it.'

'What you're saying doesn't make sense,' someone else

objected. 'We've just won a great victory, right? And – no disrespect to Sildocai here – we're all agreed that if anything it's made our position a damn sight worse. Suppose we hold still here and somehow we manage to beat off Loredan's attack; marvellous, they'll send *another* army – that's as well as this enormous bloody army that Loredan's supposed to be waiting for. It's pointless; for every one of them we kill, we get three in his place. Are you suggesting we kill every adult male in the Empire? Even if we could, there's so many of them our children would be old men before they were through with it. We can't win; and if you can't win, you either give up or try to run away. Let's at least *try* to run away, Temrai, while we still can. We've got nothing to lose.'

Temrai shook his head, without stopping to think. 'No,' he said. 'We stay here. If we run away across the mountains, he'll follow us. He'll always be there. We'll fight him here, and we'll win; then we'll decide what to do next.' He frowned, as if trying to hear something. 'They know that if he fights us here, he may lose – that's why they tried to stop him. So we'll do what they don't want us to do; first rule of war, that is.'

Sildocai looked up in surprise. 'You've changed your tune, haven't you? A moment ago, the letter not getting through was a disaster.'

Temrai smiled. 'I've had a few minutes to think about it,' he said. 'Actually, it's an opportunity; it just looked like a disaster until I had a chance to get the skin off it. No, they specifically said in the letter don't engage the enemy, we can't risk any more defeats. You said yourself a moment ago, we outnumber them. Loredan will be attacking a defended position with inferior numbers. We can win this.'

'Have we actually established that he's going to attack?' somebody asked. 'I wouldn't, for the reasons you've just stated.'

'Of course he'll attack,' Temrai replied. 'Otherwise they wouldn't have written and told him not to. No, he's coming, and that's good. We'll beat him, and then we'll go.'

'You're wrong—' Sildocai started to say.

Temrai held up his hand. 'Trust me,' he said. 'That's all you've got to do. I know I can beat him; I've done it before, when the odds were against me. I can do it again. Don't ask me how I know, I just do.'

After that, there didn't seem to be much point continuing the discussion.

CHAPTER SEVENTEEN

'It's an awkward one, and no mistake,' said the engineer, scratching his head. 'You can see where they've dug a canal to bring the river round the other side; they've made it into an island, effectively. Suppose we bridge the river; there's a stockade tight up against the water – well, we can breach that with our artillery – assuming they let us, they've got more engines than we have and better ones, too – and then we've got the cliffs to get up. There's only the one path and that's going to be no fun at all with all those gates and traps. But say we get up the path to the plateau; there's two more stockades, out of range of our artillery so we can't lay down a barrage first, and then – assuming we get that far – a straightforward pitched battle on the top where they'll outnumber us at least three to two, depending on how many we've lost getting that far. If you want my considered opinion, forget it.'

The wind was fierce and fresh on the hilltop they were standing on. At this distance, the fortress looked beautiful, with the sun glinting on the water.

'It can be done,' Bardas replied. 'I know it can be done, because he's done it.'

The engineer frowned. 'I'm sorry,' he said, 'I don't follow.'

Bardas pointed. 'You see that?' he said. 'That's as close as he could get to a replica of the City; he's effectively rebuilt Perimadeia, right here on the plains. And whatever else that might be, it's as clear an admission of defeat as you'll ever want to see.'

'I don't know about that,' the engineer said doubtfully. 'I never saw Perimadeia. All I can tell you is, it's as near as dammit the perfect use of position and resources. Besides,' he added, 'wasn't the only reason the City fell because some bastard opened the gates?'

Bardas shook his head. 'It should have fallen before that, only I cheated.' He sat down on a rock, picked a stem of grass and chewed it. 'We'll start with a bombardment, all around where they've got the swing-bridge; we'll bring up siege towers and – what do you call them, those roofed-over sections, like the tops of wagons, made out of hides stretched over hoops?'

'I know what you mean,' the engineer said.

'Anyway,' Bardas went on, 'them; there's a blind spot, see? If we concentrate our artillery and knock out the trebuchets covering the point, and then bring them forward to take out the defences on the path—'

'But he'll just bring up more engines,' the engineer objected. 'Take 'em to bits, carry 'em round, put 'em back together again; they'll have it down to a fine art by now, being a nomadic people and all.'

'You'll just have to make sure they don't get the chance,' Bardas replied. 'And it oughtn't to be a problem. There simply isn't enough room to put in enough engines where they need to go. His mistake is, he's gone for a circular ground-plan. He can have as many engines as he likes around the other two hundred and forty degrees of the circle, but they won't be any danger to us because the angles are wrong.'

The engineer thought for a minute or so. 'You may be right,' he said. 'If we can get in tight to the river, the engines on the plateau'll all be overshooting. Yes, I can see it now.' He grinned. 'I'm surprised he didn't think of that.'

'I'm not.' Bardas stood up. 'He was rebuilding Perimadeia, but he's made it too small, too cramped-up; and the angles are wrong. He's forgotten about the bastions I built out from the old wall, specifically to allow us to enfilade them and stop them doing what we're going to do now. You see,' he went on, climbing into his saddle, 'that's what comes of living too much in the past – you make unnecessary difficulties for yourself.'

The engineer hauled himself clumsily on to his horse and sat for a moment, catching his breath. 'I hope you're right,' he said. 'So what happens as and when you do make it to the top? There's still more of them than us.'

'So what?' Bardas stood up in his stirrups for a last look at the fortress. 'I was winning battles against superior numbers of these people when you were still playing with clay soldiers. You worry too much, that's your problem. How soon can you have my siege towers and—'

'Mantlets?'

'That's the word. Mantlets. How long?'

The engineer stroked his beard. 'Three days,' he said. 'And I mean three days, so don't go telling me they've got to be ready in two.'

'Three days will be fine,' Bardas replied. 'Just make sure you do a good job.' He sat down again and turned his head away, but in his mind's eye he could still see the shape; the encircling moat, the three levels – he knew it was an illusion, but he felt as if he was home again after a long and exhausting campaign, that first thrilling glimpse of the City. Which was strange, because in all the time he spent there, he'd never once thought of it as home, just as somewhere he happened to live.

'I had a friend,' he said – he knew the engineer wasn't really interested, but he wasn't bothered by that – 'who was a philosopher, or a scientist, or a wizard; I'm not sure he knew himself what he was. But he used to reckon that there are these crucial moments in history, when things can go one way or another, leading to entirely different outcomes; identify one of these moments, he believed, and you can control it.' He lifted his feet out of the stirrups and let them swing. 'I'll be honest with you, I thought the whole business was a mixture of rather idiotic mysticism and the glaringly obvious. Come to that, I still do. But just suppose there's something in it; what are you supposed to make of it when you seem to be getting the same crucial moment, over and over again? If he was still alive, I'd be interested to hear him talk his way out of that one.'

The engineer shrugged. 'If you're asking my opinion on a point of mechanics,' he said, 'I'd say that you're talking about a camshaft.'

Bardas opened his eyes a little wider. 'Explain,' he said.

'Simple, really.' The engineer tied his reins in a knot and tucked them under the pommel of his saddle, to leave both his hands free for making explanatory gestures. 'The cam,' he said, 'is an absolutely basic, fundamental piece of design; it turns your standard rotary movement –' (he drew a circle in the air) '– into a linear movement –' (he drew a straight line) '– which is obviously very important, right? Because all your sources of power, your prime movers – waterwheels, say, or treadles – they're repetitive, so they describe a rotary movement, a circle going round and round for ever. Your cam, which is nothing more than a link attached to one point of the circle, turns that into a straight-line push. Add a simple ratchet and you don't have to be a genius to have your wheel, endlessly going round and round the same axis, slaved to give you a progressive linear movement, such as pushing something along. It follows that the bit that does all the work, makes the connection, is the link between the wheel and the workpiece. If I was your mate, the philosopher, I'd be looking for a camshaft.'

Bardas frowned. 'The camshaft of fortune,' he said. 'Well, it's a thought. Of course, to complete the analogy, you'd have to have some way for it to change direction while still going round and round in circles. Is that possible? Mechanically speaking, I mean?'

The engineer grinned. 'Of course it is,' he replied. 'All you do is, you whack it bloody hard with the big hammer.'

'What do you mean, junk?' Temrai demanded, wincing as Tilden tightened a strap. 'I've been told by experts that this is probably the finest armour money can buy.'

'Experts,' Tilden sighed. 'You mean that lying thief who sold it to you. Hold still, will you? Either this strap's shrunk or you've put on weight.'

Temrai scowled. 'There you go again,' he said. 'Anything I say or do, you've got to belittle it. If this stuff isn't any good, then why would he give it an unconditional lifetime guarantee?'

'Oh, come on,' Tilden replied, smiling. 'A guarantee that lasts as long as you live. So when, five minutes after the start of the first battle, it falls to bits on you and you die ...'

'Ouch.'

'Sorry. It's your own fault. I did say hold still.'

First, the greaves, covering the leg from ankle to knee. They reminded Temrai of two pieces of guttering joined with

382

a hinge. 'There's got to be some way,' he said, 'of stopping these things from sliding down and trapping your foot. See that bruise? After an hour it's so bad I can hardly walk.'

'But you don't walk when you're fighting, you sit on your horse. So it doesn't matter.'

'Yes, but I've got to walk from the tent to the horse, then from the horse back to the tent ...'

After the greaves, the poleyns and cuisses, to cover his legs from knee to groin; they hung by straps from his belt, and were held in place by more straps around the knee-joint and thigh. Next the mailshirt –

'I can't lift this,' Tilden said.

'Of course you can. Don't be so feeble.'

Tilden grunted, trying to hoist the shirt over his head so that he could wriggle his hands through the armholes. He found them just in time, before she let go. As he pushed his head through the neck-hole, his hair snagged in the rings, making him curse. 'Don't call me feeble,' Tilden said, 'or you can put on your own silly armour.'

'I'm sorry,' Temrai said unconvincingly. 'Right, what comes next? Breastplate, I think.'

Breastplate and backplate, connected at the top by two straps, one on either side of the neck, like the shoulder-straps of a soldier's pack, and two more at waist level. 'Lift your arm a bit more,' Tilden muttered, straining at the left-hand side buckle, 'You aren't giving me enough room – there we are. Is that tight enough?'

'Too tight. Let it out a hole before I choke.'

'You might have said, instead of letting me hurt my wrist tightening the horrid thing.'

Next the arm-harness; vambraces from wrist to elbow, cops to protect the elbow itself, rerebraces from the elbow to just below the shoulder – more straps, more buckles. 'What happens when you need a pee?' Tilden asked sweetly. 'Do you stop the column and summon a couple of armourers?'

Temrai looked at her, frowning. 'No,' he said.

'Oh. Then what's to stop it getting all rusty, right down the inside of your leg? You could seize up at the knees, and then where'd you be?'

'Thank you,' Temrai said.

'And it must be really sordid when you need a—'

'All *right*,' Temrai said. 'And yes, it is. Now undo the shoulder buckles—'

'But I've just done them up.'

'Well, undo them again, and you see those loops at the top of the pauldrons? You thread them through so they hang over the rerebraces—'

'The whats?'

'These bits –' Temrai tried to move his arm to point at them, but he didn't quite have the freedom of movement. Tilden giggled. 'So they hang over my upper arm,' he said severely. 'That's it, you've got it.'

'Is it all right to do these buckles up now?'

'Yes.'

'You sure? Only I don't want to have to do them again.'

'Positive. Now put on the gorget – there's a little catch at the side, look ...'

'You mean this collar thing?'

'That's right,' Temrai said patiently. 'The gorget.'

Tilden raised an eyebrow. 'I don't see why you can't just call it a collar.'

'Because it's a gorget,' Temrai said. 'You've found the little catch? That's it. Right, now all I need are the gauntlets and the helmet, and that's that done.'

'You mean the gloves. And the hat.'

'Quite right. The gloves first, then the hat.' He held out his hand. 'You've got to pull it on by the cuff – no, not the metal cuff, there's a leather lining, see?'

'It must be awfully hot in all that lot.'

'Yes, it is. Now hold it firmly while I wiggle my fingers in place – I said hold it, for pity's sake.'

'I'm doing my best,' Tilden said. 'Try again.'

'That's better – no it's not, the useless bloody thing's not on straight, it's slipping round the side of my hand. Pull the *cuff* —'

'I'm pulling. It's stuck.'

'What? Oh, right. I'll bend my thumb a bit, see if that makes any difference. Try it now.'

Eventually the gauntlet was persuaded into place – 'It's pinching my wrist, there, between the cuff and the vambrace,' Temrai complained. 'I'll just have to make sure I only fight against southpaws' – and Tilden picked up the helmet; a one-piece sallet that came down over Temrai's face like a steel pudding-basin, with one narrow slit to see out of. She settled it on his head and stood back.

'Temrai?' she said.

'What?' His voice sounded far away and faintly comic; but the fact remained that Temrai wasn't there any more. The steel had finally closed around him, like quicksand.

'Nothing,' Tilden said. 'Can you manage to stand up in all that?'

'I think so,' Temrai's voice bumbled through the steel, 'if I take it slowly.'

As he stood up, Tilden watched the joints, the layers of articulated lames, rippling like the muscles of a scale-skinned dragon. There was nothing human there, except for a vaguely familiar shape. 'You forgot the shoes,' she said.

'Sabatons.'

'What?'

'Sabatons. That's what they're called.'

'Fine. Do you want them or not?'

'Can't be bothered,' said the echo of his voice. 'What I do need, though, is my sword. Over there, by the wash-stand.'

Tilden brought it to him. 'Does that tie on as well?' she asked.

The helmet nodded; up, flexing the lames of the gorget, and ponderously down. 'Over my shoulder and round,' it said, and the left-hand vambrace, cop and rerebrace lifted into the air. 'Come on,' it said, 'I can't stand like this indefinitely.'

'Can you get it out of the scabbard?' Tilden asked dubiously as she fastened the last buckle.

'Probably not, but who cares? It's just a fashion accessory anyway. With these bloody gauntlets on, I'd need someone to fold my hand around the hilt before I could hold it.'

'You look very funny,' Tilden said. She didn't think he looked funny at all; quite the opposite. But she had an idea he wouldn't want to know what she really thought. 'Don't fall over, whatever you do.'

'I'll try not to.'

By the time he'd walked from his tent to the gatehouse, Temrai felt much more at ease. It was as if the armour was growing on him, like a cutting grafted on to a tree. It was awkward rather than heavy, until he made an injudicious movement and upset the balance; then he had to make an effort to get his weight back on the soles of his feet. He wondered if that was how he'd felt when he was a child, learning to walk for the first time.

They were waiting for him; Sildocai, his second in command Azocai, most of the general staff. 'Very smart,' someone said. 'Can you breathe in there?'

'Yes,' Temrai said, 'but I can only just hear you. Get this helmet off me, someone.' As he emerged he took a big gasp of air, as if he'd been under water, or in the foul air of the mines. 'That's better,' he said. 'So, what's happening?'

Sildocai, who'd been looking at him as if he'd never seen the like, pointed at the tiny figures moving about below them. 'That's his siege train there,' he said. 'Well out of range still; we'll let them know when they've come too close. He's got his cavalry out front in case we make a sortie, try to run him off, so I wouldn't recommend that. They'll probably spend the rest of the day pitching camp, making themselves feel at home.'

Temrai tried to make out what he was pointing at, but all he could see were dots and blurs. 'He's welcome,' he said. 'What about a night-raid, like we've been practising?'

'Could do,' Sildocai replied, without much enthusiasm. 'I'd prefer to wait a day or so, until they've deployed their artillery. I'd like a chance to cut a few ropes, do a bit of damage before they start the bombardment.'

Temrai nodded; the gorget creaked and graunched. 'Fair enough,' he said. 'Are they using the river at all?'

'Haven't seen any signs as yet,' replied a man whose name Temrai couldn't quite remember. 'Probably he doesn't want to risk fire-ships.'

Sildocai grinned. 'Very sensible of him. Well, they're worth keeping in reserve, in case he tries to build a causeway across the river. We'd better keep a few surprises up our sleeves.'

'He won't build a causeway,' Temrai said. 'He'll use boats; that's after he's shot up our engines. That's when we'll use the fire-ships. Of course he'll be expecting that, too; but there's not a lot he'll be able to do about it.'

Sildocai looked at him. 'You seem pretty sure about that,' he said.

'I am sure,' Temrai replied. 'We've been through all this before, if you recall.'

'Have we?'

Temrai nodded. 'Oh, yes. Different war, same situation. Unless he's better at being me than I was, I know exactly what he's going to do. And he knows what I'm going to do, of course.'

'Right. Do you fancy sharing any of this with us, or is it a secret between you and him?'

'For the last time,' Venart protested wearily, 'I am not the government. We haven't got a government. We've never had a government before.We don't need a government now. Can you understand that?'

The man looked at him for a moment. 'All right,' he said. 'So you're not *officially* the government; but you led the revolution and chucked the bogies into the sea, so like it or not you're in charge. And what I want to know is, when am I going to get my compensation?'

Venart was ready to burst into tears. 'How the hell do I know? And who started this rumour about compensation anyway? I didn't.'

'So you're saying there isn't going to be any compensation?' said one of the other faces in the crowd. 'Is that right?'

'Yes.'

'Well, you may think it's right, it wasn't your warehouse that got burned down. You want to come with me now and explain to my creditors that it's all right?'

'No, I didn't mean right like you're saying—'

'Perhaps you should say what you mean, then,' said the face, scowling furiously at him. 'You could start by telling us why you've suddenly decided there isn't going to be any compensation.'

'I haven't decided anything,' Venart groaned. 'It's not up to me—'

'So you haven't decided yet. Any idea when you're likely to decide?'

Vernart took a deep breath. 'No,' he said. 'Now for gods' sakes, let me through.'

That didn't go down well. 'You're just going to walk away and leave us here guessing, are you?' someone shouted.

'I'm going to walk into my house and take a leak,' Venart replied, 'like I've been wanting to do for the last half hour, only you won't let me. Now get out of my way or get wet, the choice is yours.'

When he'd finally managed to close the door behind him, he sprinted/hobbled round the courtyard to the outhouse as if pursued by wolves. When he came out again, he felt much better. *Remarkable*, he thought, *how so simple an act can impart such a feeling of well-being.*

It didn't last, though. 'Ven, where the hell have you been?' Vetriz ambushed him as he walked back across the courtyard. 'Ranvaud Doce is here, he's been waiting for nearly an hour.'

Venart stopped and looked at her. 'Who?'

'Ranvaud Doce. You idiot, he's the new chairman of the Ship-Owners'.'

'Oh. What does he want to see me for?'

Vetriz didn't even bother to answer that. 'And you'd better get rid of him quick, because Ehan Stampiz'll be here at noon, and if those two run into each other, I don't want to be anywhere near. And when are we going to write your speech?'

Venart glowered at her. 'I am not making a speech,' he said.

'I haven't got time to argue with you now,' Vetriz said. 'Doce is in the counting house. Oh, don't just stand there looking pathetic.'

Ranvaud Doce turned out not be Ranvaud Doce at all; he was Ranvaut Votz (Vetriz had got the name wrong; she wasn't very patient with names), and of course Venart had known him for years. 'Gods, you look shattered,' Votz said. 'Sit down before you fall down, and have a drink.'

'Brandy,' Venart replied. 'The white jug, on the side there.'

'Say when.'

'Whenever.'

The brandy helped, to a certain limited extent; but it was the kind of help that's probably counterproductive before noon on a busy day. 'Better not have any more,' Venart said ruefully, after he'd recovered from the burn, 'or I'll go straight to sleep. So, what can I do for you?'

Votz raised his eyebrows. 'Full marks, Ven,' he replied. 'You said that as if you really don't know.'

'Excuse me?'

'Don't be aggravating. Playing games is fine for business negotiations, but it's not really appropriate for a head of state.'

'Oh for—' Venart slammed his cup down a little too hard, and the thinly skived horn cracked under the pressure of his thumb. 'Not you as well. Come on, Ran, you know perfectly well I'm not the head of anything. For gods' sakes, I'm not even head of this household; you've seen how Triz pushes me around—'

'Proves nothing.' Votz took the smile deliberately off his face. 'I know,' he went on, 'the truth is, you had next to nothing to do with what happened. You didn't even show up till halfway through – not that I'm blaming you, that's just the way it was. But for some reason, people think you were the leader of the rebellion, and now they think you're leading some kind of state-of-emergency government. And what I say is, why not? I mean, you're a pretty harmless sort of man, you won't try to do anything silly or throw your weight around – just the sort of leader this country needs.'

'Thank you very much.'

'You're welcome. But we do need a little bit of a government, Ven; just the ears and the tip of the tail. Otherwise, how's the Ship-Owners' going to get things done?'

Venart frowned. 'Oh, I see,' he said. 'You and your bunch of deadheads from the back bar of the Fortune and Favour are going to be the real government, and I'm going to get all the blame. No, thank you very much. Weren't you bloody Ship-Owners the ones who started all this off by trying to shaft the provincial office for more money?'

Votz held up his hand. 'That was then,' he said. 'And you were one of us, remember; just as much to blame as anybody. But,' he added, as Venart tried to object, 'agonising over that isn't going to get ships on the water or food in the barns. You do realise there's next to nothing left to eat on this confounded island? Not after those bastards took it all with them.'

Venart stayed quiet. He hadn't thought about that.

'So,' Votz went on, 'we need to do something quick, before the situation gets dirty on us. The question is, who's "we" in that context? One thing's for sure, we can't go merrily sailing off into the wide blue yonder on our own, not if we want to have a mayfly's chance of coming back; put in anywhere where the provincial office has so much as a commercial attaché, and the next thing you'll see is the inside of a cell. So, if we want to go anywhere, we've got to go in strength, in convoy; but we can't all go, or who's going to stay here and make sure there'll be somewhere for us to come back to? We need to be organised; and that's precisely the sort of job the Ship-Owners' is for.'

Venart nodded. 'All right, I agree,' he said. 'So go away and form a government. Who's going to stop you, since it's in everybody's interest? Not me, for sure.'

'You really don't know, do you? The Guild, that's who. Now, if you're looking for a genuine threat to our way of life, you wander down to the Drutz and take a good look.'

Venart looked confused. 'Who's the Guild?' he asked.

'Oh boy.' Votz shook his head. 'As head of state, if any-thing, you're *over*qualified. The Merchant Seamen's Guild, my friend; a nasty rabble of ungrateful rope-jockeys and cabin rats who've already stated their intention of stealing our ships – commandeered for the public good, they're calling it, which is pig-Perimadeian for "steal" and that's all there is to it – and making us pay them taxes for the privilege. *That's* why we need a head of state, my friend; someone who's not the Ship-Owners' who'll tell them not to be so damn stupid. And who better than the inspirational leader, war hero, architect of victory—'

'Oh, shut up, Ran.'

'Yes, but they don't know that.' Votz shrugged. 'The people out there on the streets believe all that stuff is true, and really, that's what matters. Do you want them stealing your ship and taking your money off you at spearpoint? Might as well ask the Empire back again and have done with it.'

'All right,' Venart sighed, 'you've made your point.' He slumped back in his chair, looking wretched. 'Just out of interest,' he continued, 'do you and your chums in the Ship-Owners' have any constructive, practical ideas about how to get some food? Or haven't you got around to the finer points yet?'

Votz clicked his tongue. 'There's no need to be sarcastic,'

he said. 'As a matter of fact, we have.'

'All right. If I'm your new Crown Prince, the least you can do is let me in on the secret.'

'Simple,' Votz said. 'It stands to reason, if Gorgas Loredan went to all that trouble to help us get rid of the Imperials –'

'Have you any idea *why—*?'

'– Then he won't be averse to selling us a few shiploads of grain and salt pork, especially if the price is right. And Tornoys is in the right direction, away from the Empire; we'll have to sail pretty close to Shastel, of course, but if we're in a convoy that shouldn't be a problem.'

'I suppose not,' Venart conceded. 'But he gives me the creeps, that man. I'm not sure why, he just does.'

'Well, that's your problem. While we're there, I fully intend to talk to him about hiring a few of those crackerjack archers of his; another thing we're definitely going to need is some sort of militia, and since none of us know squat about the trade, it'd be a good idea to hire someone who can teach us.'

Venart closed his eyes. 'Steady on,' he said. 'Exactly who did you have in mind for this army of yours?'

'Well, us, of course,' Votz replied patiently. 'And it's not an army, it's a militia. Quite different.'

'All right, it's different. But by "us", do you mean us Islanders, or us Ship-Owners, or what?'

'Well, I'm not going to put weapons into the hands of the Guild, if that's what you mean,' Votz replied, as if explaining to a small child that fire is hot. 'I mean *us*, the responsible adult male population of the Island. We don't need those layabouts in the Guild; I mean, when the fighting was on, where were they? Cowering in a lock-up. Fat lot of good they were, until *we* came along and turned them loose.'

'Wonderful,' Venart muttered. 'First you want a government, then an army, now you're planning a civil war. This state of yours is growing faster than watercress. All right,' he added quickly, 'spare me the reasoning. I agree, yes, it does seem like ordinary common sense to be able to defend ourselves if we're likely to have the provincial office coming after us any time soon. Though to be honest with you,' he continued, frowning, 'if they do decide to come back, I can't see that we stand a chance. We were lucky the last time, and they were disgracefully complacent. I think fighting them once they've got their act together really would be asking for trouble.'

'Really? So what would you suggest?'

Venart stood up and turned to look out of the window. 'Leaving,' he said. 'Packing up everything we can move, setting sail and putting as much sea between us and them as we possibly can.'

Votz glared at him. 'You're joking,' he said.

Venart shook his head. 'Actually,' he said, 'I think it's an inspired idea. We aren't farmers or manufacturers, we're traders; most of us spend as much time on our ships or abroad as we do at home. If ever there was a – a nation that could afford to up sticks and sail away, it's us. If the worst comes to the worst, we could simply live on the ships, keep moving about like nomads.'

Votz grinned unpleasantly. 'Like King Temrai's lot, you mean. Oh, yes, guaranteed absolute safety, no need to worry ever again.'

'That's on land. It's the ships that make it different.'

'Until they start building ships of their own.' Votz stood up too. 'Running away isn't going to solve anything; we've got to make a stand and fight. And if we're going to fight, where better than here? We've got a superb natural fortress, even better than Perimadeia was. We've got a fleet of ships, which they haven't.' He grabbed Venart by the shoulder and turned him round. 'We can win this,' he said.

'I don't think so,' Venart replied. 'And since you've just made me the head of state—'

'That's the thing about heads, they can come off.'

At first Venart looked startled; then he giggled. 'Oh, come *on*, Ran,' he said, 'don't be so bloody melodramatic. Government, army, civil war *and* palace coup, and we haven't even told anybody else about it yet.' He pulled away and grinned. 'Just think what fun we could have if there were *three* of us playing.'

There was a brisk cool wind, which was a mercy; Bardas remembered all too well how quickly the midday heat of the plains could drag a man down before he even realised it. Fortunately the army of the Sons of Heaven had been recruited in many places, most of them far away, nearly all of them hotter than this. At the point where he collapsed in a sweaty heap, at least half his men would still be snuggling into their cloaks and blowing on their hands.

The sun had already whisked up a fine heat-haze out of the river, smudging the sharp edges of the fortress until it looked vague and ill-defined, like the background in a painting. The sunlight burned on the water like some kind of incendiary; he could still see the red glare when he closed his eyes.

'All done?' he asked. The engineer nodded. 'Very well.' He positioned himself behind the cocked arm of the trebuchet and looked over it at the distant fortress. It was all very still and quiet, as if the world was waiting for him to make a speech. 'I hereby declare this war open for business,' he said. 'In your own time.'

The engineer nodded, once to him and once to the artilleryman with his hand on the slip. The artilleryman jerked hard on the rope and the arm reared up into the air like a man suddenly woken up in the middle of a dream; the long square-section beam bowed under the inertia, straightened and stopped hard as it reached the point of equilibrium, the counterweight lurching wildly on its cradle beneath. With a crack like a slingshot, the rope net gave the stone roundshot a final, crucial flick and fell away –

('Here goes nothing,' muttered the engineer.)

– While the projectile rushed with absurd speed up into the air, dwindled into a black dot, slowed to a stop, hung in the air for a moment and started to come down –

('Let's see what they make of that,' said the chief bombardier, grinning. 'If they've got any sense, they'll ask if they can move their fort a hundred yards back.')

– And pitched, with a sound like a child's face being slapped, in the river. The dazzling white fire was punctured, like a sheet of steel shot through with an arrow.

'Told you it'd drop short,' sighed the bombardier. 'All right, up five and try again.'

Upgrading the counterweights had been Bardas' idea; after all, Temrai had done the same thing, building trebuchets that outranged their counterparts on the City wall. Now he had at least fifty yards of clear ground over his enemy (his counterpart; himself in a previous revolution of the wheel); he could hit them and they couldn't hit him back. The further along the rack you travel, the greater the stress; the greater, too, the mechanical advantage.

'Number-two engine, elevation up five,' the engineer called out. 'Make ready.'

An artilleryman turned a handwheel, a ratchet strained and clicked. 'Ready.'

'Loose,' the engineer said; and the arm bent, straightened and threw. 'Damn,' the engineer added, as the shot scuffed a cloud of dirt out of the bare rock of the slope, 'now the windage is off. Number-three engine, elevation up *four*, bring her across left two. Make ready.'

At this distance, of course, it was an exercise in skill, the scientific application of force to a precise spot on a virgin plate. One tap to begin with, to start off the bowl; start at the edges, work your way round the outside, gradually move inwards to the point where the dishing needs to be deepest; that's the way to force stress into the workpiece.

'On the money,' said the chief bombardier. 'All right, let's keep them there or thereabouts; that's –' he laid his knife alongside the lead screw; like all good artillerymen's knives, it had a precisely calibrated scale engraved on the blade '– let's see, that's twelve up from zero, six across left. Each of you loose three, mark your pitches and adjust for zero.'

When each trebuchet had shot three times, and the bombardiers had made the necessary corrections to compensate for the slight differences in cast and line of their respective engines, the bombardment fell into a pattern. Bardas recognised this phase; it was the stage when the hammer bounced off the work, up and down in its own weight (like a trebuchet, weight and counterweight), with the craftsman's left hand moving the workpiece into position under the hammer. One blow doesn't impart the desired stress; many blows, a controlled, continuous hammering and pounding, are needed to impact the material into strength. 'It's a shame there's all that dust,' the chief bombardier lamented, 'I can't see a damn thing. For all I know, we could be dropping them all in the same hole.'

'Good point,' Bardas said. 'But let's keep it up a while longer. I want them to feel the pressure.'

So this is what it was like, Temrai said to himself, waiting for the next shot to fall. *Well, now I know.*

The shot landed, a heartbeat late, making the ground shake. Because of the dust-cloud, he couldn't see where it had pitched or whether it had done any damage; it was as bad as being in the dark. But he could hear shouting, implying an emergency – someone was giving orders, someone else was contradicting him; there was an edge of raw urgency to their voices that didn't inspire confidence. *Should have anticipated this,* he thought. *Didn't. My fault, ultimately.*

He counted down from twelve, and the next shot pitched. He could feel where that one went (when you're in the dark, the other senses adapt quickly) – presumably an overshot, strictly speaking a miss, but it felt like it had landed on one of the stores. *I'd rather it was the biscuits than the arrows; we can eat broken biscuits if we have to.* He started counting again.

'Temrai?'

Damnation, lost count. 'Over here,' he called out. 'Who's that?'

'Me. Sildocai. Where are you? I can't see a thing.'

'Follow my voice, and keep your head down; one's due any second now.'

Another overshot; no prizes for guessing where it had gone either, as it sprayed sharp-edged chips of rock across the catwalk. 'Their settings must be shaking loose,' he observed. 'They can't see the pitches, so they don't know they're going high.'

'I preferred it when they were on target.'

'So did I.'

Sildocai materialised in front of him, as if he'd been moulded out of the dust. 'I've been down there,' he said. 'Since they started shooting high, I reckoned it was the safest place to be. They've smashed up four trebuchets and half a dozen of the scorpions, two more of each out of action for now but fixable. The worst part is, there's a damn great hole in the path which we're going to have to fill somehow.

Otherwise we're completely cut off from the lower defences.'

Temrai closed his eyes. 'Well, there ought to be enough loose rock and spoil,' he said. 'You'll need to lay timbers to hold the loose stuff in, anchor them with pegs like you're building a terrace.'

'All right,' Sildocai said, coughing. 'When we've done that, what about hauling some of the engines up out of the way? They're doing no good down there, just waiting to be smashed up.'

Temrai shook his head. 'No, we won't do that,' he said. 'They'll just bring theirs up closer. We need to shut those trebuchets down for a while, and if we can't reach them with artillery, we'll have to go over there and do it by hand.'

Sildocai frowned. 'I'd rather not do that,' he said, 'even with the light cavalry. It's a bit too flat for charging down the enemy's throat.'

'We haven't got any choice,' Temrai replied, as another shot pitched, scooping up loose dirt and sprinkling it over their heads, the way the chief mourner does at a funeral (*although it's customary to die first*). 'We're outranged. If we sit here and do nothing, they'll flatten the whole thing.'

'All right,' Sildocai replied doubtfully. 'But let's at least wait until it gets dark and they stop shooting.'

'What makes you think they'll stop when it gets dark? I wouldn't. If they fix their settings, they don't need to see us in order to smash us up. They're doing a pretty good job as it is, and this dust is as good as a dark night.'

'Yes, but it's only dusty over here. I'd rather not ride up on their archers in broad daylight, thank you very much. You may not remember, but there's bright sunlight outside all this muck.'

Temrai thought for a moment. 'Fair enough,' he said. 'I'm not thrilled at the thought of having to sit through three more hours of this, but you're right, we don't want to do their job for them by making silly mistakes. Get a raiding party organised, and then put someone on making good that path. Nobody's going anywhere till that's fixed.'

Sildocai scrambled away, trying to keep his head down below the level of the earth bank into which the stakes of the stockade had been driven. It meant scuttling like a crab, or a man in a low-roofed tunnel. Another shot pitched, but too far away to be a danger to him. *Very erratic now*, Temrai decided, *but I don't suppose they care; this is just to make us feel miserable. The damage is probably trivial, but this dust is starting to get on my nerves.*

'No mucking about,' Sildocai said, a stern, parental expression on his face. 'The only thing we're interested in is the trebuchets; cut the counterweight cables, then when the beam comes down cut the sling cables, and that's it. Just this once, getting back in one piece is more important than killing flatheads, so no wandering off, no hot pursuit and categorically no looting. Understood?'

Nobody spoke. By the look of it, his dire warnings had been largely unnecessary. Chances were they'd only volunteered in the hope of getting away from the dust for an hour.

It was a typical plains moon, bright enough to cast shadows. That was good. From here he could see the campfires across the river, where they were going. Men sitting in the firelight don't have good night vision, whereas his men would have had time to get accustomed to the dark; they'd be able to see the enemy, and the enemy wouldn't see them. He gave the sign, and the winch crew started to wind the swing-bridge into place.

Sildocai went first. It was tradition in his family, which had produced more than its share of commanders; so many, in fact, that it was remarkable that it had lasted this long. His own father had been killed fighting this same Bardas Loredan, shortly after Maxen died. His grandfather had also fallen in battle against the Perimadeians. His great-grandfather had gone the same way, though nobody could remember who he'd been fighting against. Four generations of brave leaders who always led from the front. Some people never learn.

Getting there was no problem; just head for the nearest cluster of camp-fires until he could make out the trebuchets, silhouetted against the blue-grey sky. There was just enough wind to carry away the sound of the horses' hooves on the dry grass. All in all, ideal conditions for a night attack; it was almost enough to tempt him into ignoring his own excellent advice and go looking for a fight, except that he didn't want one. There'd be plenty of time for that sort of thing later;

besides, his men were tired after a bad day divided between cowering under the dust-cloud and hauling dirt in buckets to fill in the hole in the path uphill.

They did better than he'd expected; they were fifty yards from the nearest fire by the time someone saw them and shouted. Sildocai drew his scimitar, called out, 'Now!' and kicked his horse into a gentle canter.

It started well. Understandably, the enemy ran away from the suddenly materialising horsemen, heading for the weapons stacks, away from the trebuchets, and nobody bothered the raiding party until they'd done some useful work among the trebuchets. That would have been a good time to quit.

Sildocai was the first to cut a rope; it took him three attempts. It was almost comical. Somehow he'd pictured himself cleaving the rope with a single blow, slicing through the taut fibres almost without effort. Instead, he caught it at an awkward angle, jerked his wrist and nearly dropped the sword. He'd have been better off with a bill-hook or a bean-hook, a heavier, more rigid blade. His adventure nearly ended there; in his grim determination to hack through the rope he forgot that cutting it would result in a long, heavy piece of wood pivoting sharply downwards – the beam missed his shoulder by no more than a couple of inches, and startled the life out of him. Then, as he pulled his horse round, he found he couldn't quite reach the sling on the other end; he had to jump off his horse, kneel down, saw through it with the forte of his sword blade, and then hop back up again (except that his horse was spooky and didn't want to hold still, and he spent an alarming moment or two dancing beside a moving horse, one foot in the stirrup, the other dragging on the ground while he clung to the pommel of the saddle with one hand and tried not to drop his scimitar with the other).

But he was a grown-up, he could cope; and he made a rather less messy job of the next two trebuchets. In fact, he was feeling confident enough to be toying with the idea of trying to get the things to burn when the enemy finally showed up. That was the point at which he should have let it alone and gone home to bed.

The enemy didn't want to be there, it was obvious from

the way they advanced; crab-fashion, their halberds and glaives thrust out well in front, sheer terror on their faces. Urging them on were a couple of officers, beside themselves with fury, like apple-growers whose trees are being robbed by the village children, but not quite furious enough to lead from the front. The job was about half-done; Sildocai called the first and second troops to follow him, and kicked up his favourite slow canter – quick enough to have momentum but slow enough to maintain control. There wasn't a line – the enemy were slouching towards him in a huddled bunch, the men on the ends trying to snuggle towards the centre – so he waved the second troop out wide left, and took the first troop wide right. The plan was to hit them hard in flank, turn them back on the camp in a confused mob so they'd get under the feet of any further, better-organised relief party. There was just about enough light from the camp-fires to see what he was about. It should have worked fine. It did –

– Except that, as he bent down over his horse's neck to deliver a straightforward diagonal cut along the line of some footslogger's collar-bone, his saddle-girth snapped, sending him sliding helplessly down the vector of the stroke. He landed with his shoulder in the dead man's face, with his saddle still gripped between his thighs.

If it had happened to somebody else he'd probably have wet himself laughing as he rode to the rescue; but comedy is relative, and when he looked up, the first thing he saw was a man standing over him. He was wearing a shirt, a kettle-hat and nothing else, and he was just about to stick a halberd into Sildocai's chest.

There wasn't a lot he could do about it; the damned saddle stopped him moving his legs, so all he was able to do was throw up his left arm in the way of the halberd. He had a boiled leather vambrace on his forearm; the cutting edge of the blade slid across it like a skater on ice and came off at an angle, making contact with his face at the point of his cheekbone and slicing off the top of his ear. That left his hand in good position for grabbing hold of the halberd shaft; but what with the shock and all he muffed it a bit, and the blade slit the web between his thumb and forefinger before he was able to tighten his grip and pull.

The manoeuvre was a qualified success; he got the halberd

away from the man, but he pulled it down across his own face, cutting another line more or less parallel to the first, from the corner of his eye across the lower part of his scalp. He couldn't keep hold of the halberd, and dropped it. The man stared at him, then kicked him in the face – not a good idea for either party, since the man wasn't wearing anything on his feet. Sildocai was sure he felt one of the man's toes break at the same time he felt the bone go in his nose.

He had his right arm free by now, and he used it to grab the man's ankle and try to pull him down; but he muffed that too and was left gripping a flailing leg, hardly able to see because of all the blood in his eyes. There didn't seem much point in holding on, so he let go, at which point the man suddenly threw his arms wide and fell on top of him.

He'd been hit hard, but not hard enough to kill him; at a guess, a scimitar-cut slantwise across the base of his neck under the rim of the kettle-hat. Now the bastard was lying right on top of him, their mouths almost touching, like lovers; the man's eyes were open wide and he was making some sort of stupid glugging noise; he was trying to say something, but Sildocai wasn't interested. 'Get off me!' he screeched, and jerked and pulled at his trapped left arm until he had it free. The fingers were stiff and tight (*Permanent disability*, Sildocai noted, *worry about it later*) but he had enough use of it to get a grip on the man's shoulder and push. He didn't want to go, but it turned out he didn't have much choice; he rolled on to his back without moving, except for more eye-rolling and gurgling. With a lot of effort Sildocai found a way to scrabble himself up on to his knees, but things weren't getting any better; a man running past him rammed him in the back, knocked him on his face and went sprawling down beside him. *Damn*, Sildocai thought, *this is hopeless.* The man was picking himself up; there was a sword lying beside him where he'd dropped it. But he left it there and skittered away, running very fast, which at the time seemed like a piece of luck.

Bad luck, as it turned out. The reason he'd bolted without even picking up his sword became horribly obvious as Sildocai lifted his head in time to see a horse's hooves rearing up over his head. He dropped down again, but that didn't help; he felt an unbearable pain in his back, felt something give way as the horse trod on him. He tried to shout, but his mouth was full of dirt and besides, all the air had been squeezed out of him. It took a lot of painful effort to put some back in its place.

Broken ribs, he diagnosed, with the part of his mind that somehow wasn't involved, *this isn't getting any better*. For two pins he'd have stayed where he was; but he could still recall a time when he'd been in charge of this situation, and one of the things he could remember about it was that as soon as the job was done, they were getting out of there and going home. Sildocai didn't want to be left behind, so it was very important to stand up, find his horse (or any damned horse) and get back to the fortress.

The man next to him was still making that ridiculous gugging noise, like a fractious baby. Sildocai rolled over on to his right shoulder, kicked with his legs and jack-knifed himself on to his feet; he staggered, nearly went over again, caught his balance just in time. The operation was unbelievably painful – *I shouldn't have to be doing this, a man in my condition* – and breathing had become a test of character. He took a step forward, but apparently someone had stolen the joints out of his knees while he'd been sprawling in the dirt. He managed to stay upright, but that was about the best he could do.

'Steady now, chum, it's all right.' Whoever he was, Sildocai hadn't seen or heard him coming; he was just there, a man to his left grabbing and holding on to his arm. 'It's all right,' he repeated. 'Let's get you out of this before you fall over.' It was a horrible sing-song voice – the Perimadeian accent had always grated on Sildocai. 'Come on, this way.'

The bastard was trying to make him go back, towards the camp; that wasn't the right direction, so why was he doing it? Then it made sense. This was the enemy, mistaking him for a friend (like the man lying blubbering in the dirt, who'd expected him to help) – well, that was just fine, but it was the wrong direction. Fortunately, the man was an idiot; there was a knife hanging from his belt, just handy. Sildocai pulled it out and stuck it between his shoulders. For once, something went in the way it was meant to, but he'd missed the spot he'd been aiming for. The man gasped with pain and shock, but stayed on his feet. 'Oh gods,' the poor fool said and grabbed at Sildocai for support – he hadn't realised that Sildocai had stabbed him, must be thinking he'd been hit by an arrow or something. He took the man's weight on his shoulder as best he could, though it was nearly enough to bring him to his knees; then he pulled out the knife and stuck it in under the man's ear.

This time he did go down, but of course he was clinging on to Sildocai's shoulder, and so they hit the ground together. This one was easier to shove off – he was dead, which helped – but getting up again was probably going to be too hard for him to manage. Well, he'd tried; and, as his father used to say, if you've done your best, they can't ask any more of you.

Breathing was becoming harder, if anything. It was as if he had a big carpenter's clamp screwed across him, pressing his chest and back together while the carpenter waited for the glue to dry. But some people never learn (four generations of leaders). He dragged his elbows towards his knees, pushed his knees forward, tried to straighten his back – no future in that. *Thanks for nothing*, he thought bitterly, aiming his displeasure at the man he'd just killed. *I'd have been just fine if you hadn't interfered.* Then he straightened his legs and arms, probably the most gruelling physical effort he'd ever made in his life. It got him on his feet again. It was worth it.

Now then; all I've got to do now is find a horse, get on it . . . There didn't seem to be much in the way of battle-noises, he noticed with dismay. He had no idea how long it had been since he'd come off his horse. It felt like his whole life, of course, but that was subjective time. Quite possible, likely even, that his men had done as they were told and pushed off as soon as the job was done. In which case he needn't have nearly killed himself getting up.

He took three steps forward – a technique of controlled falling, whereby he aimed himself at the ground and stuck out a leg at the last moment. His left hand was hurting almost as much as his back – a different sort of pain, throbbing instead of sharp. Dragging in breath was getting to be more trouble than it was worth.

And then he saw the horse. Amazing creatures; in the middle of a battle, with all that death and pain around it, a riderless horse will still stop, put its head down and nibble at the grass. Sildocai looked at it for ten seconds, a long time in that context. He was trying to work out, from first principles, how to walk over to where the horse was standing, get on its back and make it go where he wanted it to. He knew the project was possible – *we can win this*, as Temrai would say – but at that particular moment he couldn't quite see how to go about it.

Sheer hard work and application, in the end. Luckily, the horse had the grace to hold still until he reached it, and then at least he had something to lean against while he bent down and lifted his foot up to the stirrup with his now mostly useless left hand. Getting into the saddle was always going to be the hardest part. No grip in his left hand, so pulling on the saddle was out. The best he could do was try to force his left leg straight and hope momentum and body weight would do the rest. It nearly worked; but while he was standing with one foot in one stirrup the horse decided to move, and it took him a long time to find the strength to get his leg over the horse's back and down the other side. When he'd accomplished that, he found that he had nothing left; he slumped forward against the horse's neck, his nose buried in its mane, and tried for one last breath. The horse kept walking; and since it was just a horse, and the enemy were too busy to bother with stray livestock, it carried on walking in the direction it remembered home used to be, until it came to a river. There it stopped to drink; and after that, it wandered a short way, snuffling for grass, until dawn; at which point someone on the other side of the river noticed it and started making a fuss. They swung out the bridge and sent some men to catch it; the horse didn't mind that, and they led it over the bridge and took the load off its back.

'It's Sildocai,' someone said.

'Is he still alive?' Sildocai heard that. *Good question*, he thought.

'I think so. Get him down.'

In the event, Sildocai decided that he was still alive, because it doesn't hurt if you're dead. He slipped away from the pain after a while, and when he woke up someone whose name was something like Temrai came and stood over him and told him the raid had been successful. He wanted to ask,

What raid? but he didn't have the energy. He went back to sleep for a few hours, until the crash-thump of trebuchet shot landing all round him (the raid had been a success; it took the enemy five hours to make good all the damage they'd done) woke him up again.

CHAPTER EIGHTEEN

'We could do this for the rest of our lives,' said the engineer, 'and we'd be no better off. I say we stop mucking about and follow up; otherwise we're just wasting our time.'

It was the third day of the bombardment. The day before had been like the day before that; while the sun shone, the trebuchets had pounded the lower stockade, the engine emplacements and the path. When the sun set, Temrai's men had patched up the lower stockade, replaced the smashed and splintered sections of the engines and filled in the gaps hammered out of the path, and in the early hours of the morning his light cavalry had made a sortie and hamstrung the trebuchets. On the second night, they'd had a different leader and met with sterner resistance; but they'd learned a few things too, and the net result had been the same. For the third night, Bardas had detailed two companies of halberdiers to guard the trebuchets and had given orders for a stockade of his own, only to be told that all the timber within easy reach had been felled to build the fortress, so he'd have to make do with a ditch and bank, which would of course take time ...

'No,' he said, 'we'll keep going. Sooner or later there'll be so much damage they won't be able to patch it up any more – you can't keep patching on to patches, believe me, I've tried it. We can lose this war very easily, with just one error of judgement. I'd rather waste time than lives, if it's all the same to you.'

The engineer shrugged. 'You're the boss,' he said. 'And I'm telling you, I wouldn't have your job for anything.'

There was no cavalry raid that night, and the halberdiers, who'd been standing to arms for nine hours, went off duty with a feeling of having won the moral victory, giving place to the artillery crews. It was during the changeover, about half an hour after sunrise, that Temrai sent out his horse-archers, arguably the most effective part of his army. Before Bardas' sentries had a chance to identify them and signal in, they'd been shot down; then the three troops drew up in line and started a bombardment of their own, from two hundred yards; further than Bardas' bowmen could shoot; within range of the crossbows, but they could only loose one shot every three minutes, and the second troop was concentrating its volleys on them. Bardas called for the siege pavises, large oxhide shields designed to cover crossbowmen during siege operations, but there was a problem. The wagon master had stationed supply wagons all round them, hemming them in (after all, nobody had told him they were likely to be needed, and he had to park the damned wagons somewhere). In order to get them out, he had to shift the wagons, which in turn meant bringing about a third of them through the camp ... Within a quarter of an hour, the streets of the camp were jammed solid with wagons, impeding the shot wagons that were supposed to be fetching trebuchet shot from the dump. Not that it mattered; the first and third troops of horse-archers were shooting at the artillerymen, and those who'd managed to get under cover weren't likely to be loosing off any shot until the enemy had withdrawn.

'No,' Bardas kept saying, when they urged him to do something. 'Cardinal rule: don't charge horse-archers with heavy cavalry. I learned that the hard way. And if you think I'm sending infantry out into *that*—' (no need to ask what *that* was; the volleys of arrows were lifting, planing and dropping like spurts of boiling water from a geyser; the thought of being underneath one of those plumes was enough to make your mouth dry). 'So,' he went on, 'we sit tight. You know how many arrows a plainsman carries? Fifty; twenty-five on his back, twenty-five on his saddle. When they've used up their arrows they'll go away, and we can get on with our work.'

He was right, of course. Not long afterwards the horse-archers pulled out, leaving behind them the best part of a hundred thousand arrows that King Temrai was in no position to replace in a hurry. They were everywhere; sticking in the ground, in the timbers of the trebuchets and the wagons, hanging by their barbs from the sides of tents and wagon-covers, smashed underneath dead men, slanting upwards from the chests and arms of dead and living men; they covered the ground like a carpet of suddenly sprung flowers, the carts and engines like moss or lichen, their fletchings like the tufts of bog-cotton on the wet marshes, and the snapping of shafts underfoot as the artillerymen came out from cover sounded like a bonfire of twigs and dry grass. Like ants or mosquitos they'd got in everywhere; like bees dazed by the smoke from the bee-keeper's bellows they lay exhausted, their flight and stinging all done.

'Clear up this mess,' some officer was shouting. 'And get those engines working, we haven't got all day. Where's the chief engineer? We're going to need twelve new crews for number six battery. Casualty lists – who's got the damned lists? Have I got to do every bloody thing myself?'

Half the artillerymen out of action; more wounded than killed, but not by a wide margin. The injured lay or sat around the shot-wagons, the arrows still sticking out of them; the surgeons were rushed off their feet, sawing shafts and dragging out barbs the hard way, throwing the recovered arrowheads on to piles under the tables, and they didn't have time to look back at the work they still had to do. From time to time a man would die, quietly or making a fuss, and at intervals they came round with a handcart for the bodies.

They came and asked Bardas what they should do now. 'Carry on,' he said. 'Keep plugging away at the path and the stockade. You can put halberdiers on the engines, so long as there's an artilleryman to each team to tell them what to do.'

They went round with big wicker baskets, picking up the arrows – reasonable quality materiel that'd come in handy some time, if not in this war then in some other war, where the Empire saw fit to deploy massed archers – and when the baskets were full, they packed them in empty barrels and loaded them on to supply carts. The broken arrows were sorted into two piles; heads for scrap, shafts for the fire or the carpenters (an arrowshaft makes good dowel rod for small structures, like pavises and screens and the floors of siege-towers and the rungs of scaling-ladders). A platoon of pike-men with nothing else to do sat cross-legged in a circle, cutting off the fletchings and dropping them into big earthenware pots, ready for the quilters to use for stuffing gambesons.

'It was a gesture,' Bardas explained, 'nothing more. And the best thing to do with gestures is to ignore them, like your mother did when you were a kid and wouldn't eat up your porridge.' But all the while he was thinking about the second grade of proof, the proof against arrows; to meet the specification, an armour should turn a bodkinhead arrow shot from a ninety-five-pound bow at seventy-five yards, or a seventy-pound bow at thirty yards. Most armours fail that test and go in the scrap, along with the spent arrowheads.

They got the trebuchets going again, and the beams slapped upright like hammers on the anvil, pounding dust out of the side of the hill.

'Mostly,' someone was saying, 'we're using their shot to repair the road; those big boulders are a nice size, though they take some shifting. We could do with a few more cranes, though; they've smashed up most of the ones I scrounged from the top batteries.'

Temrai tried to concentrate, but it wasn't easy. He felt as though he'd been living with the thump of landing shot for years, and he'd gone past the point where he could ignore it. Earlier that day someone had come and told him that Tilden was dead; a splinter from an overshot that had smashed to pieces against an outcrop and sprayed debris over the back lot of tents on the far side. He heard the news but couldn't feel it; it was impossible to concentrate on anything important with this constant hammering going on, in his ears and coming up out of the ground through the soles of his feet. He knew it was all a ploy, an attempt to pull him down out of his fortress on to the flat for a pitched battle, and he wasn't going to fall for it. He'd been there before.

'What about the stockade?' he asked. 'How's the timber supply holding out?'

'It's not good,' they told him. 'We're giving priority to shoring up the path, like you said, and that's using up a lot of stock. We've started pulling stakes out of the back of the top stockade; after all, they aren't much good to us there, and so far we've been able to plug the gaps with broken stuff. Can't keep it up for ever, though; if we take out much more we'll leave weak spots, and that's asking for trouble.'

Temrai scowled; trying to keep his mind on the subject in hand was like trying to hold on tight to a rope: the more you gripped, the more it burned. 'I don't mind a few obvious weak spots,' he said. 'A weak spot in the wall is a temptation to the enemy, and sometimes it's good to offer them an opportunity, so long as you're ready and waiting when they accept it. Sometimes the best chance of winning a battle comes when you've almost lost it.'

That remark didn't win him any friends. *It's true, though*, he wanted to tell them, *you study old wars, you'll see what I mean*. Nobody seemed in the mood for a history seminar, however, so he ignored the scowls and frowns. 'Anyhow,' he said, 'carry on robbing the back wall for now. This bombardment won't last much longer. Trust me on that.'

(And why not? They'd trusted him once, right up to the walls of Perimadeia; and back then he was only a kid, with nothing about him to suggest he knew what he was doing apart from a certain ability to communicate enthusiasm. Now he was King Temrai, Sacker of Cities, so surely they ought to trust him even more.

Didn't work like that.

Nevertheless, these were his people; they'd do as they were told. The ones who wouldn't have were all dead now, killed in the civil war.)

They talked through a few minor points of supply and administration, then he dismissed the meeting and walked out of the tent into the dust. The death of his wife was somewhere quite close under the surface of his mind, like a fish feeding, but he wasn't consciously aware of any significant levels of grief or guilt. She had been just the sort of woman he could have loved to distraction in another time or another place. But now that he had to look at the world through the eyeslits of the visor of King Temrai, he found it almost impossible to let the sharp blade through;

there was no gap or seam, no weak point where he could create an opportunity.

The dead-cart trundled past him as he walked across the plateau towards the path. He watched it go, realised that he recognised a face peeping out between another man's crushed legs. For now they were piling the dead in a half-finished grain-pit; the stores that should have gone in there had been spoiled by an overshot, and it seemed a pity to waste the effort that had gone into digging it. He'd been to see it, had stood for a moment looking at the confused heap, arms and legs and heads and feet and bodies and hands jumbled in together, like an untidy store, but it hadn't meant anything more to him than the sum of its parts.

A man ran past him, heading down the hill; then two more, shapes that loomed up out of the dust and went back into it. More followed; he caught one of them by the arm and asked what was going on.

'Attack,' the man panted at him. 'Gods only know where they appeared from. They've got some kind of portable bridge for crossing the river.'

Temrai let go of him. 'I see,' he said. 'Who's in charge down there?'

The man shrugged. 'Nobody, far as I know. There's the gang-boss on the stockade detail, I suppose.'

'Find him,' Temrai said, 'tell him I'll be there as soon as I can.'

The man nodded and slipped away into the dust, like someone vanishing into quicksand. Temrai thought for a minute or so, then turned back up the hill and headed for his tent. There was nobody about to help him with his armour, but he'd got the hang of it now, and it was getting easier each time he wore it, as the metal shaped itself to the contours of his bones and muscles. He felt much better once it was on - in truth, he'd spent so much time wearing it lately that when he took it off, his arms and legs felt strangely light and feeble.

He was adjusting the padding inside his helmet when they came to tell him that the enemy halberdiers had breached the stockade. He acknowledged the news with a slight nod of his head. 'Who have we got down there?' he asked.

'The work crews, mostly,' someone answered. 'They've been fighting with hammers and mattocks. There's a few skirmishers and pickets in there as well, and Heuscai's on his way down with the flying column.'

'Catch him up,' Temrai said, 'and tell him to wait for me.'

When he found him, Heuscai looked impatient and bewildered, almost angry. 'We've got to hurry,' he said, 'the work crews can't hold them for long.'

'It's all right,' Temrai said, 'I know what I'm doing.'

He led the column down the path. It was slow going; the bombardment had raised elevation a few degrees to clear the lower stockade, with the result that the upper reaches of the path were being hammered away now, while the lower reaches were a mess. 'Take your time,' he called back as he picked his way through – it was bad luck and bad timing that a shot landed in the thick of the column just as he said it; the men were too closely packed together to have any chance of getting out of the way, and when the shot landed, it crushed three men with a dull crunch, like the noise you get when you squash a large spider. The dust was worse than ever, but at least there were the sounds of fighting below them to give them something to head for. Temrai found walking down the steep slope in heavy armour extremely awkward; the back plates of his greaves dug into his heels, pinching skin between the greave-rims and the upper edges of his sabatons.

As soon as he was close enough to the bottom of the path to be able to see what was going on, he gave the order for the work-crews to pull out. The first time he shouted they didn't hear him, or didn't recognise his voice; they were standing on the raised embankment on their side of the stockade, trying to keep the enemy from bursting through a gap about two yards wide where a shot had landed right on top of the fence. The boulder, of course, was still there; it was the main obstacle blocking the halberdiers' way. As they tried to scramble up on to it, the workmen bashed at them with their mattocks and big hammers, bouncing two-handed blows off helmets and pauldrons. Instead of ringing like a hammer on an anvil, the blows sounded dull and chunky.

He gave the order a second time, and the men did as they'd been told, sidling backwards away from the breach.

411

On the other side, the halberdiers were pushing and jostling each other, competing to get through while the way was inexplicably clear. As they oozed and bubbled through the gap, Temrai stepped back into the line and gave the order to draw bows. By *nock your arrows* there were thirty or so of them through the breach; more by the time Temrai called *hold* low and then *loose*, and the front rank let fly at no more than fifteen yards' range.

It was just as well he'd reminded them to shoot low; at such short range the arrow is still climbing, and even with his warning, a quarter of the shots went high. But three quarters of a volley was enough for the halberdiers at the breach; they crumpled up like paper thrown on to the fire, laying a carpet of obstacles directly in the path of the men following them. The next volley congested the opening even further; the pile of dead, twitching and wriggling bodies was over knee-high now, too tangled to step through, not stable enough to scramble over. Still they carried on coming though, each batch put to proof and found deficient. The handful that did manage to get through then underwent the next degree of the test as they threw themselves up the slope towards the line of archers, and what had passed the arrows went down under the pounding of the big hammers, swirling and falling like shot from a trebuchet.

Temrai had nothing to do in all this except stand still and watch; and as he watched, he thought about the fall of Perimadeia, the gate (not much wider than the breach here) that had opened and let in his men. There hadn't been a rank of archers waiting for him then, only the darkness and empty streets, nothing to prove his mettle. Now, trapped between hammer and anvil (the shot still hissed and whistled overhead, thudded into the side of the hill, ripping up dust) he felt a little easier in his mind.

When the enemy captain gave the order to break off, the gap in the stockade had been filled; not with timbers looted from the other side of the hill but with proof steel in a jumbled, compacted heap. *Saves us a job*, Temrai thought; *they've done it better than we could have* – and he paused to ask himself whether his men would have gone on squeezing and scrambling into the killing zone, the way the Imperials had done. *But we never had the chance; it's not a fair test.*

He shook his head, then signalled to the work-crew to move in and start shoring up, making good.

'You see,' he told Heurrai (who'd been one of the sullen faces at the council of war), 'give them an opportunity, they may just be stupid enough to take it.'

Heurrai didn't reply; what he'd seen was bothering him. Temrai could sympathise; at another time, in another place, it would have bothered him too. But he'd improved himself since then, made good the gaps in his defences; and now he was wondering if Bardas Loredan had felt this way when he'd beaten off the assault on Perimadeia with incendiaries, so that fire had danced on the unburnable water. It was an opportunity for a valuable insight, a sharing of experience leading to a sharing of minds – he felt like an apprentice standing at his master's elbow.

'They'll be back,' someone said; and a trebuchet shot pitched a few yards away, crushing one man and ripping a leg off another. The next shot only tore up more dust, as Temrai led the way up the path, where another crew was already starting to make good.

'Sure,' he replied, when he'd caught his breath. 'And when they try again, we'll share another opportunity. Don't worry about it. I know what's going to happen.'

Bardas hadn't expected the first sally to go home. It had been more in the nature of an experiment, a trial, a putting to proof. They'd passed the second degree. He'd have expected nothing less. Meanwhile he'd field-tested the portable bridges and was satisfied that they were up to the job. He was pleased by that.

He directed the second and third batteries to pick another point on the stockade, the rest of the artillery to concentrate on the existing breach. Then he ordered the halberdiers and pikemen to form a column, with the cavalry out of harm's way on the flanks. The crossbowmen had taken too many casualties to be much use as a field unit, so he relegated them to the rearguard, and brought up the archers to replace them. Imperial archers weren't up to much, in his opinion, or at least these ones weren't; they had seventy-pound self flatbows, thoroughly inferior to the heavy composites of the plainsmen, and their place in this army

was on the side of the plate, as salad. He was annoyed
by that. If it had wanted to, the provincial office could have
given him some of the best archers in the world, armed with
longbows, composites, northern self recurves, southern
cablebacks, on foot or mounted, light or heavy armoured,
fighting as skirmishers or volley-shooters, in the open or
from behind pavises. Instead he had crossbowmen and
rabbit-hunters, neither of which were likely to be much use
to him. But it didn't matter. He could manage perfectly well
with what he'd got.

He allowed the batteries an hour to make the breaches,
but they did the job in twenty minutes; so he reassigned them
to laying down a blanket barrage on the enemy artillery.
The dust was an unexpected bonus; he could have managed
perfectly well without that, too, but it made what he had in
mind that bit easier. As the trebuchets changed angles and
locked down on their new targets, he gave the order to sound
the advance. As they moved forward, the halberdiers started
to sing, and it no longer bothered him that he didn't understand the words.

This time, he tried a different tactic. Instead of simply
flooding the breaches with heavy infantry, he sent in a
few companies of skirmishers to set up pavises. As he'd
anticipated, Temrai's archers were there to oppose the
assault; but instead of men to shoot at, he gave them oxhides,
with his own archers returning fire through loopholes
and from behind the edges of the screens. They didn't
accomplish anything much, but he didn't really want them
to; the purpose of the exercise was to give King Temrai an
opportunity to shoot as many arrows as possible harmlessly
into the pavises. He knew that each plainsman carried
twenty-five arrows on his back, enough for three minutes'
sustained fire – after that, they'd have to rely on supplies
brought down the hill from the supply pits, along the pitted
and gouged-out path, through the dust. Once the three
minutes were up, the enemy archers wouldn't be a serious
threat; assuming, of course, that Temrai was short-sighted
enough not to realise what he was doing.

But Temrai played his part as if they'd been rehearsing
together for weeks; the pavises held up to the barrage
(they were an improved design of his own, stretched hides

backed with thick coils of the plaited straw matting the Empire issued for making archery targets with; designed by experts to stop an infinite number of arrows) and when the hail of arrows faltered and became sporadic, he opened the screens and sent the pikemen through.

It was a hedge of spears, dense as the undergrowth in an unmanaged wood. The archers carried on loosing into it, but their arrows didn't get very far, it was worse than trying to shoot through a matted tangle of thorns. The distance to be covered was only twenty yards or so; and then the pikes were close enough to touch, and the plainsmen tried to run away; but they were backed up on their own ranks, who were backed up on the supply carts bringing up more arrows, which were backed up on the reinforcements coming down the path. There was a certain limited scope for compression, as the front ranks cringed away from the spearblade hedge, like children on a beach skipping out of the way of the incoming tide. But when they'd flattened themselves against the men behind them, packed together like arrows in a barrel, there was nowhere left for them to go; all they could do was watch the pike-heads come on to them and into them.

Some of the front rank were killed outright. Others hung from the pikes still living, like the chunks of meat on skewers that the Sons of Heaven ate with rice and peppers. The force of the advance was enough to lift them off their feet, still struggling like speared fish (because the halberdiers were backed up too, the rear ranks pressing forward were still advancing, cramming into the ranks in front so that they couldn't have lowered their pikes even if they'd wanted to; so the long shafts of ash and apple bent like bows under the weight of the skewered meat, but being tested and approved to the highest specifications of the empire, they didn't break and neither did the men packed in round them). The second rank of the enemy joined the first on the spike, like a second layer of cloth joined to the first by the needle; a few pikeshafts snapped, but not enough to matter. After the first two ranks had been gathered up on the pikes, the forward progress stopped; dead or impaled, they served the third rank like a gambeson or some other form of padded or quilted armour, resisting the thrust with softness rather than strength or deflection (the padding of the gambeson smothers and dissipates the force of the thrust, clogging the advance of the blade). The forward momentum of the pikemen faltered, as the shower of arrows had done; the manoeuvre had run its course, and it was time for the next stage.

Temrai, meanwhile, had seen another opportunity. He was on the path, looking down at the compressed mass of the slaughter, when the advance stalled and the two sides stood staring at each other through the dust across the ashwood thicket, like two neighbours on either side of a hedge. He turned to the man next to him, a section leader called Lennecai, and tugged at his sleeve.

'They're stuck,' he said.

'What?'

'They're stuck,' Temrai repeated. 'They can't move, same as us. Get this path clear and bring down six companies of archers.'

They cleared the path by dumping the carts, pushing them off the crumbling track. Most of them tumbled harmlessly down, smashing into junk timber as they bounced off the rocky face of the slope; a few landed like trebuchet shot in the compacted mass of bodies, some on one side of the hedge, some on the other. Lennecai lined his archers out in a double column and ordered them to face about; enough of them had a clear shot down into the pikemen to make the manoeuvre worthwhile. Bardas' men instinctively looked up as the arrows hissed and whistled into the air, and were able to watch the arrows bank and pitch, slanting in at them like rain on a windy day. Of course there was no hope of getting out of the way; they had no choice but to stand and watch the arrows, as closely packed as rows of standing wheat. It wasn't just the front rank, or the front three ranks. The archers were raking the whole formation from front to back.

As men died or were spitted, so they stopped pushing; the momentum went out of the push of pikes like tension from a rope bridge when one of the main hawsers is cut through. The mass started to crumple, just as a crushed plate folds up under the hammer, until the pressure from the men on the other end of the spears forced them to give ground.

As they slipped back so the formation no longer supported the weight of the pikes, with their tremendous weight of meat hanging from the sharp end. The pikes went down, like trees felled in an overgrown forest, fouling and tangling in the undergrowth. *Now would be a good time for a counterattack*, Temrai observed, and a few moments later he saw it happen, as the survivors of the third and fourth ranks of his men pushed and shoved their way past the bodies of their fellows and tried to press home an attack with their scimitars. It was only a partial success; there still wasn't enough room to swing a sword, to bring down an overhead blow, and in any case the pikemen's helmets and pauldrons were easily proof against light cuts delivered with the force of the arm and wrist alone. The best they could do was trim off a few fingers, ears and noses (like foresters trimming a newly felled trunk).

'He's about to make a mistake,' Bardas said aloud.

The pikemen were slumping, falling back; and Temrai's men were pushing forward, following up an opportunity they'd never anticipated. Bardas sent a couple of runners to the sergeants of halberdiers, and another to the artillery crews.

Temrai saw it too, but not quite in time; by that stage it was out of his control, as his men surged out through the breaches in pursuit of the pikemen, and were immediately enfiladed by Bardas' archers, positioned on either side. The shock of volley fire at close range stopped them in their tracks, as men went down like cut corn; before they could turn round and go back, the halberdiers moved in to cut them off. Temrai's runners arrived in time to stop anybody else going beyond the stockade, but for those already outside nothing could be done. The work crews had started piling trash in the breaches to block them up even before the last of the pursuit party were killed. Bardas' second opportunity didn't amount to much; the trebuchets only managed two clear shots each on the archers lined up on the path before Temrai pulled them out.

They packed up the portable bridges and withdrew in good order, without interference from Temrai's battered and out-of-commission artillery. Once the assault party was safely home, the bombardiers restored the trebuchets to their previous settings, locked down the handwheels and carried on with the bombardment of the path and the engine emplacements.

'On balance,' Bardas explained, 'we came out ahead. We killed more of them, we made them waste a lot of arrows, and of course there's the morale effect of having the advantage at the end. More to the point, we learned another lesson about close fighting in the fortress, and we learned it in a practice run rather than the actual main assault. All they can say is that they're still there, and that hardly counts as progress.' He sighed; and if he could see the wounded men sprawled on the wagons outside the surgeons' enclosure, he didn't say anything about them. 'We've got a long way to go yet,' he said, 'but we're getting there. After all, Perimadeia wasn't built in a day.'

'What, me?' Gorgas looked shocked. 'Certainly not. Why should I do such a stupid thing?'

The envoy's expression didn't change – did they breed them that way, Gorgas wondered, or did they have the sinews in their cheeks and jaws cut when they were children, as part of a lifelong apprenticeship in the art of diplomacy? 'I'm only repeating what we were told,' he said. 'Our sources say that the rebellion was started by your men, acting on your orders. The fact that you're discussing the matter with me rather than twenty thousand halberdiers ought to give you some indication of how much faith we put in reports from that particular source.'

Gorgas laughed, as if the envoy had just told a funny story. 'Well,' he said, 'unless you tell me where the report came from I can't really comment. I suppose it's possible that these troublemakers you're talking about were my men, in the sense that they served with me at some time or other, but anything they may have done certainly wasn't on my orders. Perish the thought. After all,' he added, 'I may not be a genius, but I'm not stupid enough to go picking a fight with the Empire for the sake of a bunch of merchants who've never done me any favours. That'd be suicide. Can I get you something to eat?'

The envoy looked at him startled, then shook his head.

'No, thank you,' he said. 'I'm sorry to have bothered you. Obviously, if you do find out anything about who might have been responsible—'

'Of course. I'd be glad to have the chance to do something to show just how serious the Mesoge is about becoming a loyal and useful member of the Empire. I'm right in thinking, aren't I, that we're the first nation ever to join the Empire voluntarily?'

'I'm afraid I don't know,' the envoy said, standing up and brushing moss and leaf-mould rather vigorously from his cloak. 'One other thing before I go: have you by any chance heard anything from your sister or her daughter? We've had rather disturbing reports that suggest they may have been abducted.'

'You don't say,' Gorgas replied. 'It's true, I haven't heard from either of them lately. I was planning to write to Niessa soon anyway; I'll see what I can find out.'

'Thank you,' said the envoy gravely, staring pointedly at the axe lying across Gorgas' knees. 'I'll let you get back to what you were doing.'

'Gateposts,' Gorgas replied. 'It's a shame to fell this old oak – I remember climbing up it when I was a kid – but it's stone dead; better to cut it down now than have it come down on the roof some windy night. And you can't beat oak for gateposts.'

'I'm sure,' the envoy said. One of his escort held the stirrup for him and he lifted himself rather stiffly into the saddle. 'Thank you for your time.'

'Always a pleasure,' Gorgas said.

By the time the envoy and his party were out of sight, Gorgas was nearly through, so he decided to finish off before going back to the house. He'd made cuts on three sides so as to be able to dictate which direction the tree would fall in; all he had to do now was cut out the remaining quadrant until he reached the point where the narrow core at the centre could no longer support the shearing force of the tree's weight. Then he ought to be able to tip the tree down with just the pressure of his hand.

It fell well, more or less where he'd wanted it to go, and he allowed himself a moment of rest and satisfaction, leaning on his axe and listening to the soft patter of raindrops

falling from the leaves of the tall elm behind him. It had
rained all night, but the morning had been fine and fresh –
if there was one smell that meant home, it was the sweet
aftermath of rain.

It was a shame he couldn't stay a little longer; but there
was work to do indoors before he could get back to this
job (and it had waited thirty years; it'd probably keep
another hour without causing a disaster). He leaned the
axe against the elm tree and walked slowly back to the
house.

They were there, same as usual; staring at each other
across the dark room like two dogs. Why his sister and his
niece insisted on sulking like this he couldn't make out,
but he had a feeling that trying to bounce them into
reconciliation would most likely do more harm than good.

'Someone came asking after you two today,' he said. Neither
of them said anything. 'From the provincial office, letting me
know there was a chance you'd been – abducted, was the
word he used. So you'd better stay indoors a bit longer, just in
case they've got someone watching. I'm sorry,' he went on,
as both women protested angrily, 'but I don't need the
aggravation of being caught with you two, not until I've had
time to straighten things out.' He sat down and pulled the
cider-jug towards him; nothing like chopping down a tree
to raise a healthy thirst. 'I think we'll go along with this
abduction idea,' he said. 'What happened was, you were
both kidnapped by pirates; they sent to me for a ransom, I
pretended to play along, paid out the ransom, got you
back, then went after the pirates and dealt with them. When
someone gives you a perfectly serviceable lie, it's only polite
to follow it up.'

Not a word, from either of them. He sipped his drink
and smiled; it had taken a while to get used to the taste
of raw home-made cider again, but it was one of those
flavours that grew on you, a sort of comfortingly familiar
unpleasantness. 'Mostly,' he went on, 'I don't want to cause
any upsets until Bardas has beaten Temrai; it can't be much
longer, so we'll just have to sit tight. That damned Imperial
was sniffing about that, too, but of course they can't prove
anything.'

Niessa turned and looked at him. 'What was all that about,

anyway?' she said. 'Someone told me you'd sent soldiers to the Island—'

'Who told you that?' Gorgas asked.

Niessa frowned. 'One of the sergeants who came up here the other day, the tall ginger-haired one—'

Gorgas nodded. 'I know who you mean,' he said.

'He assumed I knew all about it,' Niessa went on. 'I hope I haven't got him in trouble.'

'It's understandable,' Gorgas said. 'After all, it's not so long ago they were taking their orders from you, not me. It's all right, I'll deal with it.'

That didn't sound very hopeful for the red-headed sergeant, who really had been most reluctant to tell her anything, but Niessa wasn't going to let herself get sidetracked. 'So what have you been up to?' she asked. 'You really shouldn't play power-politics, you know. You aren't very politic and you're certainly not very powerful.'

Gorgas grinned. 'It's like cutting down a tree,' he said, 'it's just a matter of making sure things fall the right way. I knew that if the provincial office had their way it'd be their general and the troops from the Island who ran down Temrai, and Bardas would only be there to round up the stragglers. Which would have been no use at all to anybody. So I made sure the fleet didn't sail on time.'

'You did?' Iseutz asked, smiling. 'Oh, sure. And how did you manage that?'

'Easy,' Gorgas said. 'I went round some of the merchants I know on the Island, put the idea into their heads of trying to hold up the provincial office for more money. I expected it to be much harder work than it actually was; for a nation that call themselves businessmen, they're as naïve as they come. Of course,' he went on, 'I knew there was a risk the Imperials would do what they in fact did – annex the Island and get hold of the ships that way; but I wasn't bothered by that, because I was figuring on Bardas catching up with Temrai in the open, rather than having to dig him out. So, when the Imperials made their move, I sent a few of my people to cause trouble on the Island; which they did, bless them, and now Bardas has the field pretty much to himself. It's all turned out much better than I thought it would, actually.'

There was a moment's silence. Niessa was shaking her head contemptuously. 'One thing that occurs to me,' said Iseutz. 'Do you actually have any proof that Bardas *wants* to be the one to bring back Temrai's head to the prefect, that it actually matters to him? For all you know, he was quite happy to potter about on the borders, well away from the fighting.'

'Don't be silly, Iseutz,' Gorgas said. 'I know Bardas, you don't. When he sees an opportunity, he makes the most of it – he's like me or your mother in that respect, I suppose it runs in the family. Look at how well he's done already since he's been in the army; he took Ap' Escatoy for them, and now he's in charge of an army with a field command and the chance to avenge a terrible defeat and restore the prestige of the Empire. They'll have to give him a prefecture after this, it'll be the making of him. And I don't suppose he'll be heartbroken at the prospect of settling the score with Temrai, either, though he's not what I'd call a vindictive person. Unlike some,' he added meaningfully, looking at Iseutz. 'No, what Bardas has got that the rest of us haven't is this strong moral sense; he'll want to see Temrai punished, not out of spite or because it'll give him pleasure, but because he knows it's something that's got to be done, and he won't feel right until it's been done and he's done it.'

'And you've taken steps to make sure he gets the opportunity.'

'It was the least I could do,' Gorgas replied. 'I wouldn't have felt right if I hadn't done it. And really, it was so easy in the end. Now then,' he went on, 'that's enough of that, I've got letters to write. Have either of you seen Zonaras? I want him to nip out to Tornoys for me.'

Iseutz shrugged. 'Which one is Zonaras?' she asked. 'I still can't tell them apart.'

Gorgas frowned at her. 'Very amusing,' he said. 'I take it that means you haven't. Well, if you do see him, I'll be in the office.'

What Gorgas called the office was a small room at the back of the house; originally it had been a smokehouse, where the hams were hung up over a smouldering cairn of oak-chips, but Clefas and Zonaras hadn't bothered much with curing meat, and they'd used it as a dump for sundry clutter. Gorgas had had it rethatched and repointed, and had knocked a doorway through and put in a window. He had plans for a new, much larger smokehouse on the other side of the yard, once he'd finished repairing the fence and restoring the woodshed and the trap-house; but that was going to have to wait.

He had a desk, rather a fine one with a slanting face at chest height (Gorgas was old-fashioned and preferred standing up to write), a lamp-bracket that swung sideways on a pivoted arm, another arm with a hole in it for the ink-horn and a tray on top for his penknives, sealing wax, sharpening stone, inkstone, sand-shaker and all the other marginally useful paraphernalia that tend to accrue to people who spend a significant proportion of their time writing. Under the face was a board that pulled out and was supported by two folding struts, just the right size for a counting board, with a rack for your reckoning counters let into the side. Needless to say it had been made in Perimadeia, about a hundred years ago; the wood was dark and warm with beeswax, and across the top was carved the motto DILIGENCE-PATIENCE-PERSISTENCE, suggesting that it had been made for a customer in the Shastel Order. Gorgas remembered it well from his childhood – where his father had got it from he hadn't the faintest idea, but he'd used it as a cutting-board for making and trimming arrow-fletchings, as witness the hundreds of thin lines scored across the face. When he'd rescued it from the dead furniture store in the half-derelict hayloft, Gorgas had intended to reface it with leather or fine-sawn Colleon oak veneer, but in the end he'd kept it as it was, not wanting to deface any of the visible signs his father had left behind.

He'd trimmed a fresh pen only the day before, out of a barred grey goosefeather; it didn't need sharpening but he sharpened it anyway, using the short knife with the blade worn paper-thin by decades of sharpening that had always been in the house for as long as he could remember (but his mother had used it in the kitchen, for skinning and jointing). Then he folded back the lid of the ink-horn (it was one he'd made himself; but Bardas had made the lid and the little brass hinge, beaten them out of scraps of brass scrounged from a scabbard-chape they'd found, green and brittle, in the bed of a stream), dipped the pen and started to write. It was a very short letter written on a tiny scrap of thrice-scraped parchment, and when he'd sanded it he rolled it up tight and pushed it into a brass foil tube slightly thinner than an arrowshaft. Then he reached under the desk and fished out an arrow.

It was a standard Imperial bodkinhead, with a small diamond-section blade and a long-necked socket. He pulled the head off without any real effort and pushed the brass tube up inside the socket as far as he could get it to go. Then he took a little leather bag from the top of the desk, opened it and tapped a few brown crystals out into the palm of his hand. There was also a small brass dish on the tray, one of the pans from a long-lost pair of scales. Having transferred the crystals into the pan he took the penknife and made a small nick in his forearm, angling his arm so that the blood dripped on to the crystals. When they were amply covered, he wrapped a piece of cloth over the cut and carefully spat into the pan until the proportions of blood and spit were roughly the same. Finally he added a fat pinch of sawdust from a twist of parchment he'd had tucked under his cuff.

Pulling the lamp-arm toward him, he held the pan over the flame and stirred the mixture with the penknife handle, dissolving the crystals (glue, extracted from steeped rawhide). When he was satisfied with the consistency he took a dollop of the glue on the tip of his little finger and smeared the end of the arrowshaft where the socket was to go. After putting the socket carefully back on and making sure it was straight, he served the joint with a length of fine nettle-stem twine, using the last of the glue to stick down the ends.

The last step was to mark the arrow; he dipped the pen back into the ink and painstakingly wrote *this one* between the cock feather and the bottom fletching, in tiny, angular clerk's letters. Then he laid it flat on the window-sill to dry.

He had other letters to write, and he was busy with them when Zonaras came in (as usual, without knocking).

'Well?' he said.

Gorgas looked up. 'There you are,' he said. 'Do me a favour and ride over to Tornoys—'

'What, today?'

'Yes, today. Go to the Charity and Chastity – I don't need to tell you where that is – and ask for Captain Mallo, who's going to Ap' Escatoy. Give him these letters and this arrow—'

'What's he want with just one arrow?'

'Just you make sure he gets it,' Gorgas said, in a tone of voice that made Zonaras open his eyes wide. 'He knows what to do. Once you've done that,' he added, reaching into his pocket, 'and not before under any circumstances, have a drink on me.' He handed over a couple of silver quarters, which Zonaras took quickly without saying anything. 'All right?'

Zonaras nodded. 'The mare's cast a shoe,' he said.

'What? When was that?'

Zonaras shrugged. 'Day before yesterday,' he said.

Gorgas sighed. 'Fine,' he said. 'Take my horse, just try not to ride her down any rabbit holes. We'll shoe the mare when you get back.'

Zonaras frowned. 'I've got a lot on right now,' he said.

'All right, *I'll* shoe the mare. Now get on; remember, Captain Mallo, going to Ap' Escatoy, at the Charity and Chastity. You think you can remember that?'

'Course.'

After he'd gone, Gorgas leaned against the desk and scowled. If anybody was capable of messing up a simple job, it was Zonaras. On the other hand, Zonaras riding to the Charity and Chastity in Tornoys and drinking himself stupid was the most natural thing in the world, a regular event these last twenty years, a sight so familiar as to be practically invisible.

Before he left the study, Gorgas paused in the doorway and looked up, as he always did, at the mighty and beautiful bow hung on two pegs over the top of the frame. It was the bow Bardas had made for him, just as he'd once made the ink-horn cover and the little copper sand-shaker and the folding three-piece boxwood ruler, which had been with Gorgas wherever he'd gone (it got broken in Perimadeia while he was there; he'd kept the pieces and, years later, had the best instrument-maker in the City put them back together again, with the finest fish-bladder glue and tiny silver tacks so small you could hardly see them; he'd had a rigid gold and silver case made for it at the same time, to make sure it didn't get broken again).

CHAPTER NINETEEN

Hoping to force Temrai into giving him an opportunity, Bardas kept up the bombardment for three days without changing the settings; he described it to his staff officers as 'planishing the enemy'. They didn't really understand what he was talking about, but they could see the reasoning behind it. The major obstacle was still the disparity in numbers; if they could force Temrai into an ill-advised sortie, they had a chance of killing enough men to bring the odds to within acceptable parameters. It was sound Imperial thinking, and they approved.

Nevertheless, the Imperial army was feeling the strain. A third of the halberdiers and pikemen had to be kept standing to at all times, in case Temrai launched a night attack; another third were fully occupied quarrying and hauling stone shot from the nearby outcrops (and the supply of useful rock was dwindling rather quicker than Bardas had allowed for); he'd had to detail two troops of cavalry to help the artillerymen. The troopers were disgusted at this reduction in status, while the bombardiers complained bitterly about cack-handed horse-soldiers doing more harm than good; the trebuchets themselves were starting to shake apart after so much continuous use, and Bardas found he was alarmingly low on both timber and rope, neither of which were available locally. He'd already given the order to break up the newly built siege towers for timbers and materials (but it didn't look like they'd be needed now, and the hide coverings could be scavenged to make up more pavises, when he could spare a few carpenters from trebuchet maintenance).

It was just as well he had Theudas to help him; he had plenty of soldiers, but only a few competent clerks, and

427

most of his work seemed to be drawing up rosters and schedules, allocating materials, updating stores manifests, the sort of thing he could do if he had to but which Theudas actually seemed to enjoy.

'Don't worry about it,' the boy told him. 'If I can help kill Temrai with a notebook and a counting-board, he's as good as dead already.' Then he launched into a high-speed résumé of the latest daggers-drawn dispute between the chief carpenters of number-six and number-eight batteries over who had a better claim to the one remaining full keg of number-six square-head nails—

'Deal with it,' Bardas interrupted with a shudder.

'No problem,' Theudas replied cheerfully.

Bardas smiled. 'It's good to see you've found something you can actually do,' he said. 'You were a pretty rotten apprentice bowyer.'

'I was, wasn't I?' Theudas shrugged. 'Still, everybody's good at something.'

Two men met in a shed on the outskirts of the sprawling Imperial supply depot at Ap' Escatoy. It was dark. They didn't know each other.

After a short interval during which they studied each other like cats, one of them reached under his coat and pulled out a bundle wrapped in cloth. 'Special delivery?' he asked.

'Yeah, that's me.' The other man reached for the bundle. 'I hope you know where it's supposed to be going, because I don't.'

'It says on the ticket.' The first man pointed at a scrap of paper attached to the thin, coarse string that held the bundle together.

'All right,' the other man replied, frowning. 'So what does it say?'

'I don't know, I can't read.'

The other man sighed. 'Give it here,' he said. He felt the package curiously. 'Feels like a stick. You got any idea what's in here?'

'No.'

'Your work fascinates you, doesn't it?'

'What?'

'Nothing.'

The next morning, someone stole a horse from the couriers' stable, using a forged requisition. He was believed to have left in the direction of the war. Nobody could be spared to go after him, but a memorandum was added to the incident log, so that the matter could be dealt with later.

Temrai had got out of the habit of keeping his eyes open. There hadn't been much point the last few days (how many days? No idea). There was nothing to see except dust, which clogged your eyes and blinded you anyway, to the point where it was easier to keep them shut and rely on your other senses for finding your way about. His hearing, on the other hand, had become an instrument of high precision, to the point where he could tell from the noise it made coming down almost exactly where the next shot was going to pitch. This method proved to be ninety-nine per cent reliable, the only serious exception being the shot that landed a few feet above him on the path, dislodging a great mass of rock and rubble and burying him.

That's strange; I thought you had to die first. He opened his eyes, but there was nothing to see. Hands, legs, head, nothing he could move; breathing was just about possible, but so difficult and time-consuming that it constituted a full-time occupation. It'd be all right, though; they'd come and dig him out in a minute or so.

Assuming, of course, that they knew where he was, or that he'd been buried at all. Now he came to think of it, there was no reason to believe that anybody had been watching when the hill fell on him; seeing your hand in front of your face was something of an achievement, thanks to the dust. How long would it take them, he wondered, to notice that he wasn't there any more? Even if they missed him almost immediately, it wasn't exactly an instinctive response to say, *Hey, we can't find Temrai, he must be buried alive somewhere.* He thought of the number of times he'd gone looking for someone, failed to find them and given up in a temper, assuming they didn't want to be found.

'It's all right,' said a voice beside him. 'They'll find us. We've just got to be patient and try to stay calm.'

Temrai was surprised, but pleased. He couldn't remember seeing anybody near him when the hill came down (but thanks to the dust, that was hardly conclusive). 'Are you all right?' he asked.

The voice laughed. 'Never better,' it replied. 'Nothing I enjoy more than being stuck in a hole in the ground under a few tons of dirt. I find it helps me unwind.'

The voice was familiar – very familiar, in fact – but he couldn't quite place it. So familiar that asking, *Excuse me, but who are you?* would be embarrassing. 'Can you move at all?' he asked.

'No. How about you?'

'Not so as you'd notice.' It was odd, Temrai reflected, that he could hear the other man so clearly, as if they were sitting opposite each other in a tent. Maybe the human voice carried well through dirt; he didn't know enough about such things to be able to form an opinion. 'Maybe we should shout or something,' he said, 'let them know we're here.'

'Save your breath,' the voice said. 'You'll just use up the air. I keep telling you, don't worry about it. They'll come and dig us out. They always do.'

That last remark was strange, but Temrai was too preoccupied to dwell on it. 'Where do you think the air is coming from?' he asked.

'Search me. Just be grateful it's coming from somewhere. And that you don't have one of those irrational fears of confined spaces – though what's irrational about being afraid of confined spaces I really don't know. I remember once I was trapped down a tunnel with a man who was that way; gods know how, but he'd managed to keep it under control for years and years, and then when we had the roof cave in on us, it all seemed to burst out of him. He died, actually; he got so frightened his heart stopped beating. Sorry, that's not a very cheerful anecdote; but it makes the point – the main thing is to stay calm. Can you smell anything?'

'What? No. I mean, nothing unusual. What sort of thing?'

'Garlic,' the voice replied. 'Probably just my imagination. Oh hell, my legs are going to sleep. Nothing like a few tons of spoil to cut off the flow of blood.'

Temrai could feel the muscles of his chest tiring from the effort of lifting the weight of the earth every time he

430

breathed in. 'Look, shall we just try shouting?' he said.
'I'd rather have a go and risk running out of air than just lie
here.'

'By all means,' replied the voice indulgently. 'After all,
it might work. Forgive me if I don't join you, though. I'm
concentrating on my breathing and I don't want to lose the
rhythm.'

Temrai tried to shout; but the volume of sound he
managed to produce was pitiful, more like a cat yowling,
and dirt was getting in his mouth. He managed to spit
most of it out and swallowed the rest. The effort involved was
shattering.

'I'd give it a rest if I were you,' the voice advised him.
'Either they'll find us or they won't; just for once, accept the
fact that there's nothing you can do. Relax. You could try
meditating.'

'Meditating?'

'Seriously. A philosopher I used to know taught me how
to do it. Basically it's all about ignoring your body, making
yourself forget it's there. Of course, the philosopher reckoned
it was all about merging your consciousness with the flow
of the Principle, but you don't have to bother with that
stuff if you don't want to. I use it to make myself go to sleep
when I'm fidgety.'

'All right,' Temrai said dubiously. 'But I don't think going
to sleep would be terribly clever right now. We might forget
to breathe, something like that.'

'You don't have to go to sleep, that's just one of the options.
You can also use it to cope with pain, for example, like if you
were laid up somewhere with a broken leg.'

'All right,' Temrai repeated. 'How do you do it, then?'

The voice laughed. 'It's hard to explain,' it said. 'Easy enough
to do when you know how, but hard to put into words. You've
got to convince yourself that your body isn't really there;
bit by bit's easiest. I usually start with my feet and work
up.'

Temrai could remember thinking. *No, I don't think I'll
bother with that*; and the next thing he felt was a surge of
panic, flaring and quickly subsiding, when he realised that
he didn't seem to have a body any more. But the sensation
was pleasant, exhilarating even; he was breathing, but he

couldn't feel the crushing weight of the earth or the pain in his chest. Nor did he have an oppressive sense of being in any one place (how tiresome that would be, to be in only one place at a time; he could vaguely remember what it had been like, and couldn't imagine how he'd managed to cope with it all these years) –

'Feeling better?'

'Much,' Temrai replied. 'I must see if I can remember how to do this once we get out of here.'

'How do you feel?'

'Like a head,' Temrai replied. 'A head without a body. But it's all right. In fact it's better. Thank you.'

'You're welcome,' the voice said. 'It's one of the more useful things I've picked up in the course of a somewhat adventurous life.'

'Really?' Temrai couldn't tell whether his eyes were open or shut. 'I could get to like being just a head,' he said.

The voice laughed; it was definitely familiar, almost disturbingly so. 'Be careful what you wish for,' it said. 'You never know who's listening. Favourite saying of my father's, that was. He was a very superstitious man, in some respects. Not that it did him much good, of course, but that's another story.'

Temrai had an unpleasant feeling that he knew whose the voice was; except that it wasn't possible. At least, it was *possible*, but highly unlikely. 'Excuse me asking,' he said, 'but who ...?'

And then he could hear something overhead; he felt himself fall back into his body (his painful, awkward body) like a boy falling out of a tree. There were voices, muffled and far away, and the scrape of metal in dirt, a ringing noise as a shovel-blade fouled a stone. He tried to call out, and realised that his mouth was full of dirt and he couldn't make a sound.

'Temrai?' someone said. 'Yes, it's him, over here. I think he's dead.'

'We'll see about that. Gods, I could do without this fucking dust.'

They had to go slowly, for fear of cutting him up or breaking his bones with their picks and shovels. For a long time he wasn't able to see anything, even though he was sure his eyes were open. He had the worst headache he'd ever had in his life.

'It's all right, he's alive,' someone called out; and a trebuchet shot pitched nearby, sending a tremor through the ground. 'Gently now, he may have broken bones. Temrai, can you hear me?'

'Yes,' Temrai said, spitting out the words along with a lot of dirt. 'And please don't shout, my head's splitting.'

They lugged him out and put him on a plank; he couldn't control his arms or legs, and they flopped off and hung over the side. 'Was there anybody with you?' one of them asked.

Temrai tried to smile. 'I don't think so,' he replied.

But he was wrong; before they took him away, he heard them shouting to each other – *over here, quick, yes he's still alive.* 'Who is it?' he asked.

One of the stretcher-bearers called out the question. 'It's the spy,' someone answered. 'What's his name? Dassascai. You know, the cook's nephew.'

Temrai frowned. 'What did he say?' he asked.

'Dassascai,' the bearer replied. 'You know—'

'The spy, yes.' Temrai sounded confused. 'Well, if it hadn't been for him— That's odd, I could have sworn it was someone else.'

'I thought you said there was nobody in there with you.'

'I was mistaken,' Temrai said. 'Look, make sure they take care of him, all right?'

They took care of him, as was only proper with someone who'd apparently saved the King's life (though how he'd managed to do this wasn't immediately obvious). They dug him out and carried him back to his tent; there were no broken bones, he'd be up and about again in no time.

An oddity, which nobody commented on, was the fact that when they pulled him out he was holding an arrow (just an ordinary Imperial-issue bodkinhead), and when they tried to take it from him he clung on to it as if his life depended on it.

One ship; not an armada or a flotilla, not a horizon crammed with sails, just one small sloop (square-rigged, primitive, limping into the Drutz after a tussle with a seasonal squall) bringing the provincial office's envoy to the Island.

There was something of a show of strength on the quay to meet him; a platoon of the newly recruited Civil Guard; another platoon from the Ship-Owners' even more recently recruited National Security Association; and a mob of cut-throats, thieves and housebreakers (by definition) from the Merchant Seamen's Guild. The three rival units stood still and quiet, staring at the incoming ship and each other with loathing and distrust, while First Citizen Venart Auzeil (in a floor-length red velvet gown and a big wide-brimmed red hat; he'd refused point blank to wear the almost-crown they'd made for him out of bent gold wire and a few scraps of salvaged rabbit fur) nervously picked at a loose thread in his cuff and wondered what was really going on. Flanking him were Ranvaut Votz (for the Ship-Owners') and a certain Jeslin Perdut (for the Guild), both grimly eyes-front for fear of seeing the other and having to acknowledge their presence. Finally, there was a band – to be precise, two flautists, a fiddler, a rebec player and a girl with a triangle. Venart had no idea where they'd suddenly materialised from, but they looked so excited to be there that he hadn't the heart to tell them to push off.

The ship nuzzled its way in, and a startled-looking man threw a rope across before scuttling away to the stern; some-thing about the expression on his face suggested that the show of strength was working rather too well. Venart noticed this and, hoping to reassure the visitors, turned to the rebec player and muttered, 'Play something.' The band immediately launched into 'Never More Will I See My True Love' (the majority choice) and 'The Sausage-Maker's Dog' (the favoured selection of the fiddler and the girl with the triangle) simultaneously. The resulting counterpoint was striking, but hardly calculated to reassure the apprehensive.

'Oh, for pity's sake,' muttered Ranvaut Votz loudly, thereby reinforcing Venart's suspicion that the band's presence had something to do with the Guild. 'Tell them to stop that awful noise before it constitutes an act of war.'

Although he didn't want to be seen to be taking sides, Venart turned the suggestion into an order, backed up by the full majesty of his office and the frantic waggling of his hands. When the noise had ceased, an extraordinarily tall, thin Son of Heaven emerged from the sloop's small cabin and walked slowly to the prow, where he stood looking impatient.

'A plank, quick,' Venart hissed. Someone brought up a plank – actually, it was a long board for gutting fish, but it was the nearest suitable object – and the envoy came ashore.

'I'm Colonel Tejar,' he announced, with a tiny nod in Venart's direction. 'I'm here on behalf of the prefect of Ap' Escatoy. I'd like to talk to whoever's in charge here.'

It took Venart a moment to realise that it was up to him to reply. He'd seen Sons of Heaven before, even spoken to a few of them, but never one quite this tall or angular or official-looking. 'That's me,' he squeaked, bitterly regretting the big red hat, which was flopping down over his left eye. 'Venart Auzeil. First Citizen,' he added.

The Son of Heaven looked at him. 'Thank you for being here to greet me,' he said. 'Can we make a start, please? We have a lot to get through.'

'Of course,' Venart said, and a moment later found himself trotting along in the envoy's wake like (for example) the sausage-maker's dog. Fortunately, the envoy seemed to know where he was going. Venart didn't.

'Do you speak for the Ship-Owners' Association?' asked the envoy over his shoulder.

'Oh, yes,' Venart assured him, taking a couple of skips to keep up. He'd never seen legs that long on a human before.

'And the Merchant Seamen's Guild?'

'Um,' Venart said. 'Yes, of course.'

'Good,' said the envoy. 'Then we won't need to have their representatives present during the talks. I assume they're aware of that?'

'What? Oh, yes,' Venart panted, and passed the message on to the relevant parties. Fortunately, since their legs were even shorter than his, he wasn't able to hang around and listen to their reaction.

He still didn't know where they were going, but it didn't really seem appropriate to ask. It was vaguely disquieting to think that the enemy knew their way round the Island better than the First Citizen did, but the sensible way to handle that was to file it under significant information and call it up again the next time he felt the slightest inclination to underestimate these people.

They stopped. To be exact, the envoy stopped (outside the Four Blazons Of Virtue, which Venart hadn't been in since he was a very young man; in fact, he had an uneasy feeling he'd been banned from there for life – or was he thinking of the Blameless Virtue in the Sheepwalk?) and waited for him to catch up.

'I took the liberty of hiring a room,' the envoy said, 'through an intermediary, of course. I hope you find it acceptable.'

'Fine,' Venart replied breathlessly. 'After you.'

The sight of a Son of Heaven in the public bar of the Four Blazons caused a considerable amount of alarm and despondency, which the presence of the First Citizen didn't do much to assuage. But Colonel Tejar obviously knew the way; he walked straight through the bar, up a short staircase, across the landing and down a corridor. The door was open, and there was a tray with food and a wine-jug on the table. *Impressive*, Venart admitted to himself, *but a tactical error, surely. Why make a display of your strength unless you want to persuade me it's greater than it is?* 'This looks fine,' he said, and sat down in the more comfortable-looking of the two chairs.

'Now,' said Coloner Tejar, perching on the other chair and taking a writing tablet out of his sleeve. 'Do you wish to start with a statement or any questions, or shall we pass straight on to our proposals?'

'Go ahead,' Venart replied; and he was thinking, *It may just be because he wanted to make sure we lost the other two, because he knows he can outsmart me, but he wasn't sure about Votz or the Guild. Well, so long as I know that, I should be able to cope.*

'I've taken the liberty of drawing up a draft agreement,' the colonel continued, pulling a little brass tube out of his other sleeve. 'If you'd care to spend a moment or so looking it over ...'

Marvellous handwriting these people had, Venart couldn't help thinking; and even for a thoroughly utilitarian document like this they've been to the trouble of illuminating the initial letter with three colours and just the tiniest touch of gold leaf.

– Item: the Island to be associated with the Empire as a protectorate.

– Item: an Imperial Protector to reside permanently on the Island.

– Item: a permanent honour guard to attend the Protector, such guard not to exceed three hundred men-at-arms.

– Item: the expenses of the Protector and his staff to be divided equally between the Island and the provincial office.

– Item: –

'Excuse me, ' Venart said, 'but what's a Protector?'

The Colonel stared at him down his nose. 'An Imperial official assigned to reside in an Imperial protectorate,' he replied.

'Ah. Thank you.'

– Item: the Protector to be consulted concerning all aspects of public, Association or Guild policy in any way having bearing upon the relationship between the Island and the Empire.

– Item: upon such consultation, the Protector to issue an official endorsement of such policy, such endorsement to be published in the same way as such policy.

– Item: in the event that such endorsement is not issued, the matter to be referred back to a committee composed equally of Imperial staff and officers of all relevant representative bodies of the Island.

(Clever; if they want to stop us doing something, they bring in the other two factions and get them to veto it.)

– Item: the Empire and the Island to join in a pact for mutual defensive and offensive military support.

(They get the fleet.)

– Item: only weights and measures specified by the relevant officer of the provincial office to be used in commercial transactions.

– Item: a full extradition treaty in the standard form issued by the provincial office to be signed between the Island and the Empire.

Well, there were several more items, and taken together it was total and abject surrender, but with honour. What more could a First Citizen ask? 'Excuse me.'

'Yes?'

'Just a small point,' Venart said, 'but you haven't actually said here that the extradition thing won't be retrospective. Do you want to put that in or shall I?'

The colonel frowned. 'That's not a standard term of provincial office extradition treaties,' he said.

So no prizes for guessing who you'll be extraditing first. 'It's pretty well standard for us,' Venart said.

'Really? I wasn't aware you had any extant extradition agreements.'

Perfectly true. 'We have arrangements,' Venart lied. 'Customary practices built up over the years. You know, precedents and the like.'

(And if he asks me to name one person we've extradited in the last six hundred years, I'll have to admit there wasn't any.)

'I see.' The envoy's face was expressionless. 'Perhaps it would be a more efficient use of our time to defer detailed discussion of treaty terms to a later date. It would be a shame to jeopardise the momentum towards an agreement by focusing too closely on individual issues. After all,' he added, looking just over the top of Venart's head, 'we don't have to finalise the whole thing here and now.'

'Of course.' Venart read the rest of the document, but he didn't really take it in. They had no choice in the matter, after all. 'One thing,' he said, as he rolled up the paper. 'I don't suppose this has even been considered yet, but it's worth asking, I suppose. Do you have any idea who they have in mind for the Protector's job? Just on the off chance that it's someone we've heard of, it could help to set people's minds at rest—'

'As a matter of fact,' the envoy replied, 'there's a recommendation in place; and yes, it's somebody you're likely to be familiar with. Captain Bardas Loredan.'

Venart did his very best not to react. 'I know Colonel – I mean, *Captain* Loredan,' he said. 'I met him during the siege of Perimadeia.'

The envoy nodded. 'I know,' he said. 'That was a factor we considered when making the recommendation. Also,' he went on, 'Captain Loredan is familiar with the area and the various issues, and he's certainly earned a promotion by his conduct of the plains war, and the business at Ap' Escatoy. He's very highly regarded by the provincial office.

You can count on the recommendation going through; assuming,' he added, 'that you're minded to accept these proposals.'

Venart took a deep breath. 'In principle,' he said. 'I mean, as a starting point for negotiations. Obviously there are a few details—'

'Of course.' The envoy stood up. 'For the time being, however,' he said, 'perhaps you'd care to sign the copy I just gave you.'

'Sign it?' Venart looked startled. 'But I thought we just agreed there were points of detail—'

The envoy almost smiled. Almost. 'Indeed. But I think it would be as well to have a signed agreement in existence, if only as a holding measure. Otherwise I couldn't absolutely guarantee that provincial office policy in this area would necessarily remain static indefinitely.' He turned his head, looked out of the window. 'Since the agreement would be subject to formal ratification by the regional co-ordinator, we can safely say that the terms of this draft aren't necessarily carved in stone, so to speak. For today, however, my primary concern is to protect both our positions.'

Venart hesitated. He knew a threat when he heard one; but surely this offer, these negotiations could only mean that the Imperials felt weak. It was tantamount to desperation on their part, anything to close off one lot of problems so as to be able to concentrate on the others. 'This extradition business—' he began.

The envoy turned back and looked him in the eye. It was like staring for too long down a well. 'I can give you my personal assurance,' he said, 'that there will be ample opportunity for discussion at all levels before any actual proceedings are put in hand.'

Bardas Loredan, Venart thought. Well, there comes a point when a man's got to believe in something. 'All right,' he said. His hands shook a little as he took the top off the brass cylinder; he hadn't put the paper back in quite right, and it was jammed. After he'd fumbled with it for a moment or so, the envoy leaned over him, took it from him and drew out the paper without any difficulty. 'Have you got something to write with?' he asked.

'Hm? Oh, yes. ' Venart felt in his pockets, then the pouch

on his belt. 'At least – yes, here it is.' He found the little writing-set Athli Zeuxis had given him, years ago; pen, inkstone, small knife, all in a dear little cedarwood box. He moistened the stone with a little wine, rubbed up some ink and signed the paper.

When Temrai felt a little better, he gave orders for a large-scale sortie.

'You've changed your tune,' they said to him.

'Yes,' he replied.

The general staff, who'd almost given up hope of being allowed to do anything, weren't too bothered to find out his motivation. They couldn't have cared less if he'd told them he'd changed his mind because he'd been told to do it by special voices that only he could hear; they'd been cleared for action, that was enough.

With both Temrai and Sildocai out of action, overall command passed to Peltecai, whose official designation was cavalry marshal; a good man but a worrier, who worried that he worried. Because he was concerned that his tendency to apprehension might result in dithering leading to disaster, he delegated command to a number of other officers, while reserving the right to override any of their orders if he saw fit. He then held a council of war.

This proved inconclusive; the general staff, it seemed to him, were in a reckless mood as a result of the frustrations of the bombardment, so he resolved to be firm and not allow them to rush him into anything. On the other hand, he had nothing concrete of his own in mind, since he'd wisely delegated planning on the tactical level to his lieutenants. Time, meanwhile, was getting on; unless something was decided soon they'd be too late for a daytime operation and be obliged to mount a night attack; Peltecai saw only too clearly the risks of being hustled into such a risky initiative without proper planning or preparation, and therefore made up his mind to attack at once, with all his available forces.

He then addressed the question of what forces were available, and by the time he'd worked out the true implications of the question it was getting on for mid-morning, and the last thing he wanted was to be bounced into fighting a crucial battle in the midday heat, so he nominated one unit in three for garrison duty and told the rest to fall in for the attack.

At this point, a message arrived from Temrai asking what all the delays were in aid of. Flustered, Peltecai sent back a reply saying that they were just on the point of setting off, and rode to the head of the column. Whatever faults he may have had as a commander, lack of individual courage wasn't one of them. He was determined to lead from the front, by example.

This turned out to be unfortunate, because, as the grand cavalry charge came into range of the enemy's weak and uncommitted archers, one of the handful of men shot from the saddle and trampled into an unrecognisable mess by the troop behind was Peltecai. By this point, of course, nobody else had a clue what the plan was or how the chain of command was supposed to work. As the plains cavalry crashed headlong into the wall of the enemy's pikes, therefore, they were operating on the default principle of *kill as many of them as you can, then go home.*

Which worked fine, at least to begin with. Temrai had decided at the start of the war that the only way to deal with the formations of massed armoured pikemen they were likely to encounter was a point-blank volley from the horse-archers to break the line, followed by an utterly committed follow-up with scimitars and battle-axes to widen the gaps and cause a panic. Once they'd achieved that, the enemy's close formation and sheer bulk would be their undoing, if anything could defeat them.

At the hundred-yard mark, therefore, the horse-archers pulled ahead of the heavy cavalry and split their column into two lines, peeling off to ride down the face of the pike formations. The volley went home at thirty-five yards, each archer loosing as he rode past the designated point in the line. The hedge of spearheads crumpled in two places, as the dead and dying pikemen swayed and fell against their comrades in the rows behind, tangling and snagging the men around them. As soon as the archers were clear, the heavy cavalry drove into the wounds in the line, their column splitting down the middle as they rode. Penetration was the key; if they could drive deep enough into the mass of pikemen, they'd be fighting unopposed – at ground level, there simply wasn't room to lower a pike or draw a sword, and the horsemen would cut the lines like a shear cutting sheet steel, using the tension of the material to make the cut possible. Meanwhile the horse-archers would stand off and shoot from as close as they could get into the rest of the line, trying to prompt them to charge and further disrupt their formation; and if they managed to do that, there were the heavy reserves and, if absolutely necessary, the infantry.

They made a very promising start; the front troops punched two deep holes in the line, like bodkinheads puncturing a breastplate. Once they were in, however, they found they had a problem; there wasn't much the enemy could do to them, but their light, sharp scimitars weren't up to the job of shearing Imperial proof. They hammered and bashed until their fine edges were blunt and the muscles of their wrists and forearms were crippled with the shock of resisted force running back up the bone, but it was like bashing with a hammer on an anvil, which is specifically designed to be bashed. Stalemate.

In a battle, however, stalemate never endures; something always happens, usually through nobody's conscious choice. While the heavy cavalry were pounding ineffectually on the anvil, the enemy cavalry (who'd been held back as a reserve; a mistake, as Bardas Loredan later admitted) sprinted up to engage them and ran into the horse-archers, who were pulling out in order to avoid them but mistimed their manoeuvre. In desperation, the archers loosed as much of a volley as they could put together on the fly; in accordance with standing orders, they shot at the horses rather than the men, and were far more successful than either party had anticipated. The front rank of Imperial troopers went down in a welter of noise and dust, and the next rank couldn't stop in time; they rode over and through the fallen horses, crashing like a runaway cart hitting a wall. Startled but greatly encouraged, the horse-archers put up their bows, drew their scimitars and charged, only to find they had the same problem as their colleagues in the heavy cavalry when it came to cutting steel. They'd anticipated rolling up the Imperials with the momentum of their charge; instead, they stalled and came to a standstill as they found out the hard way that their chain-mail and cuir-bouilli was enough to stop them getting cut by the four-pound Imperial swords but didn't do much to prevent smashed bones or concussion. At this point the back three troops of Imperials (who'd lagged behind and only just caught up) swept round their flank, cut off their escape and started hacking them down like an overgrown hedge.

The captain of the sixth reserve troop, a man called Iordecai, saw what was happening and led a charge. Through sheer carelessness the Imperials didn't see him coming until it was too late for them to get out of the way. Iordecai's men were one of the few units of lancers in Temrai's army, and they had no trouble at all punching through heavy plate. Their impact shifted the balance of the engagement; the Imperial captain panicked, imagining that he'd been set up for just such an attack, and tried to pull his men out, but they were too deeply engaged to be able to withdraw; instead, they tried to cut their way out through the horse-archers, and made an impressively good job of it. As they broke through the side of the mêlée, however, they were rammed in flank and rear by another troop of lancers, following up on Iordecai's lead.

At this point the balance of the rearguard, who could see the victory being won by the lancers but not the mess in the pike formation, decided it was time they had their turn; so they charged the pikemen, who were no longer being worried by archers and had had time to recover a little order. When the rearguard (who weren't lancers) drove their charge home, they found the levelled heads of the pikes waiting for them, by which point it was too late to slow down.

Bardas Loredan, on a low hill behind the camp, couldn't see much of the pike formation either, but he had a fine view of the cavalry battle and decided that his only chance of saving the day was to commit his halberdiers against the lancers at the charge and hope they got there in time. They did the best they could, but it was a fairly hopeless venture; by the time they'd skirted the pikemen, the enemy infantry-men had deployed across their line of advance and were manoeuvring to take them in flank. There didn't seem to be anything to be gained by slowing down at this point, so the captain of halberdiers led his column at the double into the centre of the enemy line. The effect was spectacular: they cut the line in half, routing one wing completely. That helped; they were now at liberty to hook the enemy formation and press home the attack on three sides. Their mistake was not spotting the two troops of heavy cavalry that had failed to get into the pike formation and retired to the side of the battle with nothing to do.

There weren't enough of them to cause catastrophic damage, but they carved up a lot of men. The halberdiers had a weak spot, where the pauldrons buckled over the shoulder; a cut across the exposed straps with a sharp blade left them with loose, flapping armour plates hampering their arm movements and the whole of the shoulder and the side of the neck open to attack. Not many killed, but a great many disabled, as the scimitars glanced off the angled sides of the halberdiers' kettle-hats and sliced into neck tendons and collar-bones. Where the halberdiers were able to turn and present arms, they had the better of the deal – the impetus of the oncoming horseman made a far better job of driving the halberd spike through mail and flesh than the human arm could ever do – but on balance the advantage, expressed as the ratio of casualties inflicted, was with the plainsmen.

At this point the battle was out of anybody's control; even with both sides co-operating in a spirit of friendship and goodwill, it would have been a hard job to have disentangled the component parts of the two armies to the point where a general retreat would have been possible. There were only two practical options: to fight it out until one side was wiped out, or to disengage and pull out in the nearest possible approximation to order.

For a while, it looked depressingly like the first option. The plains cavalry wedged into the pikemen were slowly being crushed in from the sides; stuck in the middle of a mêlée, the lancers no longer had any advantage from impetus or momentum and were mostly blunting their scimitars on the dented and mangled but uncompromised armour of their opponents; enough halberdiers were dead or on the ground to give their colleagues room to turn and start pushing spikes up into the plainsmen's faces; if the battle continued along this course, sooner or later the Imperials were bound to prevail, and their survivors, probably no more than a few hundred at best, would be left with the field and the monumental task of disposing of the dead.

Instead, the Imperials panicked, which was probably the best thing they could have done in the circumstances. The catalyst was a furious all-out attack by a young section leader by the name of Samzai on what he mistakenly believed was Bardas Loredan's honour guard (in the event it turned out to be the cavalry escort for a detachment of trumpeters and other musicians; but they were rather splendidly dressed and equipped, and they'd somehow ended up wedged in among the pikemen, so it was an understandable mistake). Samzai didn't make it; he fell swinging his axe – when his body was hauled out of the mess, they found seventeen holes in his mailshirt – just one rank short of his objective, but the survivors of his section managed to chop and shear their way through the pikemen and kill enough of the escort to get within arm's length of the musicians, at which point someone started shouting that Bardas Loredan was dead ... A head (nobody ever found out whose) was hoisted up on a pike, and the plainsmen, even the ones being clubbed to death while unable to defend themselves, started to cheer as if something important had just been decided. At first the reaction was just a moment of hesitation, concern that something was going on but nobody knew what it was; then the pikemen started to edge backwards, dropping their pikes (where possible) and looking for a way to get out of the press and into open ground. As the main infantry formation wavered and came apart, there was suddenly enough room for the cavalry to move; and a brief over-the-shoulder glimpse at the retreating pikemen was enough to convince the Imperial cavalry that something was badly wrong, prompting them to pull out as well. As the panic gathered momentum, so did the pace of withdrawal; men who'd been walking slowly backwards turned round and started to run, no longer remotely interested in the enemy in any capacity except that of possible obstruction. The battle seemed to come to pieces like a frail wicker basket, scattering its contents everywhere.

Two troops of plains heavy cavalry set off in pursuit of
the Imperial pikemen; they were intercepted by an equal
number of Imperials, cut to pieces and scattered. After
that, there wasn't much enthusiasm for pressing home the
advantage, and the plainsmen fell back on the fortress as
quickly as they could. As for the Imperials, they calmed
down a little when they were told that Bardas Loredan
wasn't really dead (by Bardas Loredan himself, riding up to
find out what the hell had happened) but still kept going till
they reached the camp. It's always hard to know how to act
when you've just been driven from the field, particularly if
the field you've just been driven from is now deserted.
Perhaps wisely, Bardas didn't try to make anything of it; he
went back to his tent and called for casualty lists and the
general staff; he had a lot to do, organising stretcher details
and burial details, making sure as many of the wounded as
possible at least got within sight of a doctor before they died,
posting pickets and seeing to it that the camp was properly
secured against follow-up attacks.

It took a full day to retrieve the wounded. Bardas sent a
herald to sort out the usual truce, and the officers in charge
on both sides reached a sensible understanding whereby
each side cleared up its end of the field and handed back the
other side's wounded in a reasonable state of repair. It was
harder to reach agreement on disposing of the daunting
number of dead bodies that needed to be dealt with before
they became a health hazard to both parties. Temrai's men had
to be cremated, whereas the Imperials needed to be buried,
so a reciprocal arrangement was out of the question; Bardas'
negotiators suggested taking it in turns – they'd go first,
collect their dead and then withdraw while the plainsmen
collected theirs – but Temrai's people objected on the
grounds that that would mean waiting for at least a day,
which wouldn't be advisable if the sun decided to come out;
instead they proposed having retrieval details working side
by side, but the Imperials weren't having that – too much risk
of an incident, they said, tempers flaring, fights breaking out;
instead, why not divide the field as before and each side
make two piles, ours and theirs? Time was getting on, and
Temrai's people reluctantly agreed, but the deal nearly
foundered on where the line across the field was to be drawn

- more people had died on both sides up at Bardas' end of the field, and his negotiators felt they were ending up with the rough end of the bargain, so they suggested splitting the field lengthways instead of down the middle. The plainsmen refused, but agreed to bring up the dividing line by a hundred and fifty yards, so that they took responsibility for most of the bodies from the cavalry actions, while the Imperials cleared up after the fighting around the pike formation. When the deal had been done and the work details were lining up, one of Bardas' men remarked to his opposite number on Temrai's negotiating team that whereas during the battle they'd been fighting to get as much of the field as possible, now they were struggling to give as much of it as they could away. The plainsman thought this remark in poor taste and lodged a formal complaint, which was ignored.

After the field had been cleared, the bodies removed, as much in the way of armour, arrows, horses and weapons as possible scavenged for salvage, it was finally possible to work out the score and announce the winner. It turned out to be a remarkably close thing. Purely on head-count of men killed, Temrai had lost; on percentages of total forces engaged killed, he had a marginal advantage. Broken down between cavalry and infantry, assuming cavalry to be worth more, Bardas had a slight lead, but the basis of accounting was dubious there, since heavy infantry were more useful to him than cavalry, and he'd lost rather more of them than Temrai had; besides which, properly speaking, at least three quarters of Temrai's army were theoretically cavalry, which made a nonsense of the whole calculation. Since the battle hadn't been about territory, and neither side had gained or lost an inch, that wasn't much use as a criterion of success. The last accepted category, objectives achieved, was equally unhelpful, since (when they came to think of it) nobody could clearly define what either side's objectives had been, or whether they'd had any at all; if there were any, nobody had achieved them, which meant that both sides had lost, which was plainly ridiculous.

CHAPTER TWENTY

'For pity's sake,' Venart shouted, 'will you stop that godawful noise?'

The hammering stopped. 'What did you say?'

Venart took a step forward. It was dark and gloomy inside the workshop, the only light coming from the shrouded furnace. 'I said, will you stop— Can't you keep the noise down? I'm trying to work.'

Posc Dousor, the Auzeils' next-door neighbour, stepped out from behind the furnace door. He was wearing a leather apron and holding a big hammer. 'So am I,' he said.

'What?'

Dousor nodded towards the furnace and the anvil that stood near it. 'You don't think I'm doing this for fun, do you?' he said.

Venart took a step inside and peered round. 'Excuse me asking,' he said, 'but just what are you doing? Last time I was in here, this was a cheese store.'

'Well, now it's an armour factory.' Dousor wiped his forehead with the back of his gloved hand. 'On account of I can't get any cheese to sell, but I do have this stock of steel billets I got landed with twelve years ago for a bad debt, and suddenly everybody wants to buy armour. So,' he added, 'I'm going to make some. All right?'

'I see,' Venart replied. 'I didn't know you knew how to make armour.'

Dousor frowned. 'I don't,' he said. 'But soon I will. After all, it can't be difficult, can it? You get the metal red hot, you bash it with a hammer till it's thin, then you bash it some more till it's the shape you want. And anyway,' he added, 'I bought a book. If you've got a book, you can learn anything.'

'Well—' Venart wasn't quite sure what to say. It was a very

448

big hammer, and Dousor was rather short-tempered. 'That's very enterprising of you, Posc, but do you think you could possibly do it somewhere else? Only I was up all night doing Council minutes, and—'

'Where?'

'Sorry?'

Dousor waggled the hammer impatiently. 'Where do you suggest?' he said. 'Out in the street, maybe? Or perhaps I should sling out all my furniture, lug this bloody anvil indoors and turn my front room into a smithy. Well?'

Venart's head wasn't getting any better. 'Look,' he said, 'I really don't mind what you do so long as you keep the noise down a bit. I do have a lot of rather important—'

'Keep the noise down a bit,' Dousor repeated. 'You mean, bash a bit more gently? Just sort of *pat* the bloody great iron bars into flat sheets? Don't be a prawn, Ven. Besides, you ought to be grateful.'

'Sorry?'

'War effort,' Dousor said. 'Munitions. Doing my bit for freedom and our unique cultural heritage. Doesn't look particularly brilliant, does it, the First Citizen obstructing the war effort because of some trifling personal inconvenience?'

Venart thought for a moment. 'Listen,' he said. 'What if I were to find you a nice workshop you could use - down on the Drutz, say, in one of the old bonded warehouses? You could bash away to your heart's content down there and I don't suppose anybody'd even notice.'

Dousor frowned. 'What, and pay you buggers rent when I've got a perfectly good shop of my own? Do I look like I'm stupid?'

'All right then, rent-free. Come on, Posc, it's driving Triz up the wall.'

Dousor shook his head. 'I can't help that,' he said. 'It's taken me days to lick this place into shape, put in all these fixtures and stuff. And now you want me to rip them all out again, hump all this heavy gear halfway across the Island—'

'I'll send someone to help you,' Venart sighed. 'At my expense, naturally,' he added.

'But there's still inconvenience,' Dousor persisted. 'Time lost travelling to and fro, haulage charges—'

'How much?'

'What was that?'

'How much do you want me to pay you,' Venart said slowly, 'to move all your gear over to the Drutz and leave us in peace? That's what you're getting at, isn't it?'

Dousor's brow furrowed. 'That's actually a rather offensive thing to say, Ven,' he replied. 'We've been neighbours for years, since your father was alive. Actually, I always thought we were friends. But now you're First Citizen, of course, you think you can come barging in here giving orders—'

'Twenty-five? Fifty?'

Dousor laughed. 'Do me a favour,' he said. 'There's also lost production time to consider. This window of opportunity isn't going to last for ever, you know. Pretty soon this soldiering craze is going to wear off, and if I don't get up and running pretty damn quick, I'm going to look round and see I've missed the boat. And now you're telling me to drop everything—'

'A hundred and seventy five.'

'No way,' Dousor said. 'No way I'm even going to consider it for less than three-two-five.'

'Three-two-five? You must be—'

By way of replying, Dousor picked up the hammer and started laying into the bloom of iron on the anvil; it had long since gone cold, but he didn't seem to have noticed that. Before Venart had a chance to make himself heard again over the noise, his sister pushed past him, swept into the shop and grabbed Dousor by the wrist.

'You,' she said. 'Pack it in.'

Dousor looked at her.

'Don't start,' she said. 'I've got a splitting headache thanks to you and your incessant banging. It's got to stop, understood?'

Presumably Dousor intended to explain, as he'd explained to Venart, about the war effort and his patriotic duty. But he didn't, possibly because with her other hand Vetriz had picked up the pincers, the jaws of which were red hot on account of being carelessly left in the fire, and was holding them about an inch under Dousor's beard.

'All right,' he said. 'Just as soon as your brother and I work out the compensation.'

Vetriz stared him in the eye. 'It's all right,' she said quietly, 'we don't want any compensation. Now start packing up all your silly tools and things, while Ven sends out for the carrier's cart.'

After that, there were no more loud noises from next door, and Venart was able to get back to work. Even without the ring of hammer on steel, it wasn't easy to keep his concentration; the revised heads of agreement from the provincial office were couched in such ambivalent terms that they could mean anything, nothing, or both simultaneously.

'You're going to have to tell someone about this,' Vetriz said. 'Tell him, Athli. You can't make a peace treaty with the enemy and not *tell* anybody.'

'I've told the Council,' Venart replied irritably. 'And the Ship-Owners', and the Guild. Who does that leave, really?'

'You've told the bigwigs,' Athli pointed out, 'and made them promise to keep it to themselves. That's not the same thing at all.'

'You think they can keep a secret? Come off it.' Venart allowed himself a small, weary smile. 'Telling Ranvaut Votz something and making him promise not to repeat it is the most efficient means of disseminating information the world has ever seen. I expect they know about it in Colleon by now.'

'All right,' Athli said. 'But you haven't told *us*. Which means that everybody's rushing around in a panic, not knowing what's going on. You know what Eseutz Mesatges did when she heard the news? She went out and bought up fifteen crates of swords and a dozen barrels of armour parts, on the basis that when all the swords and armour are confiscated, the government's going to have to pay compensation, and she's figuring that the difference between market value and assessed value's going to be a substantial profit. You can't let people carry on like that, there'll be chaos.'

Venart blinked, then said, 'I'm not responsible for the way people like your friend Eseutz choose to behave. I just want to keep the lid on things till we've had a chance to lick these bloody terms and conditions into shape; and I don't want to do that yet, for obvious reasons.'

'Obvious to you perhaps,' Vetriz said. 'Enlighten me.'

'Simple.' Venart put the parchment down, and it rolled

451

itself back up into a tube. 'If I can spin things out till Bardas Loredan finishes with Temrai, then we'll be talking to him and not some devious bastard of a Son of Heaven. Well? Can you think of a better way of handling it, because if so I'd love to hear it. Playing diplomatic chess with these people is way above my head, but unless we can put up some sort of a show, we're in deep, deep trouble. Or didn't you read that extradition clause?'

Neither Vetriz nor Athli seemed to have anything to say; the name Bardas Loredan had somehow put them off their stride.

'I'll take that as agreement then, shall I?' Venart said. 'Although since when I had to get your approval for acts of state I'm not entirely sure. It's bad enough trying to keep Votz and that lunatic from the Guild off the premises without you two ganging up on me as well.'

Athli seemed to pull herself back from an entirely different train of thought. 'All right,' she said. 'But really, Ven, trying to win a cleverness match with the provincial office isn't very – well, clever. You're playing on their side of the court.'

Venart nodded. 'Yes,' he said, 'but at least I know that. Remember what Father used to tell us, Triz? Properly handled, the other man's strength can be his greatest weakness? They know perfectly well they've got me completely muddled and confused; what I've got to do is find a way of staying muddled and confused long enough for Bardas Loredan to win his damned war. Look at it from that perspective, and I think you'll see what I mean.'

Athli stood up. 'I hope you know what you're doing,' she said. 'Remember, this is politics, not a sardine deal.'

Venart groaned. 'I know,' he said. 'And I'm well aware that I'm out of my depth, haven't got a clue what I'm doing and shouldn't be trusted with running a whelk stall, let alone a government. Just because something's true doesn't always mean it's helpful.'

Athli put a hand on his shoulder, then walked out across the courtyard to the small room she was using as an office. Not that there was much to do; business was at a standstill, she had no means of communicating with head office in Shastel, and nothing to tell them even if she had been able to get a message through. It was all rather depressing;

everything she'd achieved by luck, hard work and native ability had somehow managed to melt and drip out between her fingers.

Maybe— People were leaving the Island, she knew that. At first they'd been circumspect about it; they'd announced their intentions of going off to buy food, loaded everything they could aboard their ships, slipped out of the Drutz in the early morning and not come back. Now they weren't even bothering to lie. Looked at from a more rational perspective, it was remarkable that so few, relatively speaking, had done the sensible thing – of course it had been the same in Perimadeia, except that only a few hopeless pessimists had really believed the City would fall. She'd been one of them; and now it was time to go again, without shame or regret, taking with her any of her friends who chose to come with her, as calmly and sensibly as (say) Niessa Loredan abandoning Scona ...

It was true to say (she decided, reviewing the facts like a historian) that once upon a time she'd cared about Bardas Loredan; cared a lot. Loved? Sloppy, imprecise term. She'd worked with him, done what she could to keep him in one piece when the horrors of his trade started to get to him, been there for him, worried herself sick every time he'd stepped out on to the courtroom floor but never once shown it – always so confident that she knew and understood him, the way nobody else did. Now it was true to say that she didn't love him, although that didn't stop her thinking about him all the time – but that had been then and there, this was now and here, and she'd carried his luck this far, to this conclusion. She'd always known, somehow, that as long as she cared for him he would survive. It was as if she'd been keeping his life safe for him, in a stout steel-banded locked wooden box, while his body went out and did violent, irrevocable things to the world. After all, she was a banker; he'd deposited his life, his luck with her, made it her responsibility. She'd carried it safely out of Perimadeia, guarded it for him while he tried to make something of his life on Scona, been entrusted with his apprentice and his sword; she'd taken it from him again when he'd lost his last hopes and dreams in the Mesoge, and sent her away. Well; and now he was coming to the Island, where she'd set up in business on her own account as a taker of deposits and creator of opportunities. Time to hand it back, to render her accounts and be discharged; to leave it for him here, in the condition he would expect to find it, paid up, balanced and signed off, and then to go away.

Some clients are more trouble than they're worth.

Which only left the question: what should she take with her? To which question, the answer was simple. Her writing-desk and counting-board, a few changes of clothes, a small case of books and all the ready cash she could put together in the time available.

Vetriz soon got bored watching her brother fretting over his paperwork and went to her room.

It was a nice room. She had a comfortable bed, a rather grand and melodramatic chair with big carved arms and legs, a rosewood dressing table inlaid with lapis and mother of pearl (she'd bought it in Colleon and made Venart find space for it on the ship, much to his disgust; it meant throwing a whole barrel of sun-dried herrings over the side to make room), an ivory and brass mirror that gave her skin a wonderfully flattering golden tone, three chests full of clothes, a silver lamp on a turned sycamore stand that was as tall as she was, a rack for her seven pairs of shoes, a book-box, with padlock, a small stool with an embroidered seat, two genuine Shastel tapestries (one of them thought to be a School-of-Mavaut, but the other one was much nicer to look at), a writing desk and a chequer-board that doubled as a chessboard, with a set of attractively carved chessmen (horn and bone), an embossed brass water jug all the way from Ap' Elipha (a present from her father when she was six and really wanted a doll's house) – all nice things, solid things to define her life with. She had a polished marble floor (cold underfoot on winter mornings but beautifully cool in summer; sometimes she slept on it when it was really hot) and a view over the courtyard.

And that was about it.

She lay down on the bed. There was a headache gathering behind her eyes which a short nap might dissipate. She snuggled her head into the pillow and –

– 'Hello,' she said. 'I didn't expect to see you so soon.'

'I'm not here yet,' he replied.

'Ah.' She looked at him carefully. He looked older – well, that was only to be expected, he *was* older – but otherwise pretty much the same. For some reason he was dressed as a fencer, the way he'd been when she first set eyes on him in the courtroom in Perimadeia; in fact, that's exactly where he was, standing in the middle of the black and white tiled floor, like a counter on a counting-board, a reckoning piece. She wondered how much he stood for.

'How are things with you, anyway?' he asked.

'Oh, not so bad,' she replied automatically. She realised that she was standing in the middle too; she was standing a sword's length away from him, and the needle-sharp point of his vintage Spe Bref law-sword was just under her chin. If the black lines are whole units, she thought idly, then I'm a ten and he's only a five. No, that can't be right. 'What's going on?' she asked.

'A trial,' he replied; and they were standing on opposite sides of a workbench, in a dark, rather damp-smelling thatched workshop. On the bench between them was a bow – what they called a composite, if she'd got that right, the sort that's made out of sinew and horn and bone and things like that, held together with glue boiled down from skin and blood. It was fixed in some sort of wooden clamp, with a notched bar set in the middle at right angles.

'It's called a tiller,' he explained. 'It's for applying stress and tension. Now then, let's see how far this beggar'll bend before it breaks.'

– And they were in a cellar, with a high ceiling and stone floors, standing beside a pile of pieces of armour, body parts. 'A trial,' he went on, 'which is another way of saying, a putting to proof.' Gently, almost tenderly, he took her hand in his and laid it softly on the anvil. 'This may sting a bit,' he warned her, as he raised the big hammer.

'Just a moment,' she interrupted him. 'I'm sure this is all quite important and necessary, but why me?'

He smiled. 'How should I know?' he replied. 'I only work here; you want to ask the Sons of Heaven, they probably know.'

That struck her as odd. 'What've they got to do with it?' she asked. 'I mean, they weren't there in the beginning.'

He frowned. 'True,' he said. 'Hold this for me, would you? It's important you keep it steady.' He turned her hand over and put into her palm a head, a young man's head, about her age. 'King Temrai,' he explained. 'He's the plaintiff.'

'Really? And you're for the defendant, I suppose.'

He frowned. 'I'm not sure any more,' he replied. 'Still, that's all out of my hands now, thank goodness.' He brought the hammer down, using his back and shoulders to get the maximum force. The head rang, as clear and crisp as an anvil. 'Oh, well,' he said. 'All right, we'll pass that. Now let's see.' He reached down behind the anvil and produced another head. 'Of course,' he added, 'you know him, don't you?'

She nodded, as he put Gorgas Loredan's head on to the palm of her hand. 'He takes after our father,' he was saying. 'I took after mother. They say I've got her nose.'

Under the hammerfall the head split and disintegrated, like a rotten log; but he'd been slightly off his aim and knocked the head off the hammer. 'Decapitated the blasted thing,' he said irritably. 'Not to worry, though. I have a spare.'

– And drew his sword, the beautiful antique Guelan broadsword that Athli had kept for him for a time. Vetriz could feel the needle-sharp point just pricking the middle of her neck. 'Well, go on, then,' he said; and she was aware that everybody in the courtroom was staring at her, all the thousands of people packed into the spectators' galleries – plainsmen, Perimadeians, Scona, Shastel, people from Ap' Escatoy, Islanders who he'd killed over the years, all come to watch him fight. She could see herself, and Ven, up in the back gallery where they'd been sitting all those years ago. She felt the urge to wave to herself, but didn't.

'What do you want me to do?' she asked.

'How should I know?' he replied. 'You're the plaintiff.'

She shook her head and felt the sword-point nick her. 'I don't see why,' she said. 'In fact, I really don't see why I got mixed up in all this in the first place. Is it just because I can – well, see all this stuff, which other people can't? I know Alexius thought I was somehow making things happen, but—'

'You don't want to believe in all that Principle stuff,' he replied. 'If you ask me, that's making it unnecessarily complicated. You ask Gannadius, next time you see him. No, it's a question of cause; we can leave the blame and guilt out of it too, that's just lubricant. What I really want to know is, did I start it, or was it him?'

'Him?'

'Gorgas.' He lowered the sword and laid it on the anvil, next to the bow. 'Let's go through it step by step. If Gorgas hadn't killed my father, would I have left home when I did, joined up with Uncle Maxen and caused the fall of Perimadeia? (We'll leave all the other cities out of it for now – Scona, Ap' Escatoy, the Island, that pretty little model Perimadeia Temrai's built himself; they all follow on). If Gorgas hadn't done what he did, would we both still be back on the farm, mending gates and ploughing the six-acre? Or would I have left anyway? Surely that's what it all comes down to. That's probably the most important question in all history.'

She nodded. 'If Gorgas caused it, then it's his fault—'

'Not fault,' he interrupted. 'I used to think fault, but since I've been in with these people,' (he nodded towards the Sons of Heaven in their reserved seats in the front row), 'I only think cause. If Gorgas started it, then he's the cause. If I started it, then I am. What do you think?'

'I don't know,' Vetriz admitted. 'Sorry.'

'Personally, I think it was him,' he said. 'Stands to reason; he's the doer in our family, the one with the drive and the energy. On the other hand, I'm the one who brings about the consequences of his actions. Now if there really was such a thing as the Principle, that'd make sense.'

She looked at him. 'What's going to happen?' she asked.

'You don't need me to tell you that,' he said, and vanished into her pillow.

She sat up sharply and opened her eyes. She felt very uncomfortable. It was like the time she'd allowed Gorgas Loredan into her room; there was the same sense of it not being hers any more. If there was any sense to be made of it, perhaps that was where she should look; except that she couldn't see how her *mistake* with Gorgas Loredan had caused anything or made anything happen. She thought about Niessa Loredan, who'd reckoned that she could control the Principle with the help of a natural or two, and had scooped her up and tucked her away in Scona for a while. Nothing much ever seemed to have come of that. She had the feeling that he'd been right, and the Principle was nothing but a folk-tale explanation, like the far-fetched reasons you hear in stories for why the sun rises in the east, or why the moon wanes. If there really was such a thing, it was like a big machine, something like the huge rolling-mill she'd been to see in the City the first time they'd gone there, a huge, slowly turning roller that dragged in the blooms of iron, flattened them into plate and fed them out the other side; and if you weren't careful, if you leaned over the rollers, your sleeve could catch and you'd be pulled in too.

And that wasn't right, either, far too simplistic.

She got up, realising as she did so that her left foot had gone to sleep, and stumbled to the dressing table. Her face in the mirror was soft and golden, like a fond and unreliable memory.

Late in the afternoon, Bardas Loredan had a visitor. Once the stranger had convinced Bardas that he was who he claimed to be, they sat and talked in Bardas' tent for over an hour.

'You don't seem surprised,' the visitor said, after they'd talked business.

'I'm not,' Bardas replied. 'Which is odd, because I should be. But no, this seems to me to be a perfectly reasonable development.'

'Really? Well, that's your business, not mine. Anyway, you're happy with the timetable?'

Bardas nodded. 'Entirely. If I were to ask you why you're doing this, would you tell me?'

'No.'

The visitor left, and Bardas made his preparations. He called a staff meeting, explained the situation, ignored the protests and issued his orders. Then he went back to his tent.

Leaning against the bed, still in its oiled buckskin case, was the Guelan broadsword, the one Gorgas had left for him as a present, just before Perimadeia fell. Now Perimadeia fell because Gorgas opened the gates; but that didn't alter the fact that the Guelan was still a good sword (shorter in the blade than most two-handers, with a heavy pommel and the best balance he'd ever come across). He untied the strings and pulled it out of the case.

If anything, it felt lighter in his hands than ever; possibly because three years of digging in the mines had strengthened his arms and wrists, and he'd got used to the top-heavy Imperial glaives, halberds and bardiches for two-handed work. He tested the edge with his thumb, and closed his eyes.

Some time later, he put on his armour (he no longer noticed the weight), pushed the Guelan down into the belt-frog and secured it with the buckle. Then he sat for an hour in the darkness, expecting to hear voices that for once were silent; but from somewhere in the camp came the smell of garlic and coriander, flavourings often used by cooks to mask the taste of tainted meat.

(At the same moment, on the other side of the stockade, Temrai held out his plate; and a man laid on it a thin white pancake filled with spiced meat, and smiled, and went back to slicing meat with a long, thin-bladed knife.)

They came for him when it was time. As he'd ordered, the pikemen and halberdiers had smeared mud on their weapons and armour, in case the steel glittered in the starlight. He hadn't needed to obey his own order; the armour Anax the Son of Heaven had made for him was lightly browned with rust and didn't catch the light any more. Once they marched outside the circle of their own firelight it was too dark to see, but by now they knew the way with their eyes closed.

(Temrai finished his meal, got up and wandered across to the warm glow of the welding-fires, where his armourers were repairing damaged mailshirts. First they heated the new rings to a dull red, then flattened the ends, punched little holes in them, knitted them into place, closed them up with the tongs, pushed in a rivet and hammered it round over a sett. It was the warmest place in the fortress now that the nights were getting cold. There wasn't much skill in the job, not to someone who'd once earned his living making sword blades in the state arsenal of Perimadeia; the steel simply went from dull grey to blood-red. But he stood for a while watching them, not thinking of anything much – one thought that did occur to him was how convenient it would be if skin and flesh could be mended as easily as armour, by heating, softening and bashing, but it wasn't an idea worth following through.)

The swing-bridge was tied back and guarded by sentries; but in the dark Bardas' men swam across the river without making a sound (after a while it gets easy, finding your way in the dark) and cut their throats, working by feel and smell. Bardas hoped that they thanked them afterwards. Then they swung out the bridge, careful and quiet.

(Temrai went back to his tent, where Lempecai the bowyer was waiting for him; he'd glued another layer of sinew on the back of Temrai's bow to stiffen it a little more, pull it back into tiller. The glue had taken its own sweet time drying, as it always did, but it had been worth the wait. Temrai drew the bow, observing that it seemed to take less effort to draw it even though it had been made stronger, and complimented Lempecai on his work.)

Bardas led the first company over the bridge himself. It wasn't vainglory or pride that made him want to be the first man inside the fortress, more a sense of continuity, given that he and Theudas (who was beside him, in a borrowed helmet and jack-of-plates that were both a little on the small side) had been the last Perimadeians to leave the City. He'd prepared himself for the tension of waiting; but he'd scarcely set foot on the shore when a slit of light, thin and pointed as the blade of a jointing-knife, appeared down the side of the gate. He closed his eyes against the glare –

(*Bardas Loredan, Sacker of Cities.*)

– and when he opened them again, the gate was open too. He dipped his head as a sign to the men behind him, and walked into the fortress.

'As promised,' said the man standing beside the door.

'Thank you.'

'You're welcome.'

It wasn't long before the alarm was raised, but by then Bardas was leading three companies of halberdiers up the path, while the rest of the army poured in and filled up the lower level of the fortress. The plainsmen there were caught entirely by surprise – someone had taken care of the sentries on the gate – and didn't know what to do. Some of them ran towards the weapons stacks, others ran in the opposite direction, but the line of soiled black spearheads herded them like sheep, and they had no armour.

Bardas' men had made it to the top of the path unopposed by the time the shouts and screams from below attracted attention. They knew what to do and where to go; one company toward the main encampment, the other two round the sides, following the stockade, to push back the enemy as they ran. As they broke into the firelight the enemy lashed out at them, like a wave breaking on rocks and falling back.

As was only appropriate, Bardas Loredan was the first man to draw blood. His opponent was a long, thin man, wearing nothing but a helmet and waving a scimitar as if it was a charm against witchcraft. First, Bardas took off the hand holding the sword; then he rolled his wrists and brought the Guelan back for a rather showy cut across the side of the neck. The man staggered and fell over backwards, and Bardas thanked him. The next man he killed came at him with a spear and the lid of a kettle. Bardas feinted high and swept low, feeling the shock as his sword jarred on the man's shin, then drew the sword through and thrust into the ribcage. A slight twist freed it, and he was ready for the next man, who bounced a scimitar off Bardas' left pauldron before the Guelan sheared through his neck and collar-bone. The man dropped and Bardas stepped over him, muttering perfunctory thanks as he sized up the next one, a boy with a looted Imperial halberd. Bardas knew enough to respect the weapon no matter who was behind it; he watched the blade while taking a couple of short sideways steps, then lunged at the boy's heart through the crook of his elbow. He thanked him as he slid off the blade on to the ground, then ducked his head a little to the right to avoid a swing from a big hammer in the hands of a heavily built bald man who looked like a blacksmith. He watched the swing go astray, exposing the man's armpit (*the way to a man's heart is through his armpit*) but instead of lowering the sword to let the body slide off, he jerked it sharply to the right, so that it impeded the man with the long-handled axe who was next in the pile waiting for proof. Startled, the man pulled his blow and so threw himself out of position. Leaning back, Bardas swung a short cut that slit open his stomach; while he was frozen with terror and pain, Bardas put him down with a head-shot that split his skull, and thanked him.

They were loosing arrows now, close enough to test Imperial plate. But Bardas had anticipated that; on top of the plateau, hedged around by the stockade, cluttered with tents and dead men, there wasn't the room for hit-and-run tactics. He signalled the charge and his halberdiers pressed home; some of them fell, but not enough to throw out the accounts. The first archer Bardas killed held up his bow to block the thrust; the Guelan bounced off the sinewed back but Bardas turned the blade and guided it down across the man's knees, leaving his head at a convenient height. An arrow punched through his right vambrace but stopped before it reached his skin. He paused to jerk it out, then held out his sword for a man to run on to, the way he used to hold the dustpan ready for the brush when sweeping the shavings off his workbench. The next man had drawn his scimitar and was holding it in a semblance of a guard, but Bardas was too many years past fencing to bother with that sort of thing and swung down directly on the top of his head, crushing the helmet and driving him to his knees; then he kicked him in the face and finished him off with the point. *Victory to Bollo and the big hammer*, he thought as his lips shaped the words of thanks, and then he was ready for the next man, and the next, and the one after that.

Then he saw Temrai, huddled in a small crowd of half-dressed men; he'd jammed on a helmet and a pair of knee-cops, but the cop-straps weren't tight enough and they were sliding down his legs. Bardas smiled and walked towards them, but before he could start work someone ran past him, a tall man in a helmet and jack-of-plates, swinging a halberd and yelling at the top of his voice.

'Theudas,' he called out, but the boy wasn't listening; he ran straight at Temrai like an arrow, and when one of the men lunged at him with a spear, he didn't notice he'd been hit until he stopped moving, wedged up against the spear's cross-bar. He tried to turn and slash at the spearman, but the spear-shaft was too long and he couldn't quite reach, though he tried twice before he fell down. One of the other men jabbed him through the ear – the helmet had fallen off, being too small for him – and he stopped moving.

That's not right, Bardas thought, and he tried to open his eyes, but they were already open.

Temrai's party was backing away, trying to get deeper into the encampment, where there were more bodies to put between their King and the Guelan. Bardas followed them for a few yards, until something that had been chafing at the back of his mind became clear. There were, he realised, fewer people here than he'd have expected to find. Wasn't this supposed to be the entire plains nation, every last one of them? True, it was dark; but he hadn't seen more than a few hundred men –

He understood. *Very clever*, he thought. *But I should have seen it coming.*

By then it was too late. Someone down below gave some kind of signal, and the plains army broke out of cover, from tents and wagons, from supply pits and trenches; they had spears and halberds (copied from the Imperial pattern, the sincerest form of flattery) and they kept together in dense formation, pushing the Imperials away from the path and any prospect of escape. As the last of the decoys scampered out of the way (had they known that it was a trap and they were the bait? Bardas wondered; if it had been my plan, I wouldn't have told them), the lines wheeled and extended – Imperial drill-sergeants couldn't have done much better – to complete the encirclement. Meanwhile, reinforcements were coming up the path, led by Iordecai, the man who'd so helpfully opened the gates ... That didn't bode well; it implied that the pikemen who'd poured into the lower level had been driven off or killed. *Me and my sense of historical symmetry*, Bardas thought ruefully, *looks like I'm going to get what I wished for.* His wrists and forearms ached from the strain of handling the sword, all the jarring shock travelling down the blade from bone to bone (in a sense, the armour serves to prove the hammer) and the sweat, dripping down his forehead under the bevor of his helmet, was getting in his eyes. He closed them – *Now what do I do?* – but there was nobody home. From an abandoned cooking-fire nearby came the smell of coriander.

*

I hadn't thought it'd be as bad as this, Temrai thought, as they hustled him away. *I thought winning might be enough. But just knowing he's there –*

He forced himself to dismiss the image from his mind; Bardas Loredan walking towards him, armed. He wasn't sure how he'd known who it was – a man in armour, with his bevor up; but he'd known all right. It was all he could do to keep from wetting himself.

'Where's Sildocai?' he asked.

'With the reserve,' somebody answered. 'Iordecai's bringing up the main attack. Once we commit the reserve, it'll be the hammer and the anvil.'

Whatever, Temrai thought. His mind didn't seem able to hold on to a coherent train of thought; it slipped off, like a chisel point on tool steel. 'That's good,' he said. 'What about the lower level? Any word from Gollocai and his people?'

'Last I heard, it was all under control.' He couldn't see who was talking to him, and he couldn't recognise the voice. 'The rest of the army's fallen back on the camp, and there's absolutely no way this lot are going anywhere. It's only a matter of time now.'

Temrai shivered. 'Make it as quick as you can,' he said. 'And whatever else you do, make sure you get *him*, understood?'

'Sure. Alive?'

'Good gods, no. As dead as possible. I want to know his head's been cut off before I go anywhere near him.'

Someone laughed, assuming Temrai had meant it as a joke.

'By the way,' someone else said. 'That kid who made the suicide run just now; you know who that was?' Nobody said anything, and the voice continued, 'I recognised him; it was Loredan's nephew. You know, the one who showed up a while back with the wizard.'

'He wasn't Loredan's nephew,' someone else pointed out. 'I don't think they were related at all, actually.'

'Theudas Morosin,' Temrai said.

'That's him. Anyway, that was him.'

'Fine,' Temrai said. 'Now get me out of here.

The line of spearpoints crowded in close, probing and groping for the joints and gaps in the Imperials' armour – the inside of the elbow joint, the gap between breastplate and gorget, gorget and helmet, the inside of the thigh, the armpit. For their part, the halberdiers were fighting hard (the anvil proves the hammer), crushing helmets and smashing bones and blood vessels under the proof skin of mail. But the line had momentum, impetus; and as they advanced over the dead and fallen, like the sea washing round rocks on the seashore, the axemen and hammermen cracked open helmets and armour like thrushes knocking open snails, or a man at a good dinner-party prising open oysters. If Anax had been alive to hear them he could have told the story of the battle from the sounds alone; the clear ringing of the blade on sound armour, the duller clack on compromised armour, the wet crunch when there was no armour left. The battle was mostly in the dark now; Bardas' men fought with their backs to the camp-fires, masking the light. There wasn't much need to see when the enemy was all around, precisely a spear-length away.

As the enemy closed around him like a gallery collapsing, Bardas swung and cut to dig himself out. His helmet was long gone, the rivets of his gorget and pauldrons cut through by deflected axe-blows glancing off the convex surfaces, so that the plates sagged from the points and straps like overripe fruit bending the branches of a tree. His right gauntlet had become so distorted with the shock of the blows he delivered that its lames had bent and jammed, so he'd discarded it at the first opportunity. Behind him and on either side the bodies and parts of bodies fell; he was carving and jointing, as skilful and quick with his blade as a cook preparing for a banquet, and the blows of his enemies planished his steel skin. It was almost like old times, fighting in the dark; this was dull, hard work, like kicking clay, the cutting out of waste and spoil from the wall in front of him. The sounds and smells, though, were so rich and varied that they bewildered him, a banquet for the senses; sweet blood and piquant steel, heady sweat, garlic and coriander on the last breath of a man falling across him, and all the Imperial music of the proof house.

There was a man who was wearing an old-fashioned four-panel helmet, crossed with straps; having parried his spear, Bardas took the obvious shot, an over-the-shoulder cut to the man's temples. But the noise as the man dropped was wrong, there was a tiny flaw in the crisp ring of the Guelan. He noticed it, but then he had to step across and parry a halberd-cut, which left an opening across the side of a captured Imperial kettle-hat. He made the blow, and the sword snapped in two, a handspan and a half up from the quillons. *Not again*, he thought, as he dropped the hilt; then a man came at him with a spear, and he had nothing to parry the blow with. Instead he turned sideways, using the contour of his breastplate to deflect the blow, reached out with his left hand and drove his gauntleted fist into the man's face. He saw blood well up along the lines scored by the edges of the lames, straight as a well-ploughed field (Clefas was best at ploughing, but lazy; Gorgas was almost as good, and always willing to do his share) but the man didn't drop; he drew the spear back for another lunge, which would've gone home if Bardas hadn't managed to grab the spearhead around the socket and pull it clear. He tried to hold on, but the man jerked back hard, drawing the sharp edges of the spearblade across Bardas' palm and the base of his fingers –

(*Well; there's no such thing as proof, just an infinite variety of ways of failing.*)

He let go, and just had time to stamp on the man's knee-cap. Down he went this time, and all Bardas could do was grind his heel in the man's face, there simply wasn't time to pick up the spear and do a proper job. There were more of them pressing in on him, and he was unarmed. A pity; he'd dug three-quarters of the way through the enemy line, the seam, to the point where he could see still darkness above the moving shadows. Without something to fight with, however, he was only an anvil. He backed away until he could turn round, and started to run –

Which wasn't as easy as it should have been. His greaves and cuisses were mangled and jammed, and the hinge-pin of his left knee-cop was curved so wide that he knew he'd have to cut the thing off piecemeal, if ever he got out of this. Even without the armour, he wouldn't have got far before tripping and falling.

He landed badly, cracking the side of his head. When he opened his eyes again, he saw what he'd fallen against – a supply wagon with a high bed and not much in the way of suspension. He knew without needing to prove the matter that he wasn't going to be able to pull himself upright for a while, so he flattened himself on his belly and crawled painfully under the cart.

He was so tired he shut his eyes for a moment –

– And he was back in the mines, as usual; but he could see (it was pitch dark) an abandoned dolly-truck; and underneath it, staring up at him with all the fear there ever had been, was a boy's face. Sure enough it was Temrai who was staring at him, but it was also Theudas, whom he'd pulled out from under a cart during the Fall. *Why are you frightened of me, Theudas?* he asked, but the boy didn't move or say a word –

– 'There he is.' Bardas' eyes snapped open; and there, across twenty yards or so of the battle, was Temrai's face again. 'Over there,' Temrai was screaming, 'under the wagon, see? Kill him, for gods' sakes. Kill him now!'

They came for him; three plainsmen with pikes and scimitars, men of Temrai's personal guard. When they were right up close to the cart, fishing for him under the bed with their spears like a man trying to reach a coin that's rolled under a table, he convulsed away; a spear-blade stroked his cheek, slitting the skin, as he shuffled backwards (he'd learned how to do it in the mines) and then he was out the other side, with the cart between him and them. He pulled himself up against the cart's rear wheel and started to run. When he looked over his shoulder he could see them clambering over the cart, following him up with a degree of professional zeal that he'd not come across since Maxen's war, when the young man who'd eventually grown into this snake's second skin had followed up a group of running plainsmen into the dire and noisy nightmare of the dark, while all around the firelight roared and smelled at him like the gatekeepers of paradise.

Time to do something clever. He slowed right down, waited till the first of his pursuers was almost on top of him, then dropped down into a crouch. The plainsman crashed into him and went tumbling over his shoulder in a tange of arms and legs, as Bardas stood up and smacked the second man smartly across the face with his remaining gauntlet. He could feel the man's nose crack, the failure of the bone transmitted

467

to his own bones through the steel; the look on the poor man's face was priceless, a sort of dumbstruck horror. Then he took away the man's scimitar and chopped open his neck with it.

Now that he had a weapon again, he wasn't bothered about the third man, whose pike he parried in a preoccupied sort of way before slashing off his left ear and bringing the scimitar back horizontal to cut his throat. It wasn't a class of weapon he was terribly familiar with – the curved blade wasn't meant for thrusting, the hilt was too small for his hand and the large flat pommel chafed his wrist – but it had all sorts of advantages over nothing at all. He took half a second to decide what to do, then headed back towards Temrai at a comfortable trot.

A couple of optimists got in his way, but not for very long. Temrai looked as if he'd taken root; even in the red glow of the camp-fires, his face was as pale as death and his eyes were wide open, like a rabbit's. Bardas was only a few yards away by now; a guardsman blunted a scimitar on his left rerebrace and earned his thanks, leaving only two men between him and the enemy king. Of course, killing Temrai wouldn't solve anything (it'd probably win the war, but that was the last thing on his mind) but at least he'd restore the symmetry of the situation a bit. He had nothing better to do. A high right parry, wrist turned, blade down, followed by a flicked cut just under the chin; that was one less. *Thank you*, he muttered; and then he saw something that made him forget all about Temrai, the war and patterns in history. He saw a gap.

It was only a very little gap, between the tail end of one line and the front of another, and it was closing fast; but if he was very quick, he might just be able to slip through and get down the path without having to fight for every step.

'After him,' someone was screaming (Temrai, probably). An arrow glanced off his left elbow-cop and jagged sideways into the advancing line. He nearly lost his balance twice – once when he trod on a dead man's head he hadn't noticed was there, once when he stumbled on the lip of a trebuchet-shot crater – but the weight of his armour gave him so much momentum that he was able to correct the errors and keep going, almost bouncing off the ground (like a hammer on an anvil). In the event, he had to push one man out of his way and carve a chunk off the shoulder of another, but he made it. He was on the path –

– Which was, of course, in a deplorable state after days on end of constant bombardment. The crumbling dirt gave way under his weight and suddenly he was sliding on his backside down the slope. He managed to slow himself down by digging into the piled-up spoil with his heels before he veered off the verge and over the drop, and used the momentum to bounce himself back on to his feet and on to the path. After that he took it rather more slowly; his pursuers were doing the same, so it didn't matter much. He crashed into one fool of a plainsman who didn't get out of the way in time, sending him sprawling over the edge. *Clumsy*, he thought, as he wobbled himself back upright. *A menace to traffic, that's what I am.*

At the bottom of the path there was a confused mess of bodies, like sandbags piled up to keep the rainwater out of the house; he had to stop and lift his legs over with his hand. That gave the two men chasing him time to catch up, an opportunity they didn't live long enough to regret. They were still fighting down in the lower circle. There were too many bodies lying about to allow for organised manoeuvres (it reminded Bardas of the parts of the plains where the tussocks of couch-grass made it nearly impossible to walk) and the combatants were picking their way through the litter towards each other and then trading blows from a standstill. The gate, of course, was shut and barred; but he could see a clear path to the ramp that led up to the catwalk running around the inside of the stockade. He shuffled his way towards it, fending off a few half-hearted attacks, and dragged himself wearily up the ramp. He couldn't see anybody else up there with him, so he leaned the scimitar against the log wall and set about unbuckling his armour.

A full set of plate is far easier to get out of than into, and where a buckle was jammed or twisted, he simply cut the strap. He'd just discarded the breastplate and was sawing through the vambrace hanger when he heard shouts not far away. There were a dozen plainsmen on the ramp, pointing at him and yelling to another group threading their way through the battle. Bardas swore under his breath and carried on sawing, cutting himself as the blade slid off a rivet. By the time they reached him he was free of all his burdens.

They stopped abruptly and stared at him down the length of their spears. He could almost taste the fear they brought with them, and he was sure that if he'd clapped his hands and shouted, at least two of them would have run away. He didn't blame them; in the middle of what was possibly the greatest victory in their nation's history, they'd been detailed to chase after defeat, humiliation and certain death. 'It's all right,' he called out cheerfully, 'I'm not stopping,' then he jumped up from a standstill, got his fingers over the edge of the stockade, hauled himself up and sat astride the fence for a moment before swinging his leg over and pushing off. He landed in the river in a sitting position and hit the water with a comically loud splash and a great plume of spray.

Shock and exhaustion caught up with him halfway between the fortress and the camp, and he dropped down in the dirt, unable to move. The extreme elation he'd felt at getting out of the trap was wearing thin. All he could think about was the weight of his legs and the pain in his knees. He lay still for half an hour, his eyes shut (if anybody stumbled over him they'd assume he was dead). There was nothing to see behind his eyelids any more, and nothing existed outside his painful, overworked body.

Then it began to rain, and when he was soaked to the skin and hardly able to see for the water running down his forehead and into his eyes, it occurred to him that there were tents back at the camp, and rather more comfortable places to rest. Standing up proved to be a major operation, involving the co-ordination of a number of complex manoeuvres that his body no longer seemed capable of. Because the rain was particularly wet and cold, however, he found a way to pull things together, and limped back to the camp dragging his left foot, which had suddenly decided that it had got itself sprained at some unspecified stage.

The bed looked wonderfully comfortable but it was too far away, so he dropped into his chair and let his head roll forward on to his chest. Nobody seemed to have noticed that he was back, which was a relief; there would be an unendurable amount of work to be done (and no Theudas to help him) and he couldn't face doing it now. He closed his eyes, glad of the dark, but the ache in his muscles and joints was far too dominant in his mind to allow him to fall asleep. Nonetheless he was just starting to slip away into an intermediate doze when he felt something pricking the back of his neck. It might have been a thorn, or a sliver of steel from his mangled armour, but he didn't think so. 'Hello?' he said.

'Hello yourself.'

The voice was familiar. 'Who is it?' he asked.

'Me. Iseutz Hedin, Niessa's daughter. Remember me?'

'Of course,' Bardas replied without moving. 'How did you get here?'

'The usual way, by ship,' she replied. 'We had the wind behind us all the way, which made for a quick but exciting trip. But I can see you're not really interested, so I'll kill you and be done with it.'

'Hang on a minute,' Bardas said, and the fear made him slur his words slightly, the way a man does when he's not drunk but not sober either. 'I can't remember, did we ever talk about this? I'd like to know why you hate me so much.'

'Easy. You ruined my life.'

'All right,' Bardas said, 'but it was a fair fight, you'd have killed me if I hadn't—'

'I'm not talking about that,' Iseutz interrupted. 'Sure, cutting off my fingers didn't exactly make me love you, but as you say, it was a fair fight; that's not the reason, as well you know.'

Bardas could feel his hands aching, weak with both exertion and terror. 'So you're still angry with me because I killed your uncle—' He couldn't remember the man's name. Something Hedin. Tactless to betray the fact he'd forgotten it. 'Really? After all this time?'

'Yes.'

'Oh. But that was a fair fight too; come on, you were a law-fencer yourself for a while. Really, I don't see the difference.'

He heard Iseutz breathe out through her nose (all terribly familiar, this; knives in the dark, not being able to see the enemy, having to rely on sounds and smells – and yes, she'd recently eaten something flavoured with coriander). 'You don't,' she said. 'I'm not surprised. You should try listening to people when they tell you things. I said I'm going to kill you because you ruined my life. And you did.'

One thing about fear he'd forgotten: the way it saturates everything else in your mind, like lamp-oil spilt on a pile of papers. 'But really, that doesn't follow,' he said. 'The City would still have fallen whether I'd killed him or not; your life would still have been messed up. Dammit, if you want to play logic games, try this: if I hadn't killed your uncle, would you have been in that alleyway the night the City fell? Because if the answer's no, you'd have been killed. I *saved* your bloody life, remember? Doesn't that count for anything?'

'You didn't do me any favours.'

The fear was getting worse, not better. There are hysterical women with knives who say they're going to kill you and then talk at you instead; they don't inspire fear in the hearts of men who can carve a path through an enemy army while thinking about something else. But he was definitely scared of Iseutz, almost to the point of speechlessness and loss of bladder control. After all, she was his niece; if there was anything in heredity, he was in serious trouble.

'You've lost me,' he said. 'Why don't you explain, instead of making me guess?'

'All right, I'll explain.' She was leaning on the knife a little harder. 'It's quite simple, really. You made me into *this*.' (Listen to the disgust she managed to load into that one little word.) 'You made me what I am today, Uncle Bardas. I'll say this for you, you're a hell of a craftsman. You made my cousin Luha into a bow, and you've made me into another sort of weapon, you made me into a Loredan. Thank you *very* much.'

Bardas' mouth was full of something that tasted foul. He swallowed it. 'Be fair,' he said. 'Your mother did that, not me.'

'Oh, she started it, which is why she's definitely not a good insurance risk. But I got away from her, I was going to be a Hedin instead, until you interfered. That's why I'm going to kill you.'

'I see,' Bardas said. 'And won't killing me just make you more of what you don't want to be?'

'No,' Iseutz said. 'Loredans don't kill family. Uncle Gorgas, now; you murdered his son and he forgave you. You had a chance to kill me, but you didn't. Mother could've had me put down any time she chose, but she didn't. It's not our way.' She laughed. 'The more I think about it, the more I get the impression I'll be doing you a kindness. Come on, Uncle Bardas, what possible reason could you have for wanting to stay alive? If I'd done half the things you've done, I'd die of exhaustion through never being able to sleep. Your life must be really horrible; I mean, mine's bad enough and I've hardly even started.'

'What a thing to say,' Bardas replied. 'Consequences aside, I can't think of a single thing I've done that I didn't do for the best.'

'That wasn't a very sensible thing to say, in the circumstances.'

'Really?' Bardas was just about able to keep himself from shaking like a dog that's just climbed out of a pond, but it was hard work. 'I don't think so. You aren't really going to kill me. If you were I'd be dead by now.'

'You reckon?' Iseutz said, and jammed the knife home.

Later, Bardas decided that it made up for all the mistakes he'd made that day, that one deftly planned tactical success. By provoking her so skilfully, he'd at least known exactly when the thrust was going to happen. This made it possible for him to jerk his head forward and sideways – he still got a horrendous gash across the base of his scalp, but it wasn't enough to die of – while simultaneously shoving hard with both feet to slam the back of the chair into where he hoped her solar plexus was likely to be. With the same impetus he threw himself to the ground, rolled and grabbed at the place where (provided nobody had moved it) Theudas' penknife ought to be, in his writing-tray on the floor. After three years in the mines it was second nature, easier to do in the dark by feel and memory than if he were in the light and able to see. The knife-hilt found his hand and the act of throwing it was a continuation of the retrieve – economy of movement, an essential in the mines. He heard the impact and the gasp of pain – bad, because if she could cry out, he'd missed – but he was already reaching for the scimitar he'd left lying on the map-table.

She said, 'Uncle Bardas, no ...' Then he heard the wet crunch of steel cutting flesh and sinew, the sharp edge compressing the fibres and shearing them. 'Thank you,' he said instinctively, and waited (always count to ten before moving; another valuable lesson he'd learned in the mines) before lowering the scimitar, getting up and groping for the tinder-box and the lamp.

She was dead by the time he had a light; cutting the neck vein is messy but quick. There was fear in her eyes too, probably that last-second realisation that she had wanted to live after all (he'd seen it so often). Her mouth was open and she'd thrown the knife away; but in the dark, of course, he couldn't have been expected to see that. Theudas' penknife had slit her cheek open, a gaudy but trivial flesh-wound like the one she'd given him. He stood and looked at her for a while. One less Loredan. Well.

So it goes on, he thought, *so it goes on. And now I've got a dead girl in my tent.* She'd fallen, needless to say, across the bed, which was now fairly comprehensively saturated with blood. So he slept in the chair instead.

Away from the fighting, in peace and quiet; he felt like he couldn't remember a time when there hadn't been dust and the constant pounding of the trebuchets.

He remembered this place from years before. He'd been about ten years old, the whole family had gone off for the day after a distant, unconfirmed rumour of geese on the flooded levels; there weren't any geese, of course, but they did find wild strawberries and some mushrooms that Uncle maintained were edible. As was usually the way on these occasions, they brought more food with them than they took back, but that wasn't really the point. Though nobody would have put it in quite those terms, it was about getting away from the rest of the clan for a while, a token act of separation. They were the only family he knew who did such things; it was regarded as a rather quaint eccentricity, and nobody ever asked if they could come too.

He remembered the cave; well, cave was an overstatement, the scrape under a rock where there'd been plenty of room for a ten-year-old to crawl in and imagine he was living in a *house*, one of those strange, non-mobile dwellings the Enemy lived in, when they weren't being the enemy.

He remembered it because of the strange feeling of security

it gave him; walls that were rock and clay, not felt. One day, he thought, I'd like to live in a *house*. And so he had, years later, until the Enemy (another Enemy, but the same one) came to Ap' Escatoy and pulled his house down into their cave.

He remembered it also because while they were away from the clan, the Enemy had raided the camp; it was the day they killed Temrai's mother and rode off most of the herd, causing the famine that killed off so many people that winter. He remembered what it had been like riding back into the camp, seeing the scraps of burned felt flapping from the charred poles, the bodies left lying because there were so many of them it would take a whole day to clear up – he frowned, superimposing that memory on what he'd just seen.

(He'd seen a lot over the years, and remembered more of it than he'd have chosen; but that's what a spy does. He sees, and remembers; and then does what he's told.)

The scrape was still there (no reason why it shouldn't be); it was smaller than he remembered, but plenty big enough to shelter him for the rest of the night and give him somewhere to work. He tied his horse to the thorn-tree (still there too; but it was nearly dead now), unslung his saddlebag and crawled into the dark tunnel.

The tinder flared at the third attempt (outside it had started to rain). He lit his lamp, then the little oil-stove that had belonged to his uncle. It flickered rather alarmingly, but he had light and enough warmth to keep his hands steady. That was enough.

He took the meat out of the bag and looked at it; then fished in the saddlebag for the little wooden box that held his uncle's most prized and mysterious treasure, the thin-bladed jointing and filleting knife. *Think twice, cut once*, he thought, then chose his spot for the first incision.

It was important to pace the work, easing the skin back with the forefinger of his left hand, working it off the bone with the flexible, razor-sharp blade in his right. He'd done similar work before, seen similar work done many times, and of course a certain degree of natural aptitude was in the blood. This was, however, an exceptional case, and it would be infinitely easier to avoid mistakes than to make them good later.

It was an awkward joint to skin, because of the curves and angles. Uncle had done harder jobs over the years – he was so good at this sort of thing that people brought him their special trophies of the hunt, their prize bucks and wolves and foxes, to be made into cloaks and rugs and blankets (though how anybody could want a blanket with the head still on he'd never been able to understand). He'd always found the sight fascinating, to see how the skin came off the bone, looking the same but completely different; and in his unformed mind he'd often speculated about that close relationship between the skin and what it covered, how the skin could be part of the whole and yet so easily separated. These reflections had led on to others – the nature of external and internal reality, the way that what lies underneath shapes the surface, the way the surface protects and contains and masks what's inside. One paradox that had always amused him was the cuir-bouilli, thick, supple oxhide stripped off, boiled in wax and moulded to make armour that was nearly as effective as steel plate (because unlike the skin of steel, the cuir-bouilli had a memory; crush it and it flexed and returned to shape). He'd had a fantasy about a man boiled in wax until his skin became armour and no blade could bite him – impractical, of course, to make a defence for the outside that killed the inside. Nobody would ever try an experiment like that, and so the theory went unproven.

He carried on peeling and shaving until the last pinch of skin came away whole, and he was left with two separate objects; skin and bone. He looked up. The water was simmering in the pot, so he dropped the bone in, to boil out the meat and tissue (the final step would be to bleach the bone and burnish it), then he laid out the skin and reached in his saddlebag for the things he needed: salt, herbs and the pot of honey. The salt he smeared in a thick layer over the raw side of the skin; then he sprinkled on the herbs and rolled the skin up tightly, like a letter. Finally he cut the wax around the neck of the honey-jar, prised off the lid and submerged the roll in the honey. The lid went back, and he melted a little knob of wax with the lamp to seal it up again.

He rested for a minute or so, as much from the effort of concentration as the actual physical work, though that had been hard enough, calling for exceptional strength and dexterity of the fingers. To wash his hands, he crawled to the mouth of the scrape and held them out in the rain, then wiped them dry on a tussock of couch-grass. The last task was cleaning off the knife (Uncle had made him promise faithfully never to let it get rusty; once that happens, he'd said, you might as well chuck it away – you'll never get it clean again).

For a while, he thought about the work he'd done. Then he lay back, stretched out his legs and went to sleep.

Gannadius.

He sat up, his head dizzy with sleep. The room was so dark that he couldn't tell whether or not his eyes were open.

'Alexius?' he said.

– and Alexius stepped out of the darkness and sat down beside the bed. 'Sorry, did I wake you?'

'Presumably,' Gannadius replied. 'But that's all right. How are you?'

Alexius frowned at him. 'Dead,' he replied.

'Sorry, it was just a reflex question, I know you're ... I'm sorry,' Gannadius added lamely.

'That's all right,' Alexius replied. 'I always thought philosophy's gain was diplomacy's loss. Think, if you'd joined the diplomatic corps instead of the Order, how many interesting wars you could have started.'

Gannadius clicked his tongue. 'That's something I've noticed, actually,' he said. 'You've got ever so much more sarcastic and waspish since you've been dead.'

'Have I?' Alexius looked concerned. 'Yes, come to think of it I suppose I have, though I hadn't noticed till you mentioned it. I can only assume it's the result of being filtered through your delightful personality and sunny disposition every time I need to talk to you. Hence also, no doubt, the increased levels of flippancy. Not that I'm complaining; I always felt I was a trifle too dry and bland in my conversation.'

'Glad to be of service,' Gannadius said. 'Now then—'

'The message, yes.' Alexius thought for a moment. 'I'm not sure how to put this without sounding deplorably melodramatic. Goodbye for ever.'

'Oh,' Gannadius replied. 'What's happened?'

'The mess we made has finally put itself right,' Alexius replied. 'Although *right* isn't perhaps the most appropriate word. Iseutz Hedin is dead. Bardas killed her a few minutes ago.'

'Oh,' Gannadius repeated. 'And that changes things how, exactly? I'm sorry, I don't quite follow.'

Alexius sighed. 'Vegetating here among the intellectual elite of the Shastel Order hasn't done much for your inductive reasoning, I see,' he said. 'Let's see. I suppose you could say that the Principle has asserted itself, or returned to its proper course – that's if we're using the river analogy, which I never liked much. If we're using the wheel analogy, I'd say it's completed a revolution and returned to top dead centre, though that conveniently ignores the fact that it was off-line for a while. Thanks, I'm sorry to say, to you and me.'

'The curse.'

'Oh dear, that word again. That diversion, or that deflection – or should it be eccentricity? Although on balance I'd settle for that bloody stupid mistake.' He shook his head. 'It's been resolved, in any event. In a sense, we're now back to where we would have been if we hadn't interfered – except, of course, that we're nowhere near, because the city that hasn't fallen isn't Perimadeia, it's a fortress out on the plains somewhere that Bardas has failed to capture; and it's Iseutz, not Bardas, who's been killed; and of course, because the wheel's turned an extra turn and covered that much more ground, any number of people have been involved who needn't have been. But it's over, which is the main thing. Now all that's left is for you to write up the experiment as a paper. Not meaning this unkindly,' he went on, 'but I'd get someone to work on it with you, just to add that objective angle that makes all the difference. What about that confounded gifted student of yours, the girl—'

'Machaera?' Gannadius shook his head. 'She changed course last year. She's in Commercial Strategy now, doing rather well.'

'Really? Shame.' Alexius sighed. 'Well, you'll find someone, I expect. And you won't be in a position to start work until everything's calmed down anyway, so—'

K. J. Parker

'What do you mean exactly,' Gannadius interrupted, 'by "calmed down"?'

Alexius made a vague gesture with his hands. 'Worked itself out, found its own level. You'll see.' He stood up. 'Well, old friend, this is one of those acutely embarrassing moments we try so hard to avoid; it's been a pleasure working with you, and I've enjoyed our friendship very much (even if the consequences for hundreds of thousands of people were fairly catastrophic). It'd be nice to think we might meet again some day, though I have to say that in my interpretation of the Principle, that's extremely unlikely.' He pulled a face. 'I know that sounds dismally formal, but you and I aren't the sort to make big emotional speeches. More's the pity, probably.'

Gannadius nodded. 'I shall miss you,' he said. 'But I suppose I'm glad, if it really is over; except that I'm not, because things have turned out so terribly badly, and it *was* our fault—'

'Partly our fault. We didn't make people the way they are, or cause the problems that started it all. In a sense, all this would have happened anyway; because it has happened—' He broke off, scratched his head, and smiled ruefully. 'Do you know,' he said, 'I had hoped that death would clarify my thinking in this area, but I'm afraid it hasn't. I never did understand the Principle, and I don't now.'

'There were two alternative courses, each equally valid,' Gannadius said slowly. 'We chose. But what happened, happened.'

'If you use the river analogy,' Alexius said, 'which I've never been happy with. But I don't see how you can fit all this into the wheel analogy—'

'Unless,' Gannadius put in, 'you see the Principle not as a wheel but as a camshaft.'

'I beg your pardon?'

'Just something I heard. I don't think much of it, either.' He took a deep breath. 'Can we shake hands, or hug, or something? I feel some sort of physical expression of leavetaking—'

Alexius thought about it. 'I can leave you with an impression that there was physical contact,' he said, 'but it would constitute an unreliable memory. However, it would be impossible to prove otherwise.'

479

'And equally impossible to prove,' Gannadius replied with a smile. 'And remember, we're philosophers. Scientists. To us, proof is everything.'

'Very well then. Goodbye, Gannadius.'

– Who realised he was awake, and had been dreaming.

It was like the aftermath of a big feast, a birthday or a wedding; they felt exhilarated and exhausted, and the last thing they wanted to do was start clearing up the mess. Unfortunately, a certain amount would have to be done before they could go to bed; a careful search for enemy survivors, for instance, not to mention their own wounded.

'Iordecai, you organise some work details,' Sildocai said. 'Lissai, Ullacai, check the defences, just in case they do attack – I can't imagine they will, but it'd be a brilliant tactical move, hitting us when we're at our most relaxed. Pajai, I want you to take twenty men and make sure Loredan's body isn't bobbing up and down in the river somewhere. You never know your luck.'

'All right,' someone replied. 'And what are you going to do?'

'Report to Temrai, of course,' Sildocai replied with a grin. 'By the way, has anybody seen him? Last I saw him he was heading back to his tent, but that was when we were still mopping up by the cattle pens.' Nobody had anything to contribute, so he shrugged and said, 'I expect he's in his tent with his feet up; after all, he's not really fit again after that bashing he took when he got buried.'

There were fires burning everywhere he looked as he crossed the camp; the neatly stacked cords of firewood had got soaked in the rain, so they were using halberd-shafts and Imperial-issue boots for fuel. Everybody he saw was moving at the slow, grim pace of the bone-weary, the dogged trudge, shoes heavy with clinging mud. He knew how they felt; but he was still slightly buzzed with victory. A pity that a victory took even longer to clear up after than a defeat.

The women and children had come out and were doing their best to help; pulling shirts and boots off dead halberdiers, gathering up armfuls of arrows, bustling about the harvest of the dead, the unexpected windfalls of good things that shouldn't go to waste. There were children rolling helmets along the ground and laughing (excited to be up so late, burning off energy after being cooped up in the tents for so long); he saw a small girl stop and stare thoughtfully at the body of another child, one who'd run out during the fighting and got in the way; it was half trampled into the mud, and the small girl was studying it without any apparent emotion. Over on the other side, a few men were darting and sliding wildly about, trying to round up some horses that had got loose. One of the men had a saturated-red bandage round his head – but someone had to catch the horses; they were his living, after all. He looked down and realised that he'd just put his foot on a hand.

Ah, well, he thought; it'll probably be back to work again tomorrow, when the trebuchets start up again, but we might as well get some sleep tonight, we've earned it. It occurred to him that he was starving hungry – chances were he wasn't the only one – but that was going to have to wait too. Had anybody thought to get Temrai something to eat?

The tent-flap was pulled back, and light was soaking out. He knocked against the post, but nobody answered. Asleep, maybe. He ducked and walked in.

Temrai was in his chair, or at least his body was. But his neck had been cut through square, and his head was missing.

CHAPTER TWENTY-ONE

'Please try not to think of it as a retrograde step in your career,' the Son of Heaven said, his eyes focused an inch or so above the top of Bardas' head. 'It's nothing of the sort. As I said earlier, we're quite satisfied with your performance. In the final analysis, the war has proved successful; you may have lost a battle, but you've negotiated peace on the same terms I'd have found acceptable if you'd won. After all,' he went on, 'nobody was expecting you to kill them *all.*'

Bardas nodded. 'Thank you,' he said.

'My pleasure. We do recognise that you took over command under adverse circumstances, that you couldn't be expected to handle troops to the same level of competency as an experienced general, and that these plainsmen proved to be an unexpectedly resourceful, tenacious and difficult enemy. You weren't the only commander they beat. In fact, you did considerably better than we expected.'

'It's very kind of you to say so.'

'Not at all. Which is why,' he went on, 'I had no hesitation whatsoever in recommending you for your new position. After all, men with your depth of experience in siege mining operations are few and far between. Not that we expect the situation at Hommyra to last anything like as long as the Ap' Escatoy business,' he added. 'Once the main galleries are completed we anticipate a conclusion in a matter of months.'

Bardas nodded. 'That's good,' he said.

'And after that – well.' The Son of Heaven actually smiled. 'There will, I feel sure, always be a need in the service for a first-class sapper. I can see the possibility of great things in your future, provided you fulfil your side of the bargain.'

*

(It had been a strange meeting, almost comic; both men treating each other with exaggerated courtesy, as if the slightest false nuance would immediately result in a hail of arrows answered by a desperate cavalry charge. Captain Loredan had greeted King Sildocai with all due and proper respect, precisely quantified in provincial office protocols (an enemy general ranks above one's own immediate subordinate, equal with oneself, but is deemed to be equal-and-below for diplomatic purposes with one's immediate superior) and had offered formal condolences on the death of King Temrai. King Sildocai had thanked Captain Loredan for his most welcome sentiments, and expressed the wish that henceforth their two nations could work together in a spirit of co-operation towards finding a mutually accept-able settlement. The deal – that the clans would leave the plains, go north into officially designated wilderness and never come back – was concluded so quickly and easily that at times both of them suspected that they were reading from the same set of notes. When they parted, they were almost friends.)

'Of course,' continued the Son of Heaven, 'we never had the slightest intention of sending you to the Island.'

'Really?' Bardas said. He sounded as if the subject was of academic interest only.

'Absolutely. It would have represented a concession, almost an act of weakness. No, the Island needs – forgive me – strong, uncompromising leadership to see it through the difficult process of transition. The territory itself is, of course, hardly worth bothering with (in due course I expect we'll amalgamate it with one of the other sub-prefectures, adjust the population balance, make it a viable proposition as a designated naval base); but at this particular juncture, the first priority must be to secure the fleet. If our various unfortunate experiences in this theatre of operations has taught us anything, it's that we can no longer afford to neglect seapower.'

He's talking to me, Bardas realised, entirely as one of us – a subordinate, naturally, but *us* includes us all, even me. 'I can see that,' he said. 'As you say, it's a matter of priorities.'

Magnanimously, the Son of Heaven offered to pour him some more wine. He'd noticed that they liked to do this, either because it made some point about their relationship as servants of the Empire, or because they couldn't trust outlanders not to disturb the sediment. He nodded *thank you* politely.

'As a matter of fact,' the Son of Heaven went on, 'during my discussions with him, I found the rebel leader rather more shrewd than I'd anticipated – a bad lapse of judgement on my part, I confess. Well,' he added, pursing his thin lips, 'not shrewd, exactly; it was more that curious blend of cunning and stupidity that characterises mercantile nations. In my experience they tend to have an uncanny knack of being able to understand motivations on the individual human level, whereas larger issues that would be perfectly obvious to you and me seem to pass them by entirely. Hence,' he added, with a trace of a smile, 'the aptness of the personal approach, the misguidance – is there such a word? I wonder – that we would be sending you, somebody they could both trust and manipulate. Of course he was a fool to base his entire strategy on a wholly unsupported assurance, a vague statement of probable future intent. The remarkable weakness I've found among traders is their apparent desire, in spite of their façade of cynicism, to trust someone. Making him trust me was easy; people like that can't help trusting people they're afraid of.'

Bardas smiled, as if sharing the joke. 'What's going to happen to him?' he asked. 'The rebel leader, I mean.'

The Son of Heaven was watching him out of the corner of his eye. 'Oh, he'll be extradited, tried and sentenced; we have to balance the books, after all. Fortunately, our system of audit allows one man to bear the blame for his country's defaults; it's efficient and humane, and it simplifies performance reviews. Thus King Temrai's paid for his people, Master Auzeil and his cohorts will pay for theirs; we can draw a line under both columns and rule the page off. Similarly,' he went on, his voice so gentle that it almost degenerated into a drawl (except that no Son of Heaven would ever sink so low), 'we can conclude our rather pointless entanglement in the Mesoge with one simple act of accounting.'

Bardas kept perfectly still.

*

They had, of course, been reading his letters. It was standard operating procedure when an officer was under review following an unsatisfactory or questionable action.

The letter in question had reached him at a bad time, when he was in the middle of trying to sort out a mess he'd made with the duty rosters. 'Not now,' he'd said, and then seen the expression on the face of the man who'd brought it. He looked as if he wanted to be sick.

'What've you got there?' he asked.

'Letter for you,' the man replied. 'And that.' He pointed to a large earthenware jar, which was being held by another distressed-looking soldier. 'We've got the man who brought them in the guardhouse.'

Bardas nodded. 'Fair enough,' he said, wondering what was going on. 'Give me the letter and put the jar in my tent. I'll be along in a minute'

In the event it took him nearly half an hour to straighten out the rosters, by which time he'd clean forgotten about the letter. It wasn't until that evening, when he managed to scrape up an hour for a rest and a sit-down, that he saw the jar beside his chair and remembered.

The seal was broken – well, he was used to that – but familiar; the Loredan Bank, which meant the letter was from one of two people. And he couldn't imagine his sister Niessa sending him a letter, let alone presents.

Dear Bardas,

You're reading this, which means you've won the battle. Congratulations! Now, let's go back a bit.

When I've finished writing this letter, it'll go to my man in Temrai's camp. He's been working for me for a while now; basically, his job's been to make sure nothing happens to Temrai until you catch up with him; then to make sure, come what may, that he doesn't escape. If you get him – well, fine, you won't be reading this letter. If he's managed to give you the slip – well, it's all right.

It was the least I could do. I know how important it is for you – your career, your future – to make a success of this war. It's been touch and go, hasn't it? First they were going to send that huge great army, which would've meant you

*never got your chance. Well, we couldn't have that, could
we? Luckily, I was able to arrange a little diversion there;
the Islanders are so stupid and greedy that all I had to do
was suggest that they might consider holding out on the
deal and demanding more money, and that was that. Then,
of course, they went too far and got themselves annexed; I
felt a bit foolish when I heard about that, I can tell you.
Luckily, though, there was enough time to send some of my
people across to start a neat little rebellion – a long shot,
but it worked. I had a feeling it would work; because, you
see, I know this war is meant to happen for you, and
nothing's going to stand in your way this time.*

*I hope you like the present. You've been making things
for me ever since we were kids (you were always the clever
one with your hands). Now, you know I can't make things to
save my life, so I've got this clever fellow Dassascai to do this
for me. What with being an assassin and a cook, he ought to
have made a fair job of it. If not – well, it's the thought that
counts.*

> *As always,*
>> *Your loving brother,*
>> *Gorgas.*

Bardas rolled up the letter; then he cut the wax around the
neck of the jar, eased off the stopper and pulled out what he
found inside.

At first he thought it was a pig's head, like the ones
he'd always dreaded as a boy, though his father and Gorgas
considered them a great delicacy. The drill was to bone out
the skull, leaving the mask intact; it was then cured with
salt and stuffed with good things – cloves, allspice, basil, black
and red Colleon peppercorns, mace, cinnamon, cumin,
dried apricots and root ginger – and steeped in thin, clear,
almost white domestic honey. Even then, Bardas had been
both intrigued and disgusted by the paradox of the sweet,
delicious, fragrant inside and the grotesque, dead exterior;
he wondered who could possibly have thought up the idea
of such a bizarre combination. As a dutiful son, he'd always
made a show of tackling his share and miming enthusiasm,
trying to make himself concentrate on the gorgeous smell
and the rich, sweet taste – after all, you don't have to look at

something in order to eat it, you just reach out with your knife and cut.

It was the same recipe; he could imagine Gorgas writing it out in detail and sending it to his cook, with strict instructions not to try to improve it (Gorgas had a flair for cooking and a tremendous ability to enjoy food; details mattered to him. On reflection, Gorgas would have made a fine Son of Heaven). But it wasn't a pig's face that dangled from the mop of honey-slicked hair between his fingers; shrunken and distorted (probably by the drying action of the salt), it was the face of King Temrai.

Honey trickled down the dimpled, overripe-peach cheeks like golden tears; the eyelids were closed on the empty sockets (Bardas knew how much closed eyes could see) and the mouth was sewn up with finely twisted sinew, which had in one or two places torn through the thin fabric of the lips as the skin contracted and tightened. It was soft and yielding to the touch, like a leather bag – like the footballs they used to make out of bladders crammed with straw, or the savoury winter puddings his mother stuffed into the stomach of a sheep. Under the white-gold glaze, the skin was pale and marbled, like mother of pearl.

(How curious, Bardas thought; how curious and impractical of the makers of men to put the hard armour of the skull inside the softness of the face. Surely it ought to be the other way round, the tough, uniform bone sheltering the vulnerable, distinctive features that made one individual different from another. In that respect, if in no other, they knew better in the proof house.)

Soft and unformed, yet shrivelled and lined, Temrai looked both very young and very old. In this face he could see the boy who'd hidden from him under a cart, in a place not far away from here; and he could see the old man that Temrai would have been (the river or the wheel, unless one preferred the analogy of the camshaft) – and he thought for a moment about the process of preservation (curing the meat), which is an attempt to dam the river and stop the wheel, to find a way of failing to sack the doomed city or kill the accursed man. Someone who believed in the Principle might be inclined to make that into a theory, as if there hadn't been enough reshaping of raw material already.

'It's a bit late to worry about that now,' observed Anax, standing behind his shoulder. 'And besides, the ability to make things into other things is what makes us human. Or makes us the humans we are,' he added, with a wheezy chuckle. 'You know what,' he went on, 'dried out and properly padded you could use that as a helmet liner.'

'Go away,' Bardas said.

'You're just cranky because you never had a chance to say thank you,' Anax replied. 'And you're the man who was always bitching in the mines about never getting to see the face of his enemy.'

Bardas frowned. 'I never thought of him as that,' he said. 'In fact, to be honest with you, I never really thought about him as a human being.'

'Missed your chance for that, I'm afraid,' Anax said, in a told-you-so voice. 'Because that's not human, it's just a thing. Comes to us all in time, of course; we gradually grow these inhuman skins – a bit like trees, really, except the other way round; with us, it's the living bit that's on the inside and the dead bit that's outside. Which reminds me, was that or was that not an amazingly fine suit of armour I made for you?'

'Yes.'

'Is that all you can say, yes? Talk about passing proof; you sit there without a mark on you, and all you can say is *yes*.'

Bardas smiled. 'Ah,' he said, 'but that was just war. It never had to withstand Bollo and the big hammer.'

Anax smiled; Bardas couldn't see the smile, but he knew it was there. 'Son,' he said, 'there's nothing on earth that strong. It's like those boxing booths you used to see at fairs; rule of the house, Bollo always wins. The fun's to see how many rounds you can go.'

'Fun?'

'For want of a better word.'

A little later, Bardas went to the guardhouse.

'That man who brought the letter for me,' he said. 'Have you still got him there?'

They told him yes, he was still here.

'Fine. Have you asked him his name?'

Sure, they replied. Dassascai, he called himself. Made no secret of it. Seemed to be under the impression he had a nice reward coming.

'Absolutely,' Bardas replied. 'Now, get a couple of men and a flag of truce, and take this Dassascai up the hill to King Sildocai – I suggest you keep a tight hold of him, he might not want to go – along with this jar and this letter. Then, if I were you, I'd get out of there as quick as you can.'

The Son of Heaven leaned back in his chair. 'Just out of curiosity,' he asked, 'what was in the jar?'

'Victory,' Bardas replied, smiling weakly. 'At least, something that achieved the same result as victory. You might say it was a kind of secret weapon.'

'I see.' The Son of Heaven raised an eyebrow. 'Like the incendiary liquid you used during the siege of Perimadeia, something like that?'

'Not quite,' Bardas said, 'though of course that came in a jar too. Excuse me, please, I'm starting to say the first thing that comes into my head.' He stroked his chin, as if thinking something over. 'So, when do I leave?' he asked.

'As soon as your relief arrives; later today or early tomorrow. You're to report to him as soon as he gets here – Colonel Ilshel. Still quite young, but a certain degree of promise; we have high hopes for him. He'll supervise the enemy evacuation, escort them as far as the mountains. It should be a perfectly straightforward job.'

'Very good,' Bardas replied, without apparent feeling (and his face didn't move, as if it was already dead and pickled).

'You been on the post before, then?' the courier asked.

Bardas nodded. 'A couple of times,' he replied.

The courier seemed impressed. 'You must be important, then,' he said. 'What was your name again?'

'Bardas Loredan.'

'Bardas – hang on, that rings a bell. Ap' Escatoy. You're the hero.'

Bardas nodded. 'That's right,' he said.

'Bugger me,' the courier said. 'It's not every day I get a hero on the round. So, what was it *really* like?'

'Boring, mostly. With occasional interludes of extreme terror.'

The courier laughed. 'Oh, they all say that,' he said, 'when you ask 'em about what they did in the war. You're not allowed to talk about it, I get the picture. So, where are you off to now? Or is that hush-hush as well?'

'Some place called Hommyra,' Bardas told him, 'wherever that is. Do you know where it is?'

'Hommyra.' The courier frowned. 'Well, if it's where I think it is, it's right on the other side of the Empire, out east. I never even knew they were having a war there, though of course that doesn't mean anything.'

'They told me it'd take me six weeks to get there,' Bardas said, 'on the post. So I guess that sounds about right.'

'Promotion?'

'They're making me up to full captain.'

'You don't say. That's pretty good going for an outlander.'

'Thank you.'

Bardas had changed coaches in Ap' Escatoy. It had disturbed him to discover that the camp and the temporary city there felt something like home, that he'd almost experienced a sense of belonging. He'd tried not to dwell on that thought; just as he'd avoided going under the gate over which, some-one told him, they'd hung the heads of three notorious rebels responsible for the recent disaffection on the Island. Once he knew what they were he hadn't looked up, for fear of recognising them or catching sight of the labels pinned to them, detailing the offenders' names and crimes.

'This business with the plainspeople, now,' the courier was saying, 'of course it could have been handled a bit smarter, but in the end it all worked out; we've got rid of them, their king's dead and we picked up a fleet of ships along the way. All this talk you hear about a blow to Imperial prestige and stuff, that's just sour grapes. It's only the score at the end that matters, wouldn't you agree?'

'Absolutely,' Bardas replied.

'Just a minute.' The courier looked round at him. 'You were in that lot, weren't you? I'm sure I heard that somewhere, the Ap' Escatoy bloke was joining the plains war. Is that right?'

'I was in on the tail end of it,' Bardas said.

'Hey! See any action?'

'A little.'

'Would you credit it?' The courier grinned. 'They're saying it was the artillery did the donkey work, though the cavalry had a good war. Is that right?'

'More or less.'

'They're always the unsung heroes, the artillery,' the courier stated gravely. 'Bloody pikemen give themselves airs, say they're the ones who actually get the job done – and fair play to them, they're good, very good. But for sieges and stuff like that, you can't beat the corps of engineers. Well, look at you, for instance.'

'Me?'

'Sure. You're an engineer, after all.'

Bardas shrugged. 'I suppose I am,' he said.

'No suppose about it,' replied the courier firmly. 'My dad, he was an engineer. Fifteen years on roads and bridges, then he got his transfer to the artillery, worked his way up to bombardier-sergeant; not a sapper like you, of course, though one of my uncles ...'

'Is that the sea over there?'

'That's right,' the courier said. 'Just over the hills there, about two miles. We follow the coast right down as far as Ap' Molian, then we head inland for a couple of days to Rhyzalia, and that's as far as I go. I expect you'll be catching the Torrene coach – one of the couriers on that's my brother-in-law, so ask him if he happens to know a bloke called—'

He didn't get as far as the name; he stopped, sat bolt upright and fell off the box. *Not again*, Bardas thought and grabbed for the reins, but they were still wrapped round the courier's wrists. He was dragged along by them as the coach gradually slowed down. Somewhere on the rack behind him was a crossbow, service issue for post guards, but it wasn't where it was meant to be. His scimitar was with the rest of the luggage, somewhere in the back. No point trying to fight, then; which left him with one option, retreat. He shuffled along the box seat and reached out for the reins, overbalanced and fell. The last thing he was aware of was the front offside wheel, rushing toward him –

Bardas?

'Anax?' he said.

Alexius. I just stopped off to say goodbye.

'Oh,' Bardas replied. 'You're leaving, then.'

At long last. Now she's dead, it sort of rounds things off.

'Who's dead? You mean Iseutz, my niece?'

No. Someone else; I don't know, you may not remember her. Vetriz Auzeil. She was involved, peripherally.

There was no way of knowing where this place was; it was dark, without noises or smells. 'I seem to remember you telling me about her,' he said. 'And I met her and her brother a few times. They were friends of Athli Zeuxis.' He was about to say something else, but didn't.

Well, I know you're a sceptic, so I won't go into details. I believe she was a natural of sorts, but to what extent she played any significant part – although obviously she did have some bearing, or else her death wouldn't be rounding off the chapter, so to speak. Anyway, that seems to be that.

'Well, then.' Bardas decided to ask after all. 'Do you happen to know – what did become of Athli, in the end?'

In the end, I'm not sure. She had some part to play in the last defence of Shastel, but whether she escaped or not I never found out. There's a passing reference to her in one of the discussions of the Colleon war, but it's inconclusive; it could be either the First Colleon War, which was before the fall of Shastel—

'So it wasn't her,' Bardas said, 'above the gateway?'

Not the gateway in Ap' Escatoy; I assume that's the one you mean. No, the third head was someone called Eseutz Mesatges, and that was a case of mistaken identity – they confused her with your niece Iseutz, you see. And to be fair, it's an unusual name.

'Not someone I've heard of,' Bardas replied. 'Thank you. I feel a bit better for knowing Athli got away.'

Well . . . Anyway; I'll be seeing you again, of course, but this is the last time you'll see me as Alexius. I shouldn't really be here now, but –

Bardas opened his eyes.

'Thank the gods for that,' Gorgas said. 'I've been worried sick.'

Gorgas was kneeling over him, a bowl in one hand, a piece of wet rag in the other. The rag had been torn off his shirt; Bardas could see where he'd ripped it from the sleeve.

'It's all right,' Gorgas went on. 'You took one hell of a nasty bump on the head, but the swelling's gone down and I don't think it's bleeding inside. Bardas? You do know who I am, don't you?'

'I think so,' Bardas replied. 'You're my brother Gorgas, right?'

'Yes, that's right.'

Bardas tried to nod, but that turned out to be a very bad idea. 'We built the tree-house together,' he said. 'In the big apple tree, before it blew down. There was a squirrel that used to walk right past the window.'

'That's it, you've got it,' Gorgas said. 'Now lie still, take it easy. Everything's under control.'

'Where's Dad?'

Gorgas looked at him, then smiled. He had a big, warm smile.'He's around somewhere,' he said. 'Don't worry, things are going to be just fine.'

Bardas tried to smile back, but his head hurt. 'You're not going anywhere, are you?' he asked.

'Of course not. I'll be here. You take it easy.'

He closed his eyes again; and when he opened them, he remembered.

'Gorgas?' He tried to get up, but there wasn't enough strength in his body. He was lying on the deck of a small ship, his head on a folded-up sail, under a heap of coats and blankets. The sun was bright, sharp, almost cruel; but there was a pleasantly cool breeze.

'Bardas?' The voice came from some way away, up the other end of the ship. 'Hang on, I'll be right there.' Bardas couldn't move, but he could place Gorgas exactly by the sound of his feet on the deck, the vibrations running through the planking; it was a skill he'd acquired in the galleries under Ap' Escatoy.

'You got bashed on the head, remember?' Gorgas was saying (but Bardas couldn't see him; he was above and behind, so that his shadow fell across Bardas' face). 'You fell off the post coach. Dammit, I should have guessed something like that might happen. It's my own damn stupid fault. You could have been killed.'

Bardas took a deep breath, let it go. His mouth was dry, like hard leather. 'You shot the coachman,' he said.

'Seventy yards, if it was a step. That bow you made for me, Bardas, it's a honey. But I should have been more careful.'

Bardas frowned. 'Why?' he said.

'Why what?'

'Why did you kill the coachman?'

'I had to stop the coach, idiot.' Bardas could picture the smile; the big, warm smile. 'Too open for a road-block, and the post doesn't stop for stray fares. Would you like something to drink now?'

'No. Yes,' Bardas amended, because at that moment a drink was what he wanted most in the whole world.

'Coming right up,' Gorgas said. 'You've no idea the fun and games I've had since then; you were out cold, I was convinced I'd killed you, I was wetting myself. So I got all that trash off the coach, got you back on, set off cross-country for where I'd left the ship; and then a bloody wheel came off—'

Bardas frowned. He seemed to remember a conversation he'd been having a few moments earlier; the whole point was, it wasn't a wheel, it was a camshaft. But that didn't make sense.

'So after I dumped the coach,' Gorgas was saying, 'I had to carry you the last two miles - brother, you've put on weight since I used to carry you round the yard, though granted, you were only three then. And of course I was petrified about jogging you about, damaging something - head injuries are really sensitive things, you know, you can do all sorts of damage to someone's head if you're not careful. Dear gods; I'll tell you, it was only when I got us both back on this ship that I even remembered to worry about anybody chasing after us. But there doesn't seem to be anybody, luckily. And so,' he added cheerfully, 'here we are, on our way. You know, this is like old times.'

'Why did you stop the coach?' Bardas asked.

'Oh, for ... To rescue you, of course. You don't think I was going to stand by and let them court-martial my brother, do you? You may have faith in Imperial justice, but I don't.'

(Three heads over a gateway; it was a valid point.) 'They weren't going to court-martial me,' Bardas said. 'They're sending me to a new posting. Hommyra,' he remembered.

Gorgas laughed. 'There's no such place, you clown. Come on, you know the Empire by now; for every failure, one responsible officer. Hey, it's just as well you've got your big brother to look out for you, you're not fit to be out on your own.'

'But the coachman, he'd heard of it. I think.'

'Sure,' Gorgas said. 'Look, who'd you rather believe, the Empire or your own flesh and blood? No, here we are again. Only this time, it's going to be different. Promise.'

Bardas' head hurt. 'We're going home? The Mesoge?'

'You mean you haven't—?' Gorgas' voice became very soft. 'I'm afraid I've got some bad news for you,' he said. 'It's gone.'

'Gone? It can't have *gone*.'

'Sorry, bad choice of words. All right, no beating about the bush. The farm's been destroyed, Bardas. They did it, the provincial office.'

'What are you talking about, Gorgas?'

Gorgas was quiet for a moment. 'They sent a company of archers,' he said. 'In the middle of the night, needless to say. Surrounded the place, barred the doors from the outside, set light to the thatch. I woke up coughing my lungs out, ran to the window, nearly got shot. It was like hell, Bardas; there was smoke everywhere, you couldn't see a thing; burning thatch coming down in great bunches, timbers, the lot. I tried to get them out, I really tried; but Clefas was dead, the smoke got him while he was sleeping; Zonaras was trapped under about half the roof, he was caught there screaming and burning and I couldn't do anything— Look,' he said, and moved round, so that Bardas could see his face. For an instant, he thought it was someone else. 'I was still trying when he died,' he said. 'He kept yelling, *Gorgas, help me*, right up to the end.'

Bardas didn't say anything.

'Iseutz had already left – but you know that anyway. So it was just me and Niessa,' Gorgas eventually continued. 'Just her and me; we managed to jump out the top loft window on to the roof of the duck shed – she'd had the wit to grab the bow and some arrows, and there was light enough, gods know; we managed to crawl into the duck shed and I kept them off till I ran out of arrows – you saved our lives, boy, making me this bow, I'm telling you. Anyway, just when I thought we'd had it, I saw a gap we could get through and we ran for it. I didn't stop till I was out in Clyras' meadow – you know, the sunken cart-road; you'd never know it was there now, the hedge had grown up all round it. Then I realised Niessa wasn't with me, so I went back. She was dead. They were cutting her head off with Dad's old felling-axe.'

Gorgas was quiet for a long time.

'Well,' he resumed at last, 'there wasn't any point, was there? Maybe killing a few of them and getting killed myself, what would that have achieved? You've got to be practical. I snuck back down the sunken road, hid up for the day, walked into Tornoys that night and found this boat. It's Lyras Monedin's old lobster-boat; you remember Lyras, miserable old bugger who used to throw stones at us when we were kids.'

Bardas opened his eyes. 'Is he still alive? He must be over a hundred.'

'Still going strong, apparently,' Gorgas said, 'though Buciras and Onnyas take the boat out now. Well, before I stole it, anyway. So that's that,' he went on. 'Everything we ever had, everything we worked for, you and me, all gone up in smoke, literally. It's just you and me now, Bardas. We're the only ones left.'

'I see.' Bardas closed his eyes again. 'So where are we going?'

'Ah.' Gorgas' voice was smiling again. 'That's what I meant when I told you it was all going to be all right. You remember Fleuras Peredin?'

'What?'

'Fleuras Peredin,' Gorgas repeated. 'Used to go fishing for cod and those long wriggly buggers with the big flat heads, out beyond the sand-banks.'

'Yes, I remember. What's he got to do with anything?'

'Ah.' Gorgas chuckled. 'Well, I remembered something he told me once, about how he'd been caught in a squall and blown right out to sea; and he told me about this island he'd wound up on, a long way out. Of course I thought he was making it up, he always was a liar; and then I heard someone in the Hopes and Fears telling pretty much the same tale about a year ago, which set me thinking. Anyway, the long and the short of it is, there really is an island there; I've been there, and I know how to find it. It's nothing special, I'll grant you; lots of rocks and trees and not much else. But there's fresh water, and a flat spot right in the middle that looks as good a bit of dirt as I've ever seen anywhere; spit out an apple pip and a year later you'll have a tree. There's goats living up in the rocks, and plenty of birds; you couldn't go hungry there if you tried. There's timber for building, any god's amount of it; and to cap it all, do you know what I found, up one of the mountains? Iron ore; dirty great lumps of it, just lying on the surface. I promise you, Bardas; my strength, all your skills, there's nothing we can't have there if we want it. Just you and me, together. It'd be like old times. What d'you reckon?'

Bardas thought for a moment. 'You're crazy,' he said.

Gorgas frowned a little. 'What do you mean?'

'You're actually suggesting we could live together, build a farm, as if none of what you did ever happened. You want to go back to when we were kids, before—'

Gorgas' face seemed to be falling apart; the cracked, angry, melted skin and the look of horror. 'For gods' sakes, Bardas,' he said. 'What *I* did? I love you, Bardas, more than anybody in the whole world, but you simply can't just lie there and talk about what *I* did. One bad thing – oh, a very, very bad thing, no possible doubt about that; and ever since, every waking moment of my life, I've been trying to make up for it – to Niessa, to Clefas and Zonaras, to you. Every single thing I've done since, I've done for the three of you. And yes, I've done some bad things in that time, terrible things, but good and bad simply don't come into it when it's done for us, for family. But you – all the things *you've* done, all those people you killed – with Uncle Maxen, in the courts, during the siege, on Scona, Ap' Escatoy, the war here; who did you kill them *for*, Bardas? For whoever was paying you? Go on, answer me, I want to know.'

Bardas shook his head. 'Don't you dare say that,' he said. 'Don't you ever try to make it sound like I'm like you.'

'Oh, come on.' Gorgas was almost laughing. 'You left home to seek your fortune; that's fine. All the money you made, you sent it home for Clefas and Zonaras; you were trying to look out for them, just like me. During the siege you were fighting for your city. On Scona – well, you had the right, that's all I can say about that; but we were quits after that, and you know it. But since then; you, a soldier of the Empire? Do you sincerely believe in the manifest destiny of the Sons of Heaven?'

'What about the Islanders?' Bardas shouted. 'Killed, enslaved, because of you—'

Gorgas shook his head. 'By the Empire. The people you fight for. Please. And besides, none of it would have happened if Ap' Escatoy hadn't fallen; and who was it let the bull out of the pen? But that's all right,' Gorgas went on, speaking more softly. 'You were doing a job, just like you were doing when you were with Uncle Maxen; a soldier's not responsible for the wars he fights in, just as I'm not responsible for what the Empire did to the Islanders – or what Temrai did to the City. And besides—' He made his horrible face into a smile. 'Besides,' he said, 'we're through with all of that now, both of us. Don't you see? We can put it all behind us – dammit, if I've got one single virtue, it's being realistic. We can't put right any of the bad things we've done. Even trying to make up for them makes us do more bad things, worse things. There's got to come a time when we say enough's enough, it's time to do something *else*; something worthwhile and decent and good. I tried that, Bardas; I tried to go home, to be what I always should have been, a hard-working farmer making an honest living out of our land. I tried to wind back the wheel, if you like – and what happened? Our home's nothing but cold ashes and trash, everything ruined, burned and gone. And you – well. I don't have to say it, do I?'

Bardas was actually shaking with anger. 'Everything,' he said, 'everything bad in the whole world, is your *fault*. All the bad things, the evil things I did, are *your fault*. And I'll never forgive you. Never.'

'Oh, Bardas.' Gorgas was gazing at him, his face full of compassion. 'Do you know, what you just said, in a way, that's an act of love. All these years you've been letting me take away all the bad things you've done. You've allowed me to do that for you. And that's fine; I'm glad about that. Now let me do this one last thing, for both of us. Let's take all the evil away, shall we?' He grinned, stretching the burns and the wounds that hid his face like a visor. 'Let's rid the world of the Loredan boys, for good and all. Now wouldn't that be something, eh? Get the Loredan brothers out of harm's way, where they can't do any more damage. Can't think of a single more altruistic act than that. Think of it; we'd be as good as dead and buried.'

(*It's customary to die first; but in your case we'll make an exception.*)

'And anyway,' Gorgas went on, still smiling, 'it's not as if you've got a choice. You're too weak to fight me, or jump over the side. When we get there, as soon as I've got you and the stuff ashore, I'm going to soak down the decks with lamp-oil and set this old tub alight. You want to get off the island, you're going to have to build yourself a boat.'

Bardas was having trouble breathing. 'Or I could kill you,' he said. 'I could kill us both.'

'You could,' Gorgas conceded. 'If you wanted to; and then we'd really be alike, you and me – except that my act of deliberate evil was at the beginning, and yours would be at the end. Is that what you want?'

'No.'

'Thought not,' Gorgas said cheerfully. 'So it looks like we're going to be doing it my way. It's all right; if I take away the choice, you can carry on blaming me for everything. You can blame me when it rains, or when it doesn't; you can blame me when the goats eat off the green corn, or the hayrick catches fire; I'll be glad to take the blame, it'll be like old times.'

'No,' Bardas said softly. 'Gorgas, please.'

'Don't be silly,' Gorgas said (he was walking away; Bardas couldn't see him any more). 'I guess you've just got to trust me, Bardas. After all, I'm your big brother and I love you. And haven't I always seen you right?'